WARRIORS
GRAYSTRIPE'S ADVENTURE

CREATED BY
ERIN HUNTER

WRITTEN BY
DAN JOLLEY

ART BY
JAMES L. BARRY

HAMBURG // LONDON // LOS ANGELES // TOKYO

HARPER
An Imprint of HarperCollinsPublishers

Graystripe's Adventure

Created by Erin Hunter

Written by Dan Jolley

Art and Colorization by James L. Barry

Lettering - Mike Estacio and Lucas Rivera (vol. 1)
John Hunt (vol. 2)
Lucas Rivera (vol. 3)
Original Cover Design - Anne Marie Horne
Digital Toning Assistant - Lincy Chan (vol. 1)

Editor - Lillian Diaz-Przybyl
Digital Imaging Manager - Chris Buford
Pre-Production Supervisor - Erika Terriquez
Art Director - Anne Marie Horne
Production Manager - Elisabeth Brizzi
VP of Production - Ron Klamert
Editor-in-Chief - Rob Tokar
Publisher - Mike Kiley
President and C.O.O. - John Parker
C.E.O. and Chief Creative Officer - Stuart Levy

A TOKYOPOP® Manga

TOKYOPOP Inc.
5900 Wilshire Blvd. Suite 2000
Los Angeles, CA 90036

E-mail: info@TOKYOPOP.com
Come visit us online at www.TOKYOPOP.com

For information address HarperCollins Children's Books, a division of HarperCollins Publishers, 195 Broadway, New York, NY 10007.
www.harpercollinschildrens.com

Library of Congress Control Number: 2017930905
ISBN 978-0-06-257300-1

19 20 21 PC/LSCC 10 9 8 7
❖
First Edition

CONTENTS

WARRIORS

THE LOST WARRIOR

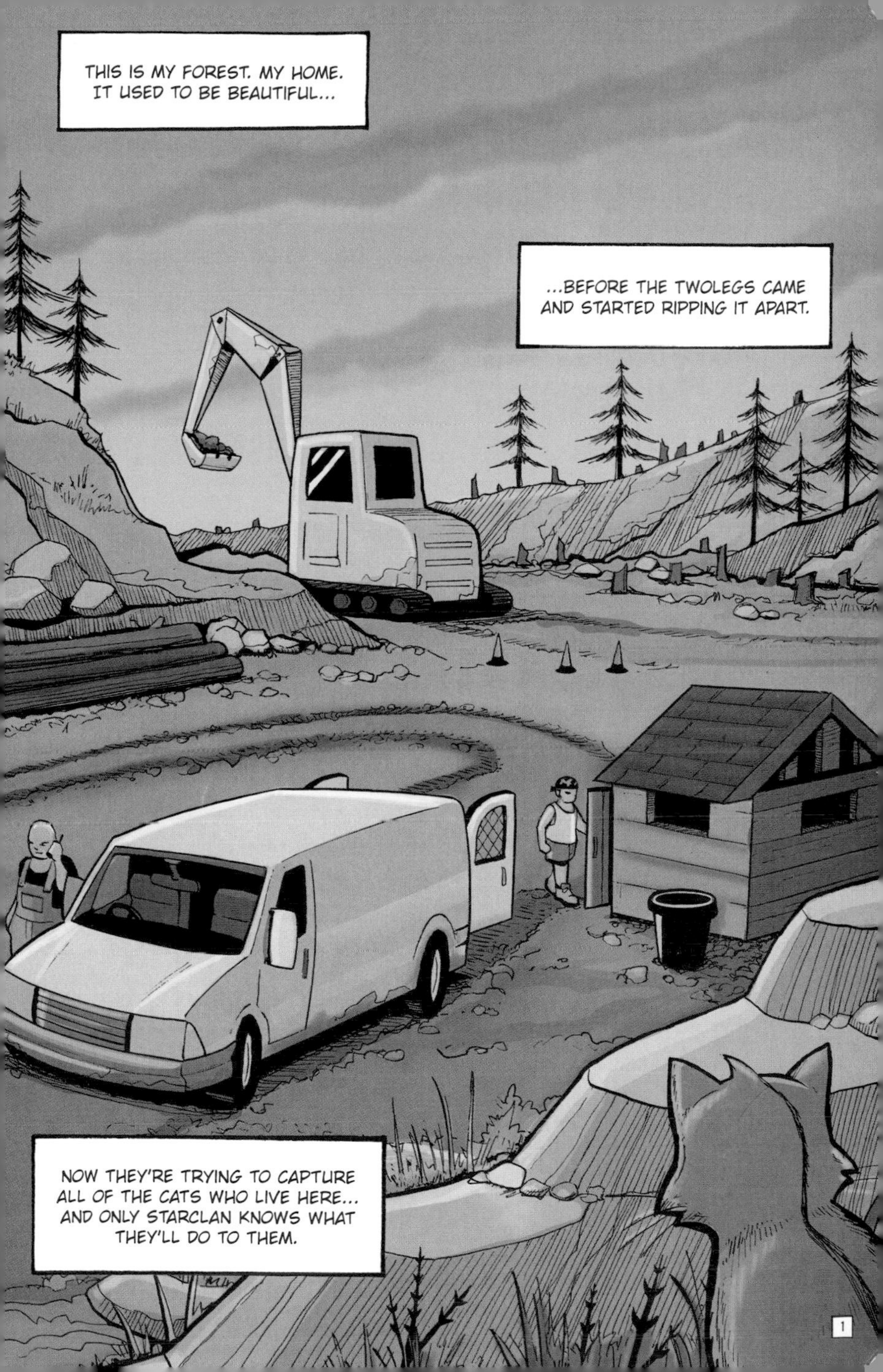
THIS IS MY FOREST. MY HOME. IT USED TO BE BEAUTIFUL...
...BEFORE THE TWOLEGS CAME AND STARTED RIPPING IT APART.
NOW THEY'RE TRYING TO CAPTURE ALL OF THE CATS WHO LIVE HERE... AND ONLY STARCLAN KNOWS WHAT THEY'LL DO TO THEM.

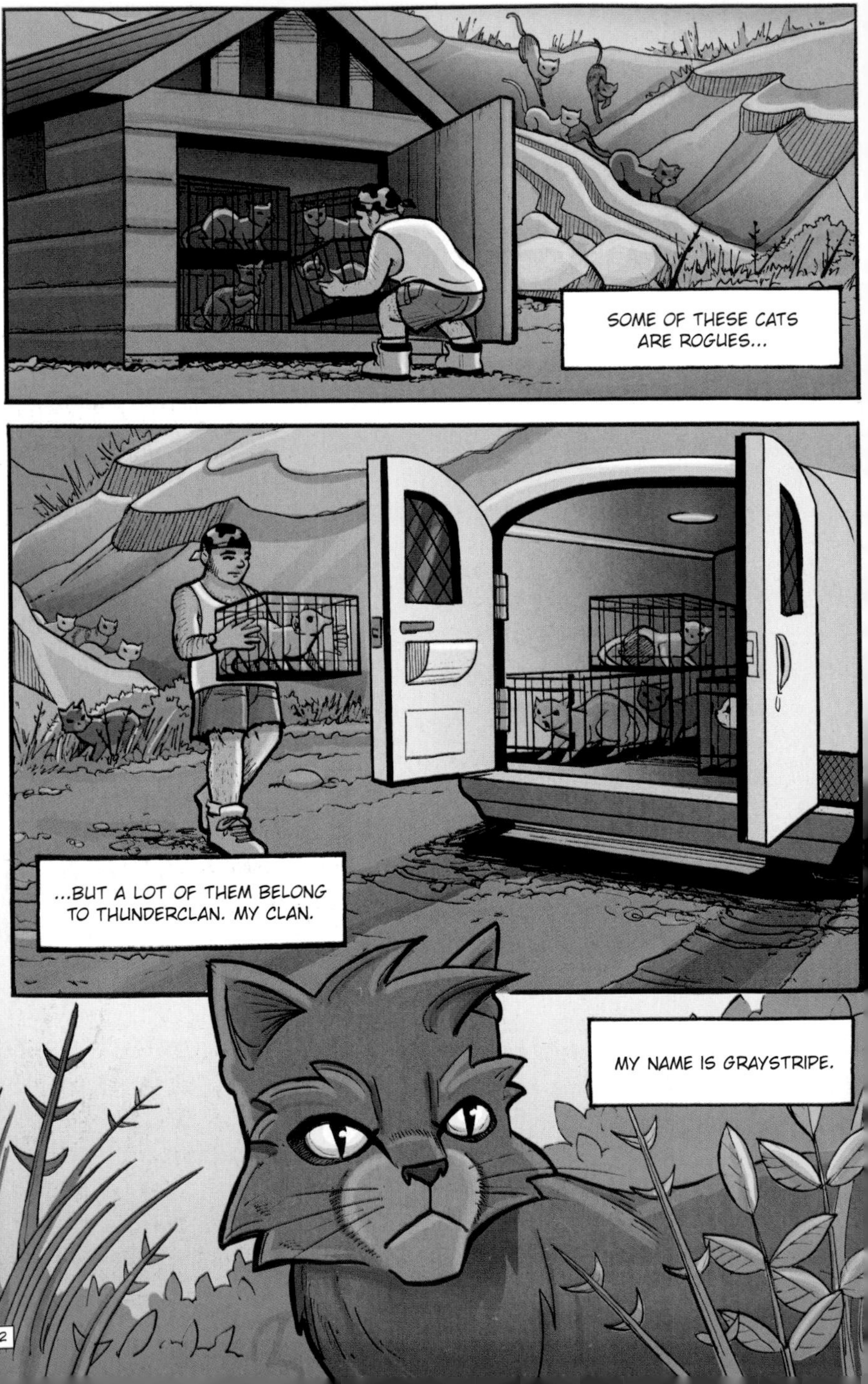
SOME OF THESE CATS ARE ROGUES...
...BUT A LOT OF THEM BELONG TO THUNDERCLAN. MY CLAN.
MY NAME IS GRAYSTRIPE.

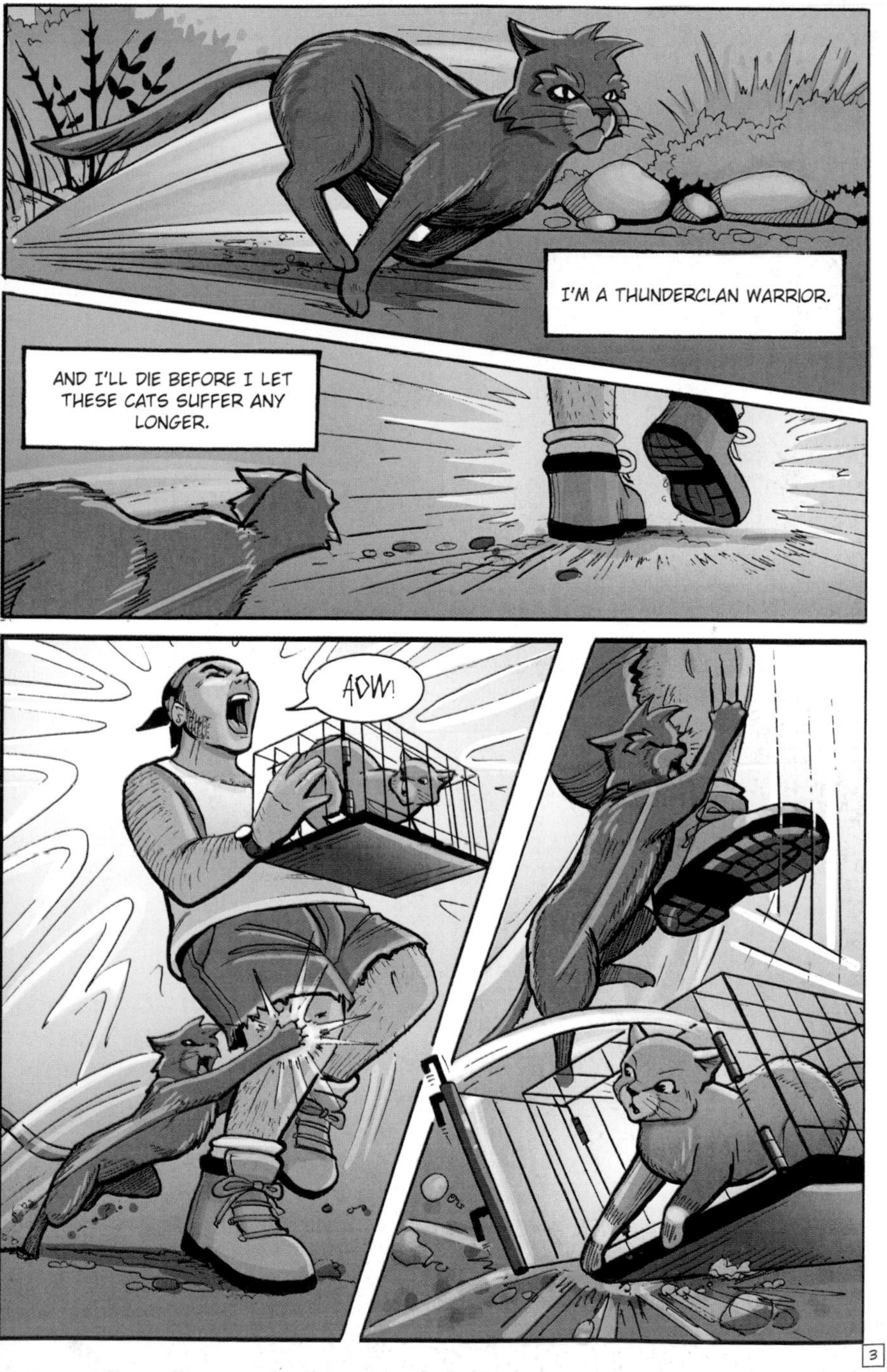
I'M A THUNDERCLAN WARRIOR.
AND I'LL DIE BEFORE I LET THESE CATS SUFFER ANY LONGER.
AOW!

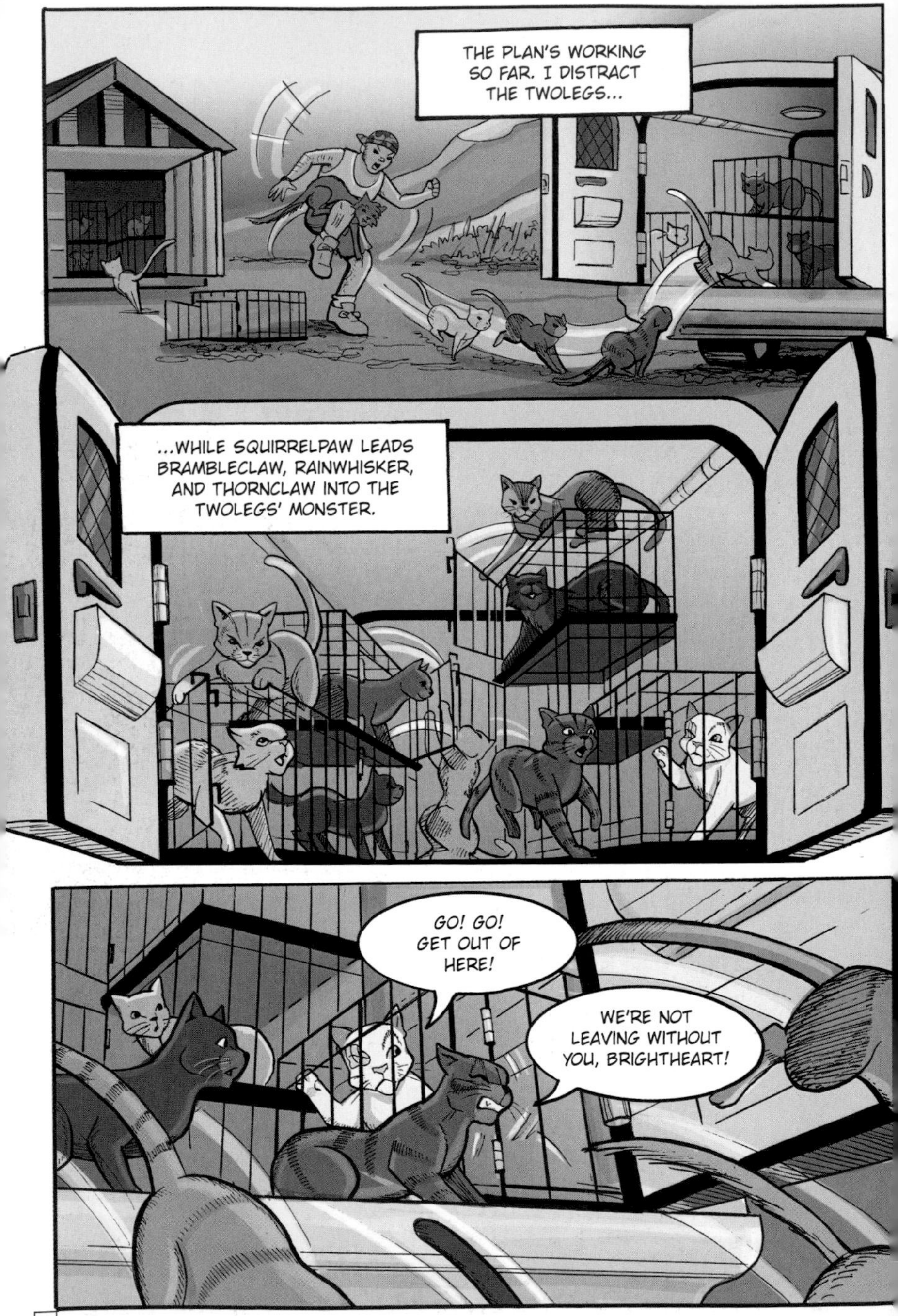
THE PLAN'S WORKING SO FAR. I DISTRACT THE TWOLEGS...
...WHILE SQUIRRELPAW LEADS BRAMBLECLAW, RAINWHISKER, AND THORNCLAW INTO THE TWOLEGS' MONSTER.
GO! GO! GET OUT OF HERE!
WE'RE NOT LEAVING WITHOUT YOU, BRIGHTHEART!

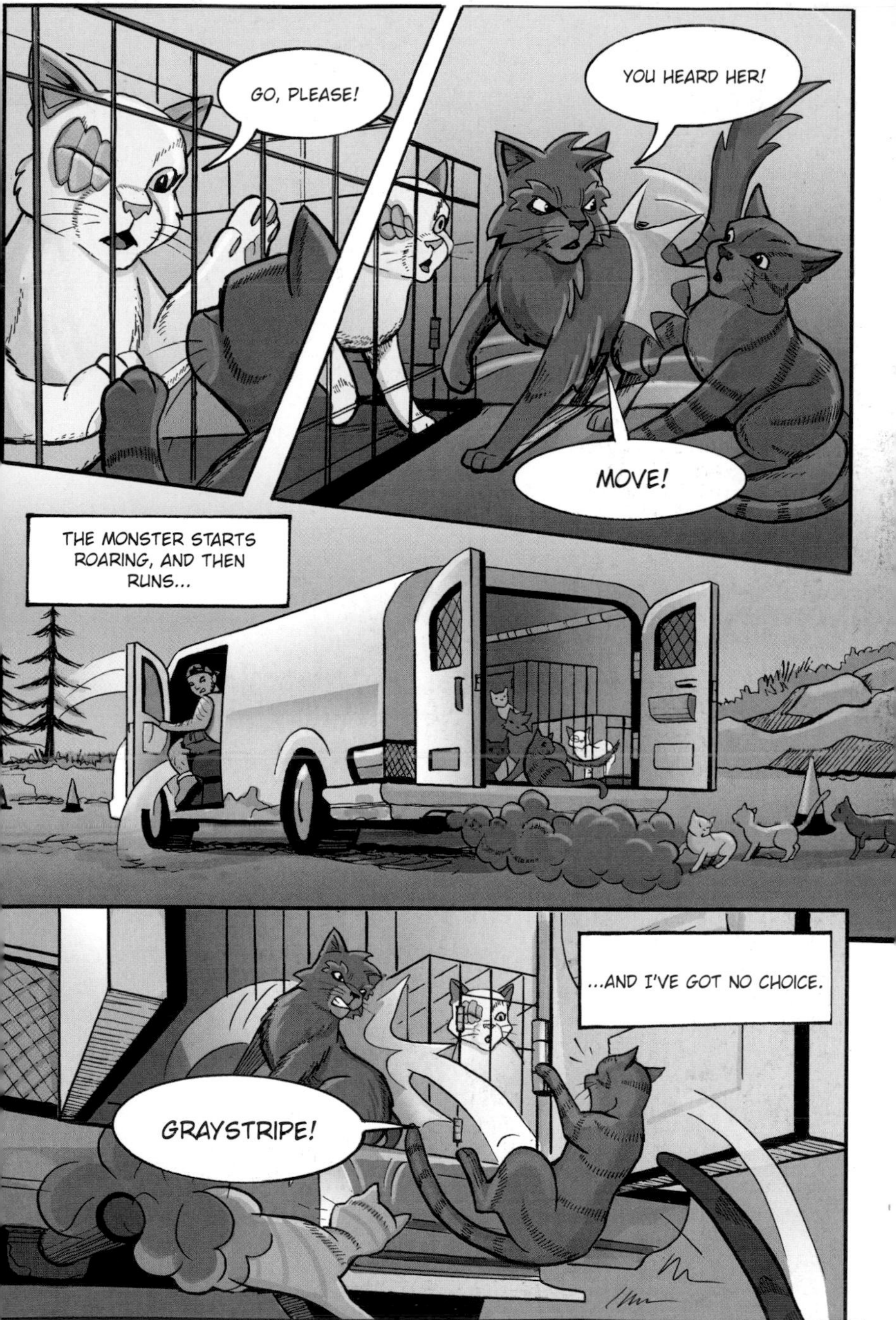
GO, PLEASE!
YOU HEARD HER!
MOVE!
THE MONSTER STARTS ROARING, AND THEN RUNS...
...AND I'VE GOT NO CHOICE.
GRAYSTRIPE!

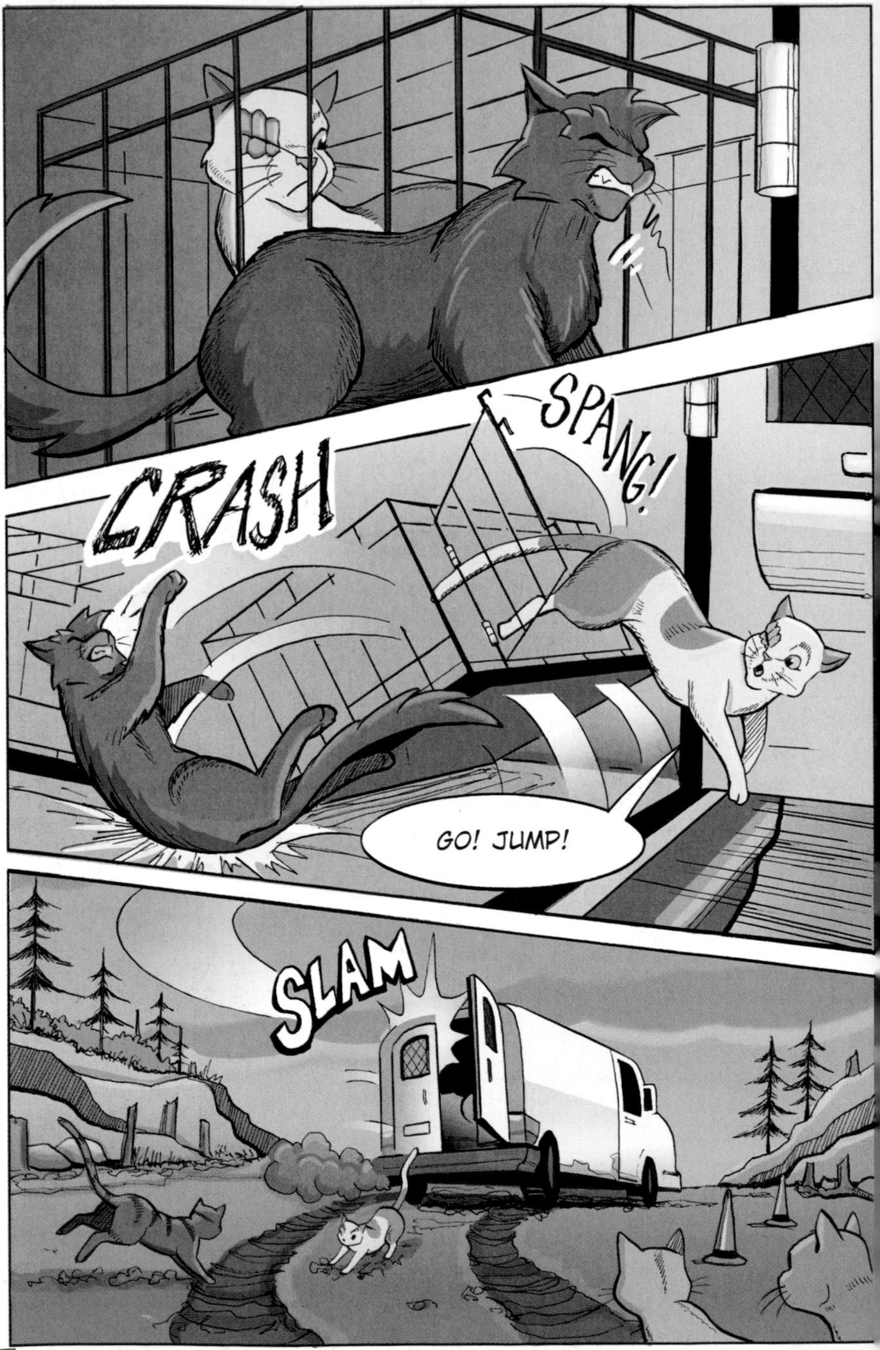
SPANG!
CRASH
GO! JUMP!
SLAM

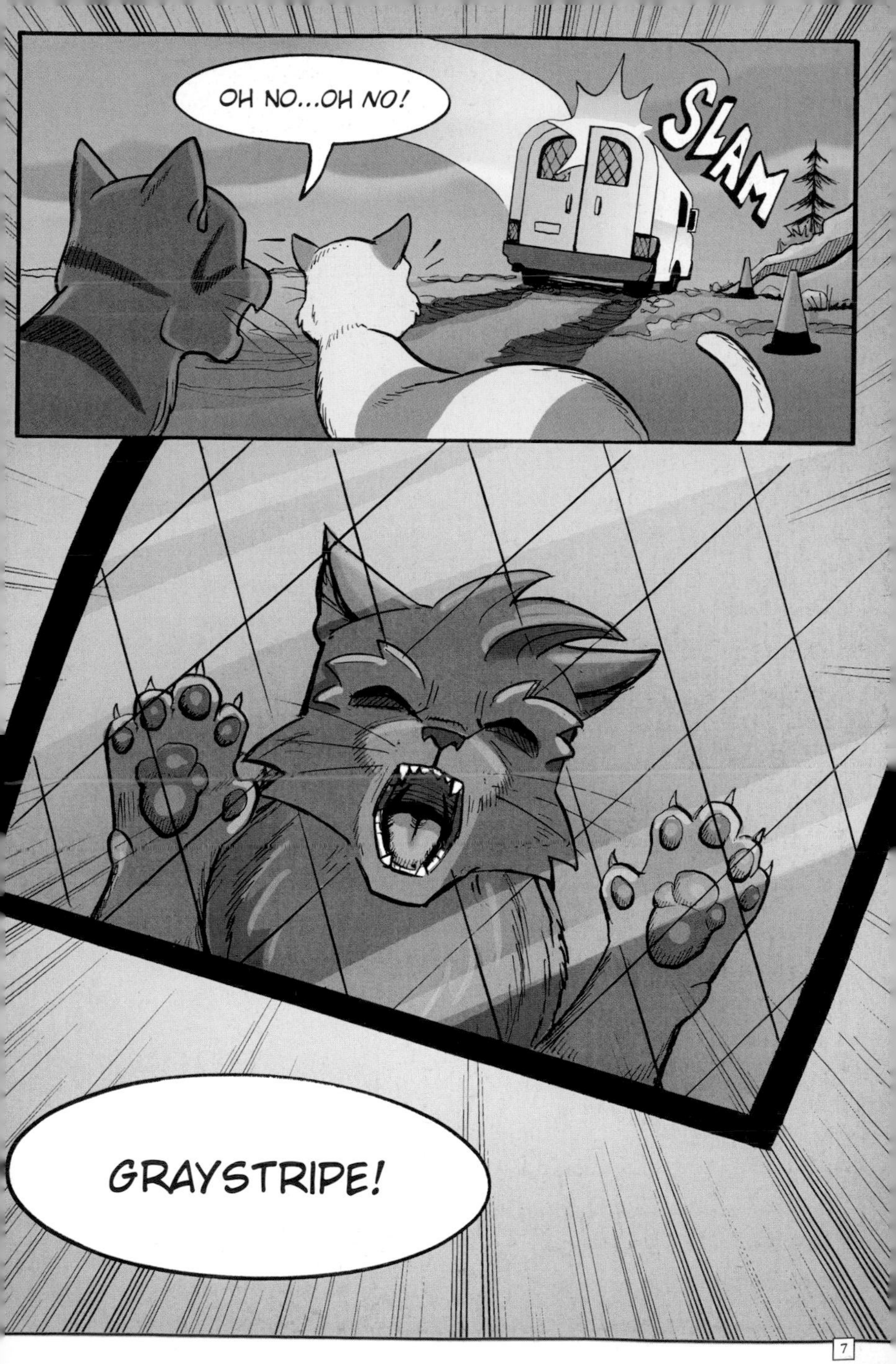
OH NO...OH NO!
SLAM
GRAYSTRIPE!

CHAPTER 1

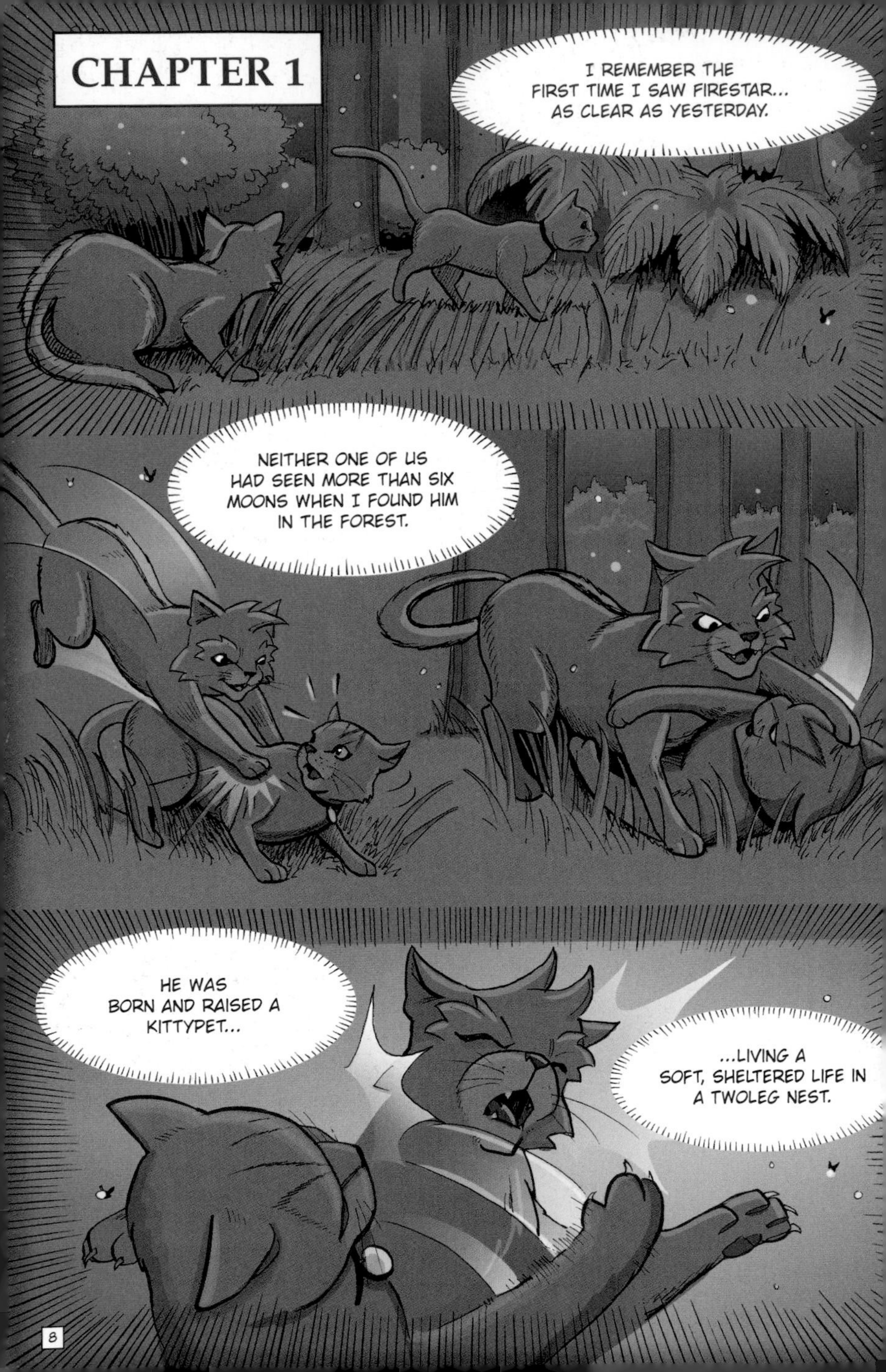
I REMEMBER THE FIRST TIME I SAW FIRESTAR... AS CLEAR AS YESTERDAY.
NEITHER ONE OF US HAD SEEN MORE THAN SIX MOONS WHEN I FOUND HIM IN THE FOREST.
HE WAS BORN AND RAISED A KITTYPET...
...LIVING A SOFT, SHELTERED LIFE IN A TWOLEG NEST.

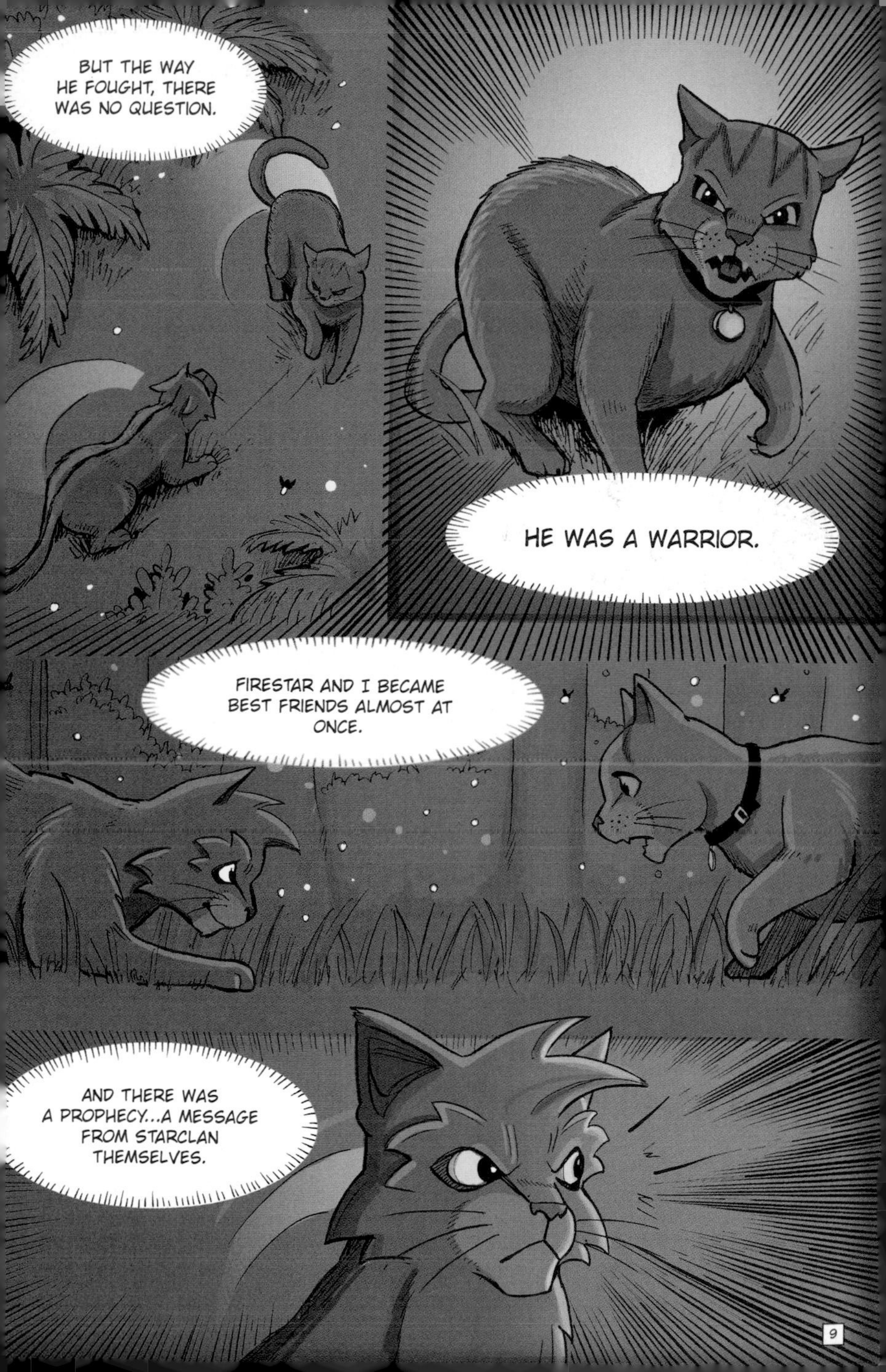
BUT THE WAY HE FOUGHT, THERE WAS NO QUESTION.
HE WAS A WARRIOR.
FIRESTAR AND I BECAME BEST FRIENDS ALMOST AT ONCE.
AND THERE WAS A PROPHECY...A MESSAGE FROM STARCLAN THEMSELVES.

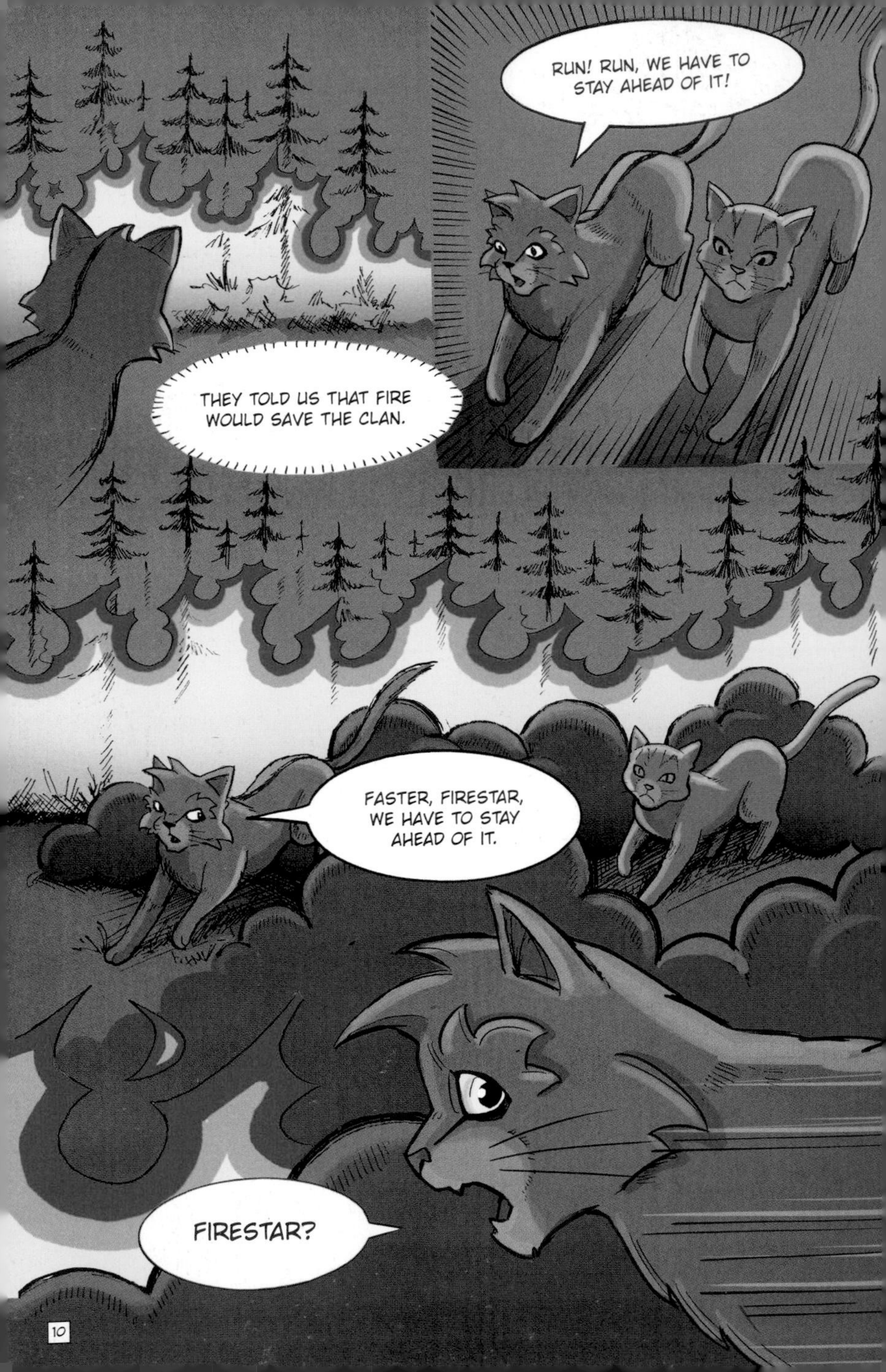
THEY TOLD US THAT FIRE WOULD SAVE THE CLAN.
RUN! RUN, WE HAVE TO STAY AHEAD OF IT!
FASTER, FIRESTAR, WE HAVE TO STAY AHEAD OF IT.
FIRESTAR?

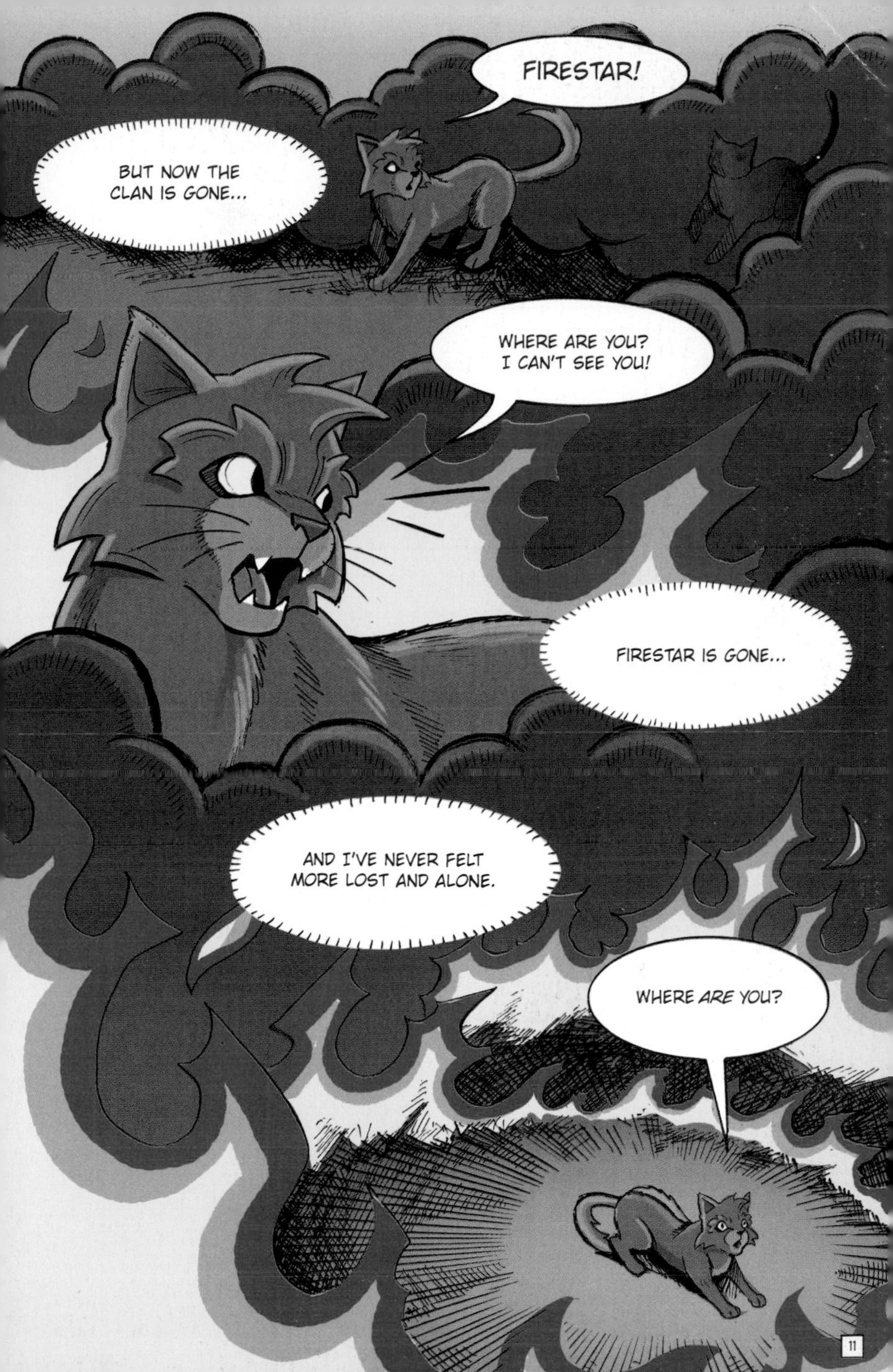
BUT NOW THE CLAN IS GONE...
FIRESTAR!
WHERE ARE YOU? I CAN'T SEE YOU!
FIRESTAR IS GONE...
AND I'VE NEVER FELT MORE LOST AND ALONE.
WHERE *ARE* YOU?

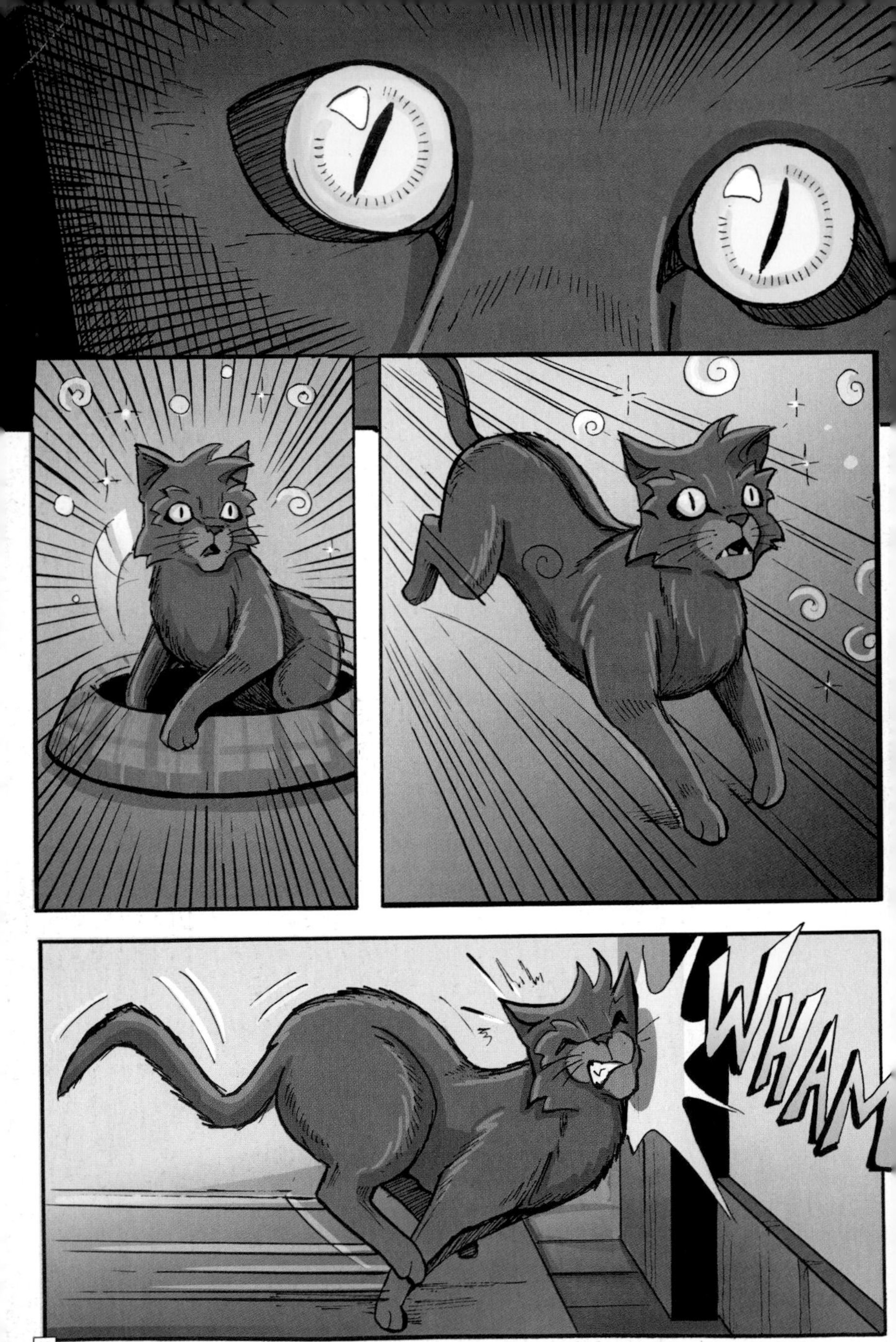
WHAM

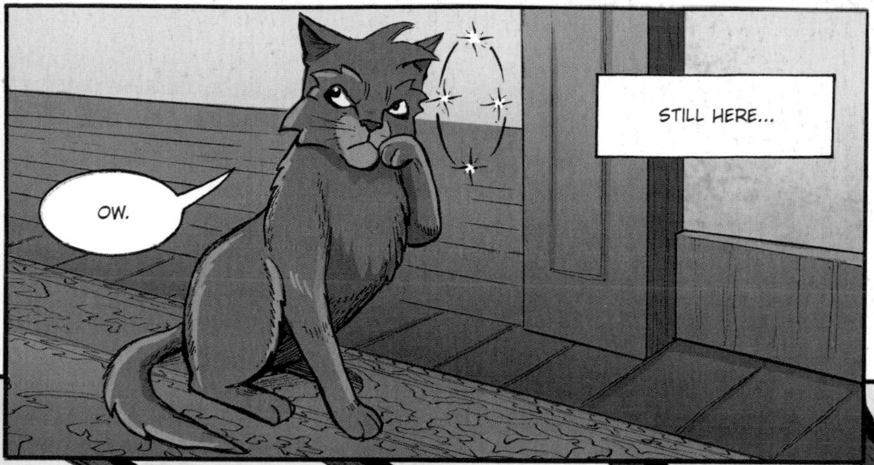
OW.
STILL HERE...
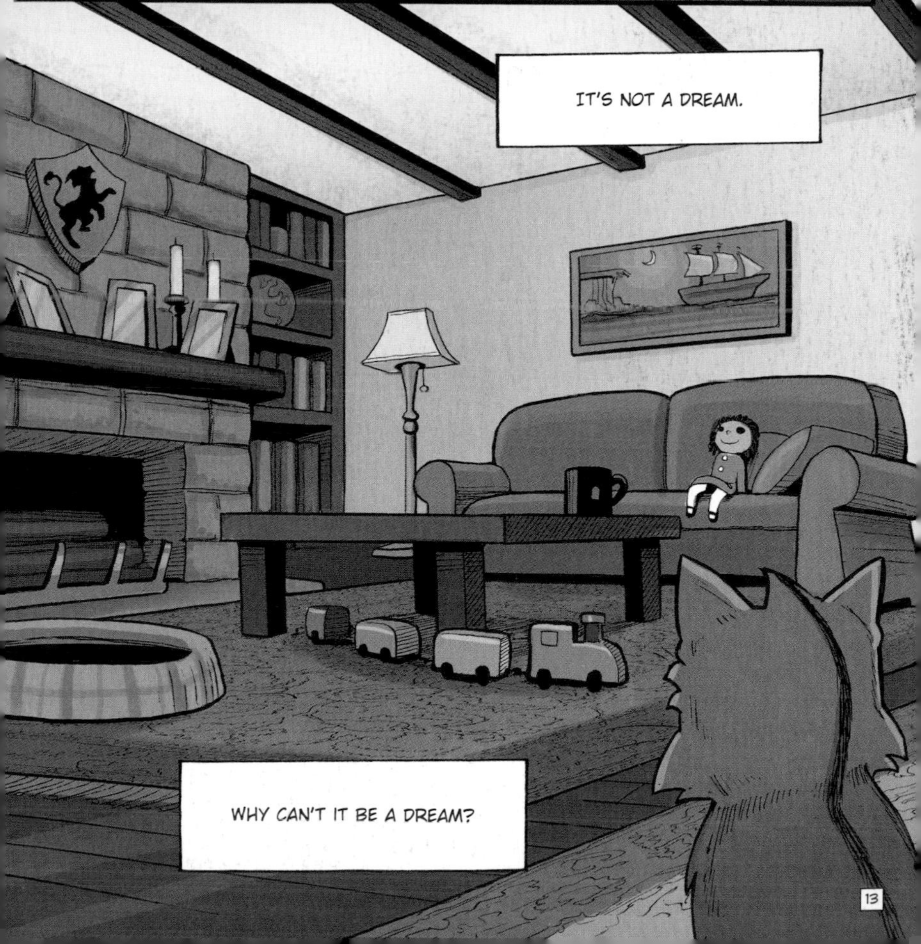
IT'S NOT A DREAM.
WHY CAN'T IT BE A DREAM?

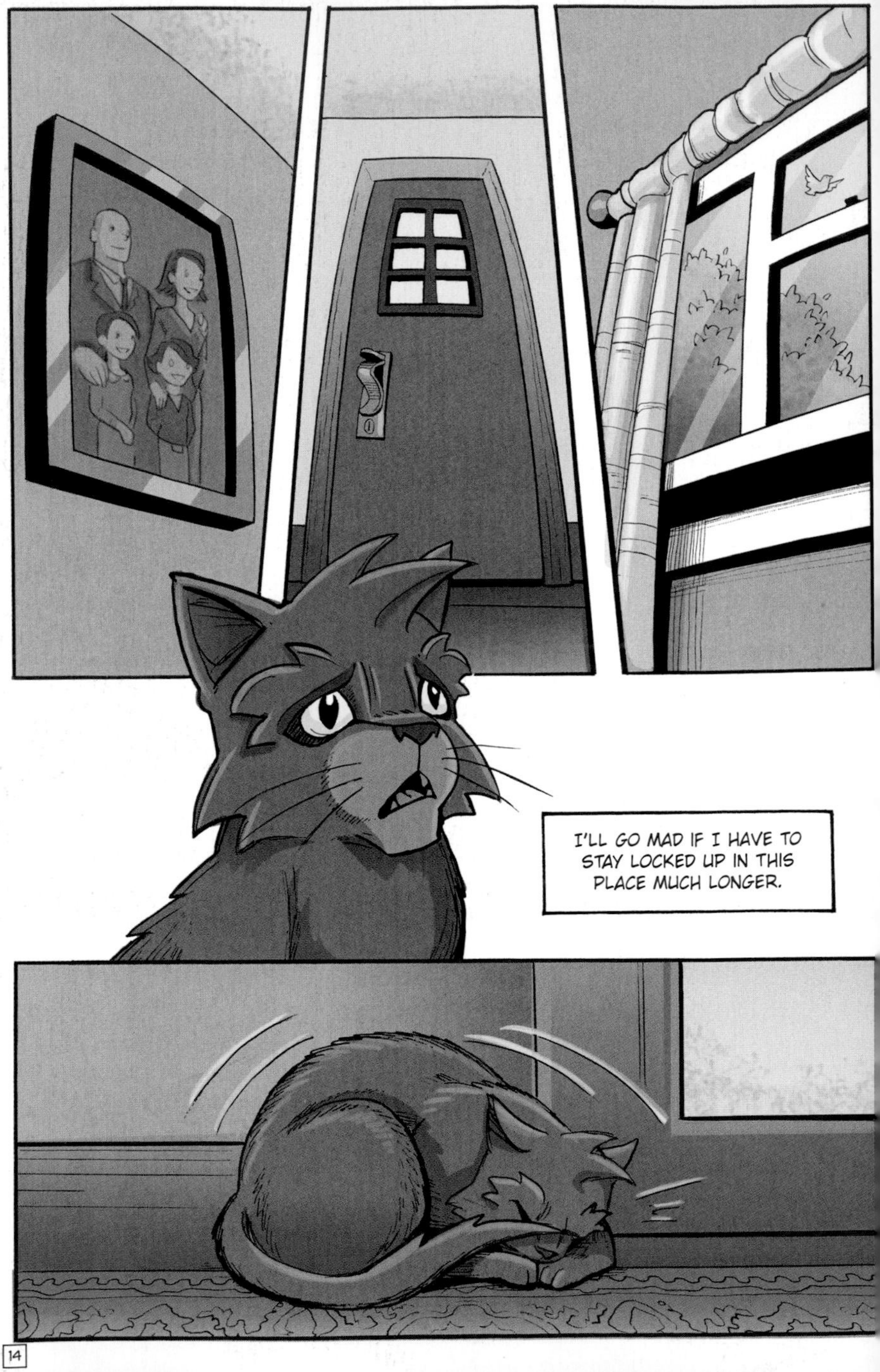
I'LL GO MAD IF I HAVE TO STAY LOCKED UP IN THIS PLACE MUCH LONGER.

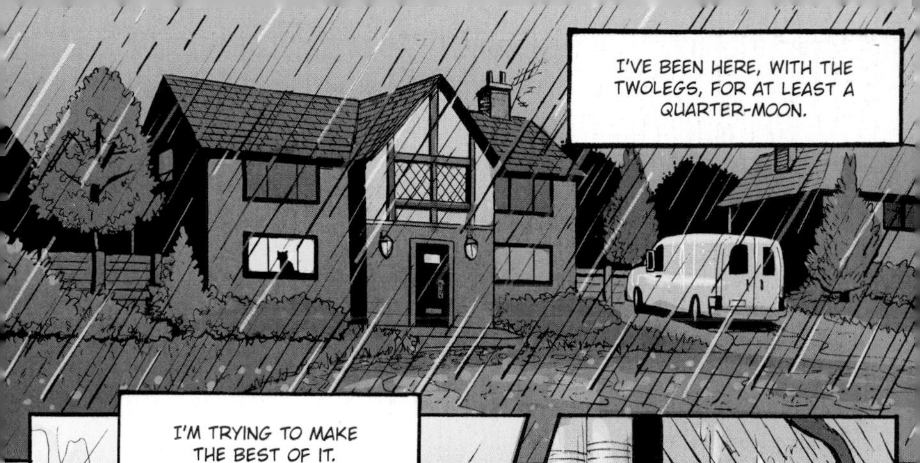
I'VE BEEN HERE, WITH THE TWOLEGS, FOR AT LEAST A QUARTER-MOON.

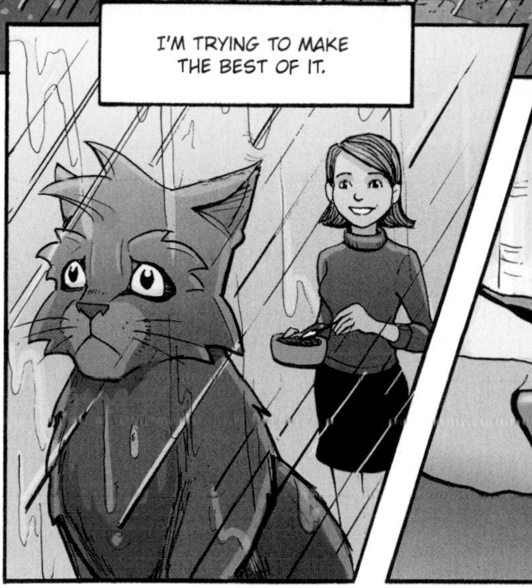
I'M TRYING TO MAKE THE BEST OF IT.

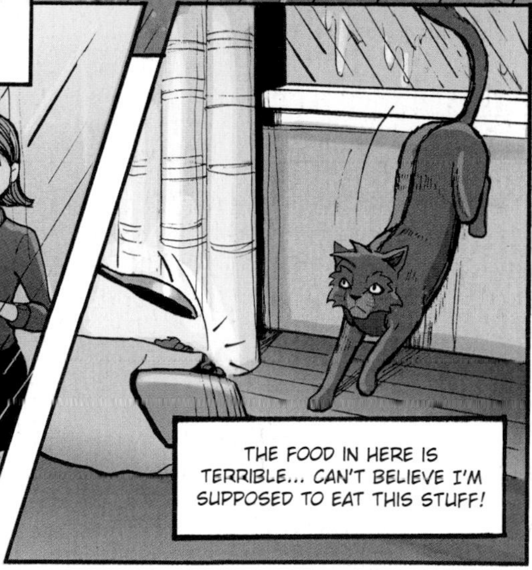
THE FOOD IN HERE IS TERRIBLE... CAN'T BELIEVE I'M SUPPOSED TO EAT THIS STUFF!

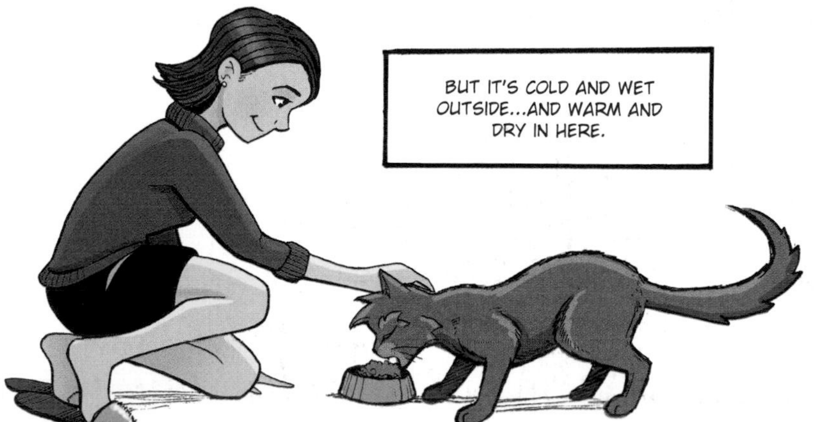
BUT IT'S COLD AND WET OUTSIDE...AND WARM AND DRY IN HERE.

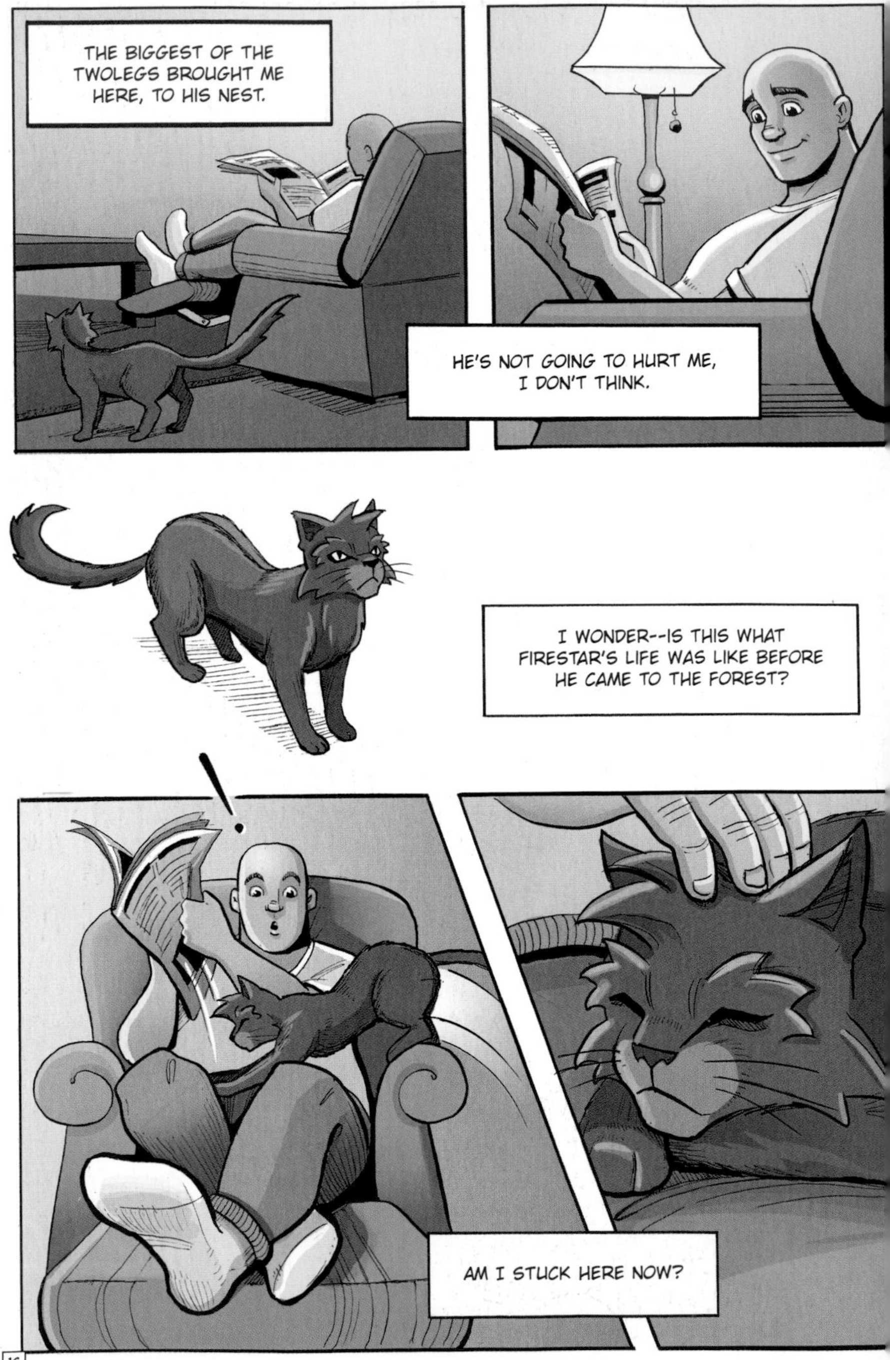
THE BIGGEST OF THE TWOLEGS BROUGHT ME HERE, TO HIS NEST.
HE'S NOT GOING TO HURT ME, I DON'T THINK.
I WONDER--IS THIS WHAT FIRESTAR'S LIFE WAS LIKE BEFORE HE CAME TO THE FOREST?
!
AM I STUCK HERE NOW?

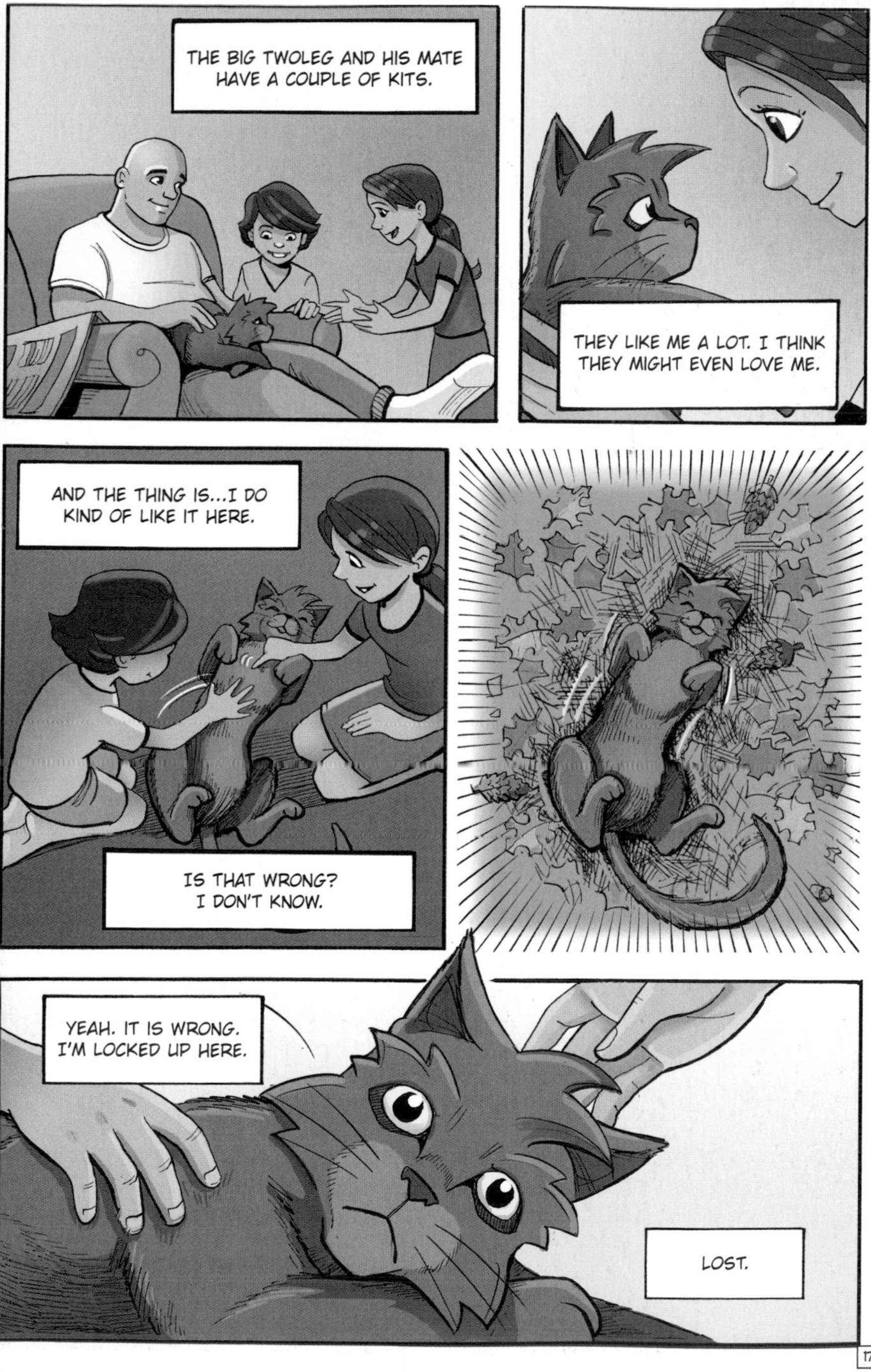
THE BIG TWOLEG AND HIS MATE HAVE A COUPLE OF KITS.
THEY LIKE ME A LOT. I THINK THEY MIGHT EVEN LOVE ME.
AND THE THING IS...I DO KIND OF LIKE IT HERE.
IS THAT WRONG? I DON'T KNOW.
YEAH. IT IS WRONG. I'M LOCKED UP HERE.
LOST.

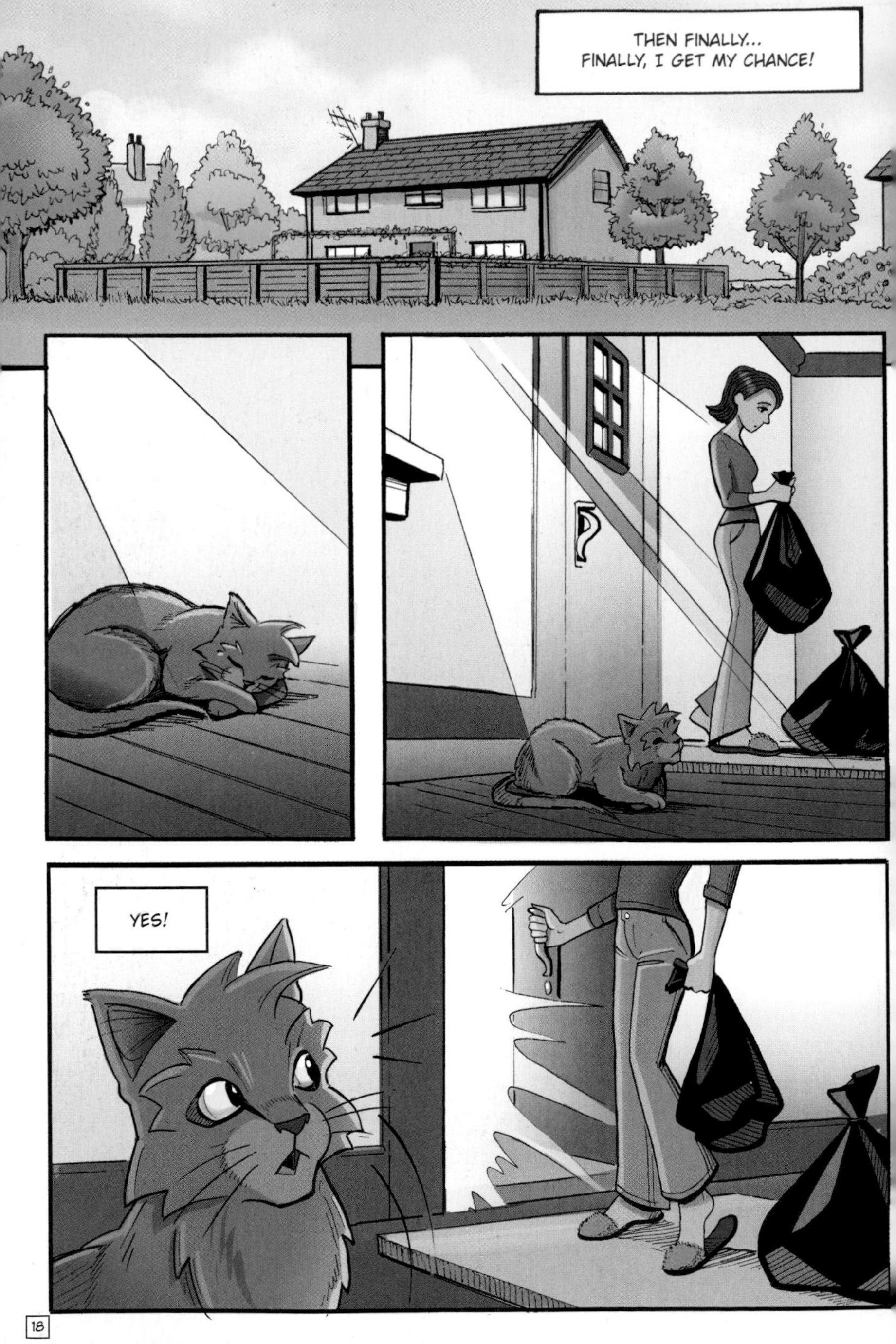
THEN FINALLY...
FINALLY, I GET MY CHANCE!
YES!

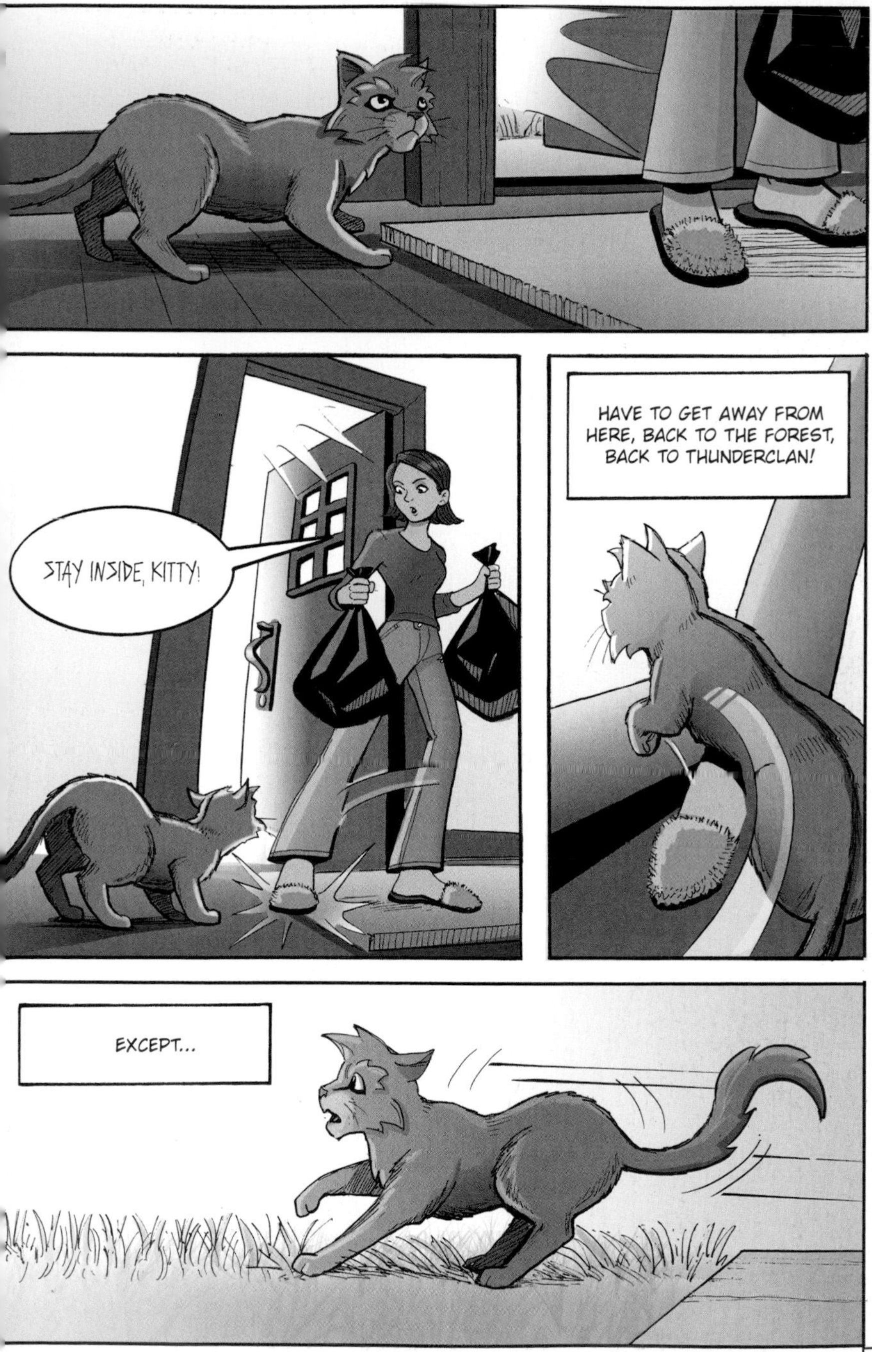
STAY INSIDE, KITTY!
HAVE TO GET AWAY FROM HERE, BACK TO THE FOREST, BACK TO THUNDERCLAN!
EXCEPT...

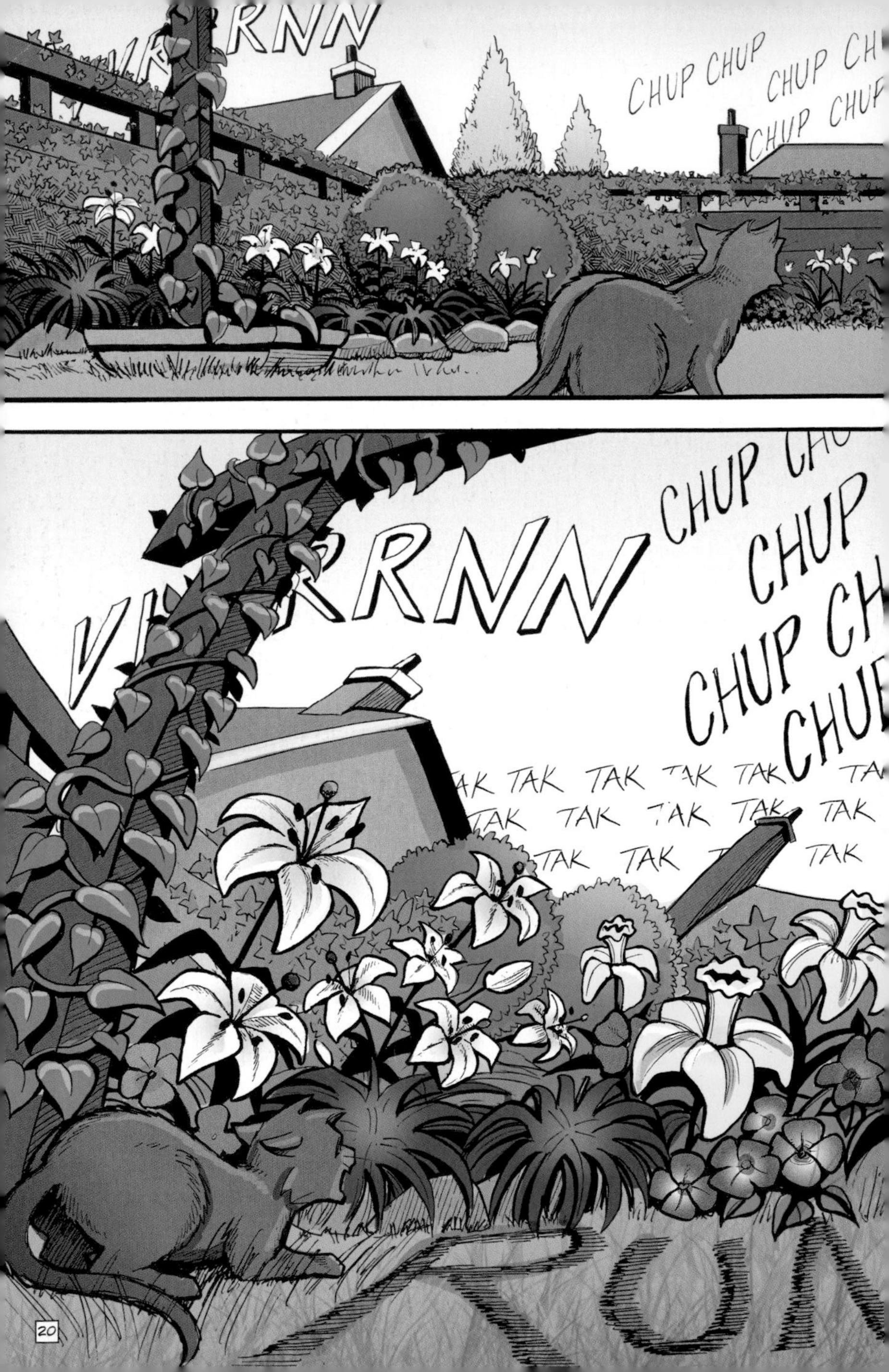
RNN
CHUP CHUP
CHUP CH
CHUP CHUP
RNN
CHUP
CHUP
CHUP CH
CHUP
TAK TAK TAK TAK TAK
TAK TAK TAK TAK TAK
TAK TAK TAK

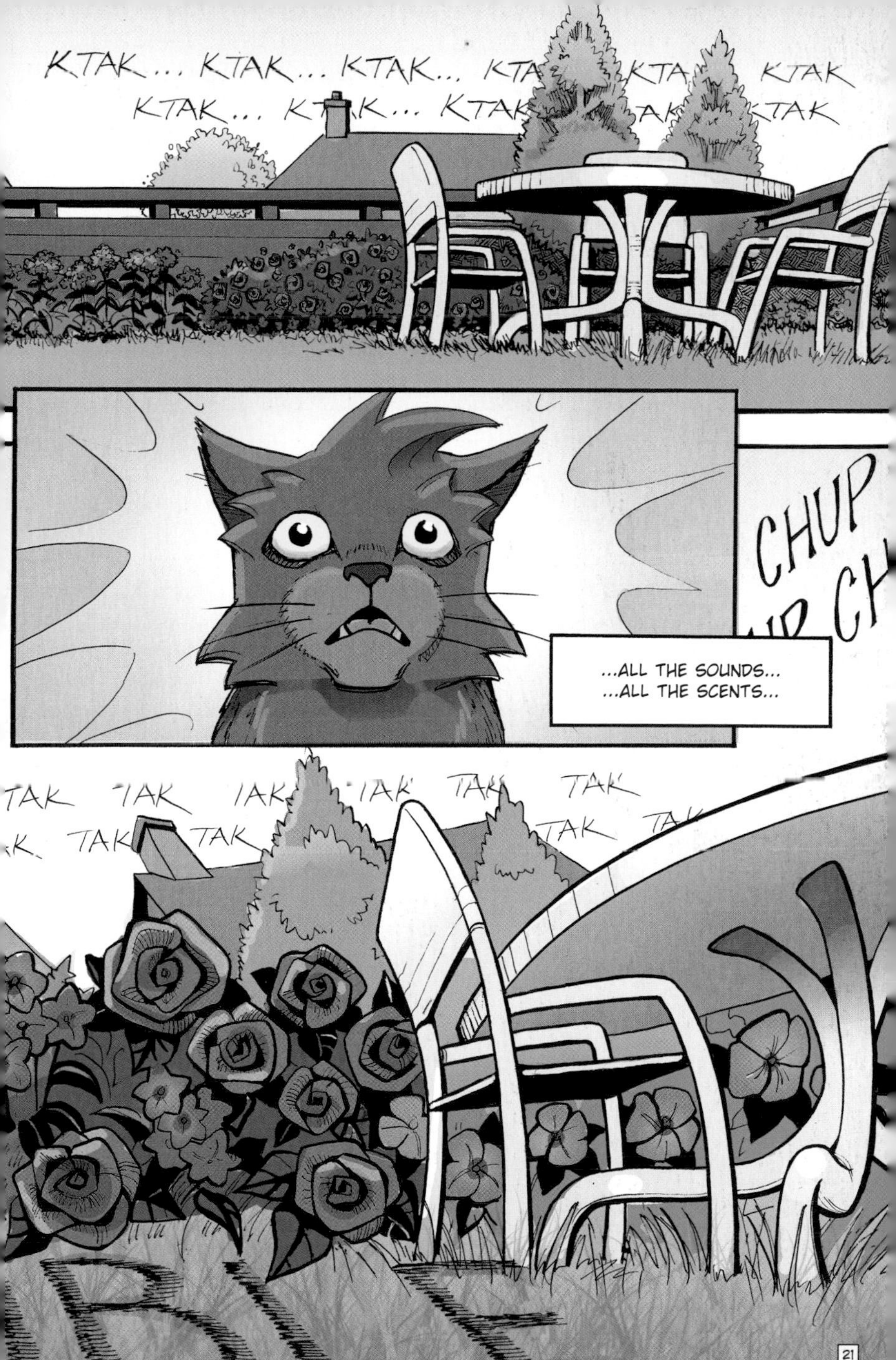
KTAK... KTAK... KTAK... KTAK
KTAK... KTAK...
CHUP
...ALL THE SOUNDS...
...ALL THE SCENTS...
TAK TAK TAK TAK
TAK TAK TAK

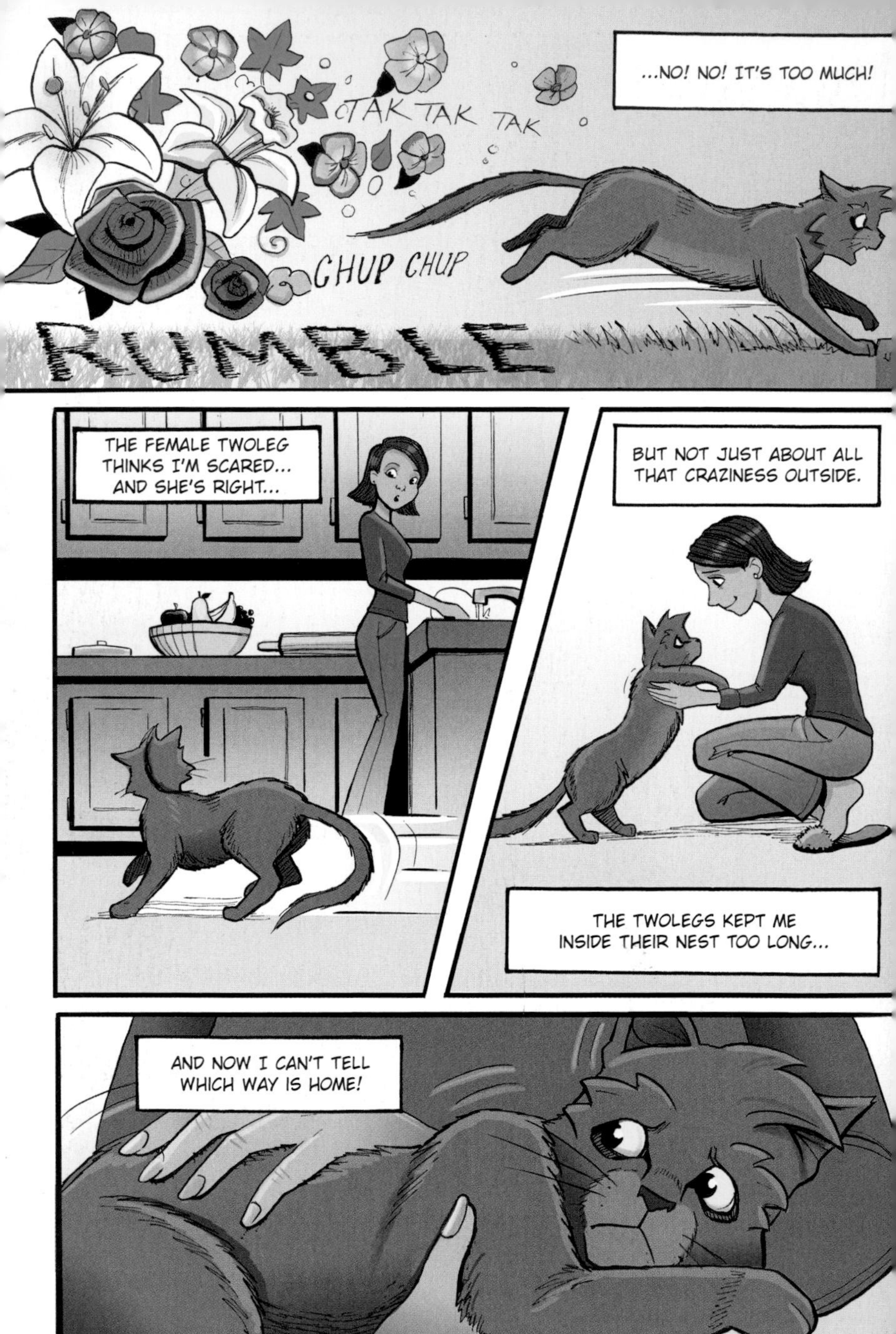
...NO! NO! IT'S TOO MUCH!
TAK TAK TAK
CHUP CHUP
RUMBLE
THE FEMALE TWOLEG THINKS I'M SCARED... AND SHE'S RIGHT...
BUT NOT JUST ABOUT ALL THAT CRAZINESS OUTSIDE.
THE TWOLEGS KEPT ME INSIDE THEIR NEST TOO LONG...
AND NOW I CAN'T TELL WHICH WAY IS HOME!

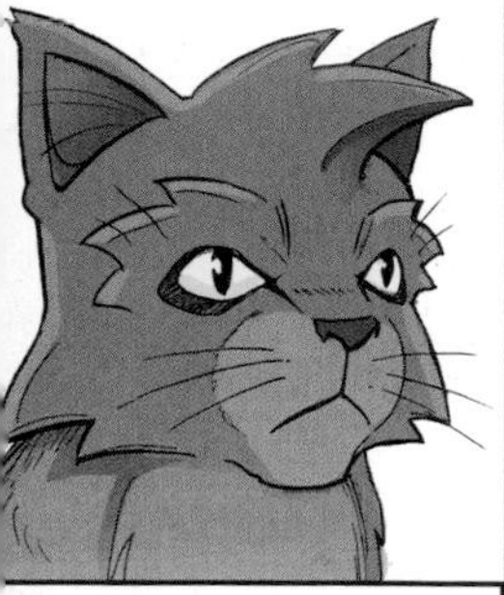

CHAPTER 2

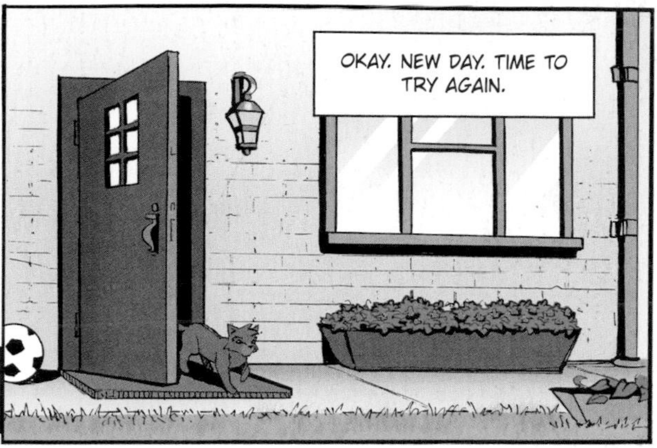
OKAY. NEW DAY. TIME TO TRY AGAIN.

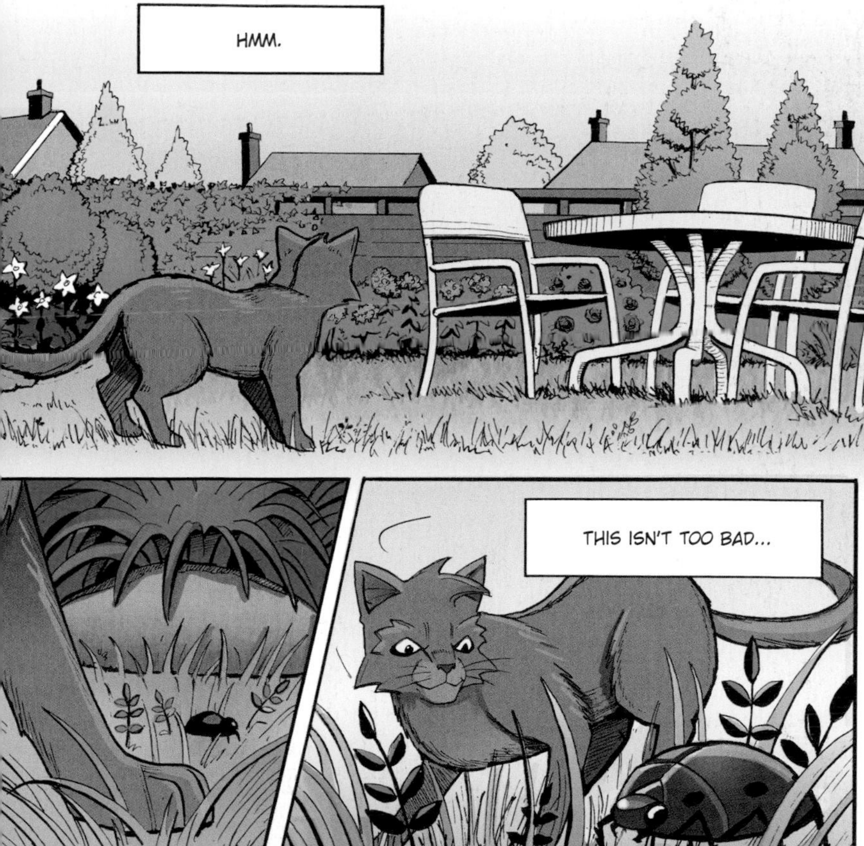
HMM.
THIS ISN'T TOO BAD...

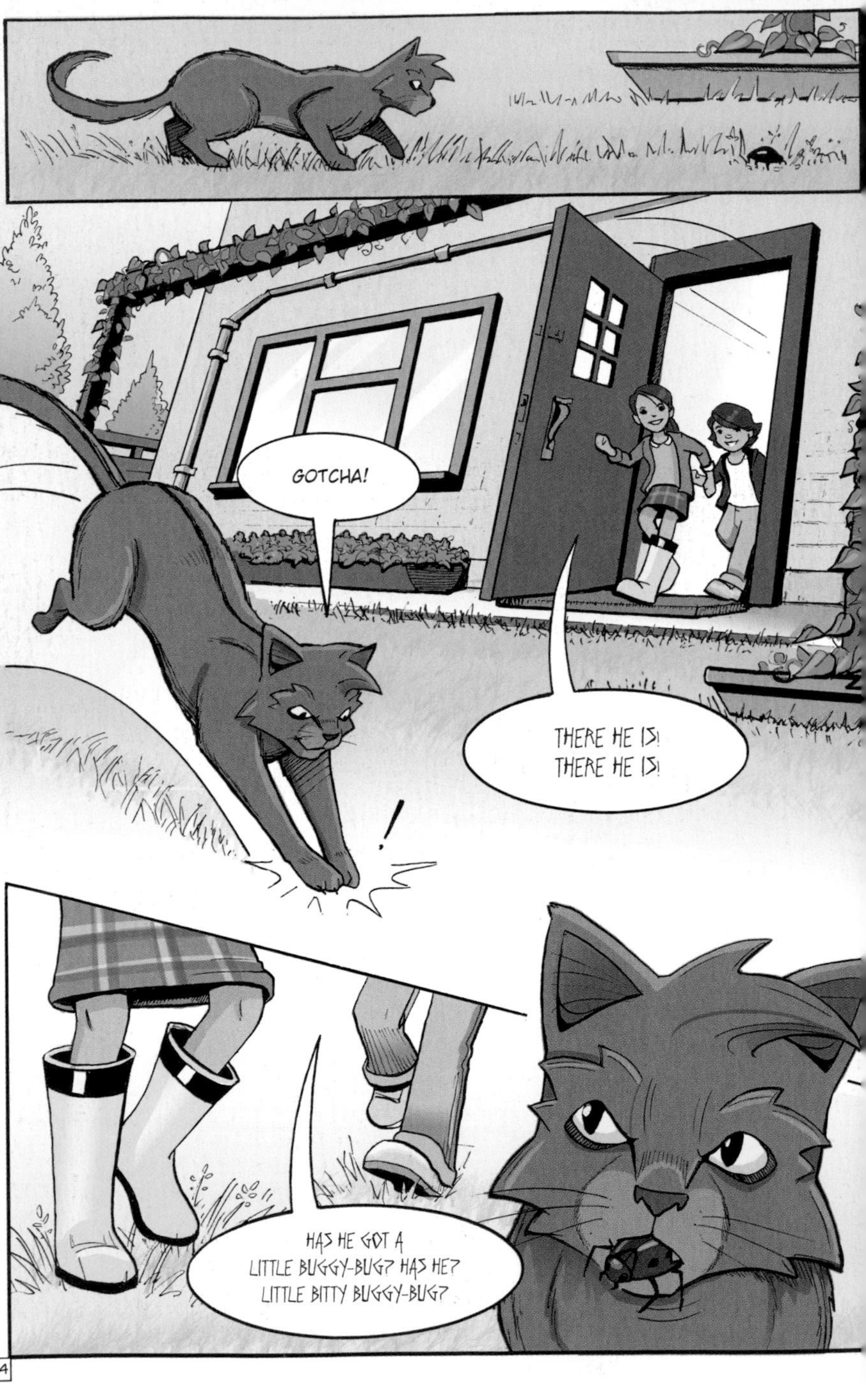
GOTCHA!
THERE HE IS! THERE HE IS!
HAS HE GOT A LITTLE BUGGY-BUG? HAS HE? LITTLE BITTY BUGGY-BUG?

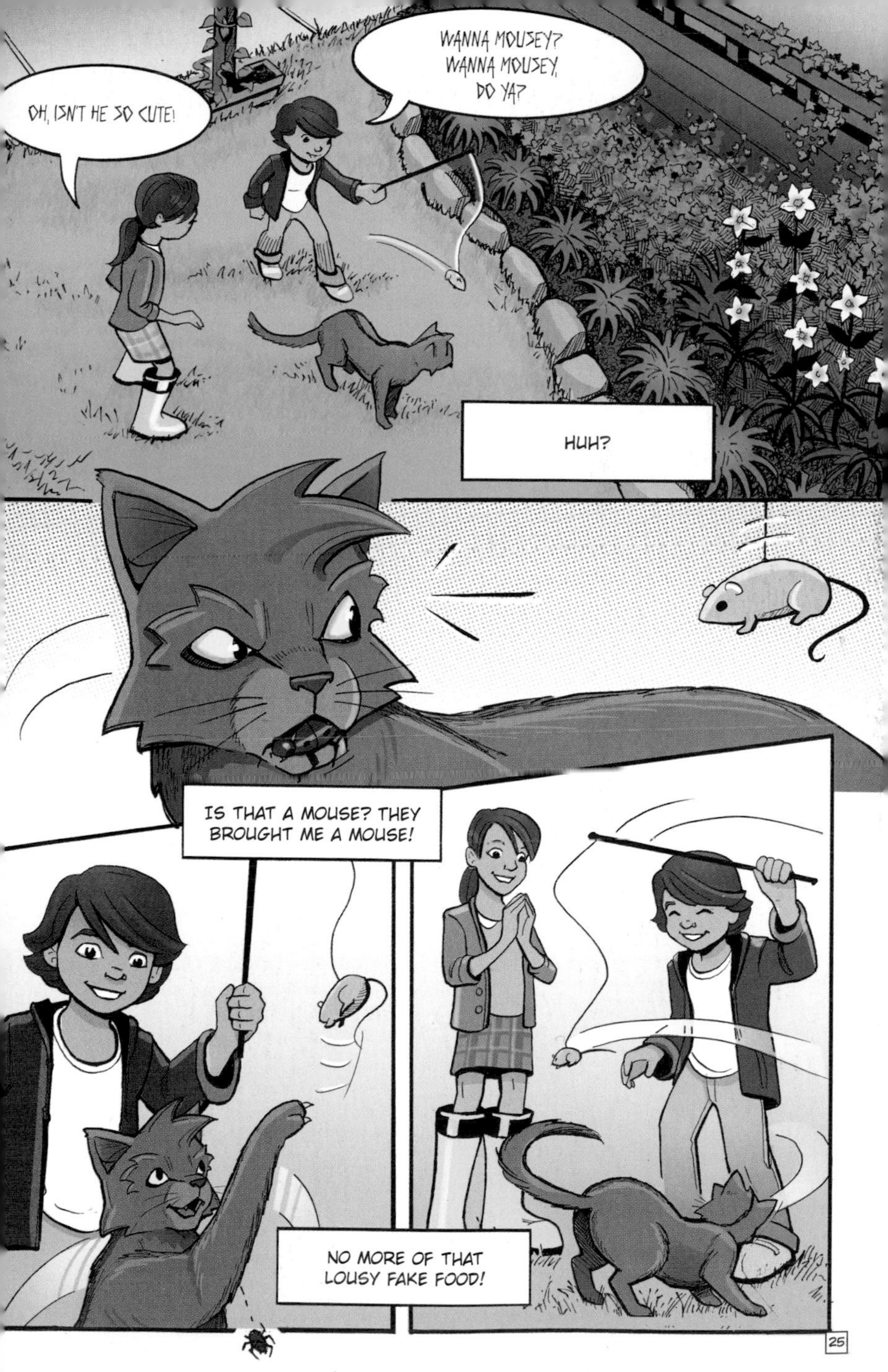

OH, ISN'T HE SO CUTE!
WANNA MOUSEY? WANNA MOUSEY, DO YA?
HUH?
IS THAT A MOUSE? THEY BROUGHT ME A MOUSE!
NO MORE OF THAT LOUSY FAKE FOOD!

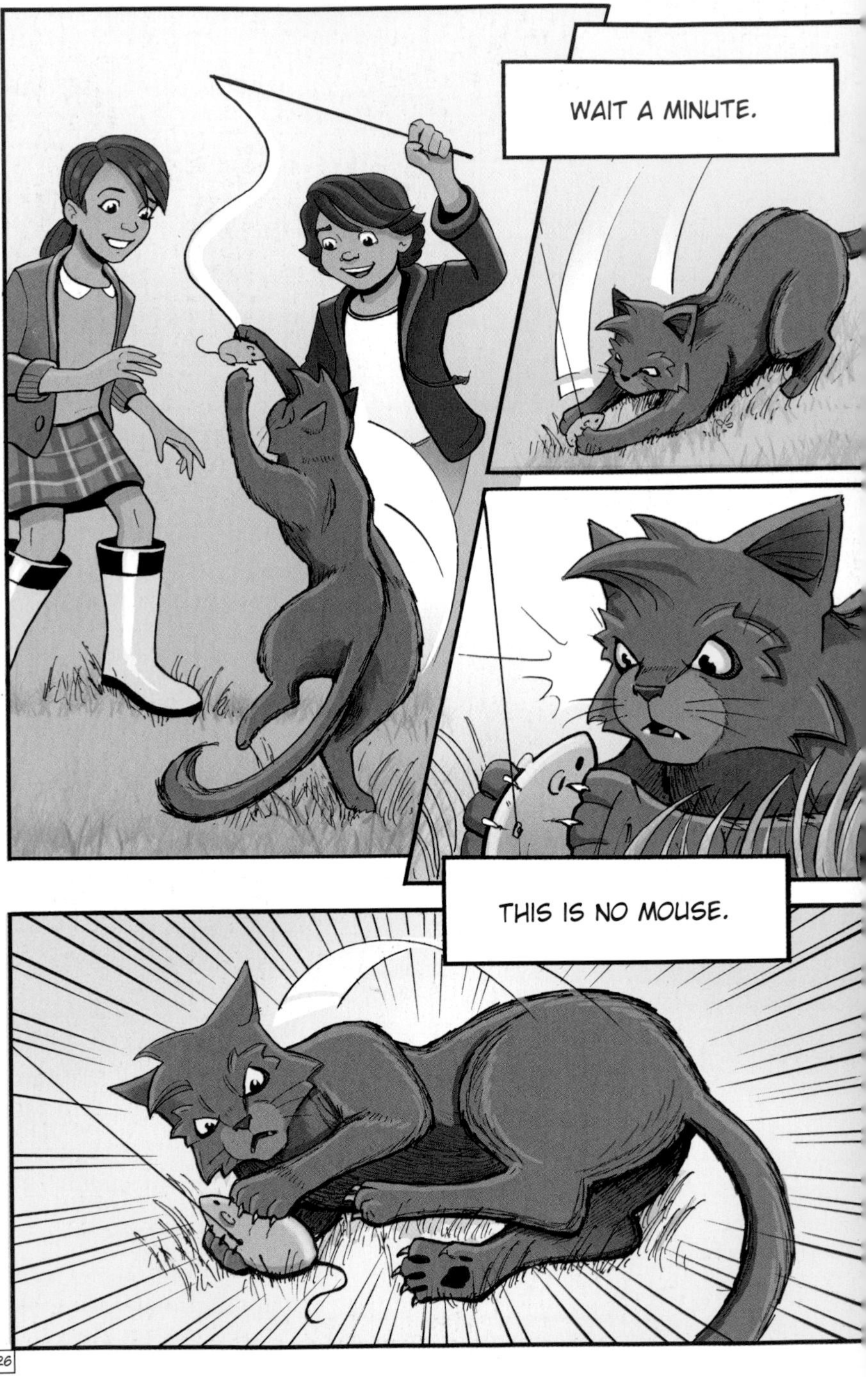
WAIT A MINUTE.
THIS IS NO MOUSE.

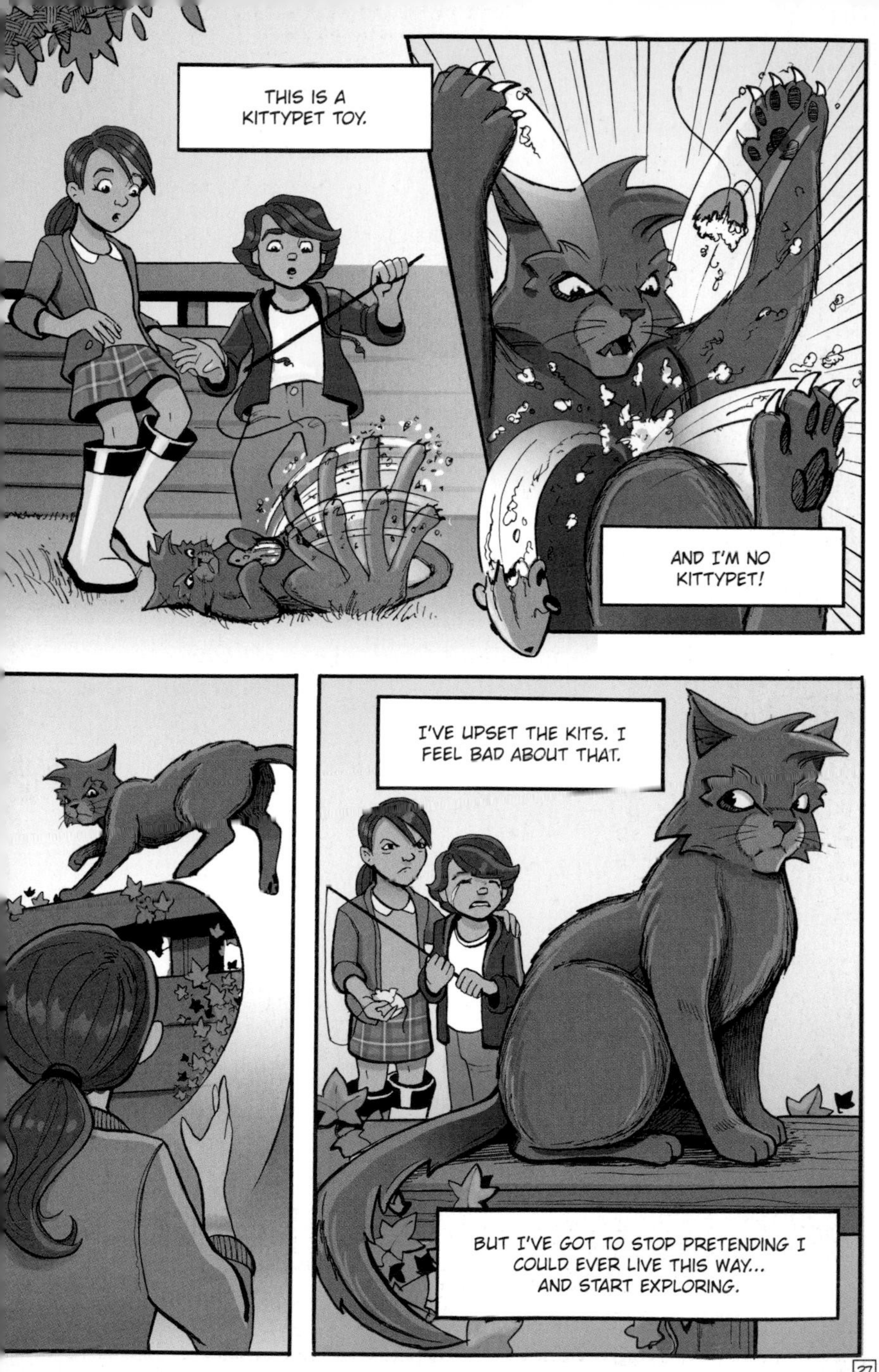
THIS IS A KITTYPET TOY.
AND I'M NO KITTYPET!
I'VE UPSET THE KITS. I FEEL BAD ABOUT THAT.
BUT I'VE GOT TO STOP PRETENDING I COULD EVER LIVE THIS WAY... AND START EXPLORING.

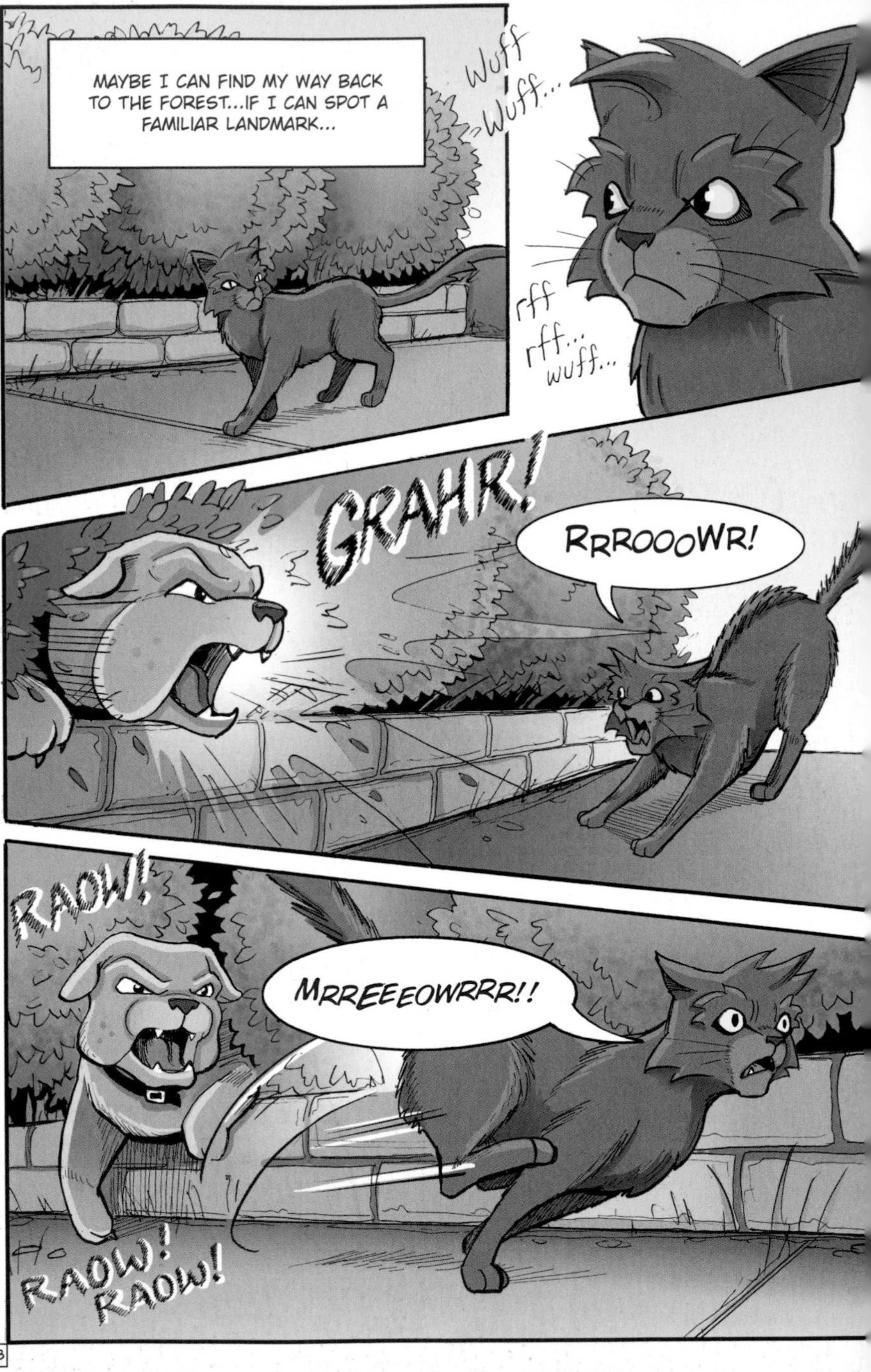

MAYBE I CAN FIND MY WAY BACK TO THE FOREST...IF I CAN SPOT A FAMILIAR LANDMARK...
Wuff
Wuff...
rff
rff...
wuff...
GRAHR!
RRROOOWR!
RAOW!
MRREEEOWRRR!!
RAOW!
RAOW!

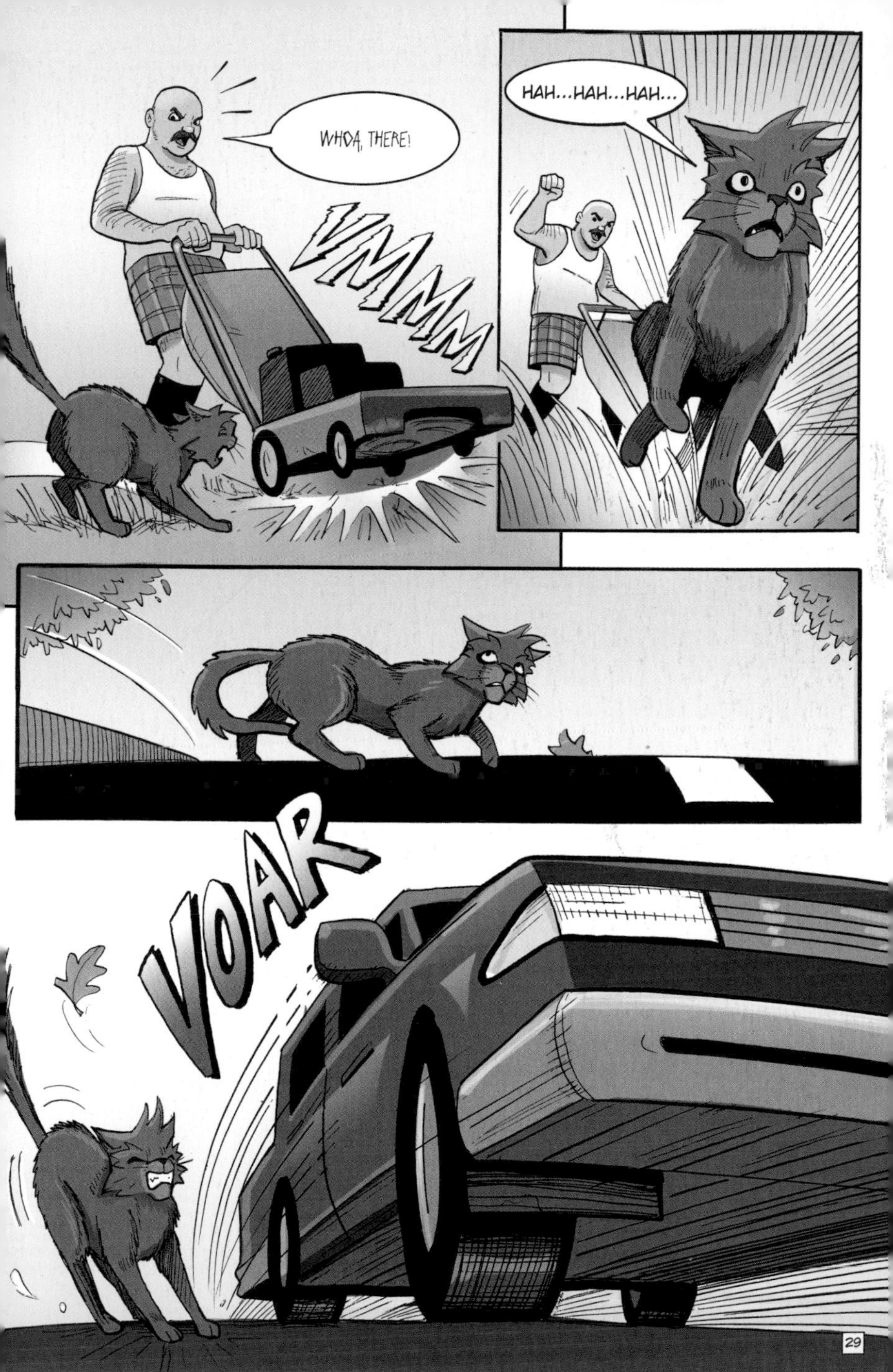
WHOA, THERE!
VMMMM
HAH...HAH...HAH...
VOAR

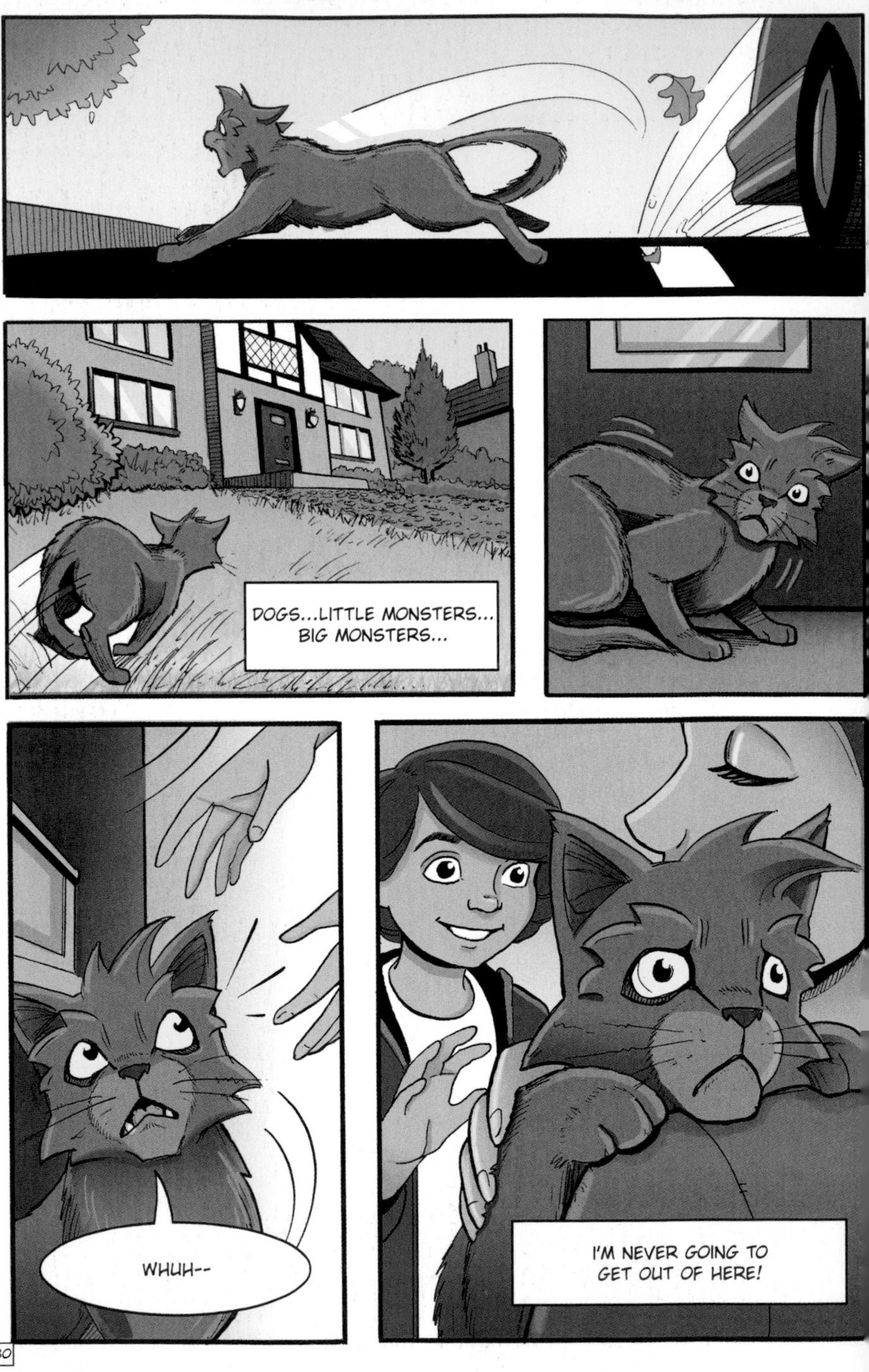
DOGS...LITTLE MONSTERS... BIG MONSTERS...
WHUH--
I'M NEVER GOING TO GET OUT OF HERE!

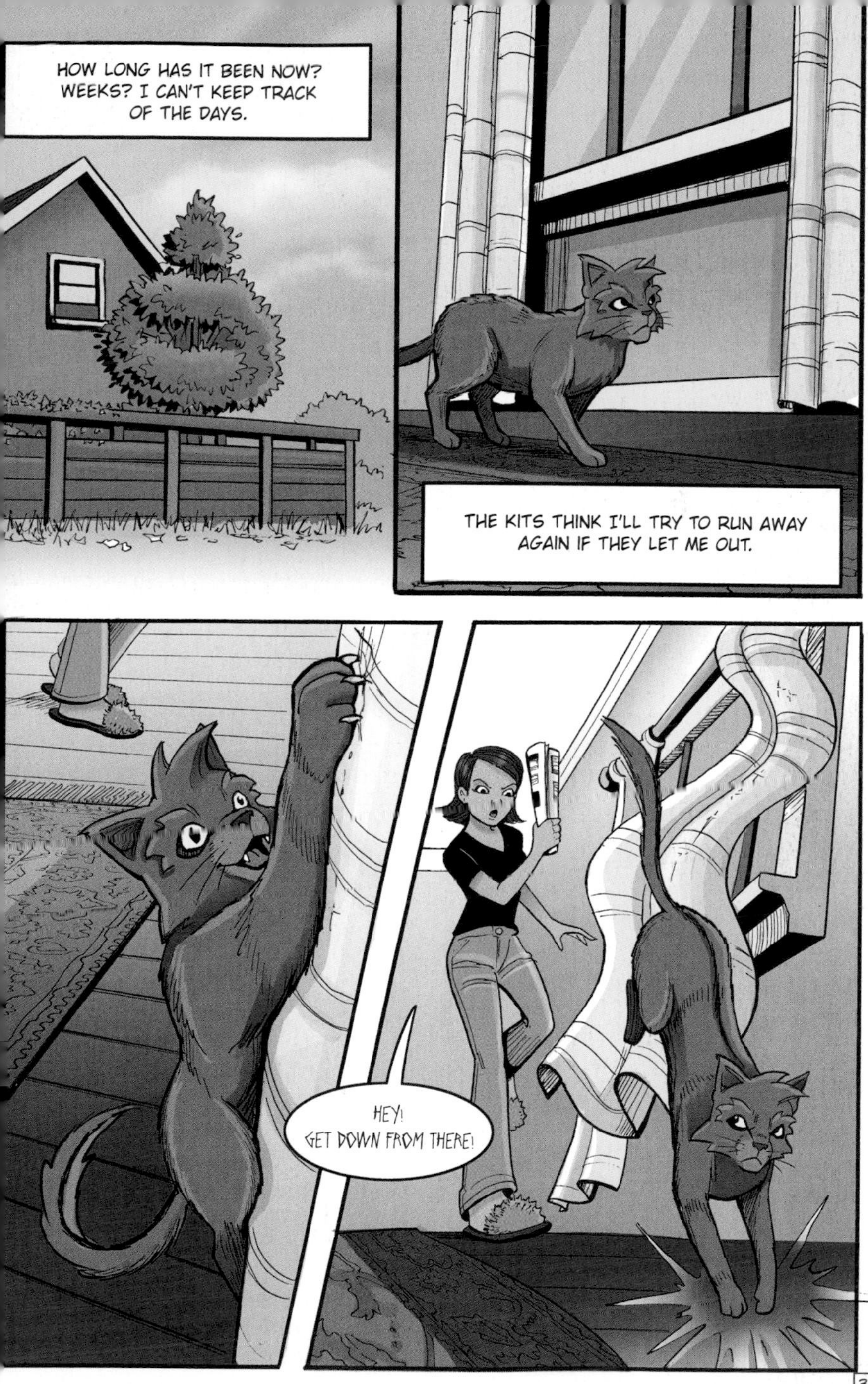
HOW LONG HAS IT BEEN NOW? WEEKS? I CAN'T KEEP TRACK OF THE DAYS.
THE KITS THINK I'LL TRY TO RUN AWAY AGAIN IF THEY LET ME OUT.
HEY! GET DOWN FROM THERE!

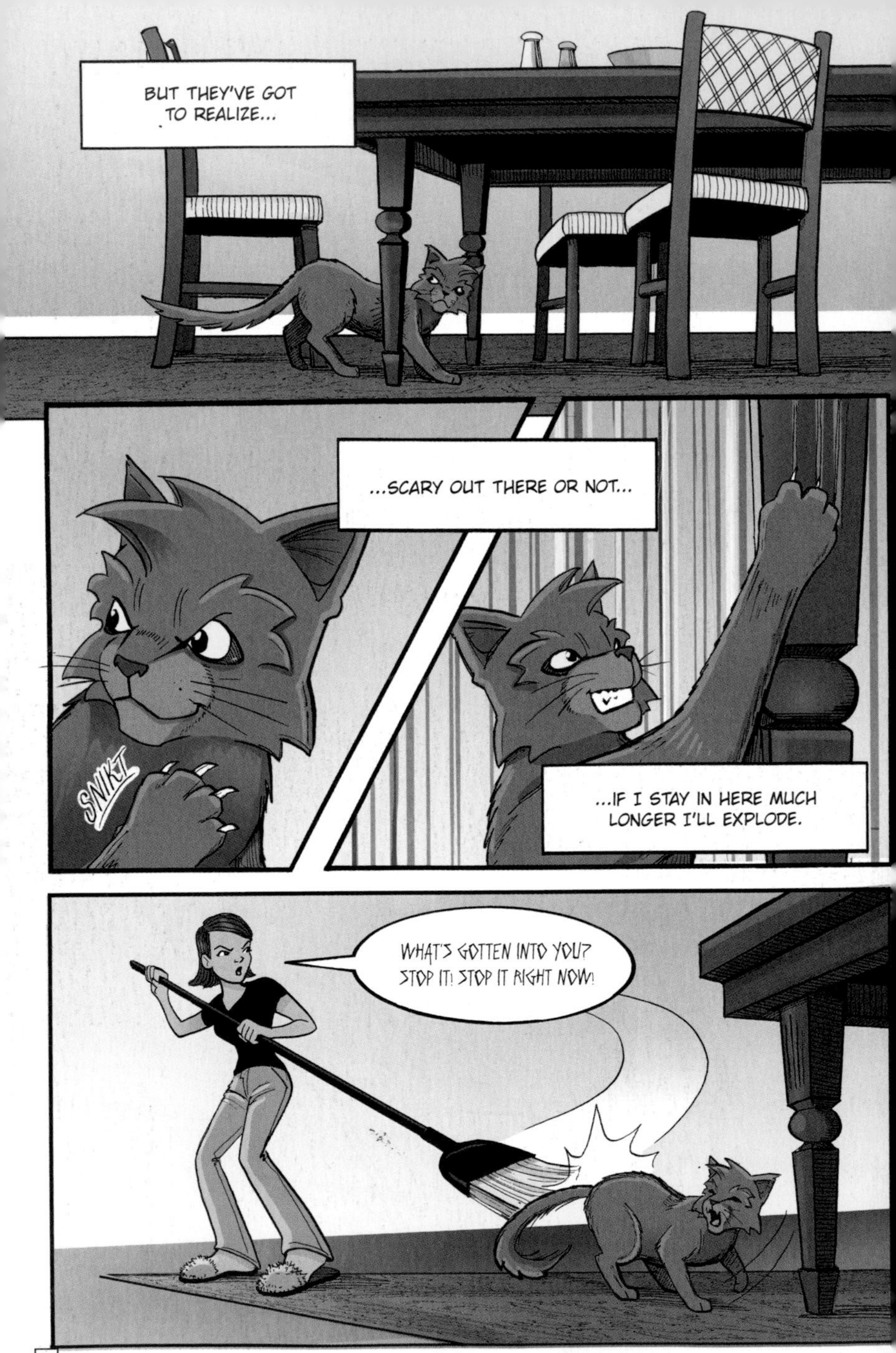
BUT THEY'VE GOT TO REALIZE...
SNIKT
...SCARY OUT THERE OR NOT...
...IF I STAY IN HERE MUCH LONGER I'LL EXPLODE.
WHAT'S GOTTEN INTO YOU? STOP IT! STOP IT RIGHT NOW!

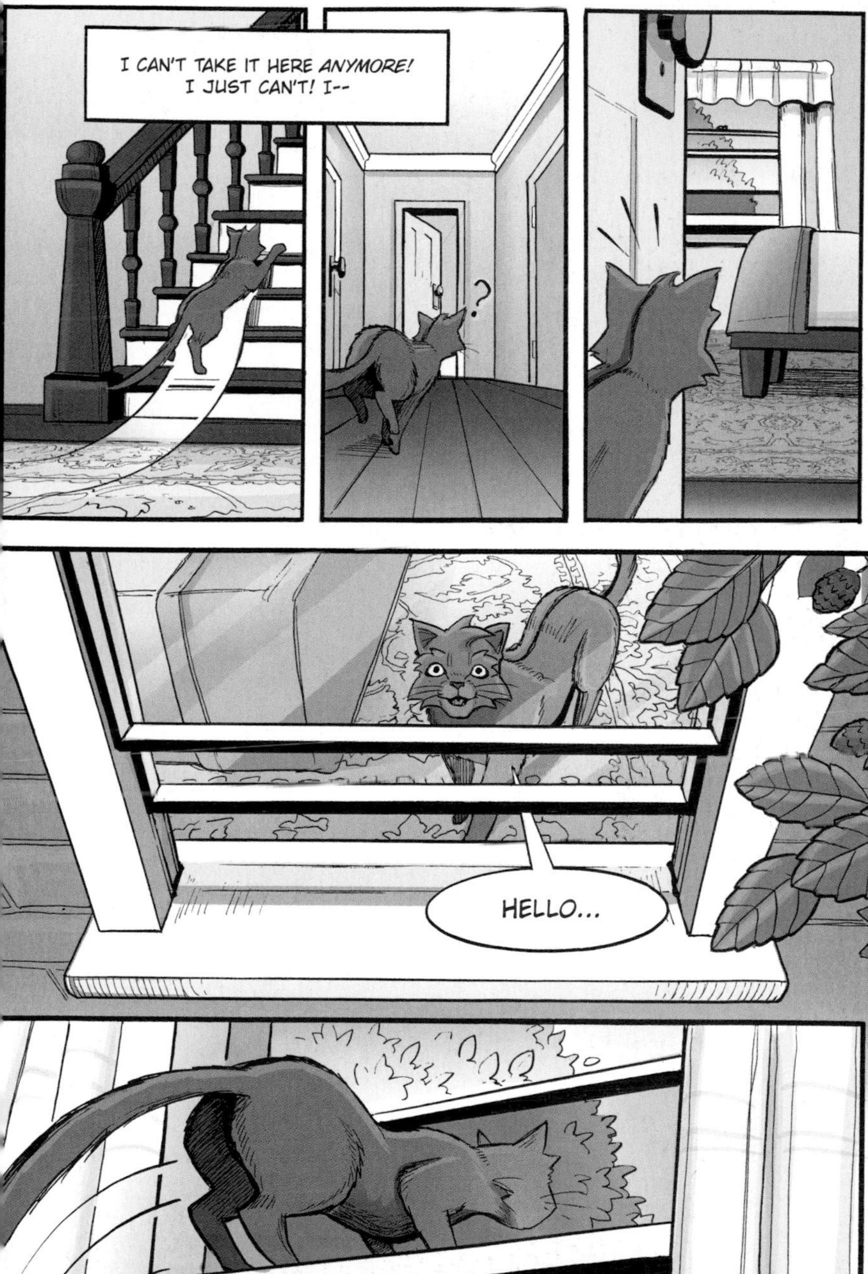
I CAN'T TAKE IT HERE *ANYMORE!* I JUST CAN'T! I--
?
HELLO...

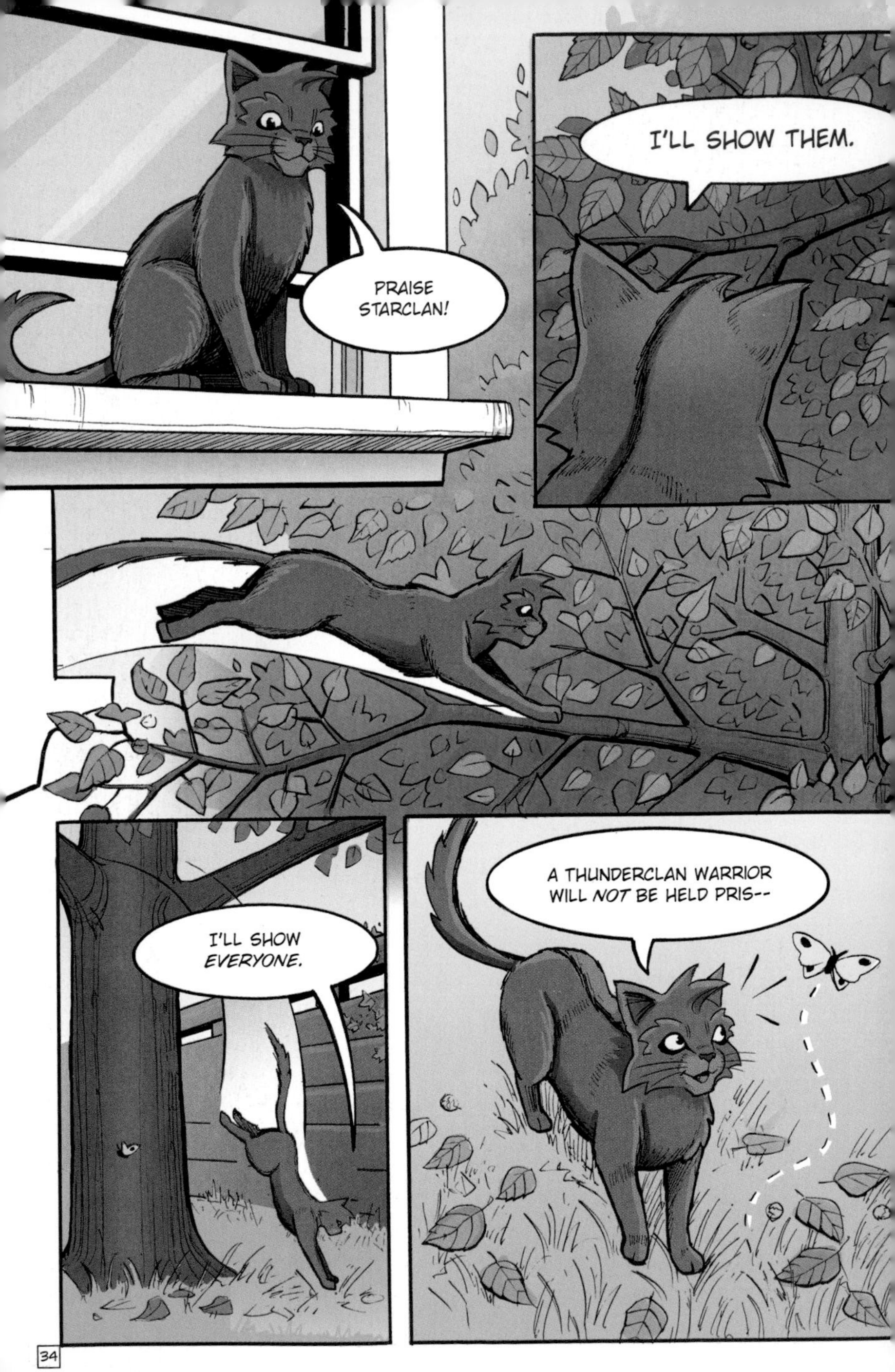
PRAISE STARCLAN!
I'LL SHOW THEM.
I'LL SHOW *EVERYONE.*
A THUNDERCLAN WARRIOR WILL *NOT* BE HELD PRIS--

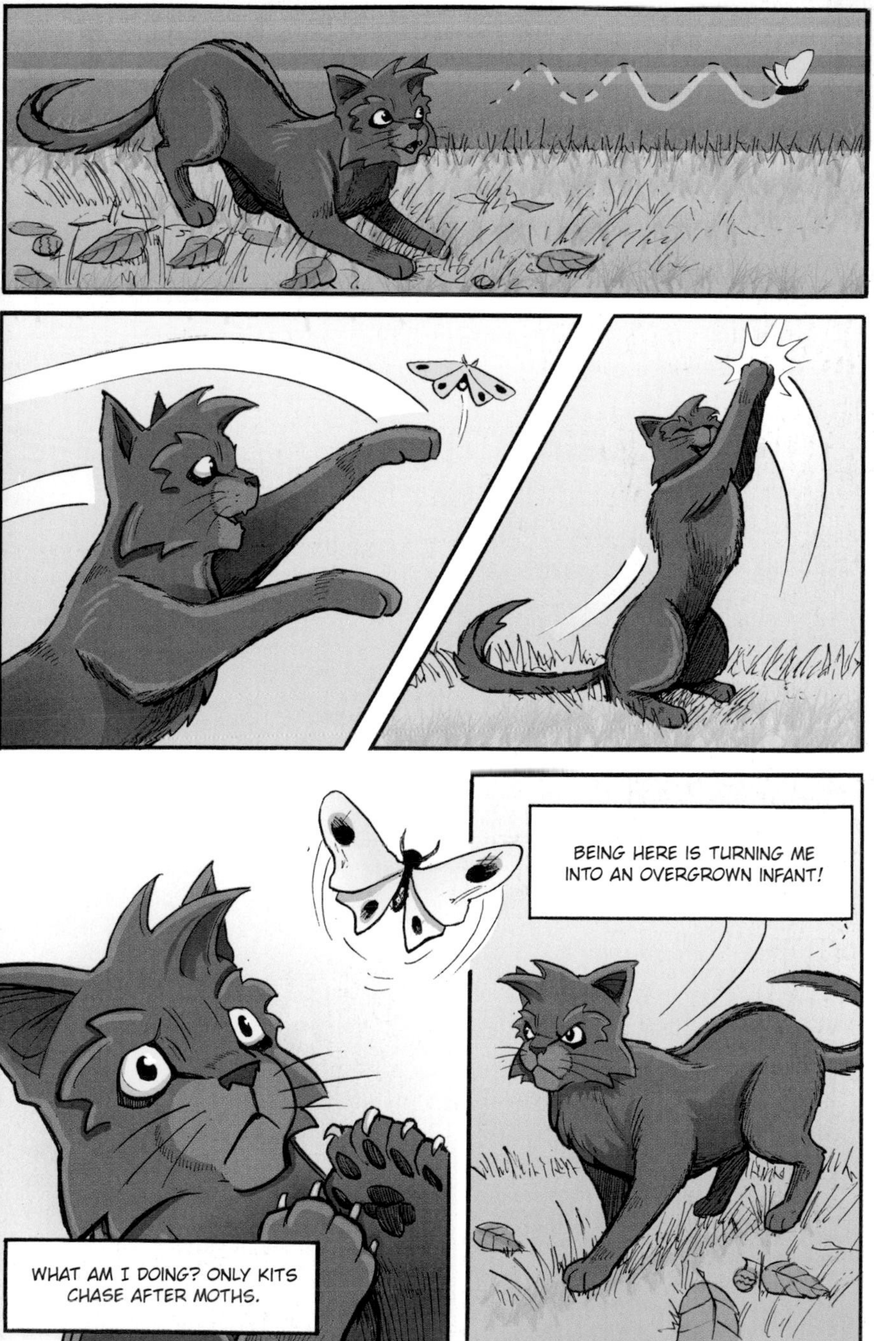
WHAT AM I DOING? ONLY KITS CHASE AFTER MOTHS.
BEING HERE IS TURNING ME INTO AN OVERGROWN INFANT!

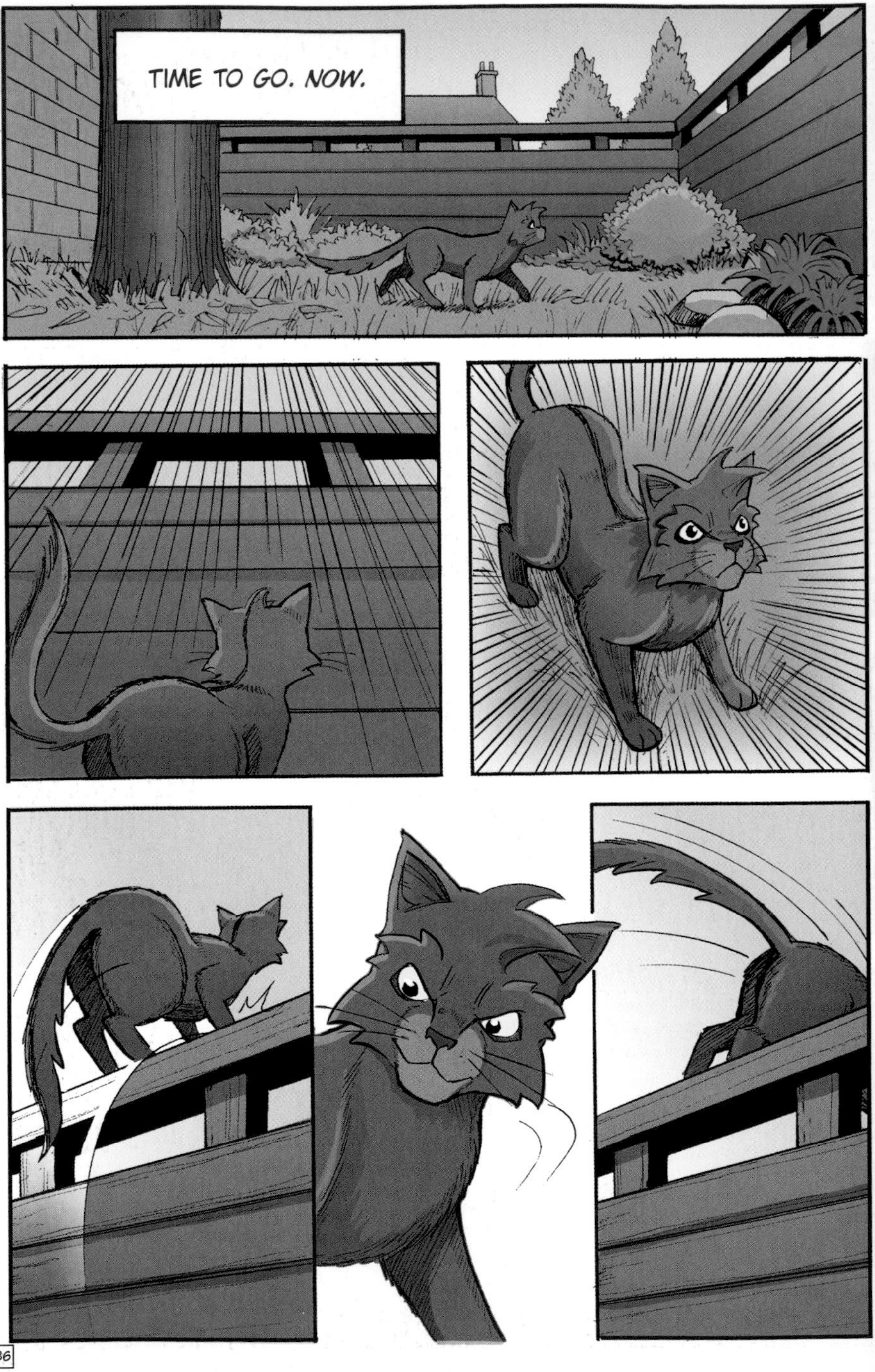
TIME TO GO. NOW.

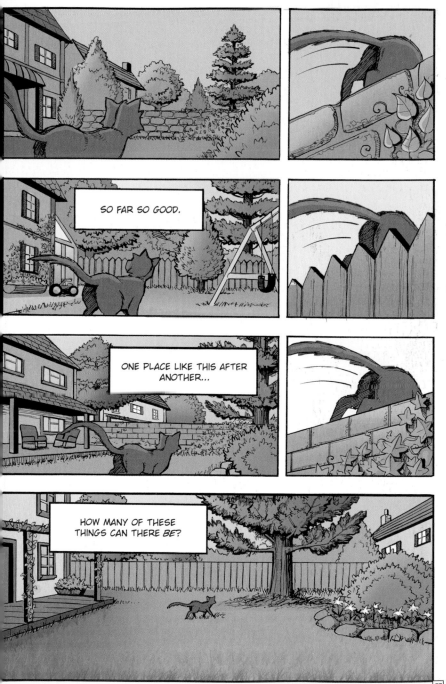

SO FAR SO GOOD.

ONE PLACE LIKE THIS AFTER ANOTHER...

HOW MANY OF THESE THINGS CAN THERE *BE*?

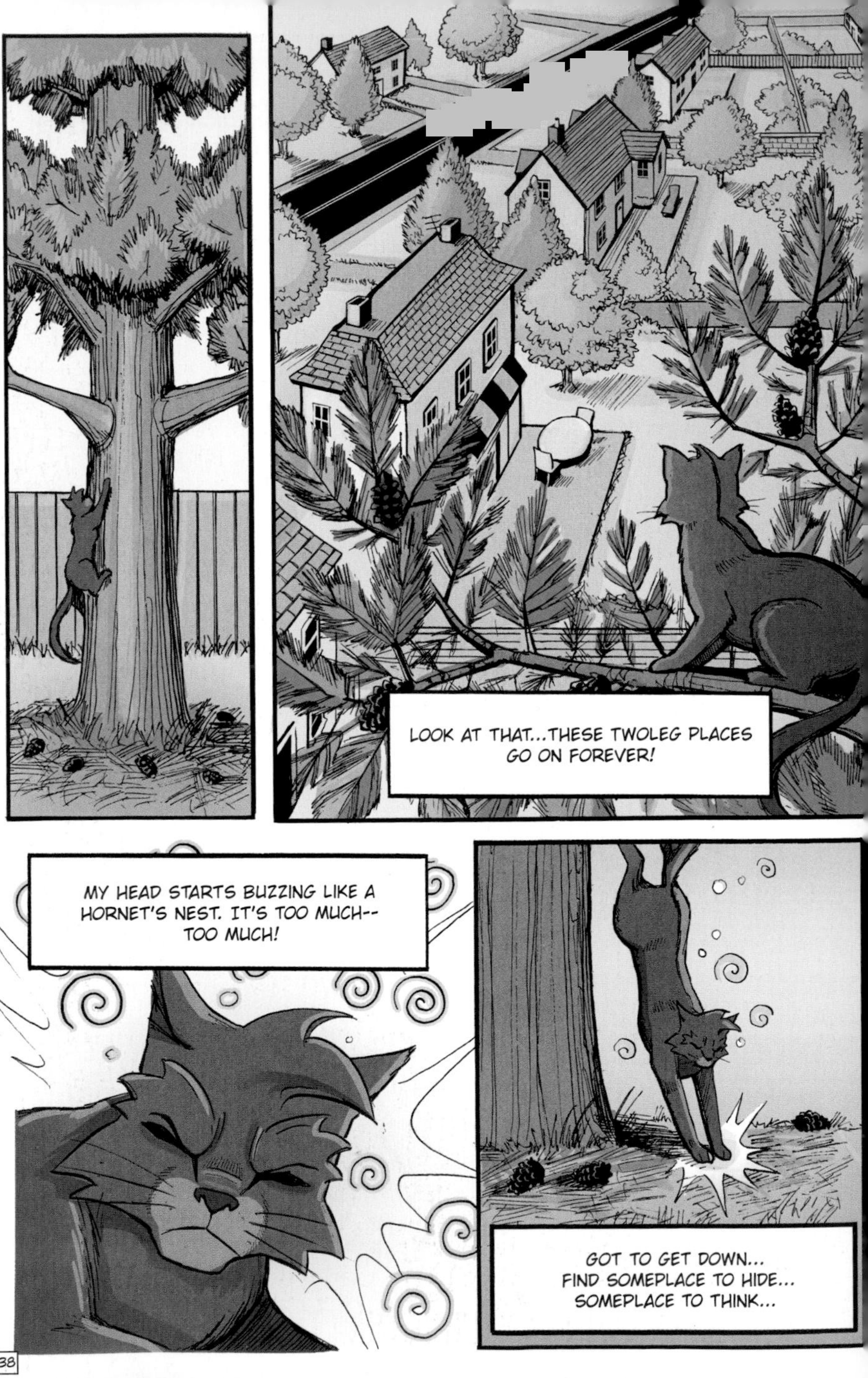
LOOK AT THAT...THESE TWOLEG PLACES GO ON FOREVER!
MY HEAD STARTS BUZZING LIKE A HORNET'S NEST. IT'S TOO MUCH-- TOO MUCH!
GOT TO GET DOWN... FIND SOMEPLACE TO HIDE... SOMEPLACE TO THINK...

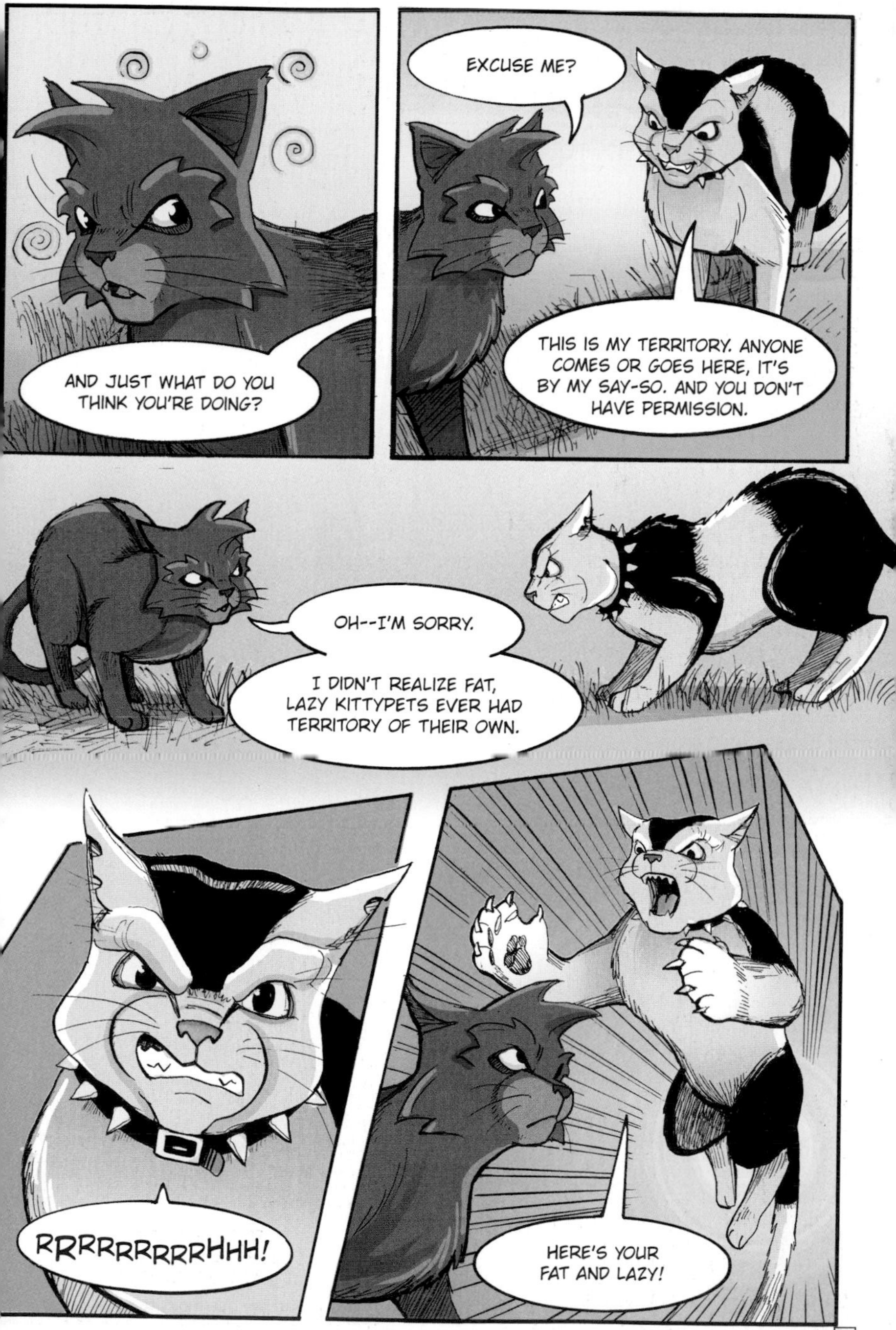
AND JUST WHAT DO YOU THINK YOU'RE DOING?
EXCUSE ME?
THIS IS MY TERRITORY. ANYONE COMES OR GOES HERE, IT'S BY MY SAY-SO. AND YOU DON'T HAVE PERMISSION.
OH--I'M SORRY.
I DIDN'T REALIZE FAT, LAZY KITTYPETS EVER HAD TERRITORY OF THEIR OWN.
RRRRRRRRRHHH!
HERE'S YOUR FAT AND LAZY!

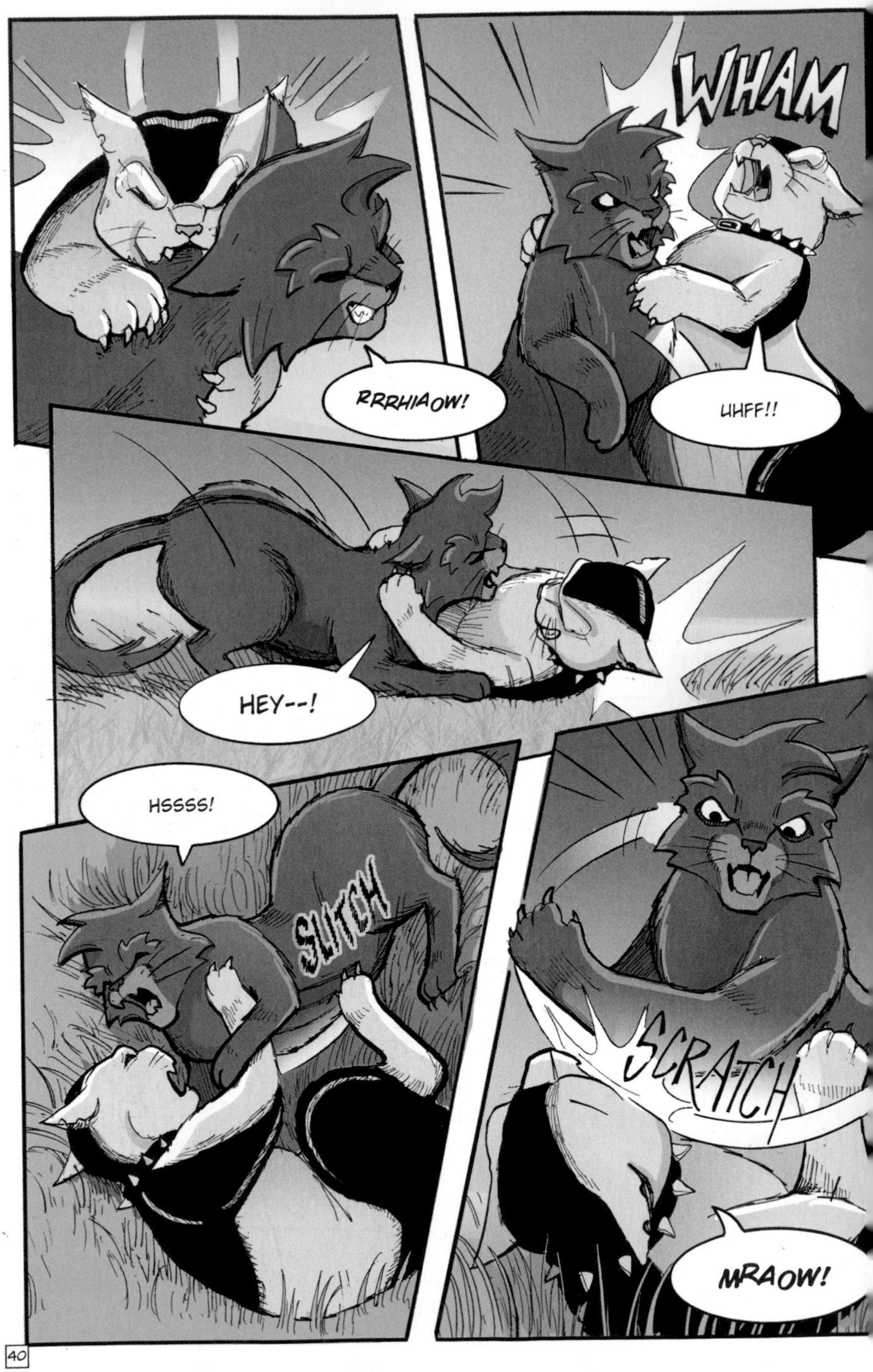
WHAM
RRRHIAOW!
UHFF!!
HEY--!
HSSSS!
SLITCH
SCRATCH
MRAOW!

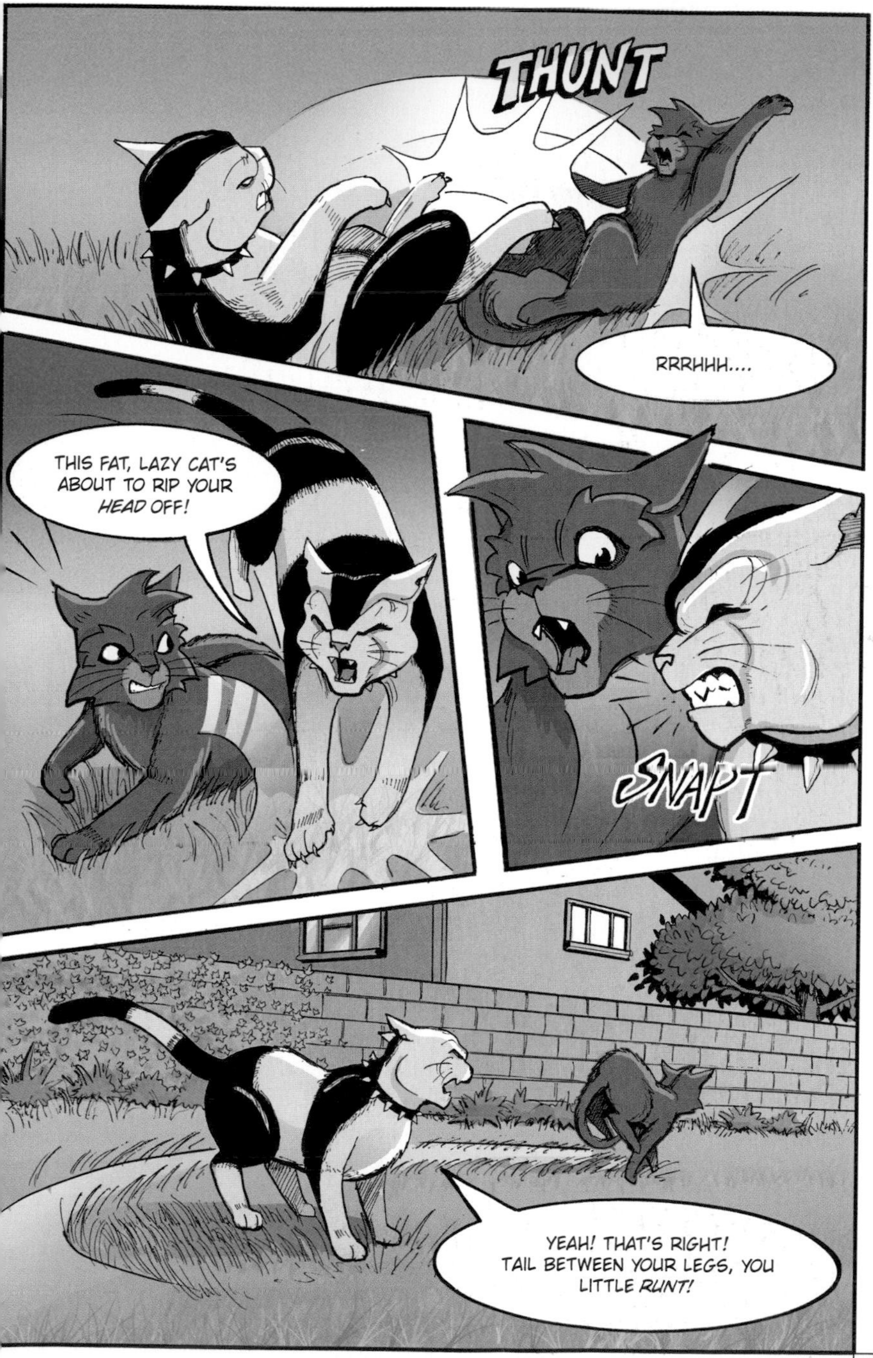
THUNT
RRRHHH....
THIS FAT, LAZY CAT'S ABOUT TO RIP YOUR *HEAD* OFF!
SNAP
YEAH! THAT'S RIGHT! TAIL BETWEEN YOUR LEGS, YOU LITTLE *RUNT!*

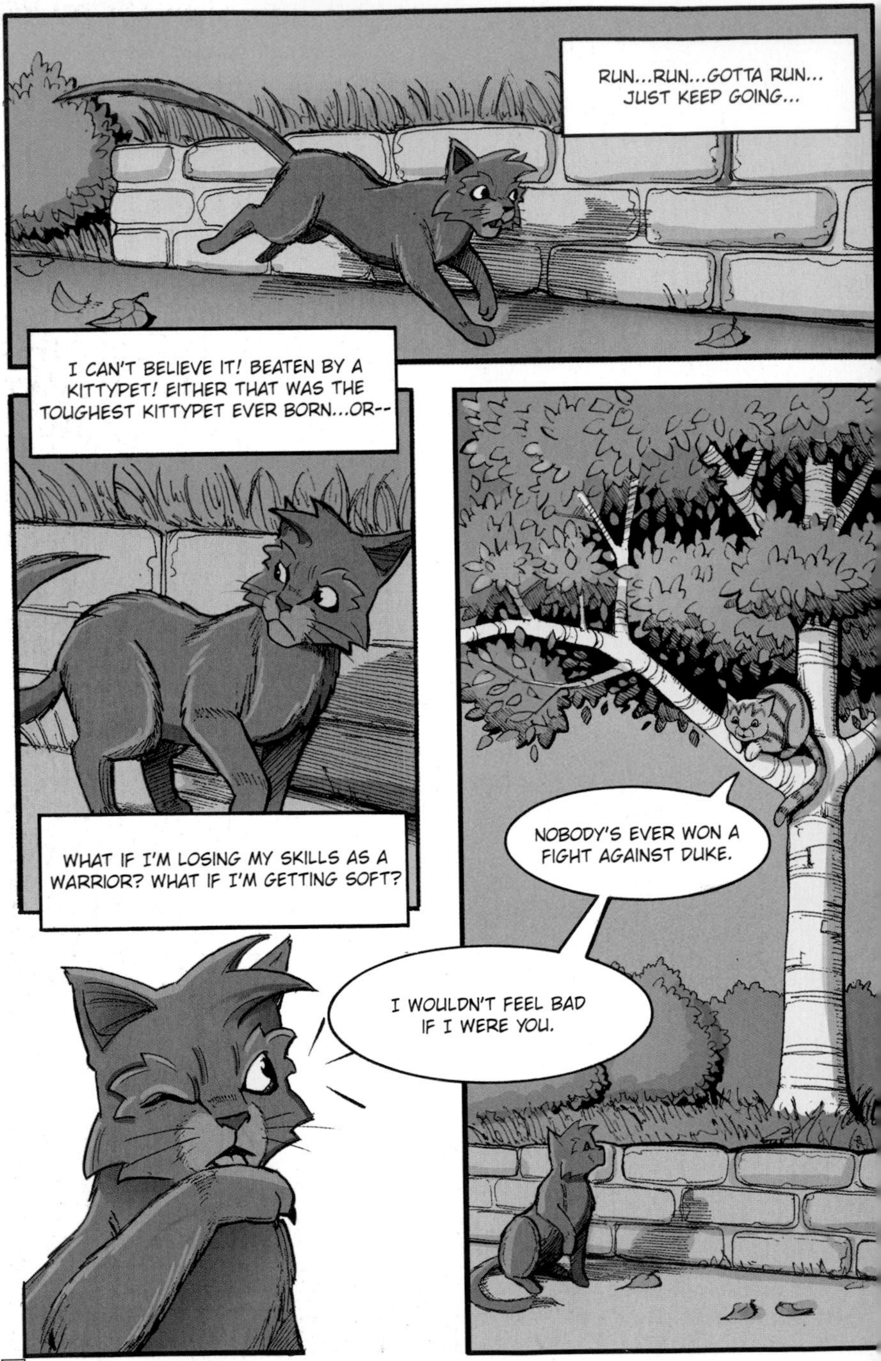
RUN...RUN...GOTTA RUN... JUST KEEP GOING...
I CAN'T BELIEVE IT! BEATEN BY A KITTYPET! EITHER THAT WAS THE TOUGHEST KITTYPET EVER BORN...OR--
WHAT IF I'M LOSING MY SKILLS AS A WARRIOR? WHAT IF I'M GETTING SOFT?
I WOULDN'T FEEL BAD IF I WERE YOU.
NOBODY'S EVER WON A FIGHT AGAINST DUKE.

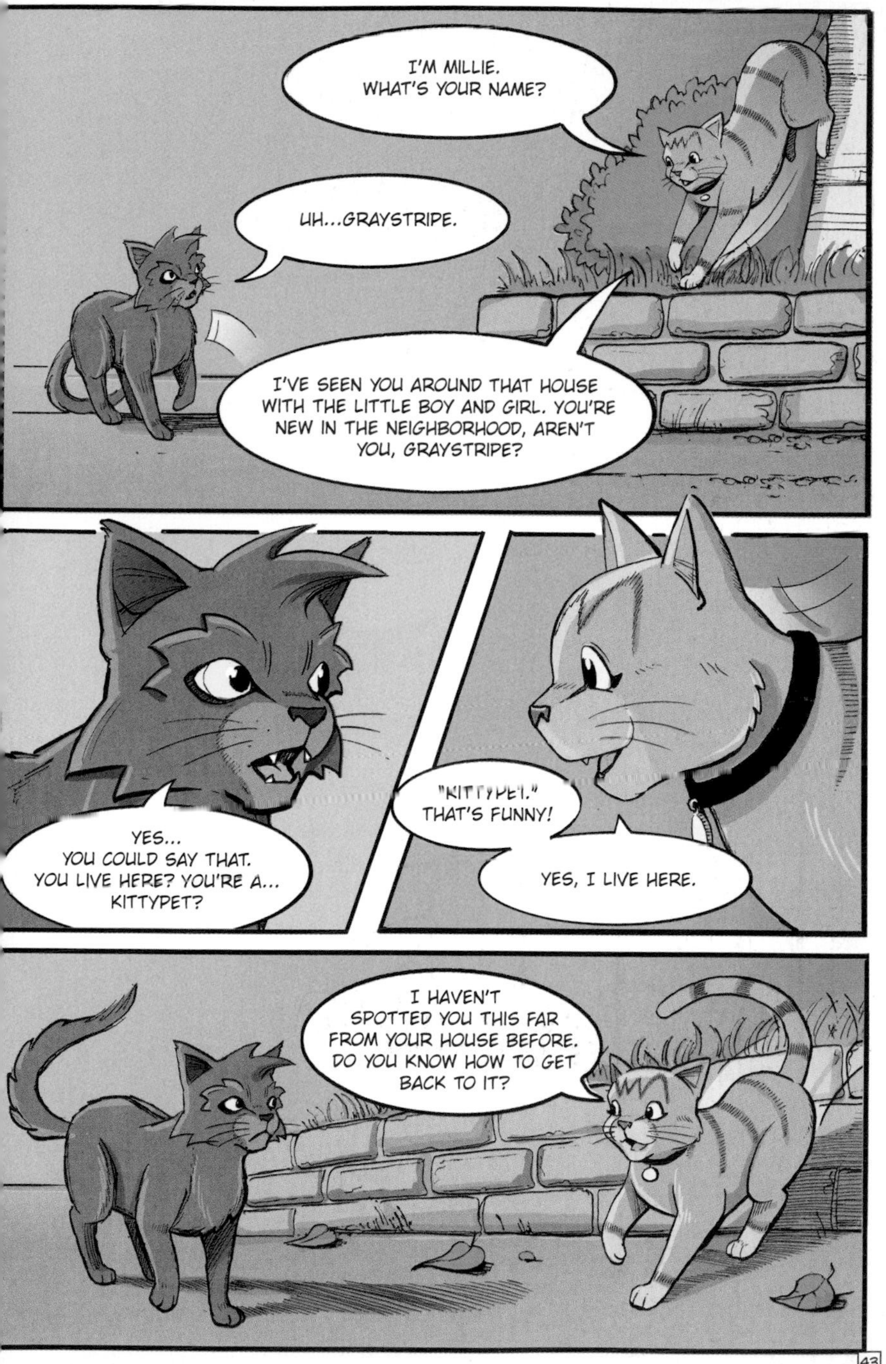
I'M MILLIE. WHAT'S YOUR NAME?
UH...GRAYSTRIPE.
I'VE SEEN YOU AROUND THAT HOUSE WITH THE LITTLE BOY AND GIRL. YOU'RE NEW IN THE NEIGHBORHOOD, AREN'T YOU, GRAYSTRIPE?
YES... YOU COULD SAY THAT. YOU LIVE HERE? YOU'RE A... KITTYPET?
"KITTYPET." THAT'S FUNNY!
YES, I LIVE HERE.
I HAVEN'T SPOTTED YOU THIS FAR FROM YOUR HOUSE BEFORE. DO YOU KNOW HOW TO GET BACK TO IT?

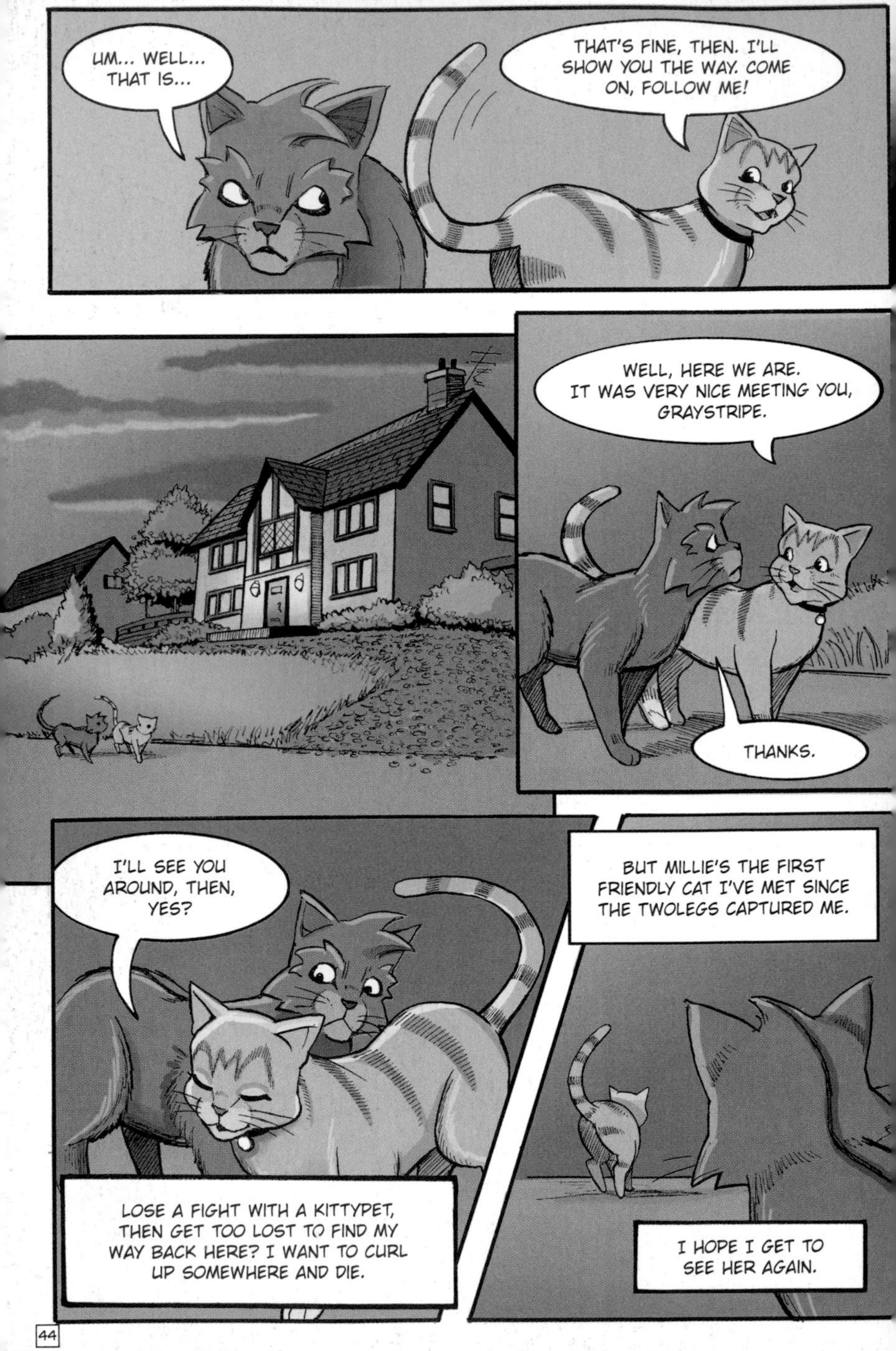
UM... WELL... THAT IS...
THAT'S FINE, THEN. I'LL SHOW YOU THE WAY. COME ON, FOLLOW ME!
WELL, HERE WE ARE. IT WAS VERY NICE MEETING YOU, GRAYSTRIPE.
THANKS.
I'LL SEE YOU AROUND, THEN, YES?
LOSE A FIGHT WITH A KITTYPET, THEN GET TOO LOST TO FIND MY WAY BACK HERE? I WANT TO CURL UP SOMEWHERE AND DIE.
BUT MILLIE'S THE FIRST FRIENDLY CAT I'VE MET SINCE THE TWOLEGS CAPTURED ME.
I HOPE I GET TO SEE HER AGAIN.

I DREAM THAT NIGHT.
PART OF ME KNOWS IT'S A DREAM, BUT THAT DOESN'T MATTER. I'M NOT ABOUT TO WAKE UP.
BECAUSE IN DREAMS, SOMETIMES YOU CAN MEET CATS WHO ARE NO LONGER WITH YOU.
AND WHEN I SEE THE SLIM, BEAUTIFUL QUEEN COMING TOWARD ME...

...PART OF ME DOESN'T EVER WANT TO WAKE UP.
SILVERSTREAM! IT'S SO GOOD TO SEE YOU... I'VE MISSED YOU SO MUCH...
HELLO, BELOVED.
I'VE MISSED YOU, TOO, GRAYSTRIPE. I WATCH OVER YOU, EVERY DAY AND EVERY NIGHT.
OH, SILVERSTREAM, I NEVER THOUGHT I'D GET TO SPEAK WITH YOU AGAIN...
ARE YOU ALL RIGHT? ARE YOU...ARE YOU HAPPY... WHERE YOU ARE?
MY SWEET WARRIOR... YOU DON'T HAVE TO WORRY. JOINING STARCLAN IS NOTHING TO FEAR.
OUR KITS GREW INTO FINE WARRIORS. I WAS SO PROUD OF THEM WHEN THEY WENT ON THE QUEST TO FIND A NEW HOME FOR THE CLANS.
YOU SHOULD KNOW, TOO, THAT I HAVE A COMPANION. SOMEONE I NEVER HAD THE PRIVILEGE TO MEET WHILE I WALKED WITH YOU.

FEATHERTAIL...! MY DAUGHTER... OUR DAUGHTER...
HELLO, FATHER. IT'S GOOD TO SEE YOU AGAIN.
I HEARD ABOUT... I MEAN TO SAY, THEY TOLD ME YOU HAD...YOU'RE AT PEACE, THEN...? YOU'RE WITH YOUR MOTHER?
YES, GRAYSTRIPE. I JOINED STARCLAN EVEN AS OUR KITS WERE BORN...BUT NOW MY DAUGHTER AND I ARE REUNITED.
FEATHERTAIL...YOUR BROTHER, STORMFUR...DID HE... HE HASN'T...ALREADY JOINED STARCLAN, TOO?
NO, FATHER. STORMFUR IS ALIVE AND WELL.
BUT NOW WE MUST LEAVE YOU.
WHAT? YOU JUST GOT HERE!
DON'T FRET, BELOVED. REST ASSURED, WE WILL ALWAYS BE WITH YOU...AND YOU WILL SEE US HERE AGAIN.

CHAPTER 3

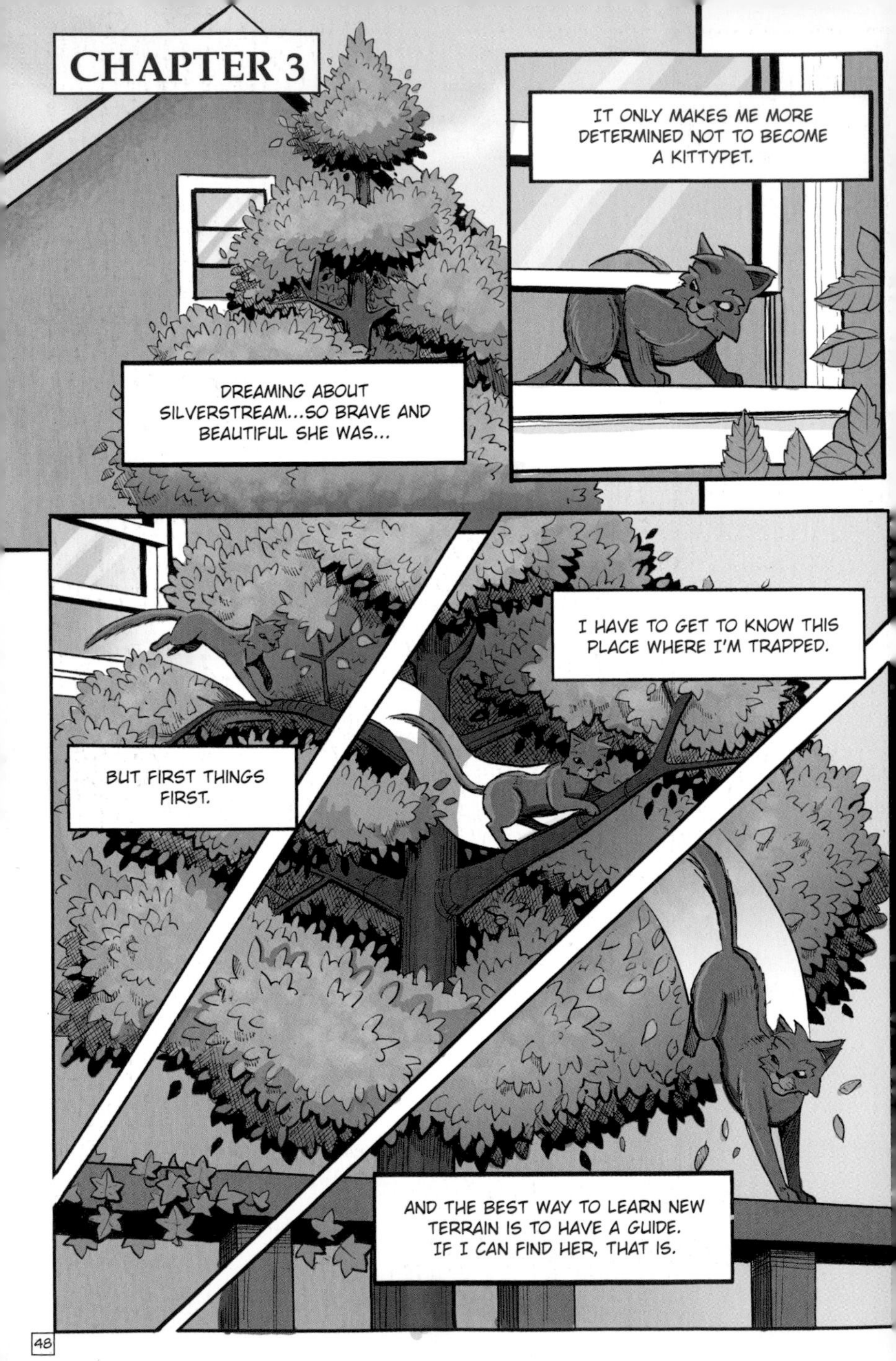
DREAMING ABOUT SILVERSTREAM...SO BRAVE AND BEAUTIFUL SHE WAS...
IT ONLY MAKES ME MORE DETERMINED NOT TO BECOME A KITTYPET.
BUT FIRST THINGS FIRST.
I HAVE TO GET TO KNOW THIS PLACE WHERE I'M TRAPPED.
AND THE BEST WAY TO LEARN NEW TERRAIN IS TO HAVE A GUIDE. IF I CAN FIND HER, THAT IS.

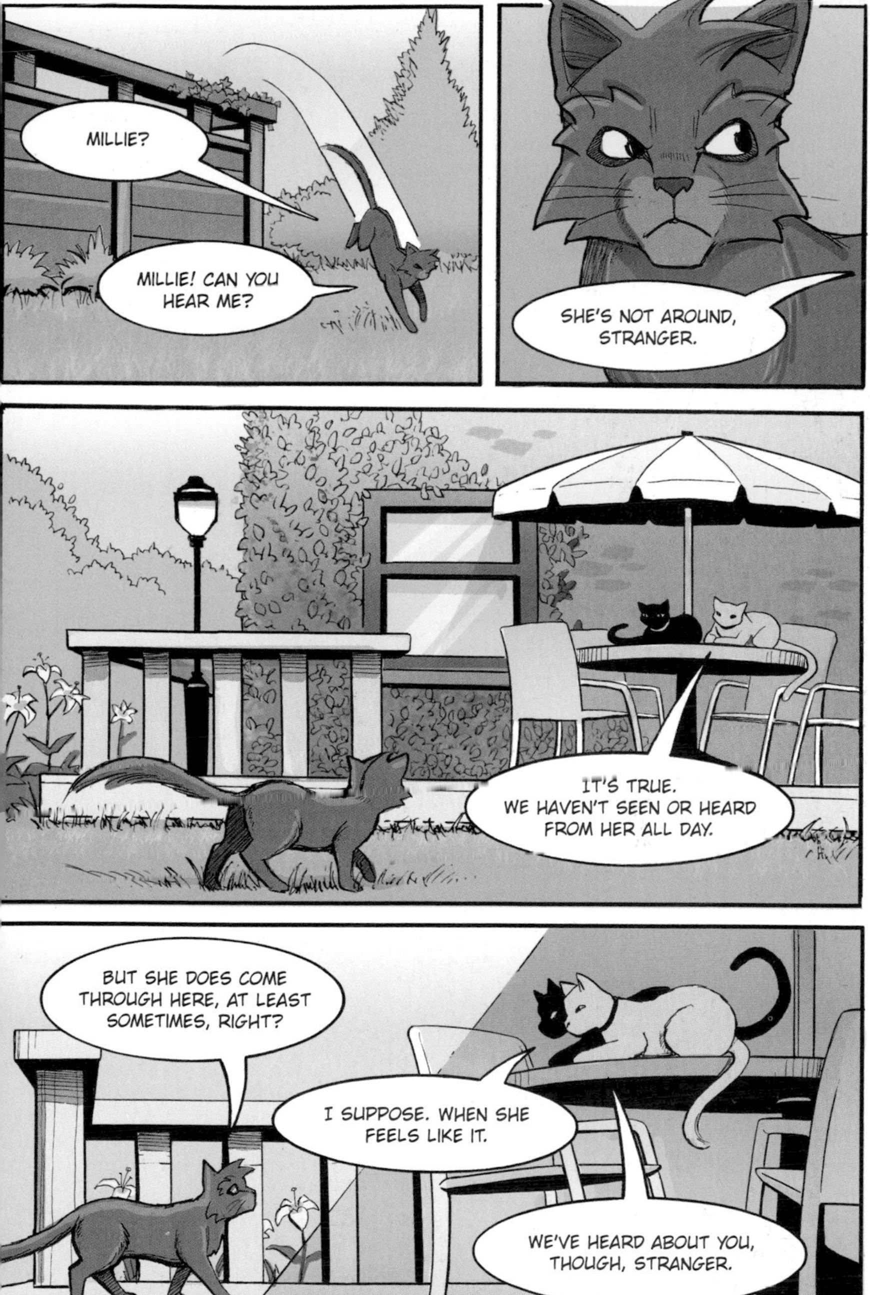
MILLIE?
MILLIE! CAN YOU HEAR ME?
SHE'S NOT AROUND, STRANGER.
IT'S TRUE. WE HAVEN'T SEEN OR HEARD FROM HER ALL DAY.
BUT SHE DOES COME THROUGH HERE, AT LEAST SOMETIMES, RIGHT?
I SUPPOSE. WHEN SHE FEELS LIKE IT.
WE'VE HEARD ABOUT YOU, THOUGH, STRANGER.

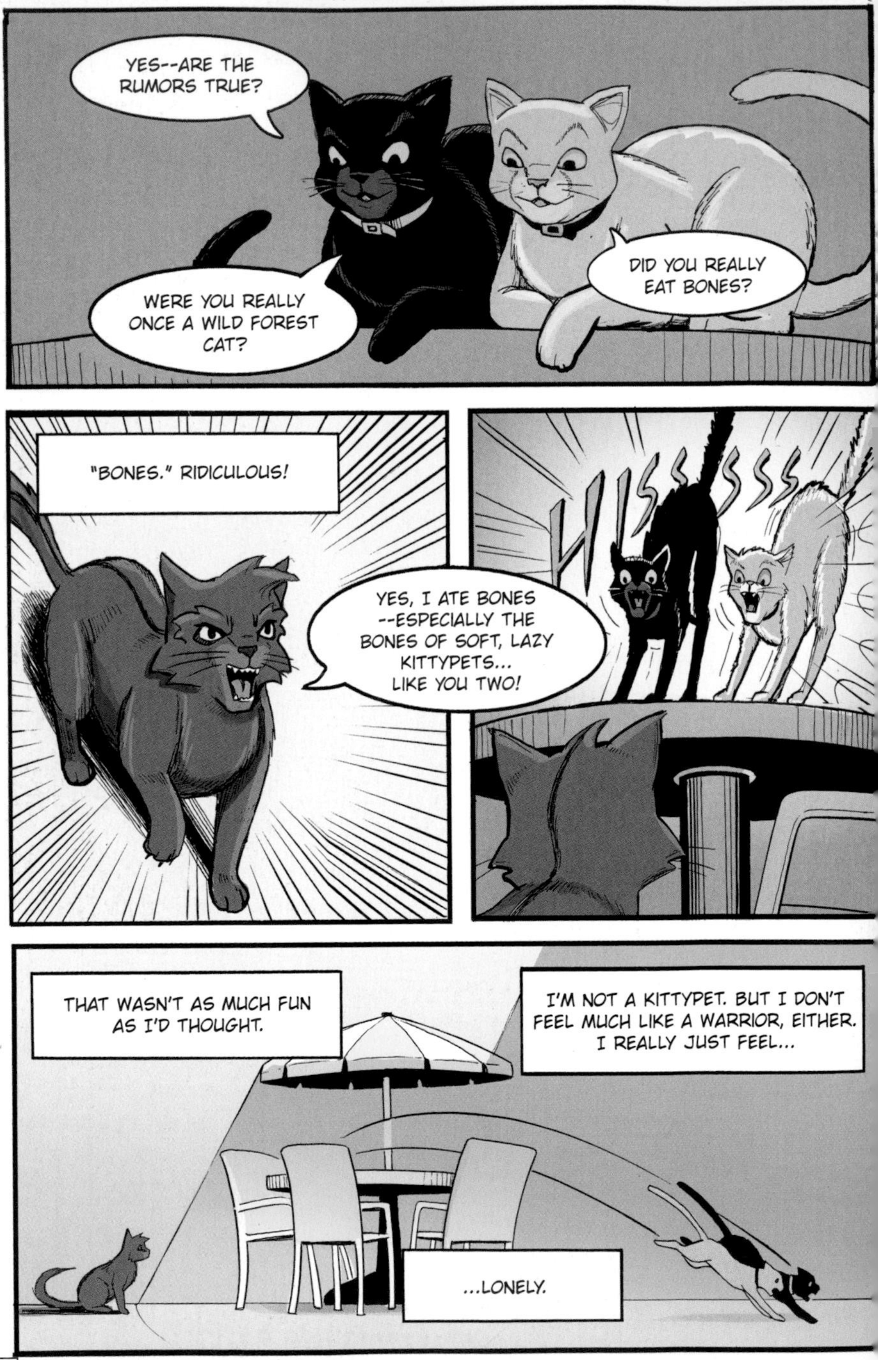
YES--ARE THE RUMORS TRUE?
WERE YOU REALLY ONCE A WILD FOREST CAT?
DID YOU REALLY EAT BONES?
"BONES." RIDICULOUS!
YES, I ATE BONES --ESPECIALLY THE BONES OF SOFT, LAZY KITTYPETS... LIKE YOU TWO!
HISSSSS
THAT WASN'T AS MUCH FUN AS I'D THOUGHT.
I'M NOT A KITTYPET. BUT I DON'T FEEL MUCH LIKE A WARRIOR, EITHER. I REALLY JUST FEEL...
...LONELY.

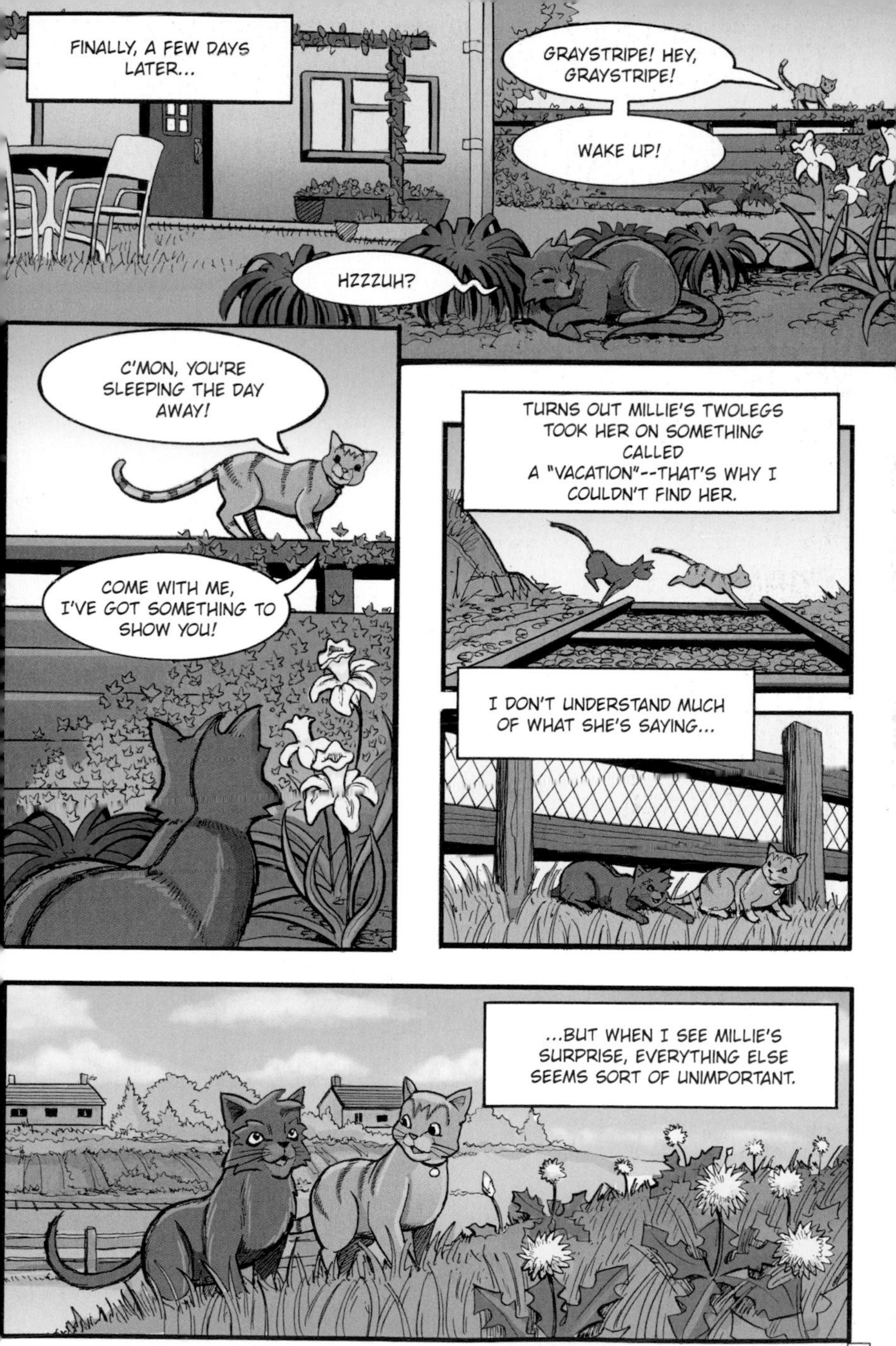
FINALLY, A FEW DAYS LATER...
GRAYSTRIPE! HEY, GRAYSTRIPE!
WAKE UP!
HZZZUH?
C'MON, YOU'RE SLEEPING THE DAY AWAY!
COME WITH ME, I'VE GOT SOMETHING TO SHOW YOU!
TURNS OUT MILLIE'S TWOLEGS TOOK HER ON SOMETHING CALLED A "VACATION"--THAT'S WHY I COULDN'T FIND HER.
I DON'T UNDERSTAND MUCH OF WHAT SHE'S SAYING...
...BUT WHEN I SEE MILLIE'S SURPRISE, EVERYTHING ELSE SEEMS SORT OF UNIMPORTANT.

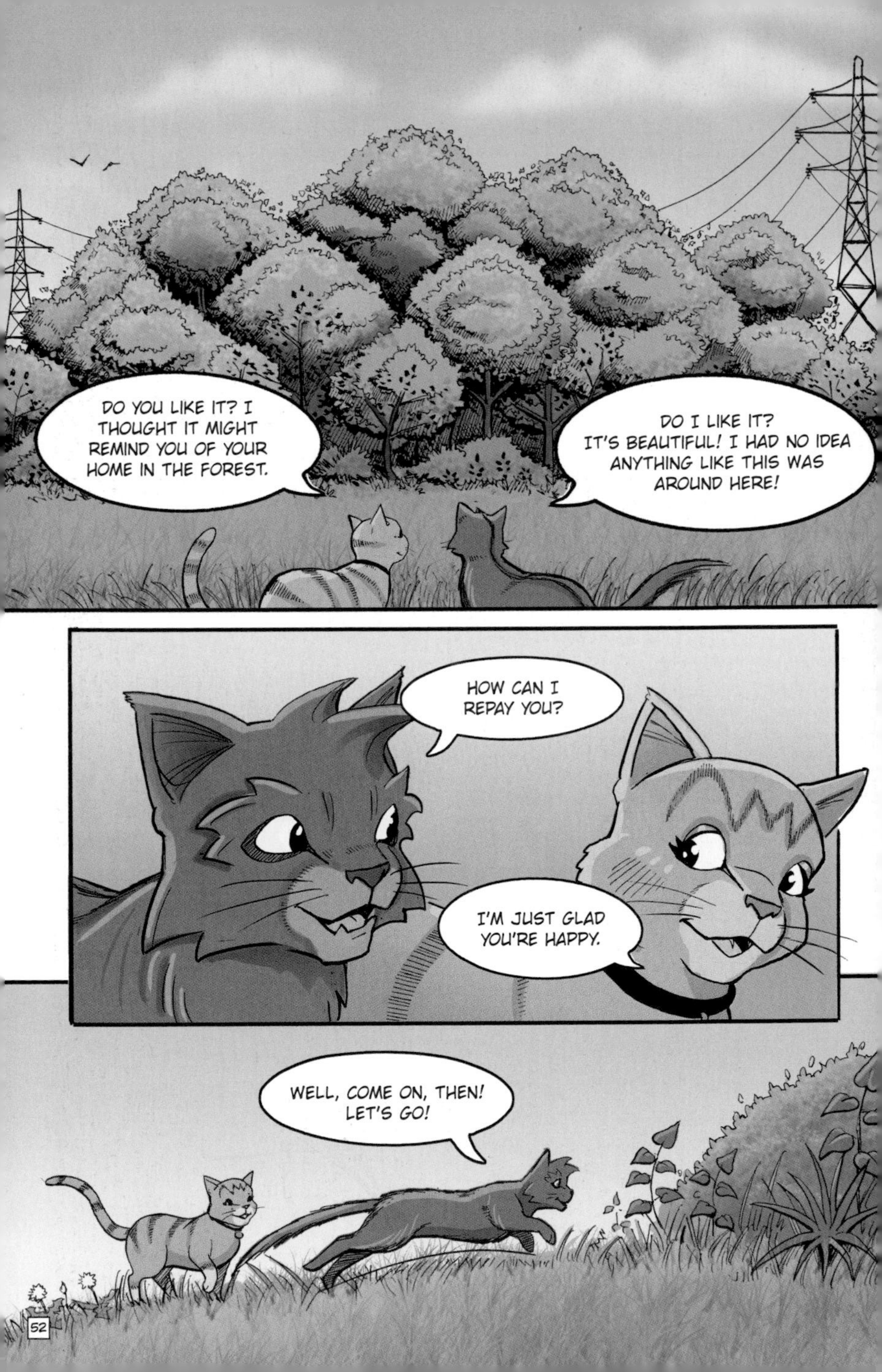
DO YOU LIKE IT? I THOUGHT IT MIGHT REMIND YOU OF YOUR HOME IN THE FOREST.
DO I LIKE IT? IT'S BEAUTIFUL! I HAD NO IDEA ANYTHING LIKE THIS WAS AROUND HERE!
HOW CAN I REPAY YOU?
I'M JUST GLAD YOU'RE HAPPY.
WELL, COME ON, THEN! LET'S GO!

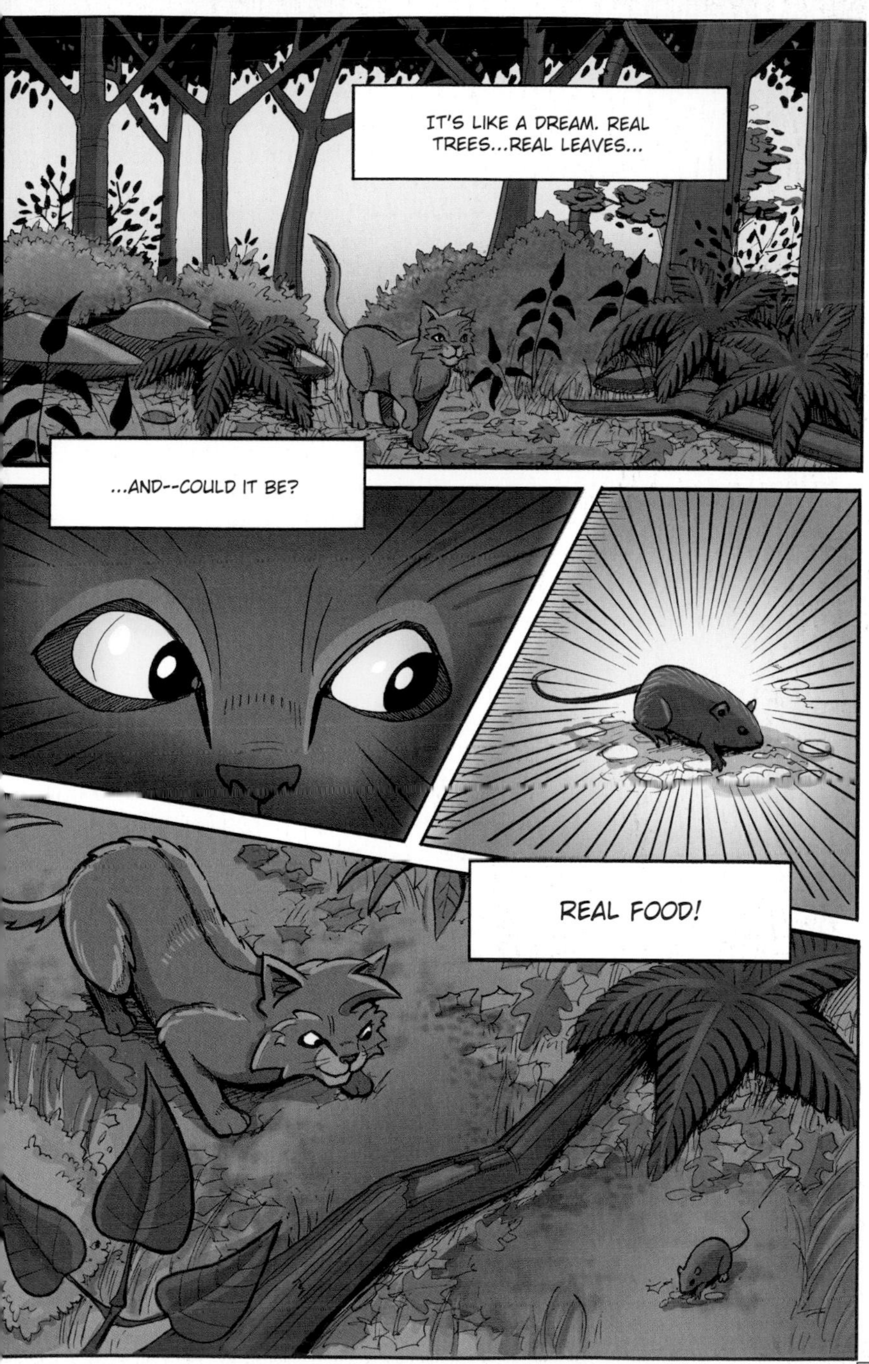
IT'S LIKE A DREAM. REAL TREES...REAL LEAVES...
...AND--COULD IT BE?
REAL FOOD!

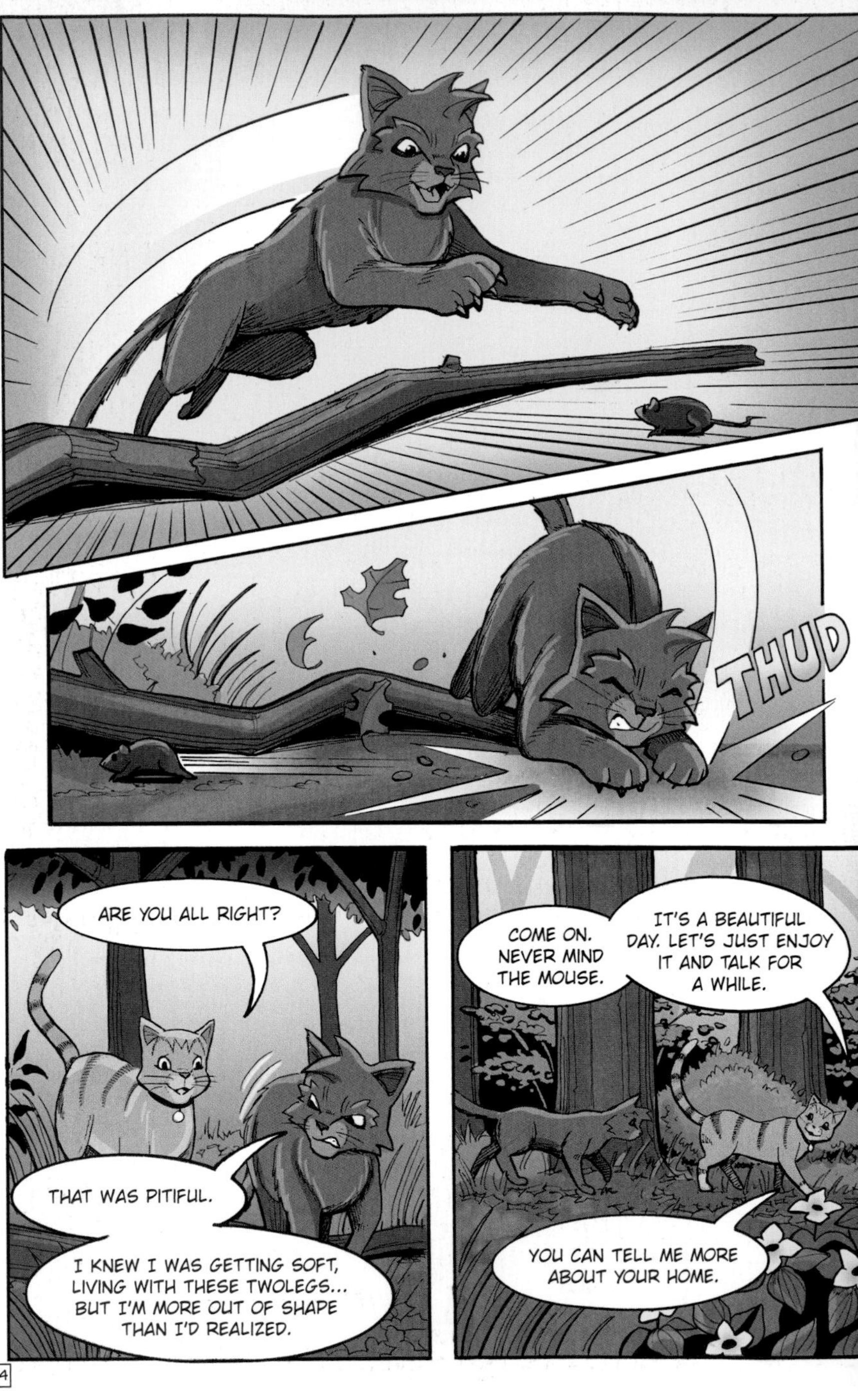
THUD
ARE YOU ALL RIGHT?
THAT WAS PITIFUL.
I KNEW I WAS GETTING SOFT, LIVING WITH THESE TWOLEGS... BUT I'M MORE OUT OF SHAPE THAN I'D REALIZED.
COME ON. NEVER MIND THE MOUSE.
IT'S A BEAUTIFUL DAY. LET'S JUST ENJOY IT AND TALK FOR A WHILE.
YOU CAN TELL ME MORE ABOUT YOUR HOME.

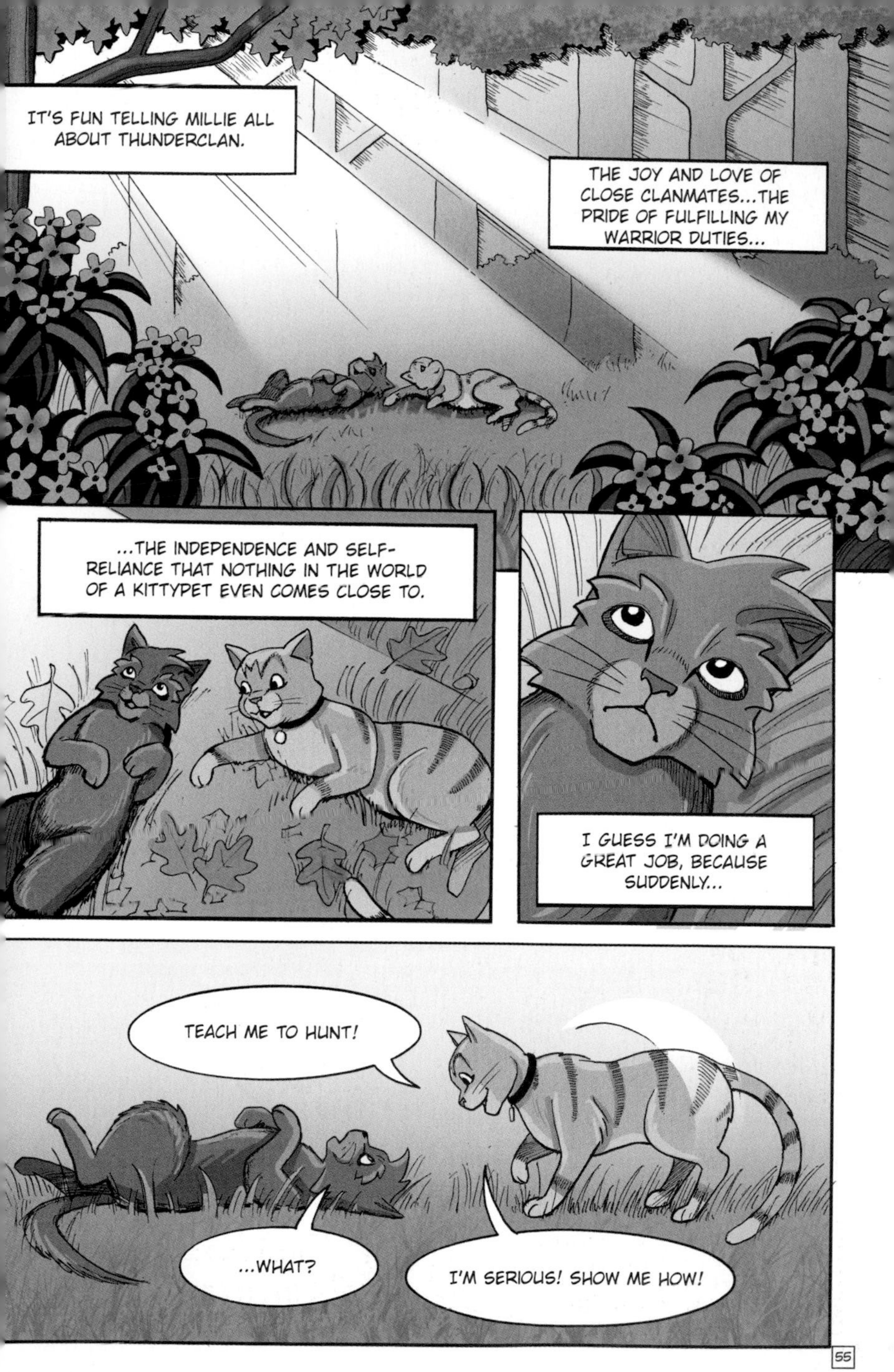
IT'S FUN TELLING MILLIE ALL ABOUT THUNDERCLAN.
THE JOY AND LOVE OF CLOSE CLANMATES...THE PRIDE OF FULFILLING MY WARRIOR DUTIES...
...THE INDEPENDENCE AND SELF-RELIANCE THAT NOTHING IN THE WORLD OF A KITTYPET EVEN COMES CLOSE TO.
I GUESS I'M DOING A GREAT JOB, BECAUSE SUDDENLY...
TEACH ME TO HUNT!
...WHAT?
I'M SERIOUS! SHOW ME HOW!

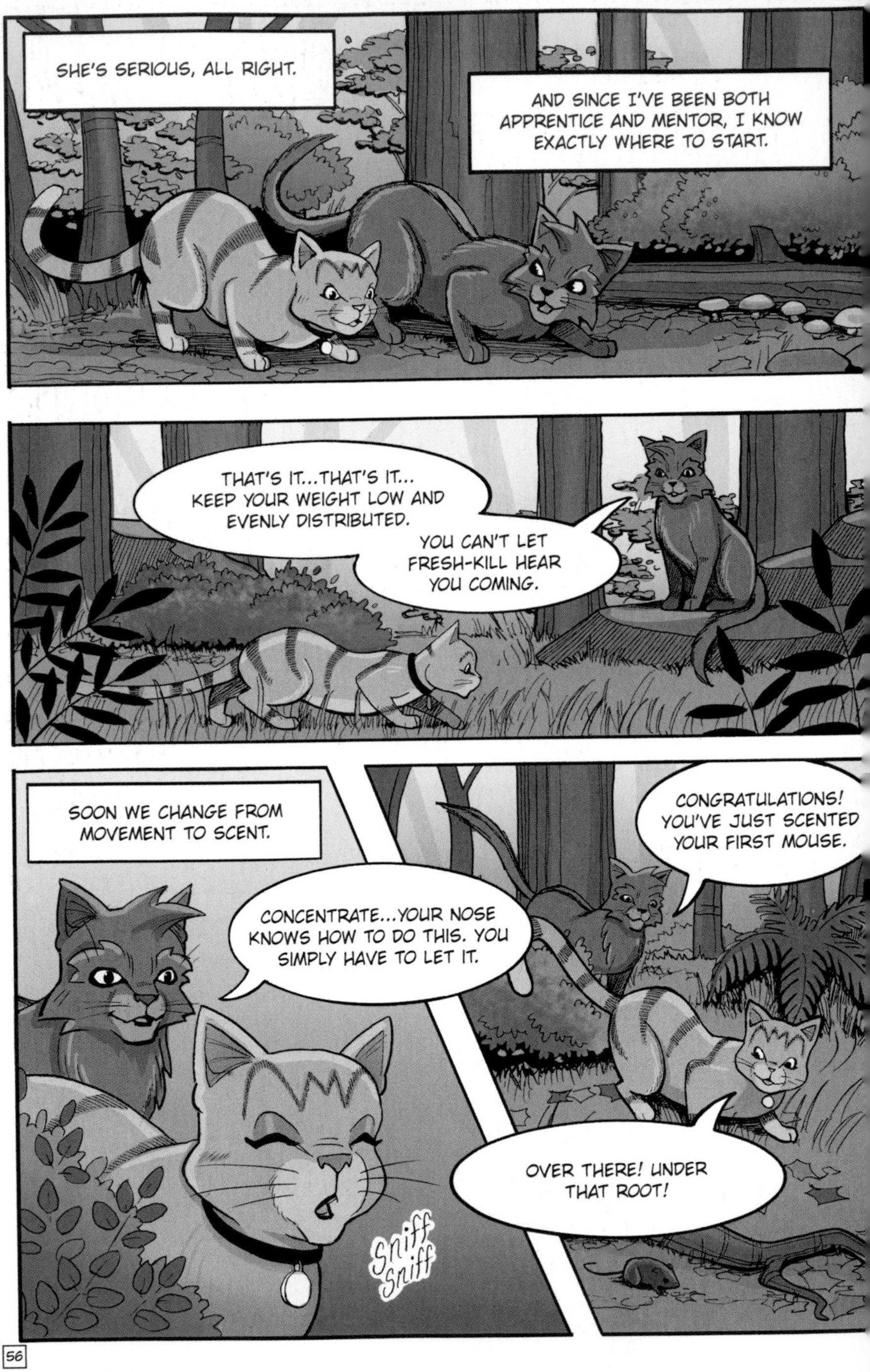
SHE'S SERIOUS, ALL RIGHT.
AND SINCE I'VE BEEN BOTH APPRENTICE AND MENTOR, I KNOW EXACTLY WHERE TO START.
THAT'S IT...THAT'S IT... KEEP YOUR WEIGHT LOW AND EVENLY DISTRIBUTED.
YOU CAN'T LET FRESH-KILL HEAR YOU COMING.
SOON WE CHANGE FROM MOVEMENT TO SCENT.
CONCENTRATE...YOUR NOSE KNOWS HOW TO DO THIS. YOU SIMPLY HAVE TO LET IT.
Sniff sniff
CONGRATULATIONS! YOU'VE JUST SCENTED YOUR FIRST MOUSE.
OVER THERE! UNDER THAT ROOT!

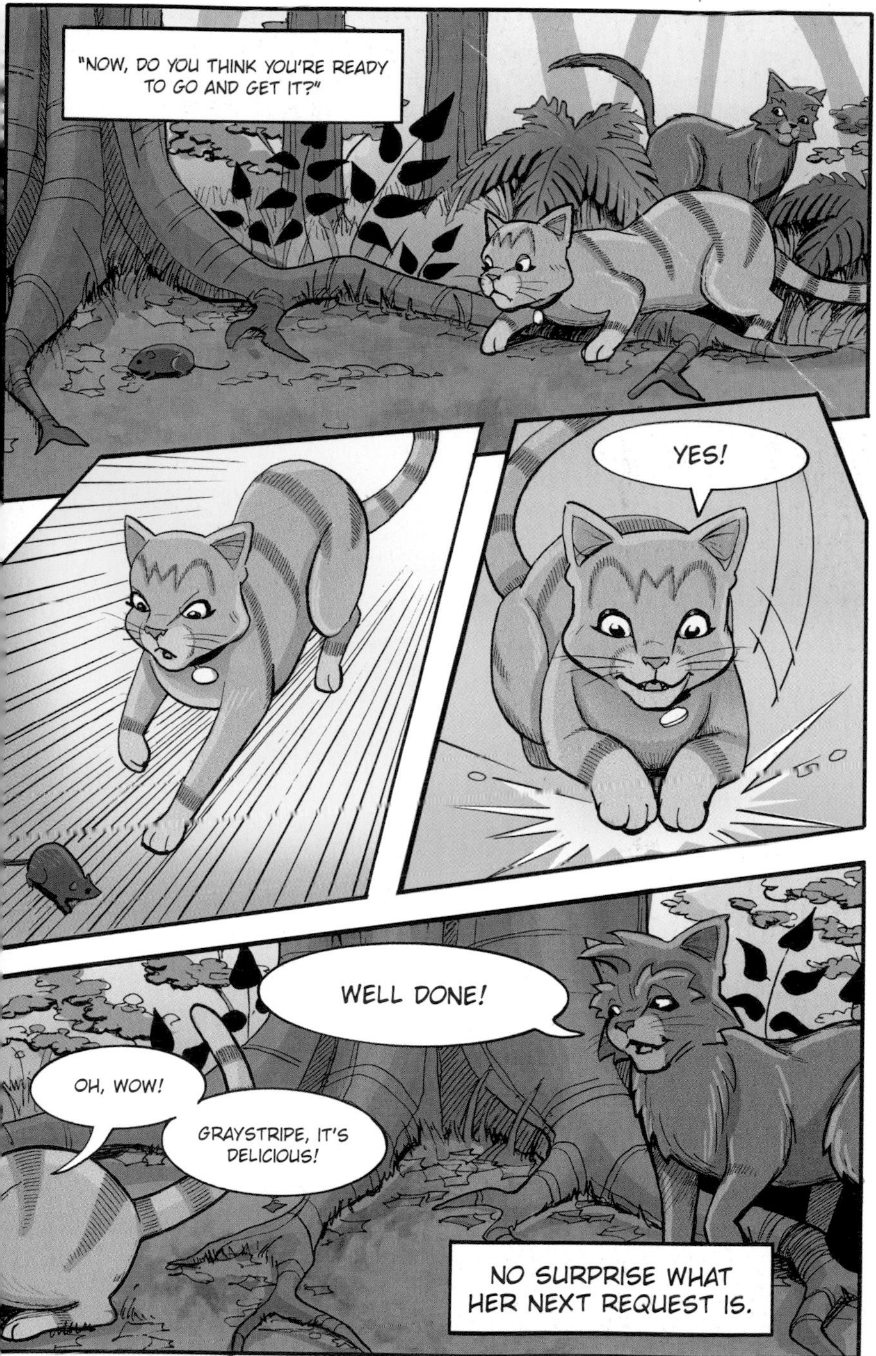
"NOW, DO YOU THINK YOU'RE READY TO GO AND GET IT?"
YES!
WELL DONE!
OH, WOW!
GRAYSTRIPE, IT'S DELICIOUS!
NO SURPRISE WHAT HER NEXT REQUEST IS.

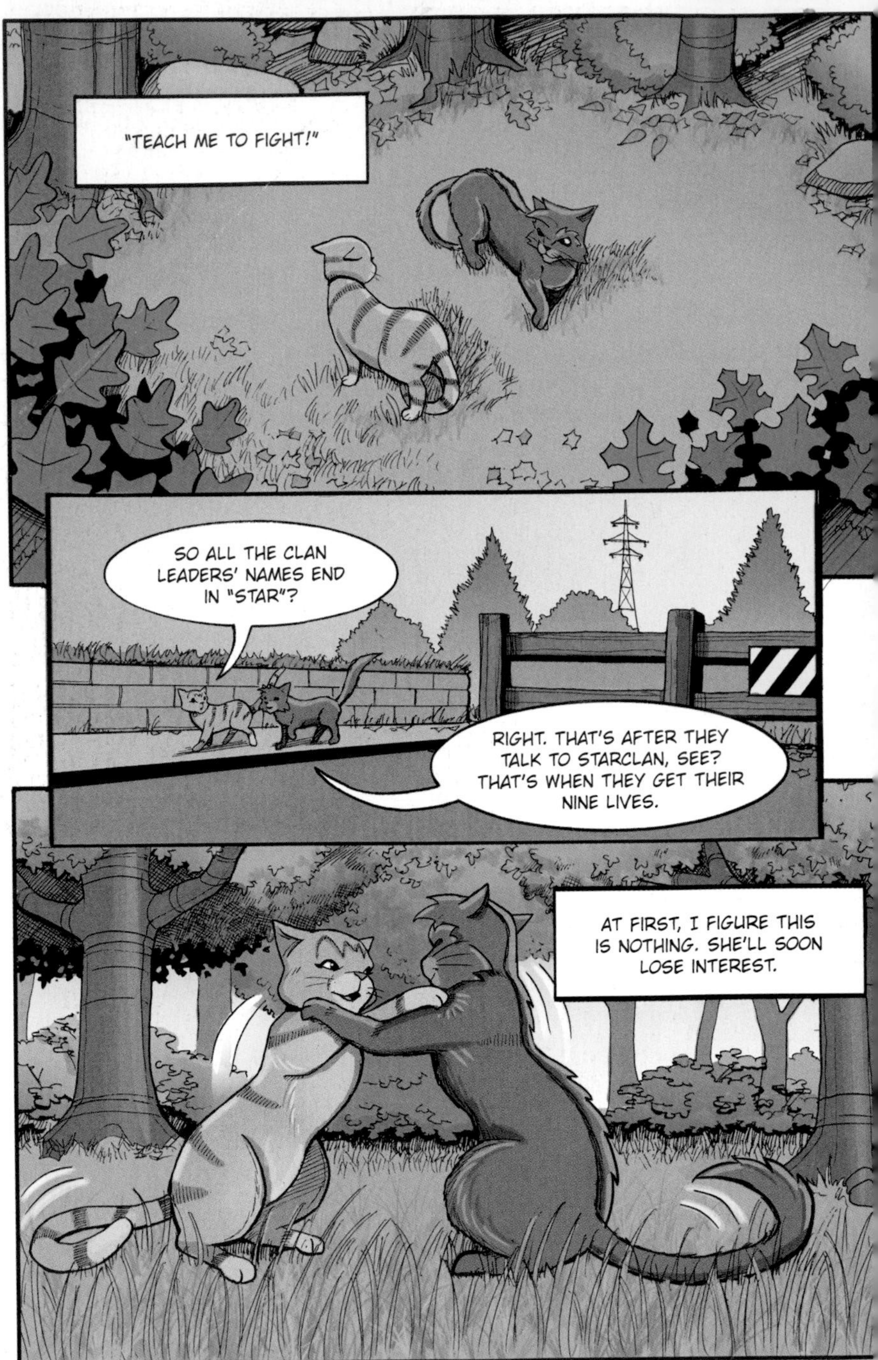
"TEACH ME TO FIGHT!"
SO ALL THE CLAN LEADERS' NAMES END IN "STAR"?
RIGHT. THAT'S AFTER THEY TALK TO STARCLAN, SEE? THAT'S WHEN THEY GET THEIR NINE LIVES.
AT FIRST, I FIGURE THIS IS NOTHING. SHE'LL SOON LOSE INTEREST.

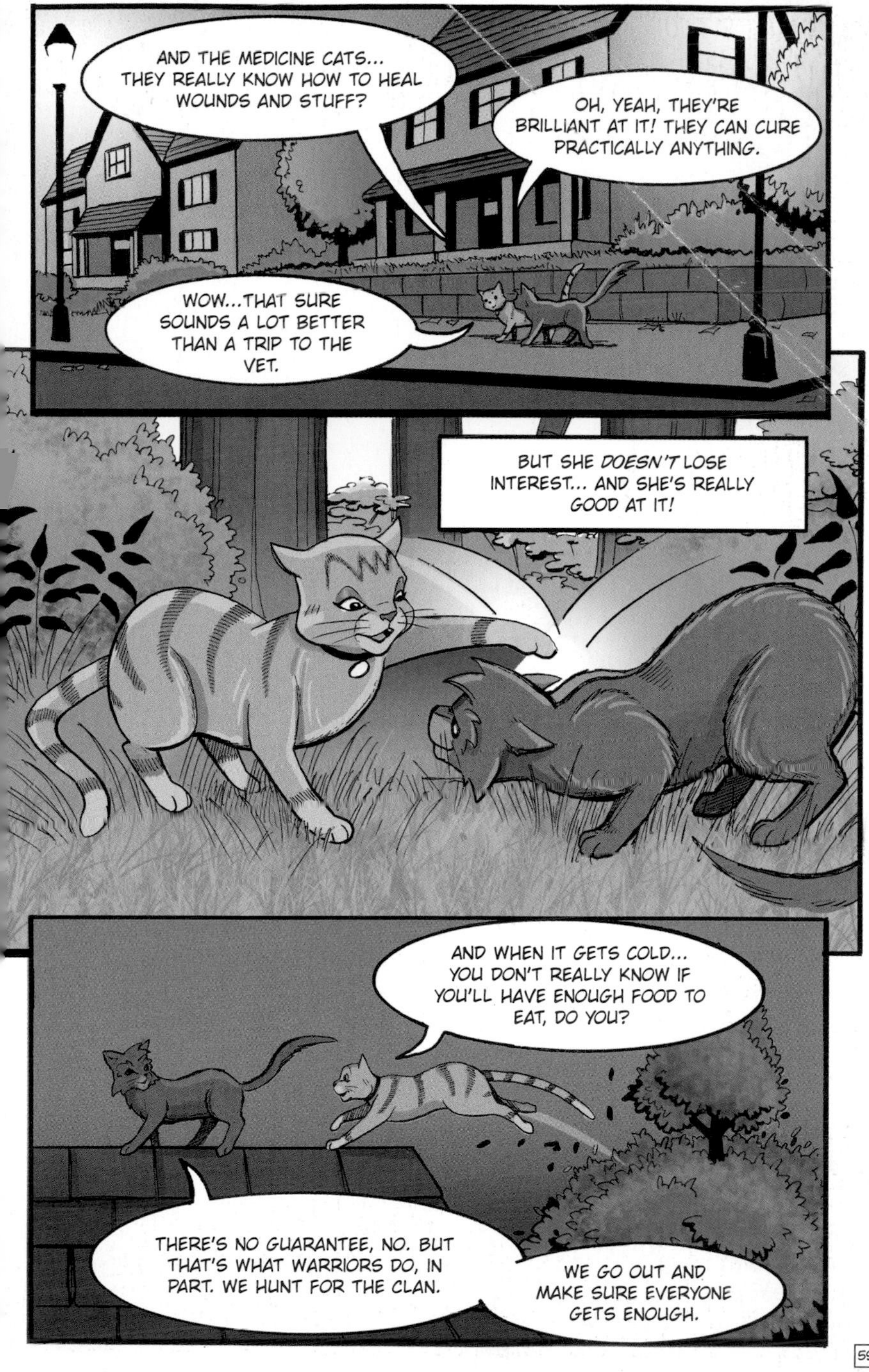
AND THE MEDICINE CATS... THEY REALLY KNOW HOW TO HEAL WOUNDS AND STUFF?
OH, YEAH, THEY'RE BRILLIANT AT IT! THEY CAN CURE PRACTICALLY ANYTHING.
WOW...THAT SURE SOUNDS A LOT BETTER THAN A TRIP TO THE VET.
BUT SHE *DOESN'T* LOSE INTEREST... AND SHE'S REALLY GOOD AT IT!
AND WHEN IT GETS COLD... YOU DON'T REALLY KNOW IF YOU'LL HAVE ENOUGH FOOD TO EAT, DO YOU?
THERE'S NO GUARANTEE, NO. BUT THAT'S WHAT WARRIORS DO, IN PART. WE HUNT FOR THE CLAN.
WE GO OUT AND MAKE SURE EVERYONE GETS ENOUGH.

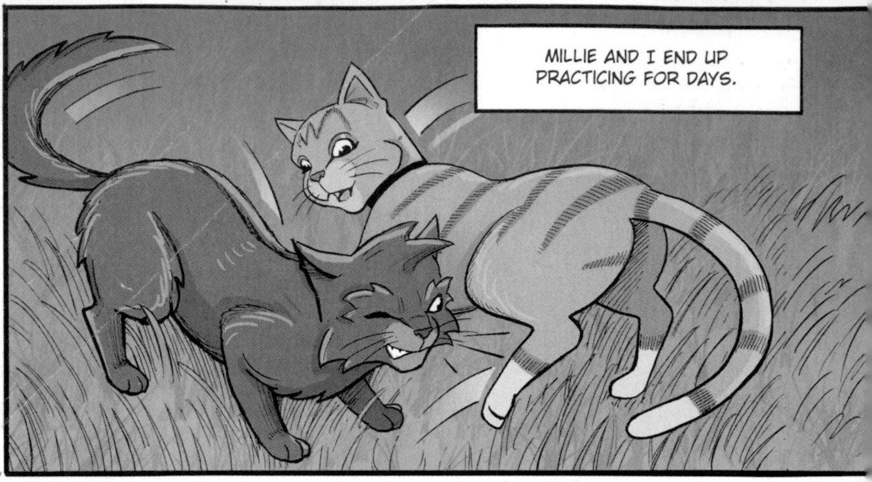
MILLIE AND I END UP PRACTICING FOR DAYS.

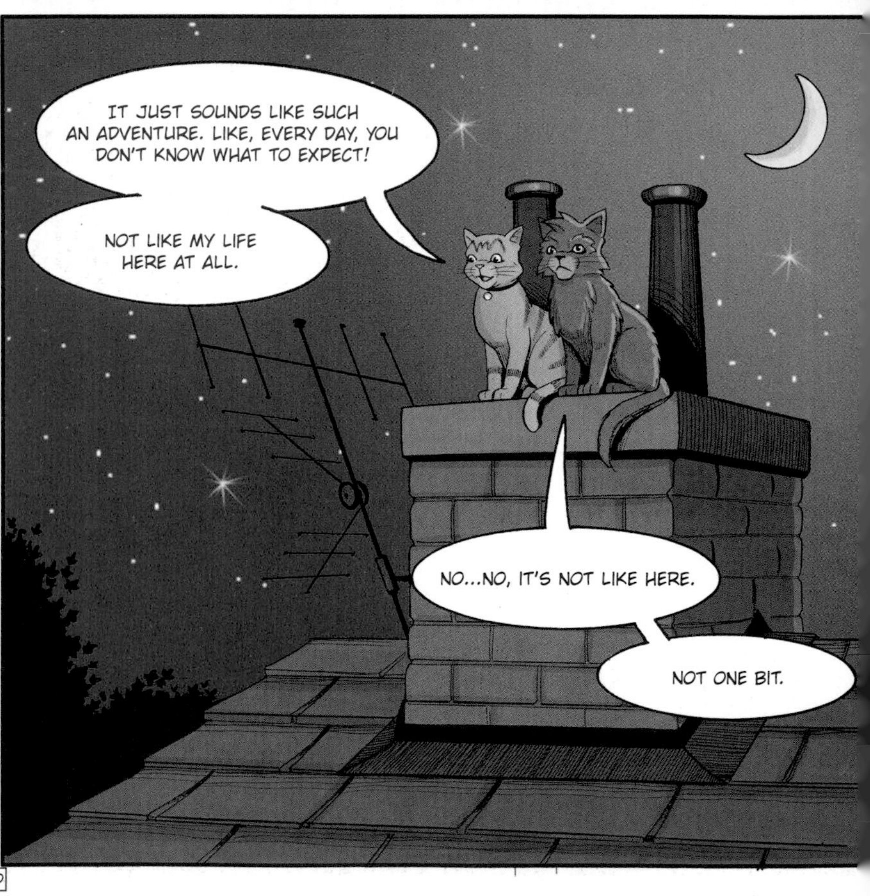
IT JUST SOUNDS LIKE SUCH AN ADVENTURE. LIKE, EVERY DAY, YOU DON'T KNOW WHAT TO EXPECT!
NOT LIKE MY LIFE HERE AT ALL.
NO...NO, IT'S NOT LIKE HERE.
NOT ONE BIT.

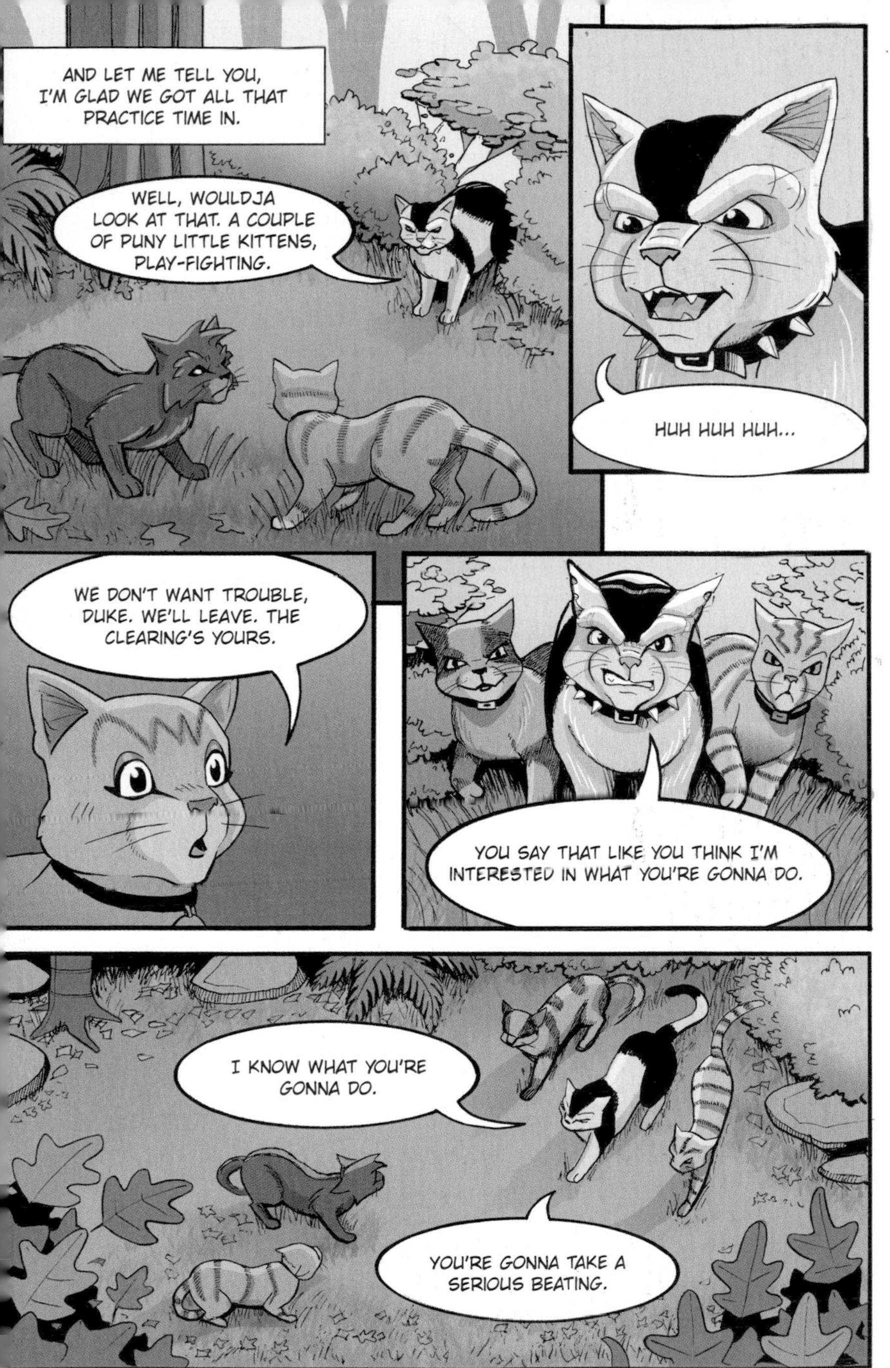
AND LET ME TELL YOU, I'M GLAD WE GOT ALL THAT PRACTICE TIME IN.
WELL, WOULDJA LOOK AT THAT. A COUPLE OF PUNY LITTLE KITTENS, PLAY-FIGHTING.
HUH HUH HUH...
WE DON'T WANT TROUBLE, DUKE. WE'LL LEAVE. THE CLEARING'S YOURS.
YOU SAY THAT LIKE YOU THINK I'M INTERESTED IN WHAT YOU'RE GONNA DO.
I KNOW WHAT YOU'RE GONNA DO.
YOU'RE GONNA TAKE A SERIOUS BEATING.

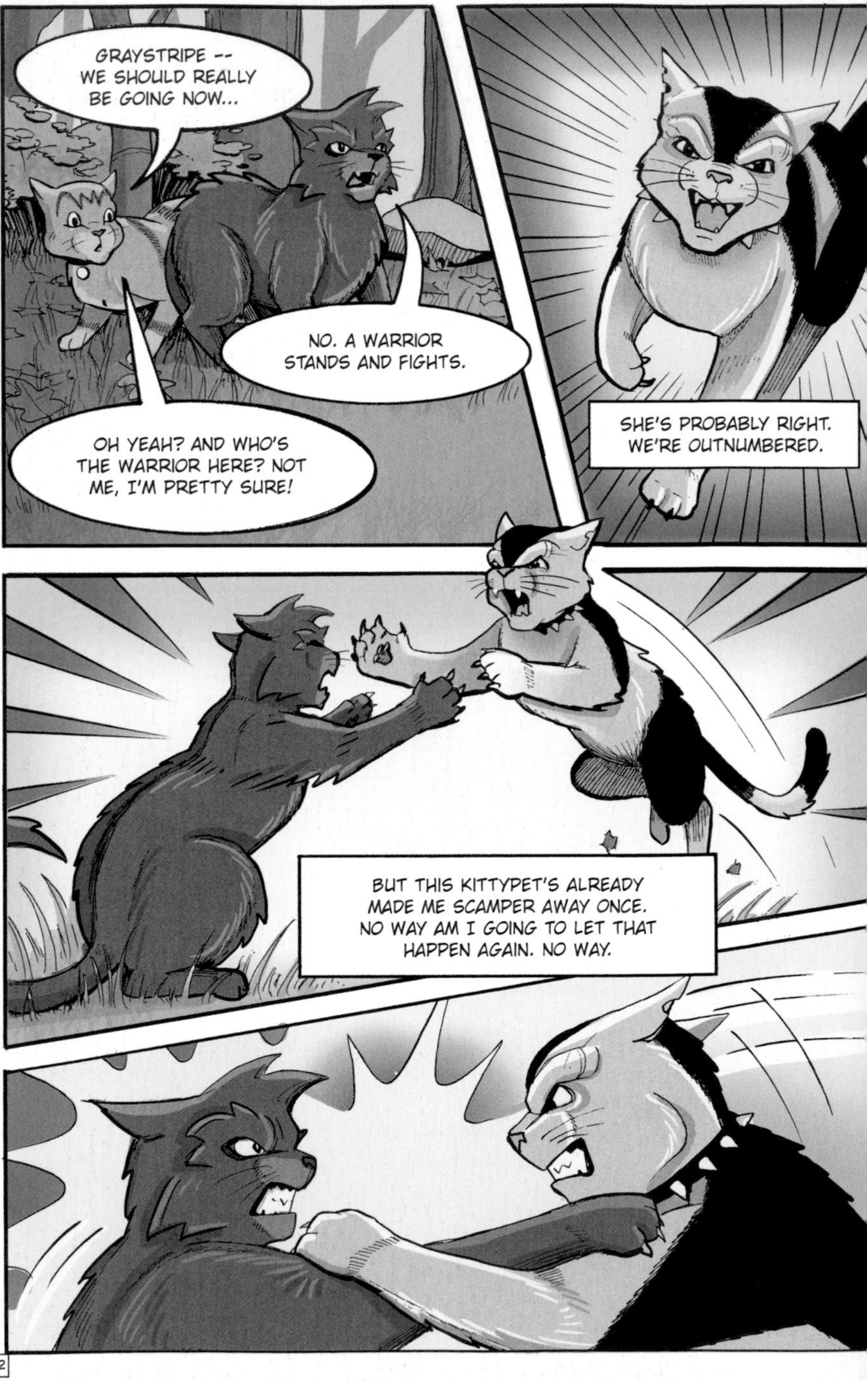
GRAYSTRIPE -- WE SHOULD REALLY BE GOING NOW...
NO. A WARRIOR STANDS AND FIGHTS.
OH YEAH? AND WHO'S THE WARRIOR HERE? NOT ME, I'M PRETTY SURE!
SHE'S PROBABLY RIGHT. WE'RE OUTNUMBERED.
BUT THIS KITTYPET'S ALREADY MADE ME SCAMPER AWAY ONCE. NO WAY AM I GOING TO LET THAT HAPPEN AGAIN. NO WAY.

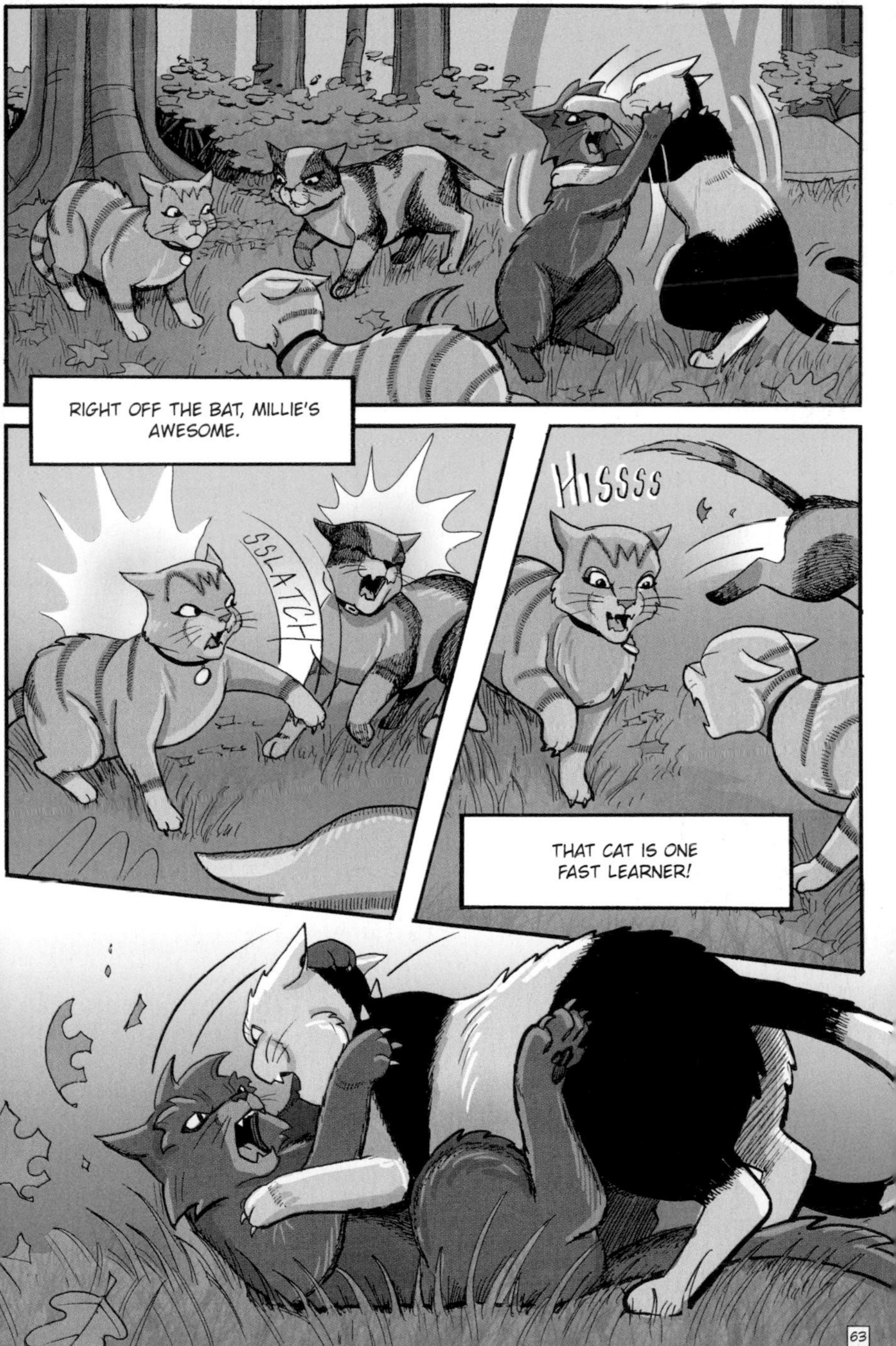
RIGHT OFF THE BAT, MILLIE'S AWESOME.
SSLATCH
HISSSS
THAT CAT IS ONE FAST LEARNER!

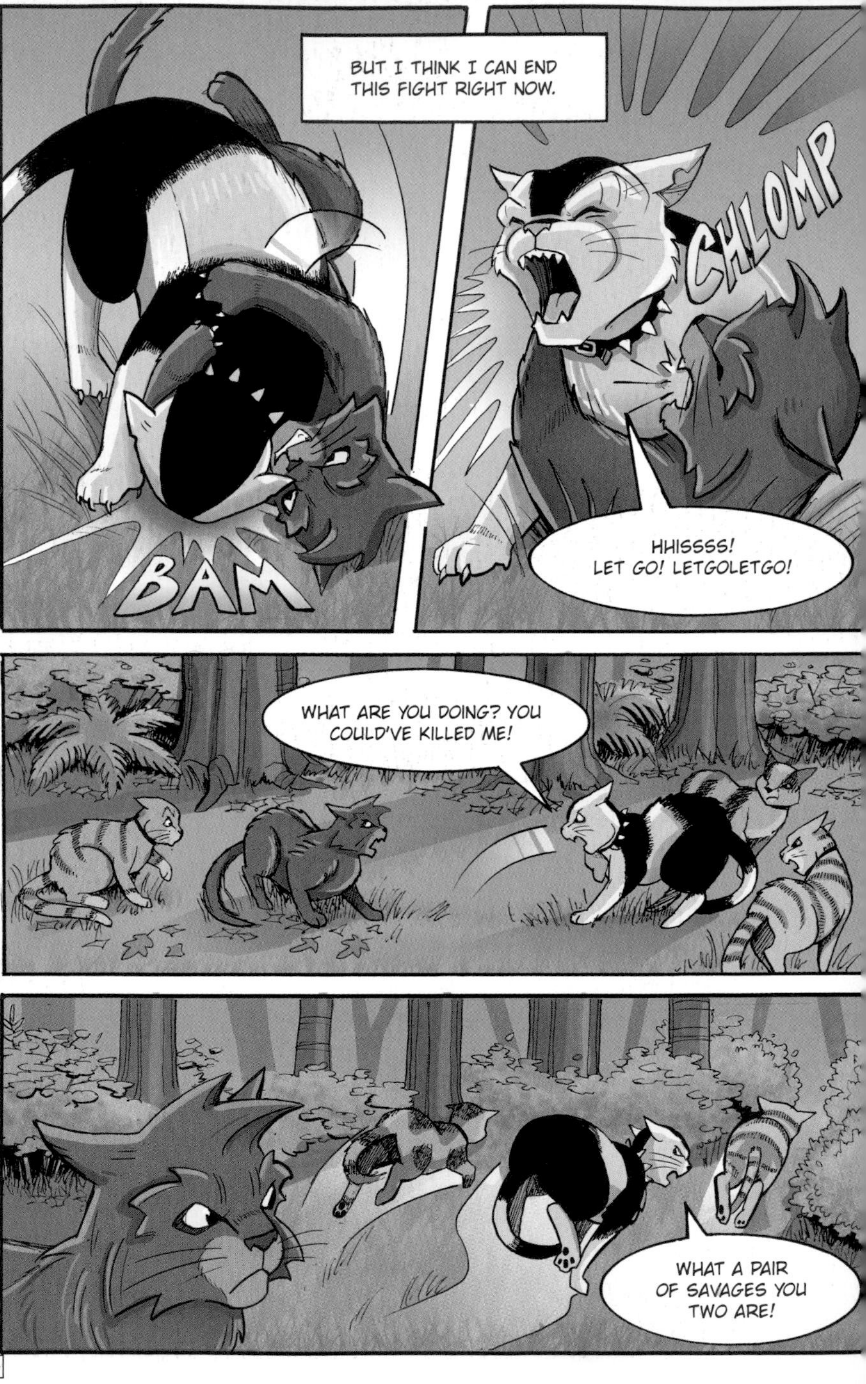
BUT I THINK I CAN END THIS FIGHT RIGHT NOW.
BAM
CHLOMP
HHISSSS! LET GO! LETGOLETGO!
WHAT ARE YOU DOING? YOU COULD'VE KILLED ME!
WHAT A PAIR OF SAVAGES YOU TWO ARE!

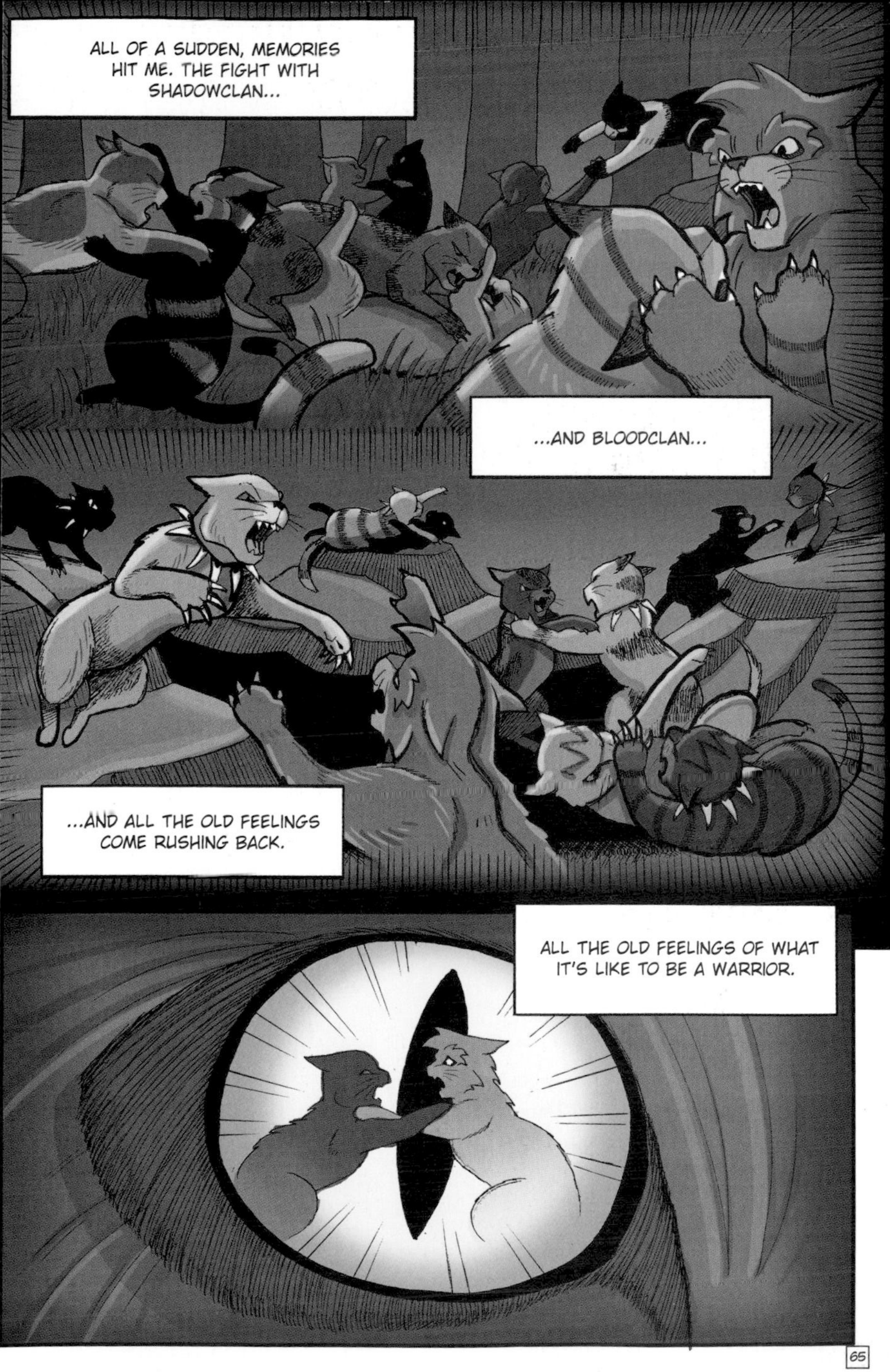
ALL OF A SUDDEN, MEMORIES HIT ME. THE FIGHT WITH SHADOWCLAN...
...AND BLOODCLAN...
...AND ALL THE OLD FEELINGS COME RUSHING BACK.
ALL THE OLD FEELINGS OF WHAT IT'S LIKE TO BE A WARRIOR.

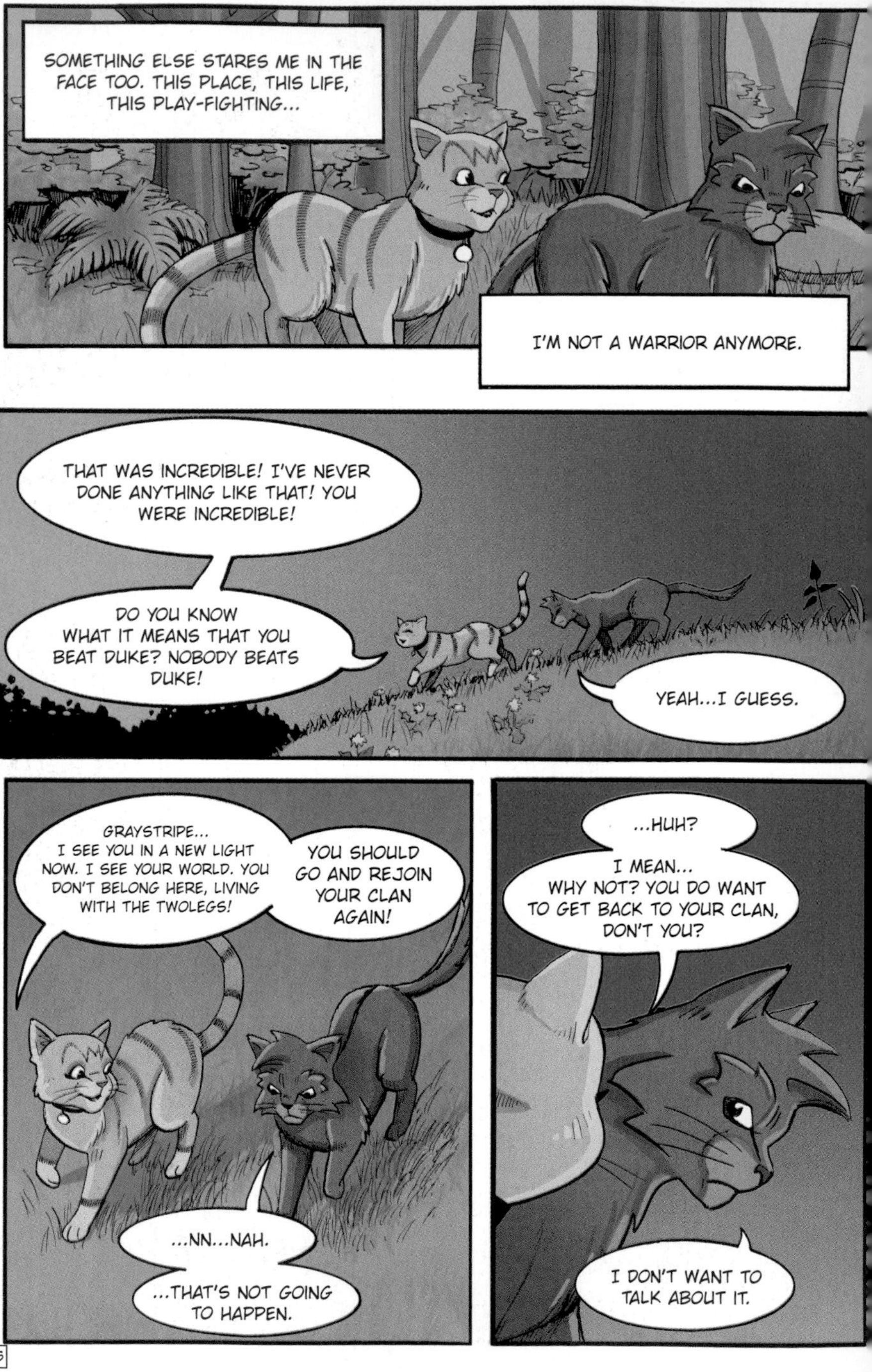
SOMETHING ELSE STARES ME IN THE FACE TOO. THIS PLACE, THIS LIFE, THIS PLAY-FIGHTING...
I'M NOT A WARRIOR ANYMORE.
THAT WAS INCREDIBLE! I'VE NEVER DONE ANYTHING LIKE THAT! YOU WERE INCREDIBLE!
DO YOU KNOW WHAT IT MEANS THAT YOU BEAT DUKE? NOBODY BEATS DUKE!
YEAH...I GUESS.
GRAYSTRIPE... I SEE YOU IN A NEW LIGHT NOW. I SEE YOUR WORLD. YOU DON'T BELONG HERE, LIVING WITH THE TWOLEGS!
YOU SHOULD GO AND REJOIN YOUR CLAN AGAIN!
...NN...NAH.
...THAT'S NOT GOING TO HAPPEN.
...HUH?
I MEAN... WHY NOT? YOU DO WANT TO GET BACK TO YOUR CLAN, DON'T YOU?
I DON'T WANT TO TALK ABOUT IT.

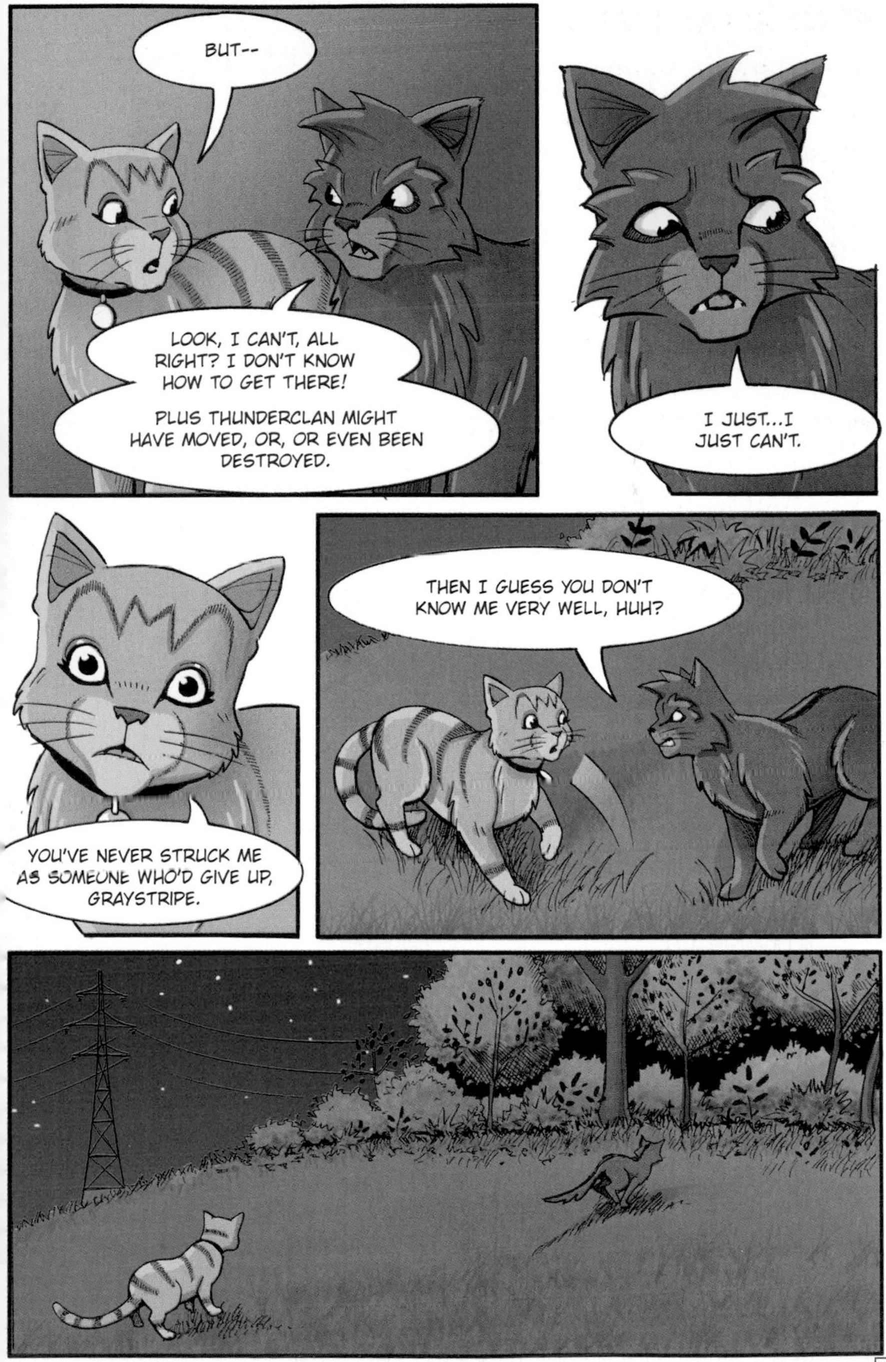
BUT--
LOOK, I CAN'T, ALL RIGHT? I DON'T KNOW HOW TO GET THERE!
PLUS THUNDERCLAN MIGHT HAVE MOVED, OR, OR EVEN BEEN DESTROYED.
I JUST...I JUST CAN'T.
YOU'VE NEVER STRUCK ME AS SOMEONE WHO'D GIVE UP, GRAYSTRIPE.
THEN I GUESS YOU DON'T KNOW ME VERY WELL, HUH?

CHAPTER 4

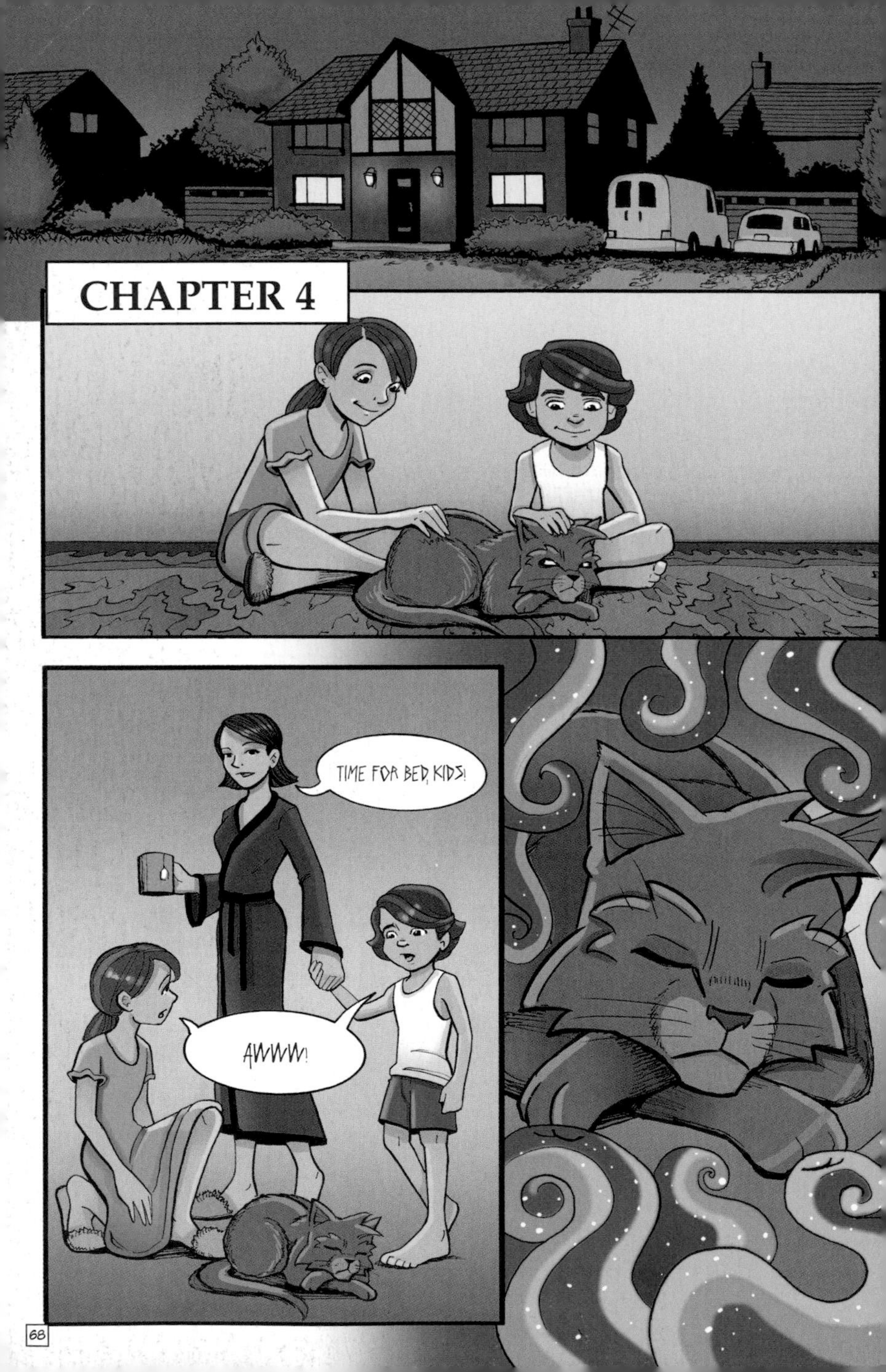
TIME FOR BED, KIDS!
AWWW!

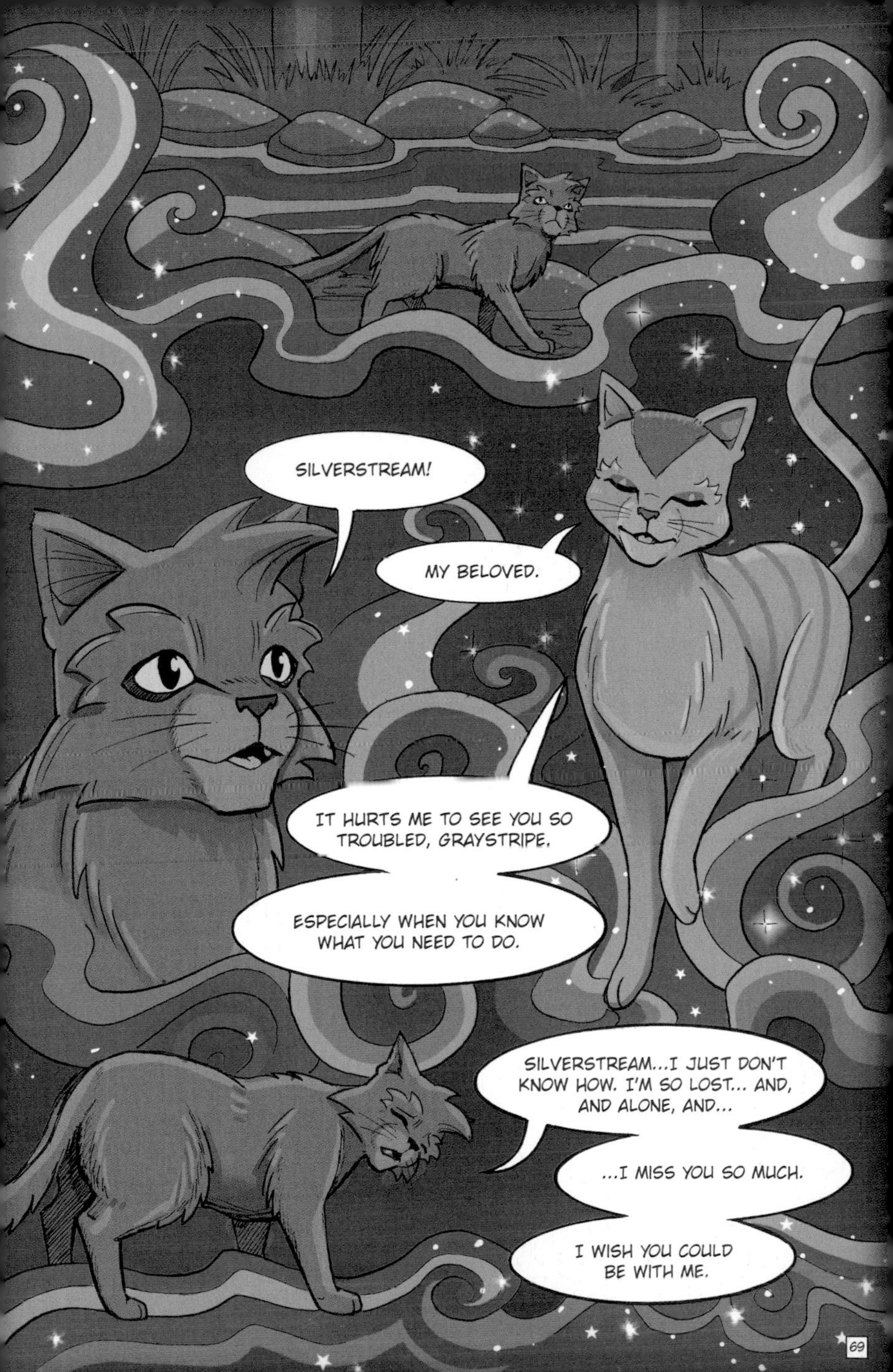
SILVERSTREAM!
MY BELOVED.
IT HURTS ME TO SEE YOU SO TROUBLED, GRAYSTRIPE.
ESPECIALLY WHEN YOU KNOW WHAT YOU NEED TO DO.
SILVERSTREAM...I JUST DON'T KNOW HOW. I'M SO LOST... AND, AND ALONE, AND...
...I MISS YOU SO MUCH.
I WISH YOU COULD BE WITH ME.

YOU ARE A WARRIOR OF THUNDERCLAN, GRAYSTRIPE. YOUR PLACE IS WITH THEM.
YOU REALLY THINK I SHOULD TRY TO FIND THEM?
I THINK YOU HAVE TO.
I WILL ALWAYS BE WITH YOU, BELOVED.
BUT I THINK YOU'LL FIND...IF YOU LOOK...
"...THAT YOU ALREADY HAVE A TRAVELING COMPANION."

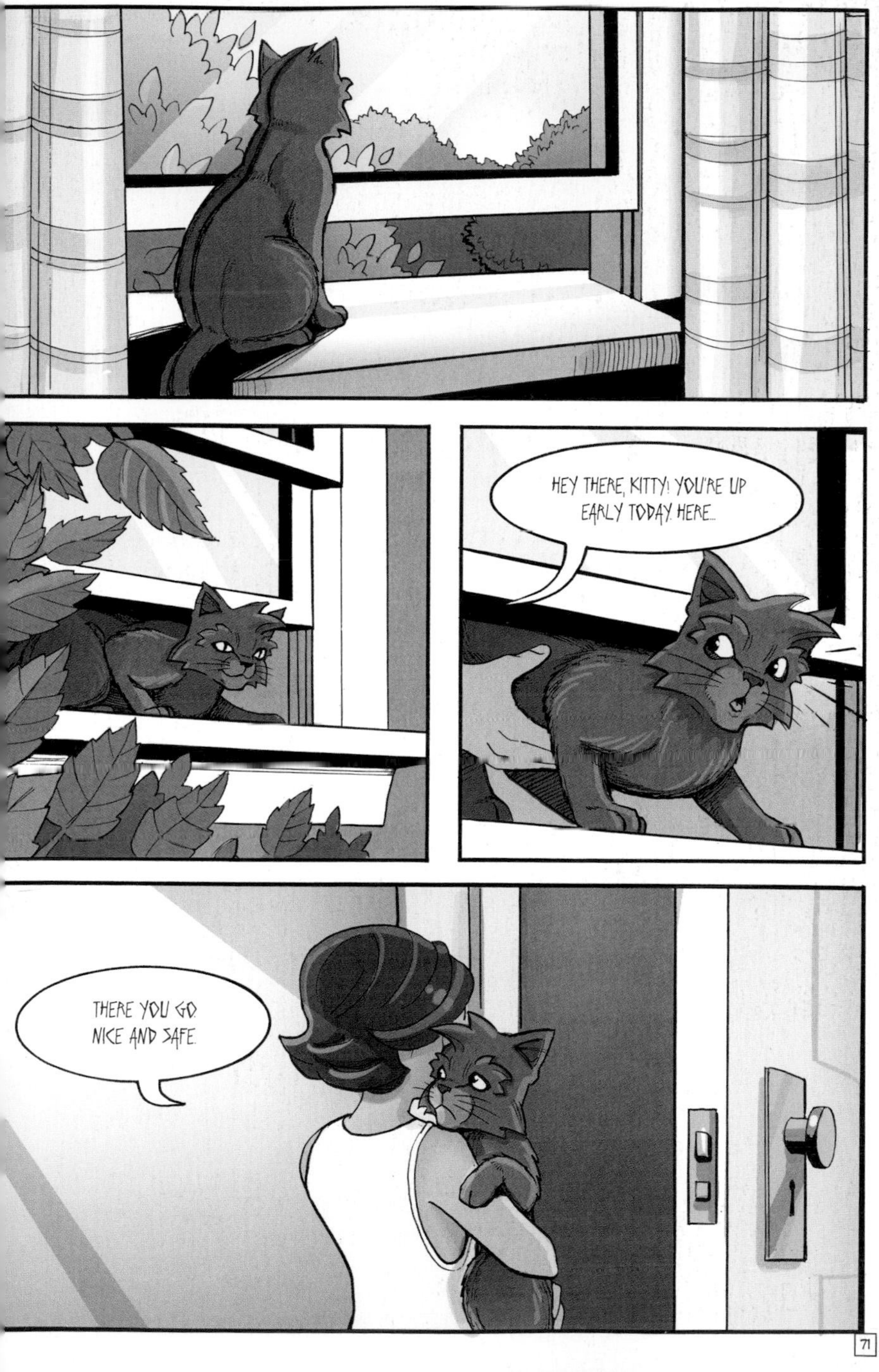
HEY THERE, KITTY! YOU'RE UP EARLY TODAY. HERE...
THERE YOU GO. NICE AND SAFE.

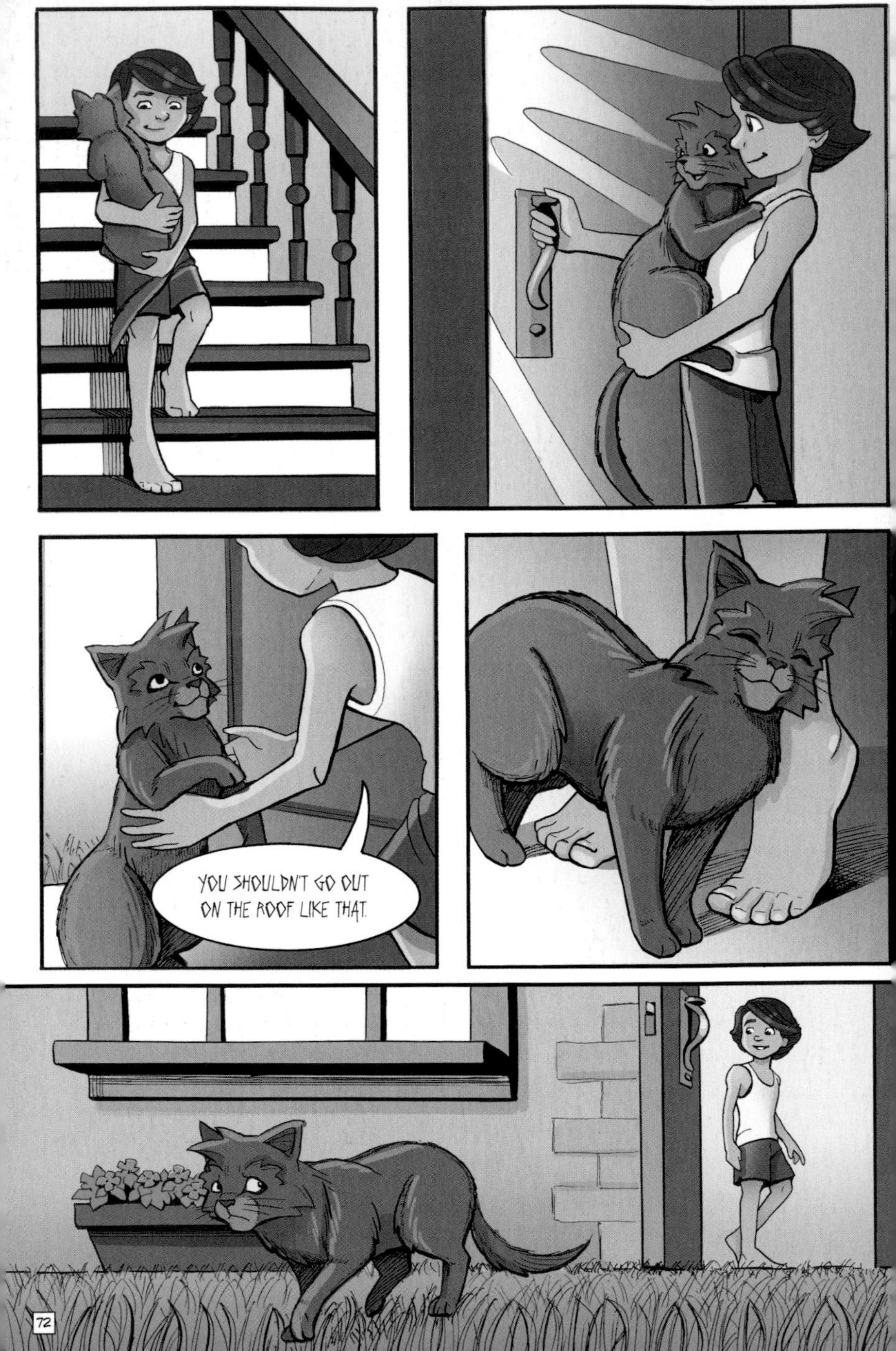
YOU SHOULDN'T GO OUT ON THE ROOF LIKE THAT.

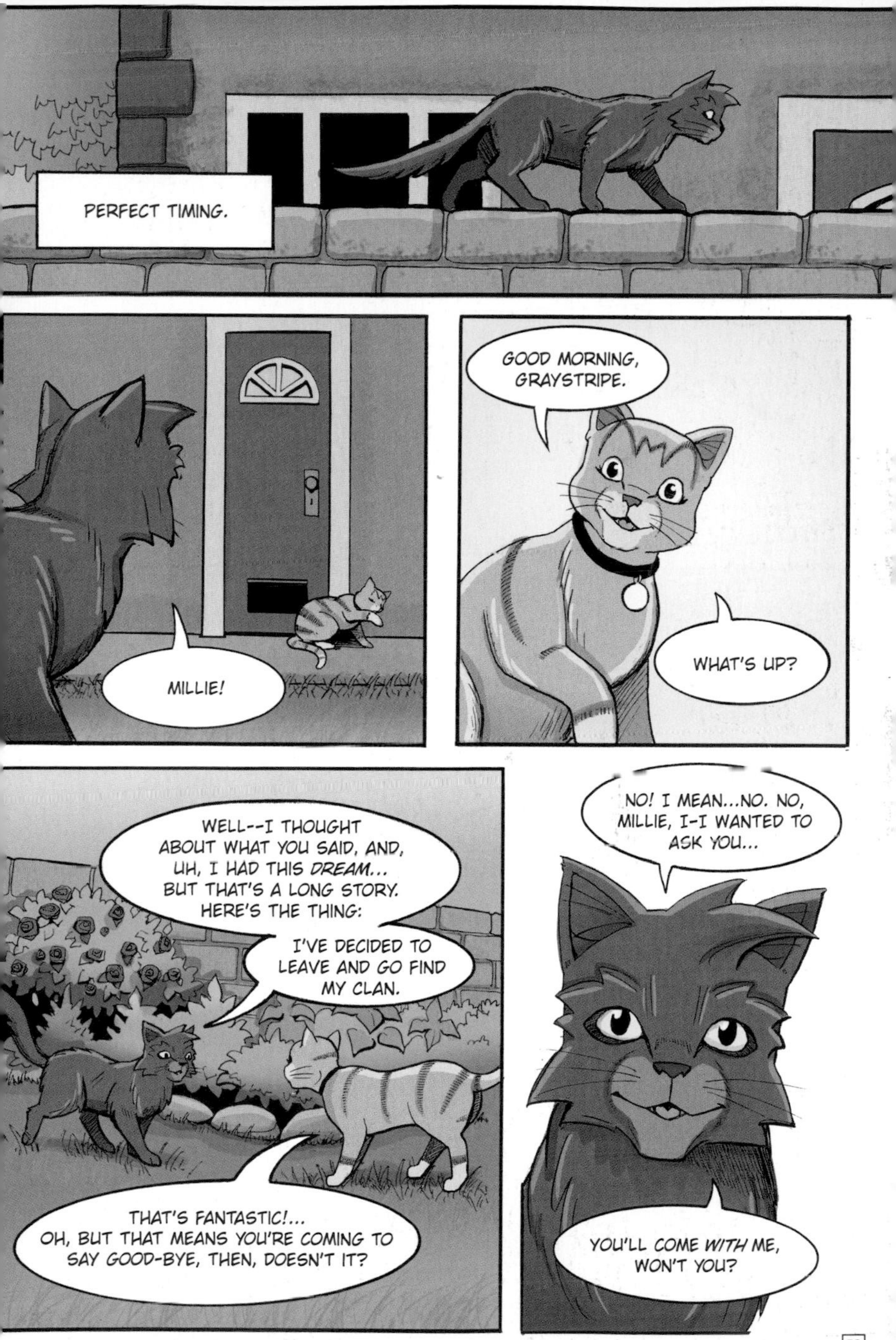
PERFECT TIMING.
MILLIE!
GOOD MORNING, GRAYSTRIPE.
WHAT'S UP?
WELL--I THOUGHT ABOUT WHAT YOU SAID, AND, UH, I HAD THIS *DREAM*... BUT THAT'S A LONG STORY. HERE'S THE THING:
I'VE DECIDED TO LEAVE AND GO FIND MY CLAN.
THAT'S FANTASTIC!... OH, BUT THAT MEANS YOU'RE COMING TO SAY GOOD-BYE, THEN, DOESN'T IT?
NO! I MEAN...NO. NO, MILLIE, I-I WANTED TO ASK YOU...
YOU'LL COME *WITH* ME, WON'T YOU?

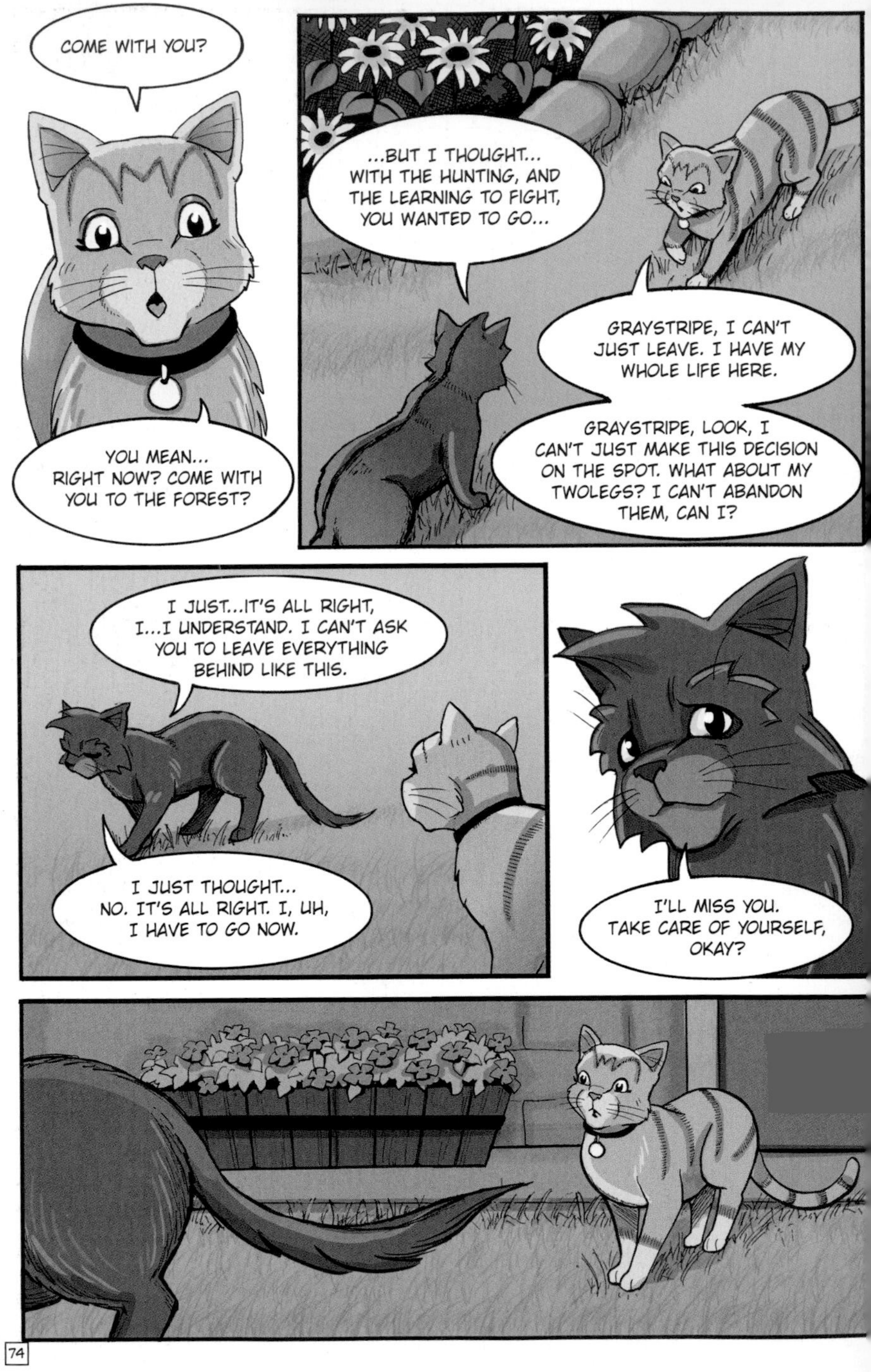
COME WITH YOU?
YOU MEAN... RIGHT NOW? COME WITH YOU TO THE FOREST?
...BUT I THOUGHT... WITH THE HUNTING, AND THE LEARNING TO FIGHT, YOU WANTED TO GO...
GRAYSTRIPE, I CAN'T JUST LEAVE. I HAVE MY WHOLE LIFE HERE.
GRAYSTRIPE, LOOK, I CAN'T JUST MAKE THIS DECISION ON THE SPOT. WHAT ABOUT MY TWOLEGS? I CAN'T ABANDON THEM, CAN I?
I JUST...IT'S ALL RIGHT, I...I UNDERSTAND. I CAN'T ASK YOU TO LEAVE EVERYTHING BEHIND LIKE THIS.
I JUST THOUGHT... NO. IT'S ALL RIGHT. I, UH, I HAVE TO GO NOW.
I'LL MISS YOU. TAKE CARE OF YOURSELF, OKAY?

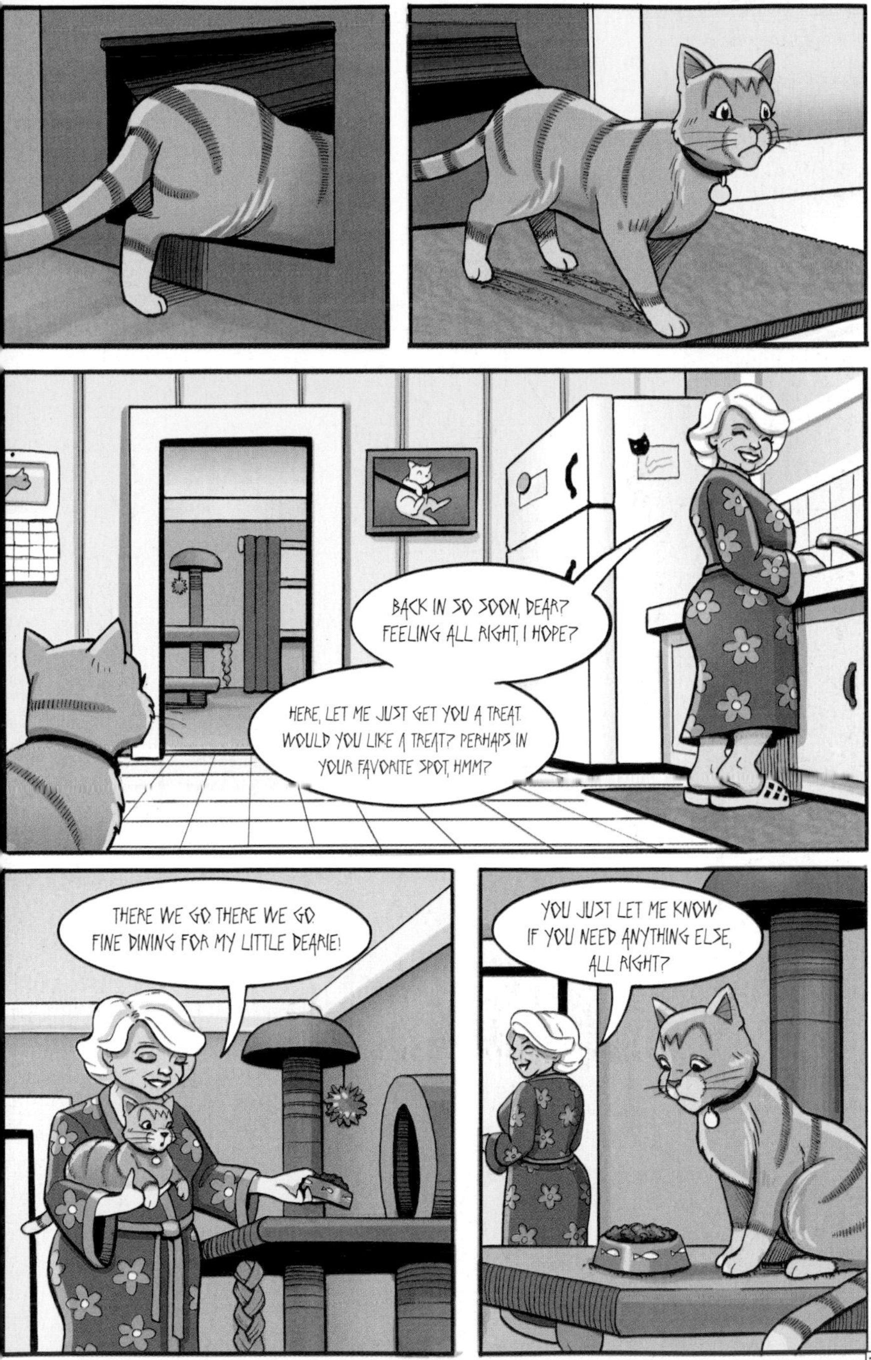
BACK IN SO SOON, DEAR? FEELING ALL RIGHT, I HOPE?
HERE, LET ME JUST GET YOU A TREAT. WOULD YOU LIKE A TREAT? PERHAPS IN YOUR FAVORITE SPOT, HMM?
THERE WE GO. THERE WE GO. FINE DINING FOR MY LITTLE DEARIE!
YOU JUST LET ME KNOW IF YOU NEED ANYTHING ELSE, ALL RIGHT?

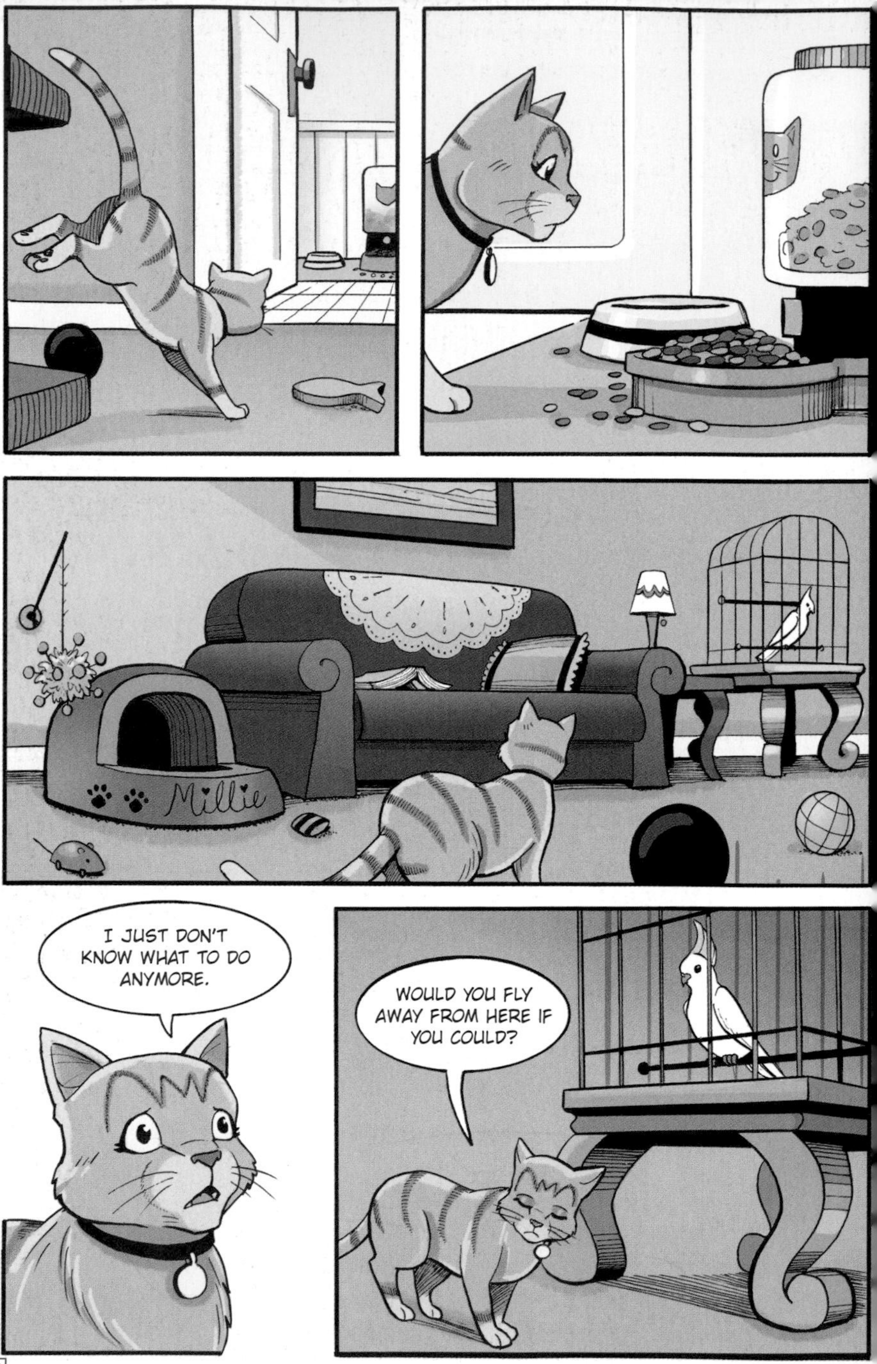
Millie
I JUST DON'T KNOW WHAT TO DO ANYMORE.
WOULD YOU FLY AWAY FROM HERE IF YOU COULD?

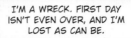

I'M A WRECK. FIRST DAY ISN'T EVEN OVER, AND I'M LOST AS CAN BE.

THIS PLACE IS NOTHING LIKE THE FOREST...

...AND I WANT TO GET OUT OF HERE SO BAD I CAN TASTE IT.

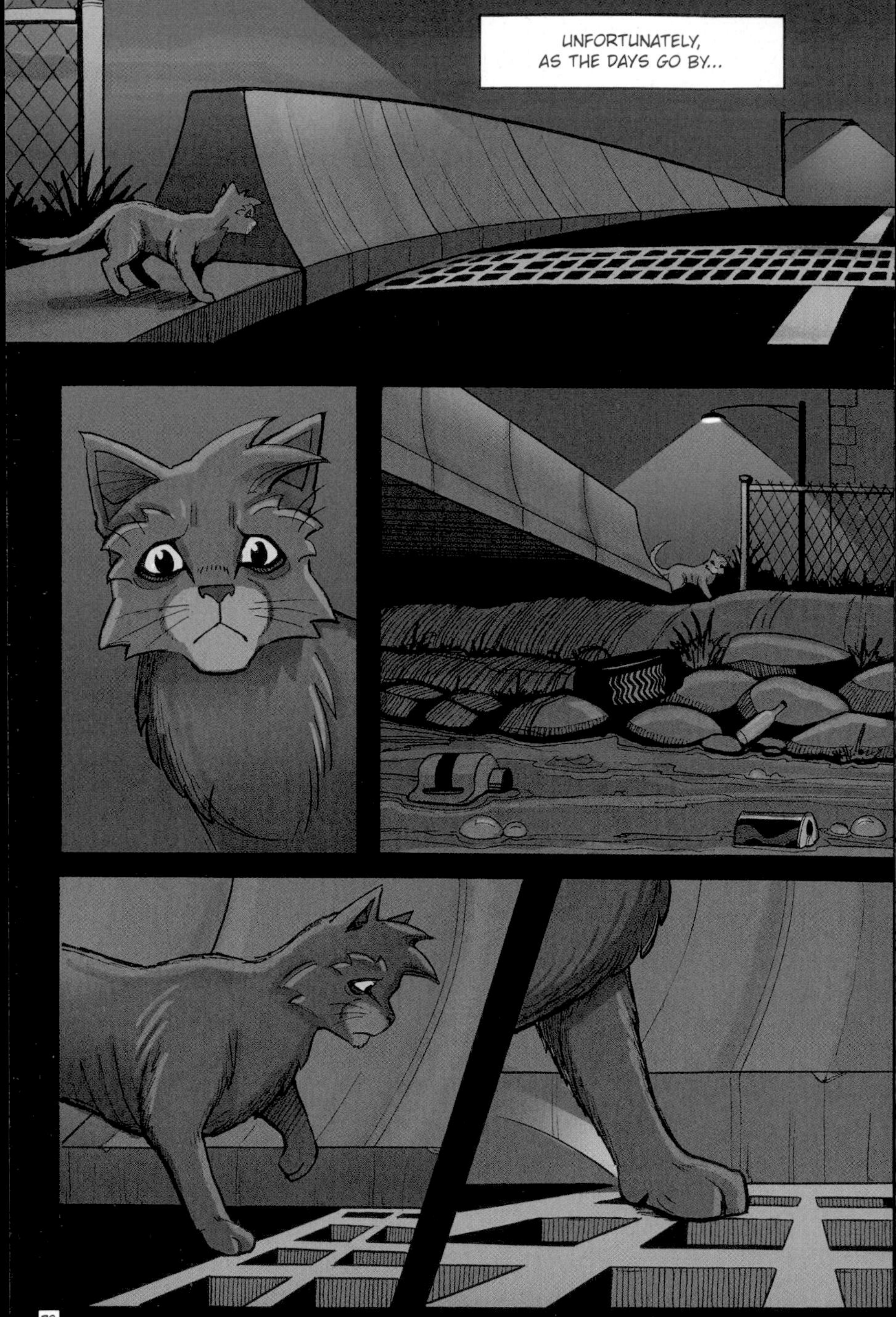
UNFORTUNATELY,
AS THE DAYS GO BY...

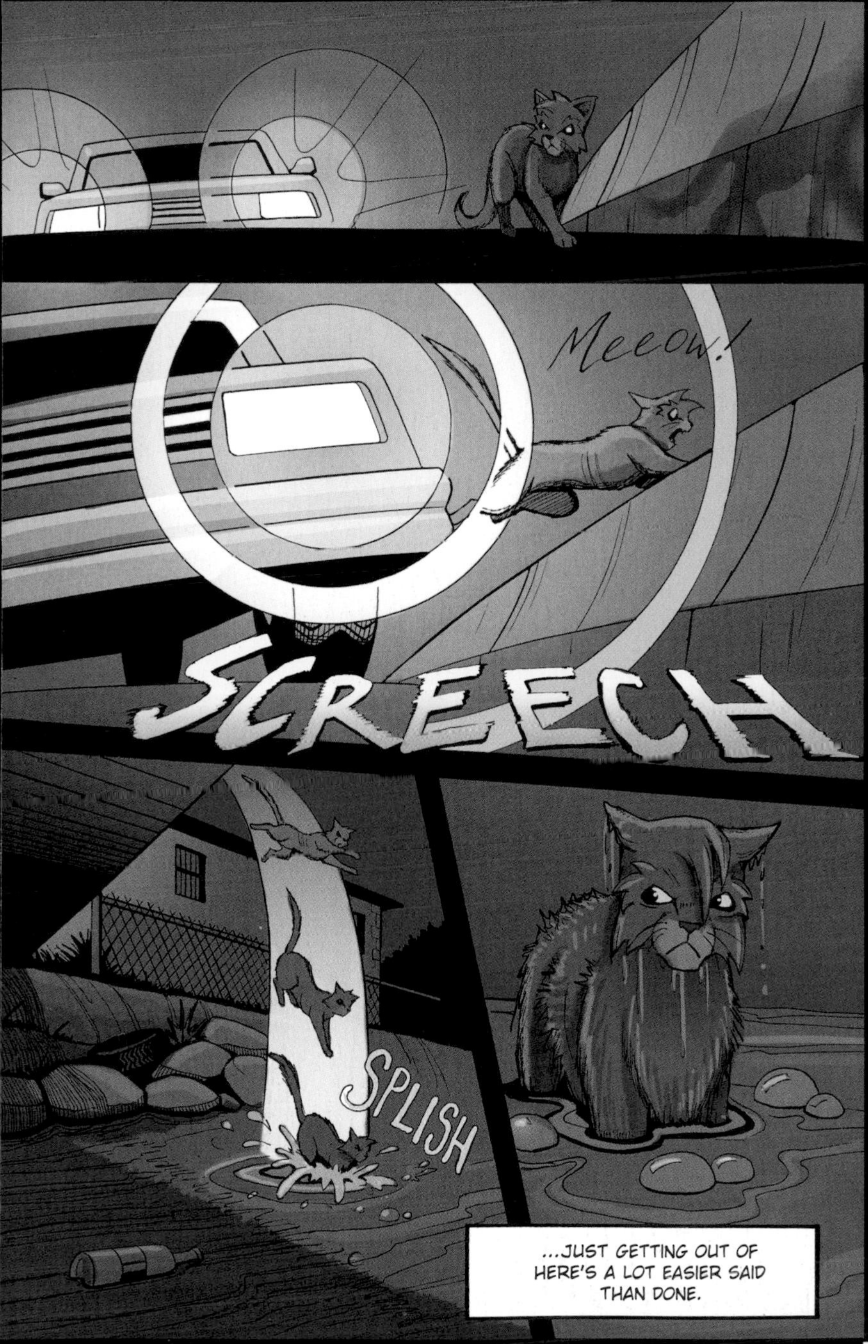
Meeow!
SCREECH
SPLISH
...JUST GETTING OUT OF HERE'S A LOT EASIER SAID THAN DONE.

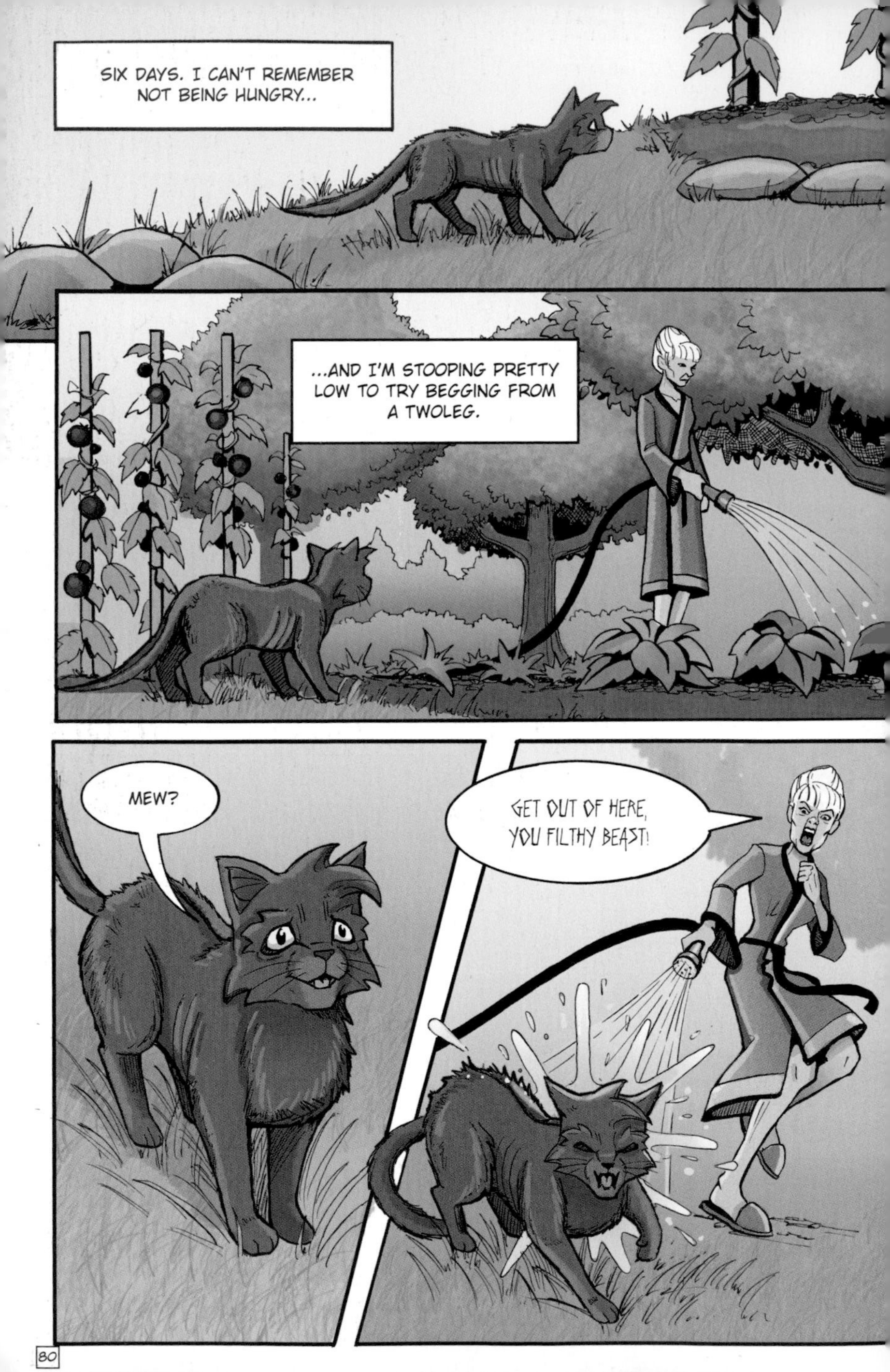
SIX DAYS. I CAN'T REMEMBER NOT BEING HUNGRY...
...AND I'M STOOPING PRETTY LOW TO TRY BEGGING FROM A TWOLEG.
MEW?
GET OUT OF HERE, YOU FILTHY BEAST!

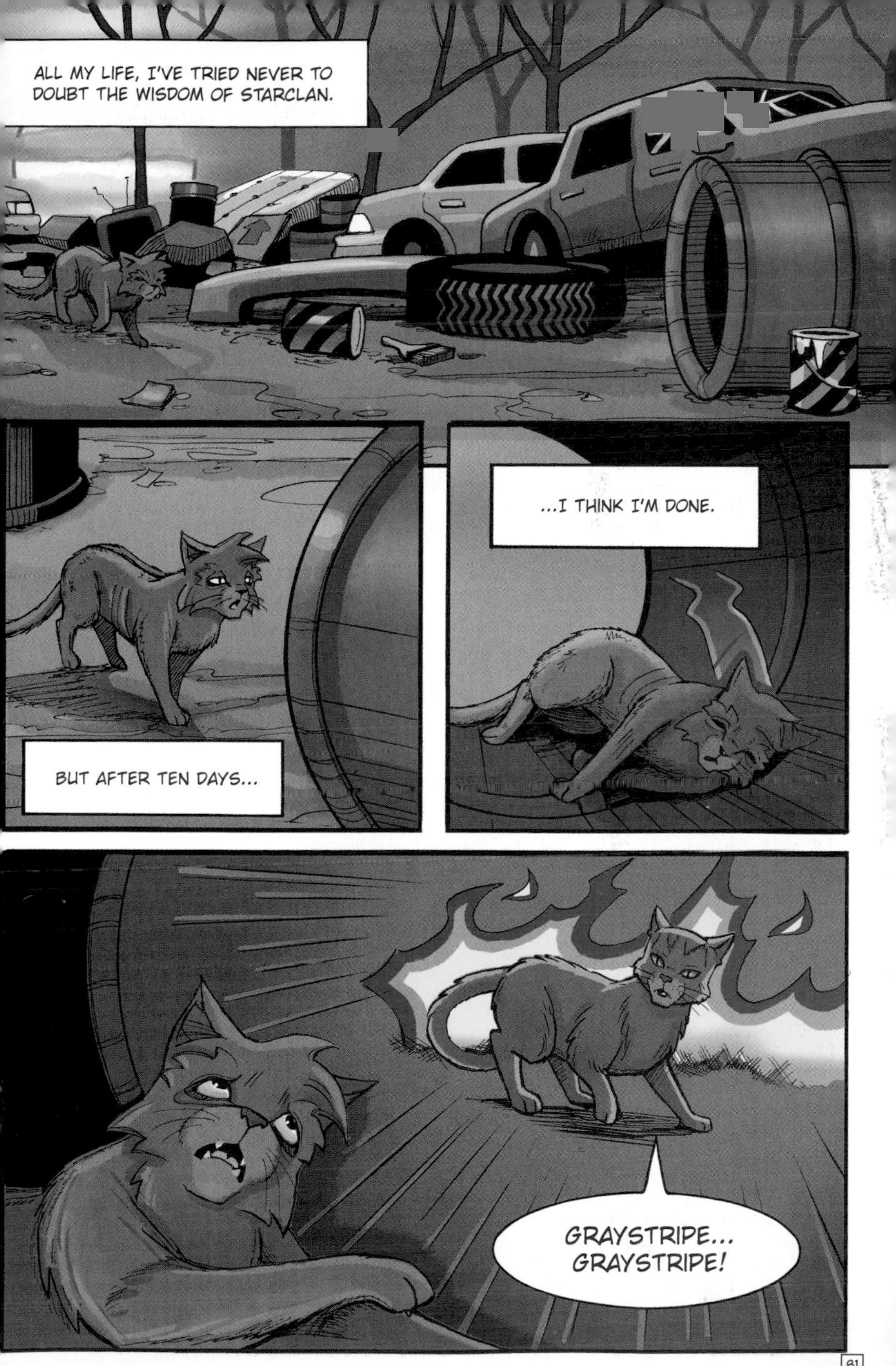
ALL MY LIFE, I'VE TRIED NEVER TO DOUBT THE WISDOM OF STARCLAN.
BUT AFTER TEN DAYS...
...I THINK I'M DONE.
GRAYSTRIPE... GRAYSTRIPE!

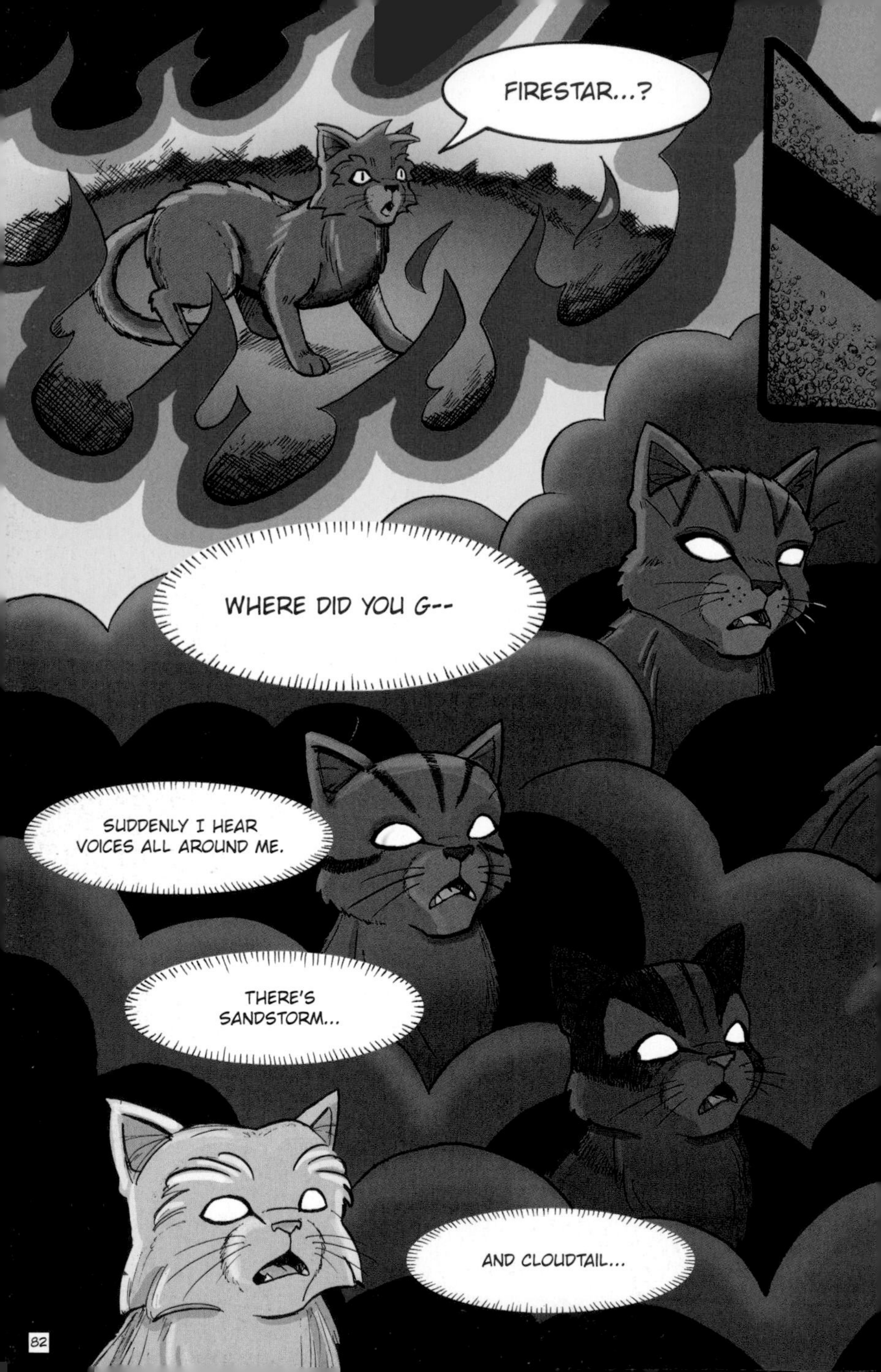

FIRESTAR...?
WHERE DID YOU G--
SUDDENLY I HEAR VOICES ALL AROUND ME.
THERE'S SANDSTORM...
AND CLOUDTAIL...

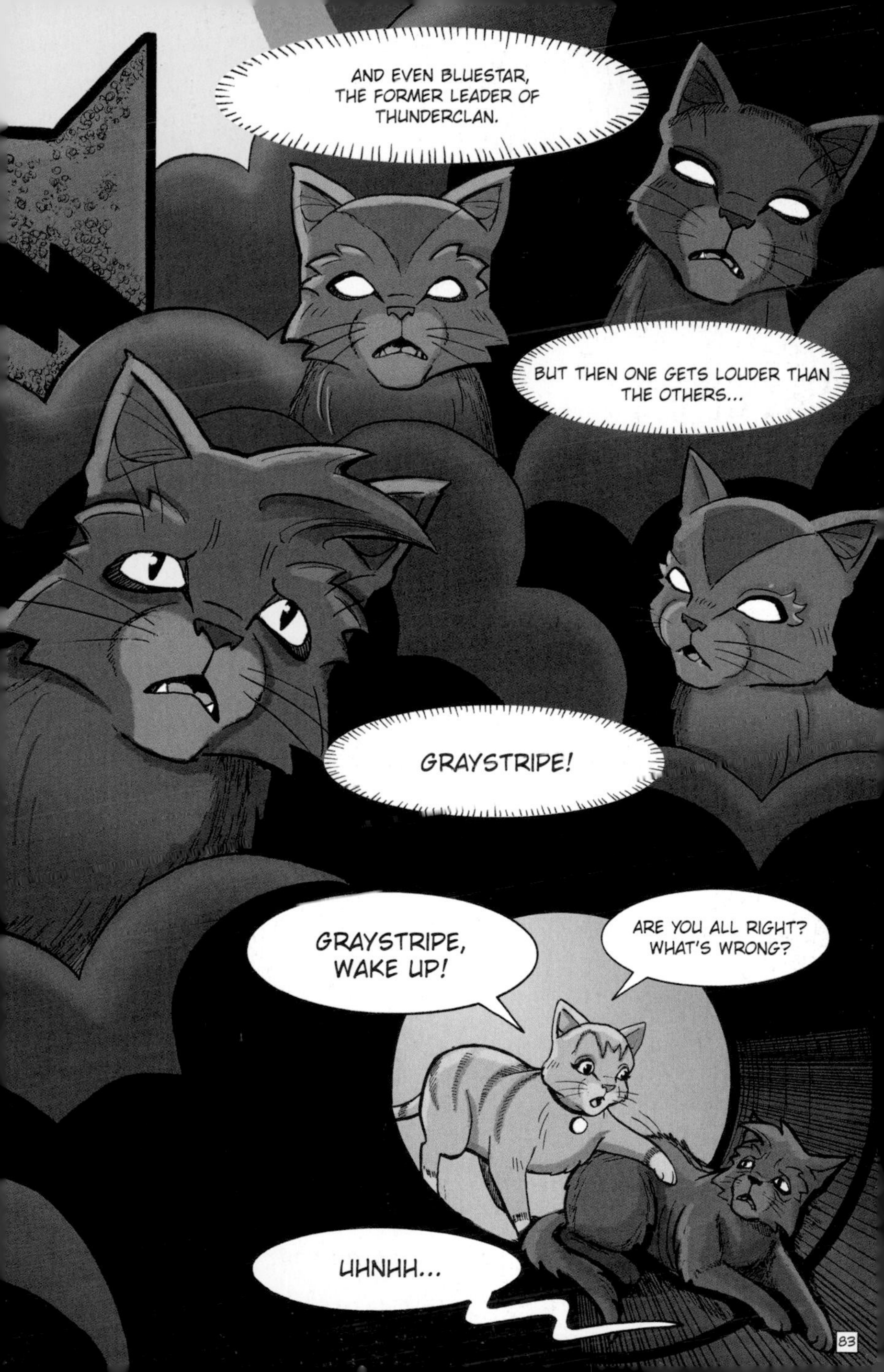
AND EVEN BLUESTAR, THE FORMER LEADER OF THUNDERCLAN.
BUT THEN ONE GETS LOUDER THAN THE OTHERS...
GRAYSTRIPE!
GRAYSTRIPE, WAKE UP!
ARE YOU ALL RIGHT? WHAT'S WRONG?
UHNHH...

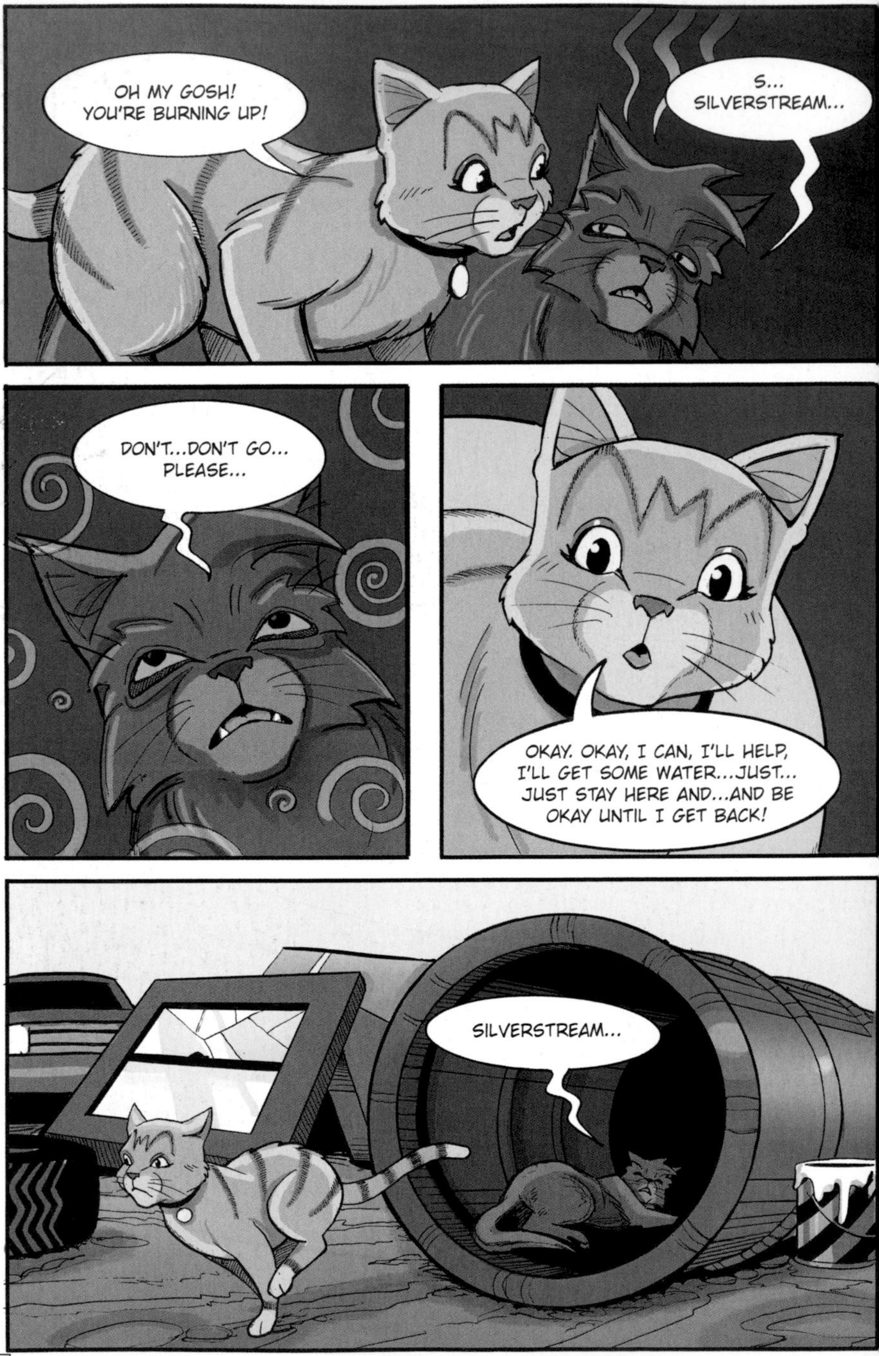
OH MY GOSH! YOU'RE BURNING UP!
S... SILVERSTREAM...
DON'T...DON'T GO... PLEASE...
OKAY. OKAY, I CAN, I'LL HELP, I'LL GET SOME WATER...JUST... JUST STAY HERE AND...AND BE OKAY UNTIL I GET BACK!
SILVERSTREAM...

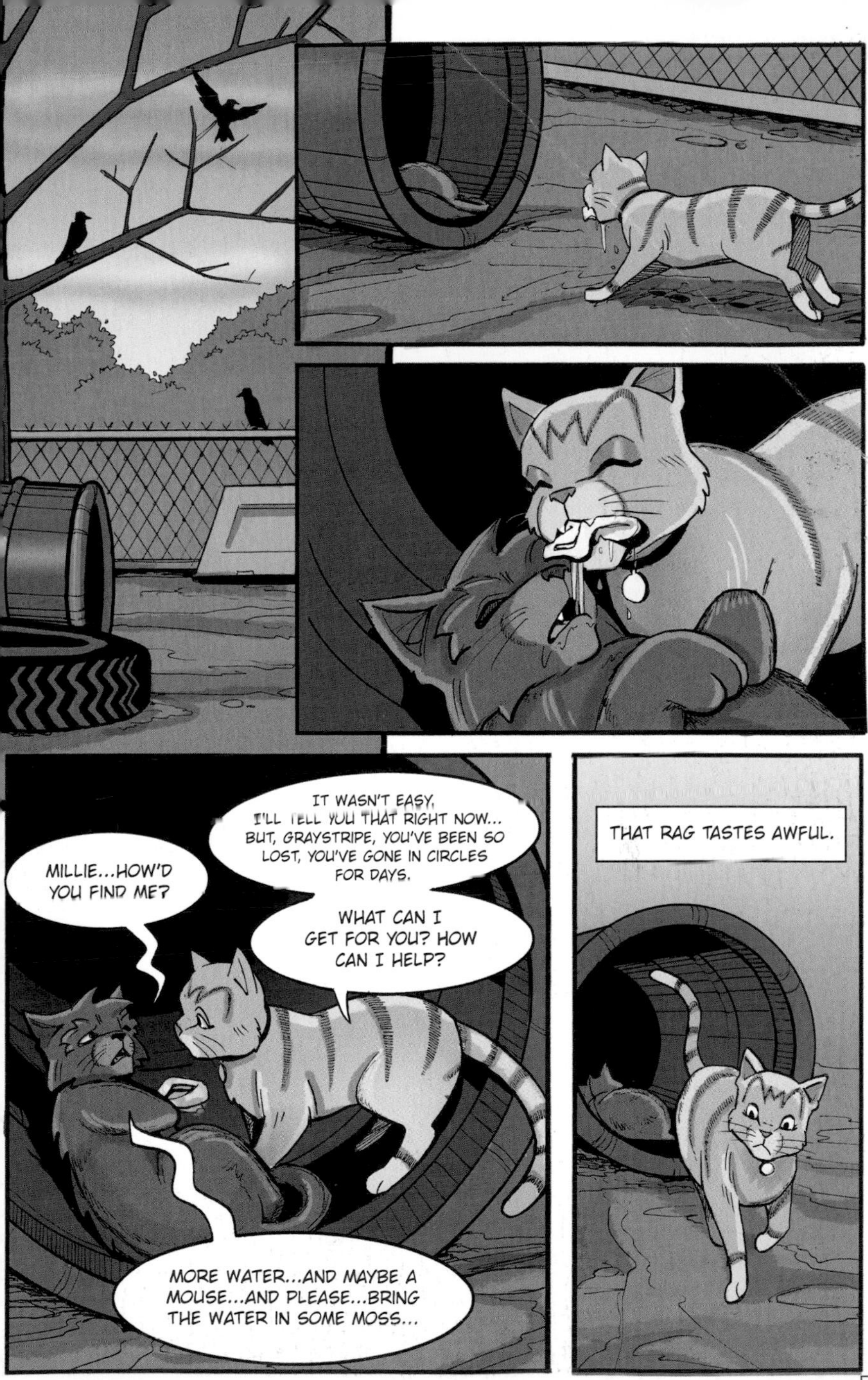
MILLIE...HOW'D YOU FIND ME?
IT WASN'T EASY, I'LL TELL YOU THAT RIGHT NOW... BUT, GRAYSTRIPE, YOU'VE BEEN SO LOST, YOU'VE GONE IN CIRCLES FOR DAYS.
WHAT CAN I GET FOR YOU? HOW CAN I HELP?
MORE WATER...AND MAYBE A MOUSE...AND PLEASE...BRING THE WATER IN SOME MOSS...
THAT RAG TASTES AWFUL.

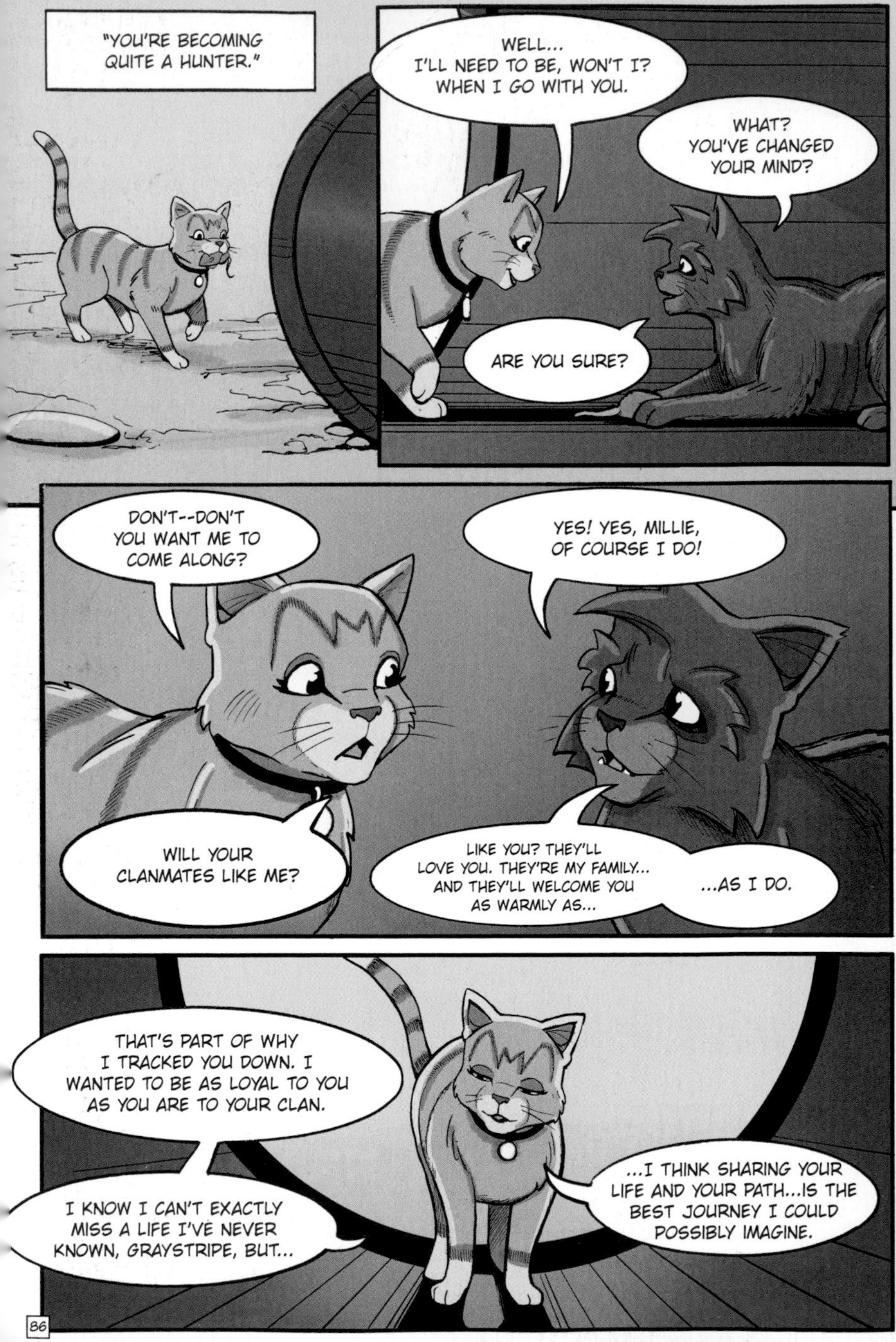
"YOU'RE BECOMING QUITE A HUNTER."
WELL... I'LL NEED TO BE, WON'T I? WHEN I GO WITH YOU.
WHAT? YOU'VE CHANGED YOUR MIND?
ARE YOU SURE?
DON'T--DON'T YOU WANT ME TO COME ALONG?
YES! YES, MILLIE, OF COURSE I DO!
WILL YOUR CLANMATES LIKE ME?
LIKE YOU? THEY'LL LOVE YOU. THEY'RE MY FAMILY... AND THEY'LL WELCOME YOU AS WARMLY AS...
...AS I DO.
THAT'S PART OF WHY I TRACKED YOU DOWN. I WANTED TO BE AS LOYAL TO YOU AS YOU ARE TO YOUR CLAN.
I KNOW I CAN'T EXACTLY MISS A LIFE I'VE NEVER KNOWN, GRAYSTRIPE, BUT...
...I THINK SHARING YOUR LIFE AND YOUR PATH...IS THE BEST JOURNEY I COULD POSSIBLY IMAGINE.

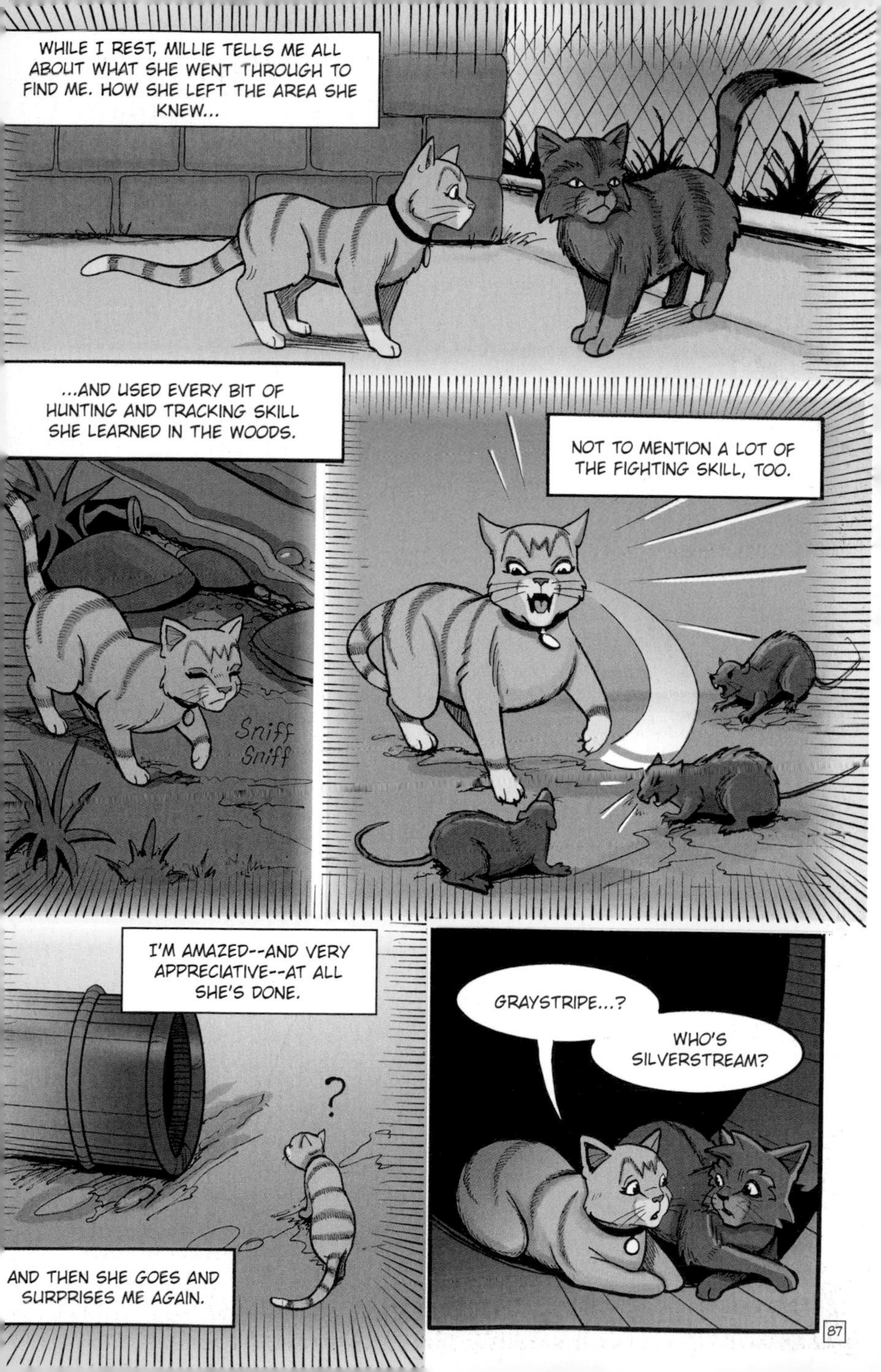

WHILE I REST, MILLIE TELLS ME ALL ABOUT WHAT SHE WENT THROUGH TO FIND ME. HOW SHE LEFT THE AREA SHE KNEW...
...AND USED EVERY BIT OF HUNTING AND TRACKING SKILL SHE LEARNED IN THE WOODS.
Sniff Sniff
NOT TO MENTION A LOT OF THE FIGHTING SKILL, TOO.
I'M AMAZED--AND VERY APPRECIATIVE--AT ALL SHE'S DONE.
?
AND THEN SHE GOES AND SURPRISES ME AGAIN.
GRAYSTRIPE...?
WHO'S SILVERSTREAM?

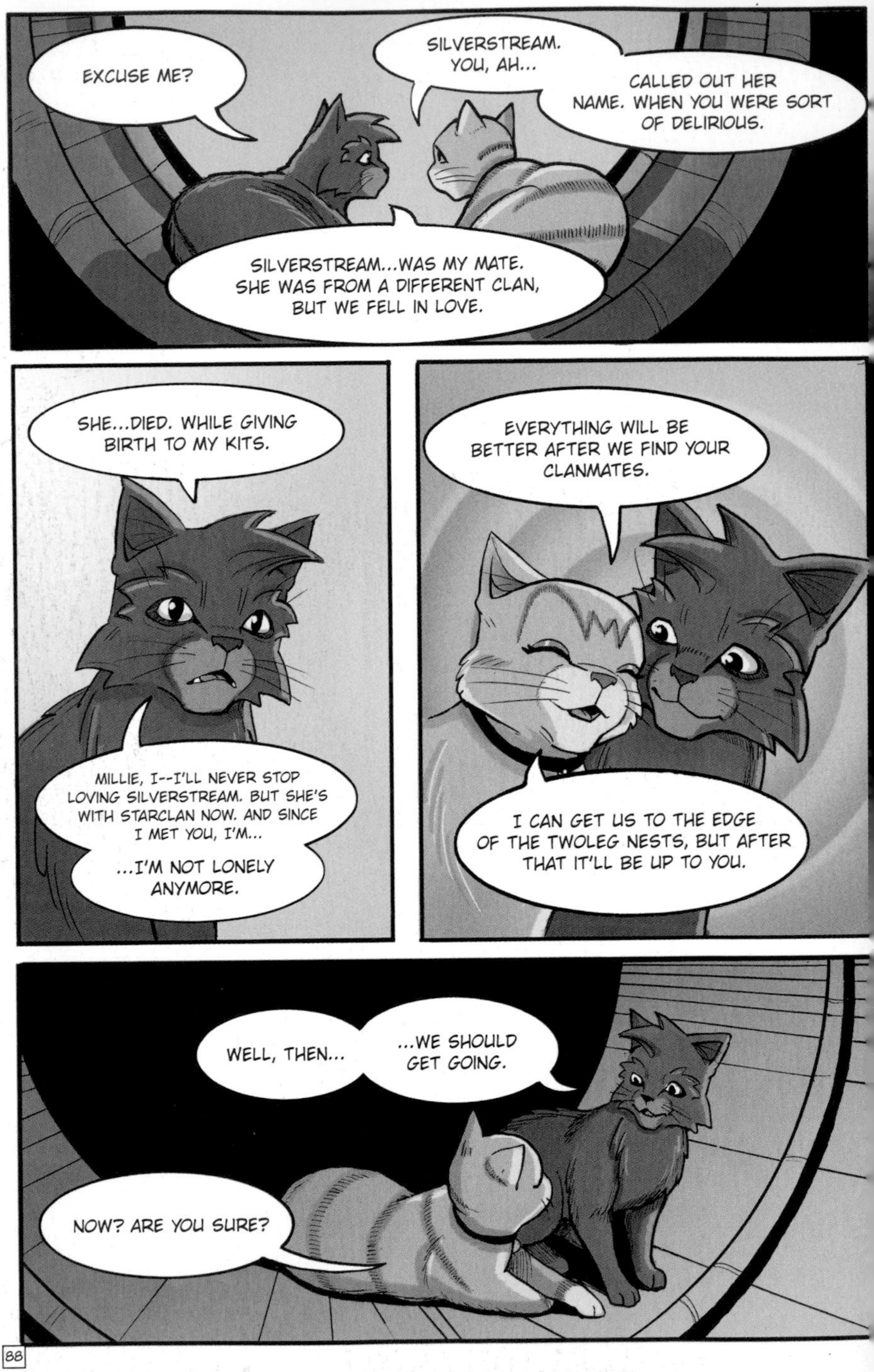
EXCUSE ME?
SILVERSTREAM. YOU, AH...
CALLED OUT HER NAME. WHEN YOU WERE SORT OF DELIRIOUS.
SILVERSTREAM...WAS MY MATE. SHE WAS FROM A DIFFERENT CLAN, BUT WE FELL IN LOVE.
SHE...DIED. WHILE GIVING BIRTH TO MY KITS.
MILLIE, I--I'LL NEVER STOP LOVING SILVERSTREAM. BUT SHE'S WITH STARCLAN NOW. AND SINCE I MET YOU, I'M...
...I'M NOT LONELY ANYMORE.
EVERYTHING WILL BE BETTER AFTER WE FIND YOUR CLANMATES.
I CAN GET US TO THE EDGE OF THE TWOLEG NESTS, BUT AFTER THAT IT'LL BE UP TO YOU.
WELL, THEN...
...WE SHOULD GET GOING.
NOW? ARE YOU SURE?

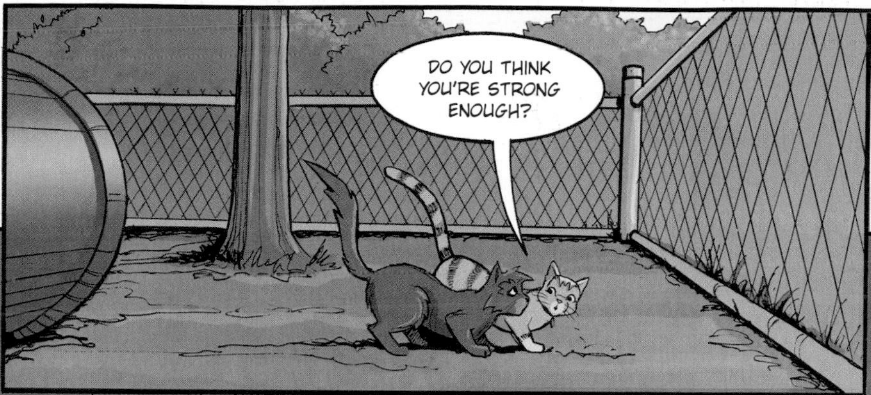
DO YOU THINK YOU'RE STRONG ENOUGH?
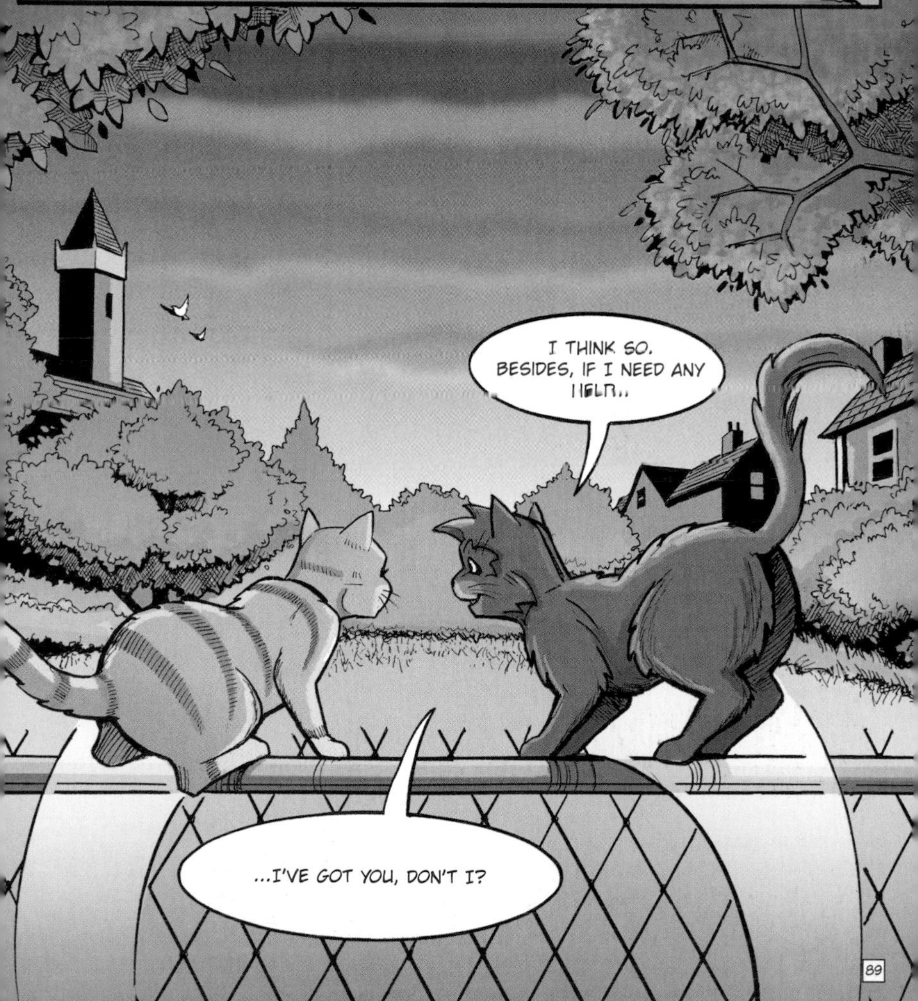
I THINK SO. BESIDES, IF I NEED ANY HELP...
...I'VE GOT YOU, DON'T I?

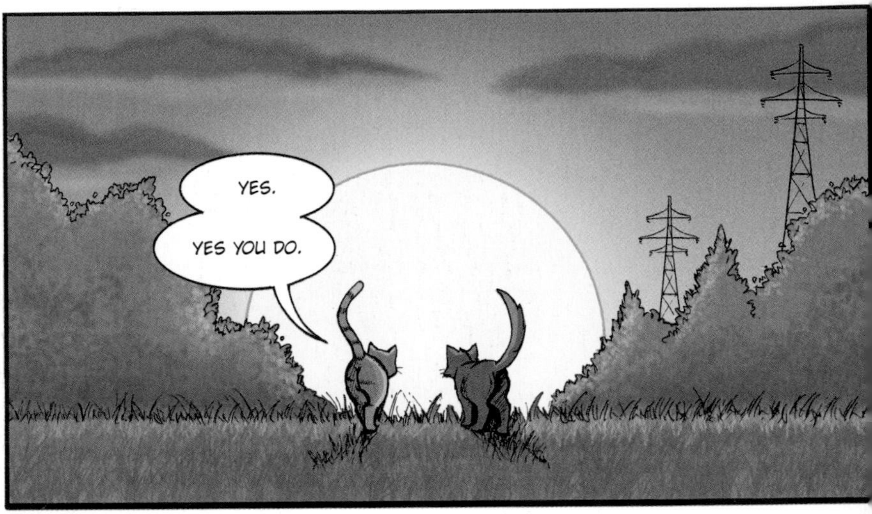
YES.
YES YOU DO.

TO BE CONTINUED

WARRIORS
WARRIOR'S REFUGE

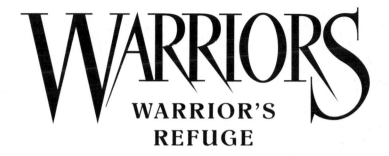

CHAPTER 1

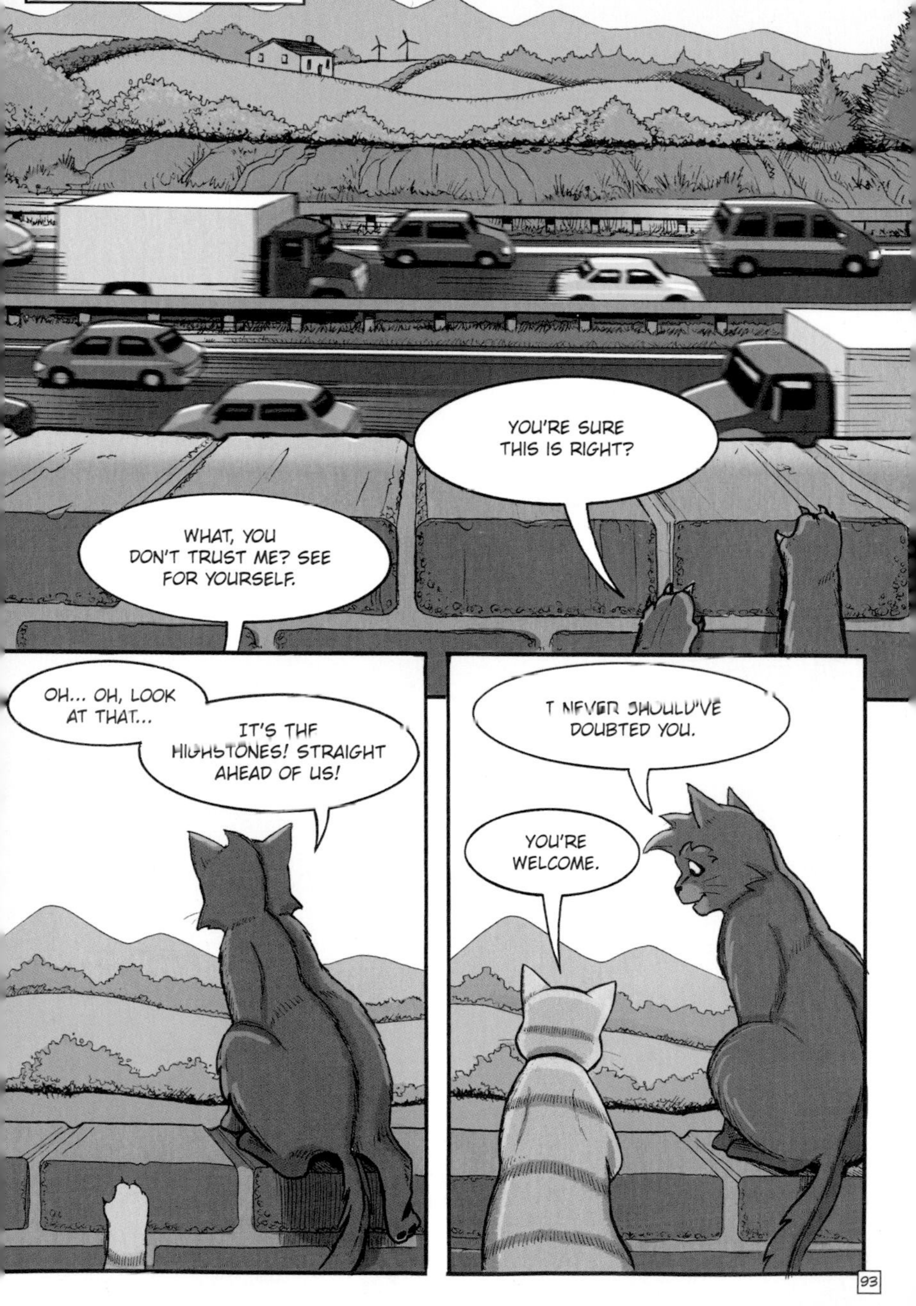

YOU'RE SURE THIS IS RIGHT?
WHAT, YOU DON'T TRUST ME? SEE FOR YOURSELF.
OH... OH, LOOK AT THAT...
IT'S THE HIGHSTONES! STRAIGHT AHEAD OF US!
I NEVER SHOULD'VE DOUBTED YOU.
YOU'RE WELCOME.

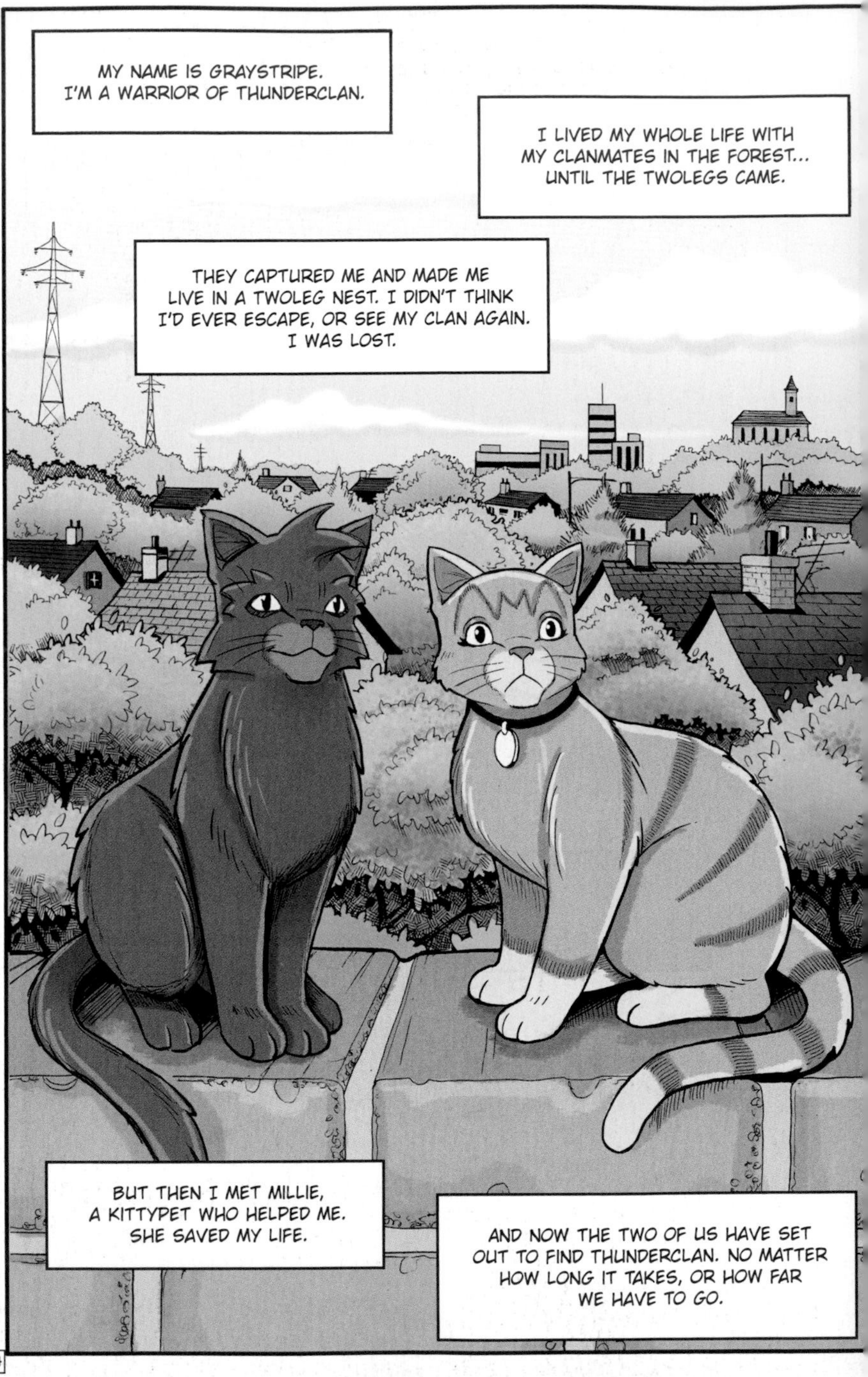
MY NAME IS GRAYSTRIPE. I'M A WARRIOR OF THUNDERCLAN.
I LIVED MY WHOLE LIFE WITH MY CLANMATES IN THE FOREST... UNTIL THE TWOLEGS CAME.
THEY CAPTURED ME AND MADE ME LIVE IN A TWOLEG NEST. I DIDN'T THINK I'D EVER ESCAPE, OR SEE MY CLAN AGAIN. I WAS LOST.
BUT THEN I MET MILLIE, A KITTYPET WHO HELPED ME. SHE SAVED MY LIFE.
AND NOW THE TWO OF US HAVE SET OUT TO FIND THUNDERCLAN. NO MATTER HOW LONG IT TAKES, OR HOW FAR WE HAVE TO GO.

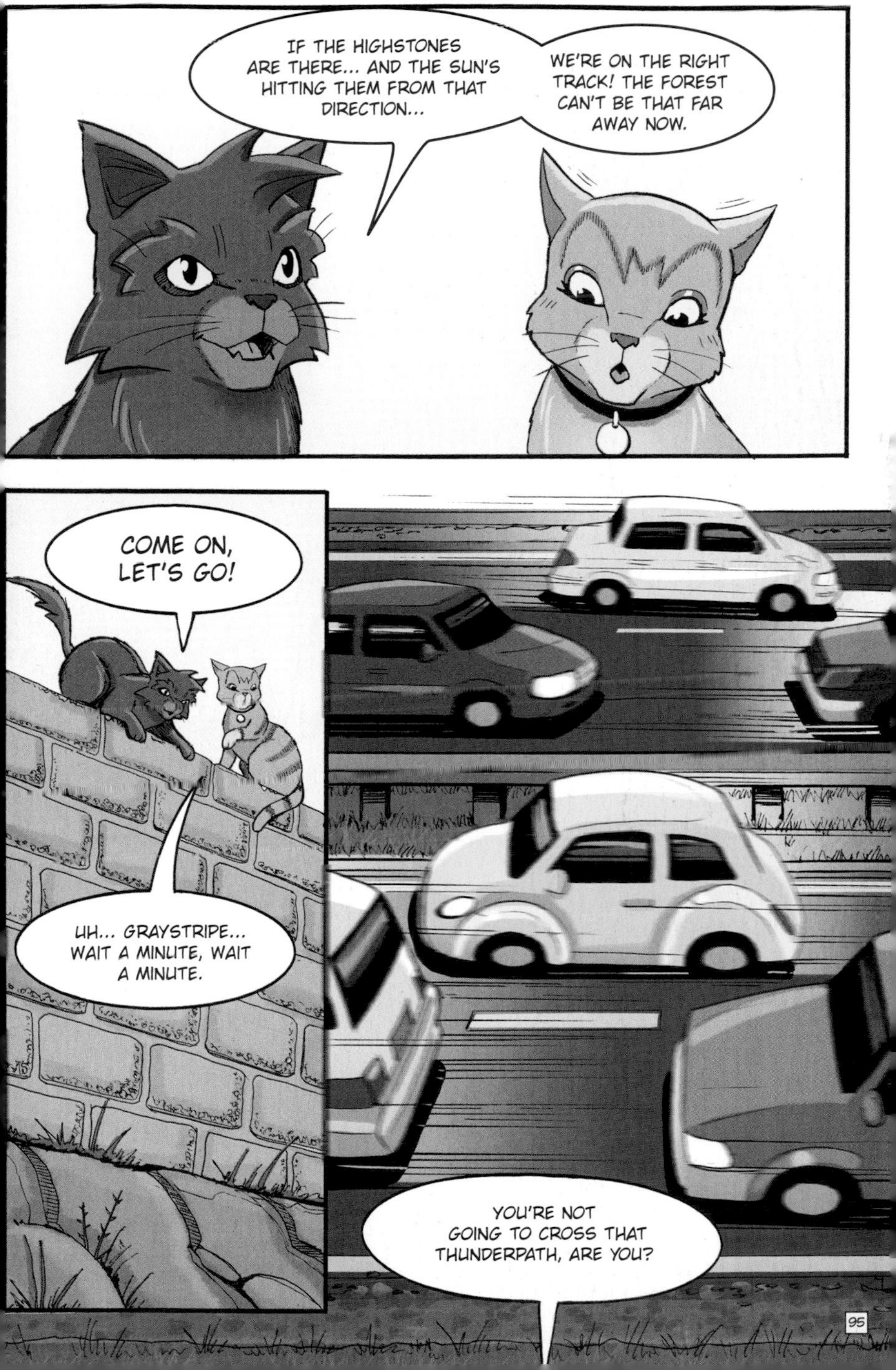
IF THE HIGHSTONES ARE THERE... AND THE SUN'S HITTING THEM FROM THAT DIRECTION...
WE'RE ON THE RIGHT TRACK! THE FOREST CAN'T BE THAT FAR AWAY NOW.
COME ON, LET'S GO!
UH... GRAYSTRIPE... WAIT A MINUTE, WAIT A MINUTE.
YOU'RE NOT GOING TO CROSS THAT THUNDERPATH, ARE YOU?

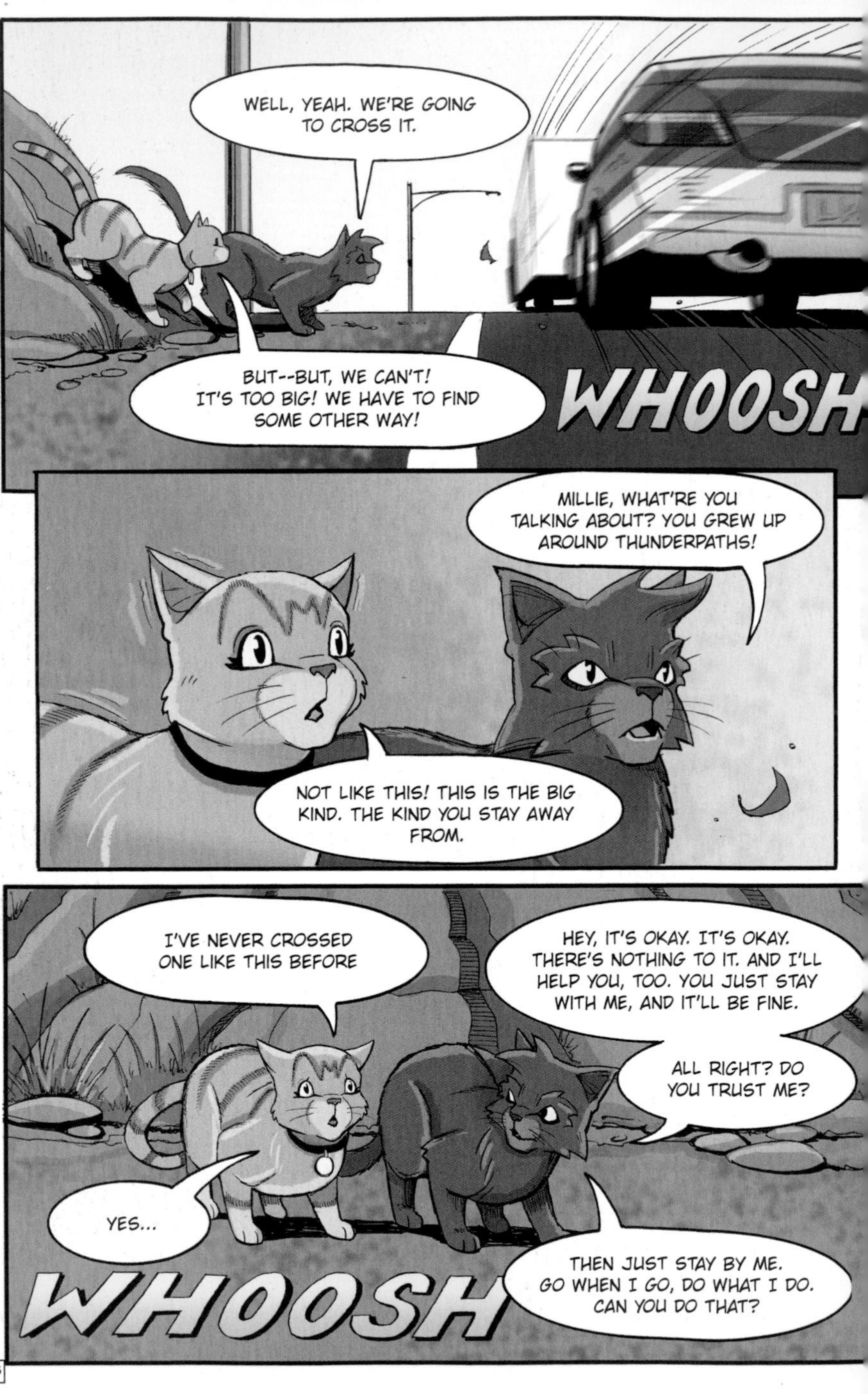
WELL, YEAH. WE'RE GOING TO CROSS IT.
BUT--BUT, WE CAN'T! IT'S TOO BIG! WE HAVE TO FIND SOME OTHER WAY!
WHOOSH
MILLIE, WHAT'RE YOU TALKING ABOUT? YOU GREW UP AROUND THUNDERPATHS!
NOT LIKE THIS! THIS IS THE BIG KIND. THE KIND YOU STAY AWAY FROM.
I'VE NEVER CROSSED ONE LIKE THIS BEFORE
HEY, IT'S OKAY. IT'S OKAY. THERE'S NOTHING TO IT. AND I'LL HELP YOU, TOO. YOU JUST STAY WITH ME, AND IT'LL BE FINE.
ALL RIGHT? DO YOU TRUST ME?
YES...
WHOOSH
THEN JUST STAY BY ME. GO WHEN I GO, DO WHAT I DO. CAN YOU DO THAT?

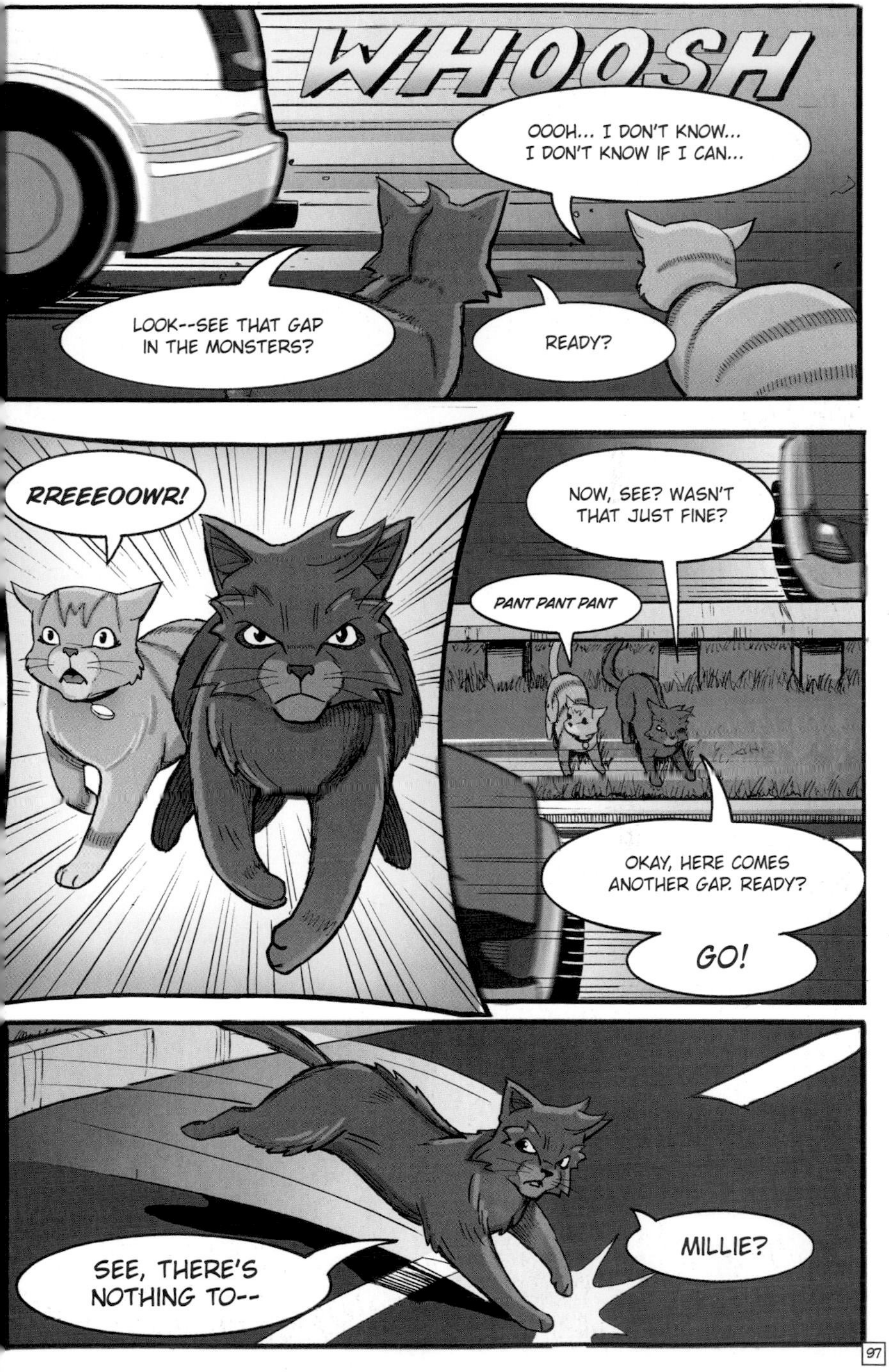
WHOOSH
OOOH... I DON'T KNOW... I DON'T KNOW IF I CAN...
LOOK--SEE THAT GAP IN THE MONSTERS?
READY?
RREEEOOWR!
NOW, SEE? WASN'T THAT JUST FINE?
PANT PANT PANT
OKAY, HERE COMES ANOTHER GAP. READY?
GO!
SEE, THERE'S NOTHING TO--
MILLIE?

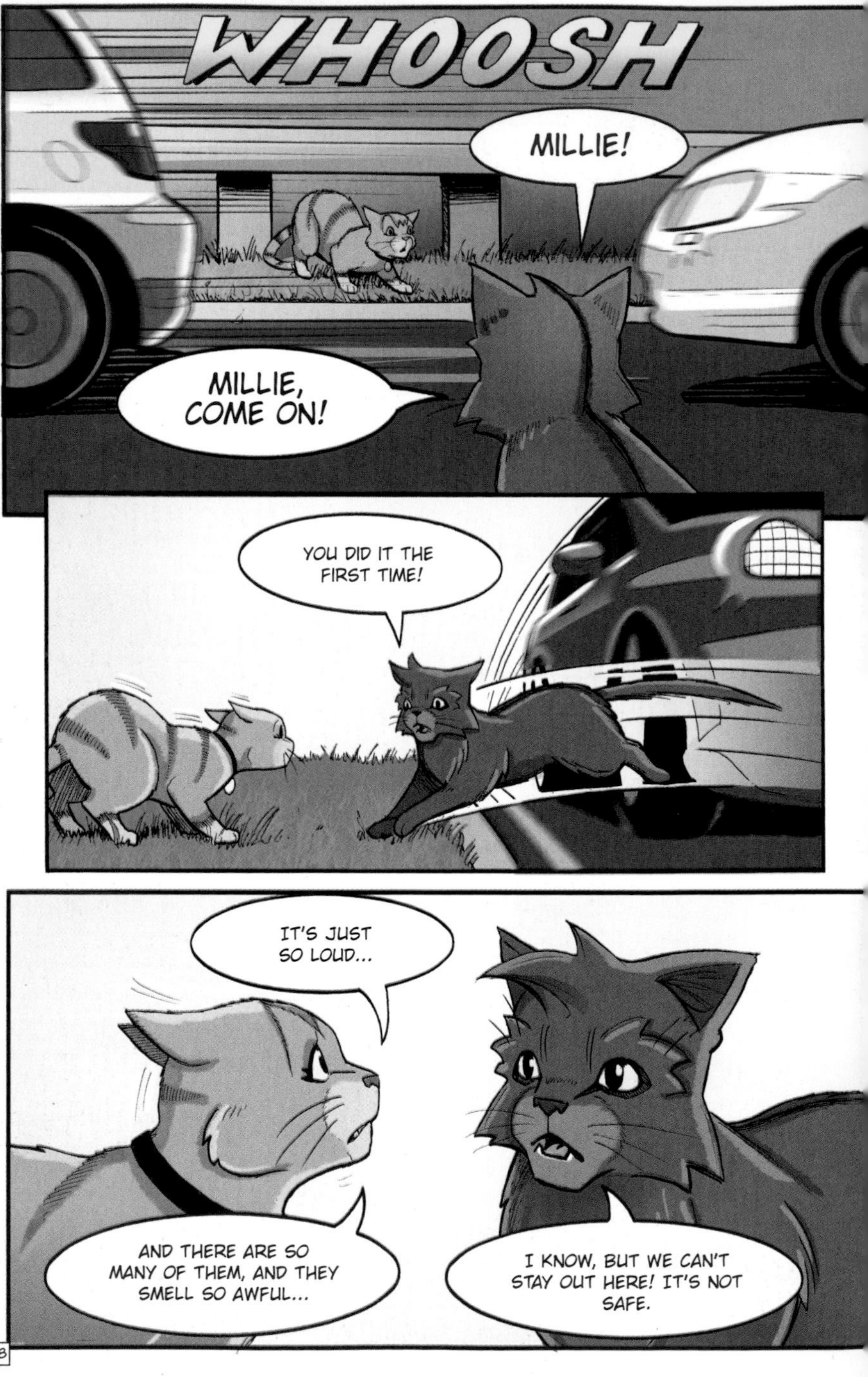
WHOOSH
MILLIE!
MILLIE, COME ON!
YOU DID IT THE FIRST TIME!
IT'S JUST SO LOUD...
AND THERE ARE SO MANY OF THEM, AND THEY SMELL SO AWFUL...
I KNOW, BUT WE CAN'T STAY OUT HERE! IT'S NOT SAFE.

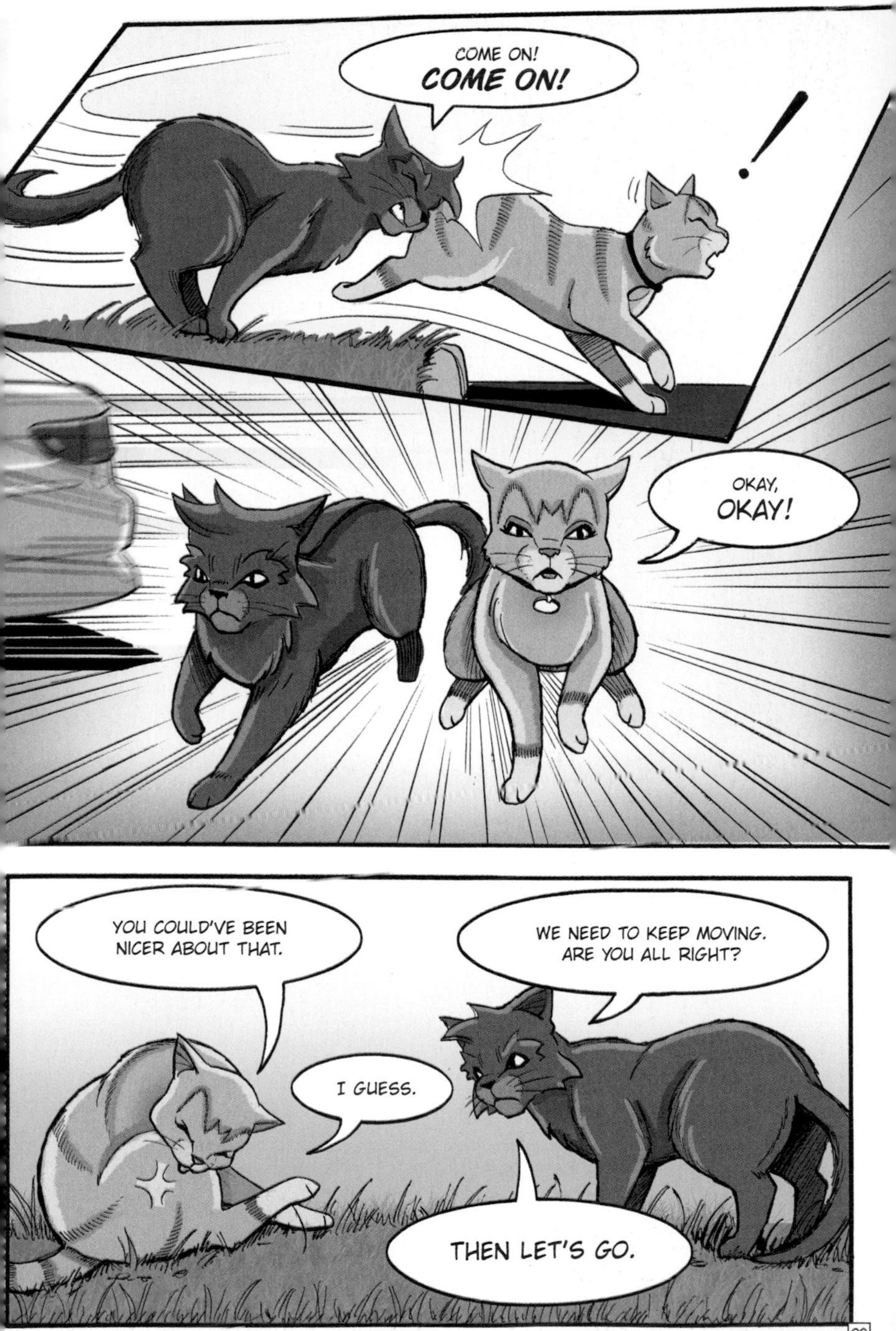
COME ON!
COME ON!
!
OKAY, OKAY!
YOU COULD'VE BEEN NICER ABOUT THAT.
WE NEED TO KEEP MOVING. ARE YOU ALL RIGHT?
I GUESS.
THEN LET'S GO.

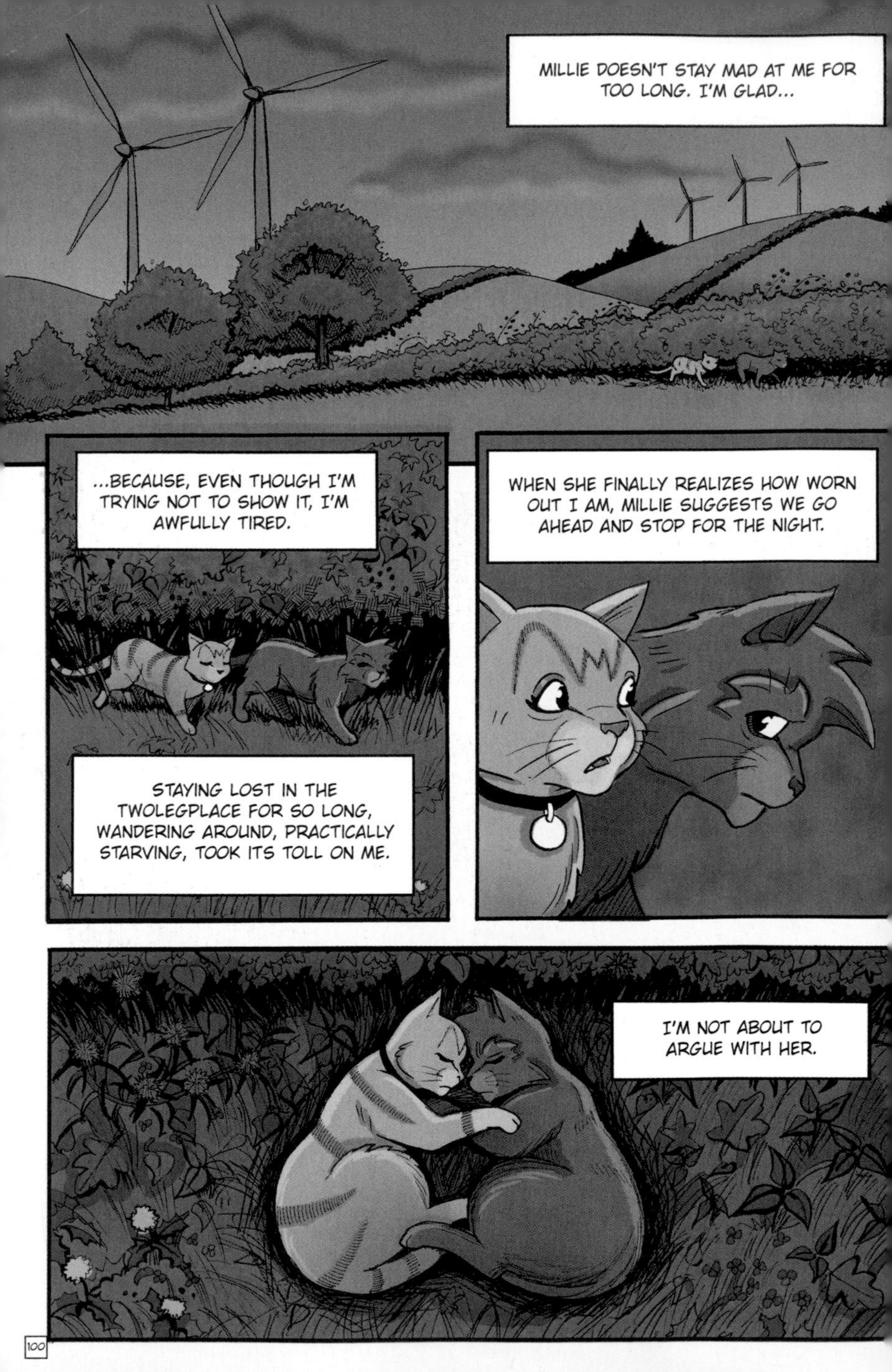
MILLIE DOESN'T STAY MAD AT ME FOR TOO LONG. I'M GLAD...
...BECAUSE, EVEN THOUGH I'M TRYING NOT TO SHOW IT, I'M AWFULLY TIRED.
STAYING LOST IN THE TWOLEGPLACE FOR SO LONG, WANDERING AROUND, PRACTICALLY STARVING, TOOK ITS TOLL ON ME.
WHEN SHE FINALLY REALIZES HOW WORN OUT I AM, MILLIE SUGGESTS WE GO AHEAD AND STOP FOR THE NIGHT.
I'M NOT ABOUT TO ARGUE WITH HER.

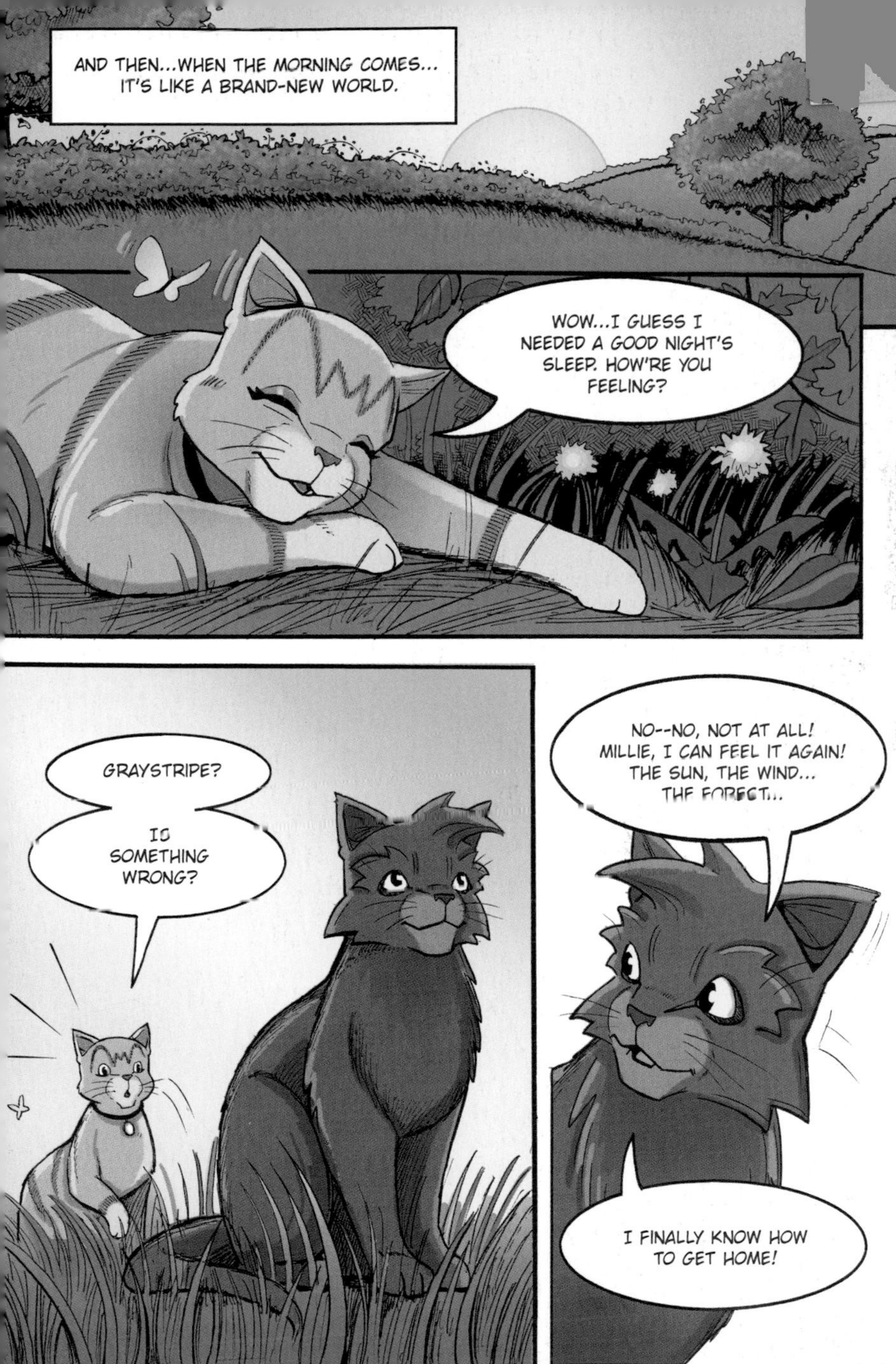
AND THEN...WHEN THE MORNING COMES... IT'S LIKE A BRAND-NEW WORLD.
WOW...I GUESS I NEEDED A GOOD NIGHT'S SLEEP. HOW'RE YOU FEELING?
GRAYSTRIPE?
IS SOMETHING WRONG?
NO--NO, NOT AT ALL! MILLIE, I CAN FEEL IT AGAIN! THE SUN, THE WIND... THE FOREST...
I FINALLY KNOW HOW TO GET HOME!

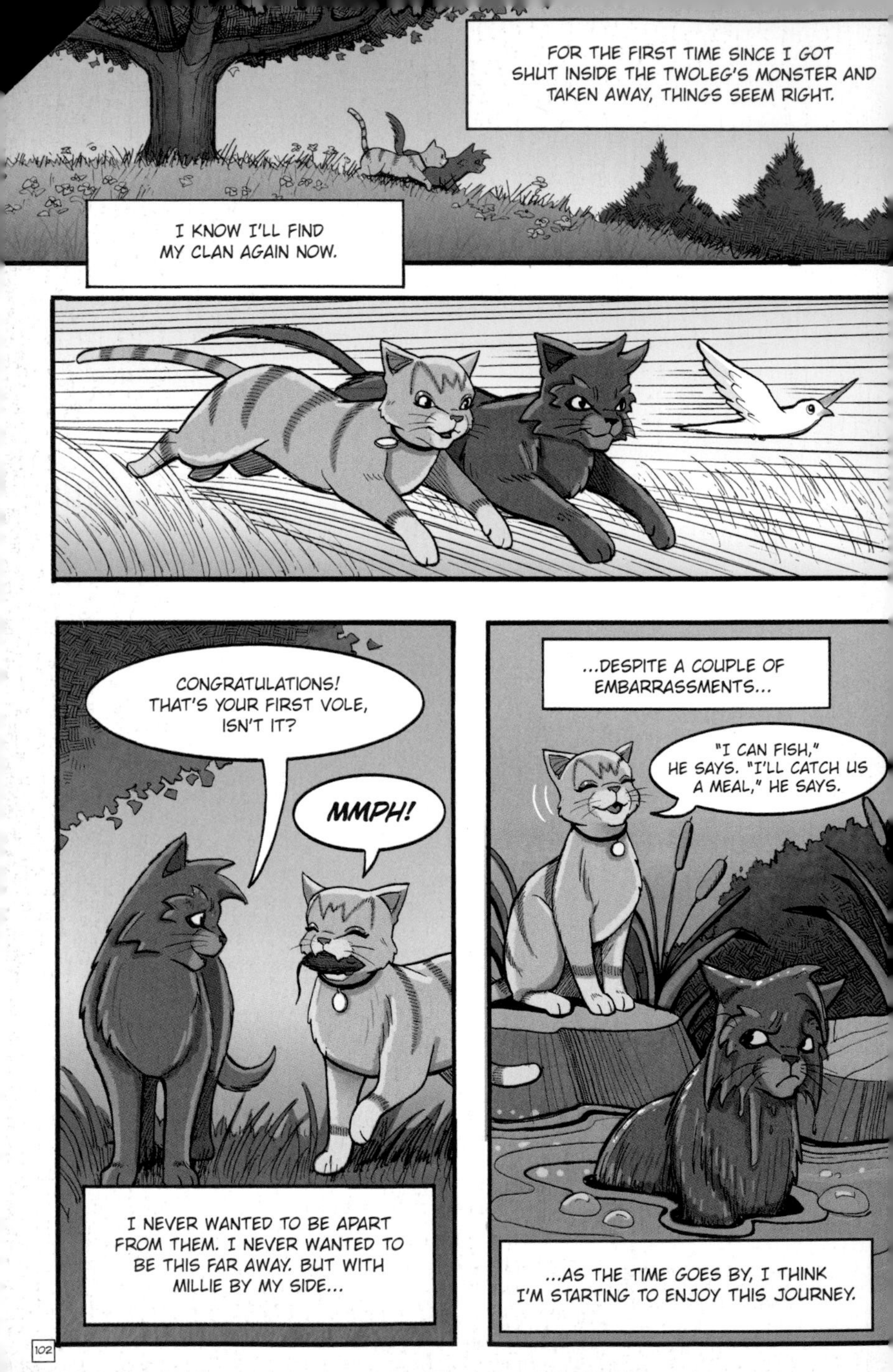

FOR THE FIRST TIME SINCE I GOT SHUT INSIDE THE TWOLEG'S MONSTER AND TAKEN AWAY, THINGS SEEM RIGHT.
I KNOW I'LL FIND MY CLAN AGAIN NOW.
CONGRATULATIONS! THAT'S YOUR FIRST VOLE, ISN'T IT?
MMPH!
I NEVER WANTED TO BE APART FROM THEM. I NEVER WANTED TO BE THIS FAR AWAY. BUT WITH MILLIE BY MY SIDE...
...DESPITE A COUPLE OF EMBARRASSMENTS...
"I CAN FISH," HE SAYS. "I'LL CATCH US A MEAL," HE SAYS.
...AS THE TIME GOES BY, I THINK I'M STARTING TO ENJOY THIS JOURNEY.

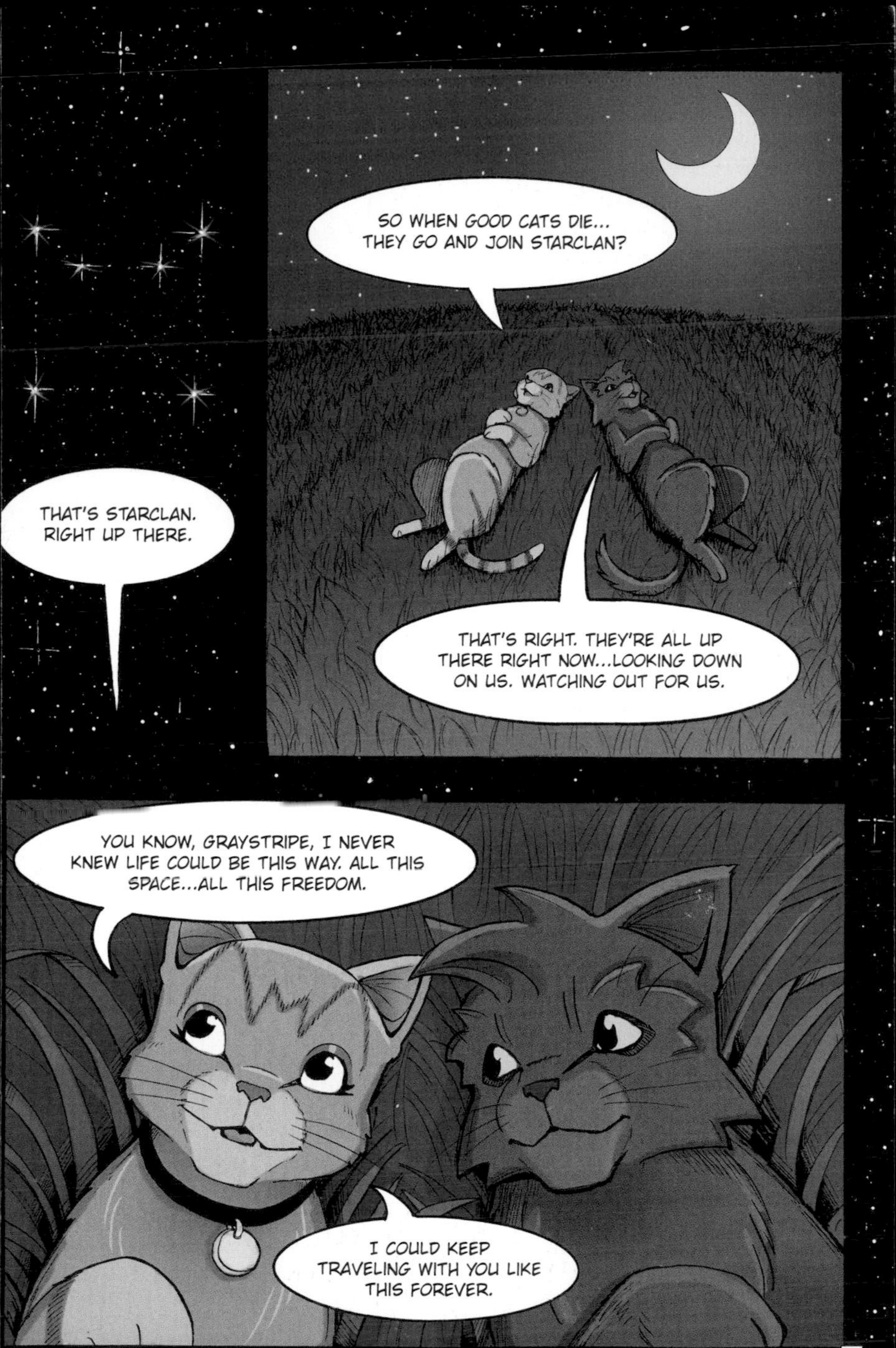
SO WHEN GOOD CATS DIE... THEY GO AND JOIN STARCLAN?
THAT'S STARCLAN. RIGHT UP THERE.
THAT'S RIGHT. THEY'RE ALL UP THERE RIGHT NOW...LOOKING DOWN ON US. WATCHING OUT FOR US.
YOU KNOW, GRAYSTRIPE, I NEVER KNEW LIFE COULD BE THIS WAY. ALL THIS SPACE...ALL THIS FREEDOM.
I COULD KEEP TRAVELING WITH YOU LIKE THIS FOREVER.

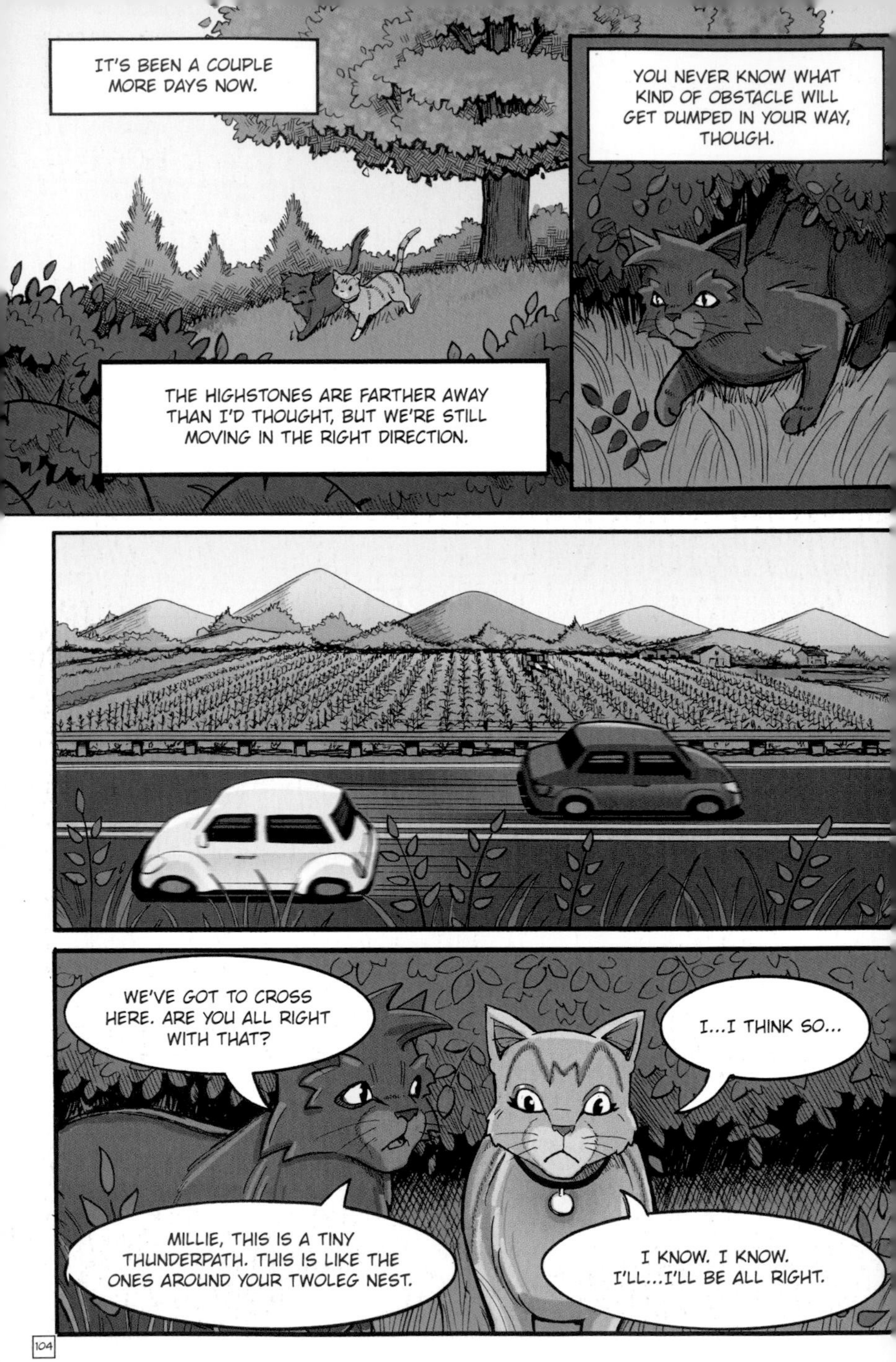
IT'S BEEN A COUPLE MORE DAYS NOW.
THE HIGHSTONES ARE FARTHER AWAY THAN I'D THOUGHT, BUT WE'RE STILL MOVING IN THE RIGHT DIRECTION.
YOU NEVER KNOW WHAT KIND OF OBSTACLE WILL GET DUMPED IN YOUR WAY, THOUGH.
WE'VE GOT TO CROSS HERE. ARE YOU ALL RIGHT WITH THAT?
I...I THINK SO...
MILLIE, THIS IS A TINY THUNDERPATH. THIS IS LIKE THE ONES AROUND YOUR TWOLEG NEST.
I KNOW. I KNOW. I'LL...I'LL BE ALL RIGHT.

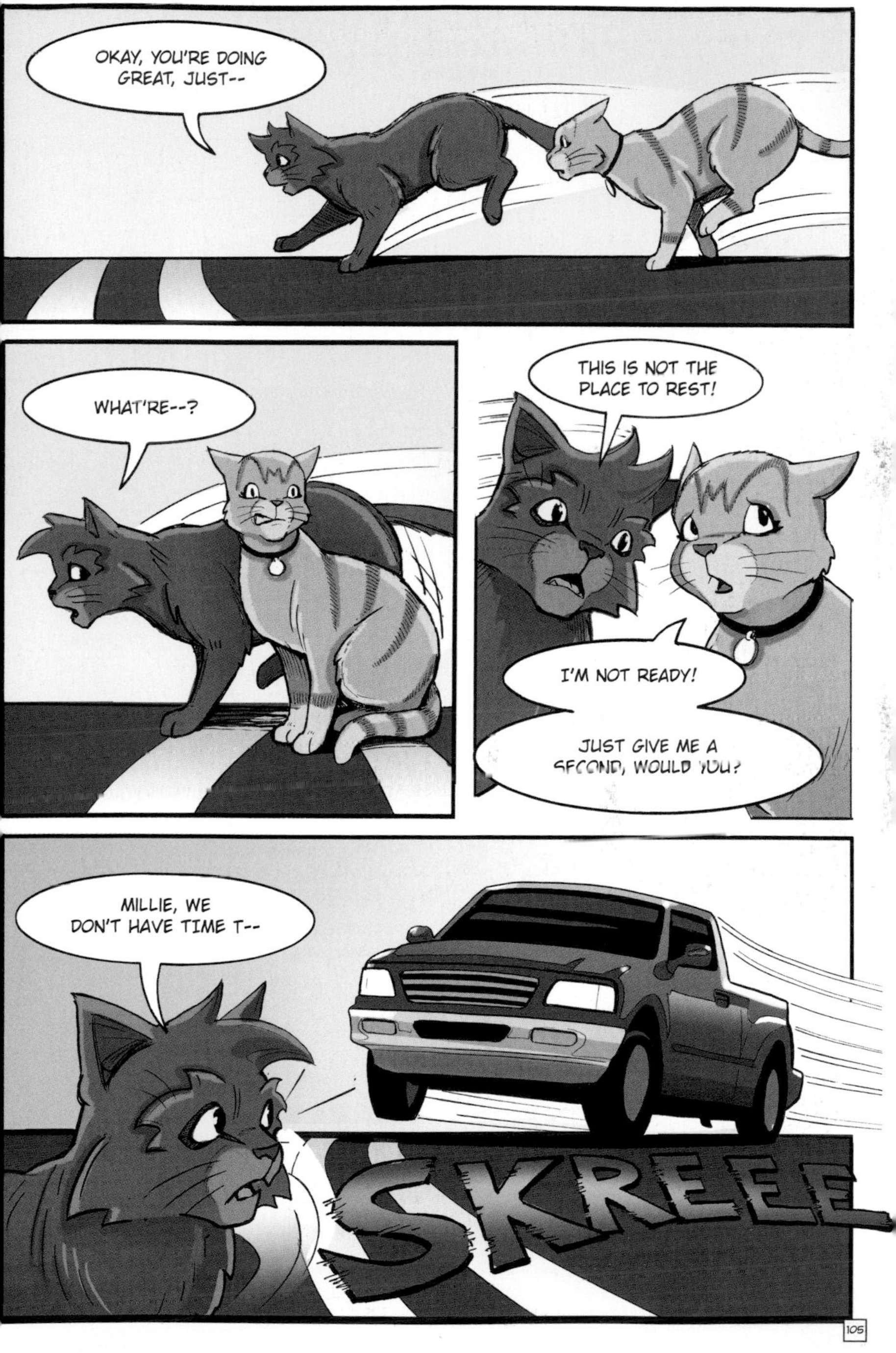
OKAY, YOU'RE DOING GREAT, JUST--
WHAT'RE--?
THIS IS NOT THE PLACE TO REST!
I'M NOT READY!
JUST GIVE ME A SECOND, WOULD YOU?
MILLIE, WE DON'T HAVE TIME T--
SKREEE

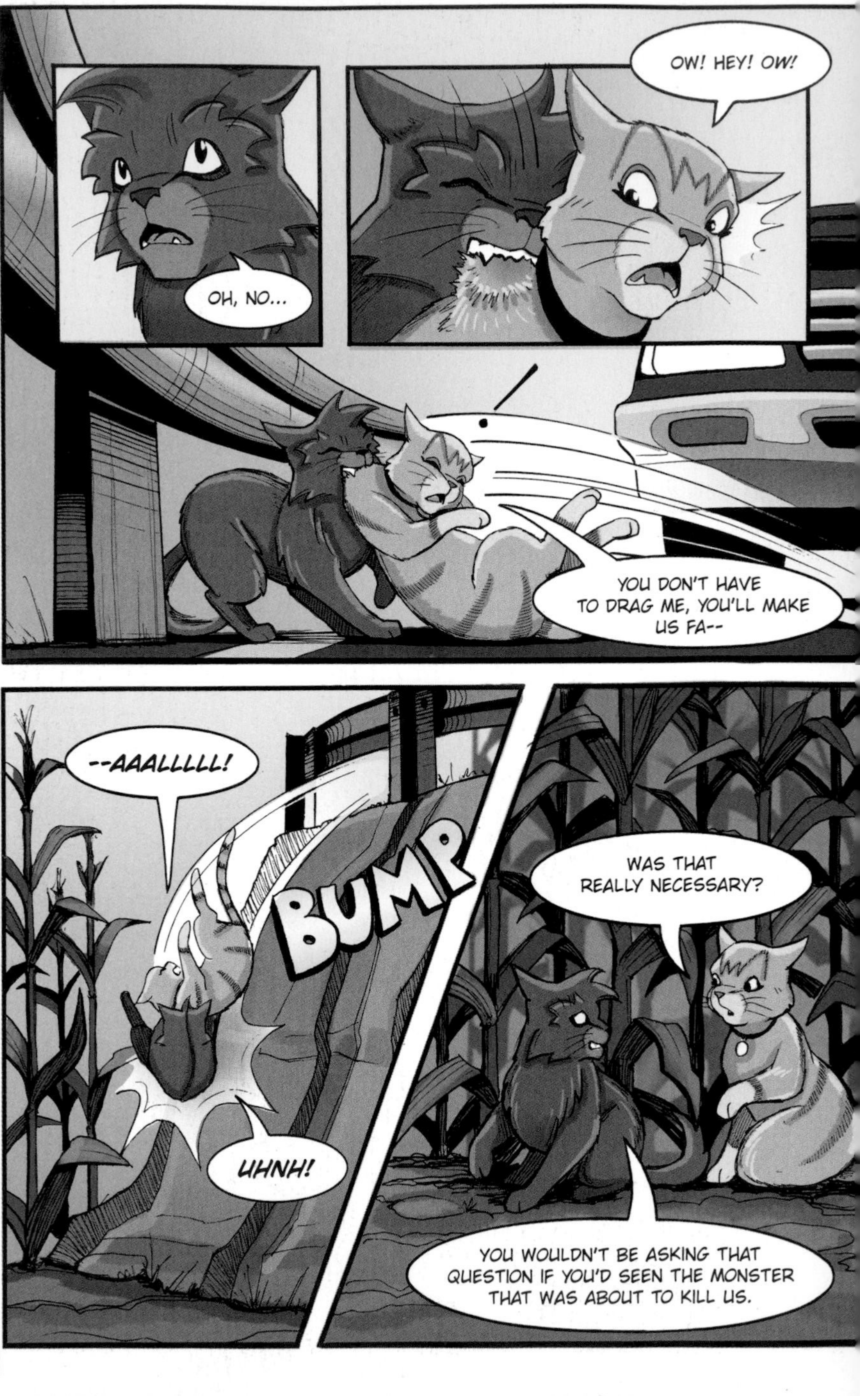
OH, NO...
OW! HEY! OW!
YOU DON'T HAVE TO DRAG ME, YOU'LL MAKE US FA--
--AAALLLLL!
BUMP
UHNH!
WAS THAT REALLY NECESSARY?
YOU WOULDN'T BE ASKING THAT QUESTION IF YOU'D SEEN THE MONSTER THAT WAS ABOUT TO KILL US.

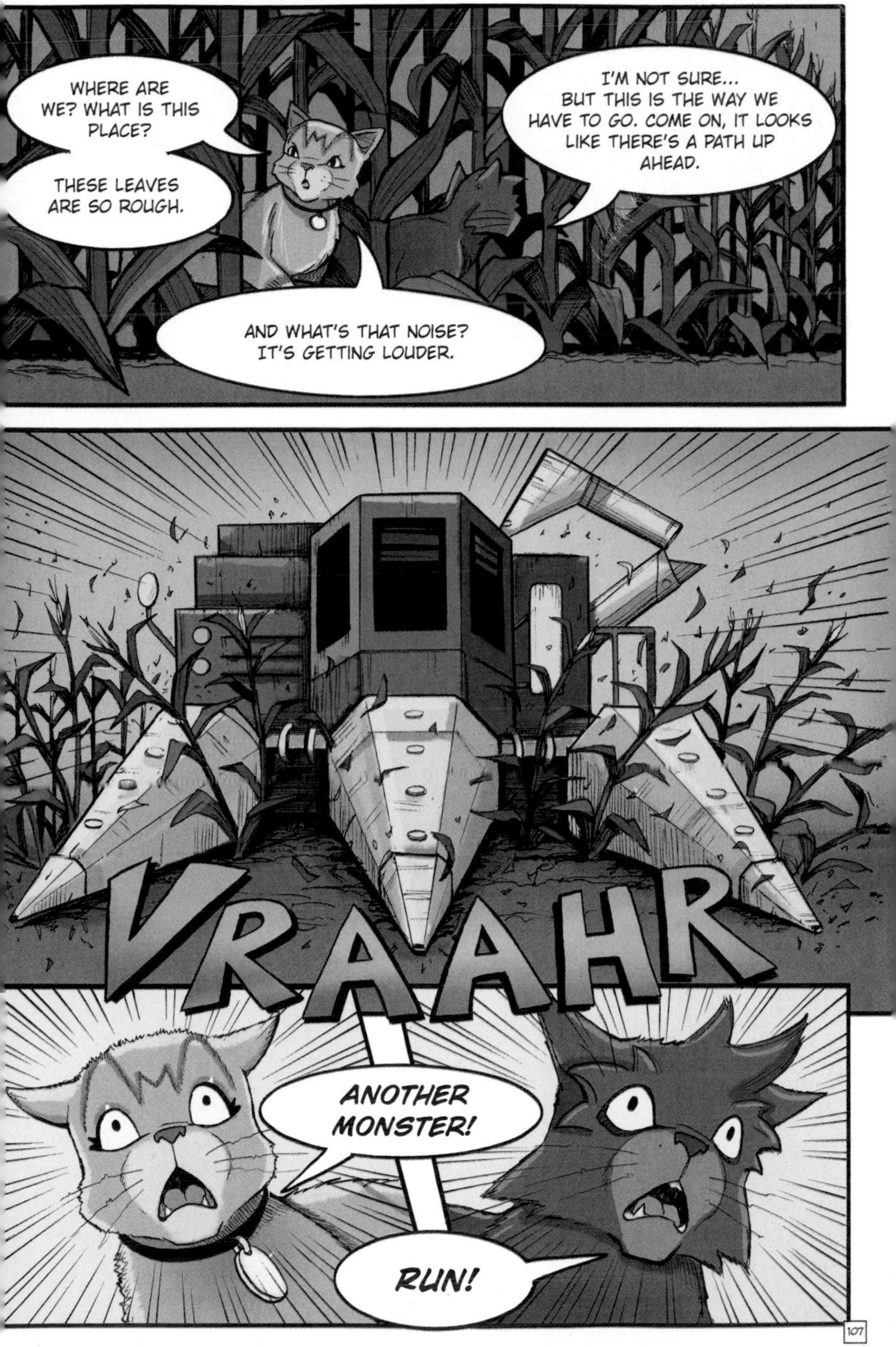
WHERE ARE WE? WHAT IS THIS PLACE?
THESE LEAVES ARE SO ROUGH.
I'M NOT SURE... BUT THIS IS THE WAY WE HAVE TO GO. COME ON, IT LOOKS LIKE THERE'S A PATH UP AHEAD.
AND WHAT'S THAT NOISE? IT'S GETTING LOUDER.
VRAAHR
ANOTHER MONSTER!
RUN!

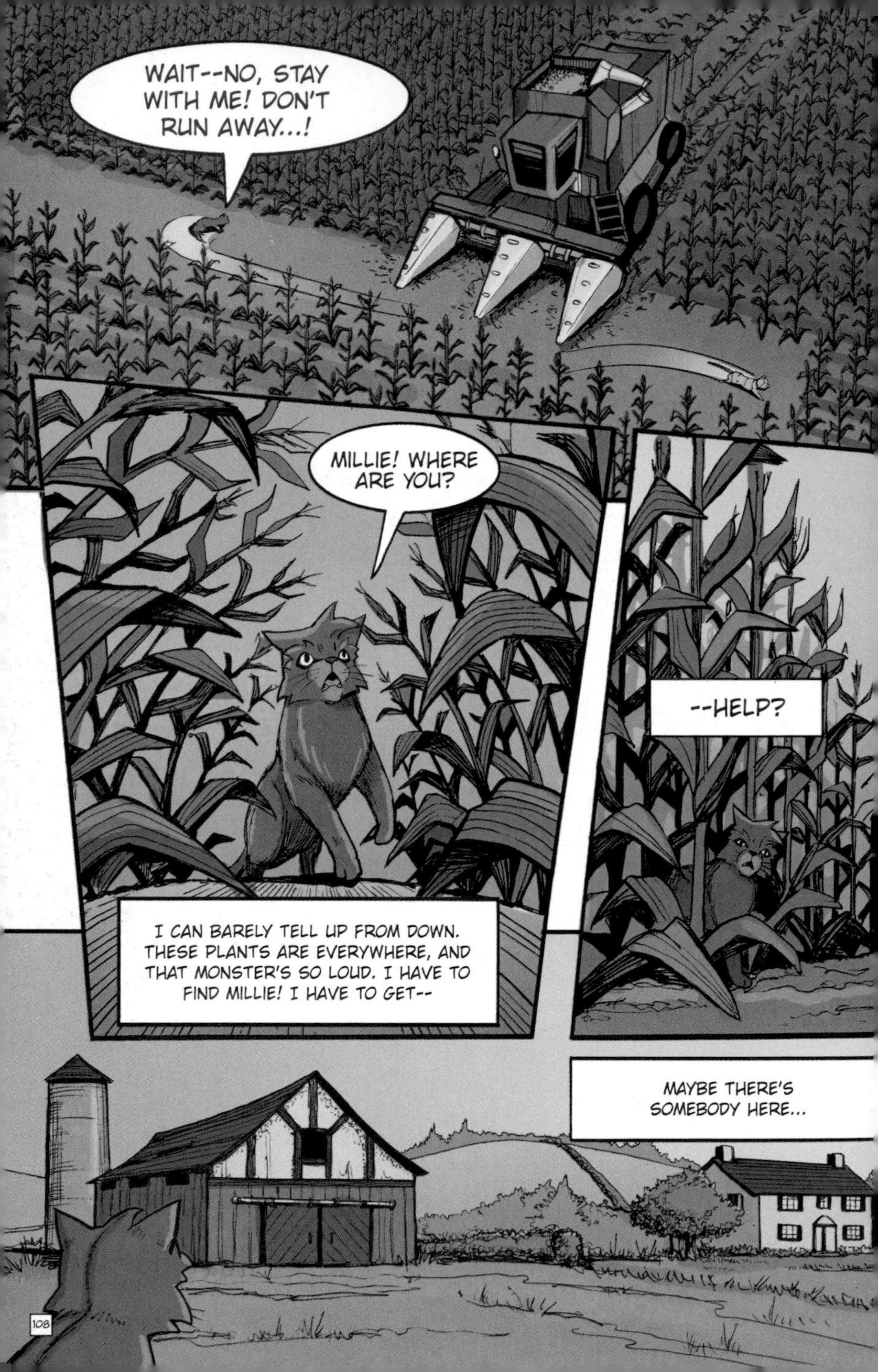
WAIT--NO, STAY WITH ME! DON'T RUN AWAY...!
MILLIE! WHERE ARE YOU?
I CAN BARELY TELL UP FROM DOWN. THESE PLANTS ARE EVERYWHERE, AND THAT MONSTER'S SO LOUD. I HAVE TO FIND MILLIE! I HAVE TO GET--
--HELP?
MAYBE THERE'S SOMEBODY HERE...

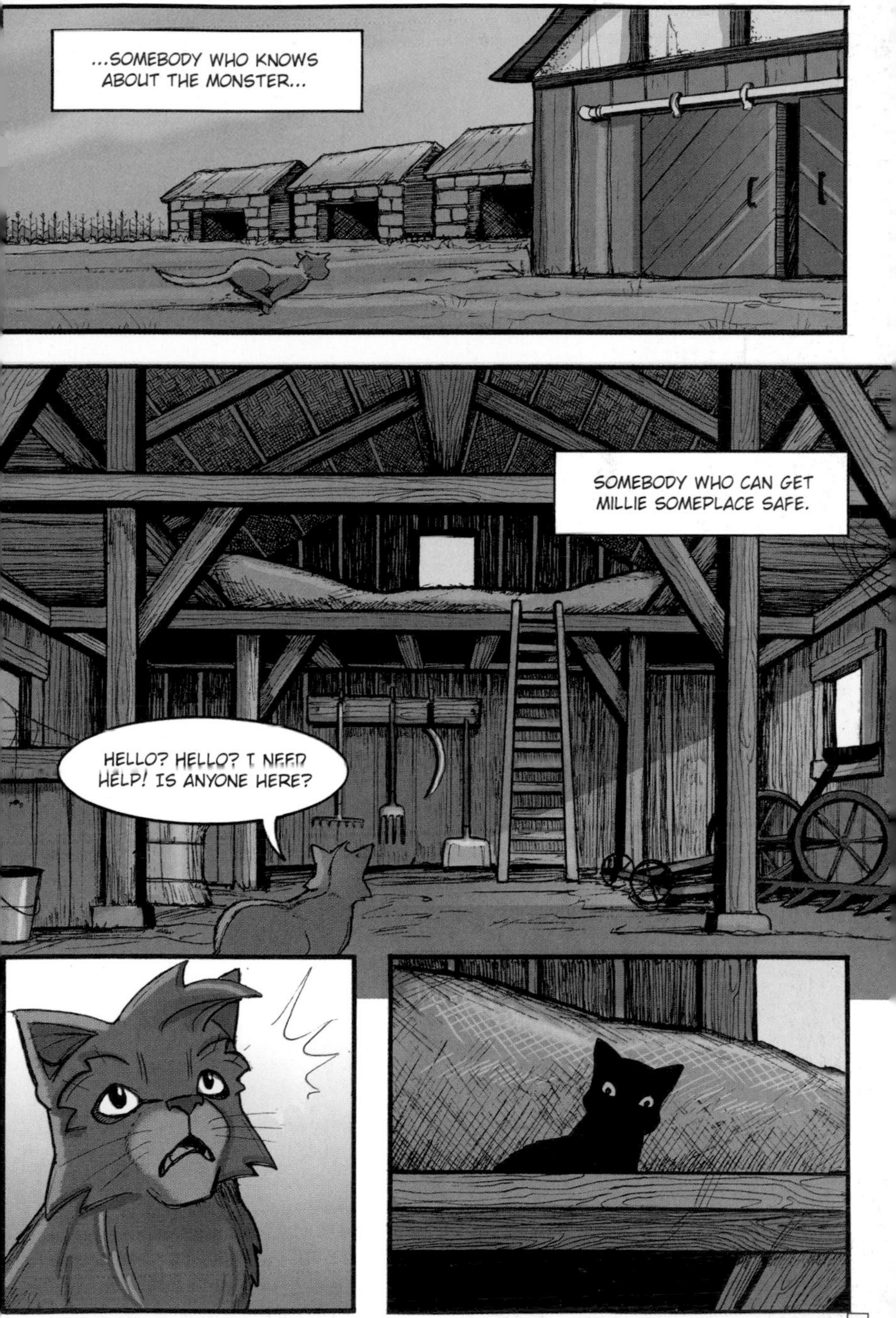
...SOMEBODY WHO KNOWS ABOUT THE MONSTER...
SOMEBODY WHO CAN GET MILLIE SOMEPLACE SAFE.
HELLO? HELLO? I NEED HELP! IS ANYONE HERE?

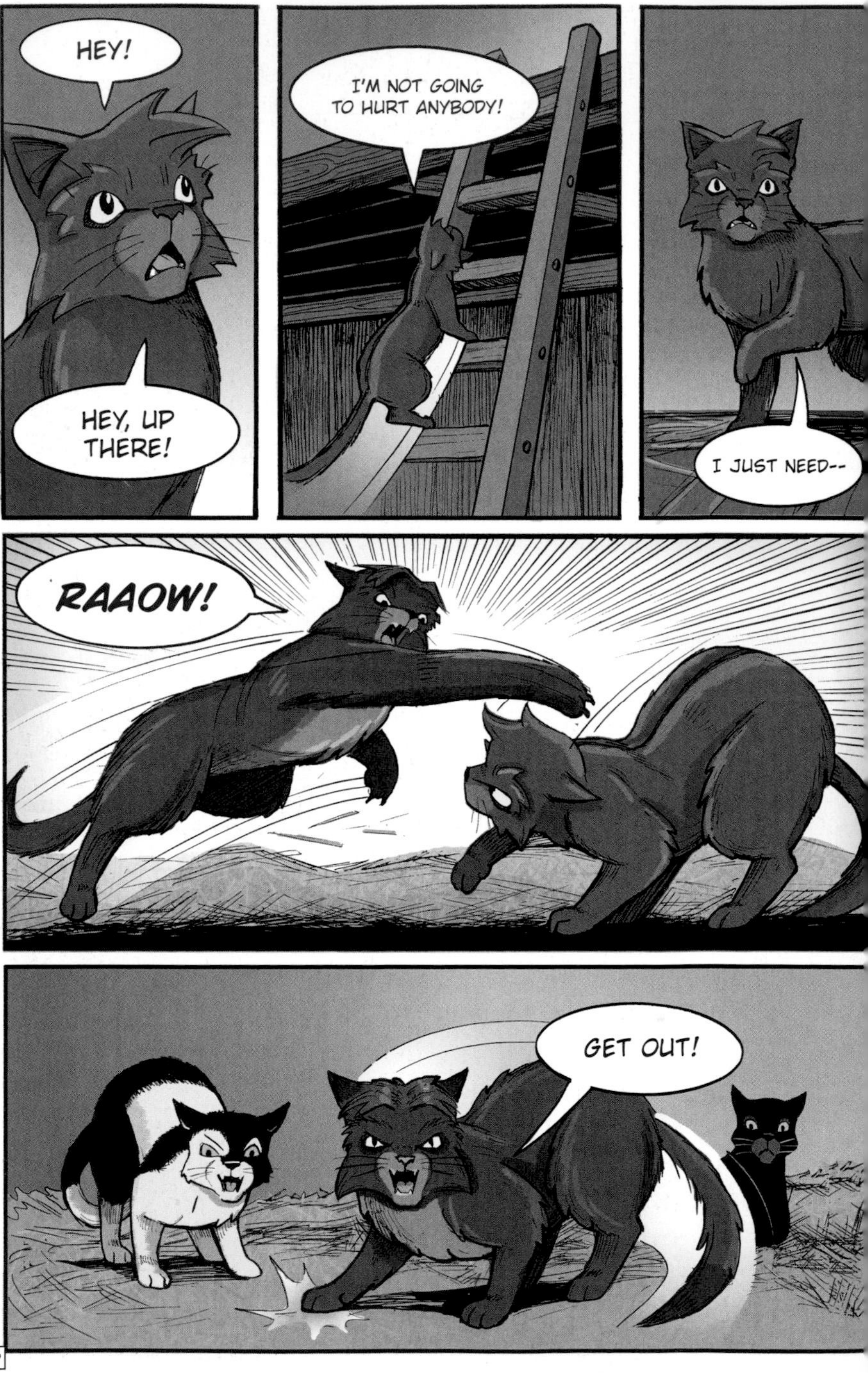
HEY!
HEY, UP THERE!
I'M NOT GOING TO HURT ANYBODY!
I JUST NEED--
RAAOW!
GET OUT!

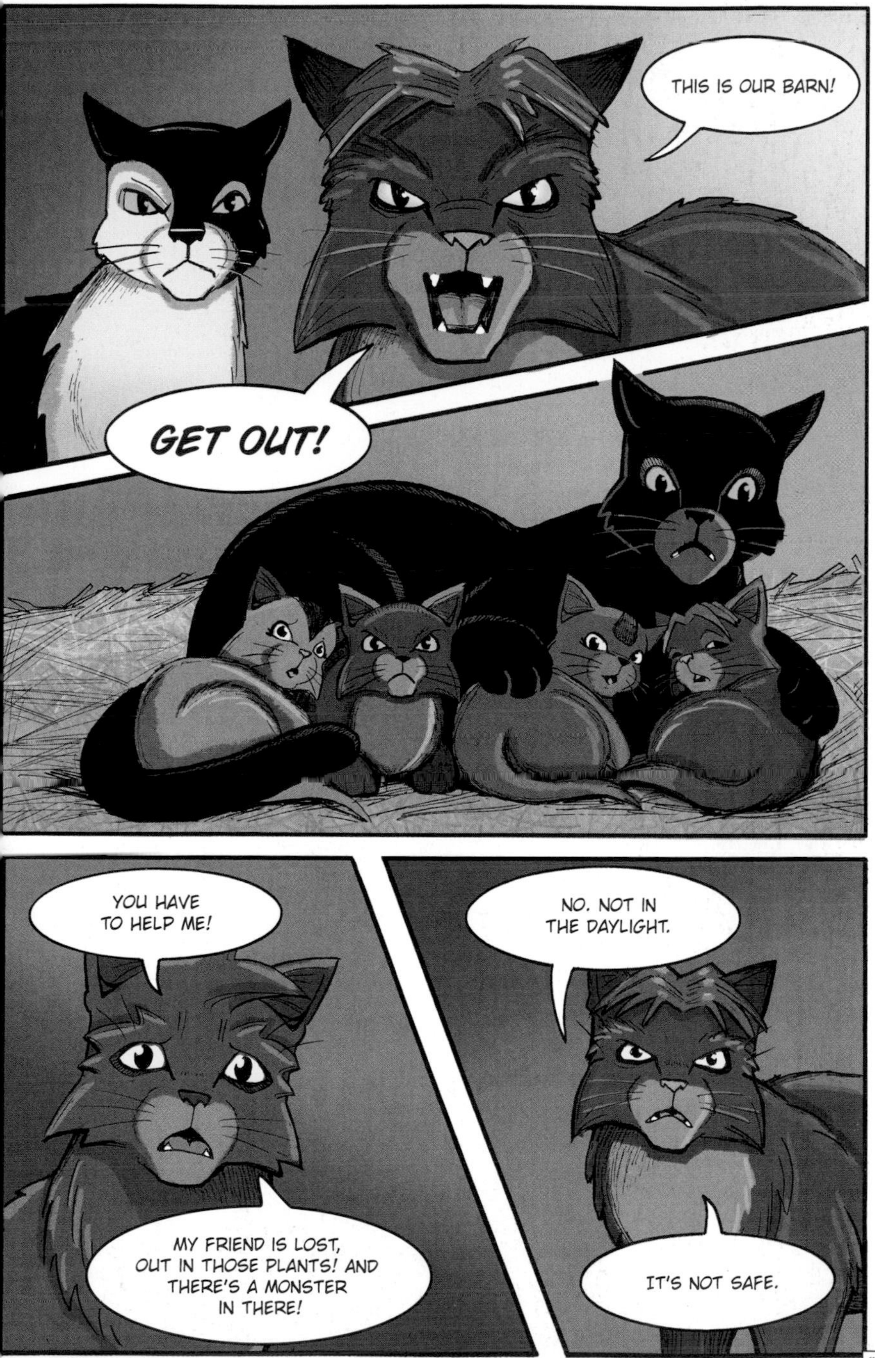
THIS IS OUR BARN!
GET OUT!
YOU HAVE TO HELP ME!
MY FRIEND IS LOST, OUT IN THOSE PLANTS! AND THERE'S A MONSTER IN THERE!
NO. NOT IN THE DAYLIGHT.
IT'S NOT SAFE.

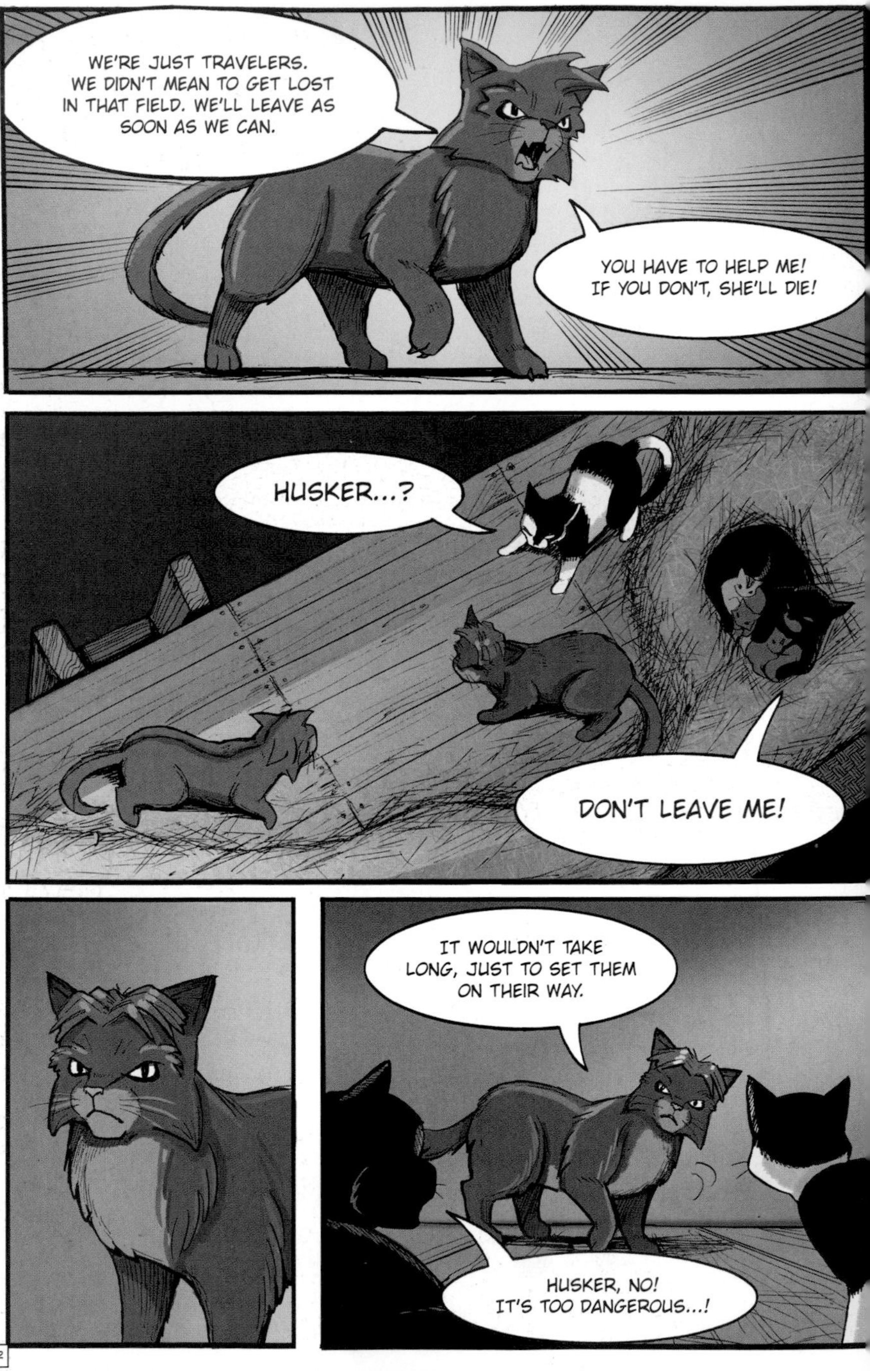
WE'RE JUST TRAVELERS. WE DIDN'T MEAN TO GET LOST IN THAT FIELD. WE'LL LEAVE AS SOON AS WE CAN.
YOU HAVE TO HELP ME! IF YOU DON'T, SHE'LL DIE!
HUSKER...?
DON'T LEAVE ME!
IT WOULDN'T TAKE LONG, JUST TO SET THEM ON THEIR WAY.
HUSKER, NO! IT'S TOO DANGEROUS...!

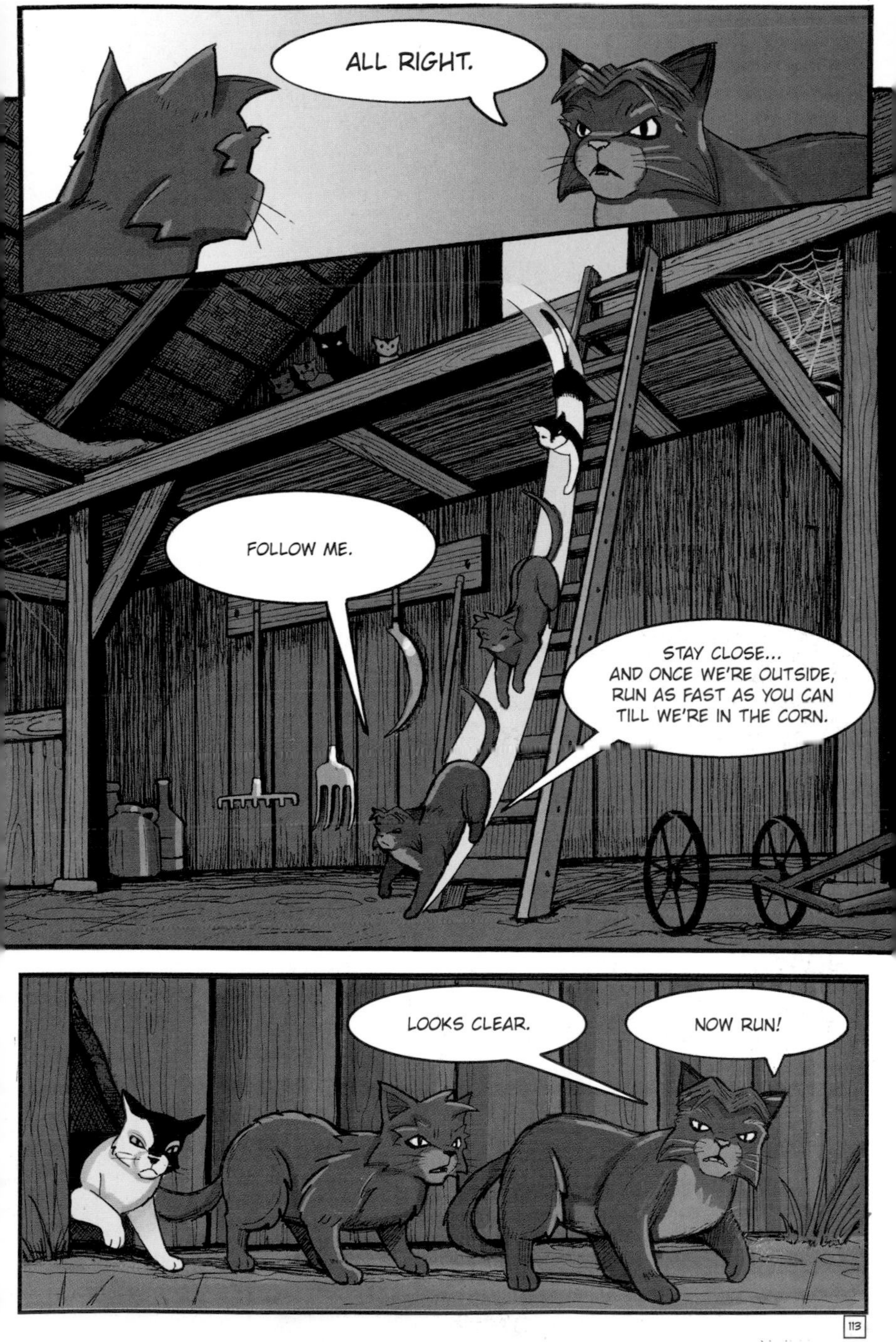
ALL RIGHT.
FOLLOW ME.
STAY CLOSE... AND ONCE WE'RE OUTSIDE, RUN AS FAST AS YOU CAN TILL WE'RE IN THE CORN.
LOOKS CLEAR.
NOW RUN!

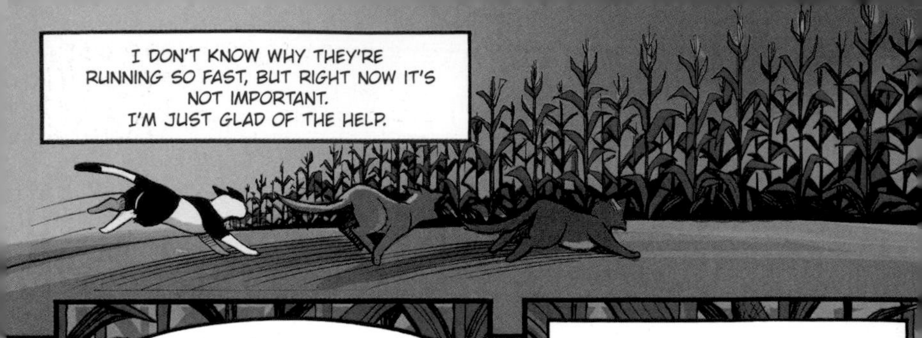
I DON'T KNOW WHY THEY'RE RUNNING SO FAST, BUT RIGHT NOW IT'S NOT IMPORTANT.
I'M JUST GLAD OF THE HELP.

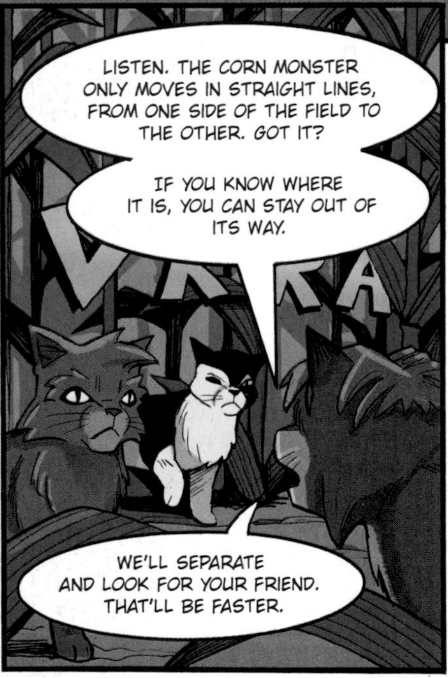
LISTEN. THE CORN MONSTER ONLY MOVES IN STRAIGHT LINES, FROM ONE SIDE OF THE FIELD TO THE OTHER. GOT IT?
IF YOU KNOW WHERE IT IS, YOU CAN STAY OUT OF ITS WAY.
WE'LL SEPARATE AND LOOK FOR YOUR FRIEND. THAT'LL BE FASTER.

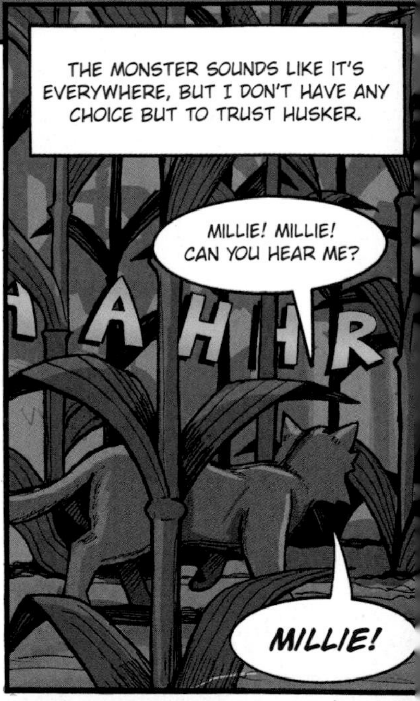
THE MONSTER SOUNDS LIKE IT'S EVERYWHERE, BUT I DON'T HAVE ANY CHOICE BUT TO TRUST HUSKER.
MILLIE! MILLIE! CAN YOU HEAR ME?
MILLIE!

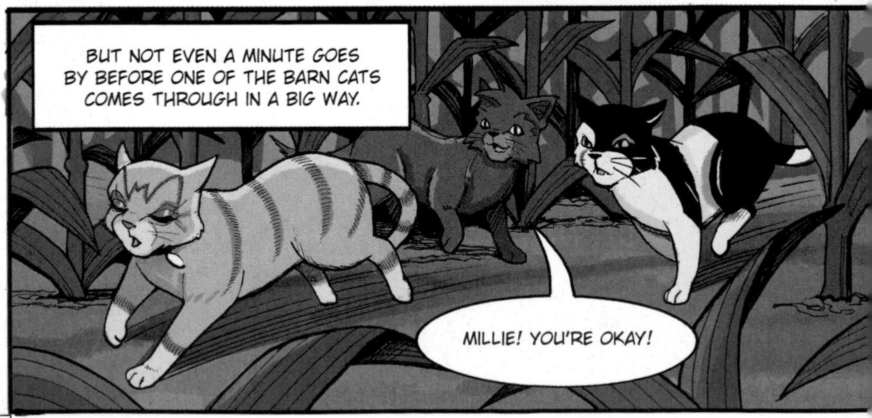
BUT NOT EVEN A MINUTE GOES BY BEFORE ONE OF THE BARN CATS COMES THROUGH IN A BIG WAY.
MILLIE! YOU'RE OKAY!

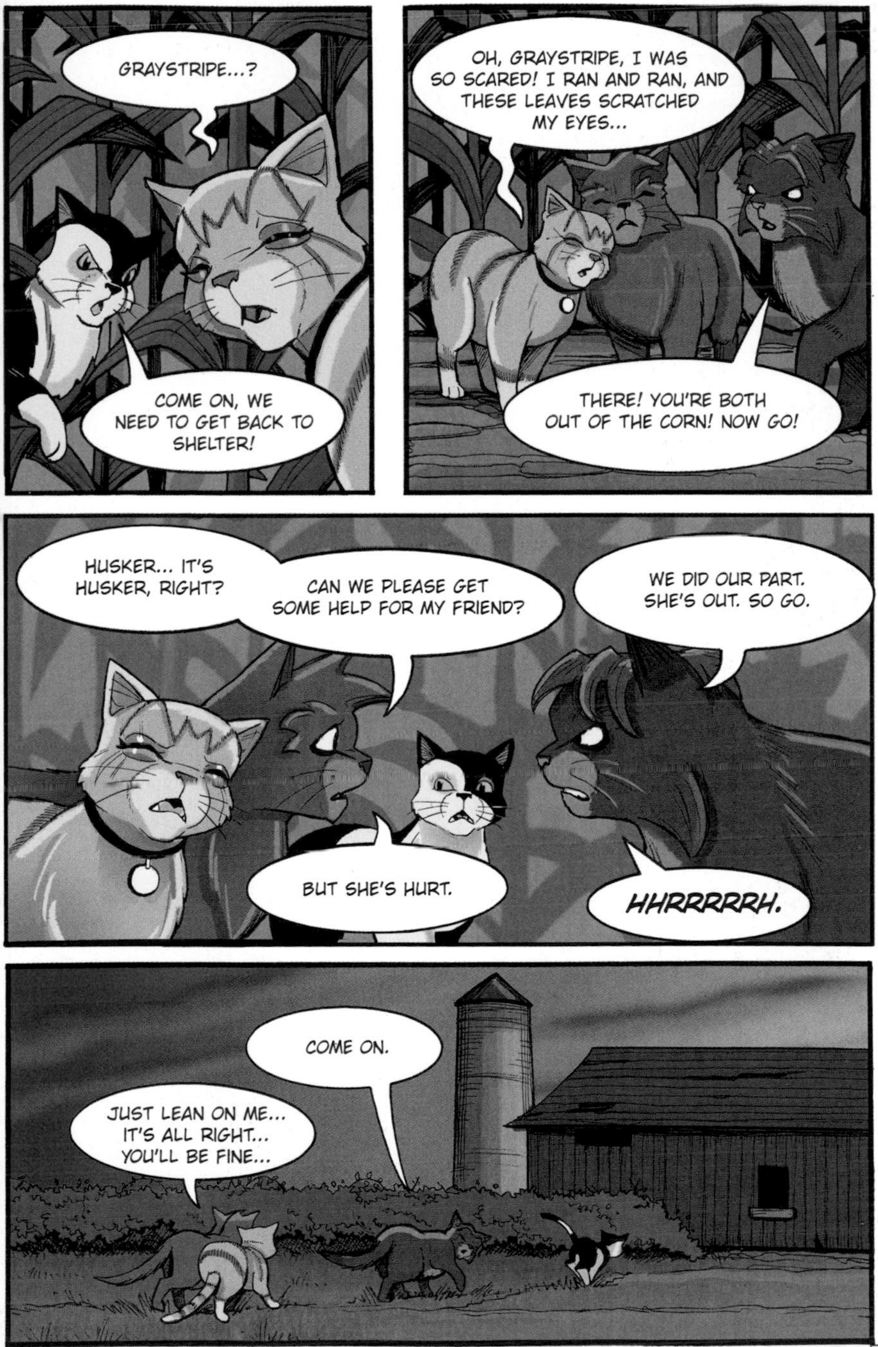
GRAYSTRIPE...?
COME ON, WE NEED TO GET BACK TO SHELTER!
OH, GRAYSTRIPE, I WAS SO SCARED! I RAN AND RAN, AND THESE LEAVES SCRATCHED MY EYES...
THERE! YOU'RE BOTH OUT OF THE CORN! NOW GO!
HUSKER... IT'S HUSKER, RIGHT?
CAN WE PLEASE GET SOME HELP FOR MY FRIEND?
WE DID OUR PART. SHE'S OUT. SO GO.
BUT SHE'S HURT.
HHRRRRRH.
COME ON.
JUST LEAN ON ME... IT'S ALL RIGHT... YOU'LL BE FINE...

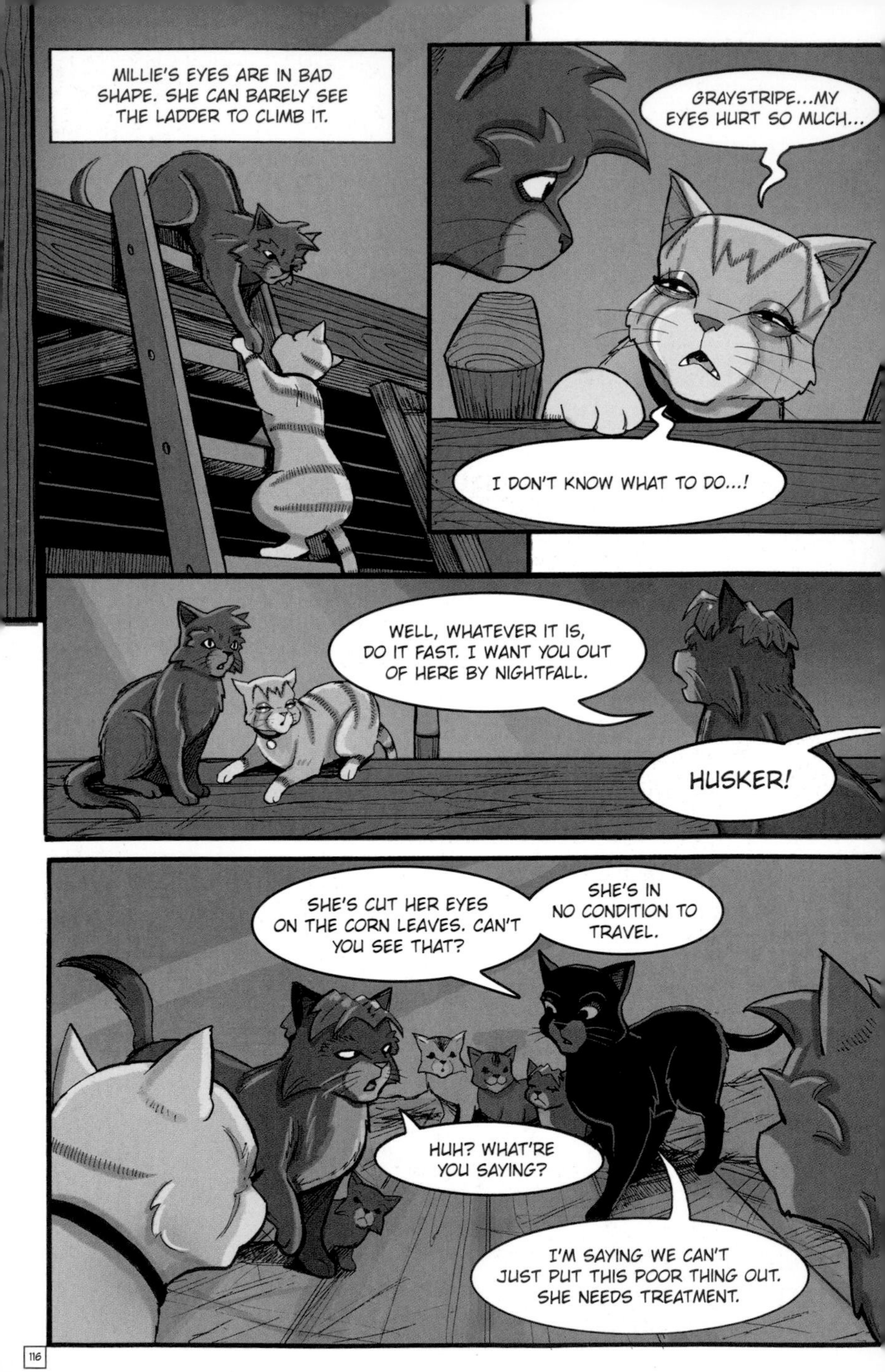
MILLIE'S EYES ARE IN BAD SHAPE. SHE CAN BARELY SEE THE LADDER TO CLIMB IT.
GRAYSTRIPE...MY EYES HURT SO MUCH...
I DON'T KNOW WHAT TO DO...!
WELL, WHATEVER IT IS, DO IT FAST. I WANT YOU OUT OF HERE BY NIGHTFALL.
HUSKER!
SHE'S CUT HER EYES ON THE CORN LEAVES. CAN'T YOU SEE THAT?
SHE'S IN NO CONDITION TO TRAVEL.
HUH? WHAT'RE YOU SAYING?
I'M SAYING WE CAN'T JUST PUT THIS POOR THING OUT. SHE NEEDS TREATMENT.

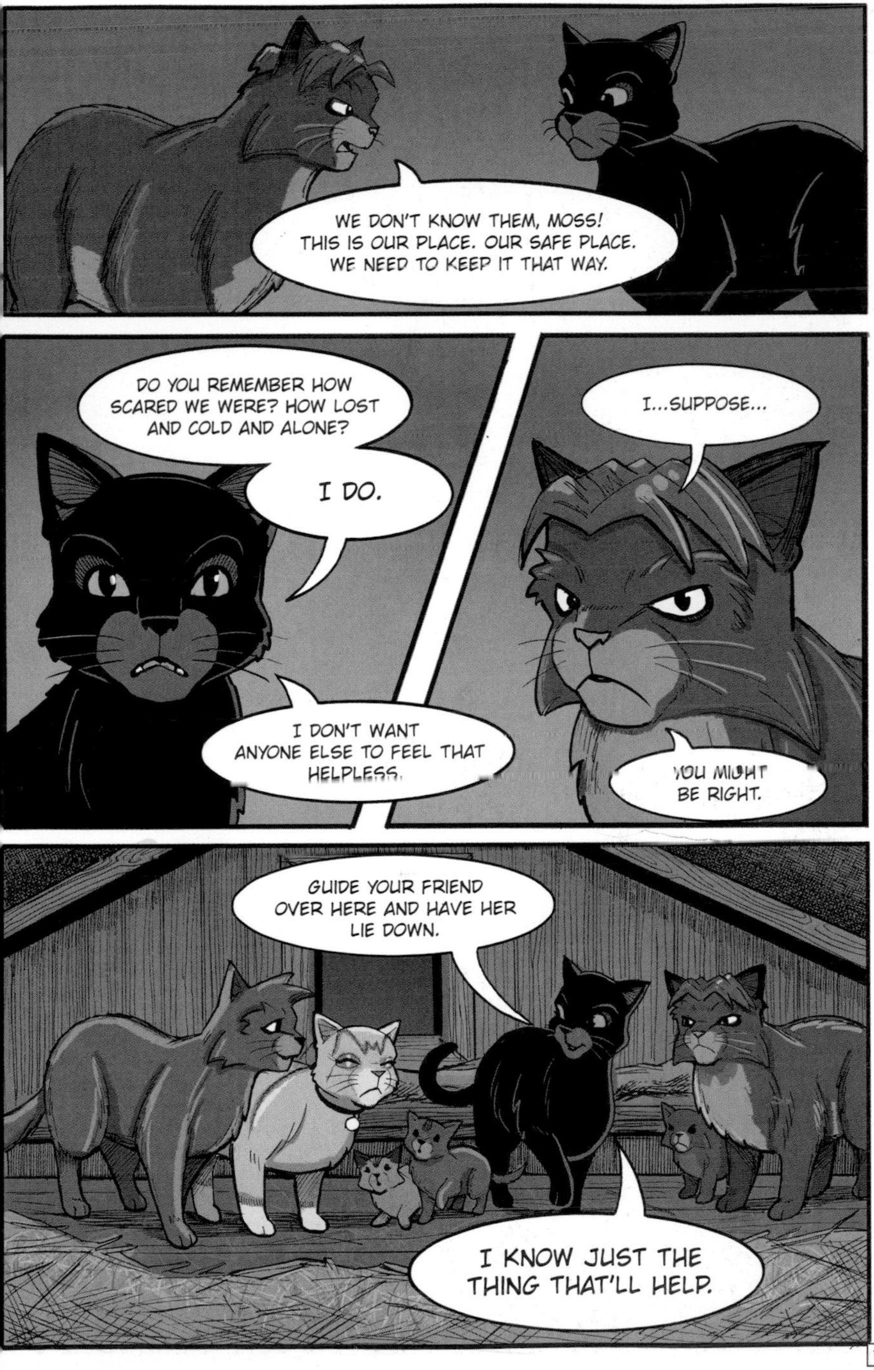
WE DON'T KNOW THEM, MOSS! THIS IS OUR PLACE. OUR SAFE PLACE. WE NEED TO KEEP IT THAT WAY.
DO YOU REMEMBER HOW SCARED WE WERE? HOW LOST AND COLD AND ALONE?
I DO.
I DON'T WANT ANYONE ELSE TO FEEL THAT HELPLESS.
I...SUPPOSE...
YOU MIGHT BE RIGHT.
GUIDE YOUR FRIEND OVER HERE AND HAVE HER LIE DOWN.
I KNOW JUST THE THING THAT'LL HELP.

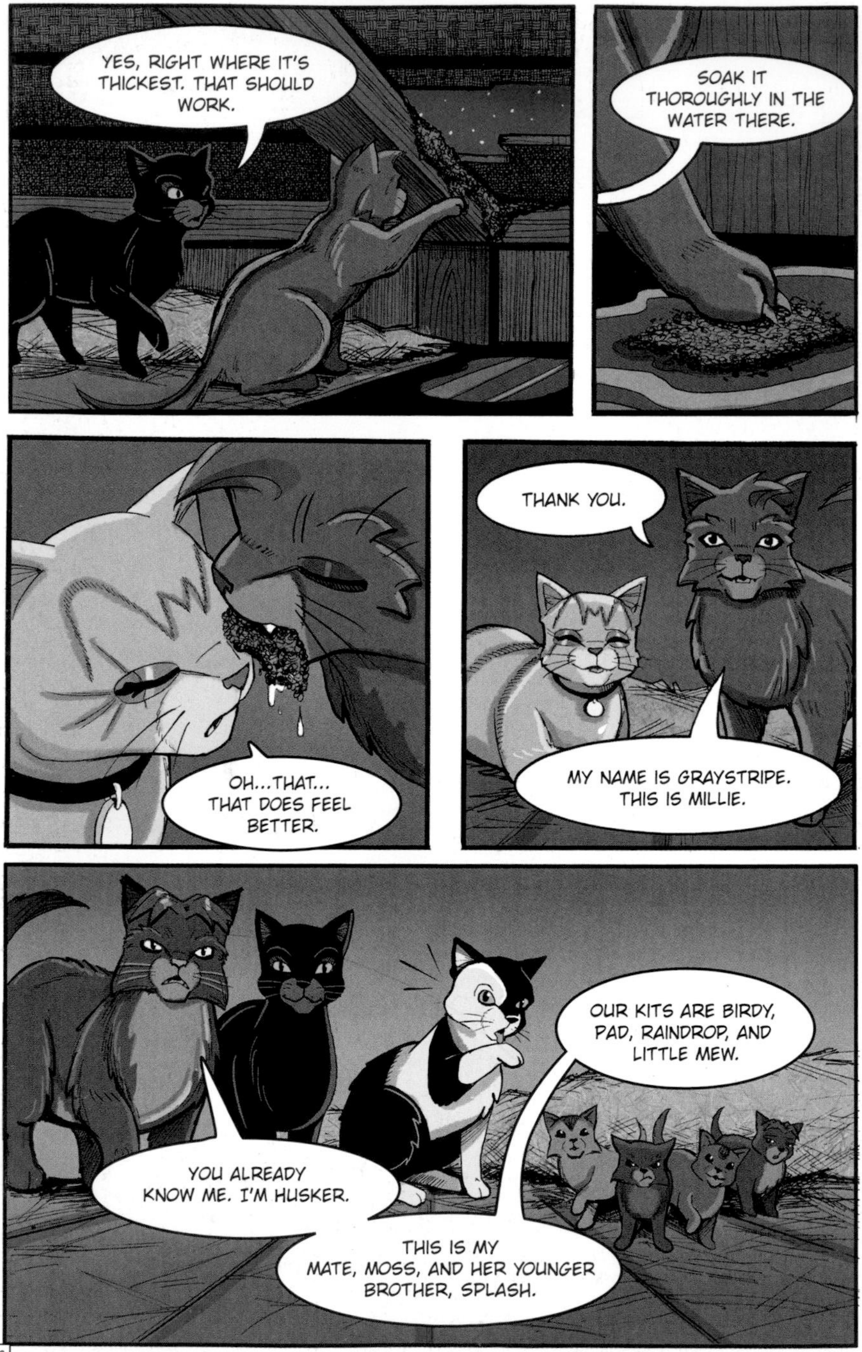
YES, RIGHT WHERE IT'S THICKEST. THAT SHOULD WORK.
SOAK IT THOROUGHLY IN THE WATER THERE.
OH...THAT... THAT DOES FEEL BETTER.
THANK YOU.
MY NAME IS GRAYSTRIPE. THIS IS MILLIE.
YOU ALREADY KNOW ME. I'M HUSKER.
THIS IS MY MATE, MOSS, AND HER YOUNGER BROTHER, SPLASH.
OUR KITS ARE BIRDY, PAD, RAINDROP, AND LITTLE MEW.

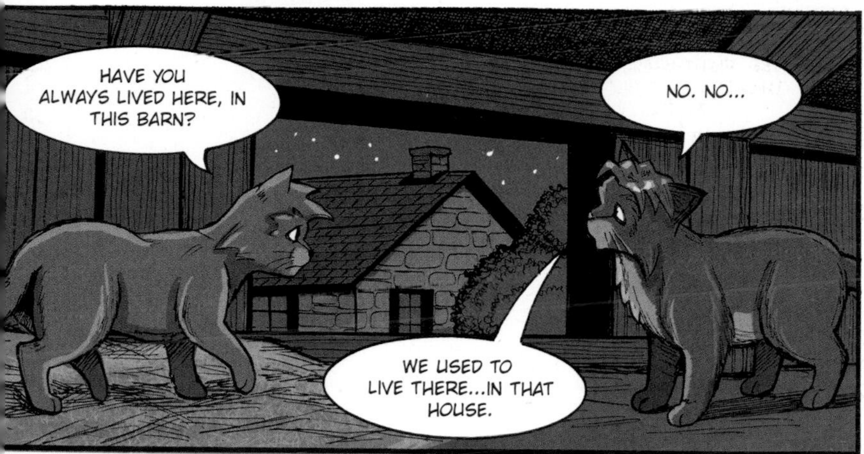
HAVE YOU ALWAYS LIVED HERE, IN THIS BARN?
NO. NO...
WE USED TO LIVE THERE...IN THAT HOUSE.

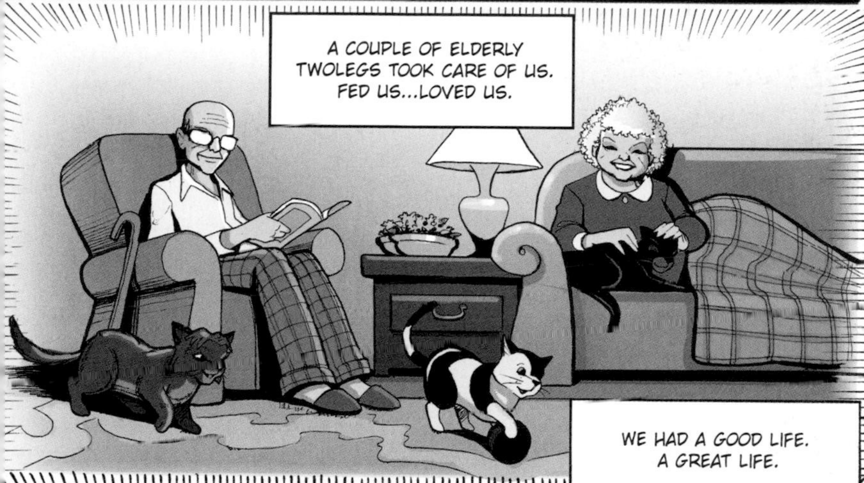
A COUPLE OF ELDERLY TWOLEGS TOOK CARE OF US. FED US...LOVED US.
WE HAD A GOOD LIFE. A GREAT LIFE.

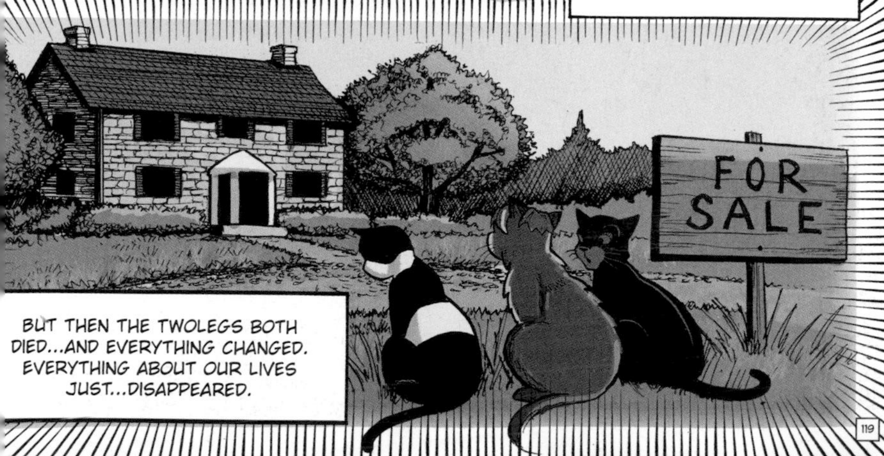
FOR SALE
BUT THEN THE TWOLEGS BOTH DIED...AND EVERYTHING CHANGED. EVERYTHING ABOUT OUR LIVES JUST...DISAPPEARED.

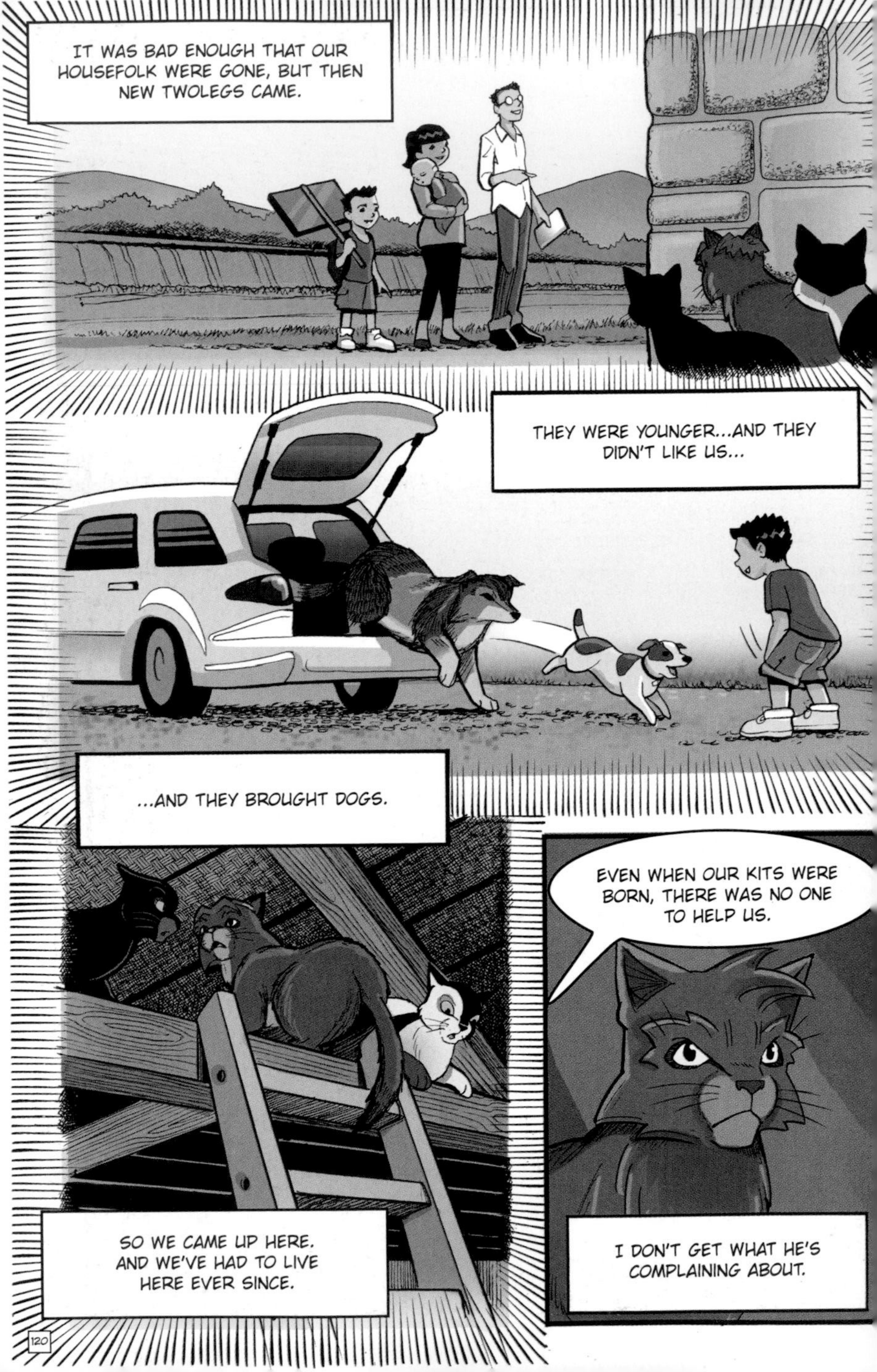
IT WAS BAD ENOUGH THAT OUR HOUSEFOLK WERE GONE, BUT THEN NEW TWOLEGS CAME.
THEY WERE YOUNGER...AND THEY DIDN'T LIKE US...
...AND THEY BROUGHT DOGS.
SO WE CAME UP HERE. AND WE'VE HAD TO LIVE HERE EVER SINCE.
EVEN WHEN OUR KITS WERE BORN, THERE WAS NO ONE TO HELP US.
I DON'T GET WHAT HE'S COMPLAINING ABOUT.

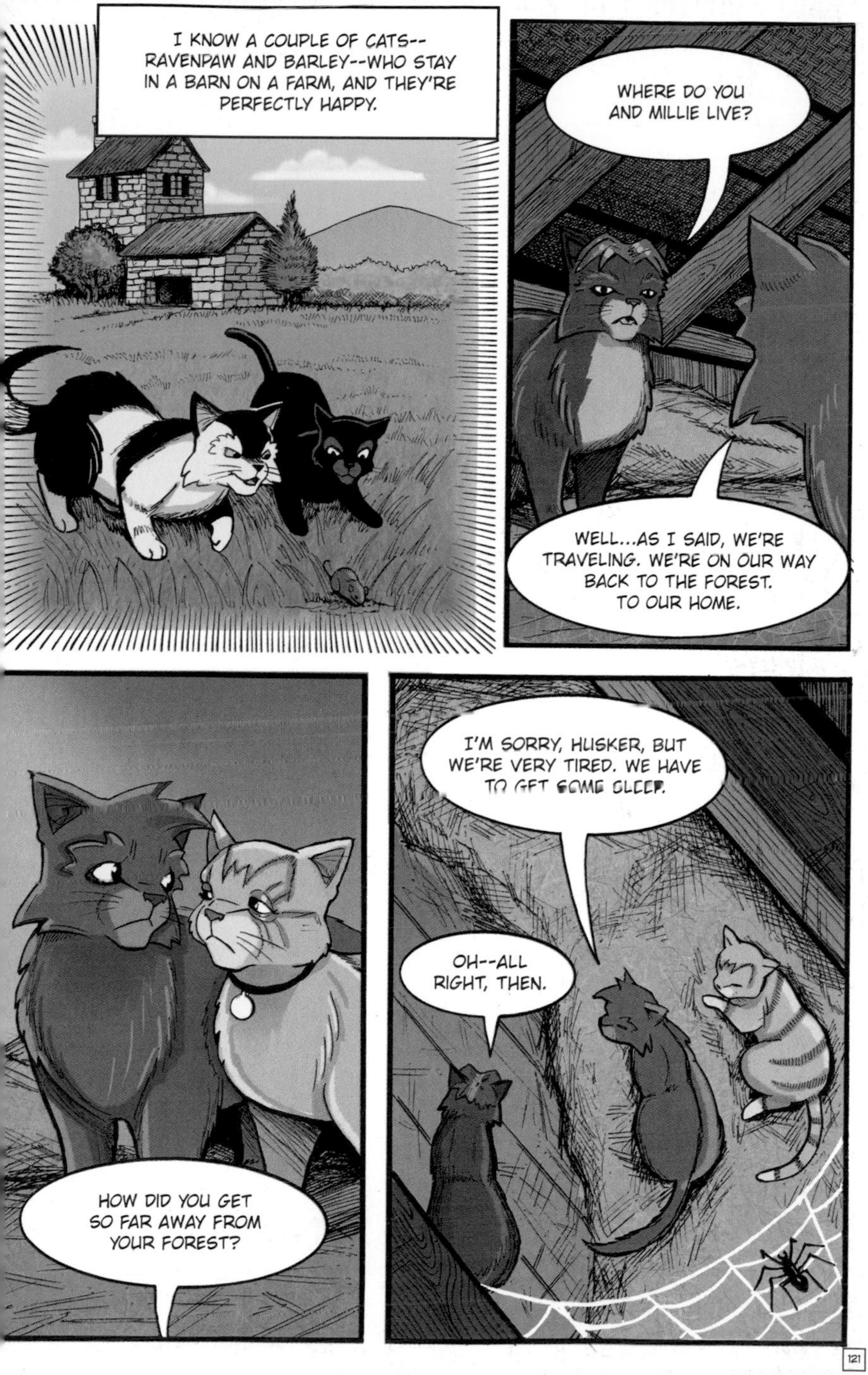
I KNOW A COUPLE OF CATS--RAVENPAW AND BARLEY--WHO STAY IN A BARN ON A FARM, AND THEY'RE PERFECTLY HAPPY.
WHERE DO YOU AND MILLIE LIVE?
WELL...AS I SAID, WE'RE TRAVELING. WE'RE ON OUR WAY BACK TO THE FOREST. TO OUR HOME.
HOW DID YOU GET SO FAR AWAY FROM YOUR FOREST?
I'M SORRY, HUSKER, BUT WE'RE VERY TIRED. WE HAVE TO GET SOME SLEEP.
OH--ALL RIGHT, THEN.

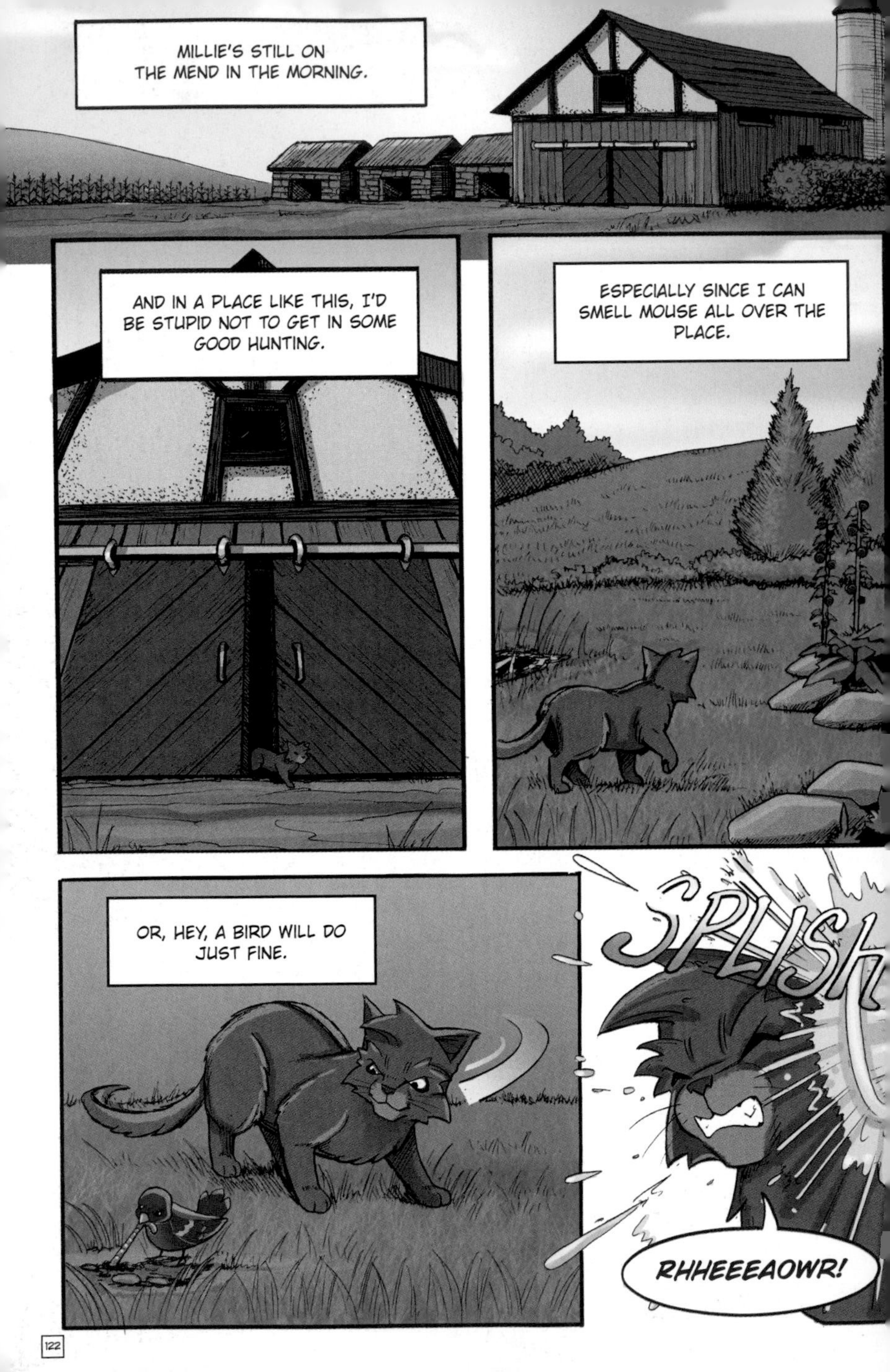

MILLIE'S STILL ON THE MEND IN THE MORNING.
AND IN A PLACE LIKE THIS, I'D BE STUPID NOT TO GET IN SOME GOOD HUNTING.
ESPECIALLY SINCE I CAN SMELL MOUSE ALL OVER THE PLACE.
OR, HEY, A BIRD WILL DO JUST FINE.
SPLISH
RHHEEEAOWR!

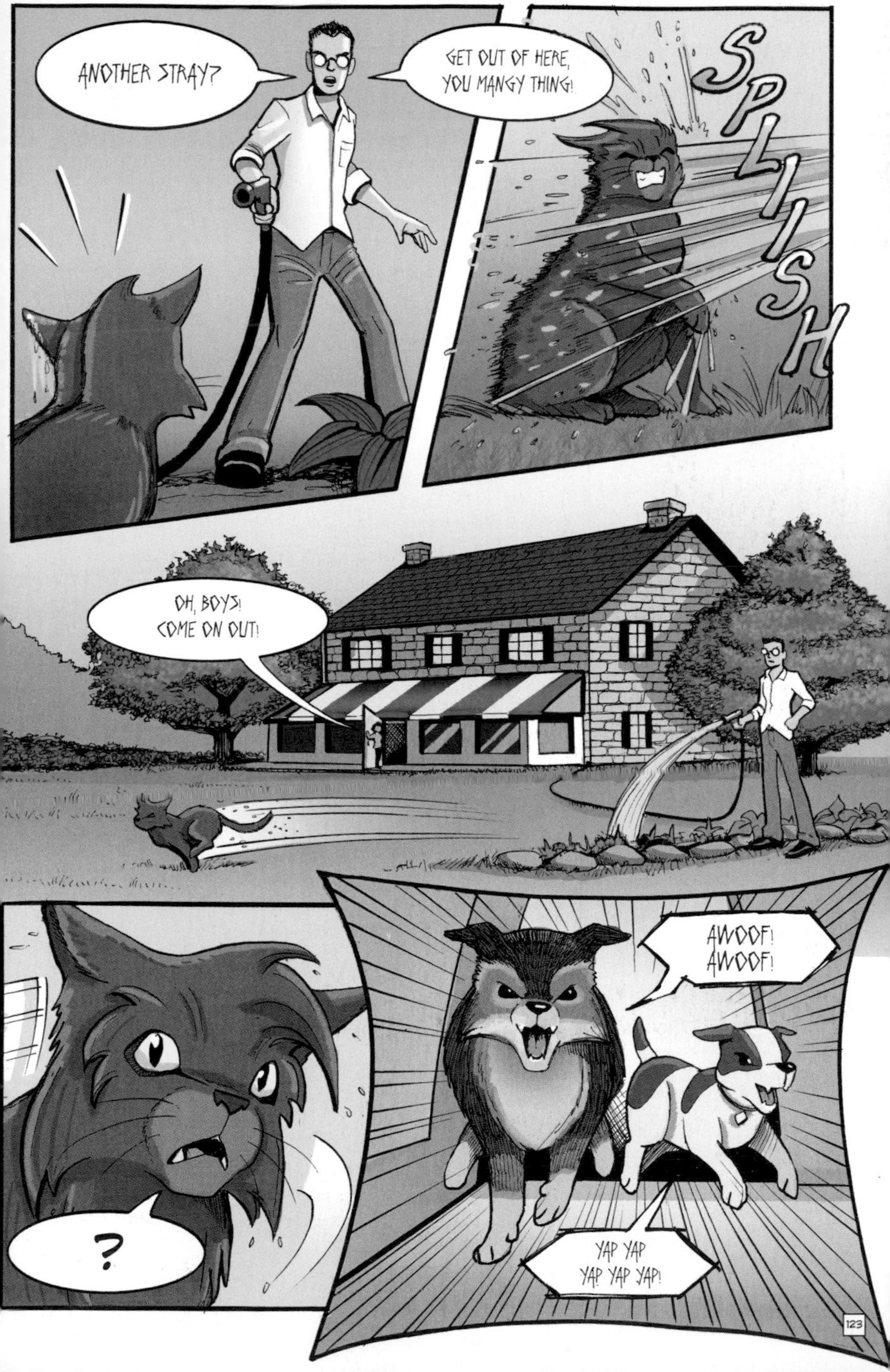
ANOTHER STRAY?
GET OUT OF HERE, YOU MANGY THING!
SPLISH
OH, BOYS! COME ON OUT!
?
AWOOF! AWOOF!
YAP YAP YAP YAP YAP!

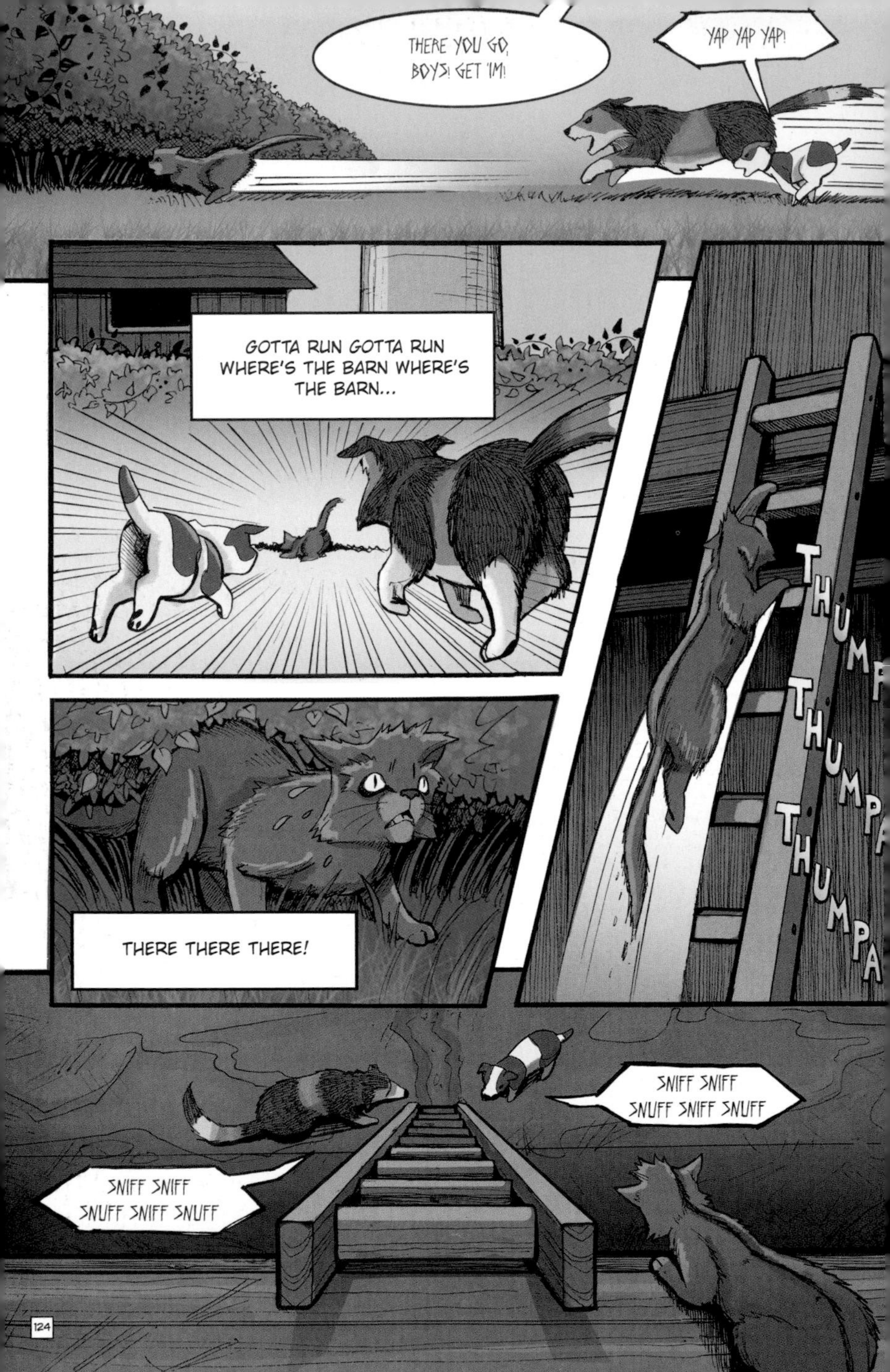
THERE YOU GO, BOYS! GET 'IM!
YAP YAP YAP!
GOTTA RUN GOTTA RUN WHERE'S THE BARN WHERE'S THE BARN...
THERE THERE THERE!
THUMP
THUMPA
THUMPA
THUMPA
SNIFF SNIFF SNUFF SNIFF SNUFF
SNIFF SNIFF SNUFF SNIFF SNUFF

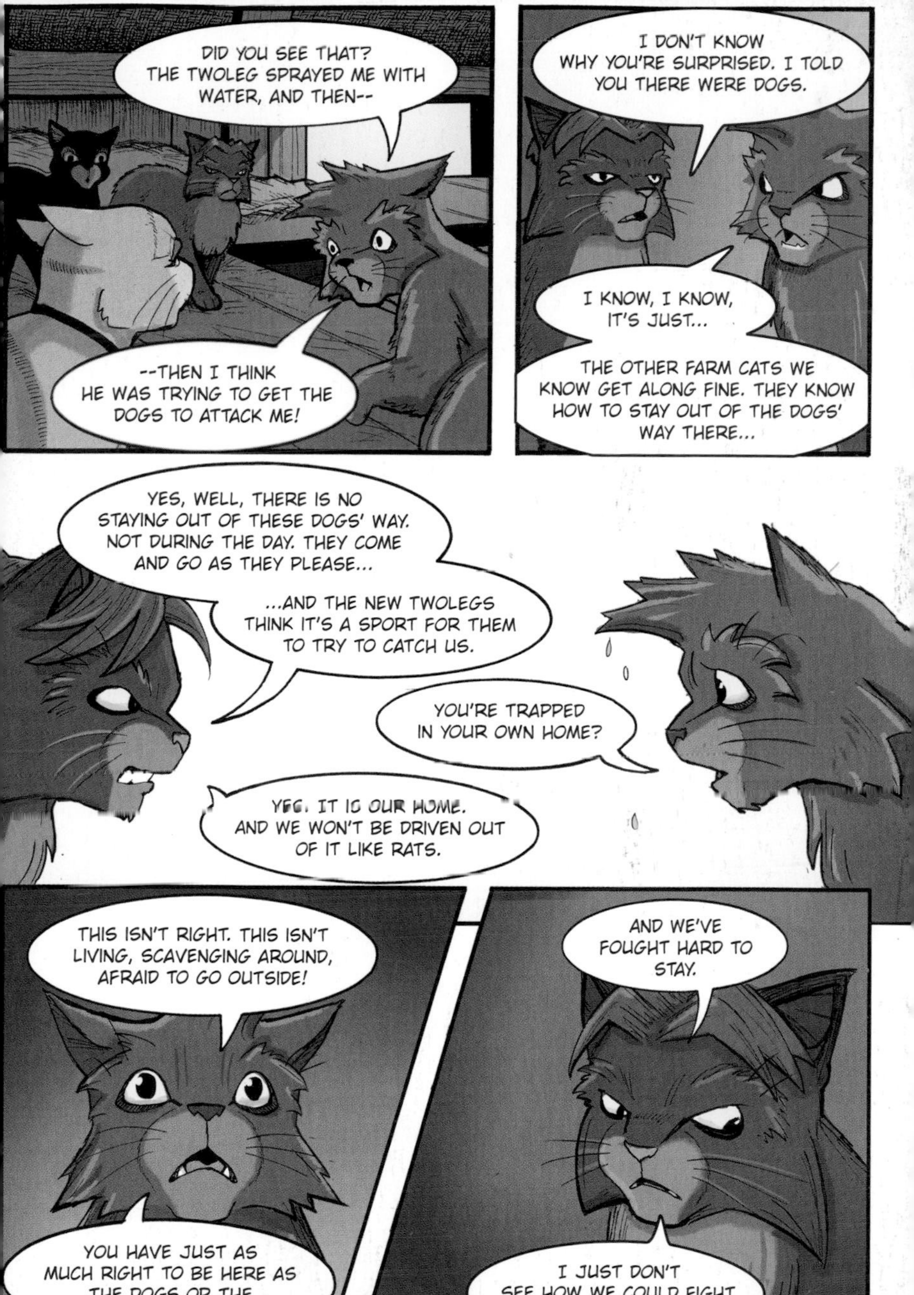
DID YOU SEE THAT? THE TWOLEG SPRAYED ME WITH WATER, AND THEN--
--THEN I THINK HE WAS TRYING TO GET THE DOGS TO ATTACK ME!
I DON'T KNOW WHY YOU'RE SURPRISED. I TOLD YOU THERE WERE DOGS.
I KNOW, I KNOW, IT'S JUST...
THE OTHER FARM CATS WE KNOW GET ALONG FINE. THEY KNOW HOW TO STAY OUT OF THE DOGS' WAY THERE...
YES, WELL, THERE IS NO STAYING OUT OF THESE DOGS' WAY. NOT DURING THE DAY. THEY COME AND GO AS THEY PLEASE...
...AND THE NEW TWOLEGS THINK IT'S A SPORT FOR THEM TO TRY TO CATCH US.
YOU'RE TRAPPED IN YOUR OWN HOME?
YES. IT IS OUR HOME. AND WE WON'T BE DRIVEN OUT OF IT LIKE RATS.
THIS ISN'T RIGHT. THIS ISN'T LIVING, SCAVENGING AROUND, AFRAID TO GO OUTSIDE!
YOU HAVE JUST AS MUCH RIGHT TO BE HERE AS THE DOGS OR THE TWOLEGS!
AND WE'VE FOUGHT HARD TO STAY.
I JUST DON'T SEE HOW WE COULD FIGHT ANY HARDER.

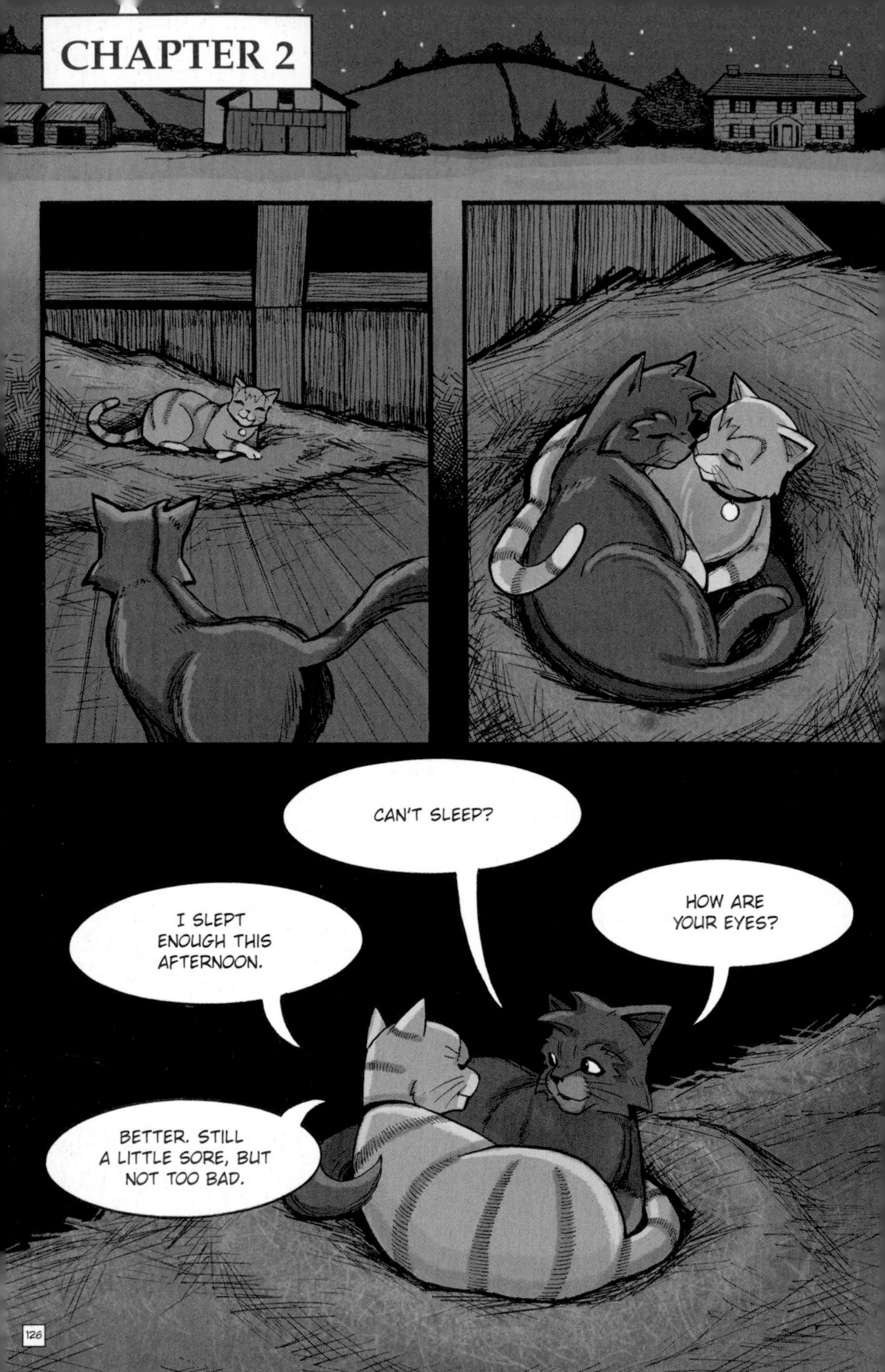
CHAPTER 2
CAN'T SLEEP?
I SLEPT ENOUGH THIS AFTERNOON.
HOW ARE YOUR EYES?
BETTER. STILL A LITTLE SORE, BUT NOT TOO BAD.

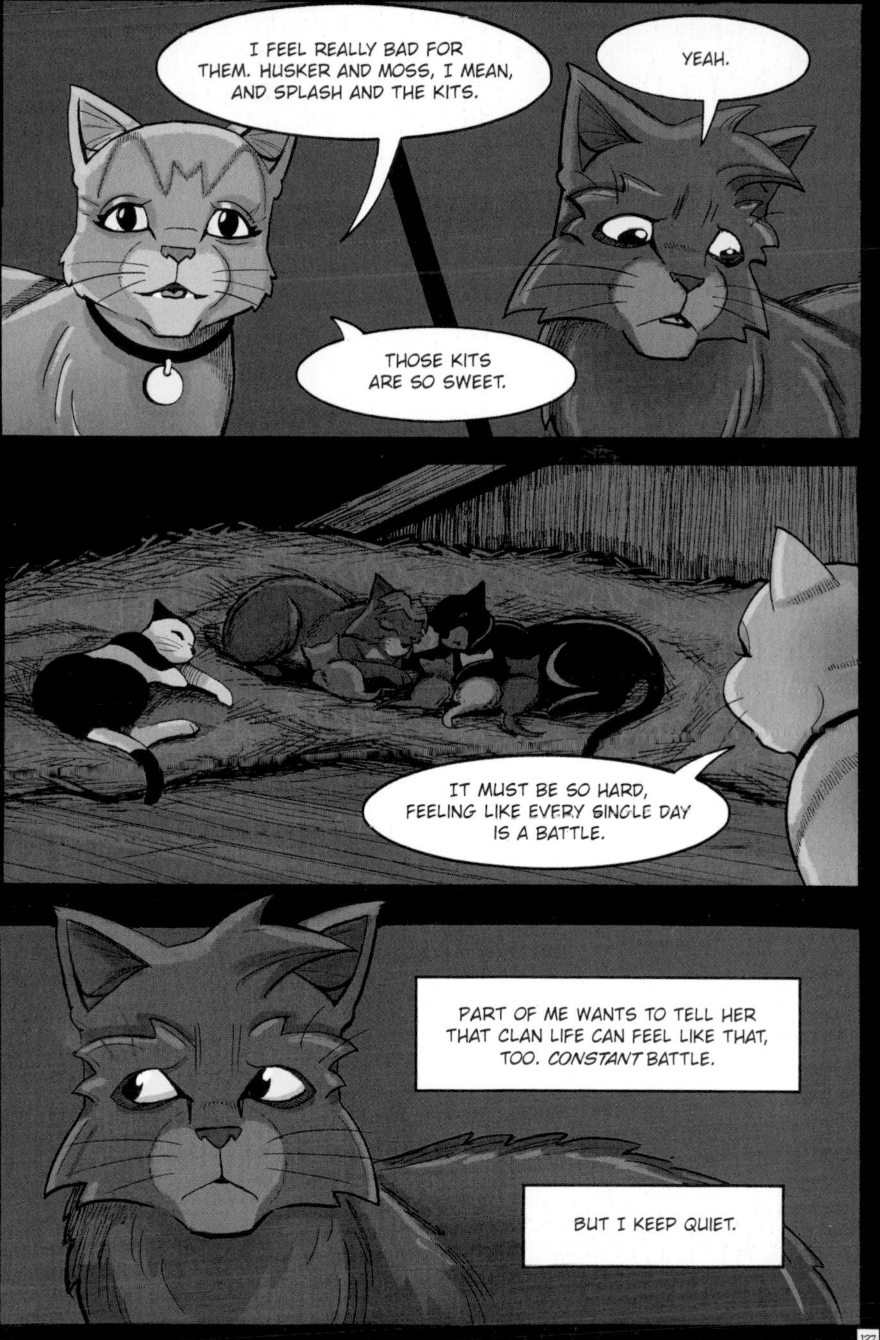
I FEEL REALLY BAD FOR THEM. HUSKER AND MOSS, I MEAN, AND SPLASH AND THE KITS.
YEAH.
THOSE KITS ARE SO SWEET.
IT MUST BE SO HARD, FEELING LIKE EVERY SINGLE DAY IS A BATTLE.
PART OF ME WANTS TO TELL HER THAT CLAN LIFE CAN FEEL LIKE THAT, TOO. *CONSTANT* BATTLE.
BUT I KEEP QUIET.

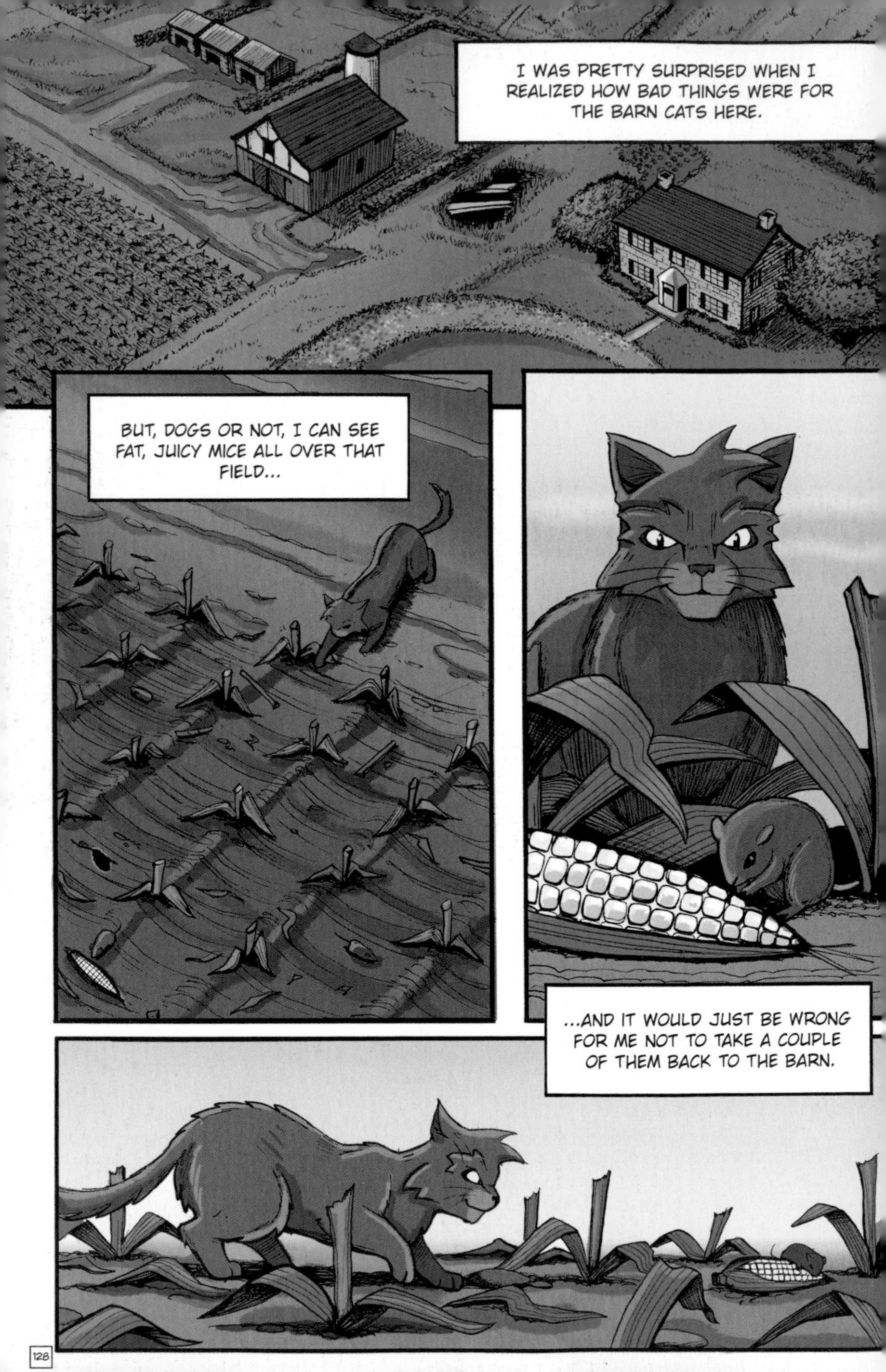
I WAS PRETTY SURPRISED WHEN I REALIZED HOW BAD THINGS WERE FOR THE BARN CATS HERE.
BUT, DOGS OR NOT, I CAN SEE FAT, JUICY MICE ALL OVER THAT FIELD...
...AND IT WOULD JUST BE WRONG FOR ME NOT TO TAKE A COUPLE OF THEM BACK TO THE BARN.

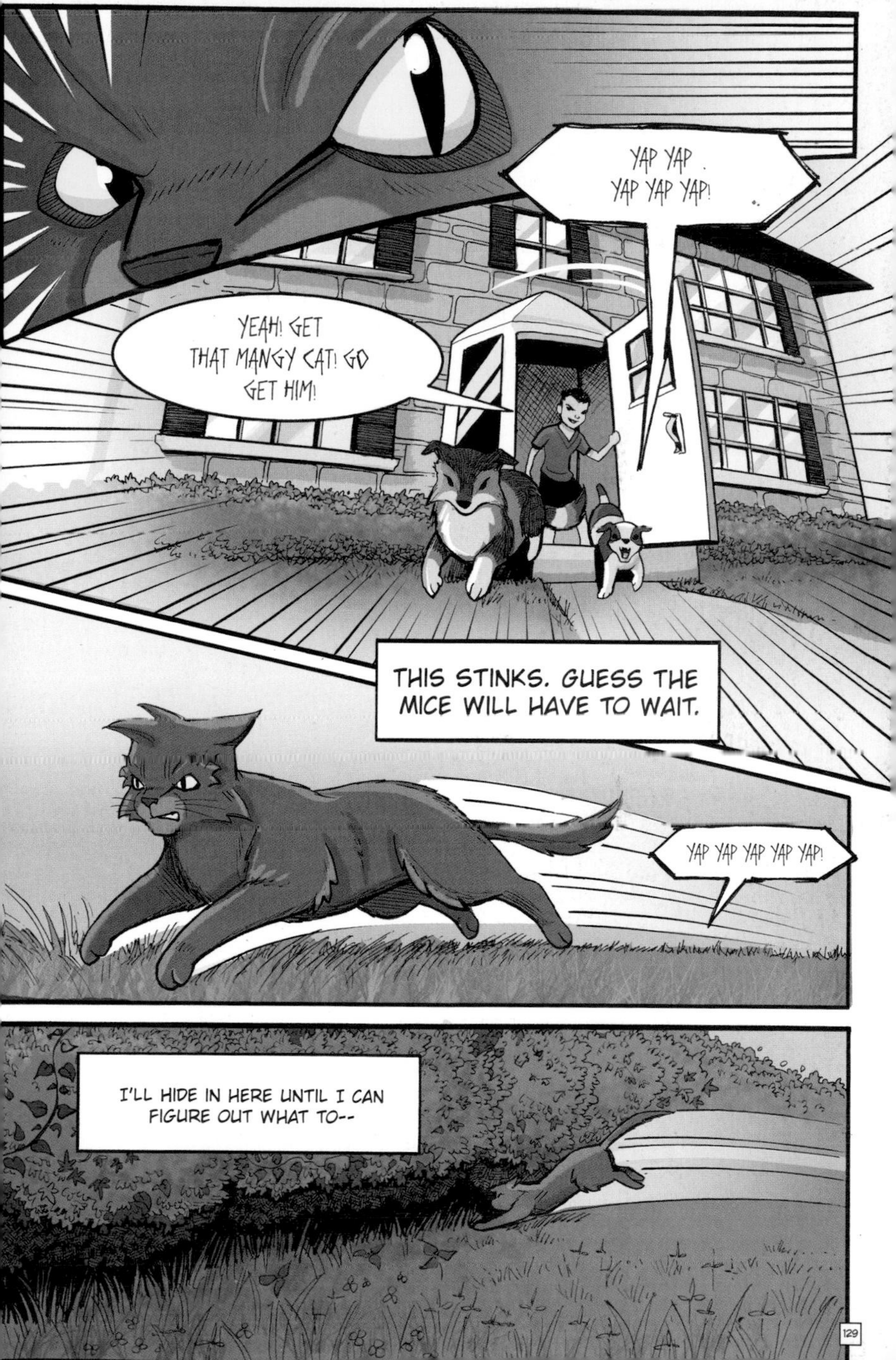
YAP YAP
YAP YAP YAP!
YEAH! GET THAT MANGY CAT! GO GET HIM!
THIS STINKS. GUESS THE MICE WILL HAVE TO WAIT.
YAP YAP YAP YAP YAP!
I'LL HIDE IN HERE UNTIL I CAN FIGURE OUT WHAT TO--

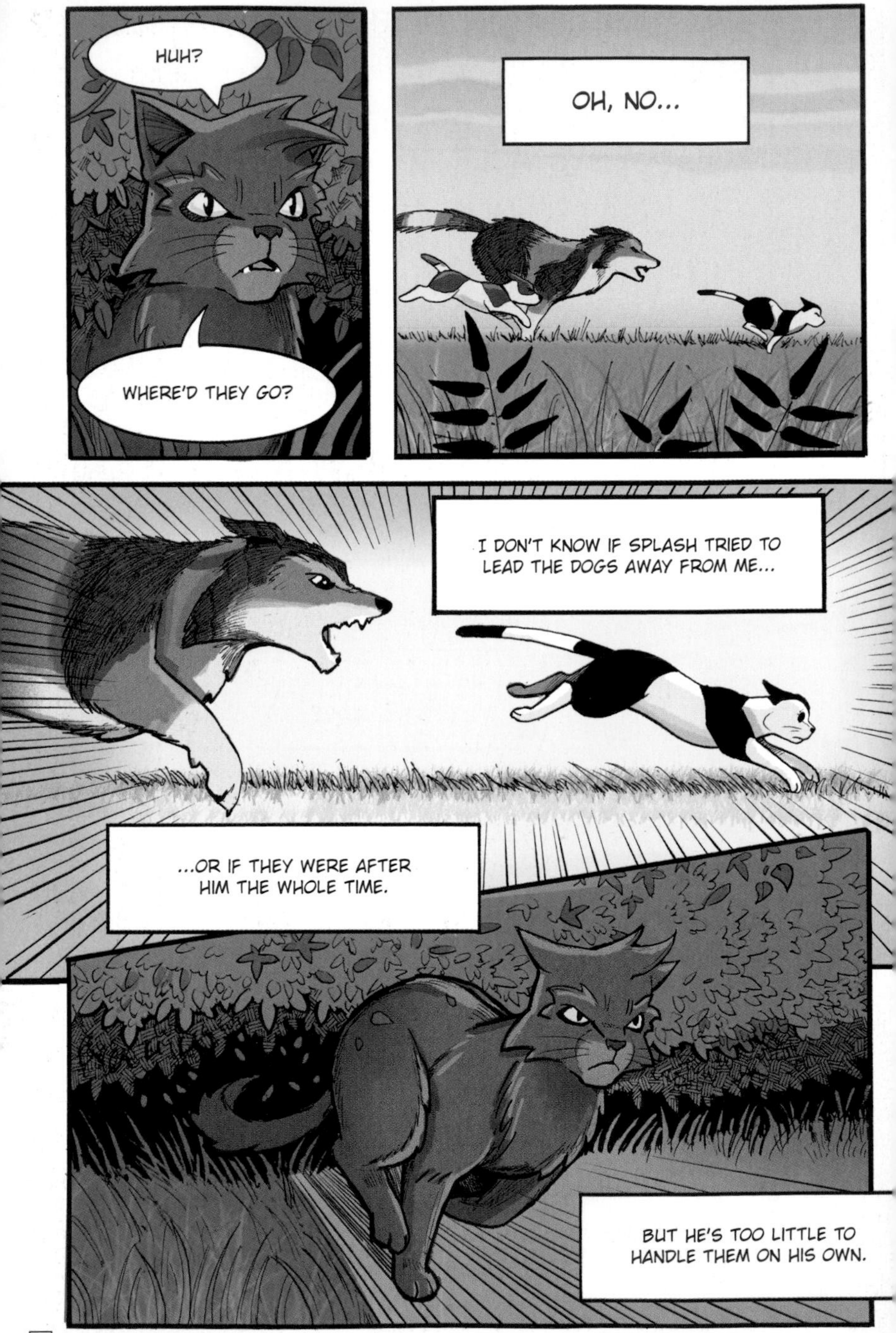
HUH?
WHERE'D THEY GO?
OH, NO...
I DON'T KNOW IF SPLASH TRIED TO LEAD THE DOGS AWAY FROM ME...
...OR IF THEY WERE AFTER HIM THE WHOLE TIME.
BUT HE'S TOO LITTLE TO HANDLE THEM ON HIS OWN.

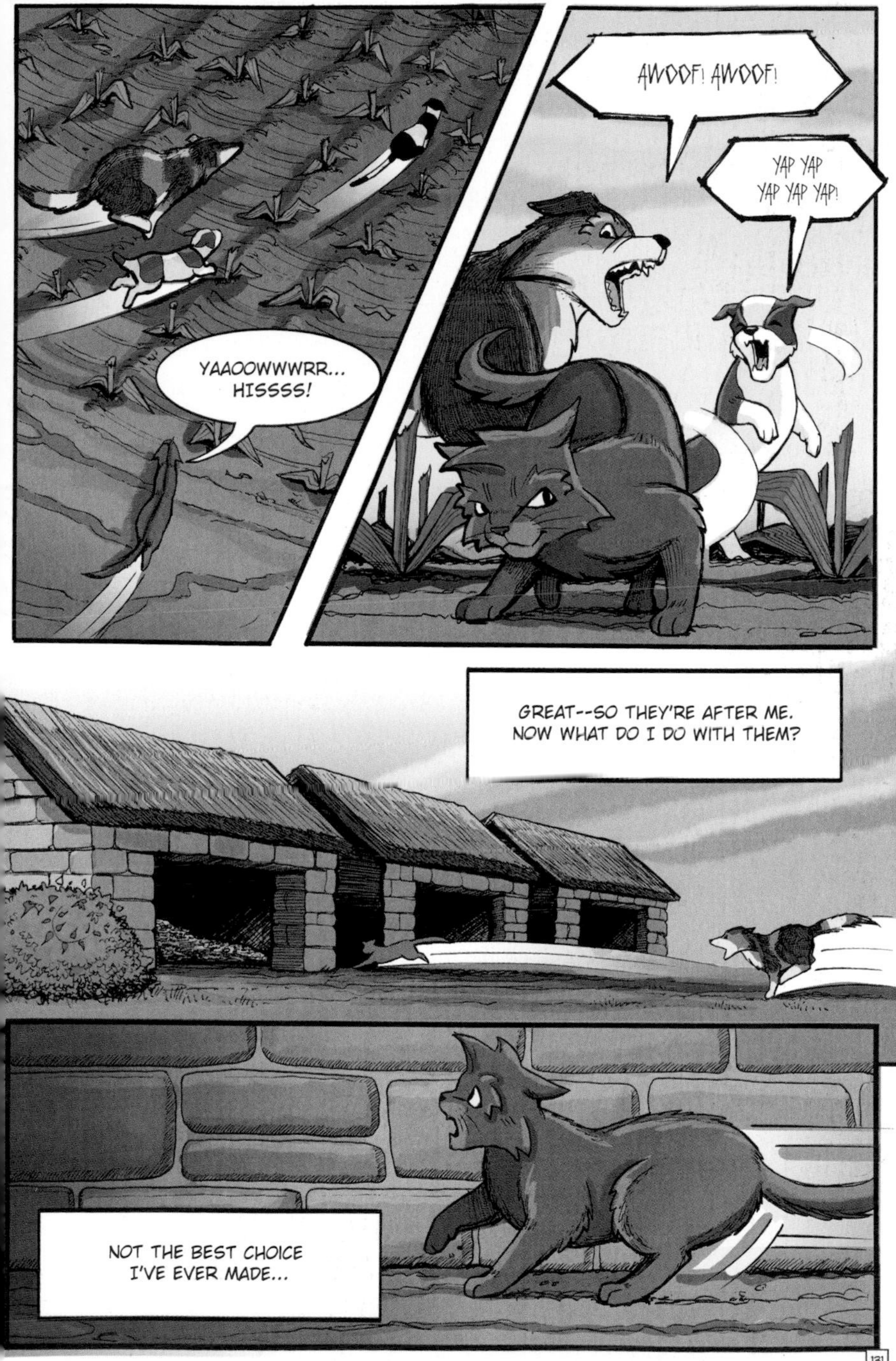
YAAOOWWWRR... HISSSS!
AWOOF! AWOOF!
YAP YAP YAP YAP YAP!
GREAT--SO THEY'RE AFTER ME. NOW WHAT DO I DO WITH THEM?
NOT THE BEST CHOICE I'VE EVER MADE...

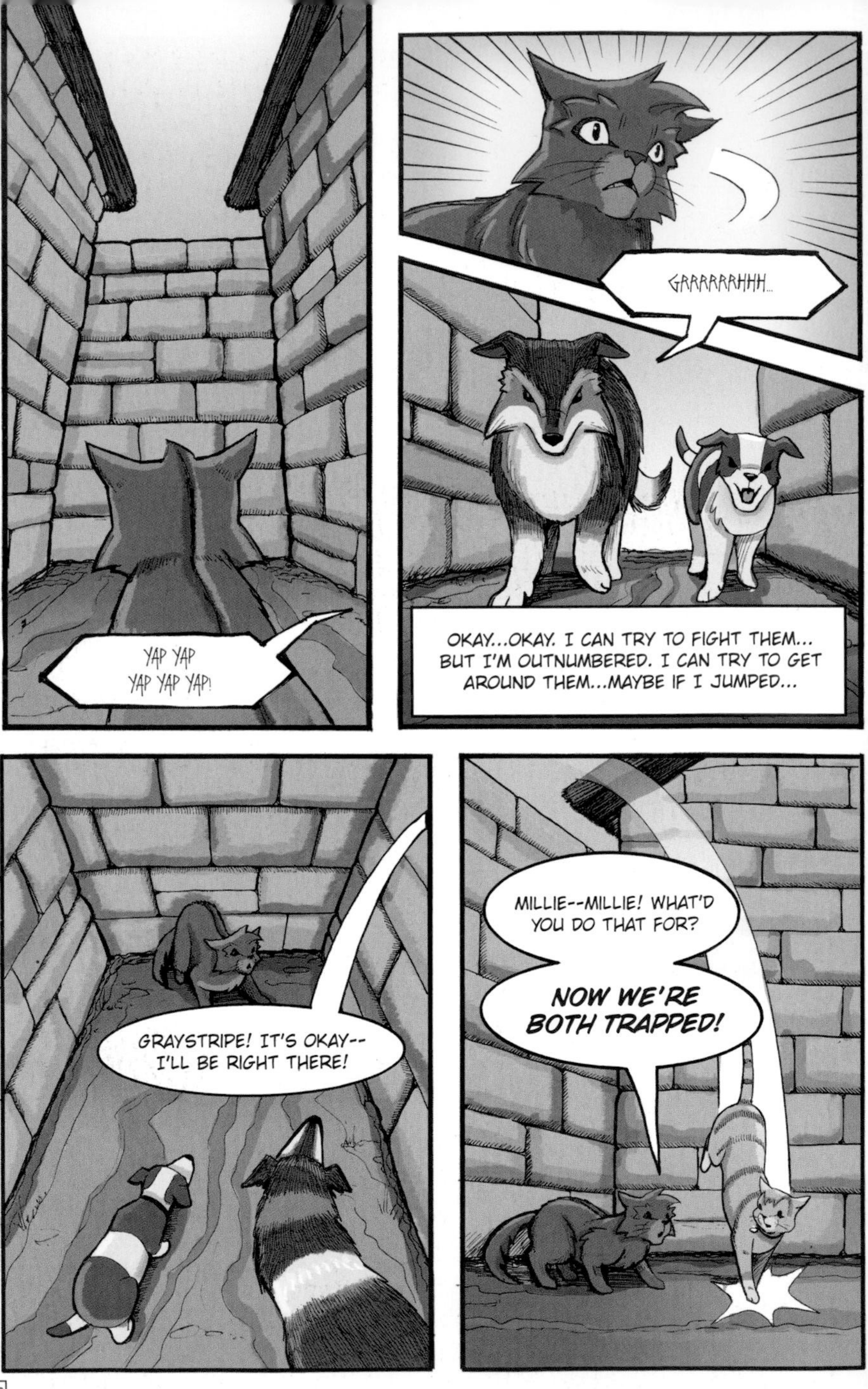
YAP YAP
YAP YAP YAP!
GRRRRRRHHH...
OKAY...OKAY. I CAN TRY TO FIGHT THEM... BUT I'M OUTNUMBERED. I CAN TRY TO GET AROUND THEM...MAYBE IF I JUMPED...
GRAYSTRIPE! IT'S OKAY-- I'LL BE RIGHT THERE!
MILLIE--MILLIE! WHAT'D YOU DO THAT FOR?
NOW WE'RE BOTH TRAPPED!

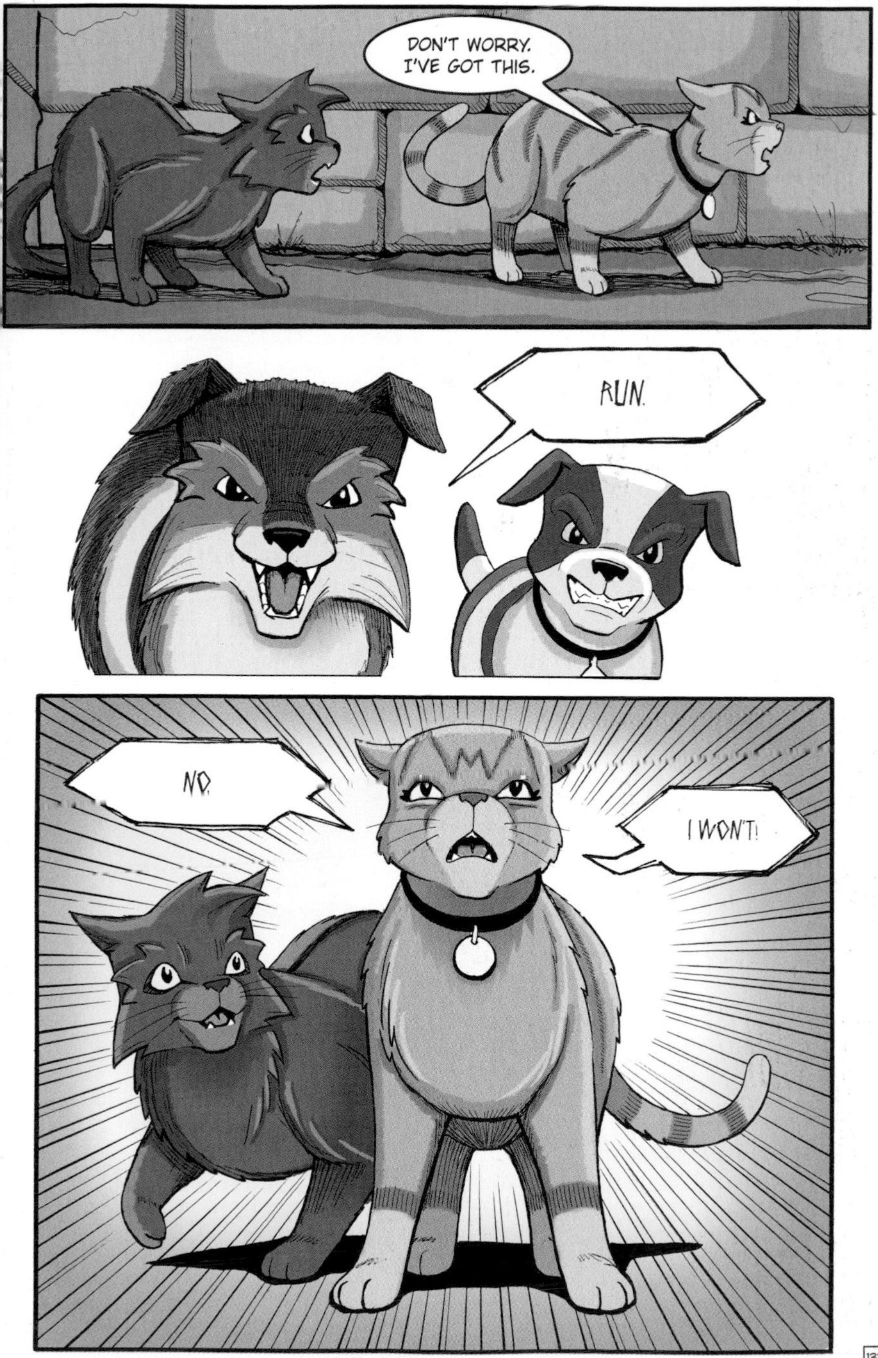
DON'T WORRY. I'VE GOT THIS.
RUN.
NO.
I WON'T!

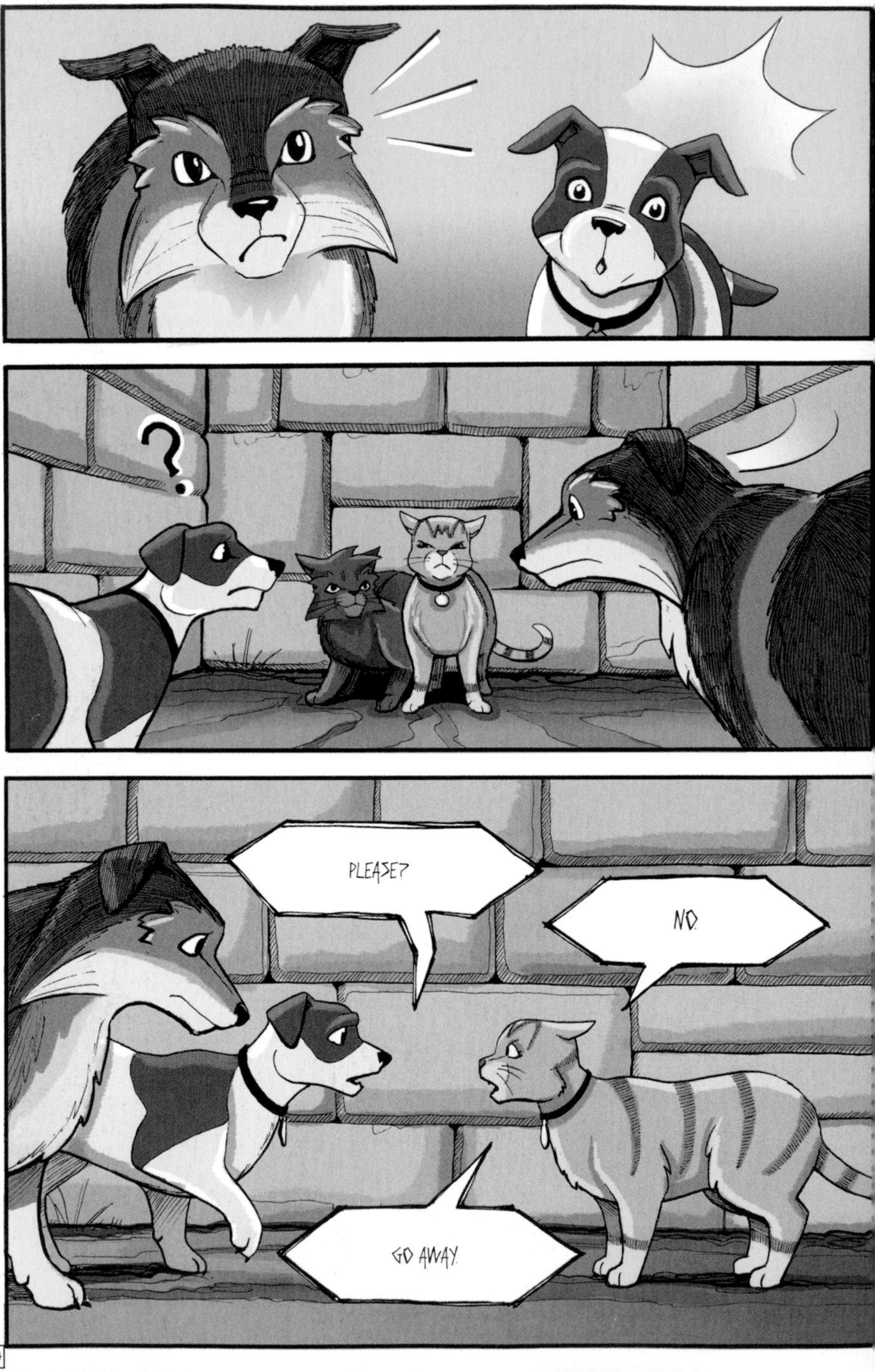
PLEASE?
NO.
GO AWAY.

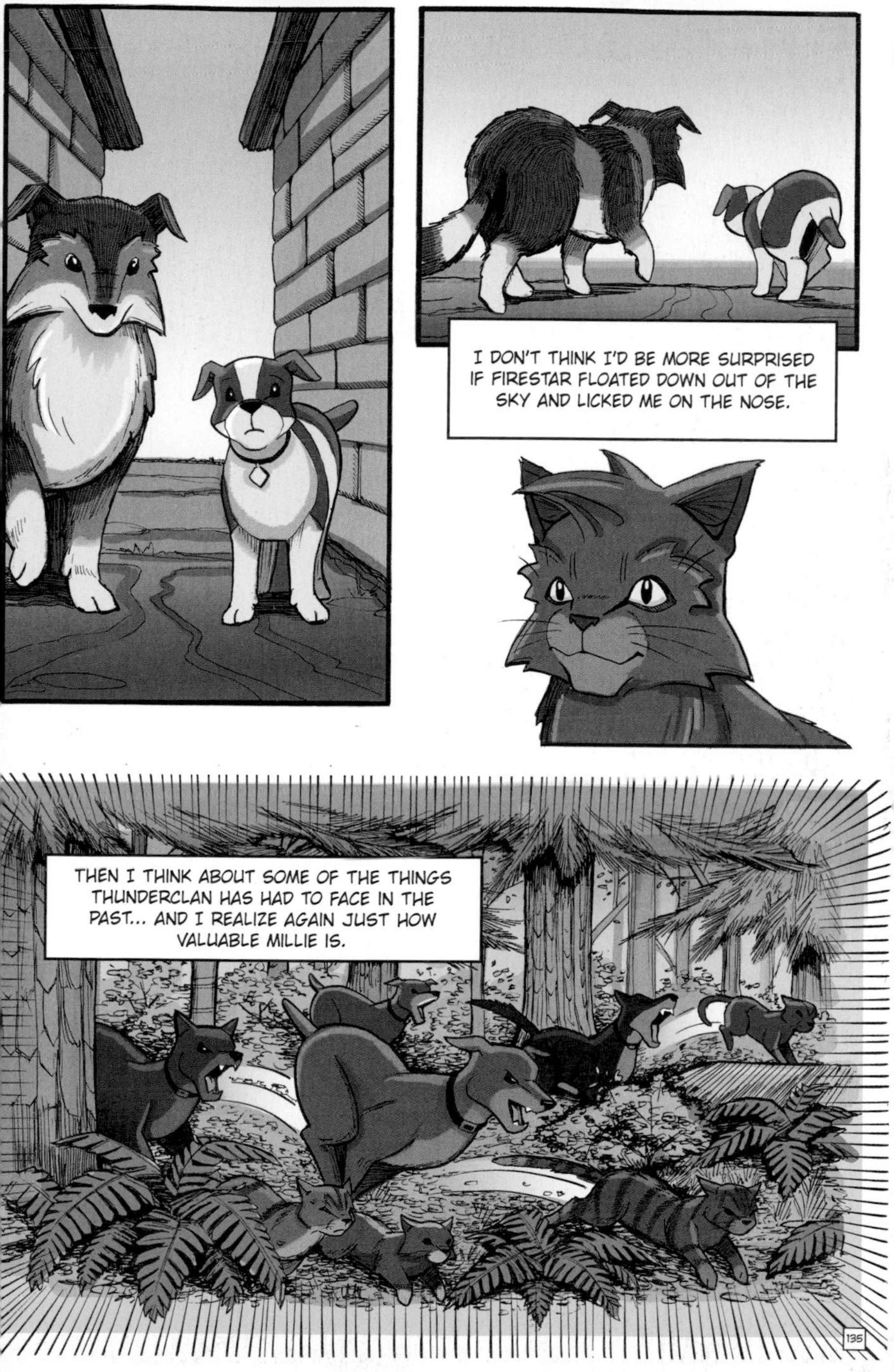
I DON'T THINK I'D BE MORE SURPRISED IF FIRESTAR FLOATED DOWN OUT OF THE SKY AND LICKED ME ON THE NOSE.
THEN I THINK ABOUT SOME OF THE THINGS THUNDERCLAN HAS HAD TO FACE IN THE PAST... AND I REALIZE AGAIN JUST HOW VALUABLE MILLIE IS.

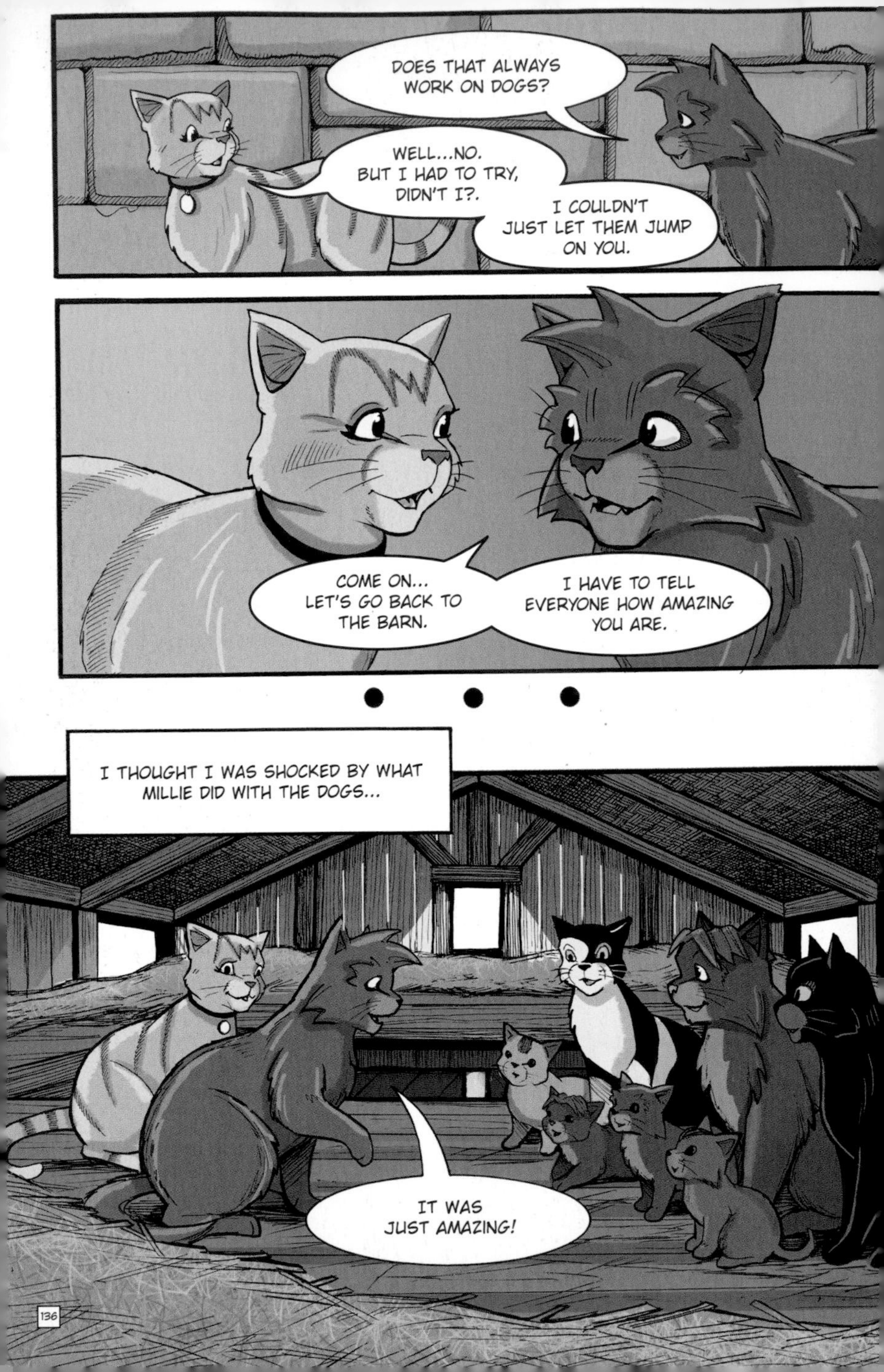
DOES THAT ALWAYS WORK ON DOGS?
WELL...NO. BUT I HAD TO TRY, DIDN'T I?.
I COULDN'T JUST LET THEM JUMP ON YOU.
COME ON... LET'S GO BACK TO THE BARN.
I HAVE TO TELL EVERYONE HOW AMAZING YOU ARE.
I THOUGHT I WAS SHOCKED BY WHAT MILLIE DID WITH THE DOGS...
IT WAS JUST AMAZING!

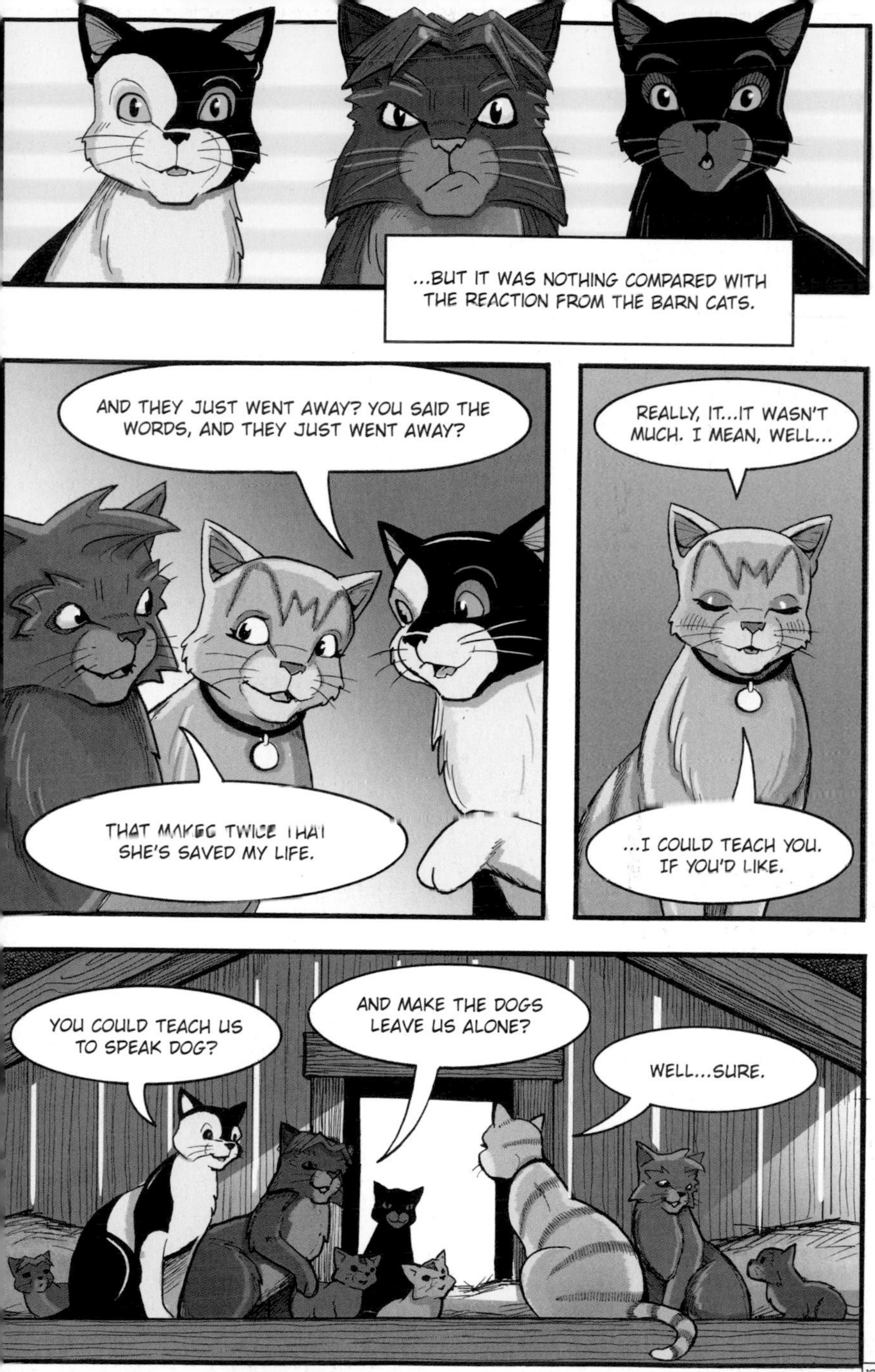

...BUT IT WAS NOTHING COMPARED WITH THE REACTION FROM THE BARN CATS.
AND THEY JUST WENT AWAY? YOU SAID THE WORDS, AND THEY JUST WENT AWAY?
THAT MAKES TWICE THAT SHE'S SAVED MY LIFE.
REALLY, IT...IT WASN'T MUCH. I MEAN, WELL...
...I COULD TEACH YOU. IF YOU'D LIKE.
YOU COULD TEACH US TO SPEAK DOG?
AND MAKE THE DOGS LEAVE US ALONE?
WELL...SURE.

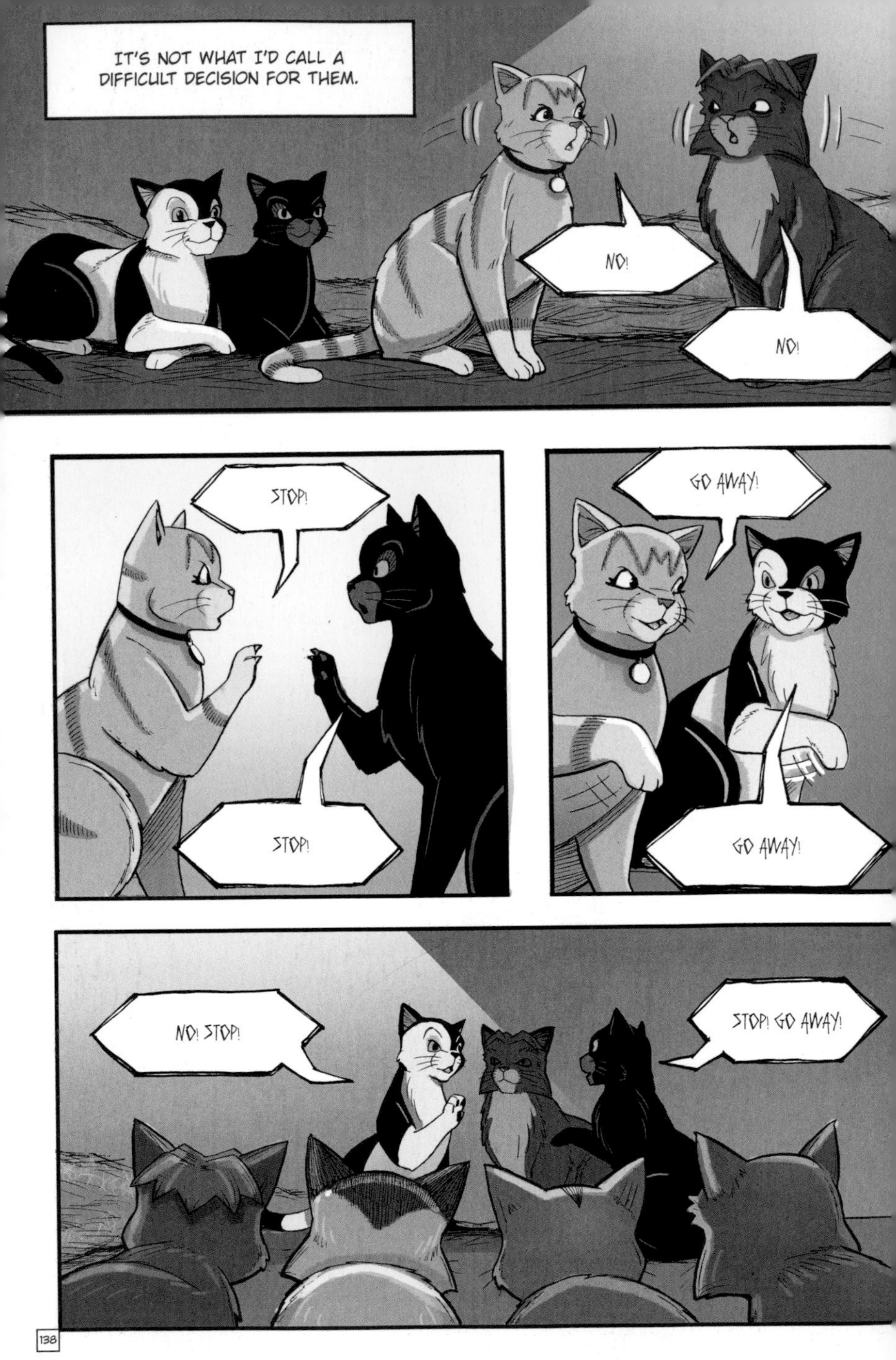
IT'S NOT WHAT I'D CALL A DIFFICULT DECISION FOR THEM.
NO!
NO!
STOP!
STOP!
GO AWAY!
GO AWAY!
NO! STOP!
STOP! GO AWAY!

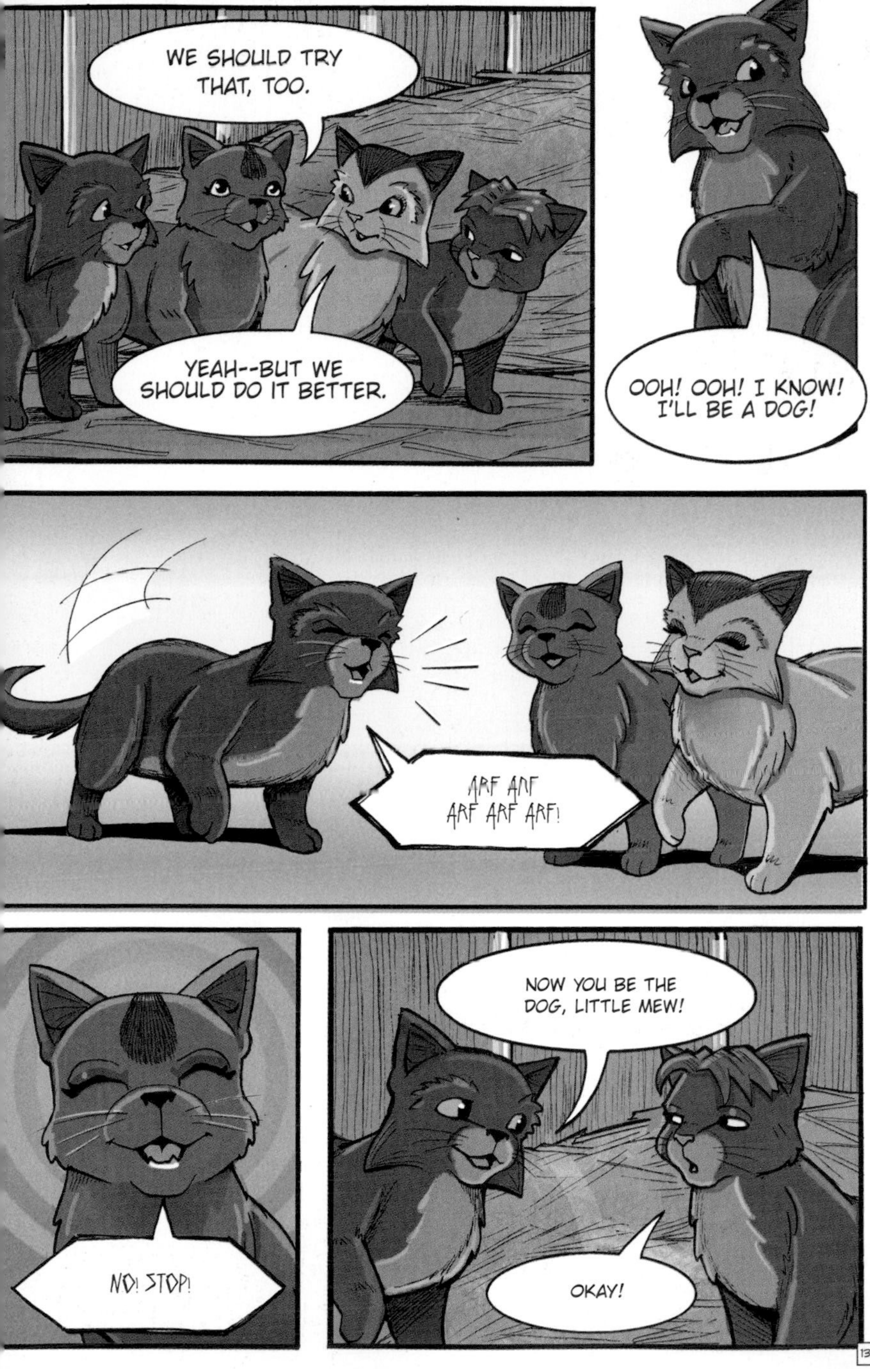
WE SHOULD TRY THAT, TOO.
YEAH--BUT WE SHOULD DO IT BETTER.
OOH! OOH! I KNOW! I'LL BE A DOG!
ARF ARF ARF ARF ARF!
NO! STOP!
NOW YOU BE THE DOG, LITTLE MEW!
OKAY!

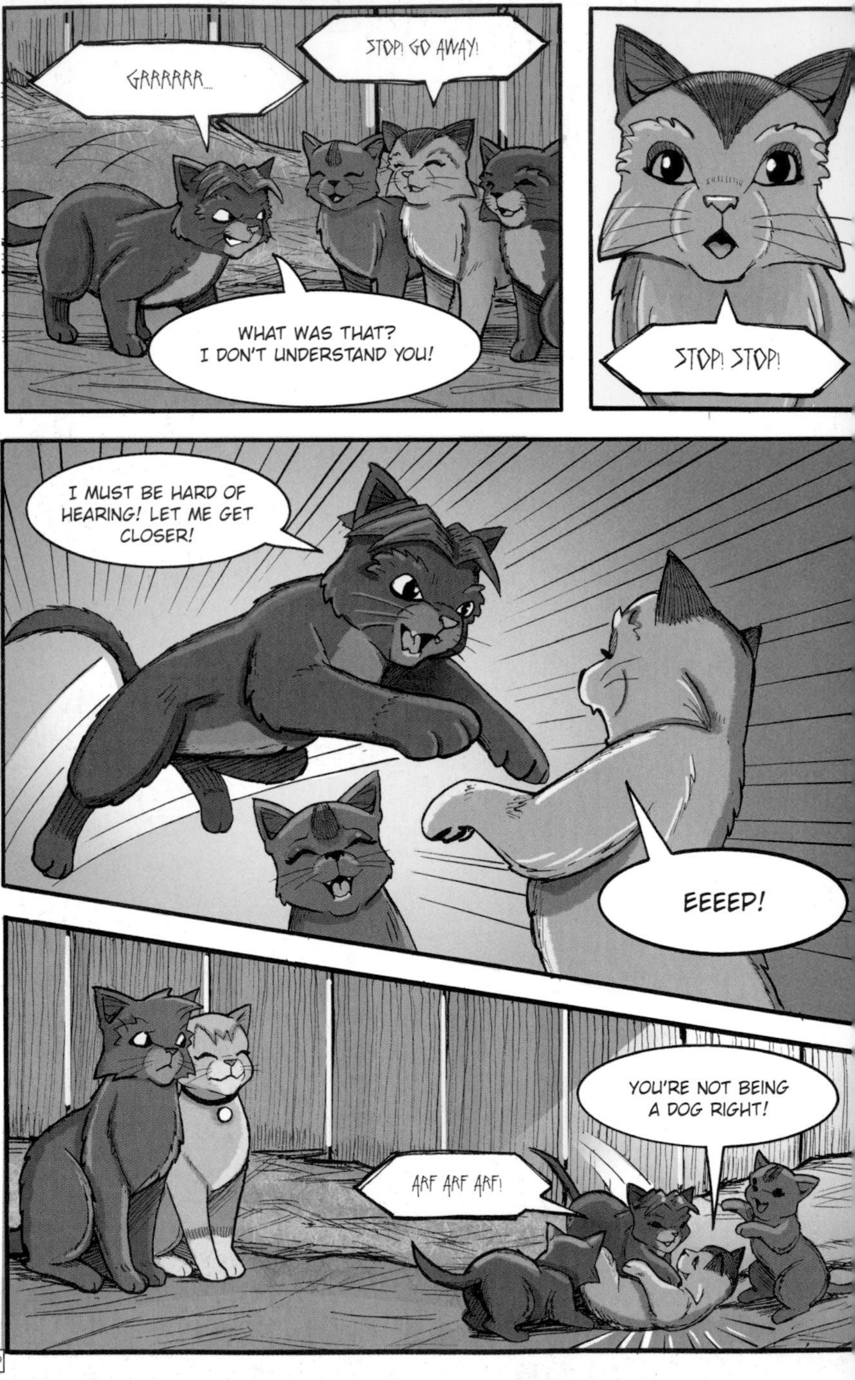
GRRRRRR....
STOP! GO AWAY!
WHAT WAS THAT? I DON'T UNDERSTAND YOU!
STOP! STOP!
I MUST BE HARD OF HEARING! LET ME GET CLOSER!
EEEEP!
YOU'RE NOT BEING A DOG RIGHT!
ARF ARF ARF!

CHAPTER 3

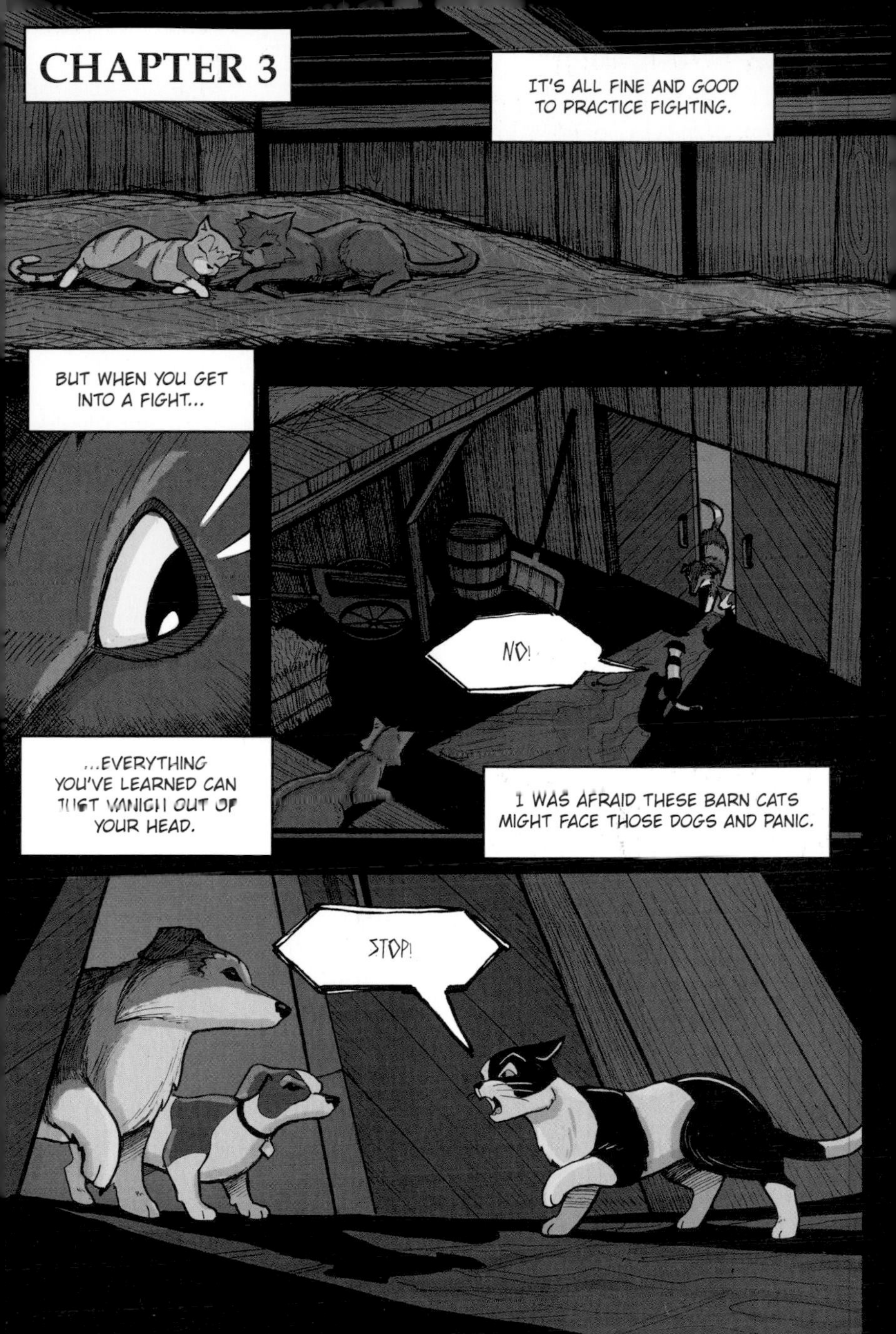
IT'S ALL FINE AND GOOD TO PRACTICE FIGHTING.
BUT WHEN YOU GET INTO A FIGHT...
...EVERYTHING YOU'VE LEARNED CAN JUST VANISH OUT OF YOUR HEAD.
NO!
I WAS AFRAID THESE BARN CATS MIGHT FACE THOSE DOGS AND PANIC.
STOP!

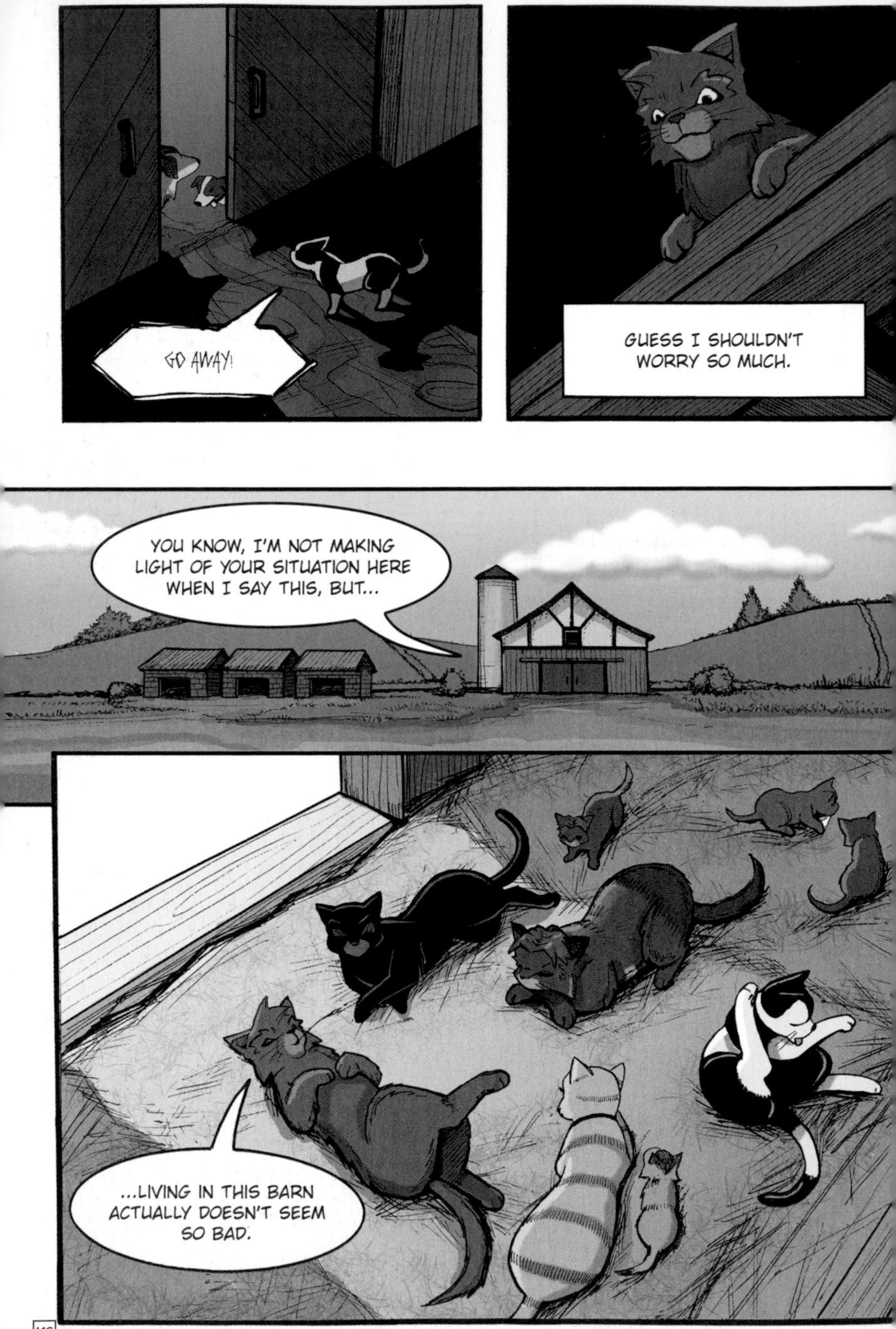
GO AWAY!
GUESS I SHOULDN'T WORRY SO MUCH.
YOU KNOW, I'M NOT MAKING LIGHT OF YOUR SITUATION HERE WHEN I SAY THIS, BUT...
...LIVING IN THIS BARN ACTUALLY DOESN'T SEEM SO BAD.

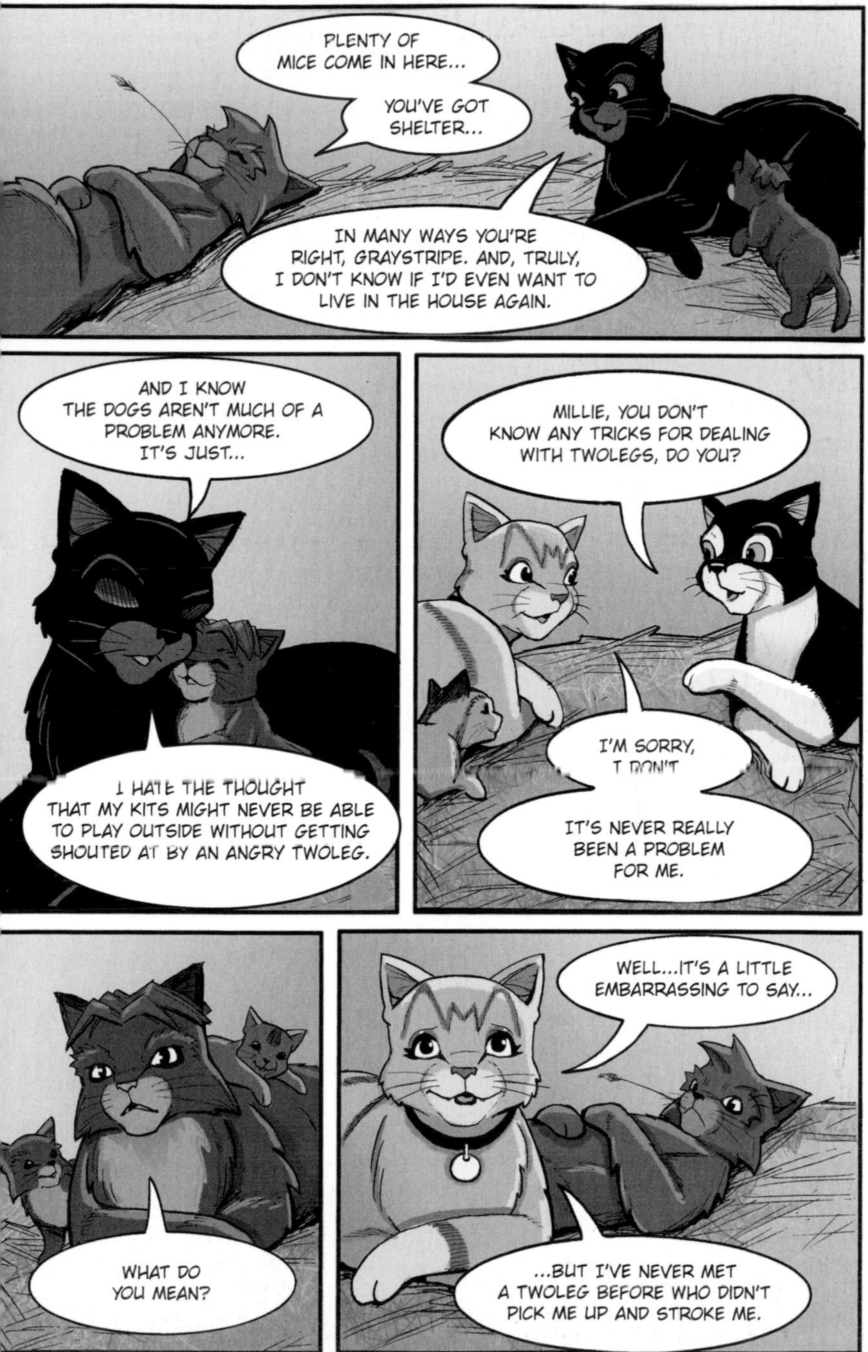
PLENTY OF MICE COME IN HERE...
YOU'VE GOT SHELTER...
IN MANY WAYS YOU'RE RIGHT, GRAYSTRIPE. AND, TRULY, I DON'T KNOW IF I'D EVEN WANT TO LIVE IN THE HOUSE AGAIN.
AND I KNOW THE DOGS AREN'T MUCH OF A PROBLEM ANYMORE. IT'S JUST...
I HATE THE THOUGHT THAT MY KITS MIGHT NEVER BE ABLE TO PLAY OUTSIDE WITHOUT GETTING SHOUTED AT BY AN ANGRY TWOLEG.
MILLIE, YOU DON'T KNOW ANY TRICKS FOR DEALING WITH TWOLEGS, DO YOU?
I'M SORRY, I DON'T
IT'S NEVER REALLY BEEN A PROBLEM FOR ME.
WHAT DO YOU MEAN?
WELL...IT'S A LITTLE EMBARRASSING TO SAY...
...BUT I'VE NEVER MET A TWOLEG BEFORE WHO DIDN'T PICK ME UP AND STROKE ME.

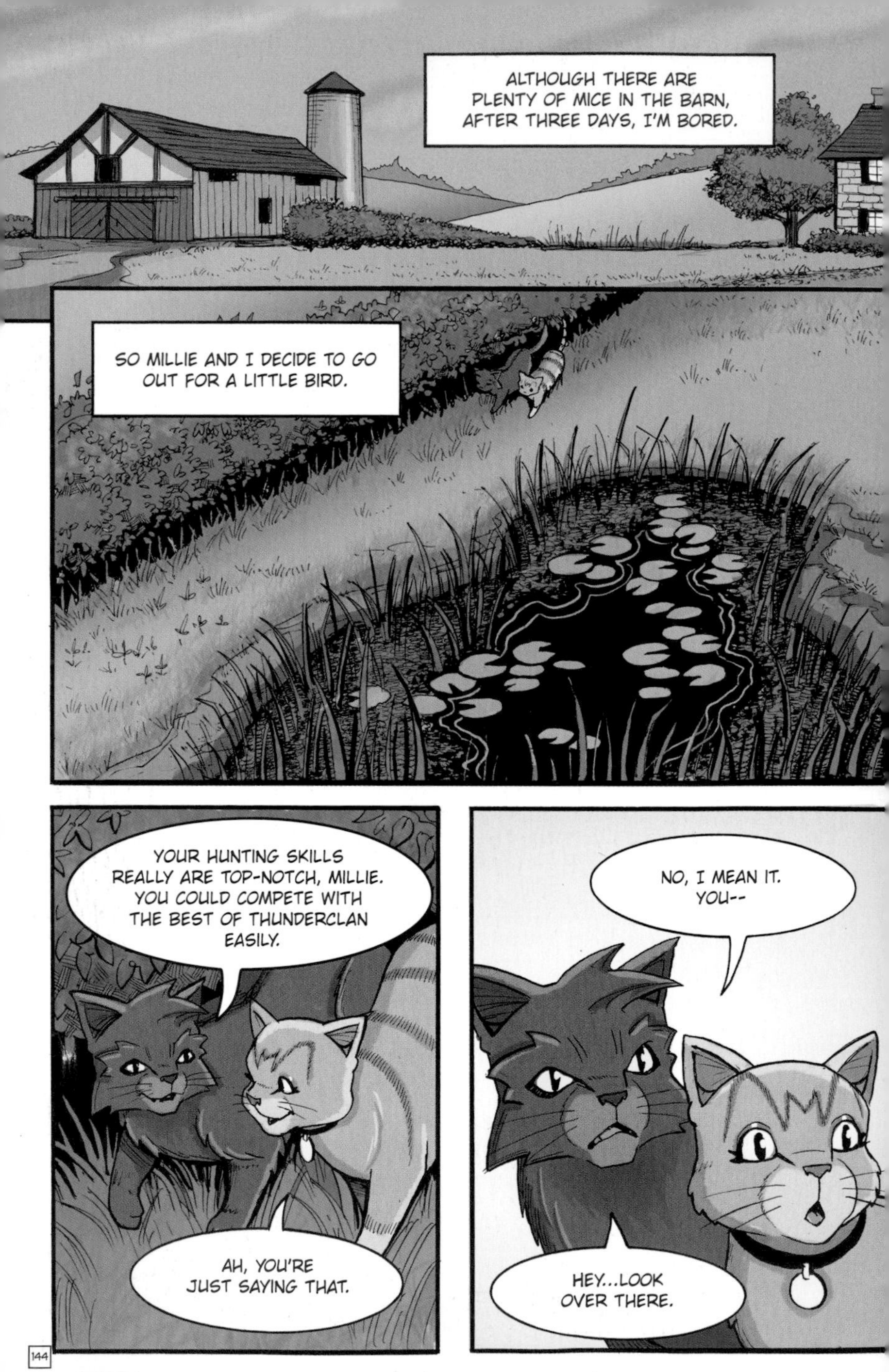
ALTHOUGH THERE ARE PLENTY OF MICE IN THE BARN, AFTER THREE DAYS, I'M BORED.
SO MILLIE AND I DECIDE TO GO OUT FOR A LITTLE BIRD.
YOUR HUNTING SKILLS REALLY ARE TOP-NOTCH, MILLIE. YOU COULD COMPETE WITH THE BEST OF THUNDERCLAN EASILY.
AH, YOU'RE JUST SAYING THAT.
NO, I MEAN IT. YOU--
HEY...LOOK OVER THERE.

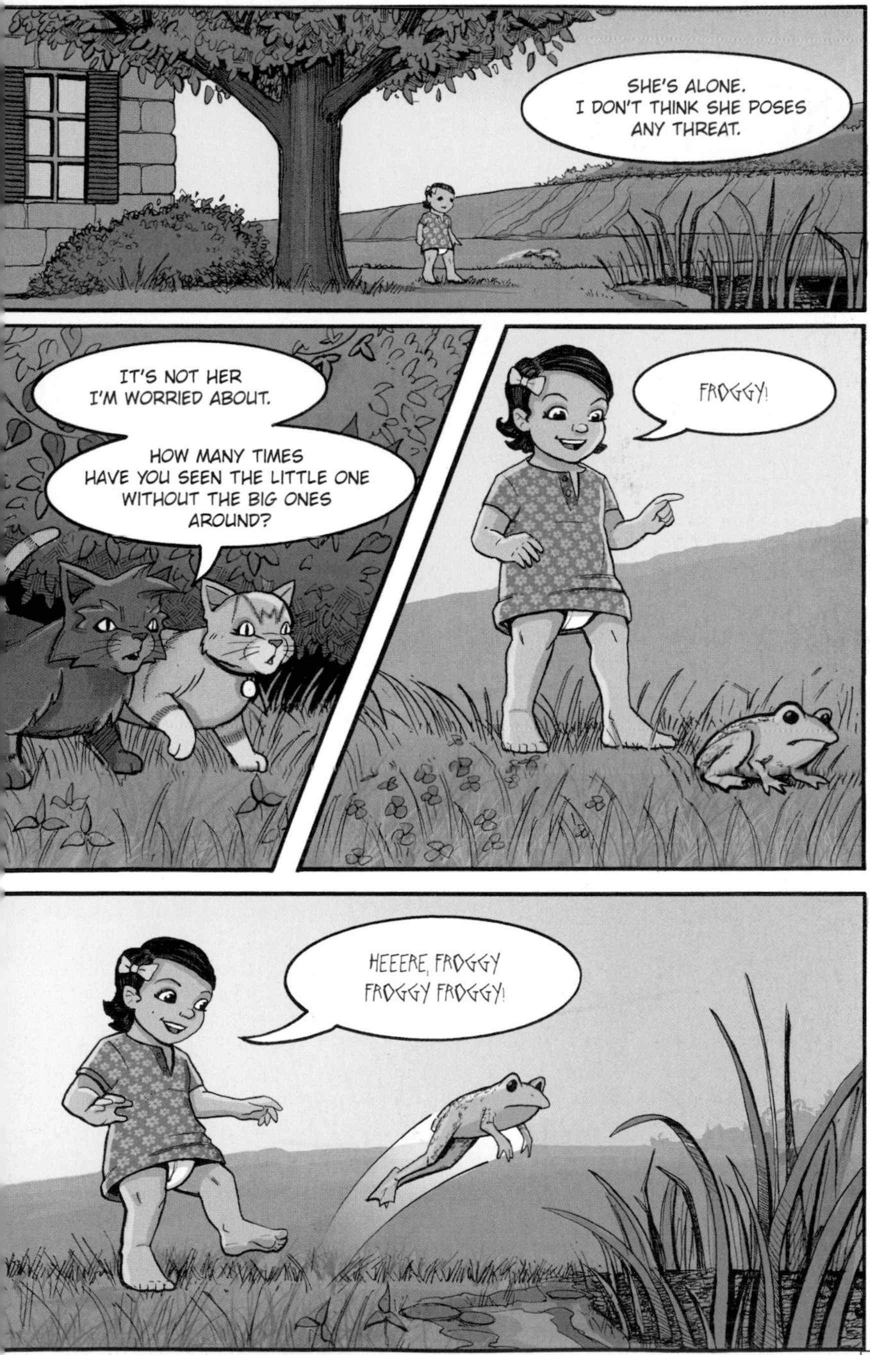
SHE'S ALONE. I DON'T THINK SHE POSES ANY THREAT.
IT'S NOT HER I'M WORRIED ABOUT.
HOW MANY TIMES HAVE YOU SEEN THE LITTLE ONE WITHOUT THE BIG ONES AROUND?
FROGGY!
HEEERE, FROGGY FROGGY FROGGY!

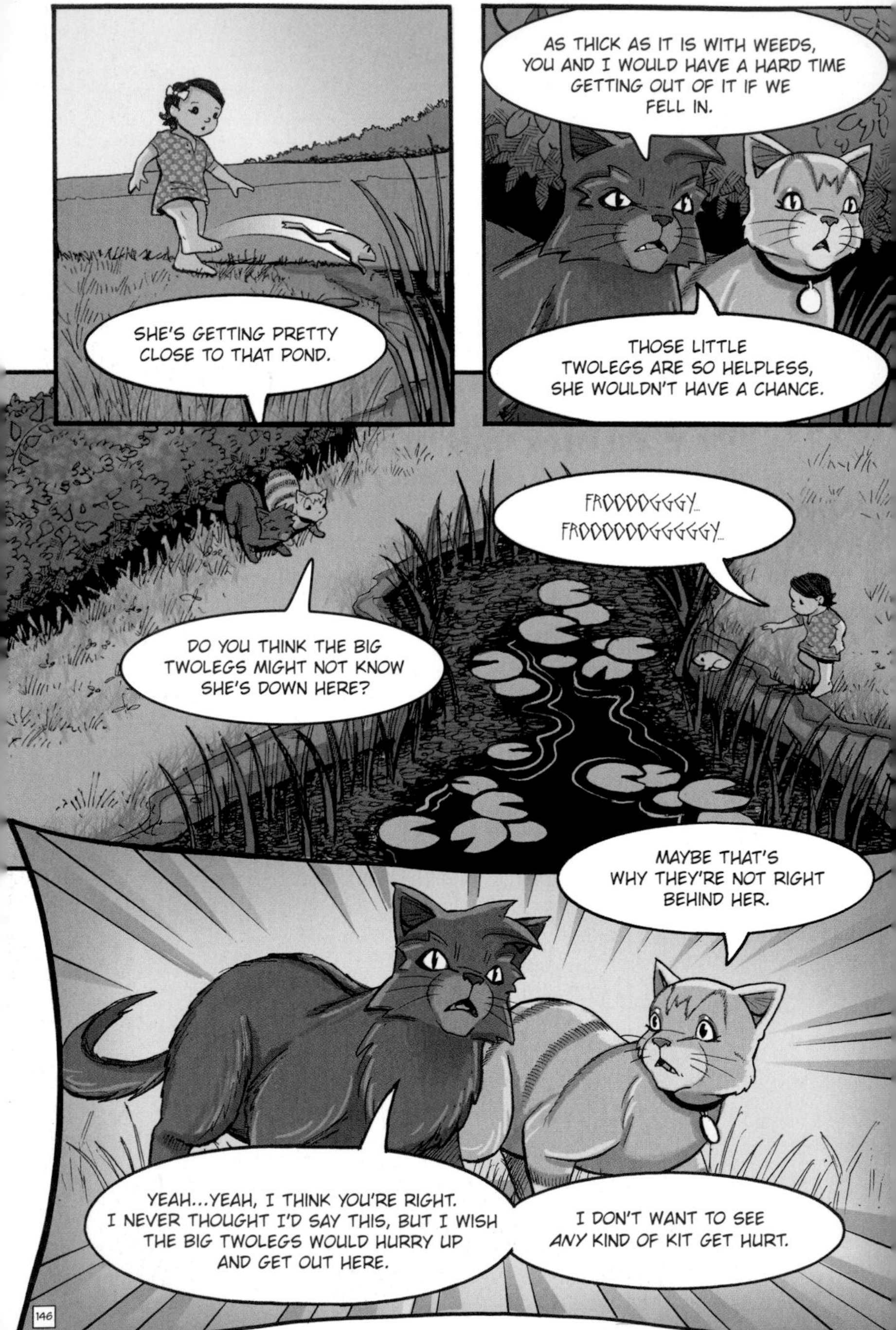
SHE'S GETTING PRETTY CLOSE TO THAT POND.
AS THICK AS IT IS WITH WEEDS, YOU AND I WOULD HAVE A HARD TIME GETTING OUT OF IT IF WE FELL IN.
THOSE LITTLE TWOLEGS ARE SO HELPLESS, SHE WOULDN'T HAVE A CHANCE.
FROOOOGGGY... FROOOOOOGGGGGY...
DO YOU THINK THE BIG TWOLEGS MIGHT NOT KNOW SHE'S DOWN HERE?
MAYBE THAT'S WHY THEY'RE NOT RIGHT BEHIND HER.
YEAH...YEAH, I THINK YOU'RE RIGHT. I NEVER THOUGHT I'D SAY THIS, BUT I WISH THE BIG TWOLEGS WOULD HURRY UP AND GET OUT HERE.
I DON'T WANT TO SEE *ANY* KIND OF KIT GET HURT.

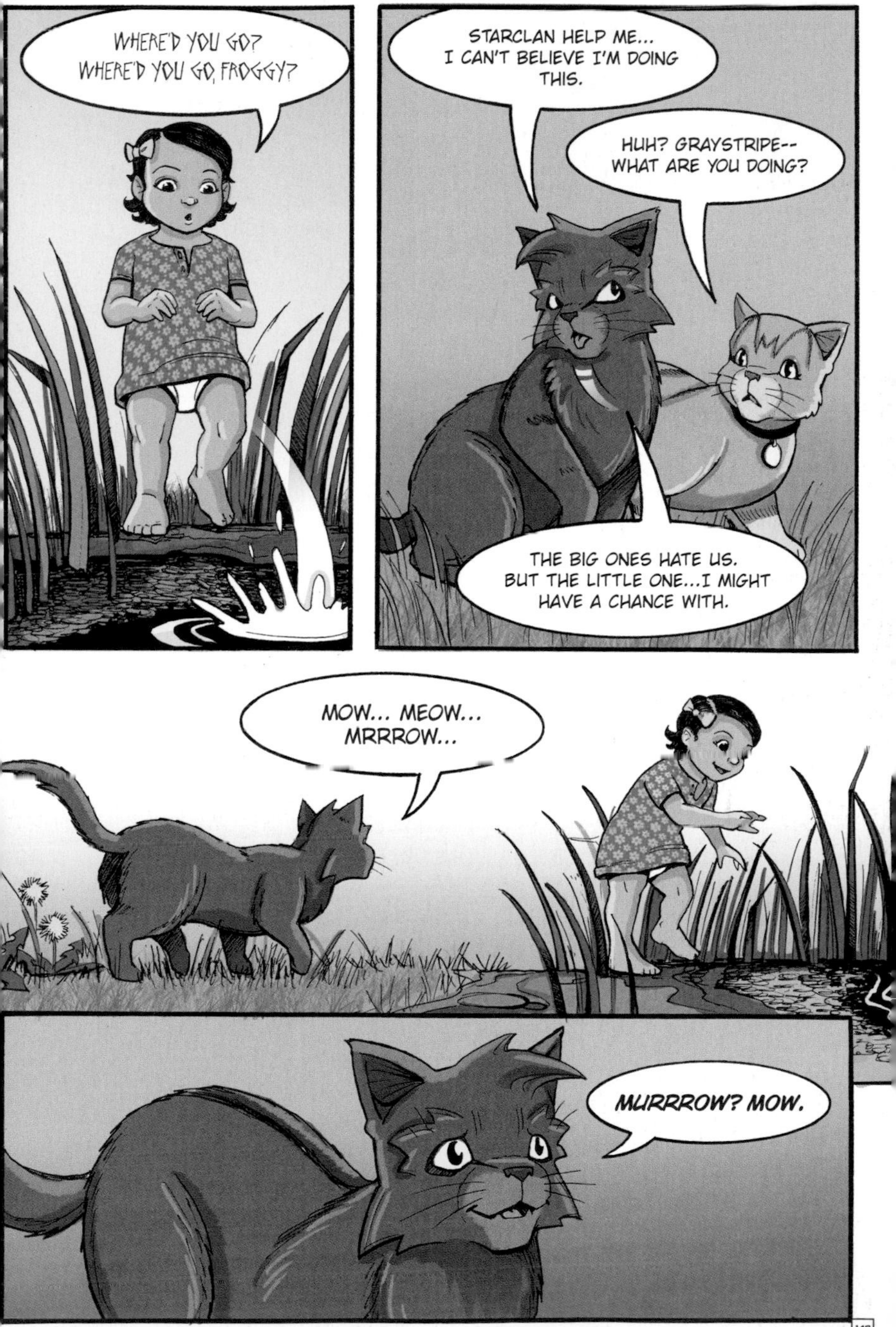
WHERE'D YOU GO? WHERE'D YOU GO, FROGGY?
STARCLAN HELP ME... I CAN'T BELIEVE I'M DOING THIS.
HUH? GRAYSTRIPE-- WHAT ARE YOU DOING?
THE BIG ONES HATE US. BUT THE LITTLE ONE...I MIGHT HAVE A CHANCE WITH.
MOW... MEOW... MRRROW...
MURRROW? MOW.

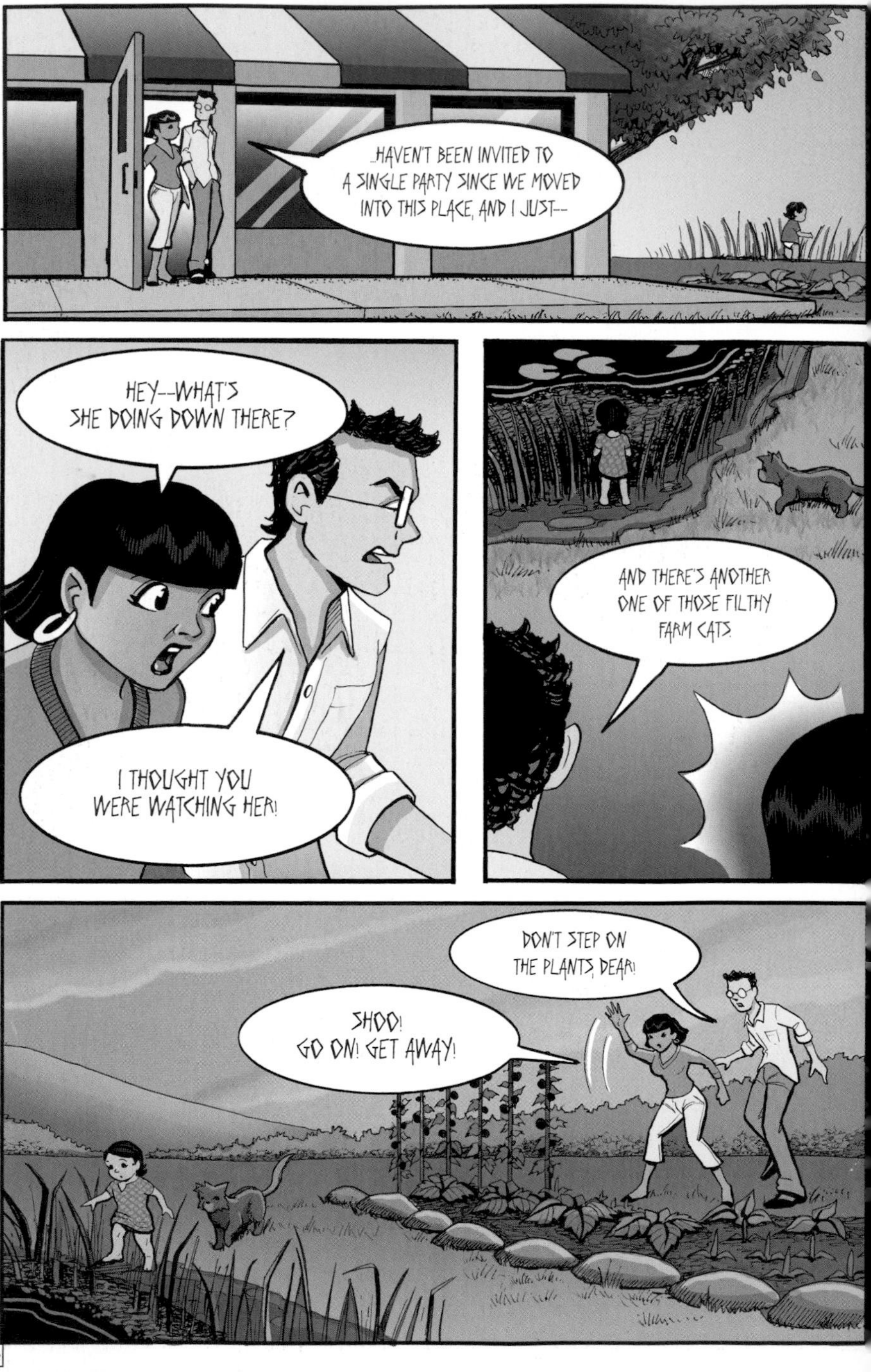
...HAVEN'T BEEN INVITED TO A SINGLE PARTY SINCE WE MOVED INTO THIS PLACE, AND I JUST--
HEY--WHAT'S SHE DOING DOWN THERE?
I THOUGHT YOU WERE WATCHING HER!
AND THERE'S ANOTHER ONE OF THOSE FILTHY FARM CATS.
DON'T STEP ON THE PLANTS, DEAR!
SHOO! GO ON! GET AWAY!

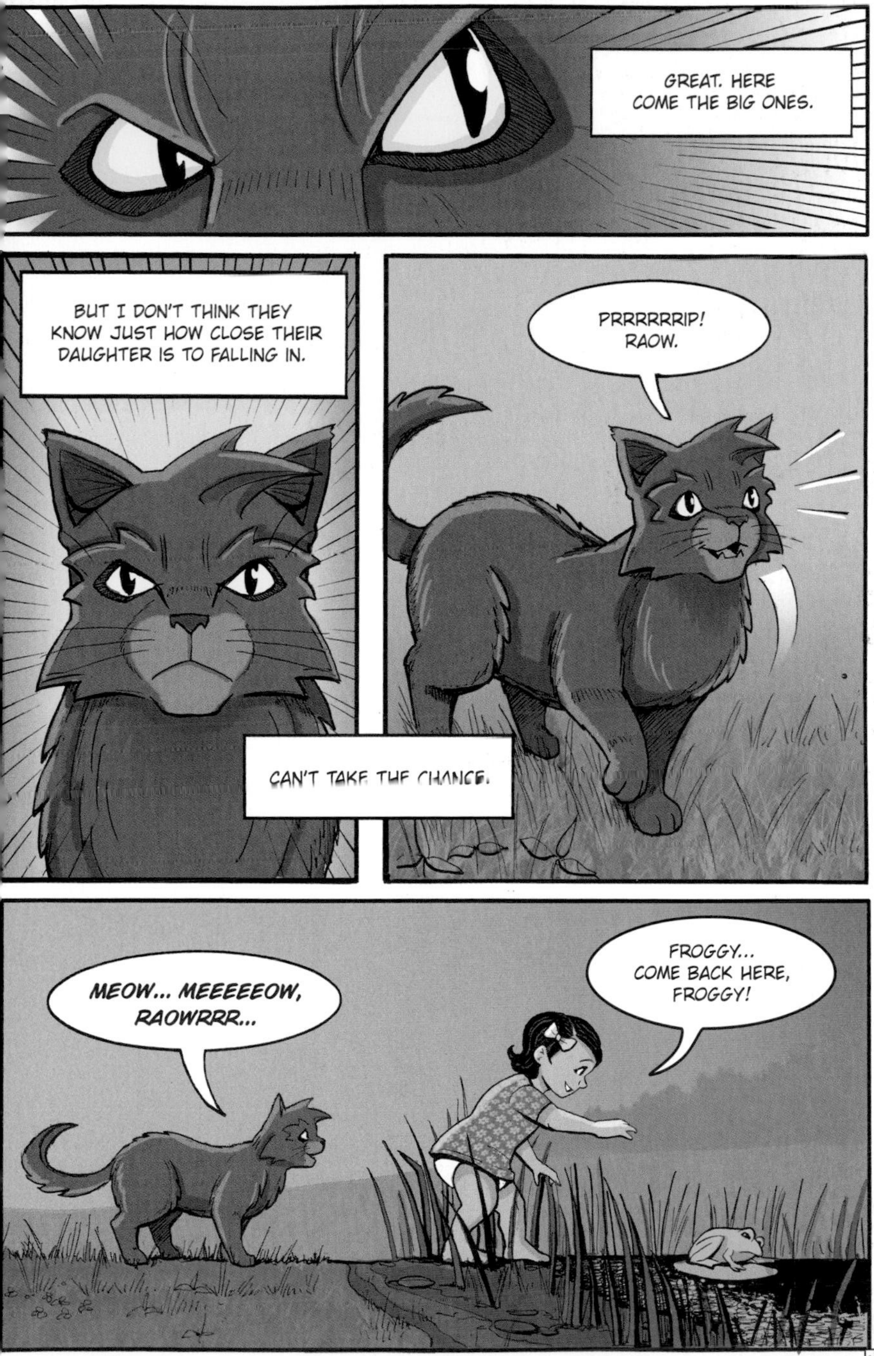
GREAT. HERE COME THE BIG ONES.
BUT I DON'T THINK THEY KNOW JUST HOW CLOSE THEIR DAUGHTER IS TO FALLING IN.
CAN'T TAKE THE CHANCE.
PRRRRRRIP! RAOW.
MEOW... MEEEEEOW, RAOWRRR...
FROGGY... COME BACK HERE, FROGGY!

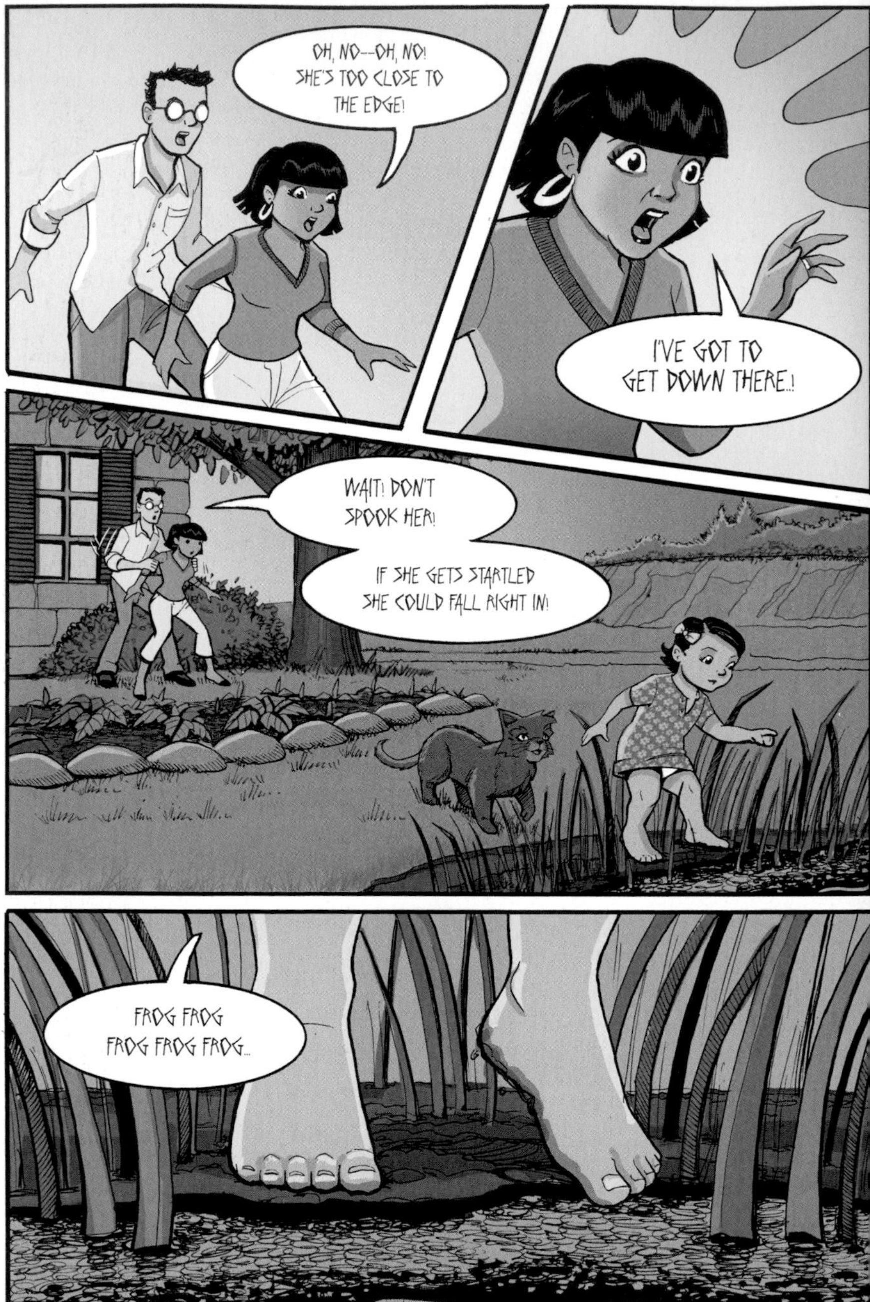
OH, NO--OH, NO! SHE'S TOO CLOSE TO THE EDGE!
I'VE GOT TO GET DOWN THERE..!
WAIT! DON'T SPOOK HER!
IF SHE GETS STARTLED SHE COULD FALL RIGHT IN!
FROG FROG FROG FROG FROG...

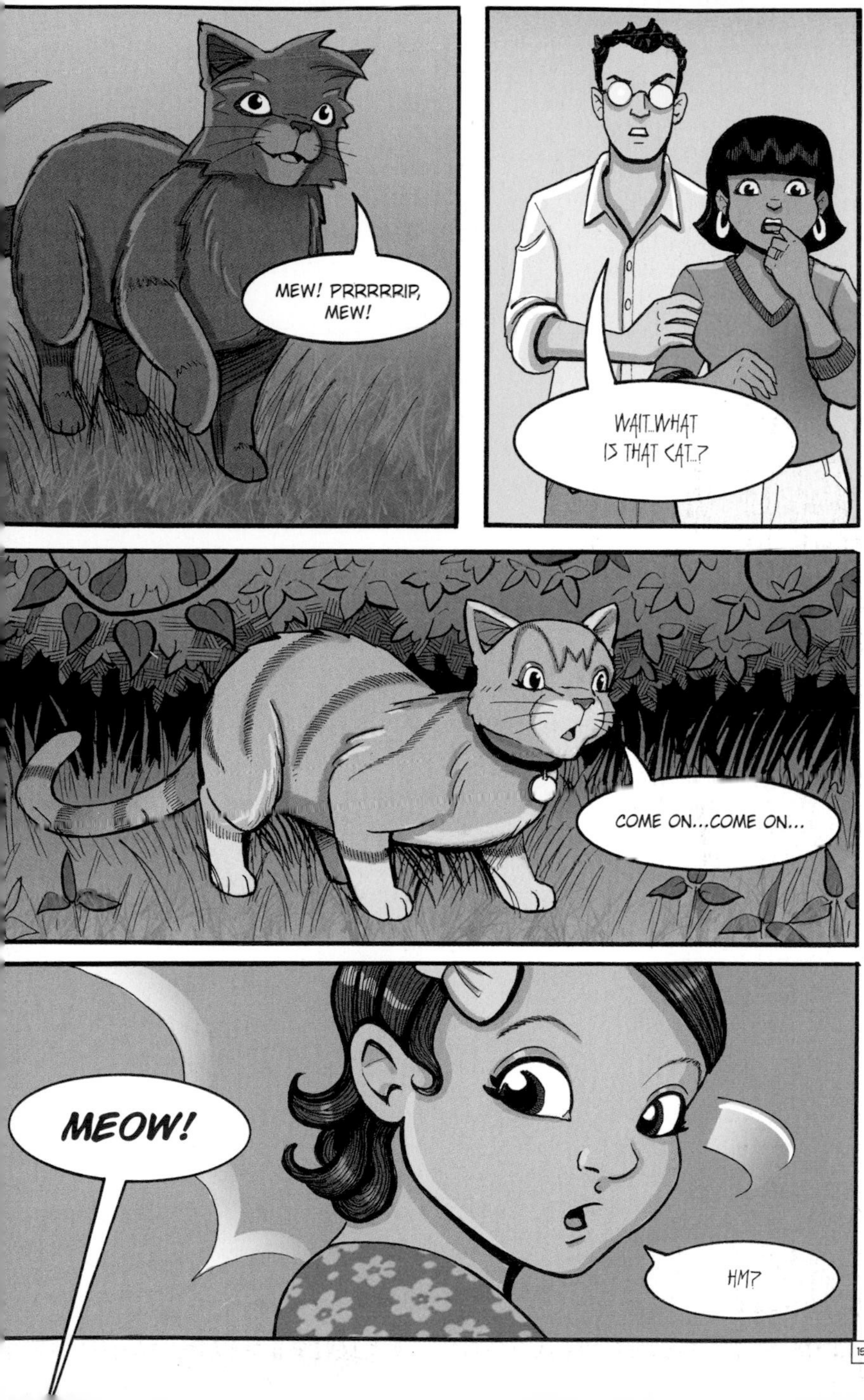
MEW! PRRRRRIP, MEW!
WAIT...WHAT IS THAT CAT...?
COME ON...COME ON...
MEOW!
HM?

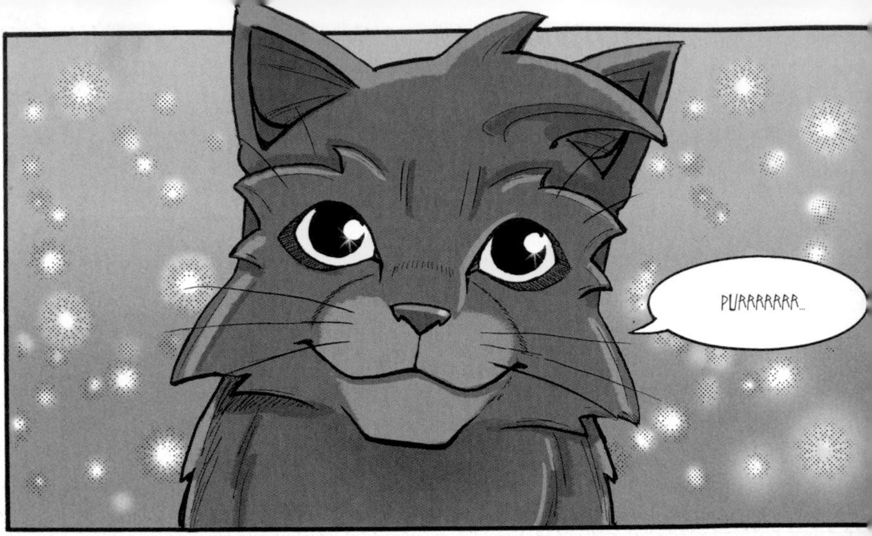
PURRRRRRR...

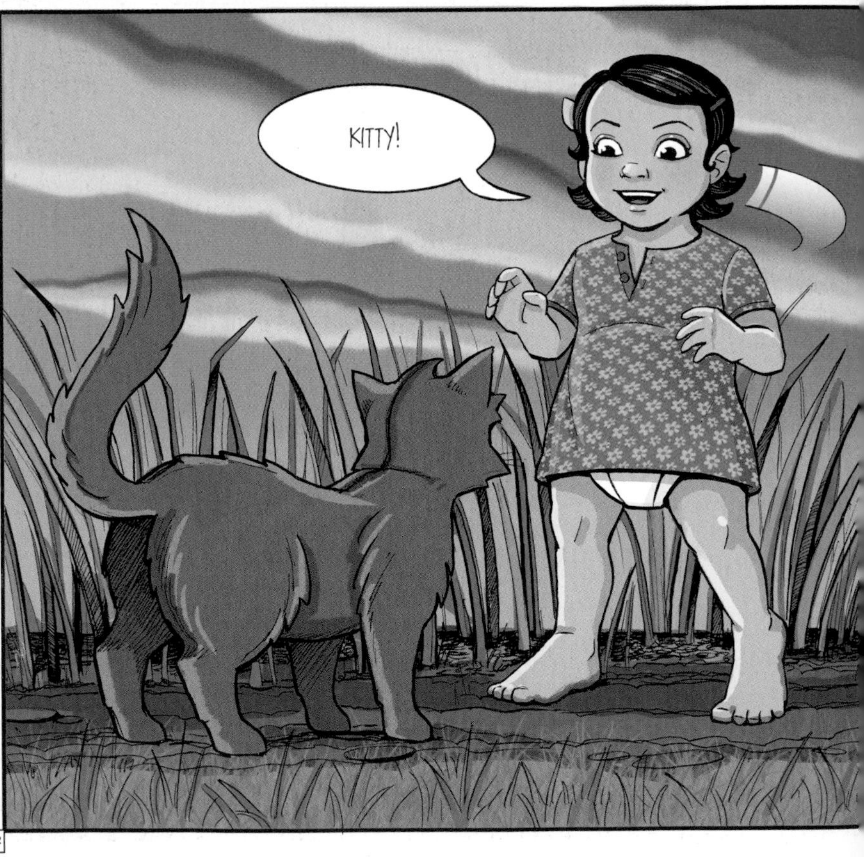
KITTY!

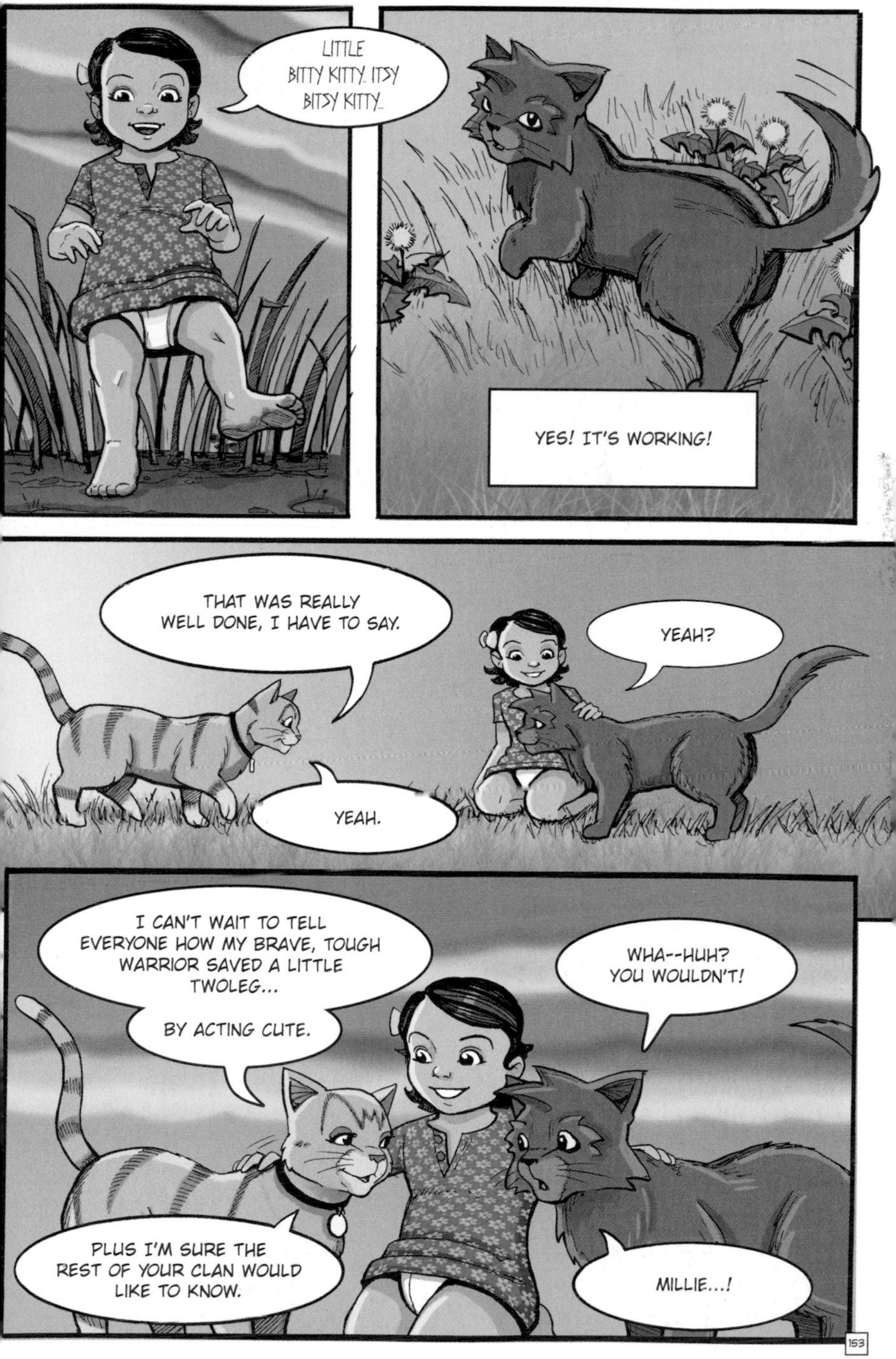
LITTLE BITTY KITTY.. ITSY BITSY KITTY...
YES! IT'S WORKING!
THAT WAS REALLY WELL DONE, I HAVE TO SAY.
YEAH?
YEAH.
I CAN'T WAIT TO TELL EVERYONE HOW MY BRAVE, TOUGH WARRIOR SAVED A LITTLE TWOLEG...
BY ACTING CUTE.
WHA--HUH? YOU WOULDN'T!
PLUS I'M SURE THE REST OF YOUR CLAN WOULD LIKE TO KNOW.
MILLIE...!

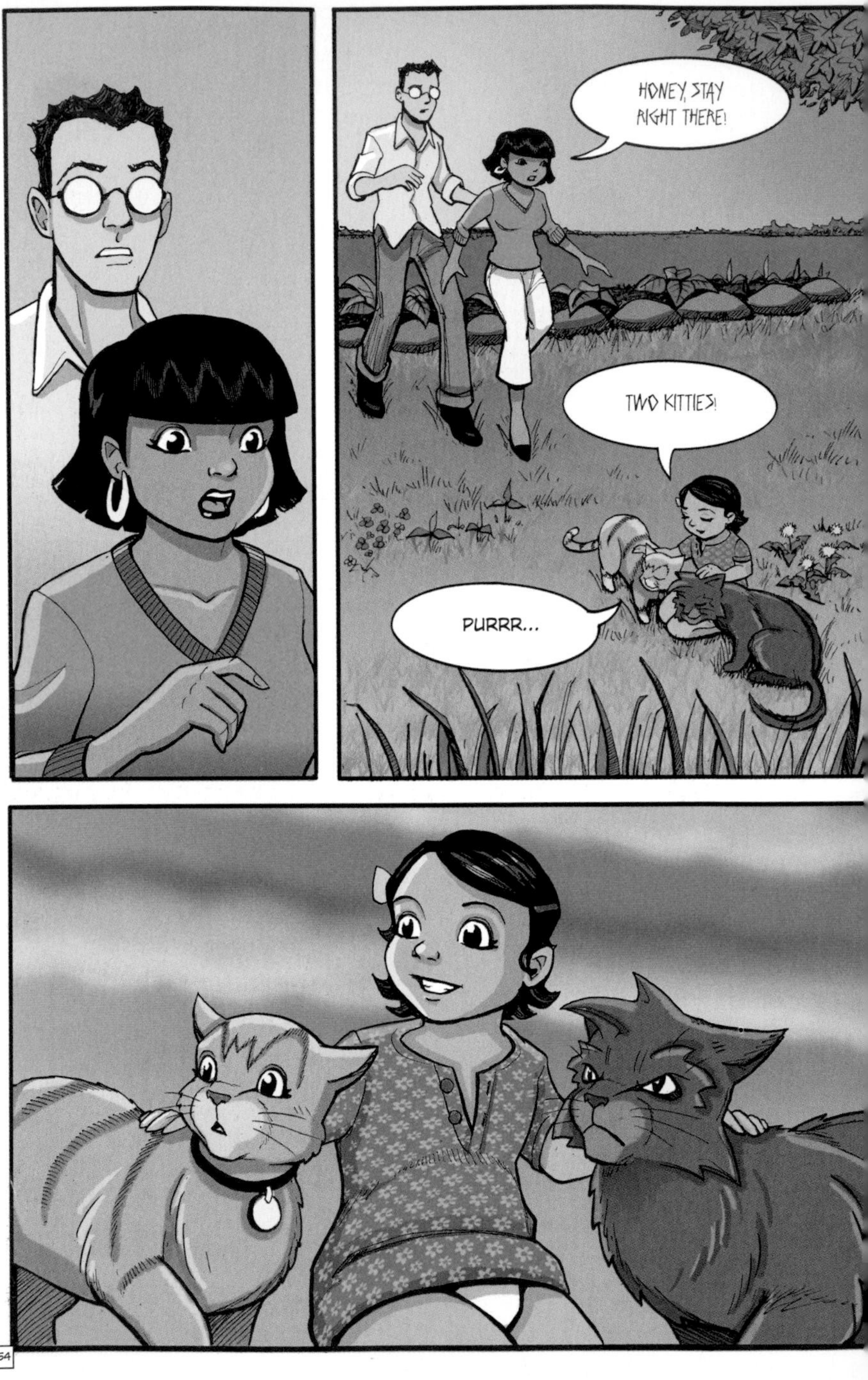
HONEY, STAY RIGHT THERE!
TWO KITTIES!
PURRR...

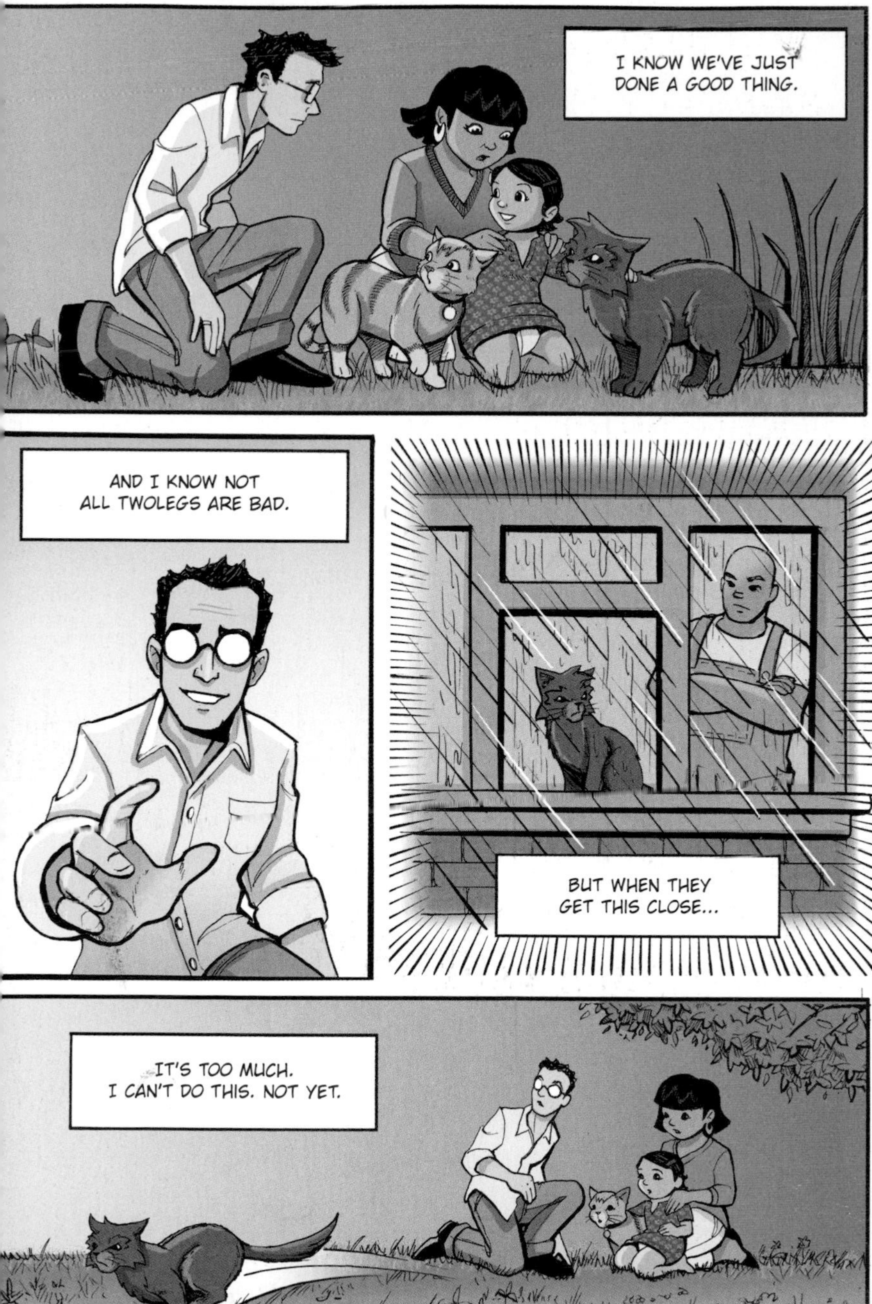
I KNOW WE'VE JUST DONE A GOOD THING.
AND I KNOW NOT ALL TWOLEGS ARE BAD.
BUT WHEN THEY GET THIS CLOSE...
IT'S TOO MUCH. I CAN'T DO THIS. NOT YET.

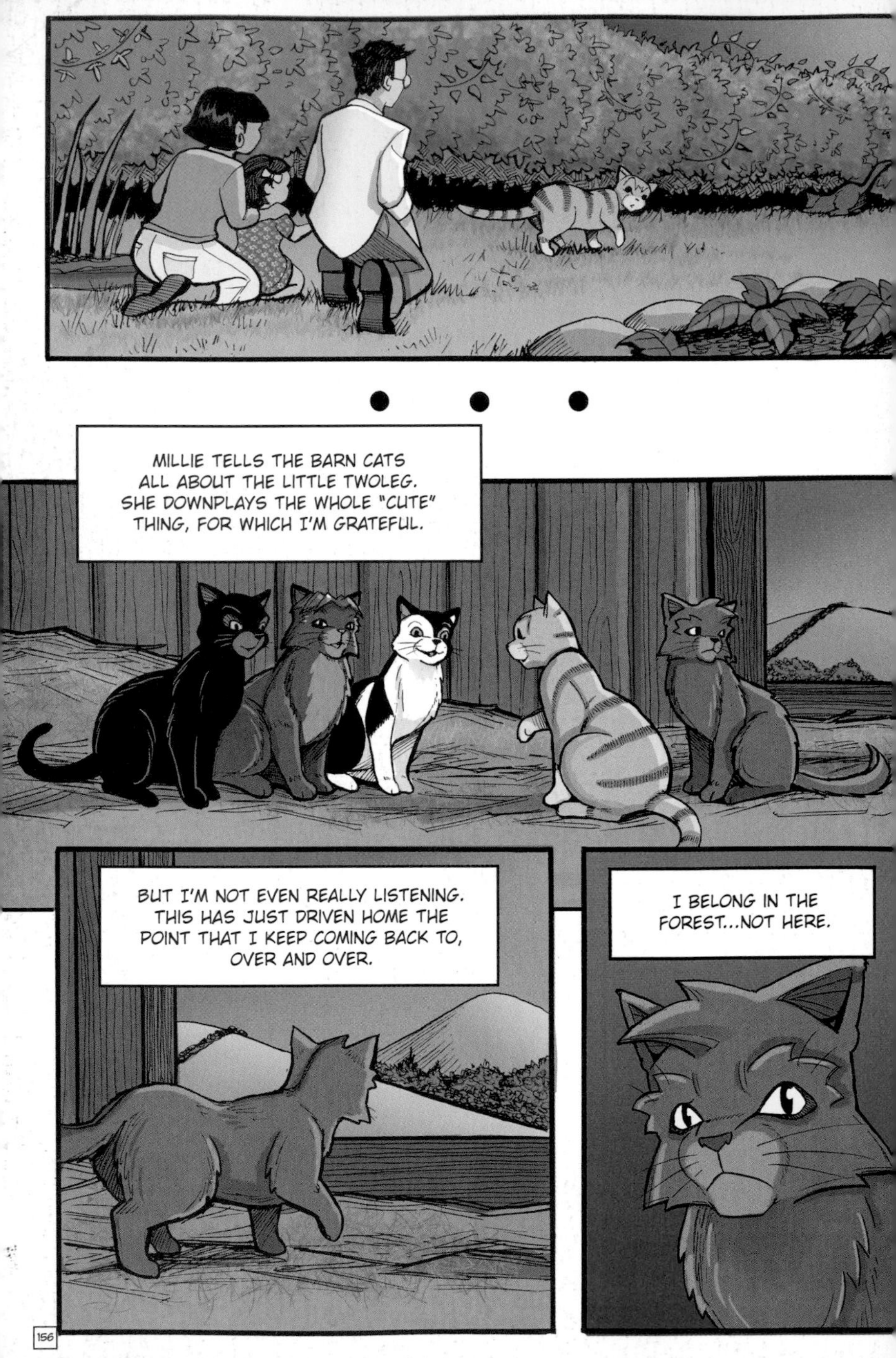
MILLIE TELLS THE BARN CATS ALL ABOUT THE LITTLE TWOLEG. SHE DOWNPLAYS THE WHOLE "CUTE" THING, FOR WHICH I'M GRATEFUL.
BUT I'M NOT EVEN REALLY LISTENING. THIS HAS JUST DRIVEN HOME THE POINT THAT I KEEP COMING BACK TO, OVER AND OVER.
I BELONG IN THE FOREST...NOT HERE.

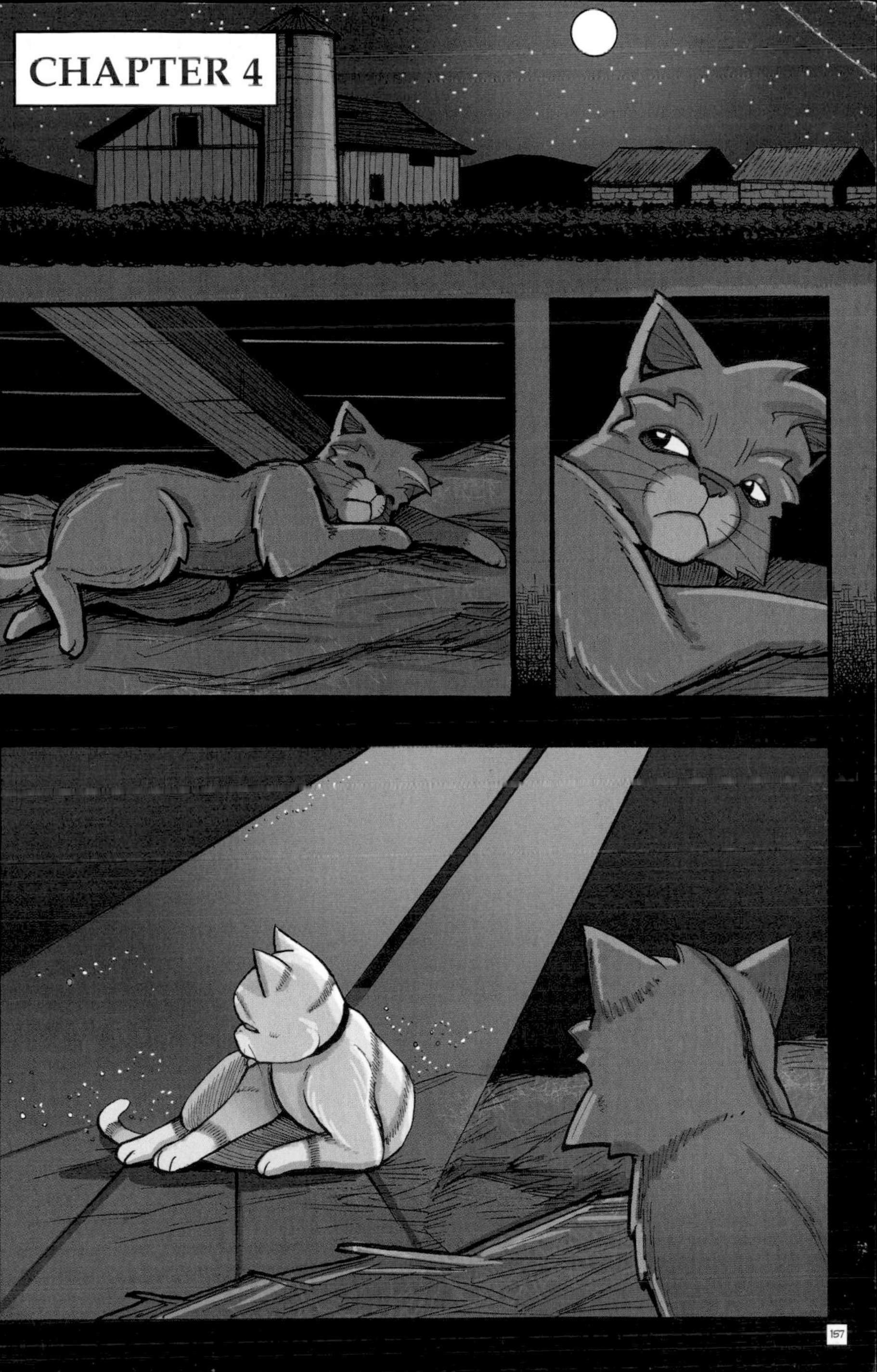
CHAPTER 4

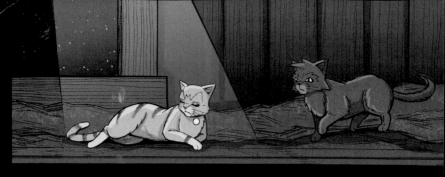

THE MOONLIGHT LOOKS GOOD ON YOUR FUR.

YOU KNOW, YOU DON'T HAVE TO COME AND COMFORT ME EVERY TIME I'M AWAKE AND YOU'RE NOT.

MILLIE, WHAT'S WRONG? IS IT...

...IS IT ABOUT THE TWOLEGS TODAY?

YOU KNOW ME PRETTY WELL.

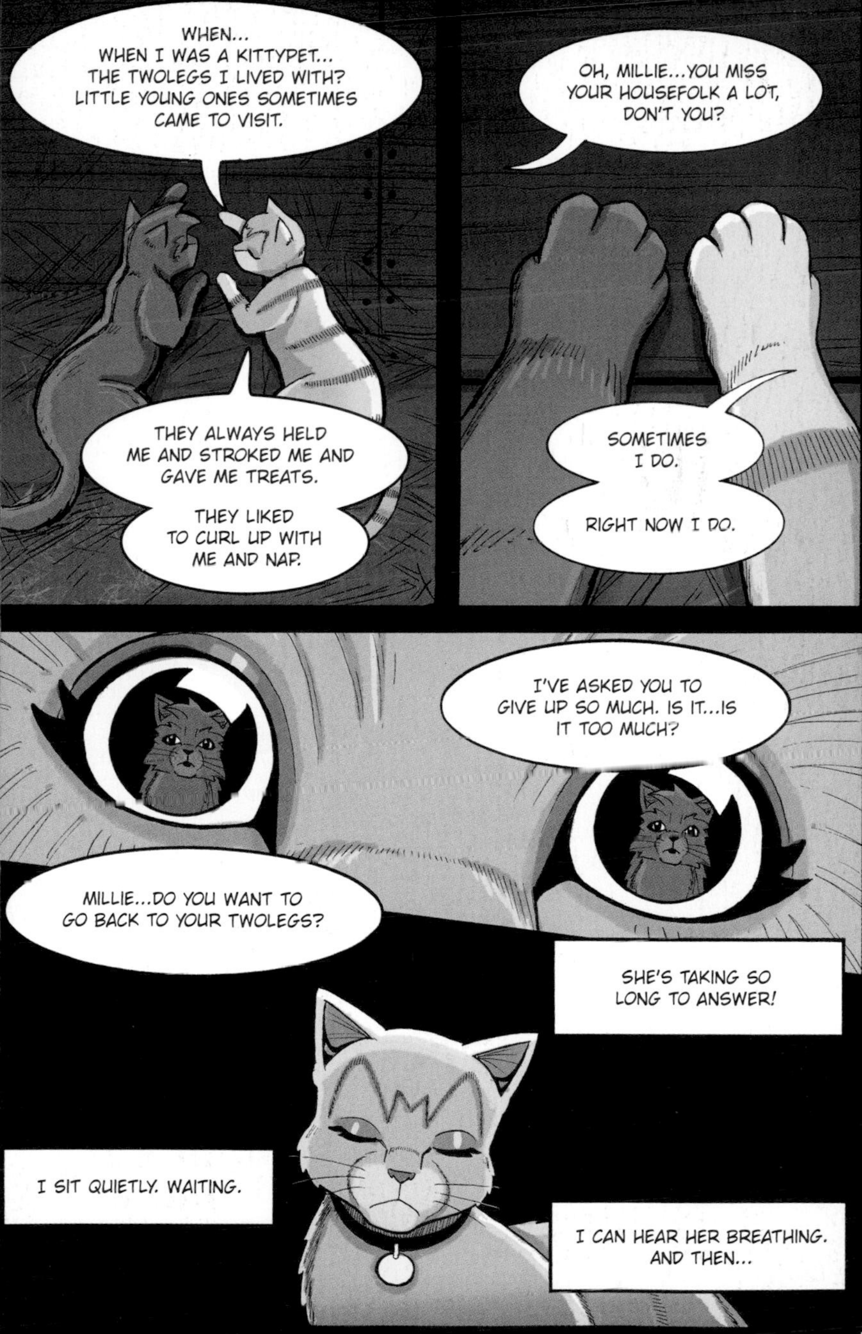

WHEN... WHEN I WAS A KITTYPET... THE TWOLEGS I LIVED WITH? LITTLE YOUNG ONES SOMETIMES CAME TO VISIT.
THEY ALWAYS HELD ME AND STROKED ME AND GAVE ME TREATS.
THEY LIKED TO CURL UP WITH ME AND NAP.
OH, MILLIE...YOU MISS YOUR HOUSEFOLK A LOT, DON'T YOU?
SOMETIMES I DO.
RIGHT NOW I DO.
I'VE ASKED YOU TO GIVE UP SO MUCH. IS IT...IS IT TOO MUCH?
MILLIE...DO YOU WANT TO GO BACK TO YOUR TWOLEGS?
SHE'S TAKING SO LONG TO ANSWER!
I SIT QUIETLY. WAITING.
I CAN HEAR HER BREATHING. AND THEN...

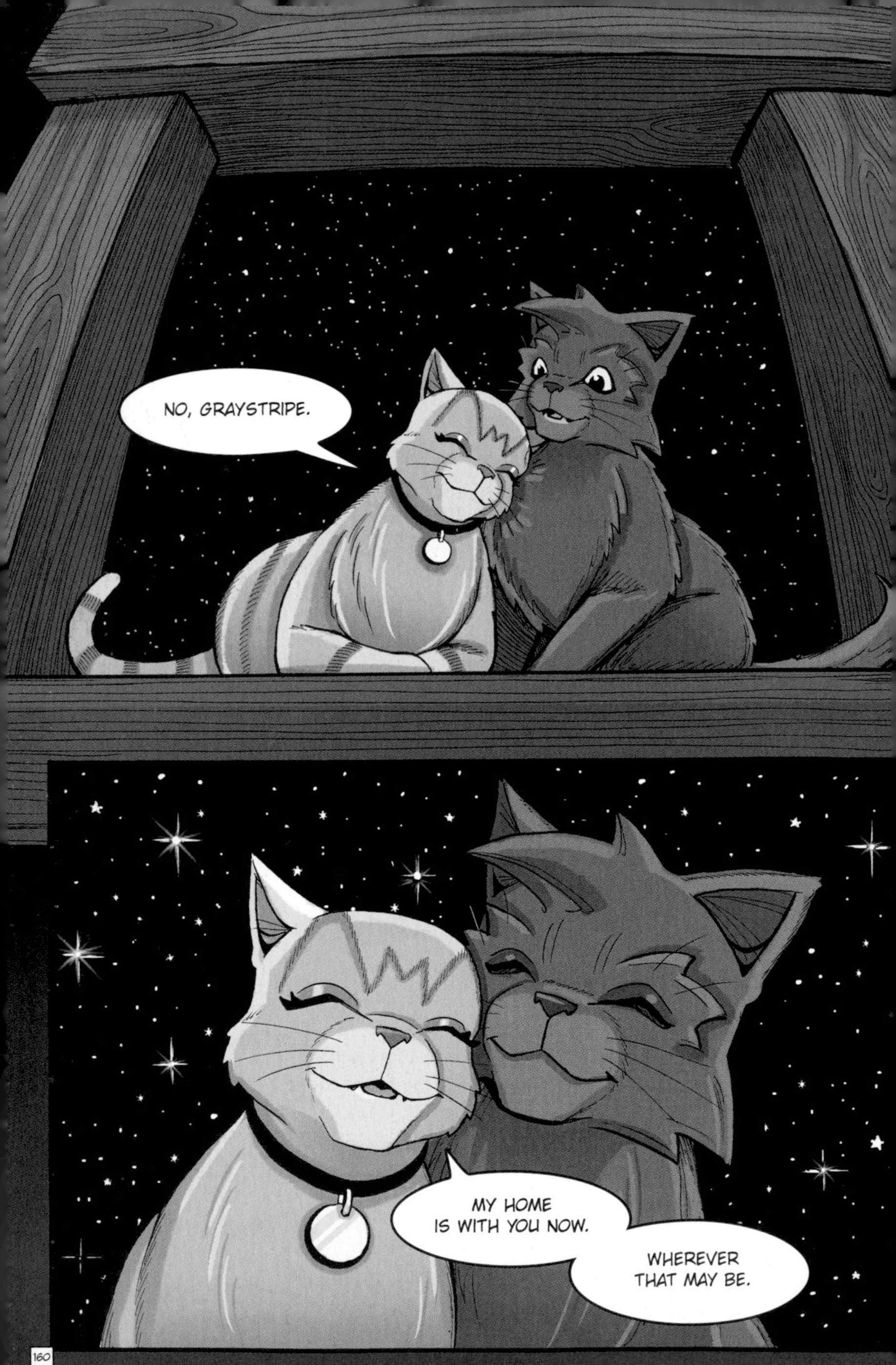
NO, GRAYSTRIPE.
MY HOME IS WITH YOU NOW.
WHEREVER THAT MAY BE.

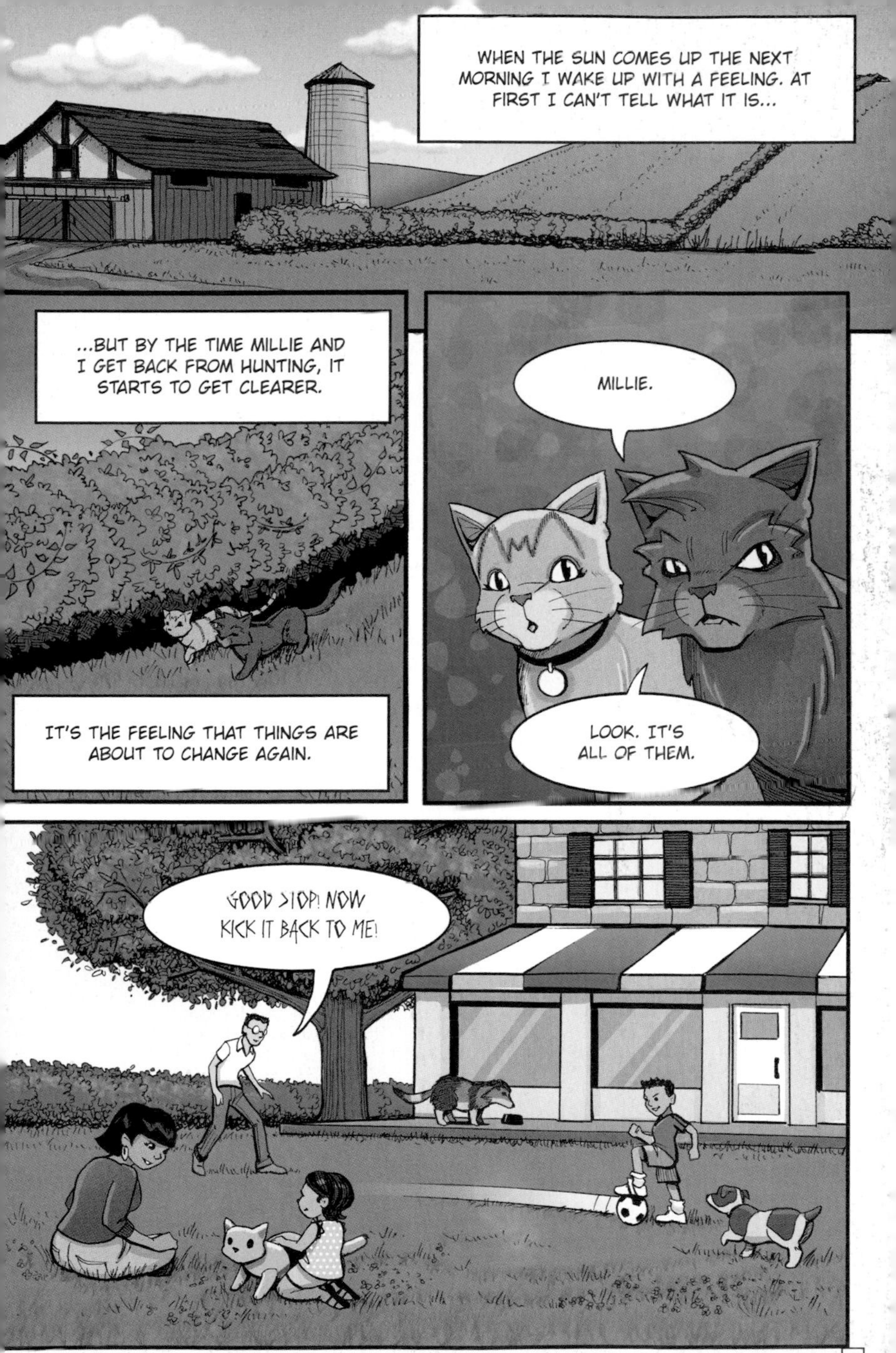
WHEN THE SUN COMES UP THE NEXT MORNING I WAKE UP WITH A FEELING. AT FIRST I CAN'T TELL WHAT IT IS...
...BUT BY THE TIME MILLIE AND I GET BACK FROM HUNTING, IT STARTS TO GET CLEARER.
IT'S THE FEELING THAT THINGS ARE ABOUT TO CHANGE AGAIN.
MILLIE.
LOOK. IT'S ALL OF THEM.
GOOD STOP! NOW KICK IT BACK TO ME!

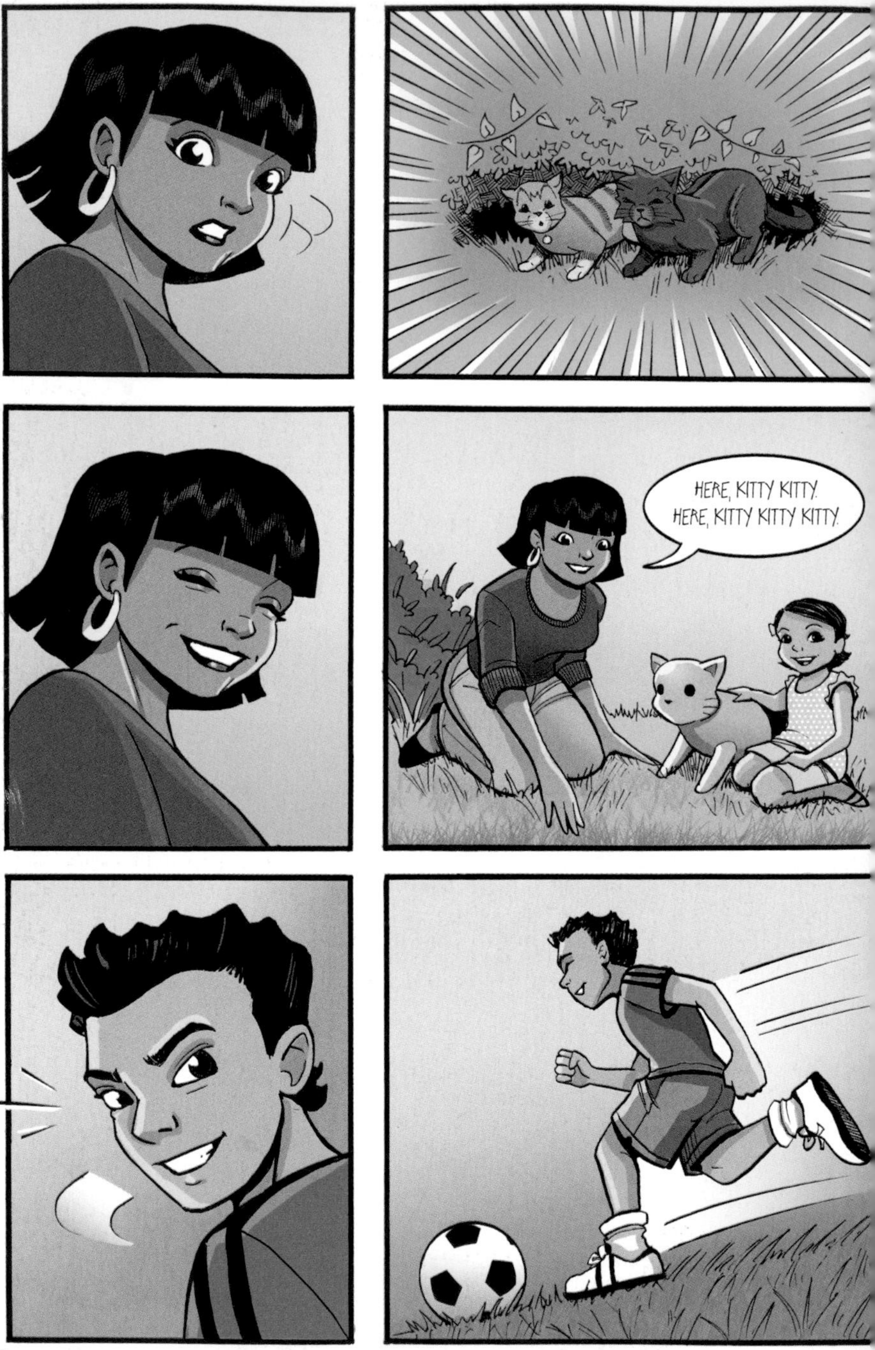
HERE, KITTY KITTY.
HERE, KITTY KITTY KITTY.

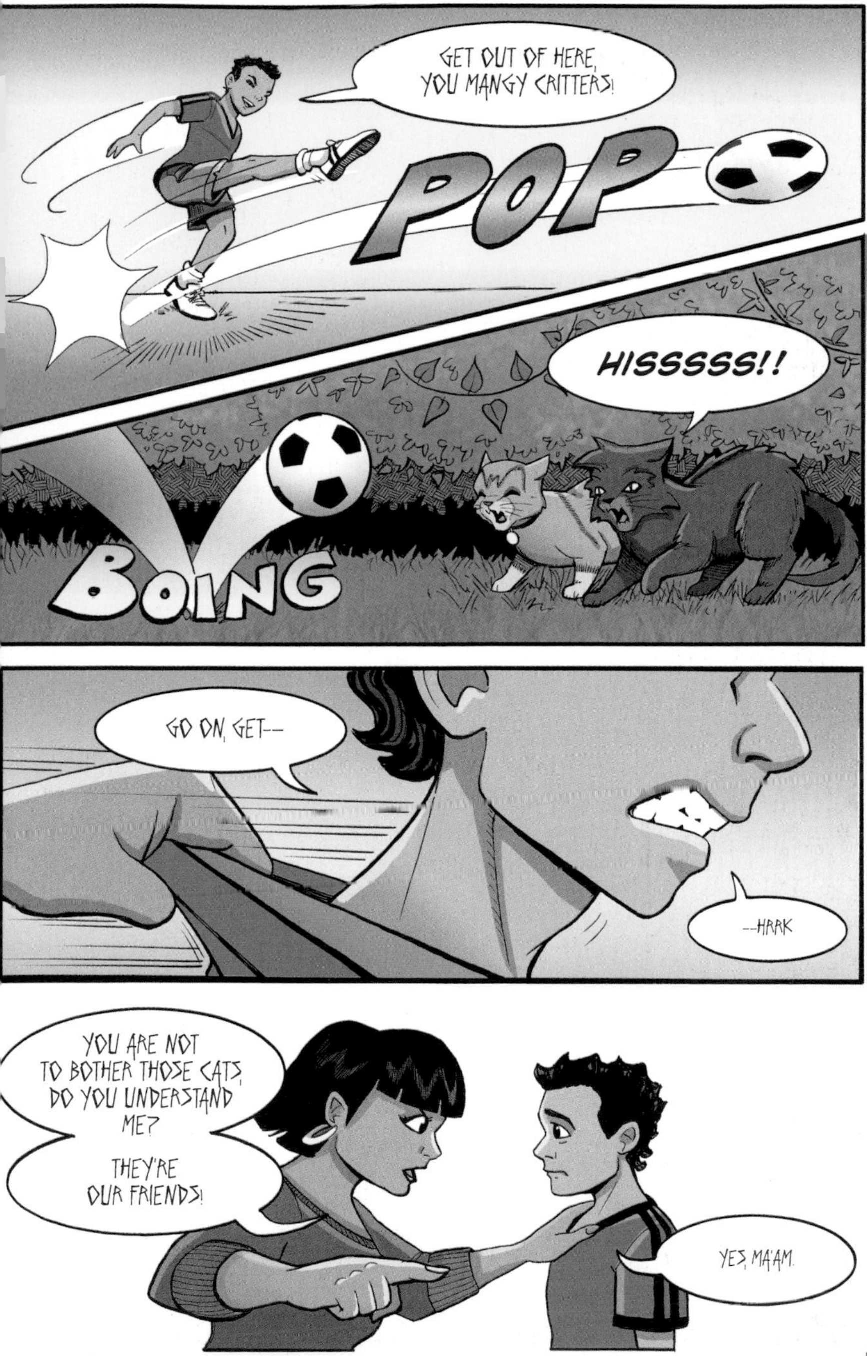

GET OUT OF HERE, YOU MANGY CRITTERS!
POP
HISSSSS!!
BOING
GO ON, GET--
--HRRK
YOU ARE NOT TO BOTHER THOSE CATS, DO YOU UNDERSTAND ME?
THEY'RE OUR FRIENDS!
YES, MA'AM.

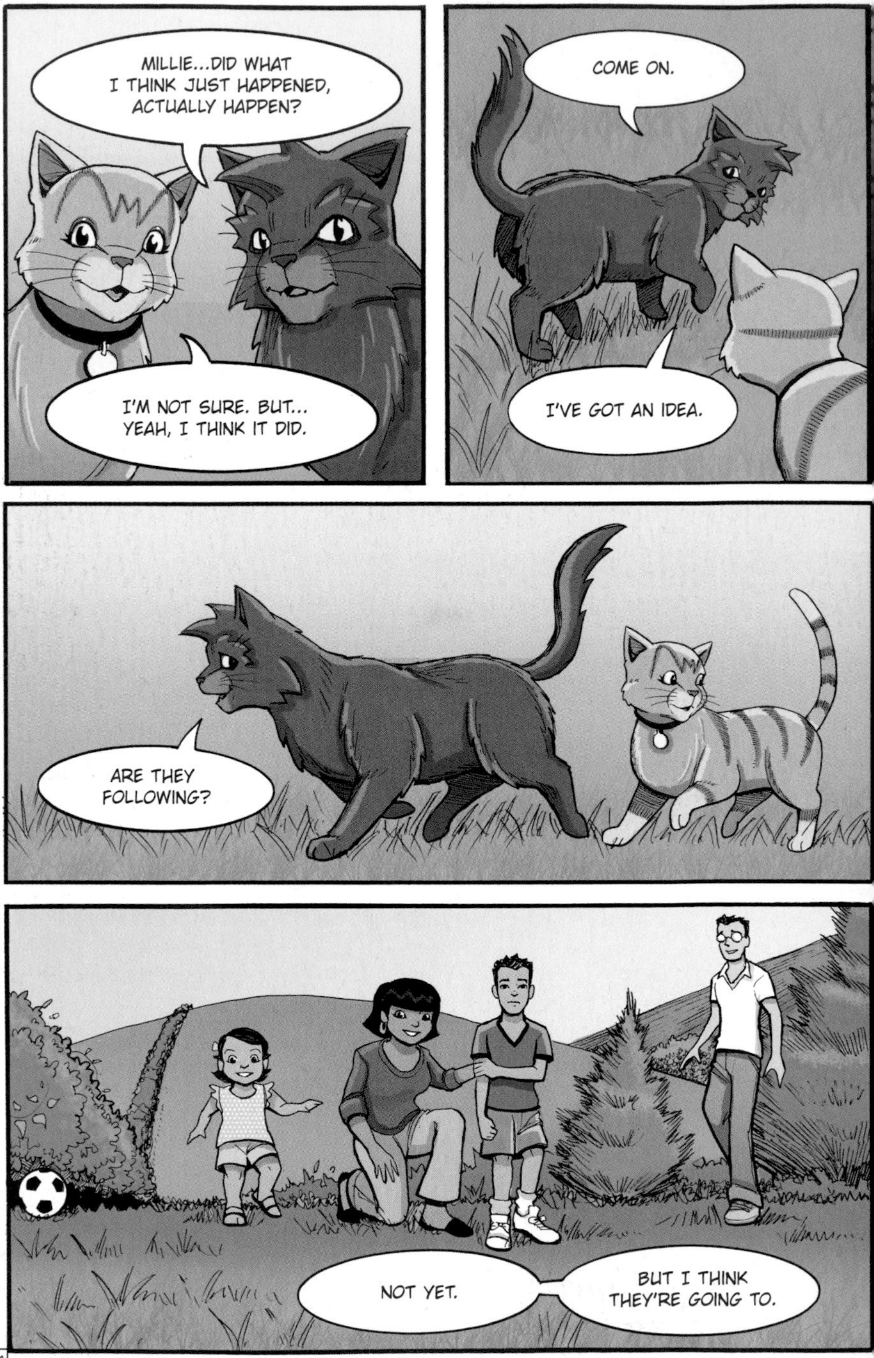
MILLIE...DID WHAT I THINK JUST HAPPENED, ACTUALLY HAPPEN?
I'M NOT SURE. BUT... YEAH, I THINK IT DID.
COME ON.
I'VE GOT AN IDEA.
ARE THEY FOLLOWING?
NOT YET.
BUT I THINK THEY'RE GOING TO.

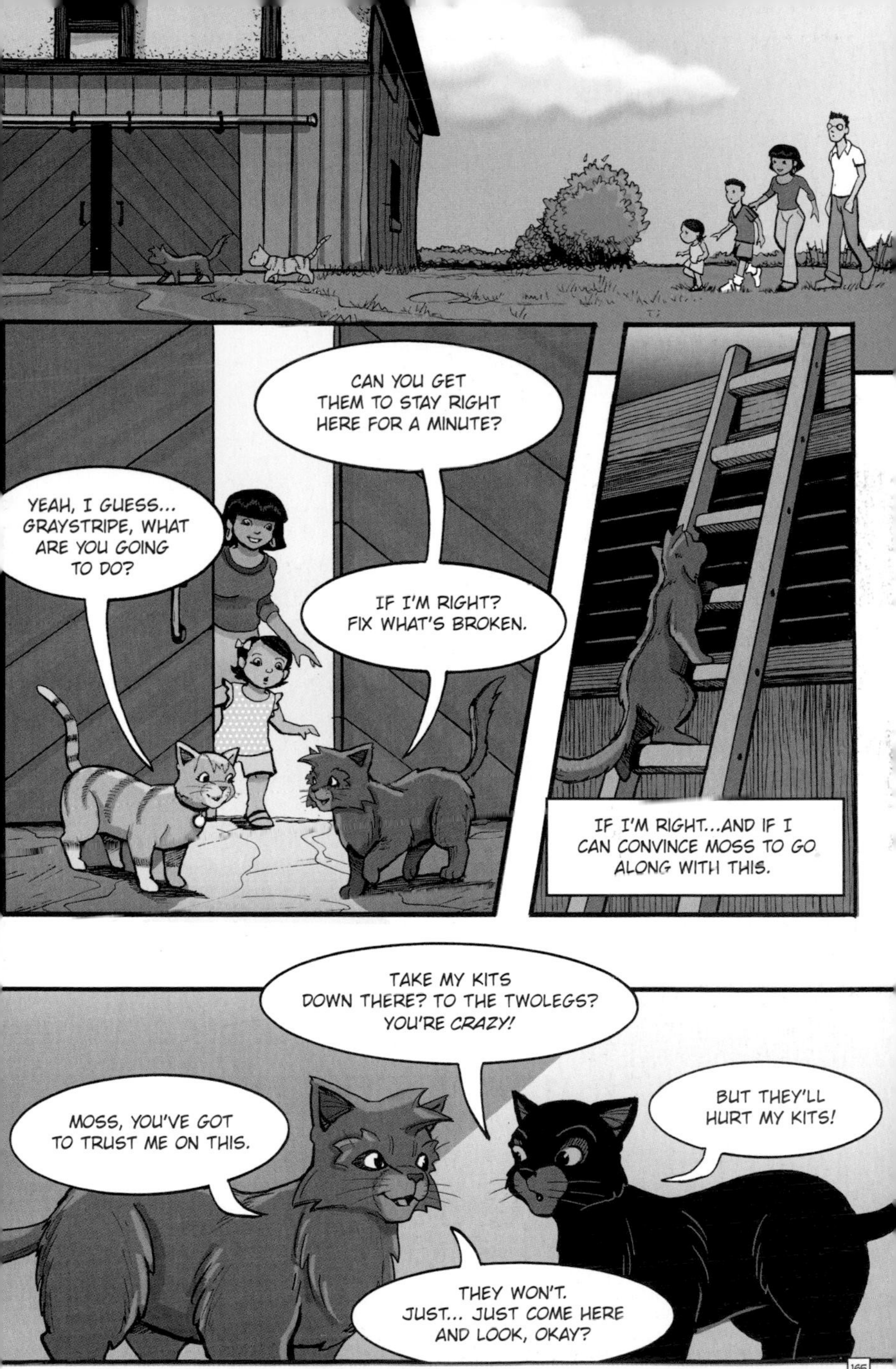
YEAH, I GUESS... GRAYSTRIPE, WHAT ARE YOU GOING TO DO?
CAN YOU GET THEM TO STAY RIGHT HERE FOR A MINUTE?
IF I'M RIGHT? FIX WHAT'S BROKEN.
IF I'M RIGHT...AND IF I CAN CONVINCE MOSS TO GO ALONG WITH THIS.
MOSS, YOU'VE GOT TO TRUST ME ON THIS.
TAKE MY KITS DOWN THERE? TO THE TWOLEGS? YOU'RE *CRAZY!*
BUT THEY'LL HURT MY KITS!
THEY WON'T. JUST... JUST COME HERE AND LOOK, OKAY?

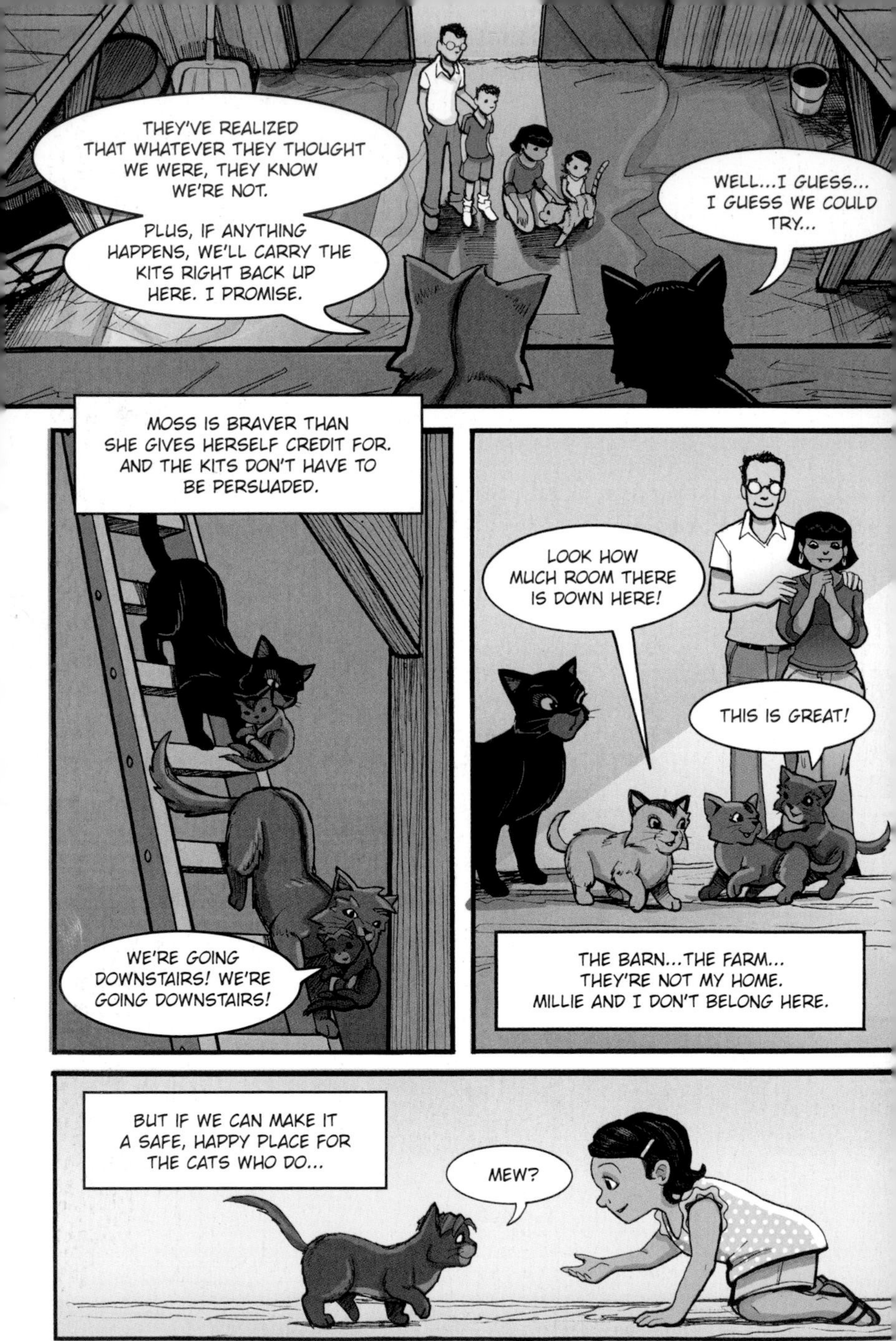
THEY'VE REALIZED THAT WHATEVER THEY THOUGHT WE WERE, THEY KNOW WE'RE NOT.
PLUS, IF ANYTHING HAPPENS, WE'LL CARRY THE KITS RIGHT BACK UP HERE. I PROMISE.
WELL...I GUESS... I GUESS WE COULD TRY...
MOSS IS BRAVER THAN SHE GIVES HERSELF CREDIT FOR. AND THE KITS DON'T HAVE TO BE PERSUADED.
WE'RE GOING DOWNSTAIRS! WE'RE GOING DOWNSTAIRS!
LOOK HOW MUCH ROOM THERE IS DOWN HERE!
THIS IS GREAT!
THE BARN...THE FARM... THEY'RE NOT MY HOME. MILLIE AND I DON'T BELONG HERE.
BUT IF WE CAN MAKE IT A SAFE, HAPPY PLACE FOR THE CATS WHO DO...
MEW?

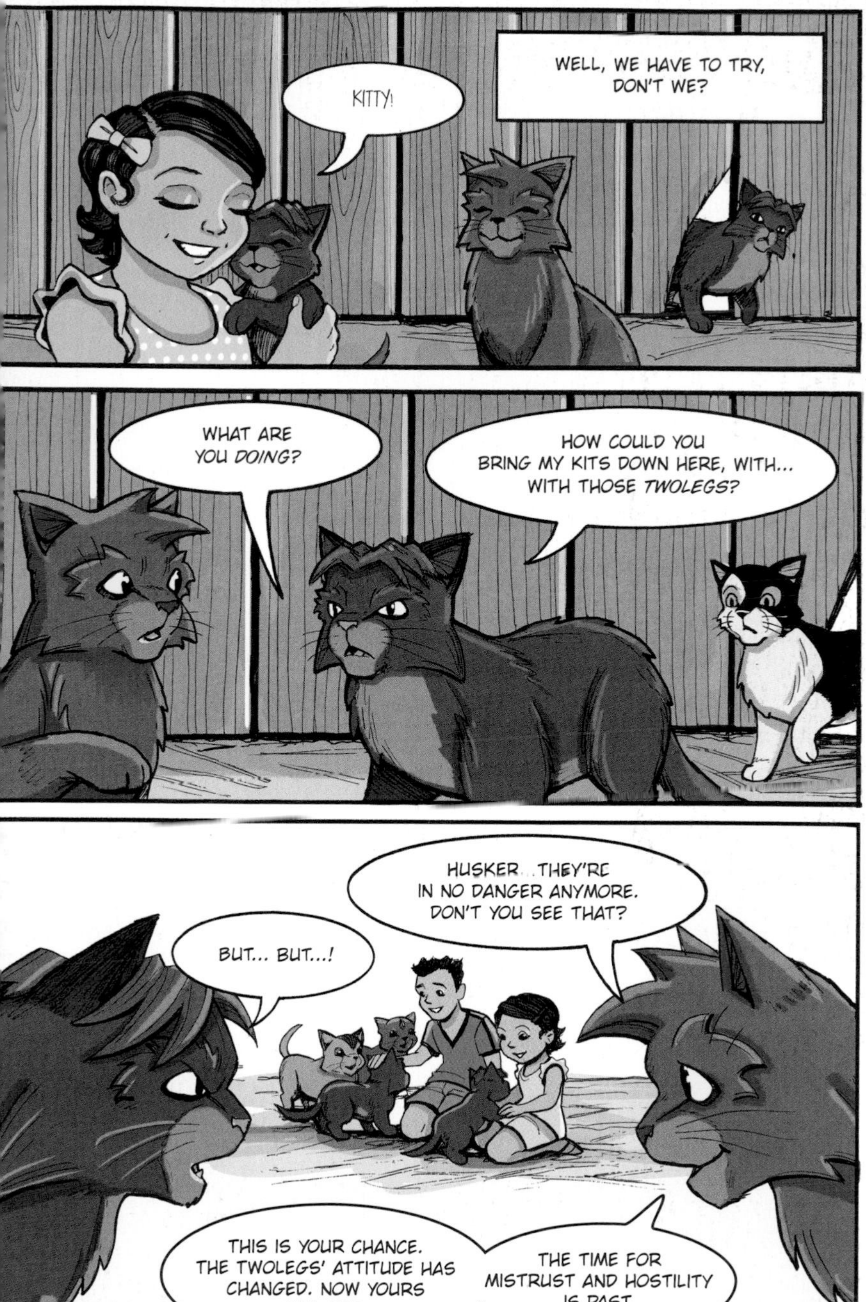
KITTY!
WELL, WE HAVE TO TRY, DON'T WE?
WHAT ARE YOU *DOING*?
HOW COULD YOU BRING MY KITS DOWN HERE, WITH... WITH THOSE *TWOLEGS*?
HUSKER...THEY'RE IN NO DANGER ANYMORE. DON'T YOU SEE THAT?
BUT... BUT...!
THIS IS YOUR CHANCE. THE TWOLEGS' ATTITUDE HAS CHANGED. NOW YOURS CAN, TOO.
THE TIME FOR MISTRUST AND HOSTILITY IS PAST.

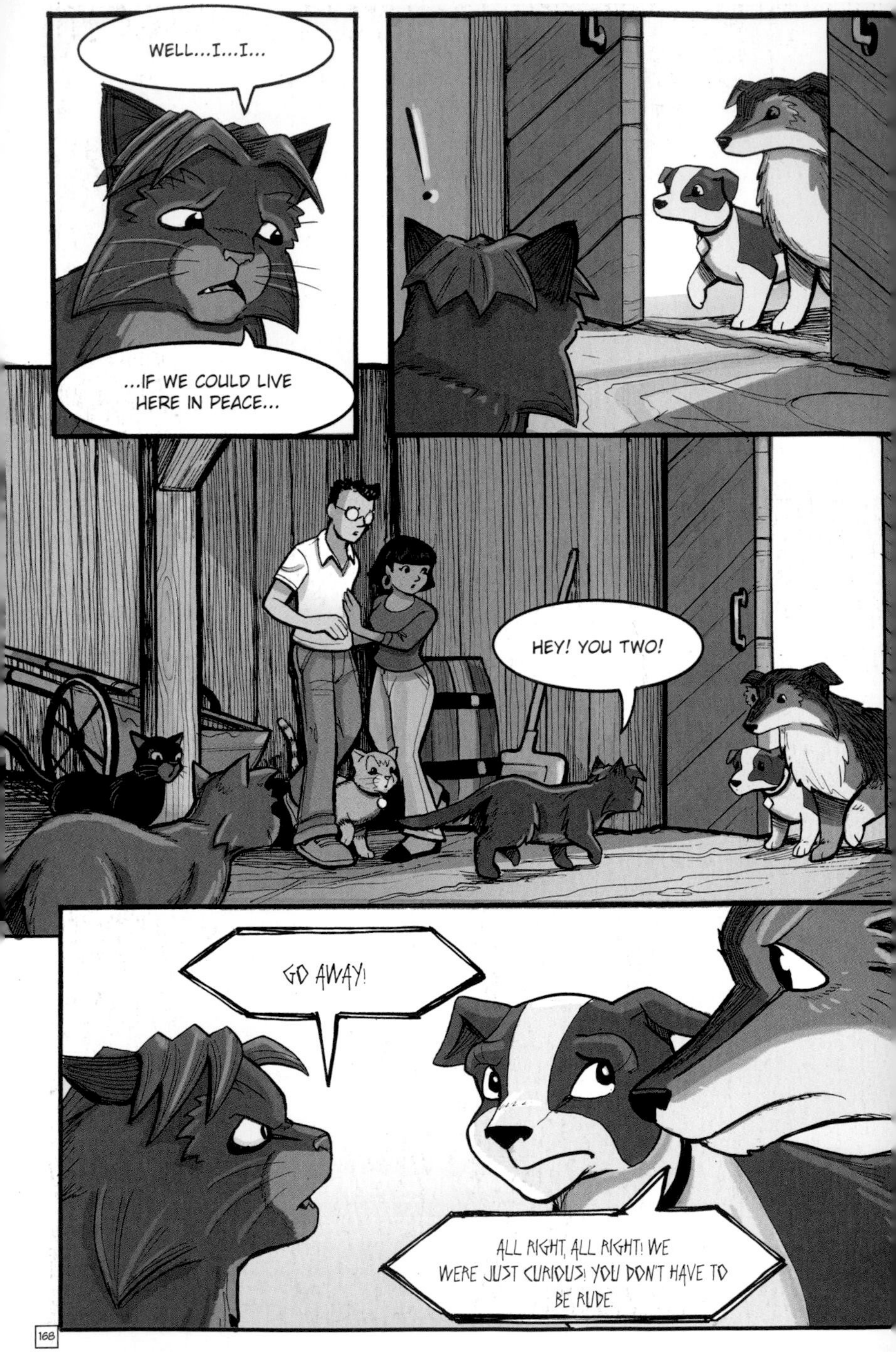
WELL...I...I...
...IF WE COULD LIVE HERE IN PEACE...
!
HEY! YOU TWO!
GO AWAY!
ALL RIGHT, ALL RIGHT! WE WERE JUST CURIOUS! YOU DON'T HAVE TO BE RUDE.

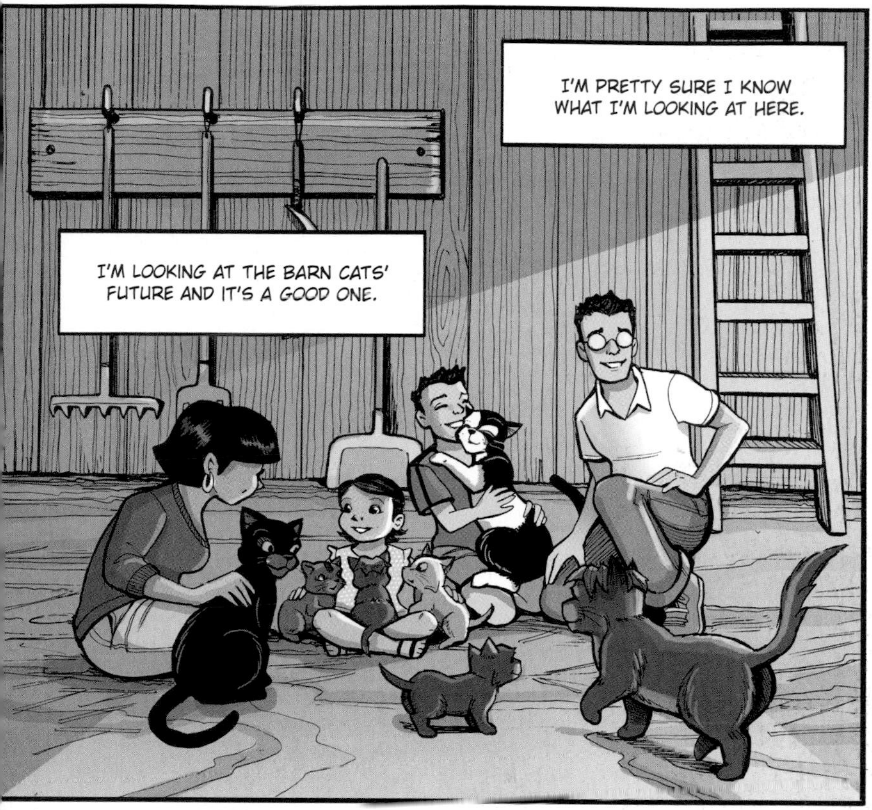
I'M PRETTY SURE I KNOW WHAT I'M LOOKING AT HERE.
I'M LOOKING AT THE BARN CATS' FUTURE AND IT'S A GOOD ONE.
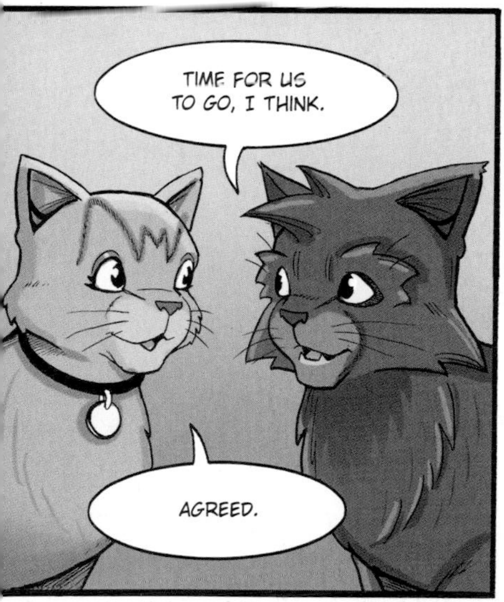
TIME FOR US TO GO, I THINK.
AGREED.
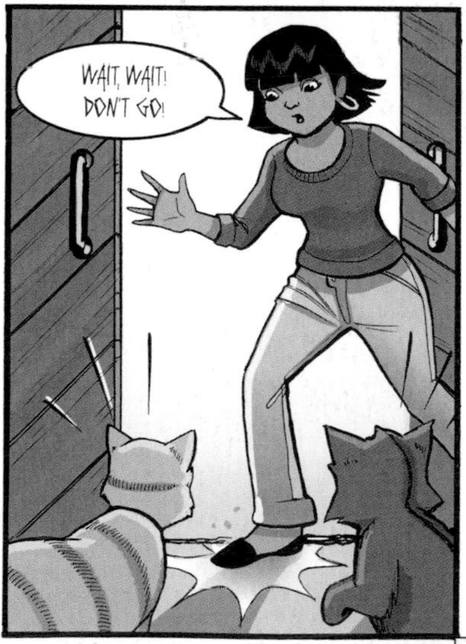
WAIT, WAIT! DON'T GO!

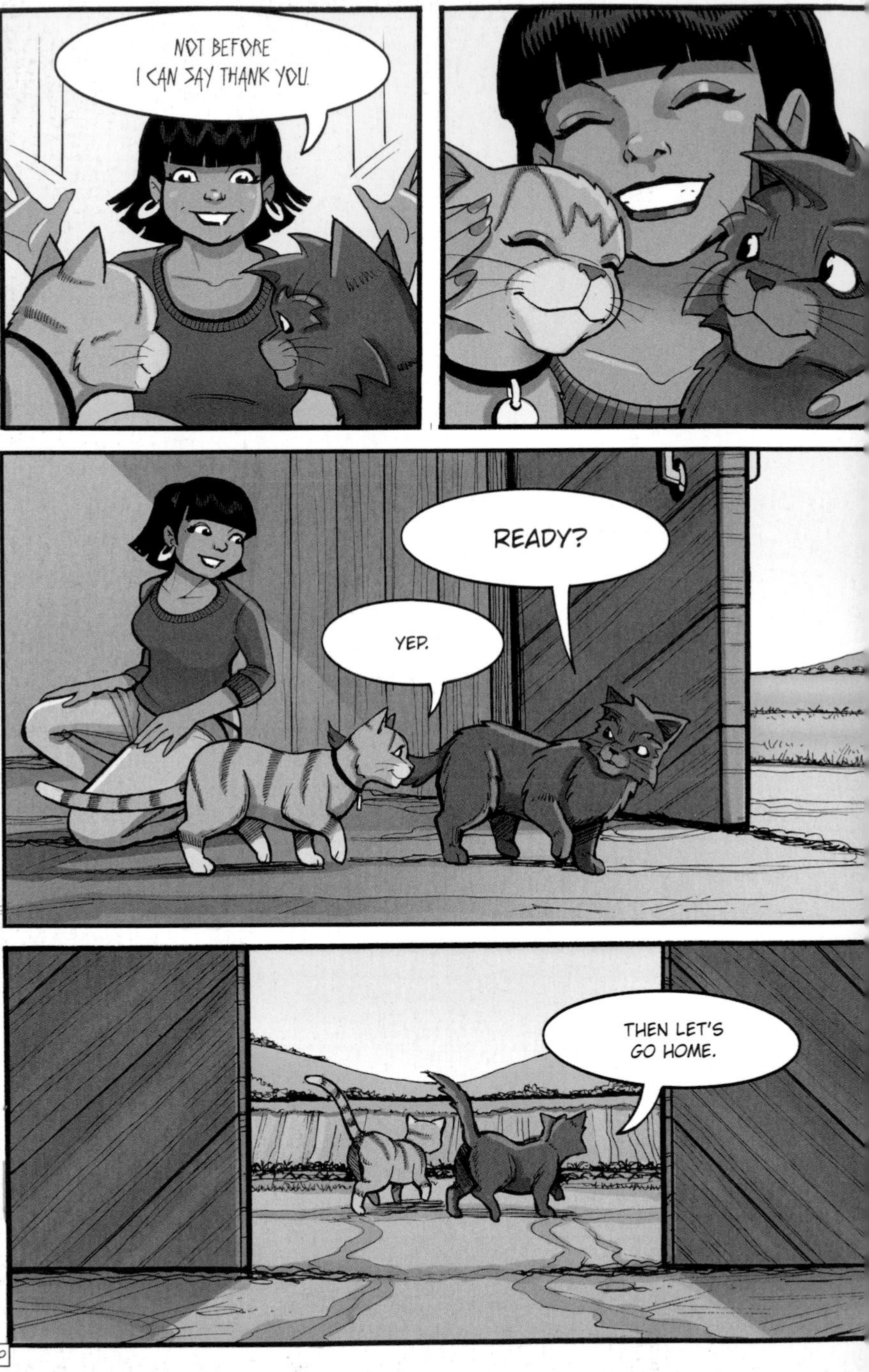
NOT BEFORE I CAN SAY THANK YOU.
READY?
YEP.
THEN LET'S GO HOME.

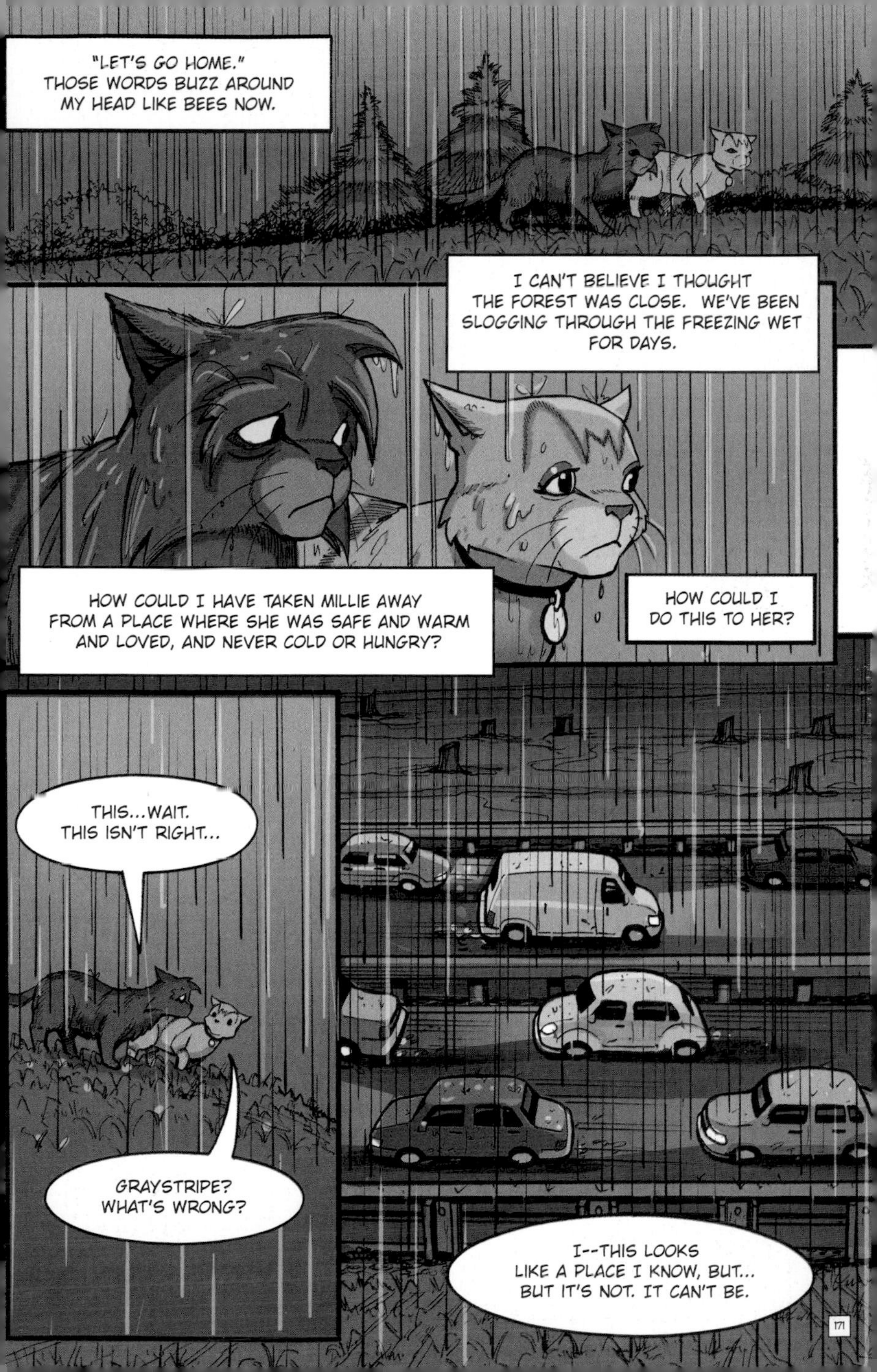
"LET'S GO HOME." THOSE WORDS BUZZ AROUND MY HEAD LIKE BEES NOW.
I CAN'T BELIEVE I THOUGHT THE FOREST WAS CLOSE. WE'VE BEEN SLOGGING THROUGH THE FREEZING WET FOR DAYS.
HOW COULD I HAVE TAKEN MILLIE AWAY FROM A PLACE WHERE SHE WAS SAFE AND WARM AND LOVED, AND NEVER COLD OR HUNGRY?
HOW COULD I DO THIS TO HER?
THIS...WAIT. THIS ISN'T RIGHT...
GRAYSTRIPE? WHAT'S WRONG?
I--THIS LOOKS LIKE A PLACE I KNOW, BUT... BUT IT'S NOT. IT CAN'T BE.

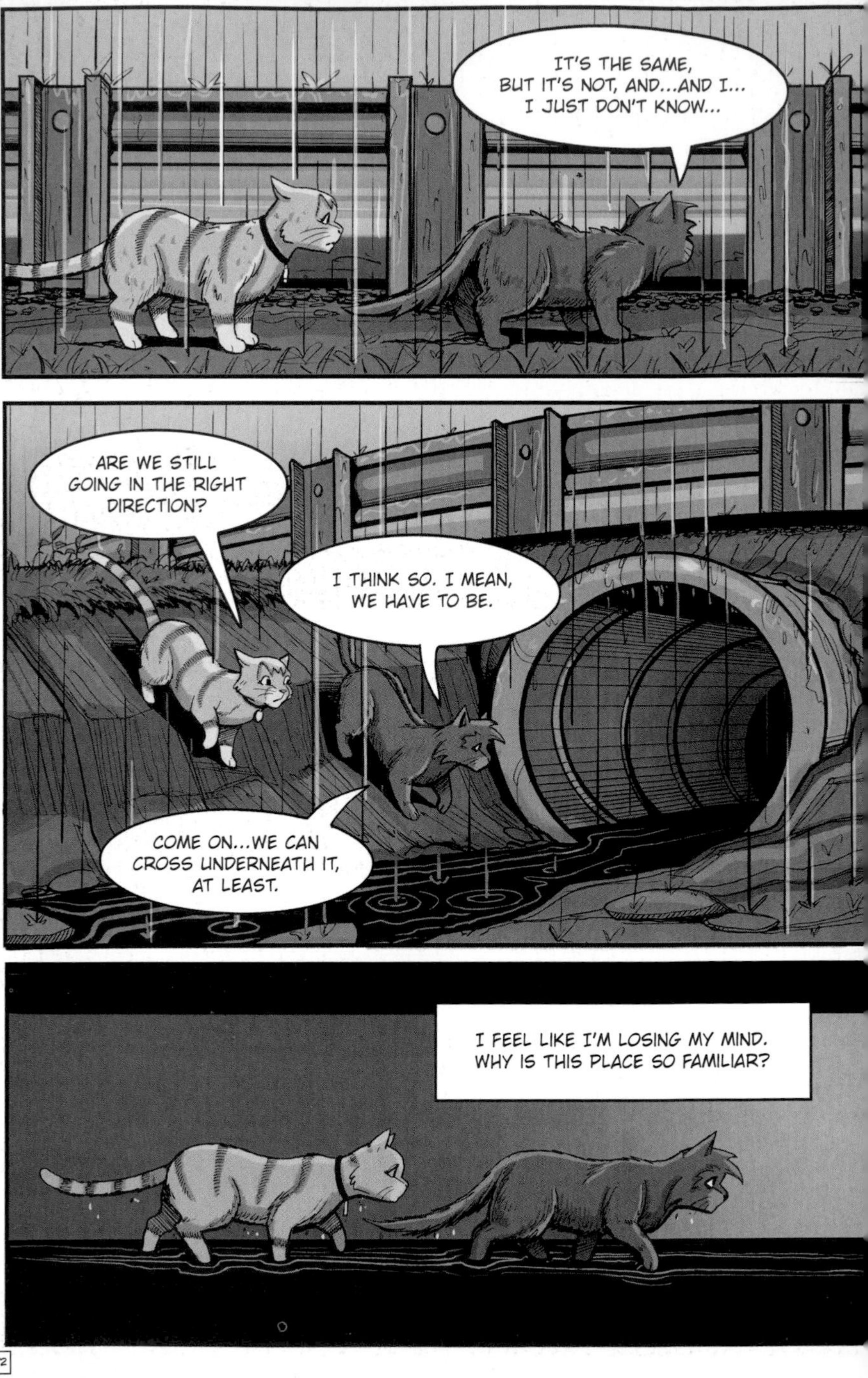
IT'S THE SAME, BUT IT'S NOT, AND...AND I... I JUST DON'T KNOW...
ARE WE STILL GOING IN THE RIGHT DIRECTION?
I THINK SO. I MEAN, WE HAVE TO BE.
COME ON...WE CAN CROSS UNDERNEATH IT, AT LEAST.
I FEEL LIKE I'M LOSING MY MIND. WHY IS THIS PLACE SO FAMILIAR?

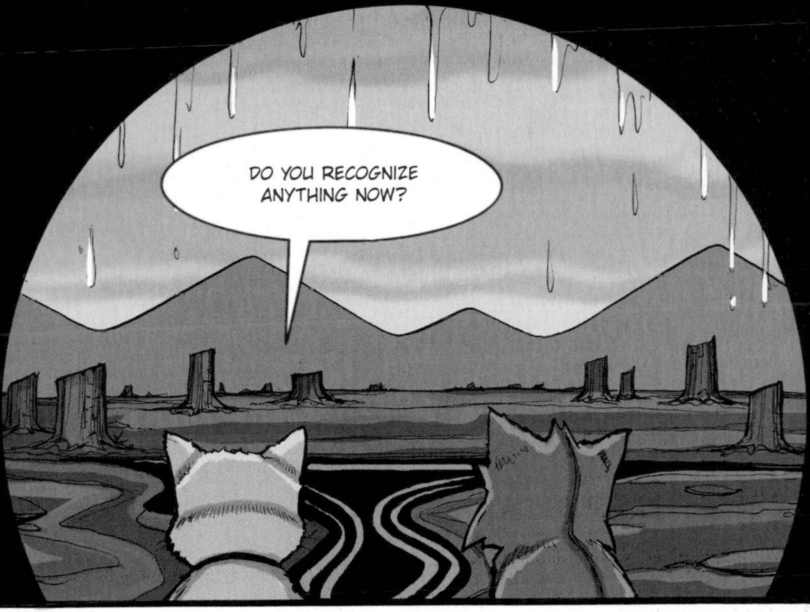
DO YOU RECOGNIZE ANYTHING NOW?

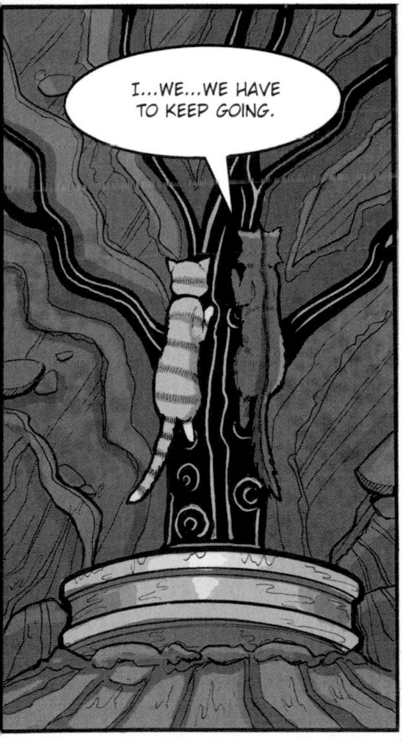
I...WE...WE HAVE TO KEEP GOING.

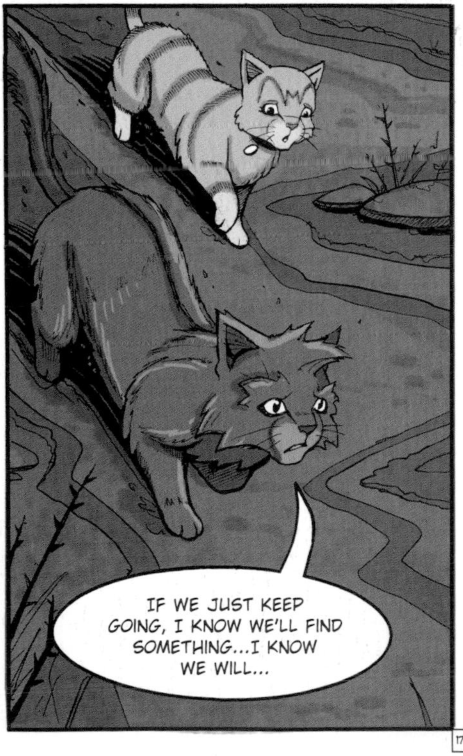
IF WE JUST KEEP GOING, I KNOW WE'LL FIND SOMETHING...I KNOW WE WILL...

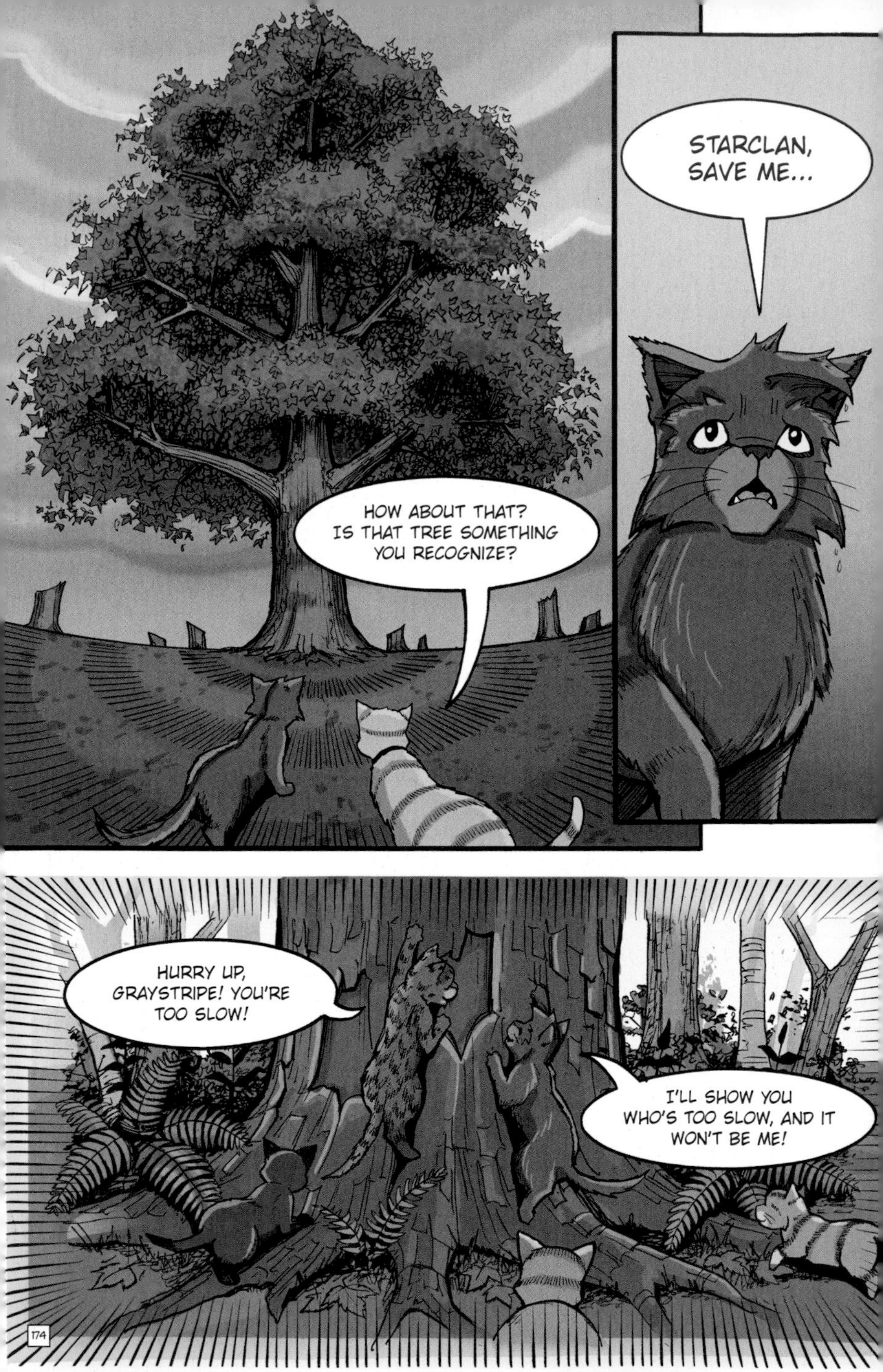
HOW ABOUT THAT? IS THAT TREE SOMETHING YOU RECOGNIZE?
STARCLAN, SAVE ME...
HURRY UP, GRAYSTRIPE! YOU'RE TOO SLOW!
I'LL SHOW YOU WHO'S TOO SLOW, AND IT WON'T BE ME!

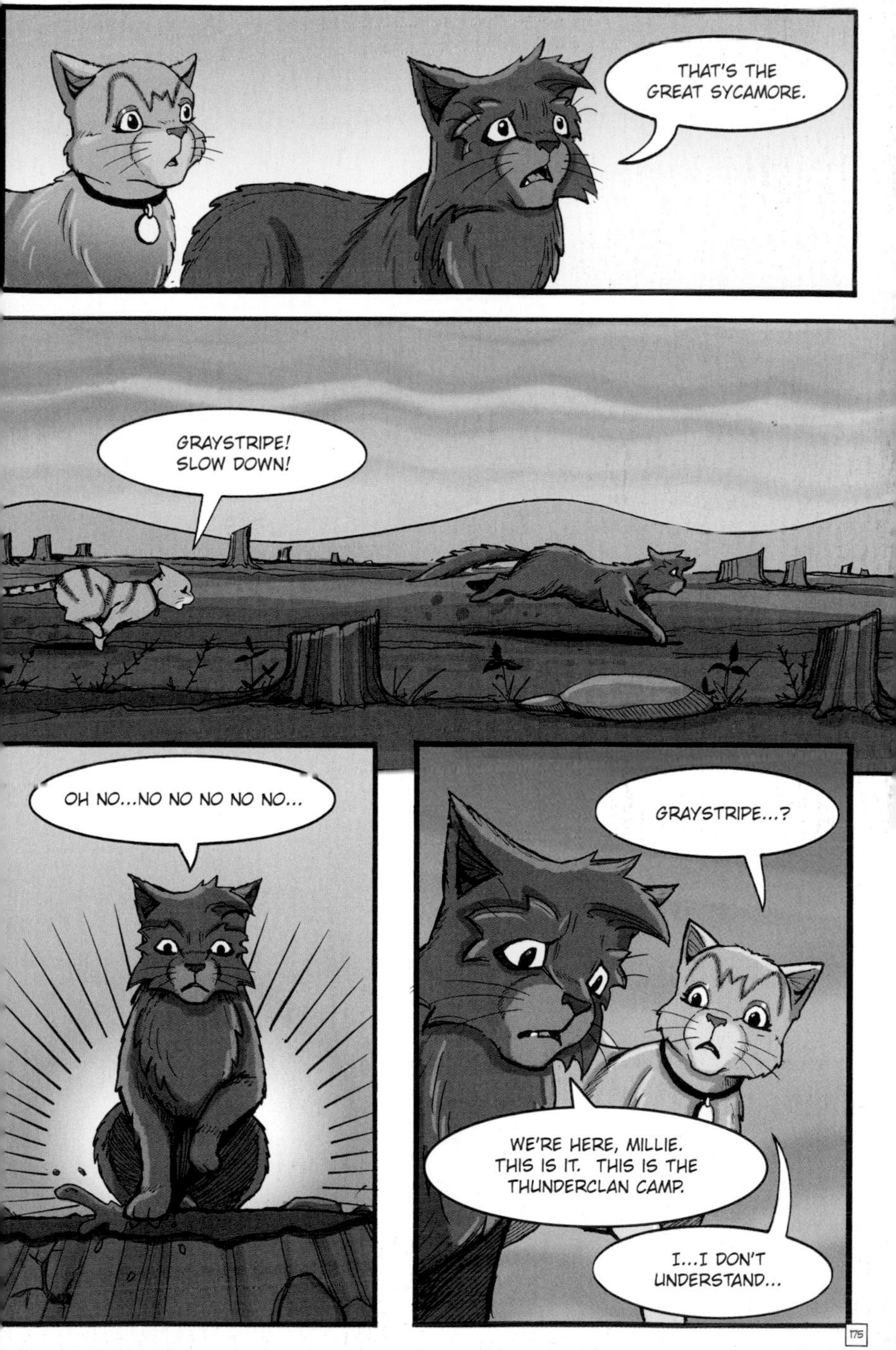
THAT'S THE GREAT SYCAMORE.
GRAYSTRIPE! SLOW DOWN!
OH NO...NO NO NO NO NO...
GRAYSTRIPE...?
WE'RE HERE, MILLIE. THIS IS IT. THIS IS THE THUNDERCLAN CAMP.
I...I DON'T UNDERSTAND...

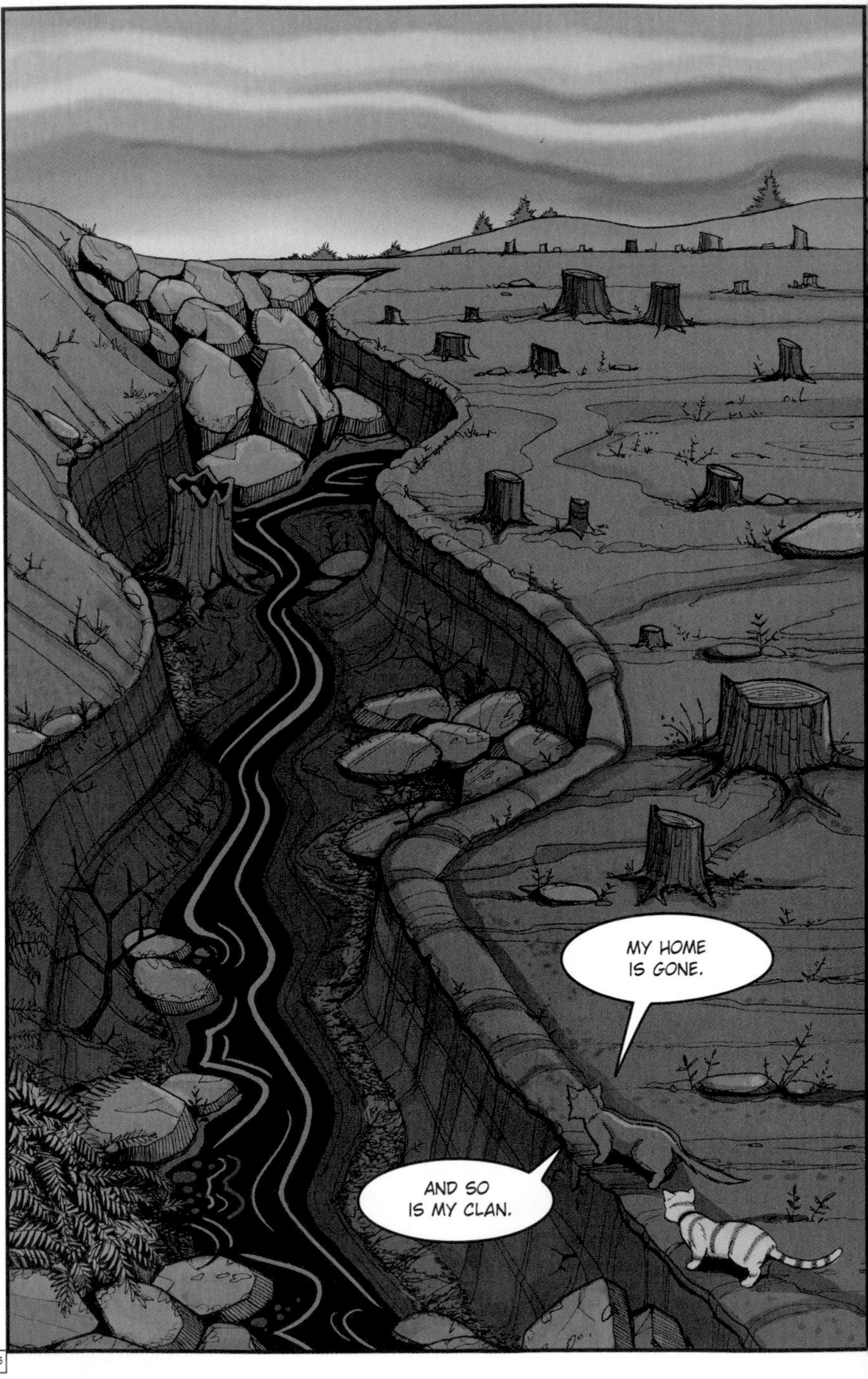
MY HOME IS GONE.
AND SO IS MY CLAN.

WARRIORS

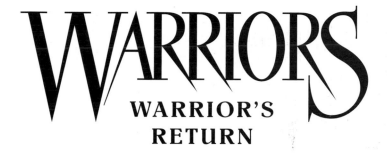

WARRIOR'S RETURN

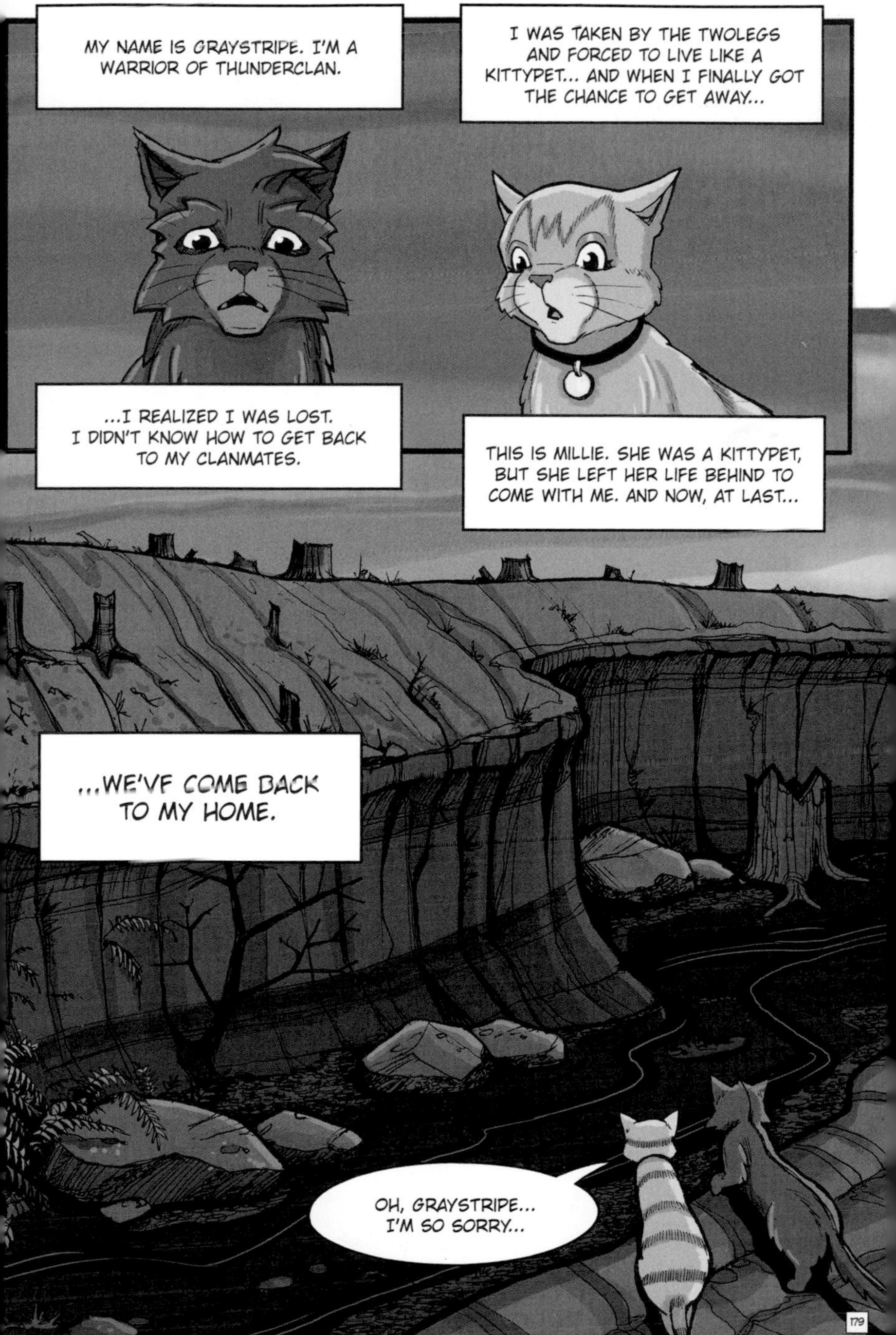
MY NAME IS GRAYSTRIPE. I'M A WARRIOR OF THUNDERCLAN.
I WAS TAKEN BY THE TWOLEGS AND FORCED TO LIVE LIKE A KITTYPET... AND WHEN I FINALLY GOT THE CHANCE TO GET AWAY...
...I REALIZED I WAS LOST. I DIDN'T KNOW HOW TO GET BACK TO MY CLANMATES.
THIS IS MILLIE. SHE WAS A KITTYPET, BUT SHE LEFT HER LIFE BEHIND TO COME WITH ME. AND NOW, AT LAST...
...WE'VE COME BACK TO MY HOME.
OH, GRAYSTRIPE... I'M SO SORRY...

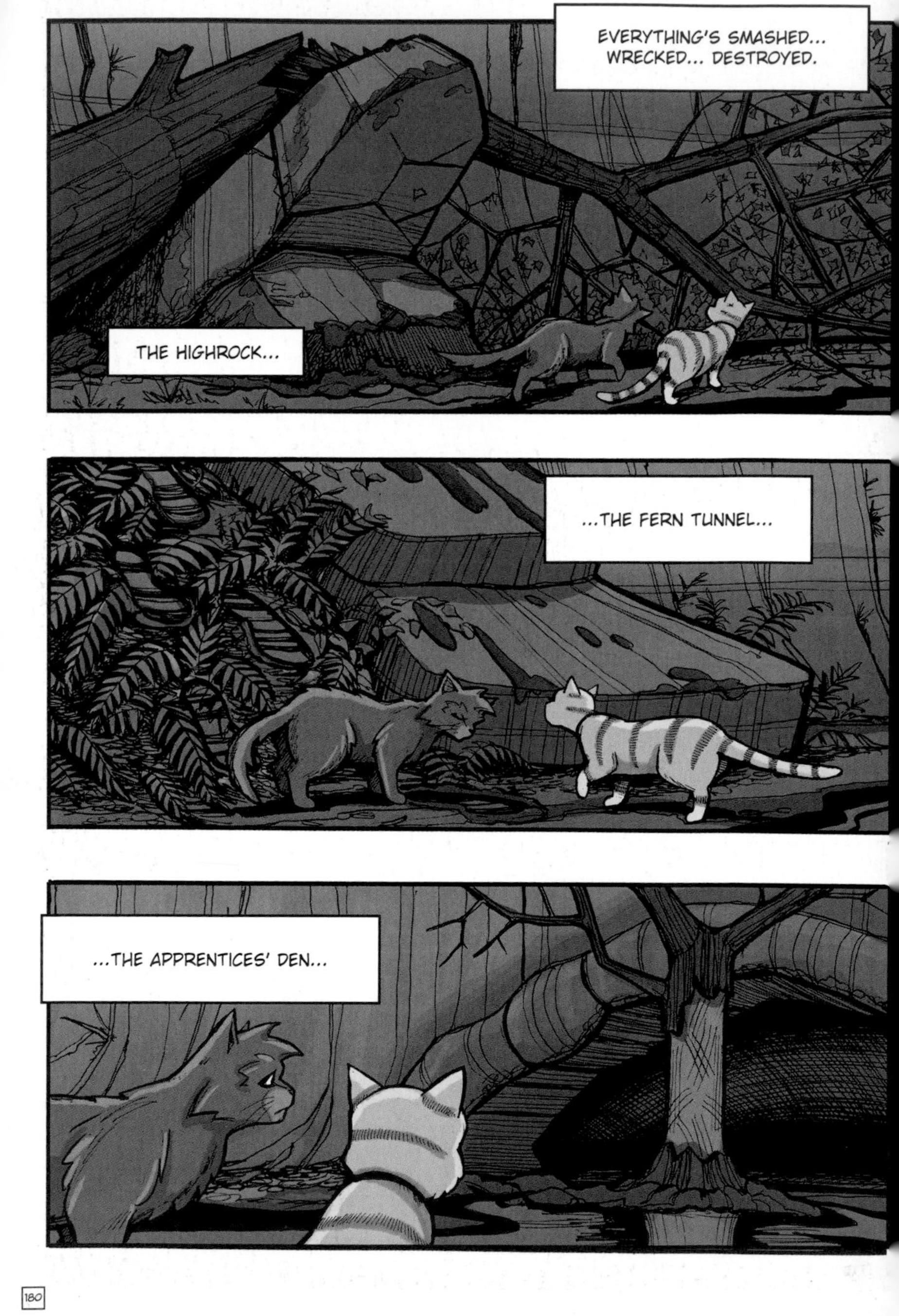

EVERYTHING'S SMASHED... WRECKED... DESTROYED.
THE HIGHROCK...
...THE FERN TUNNEL...
...THE APPRENTICES' DEN...

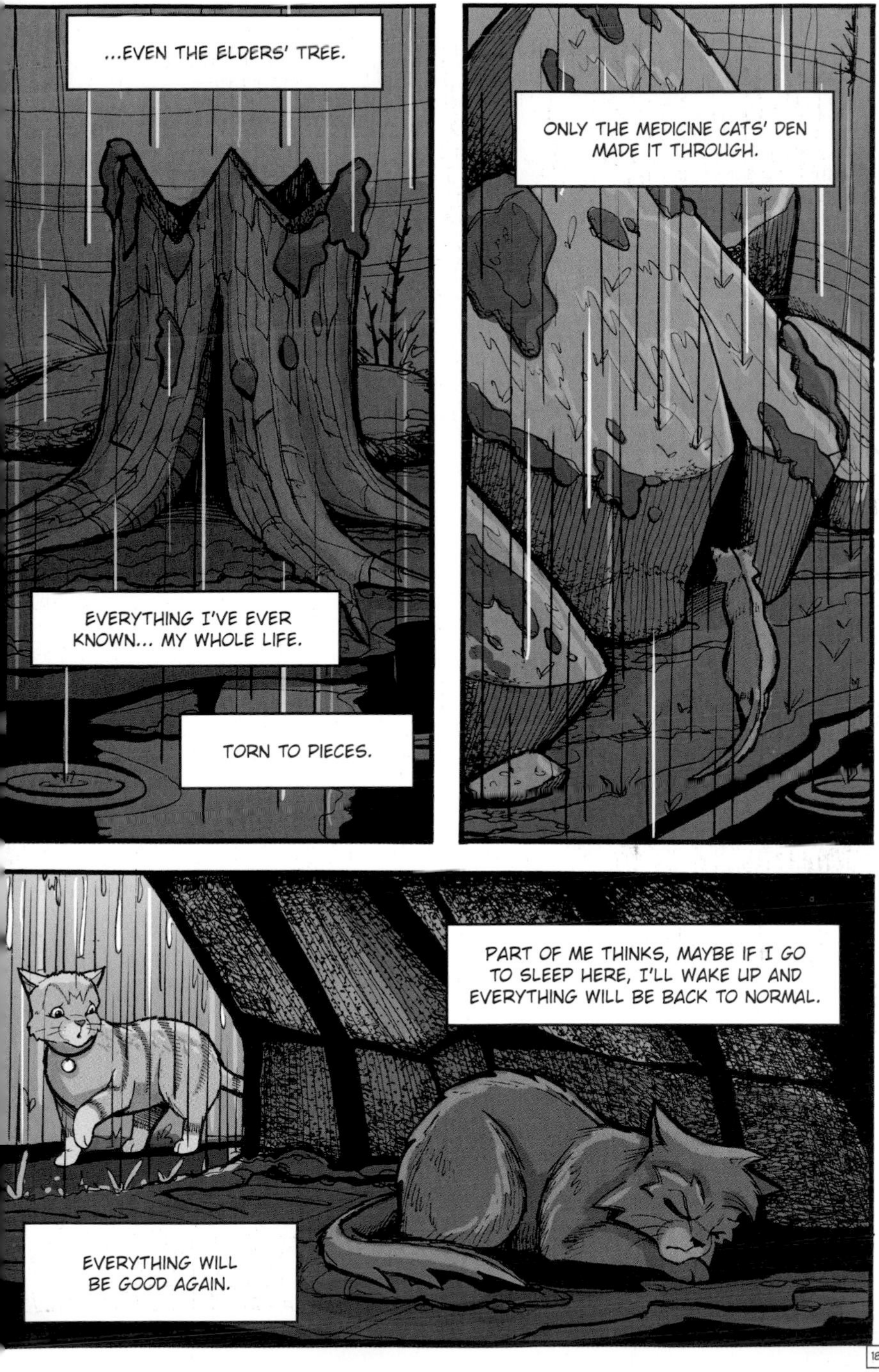

...EVEN THE ELDERS' TREE.
EVERYTHING I'VE EVER KNOWN... MY WHOLE LIFE.
TORN TO PIECES.
ONLY THE MEDICINE CATS' DEN MADE IT THROUGH.
PART OF ME THINKS, MAYBE IF I GO TO SLEEP HERE, I'LL WAKE UP AND EVERYTHING WILL BE BACK TO NORMAL.
EVERYTHING WILL BE GOOD AGAIN.

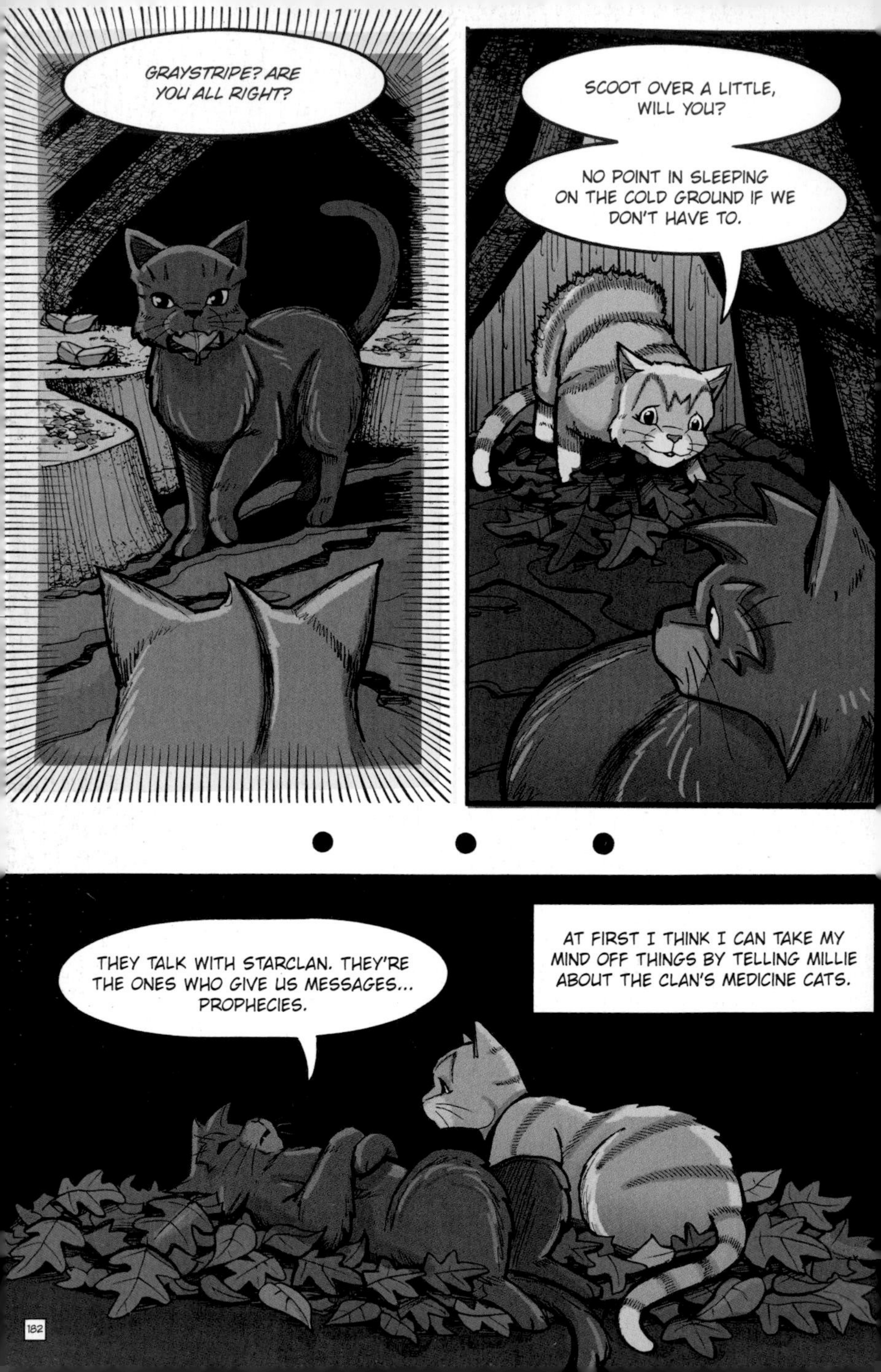
GRAYSTRIPE? ARE YOU ALL RIGHT?
SCOOT OVER A LITTLE, WILL YOU?
NO POINT IN SLEEPING ON THE COLD GROUND IF WE DON'T HAVE TO.
THEY TALK WITH STARCLAN. THEY'RE THE ONES WHO GIVE US MESSAGES... PROPHECIES.
AT FIRST I THINK I CAN TAKE MY MIND OFF THINGS BY TELLING MILLIE ABOUT THE CLAN'S MEDICINE CATS.

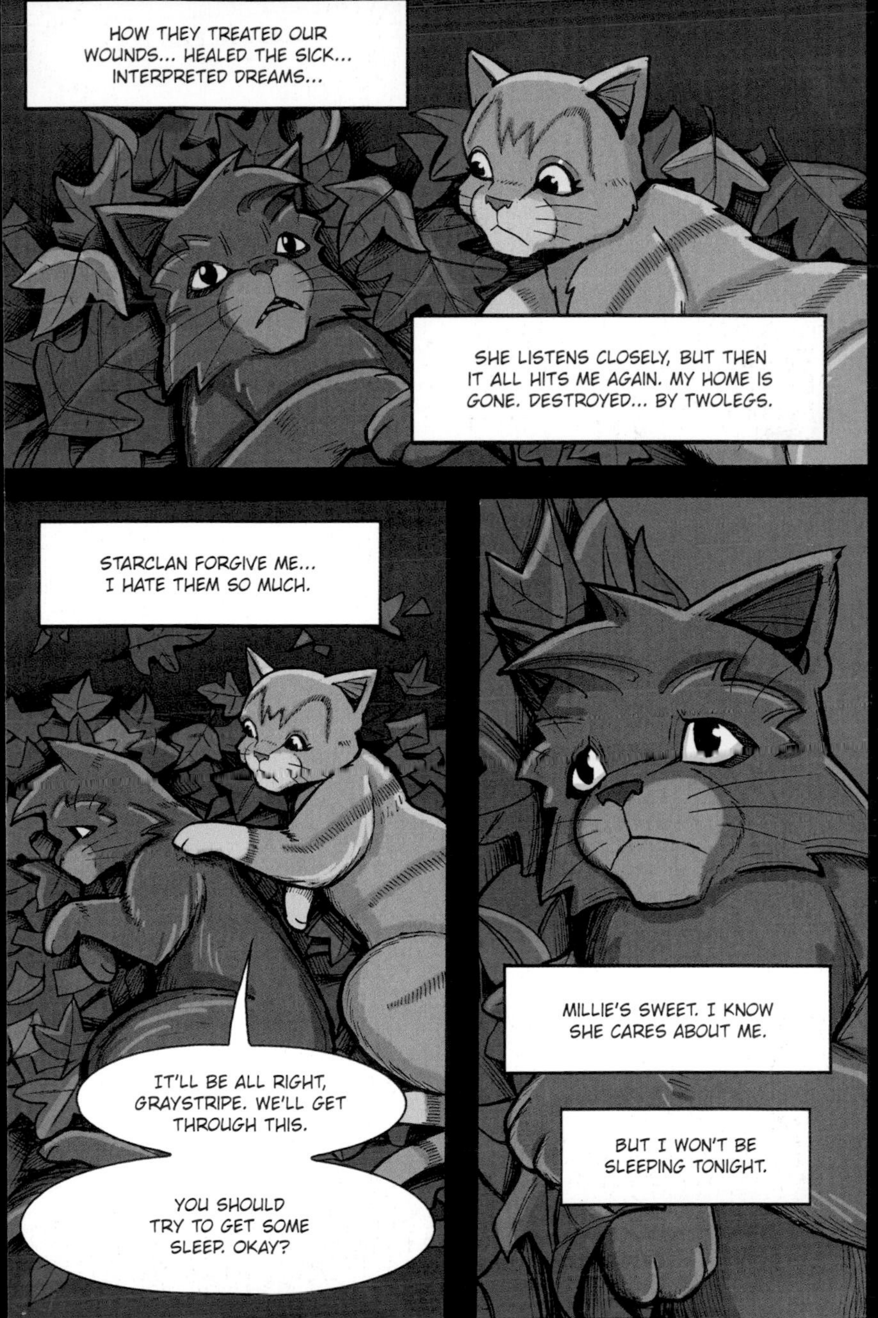
HOW THEY TREATED OUR WOUNDS... HEALED THE SICK... INTERPRETED DREAMS...
SHE LISTENS CLOSELY, BUT THEN IT ALL HITS ME AGAIN. MY HOME IS GONE. DESTROYED... BY TWOLEGS.
STARCLAN FORGIVE ME... I HATE THEM SO MUCH.
IT'LL BE ALL RIGHT, GRAYSTRIPE. WE'LL GET THROUGH THIS.
YOU SHOULD TRY TO GET SOME SLEEP. OKAY?
MILLIE'S SWEET. I KNOW SHE CARES ABOUT ME.
BUT I WON'T BE SLEEPING TONIGHT.

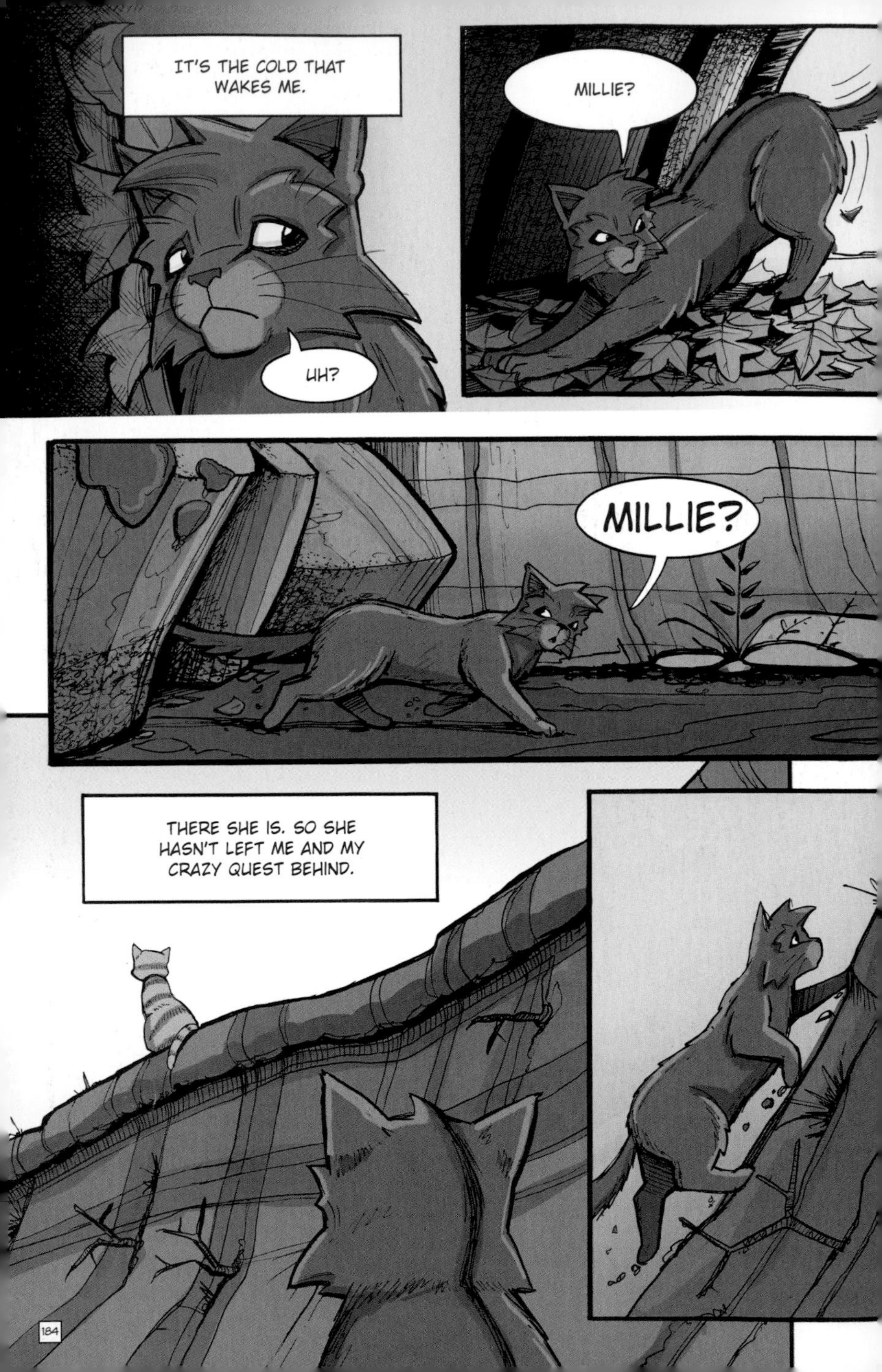
IT'S THE COLD THAT WAKES ME.
UH?
MILLIE?
MILLIE?
THERE SHE IS. SO SHE HASN'T LEFT ME AND MY CRAZY QUEST BEHIND.

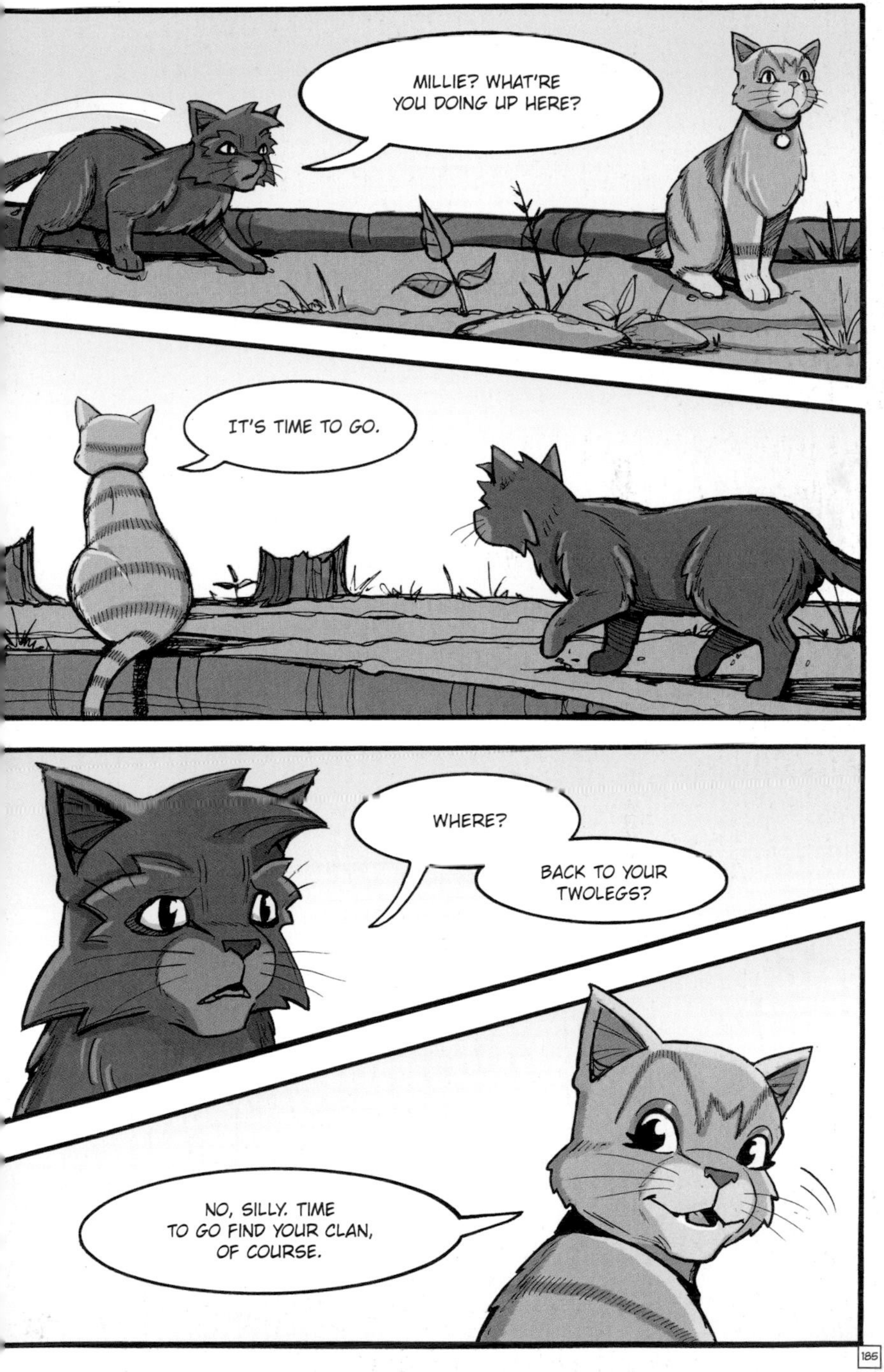
MILLIE? WHAT'RE YOU DOING UP HERE?
IT'S TIME TO GO.
WHERE?
BACK TO YOUR TWOLEGS?
NO, SILLY. TIME TO GO FIND YOUR CLAN, OF COURSE.

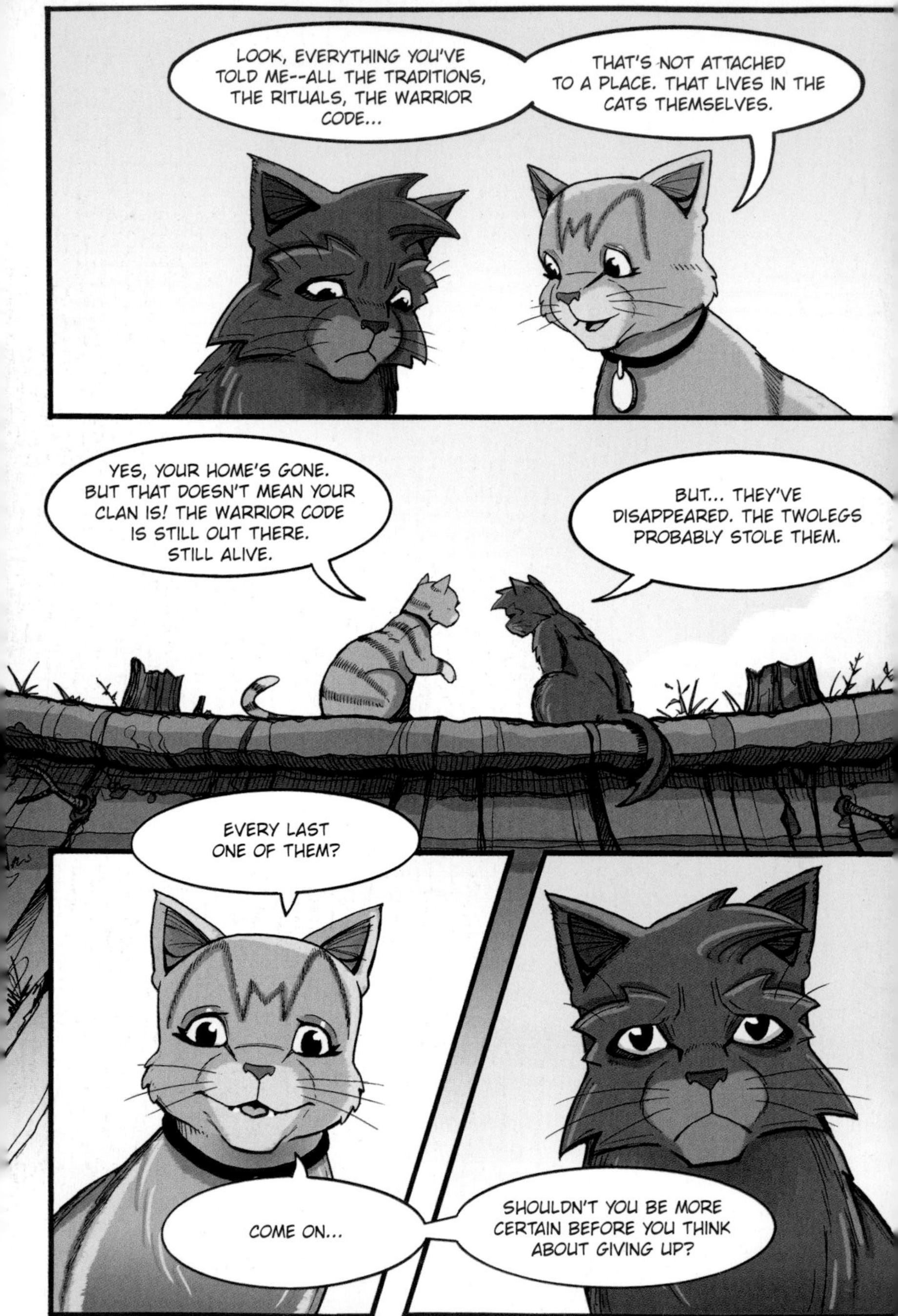
LOOK, EVERYTHING YOU'VE TOLD ME--ALL THE TRADITIONS, THE RITUALS, THE WARRIOR CODE...
THAT'S NOT ATTACHED TO A PLACE. THAT LIVES IN THE CATS THEMSELVES.
YES, YOUR HOME'S GONE. BUT THAT DOESN'T MEAN YOUR CLAN IS! THE WARRIOR CODE IS STILL OUT THERE. STILL ALIVE.
BUT... THEY'VE DISAPPEARED. THE TWOLEGS PROBABLY STOLE THEM.
EVERY LAST ONE OF THEM?
COME ON...
SHOULDN'T YOU BE MORE CERTAIN BEFORE YOU THINK ABOUT GIVING UP?

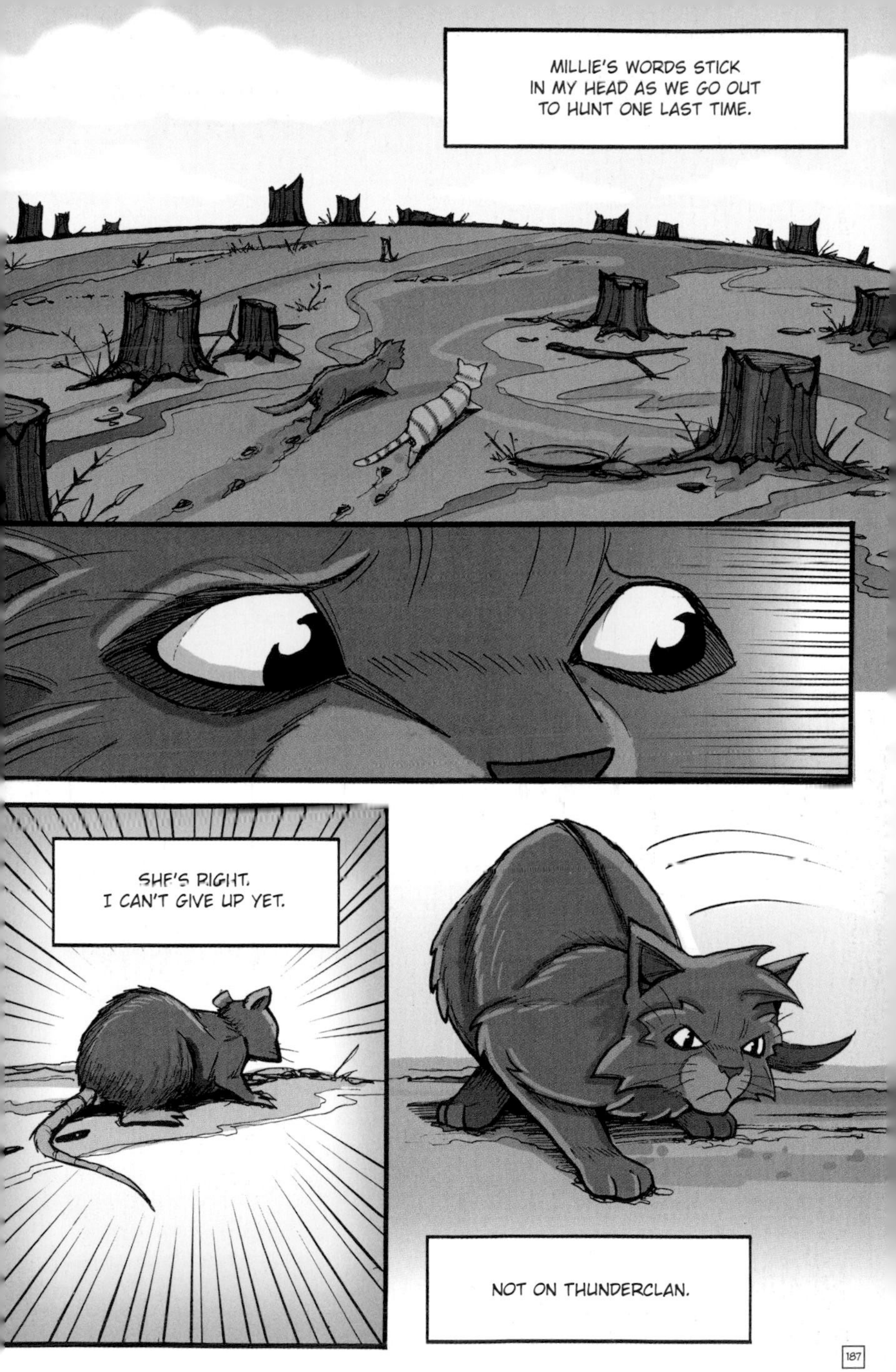
MILLIE'S WORDS STICK IN MY HEAD AS WE GO OUT TO HUNT ONE LAST TIME.
SHE'S RIGHT. I CAN'T GIVE UP YET.
NOT ON THUNDERCLAN.

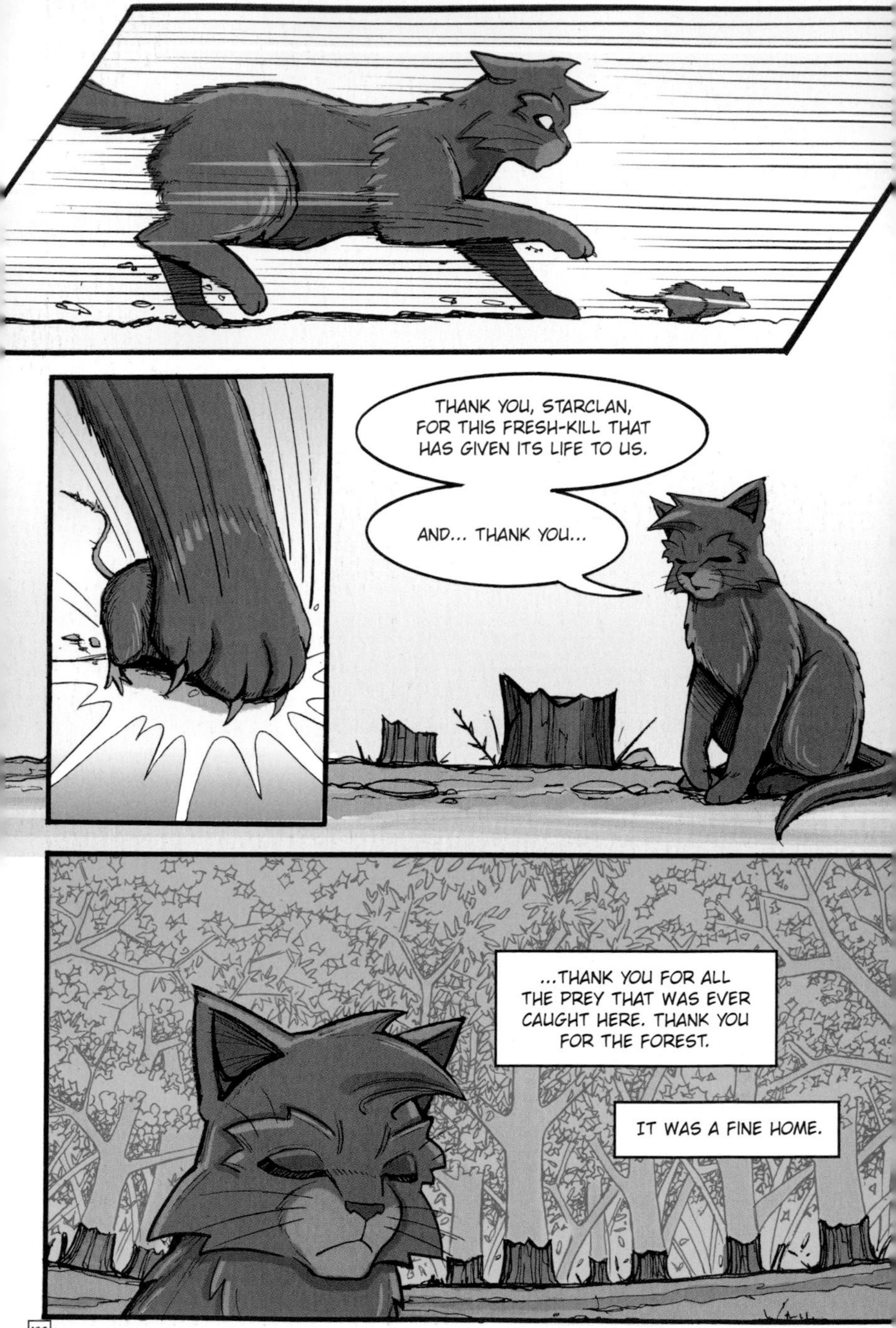
THANK YOU, STARCLAN, FOR THIS FRESH-KILL THAT HAS GIVEN ITS LIFE TO US.
AND... THANK YOU...
...THANK YOU FOR ALL THE PREY THAT WAS EVER CAUGHT HERE. THANK YOU FOR THE FOREST.
IT WAS A FINE HOME.

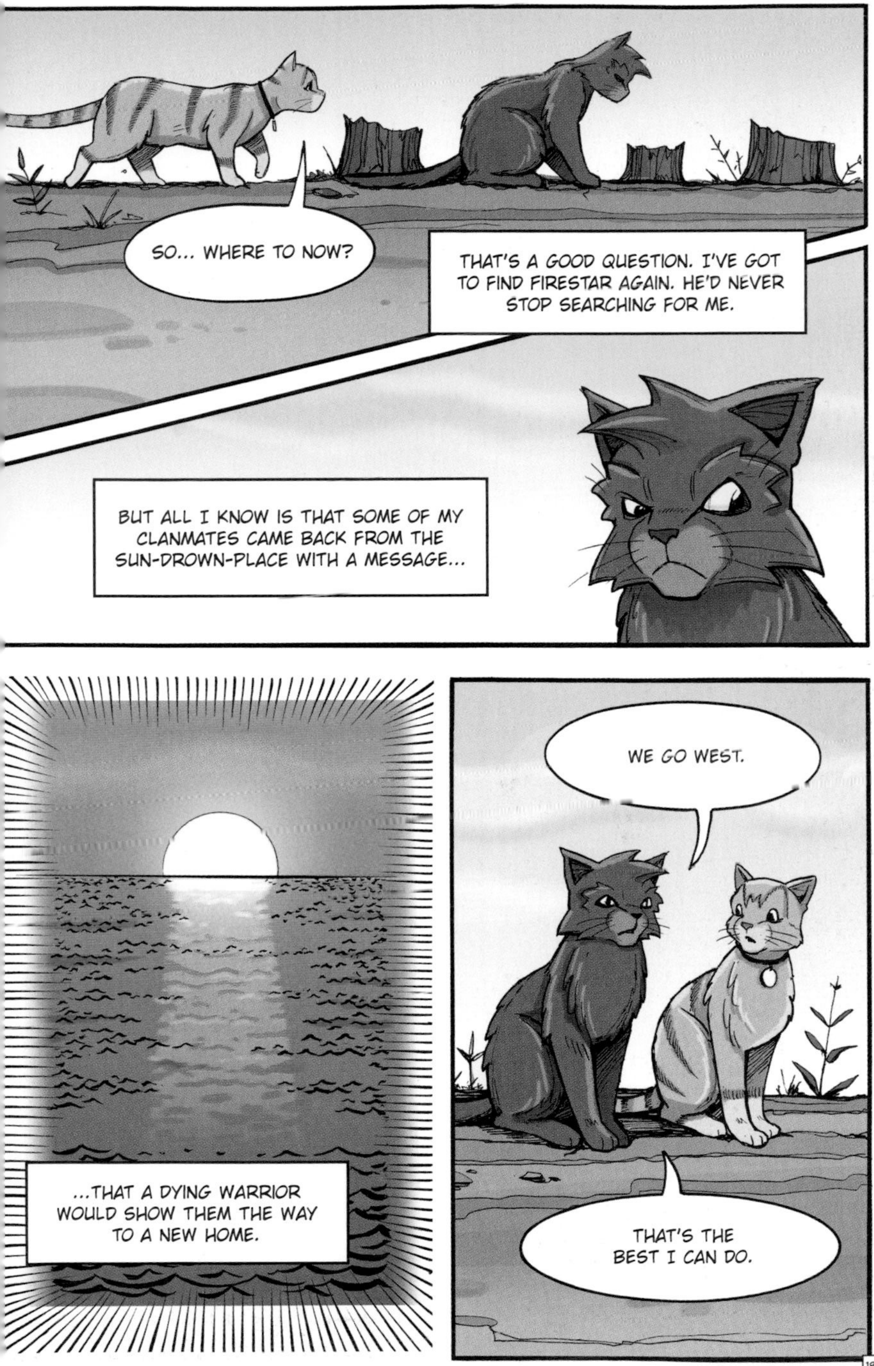
SO... WHERE TO NOW?
THAT'S A GOOD QUESTION. I'VE GOT TO FIND FIRESTAR AGAIN. HE'D NEVER STOP SEARCHING FOR ME.
BUT ALL I KNOW IS THAT SOME OF MY CLANMATES CAME BACK FROM THE SUN-DROWN-PLACE WITH A MESSAGE...
...THAT A DYING WARRIOR WOULD SHOW THEM THE WAY TO A NEW HOME.
WE GO WEST.
THAT'S THE BEST I CAN DO.

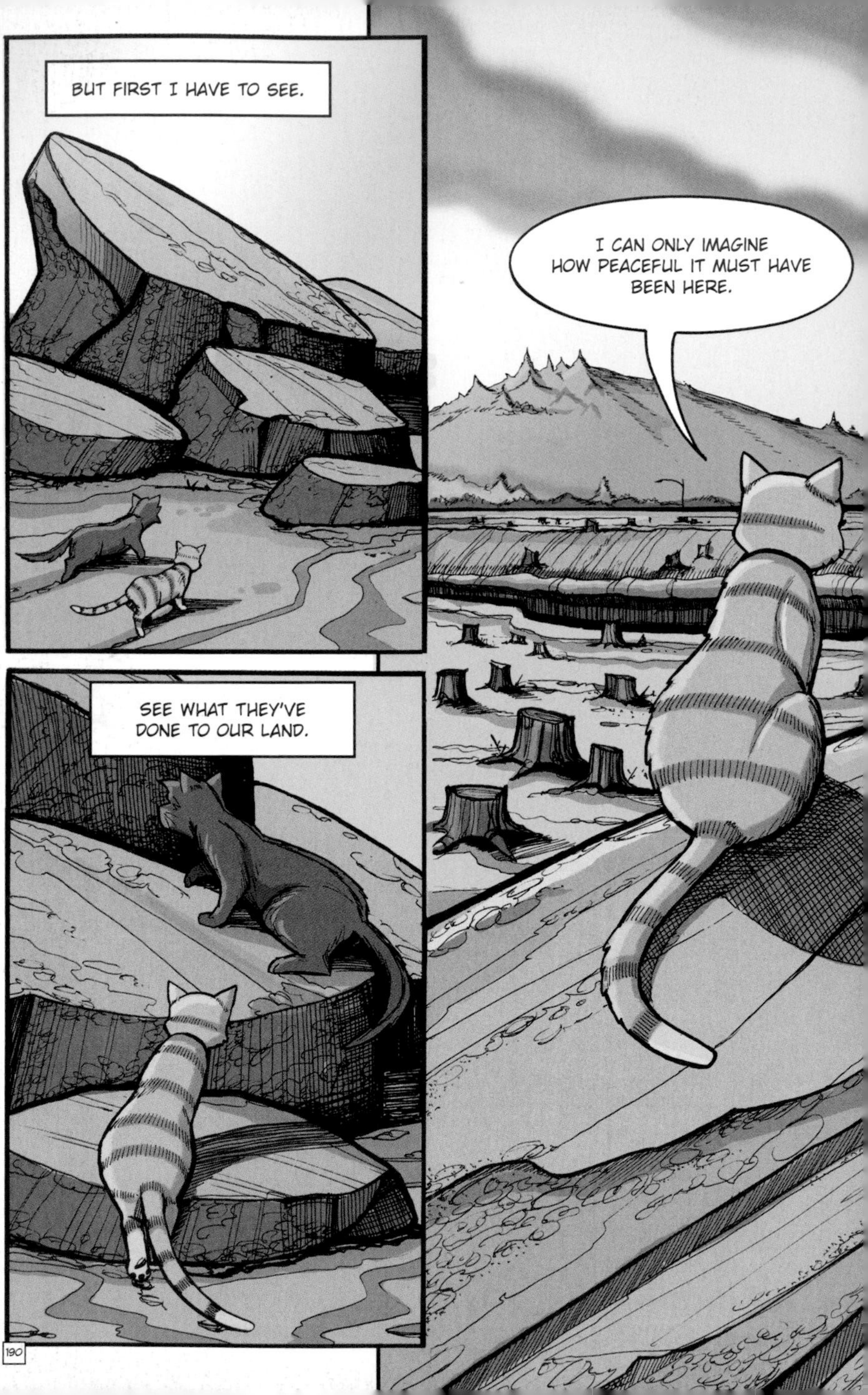
BUT FIRST I HAVE TO SEE.
SEE WHAT THEY'VE DONE TO OUR LAND.
I CAN ONLY IMAGINE HOW PEACEFUL IT MUST HAVE BEEN HERE.

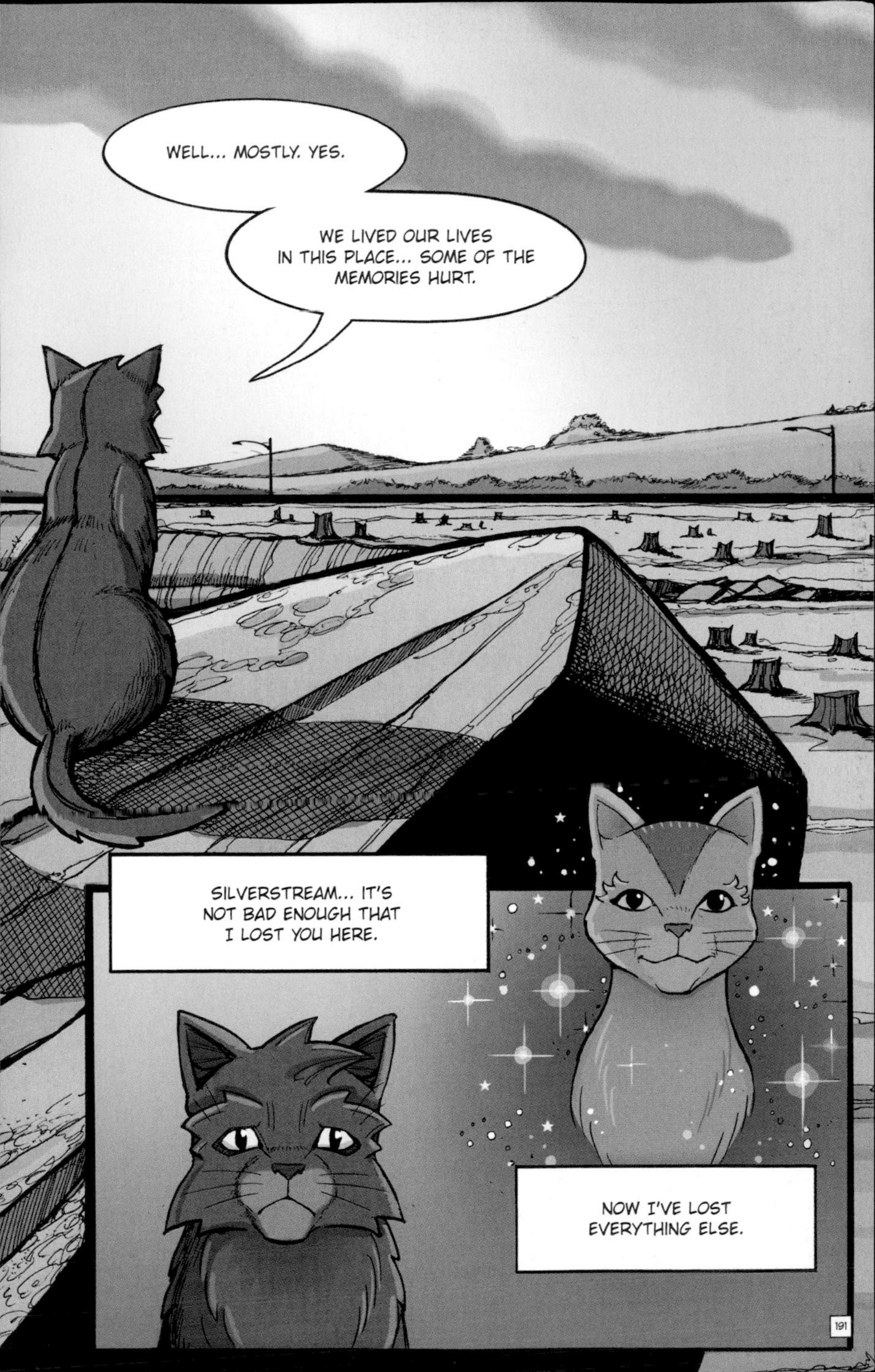
WELL... MOSTLY. YES.
WE LIVED OUR LIVES IN THIS PLACE... SOME OF THE MEMORIES HURT.
SILVERSTREAM... IT'S NOT BAD ENOUGH THAT I LOST YOU HERE.
NOW I'VE LOST EVERYTHING ELSE.

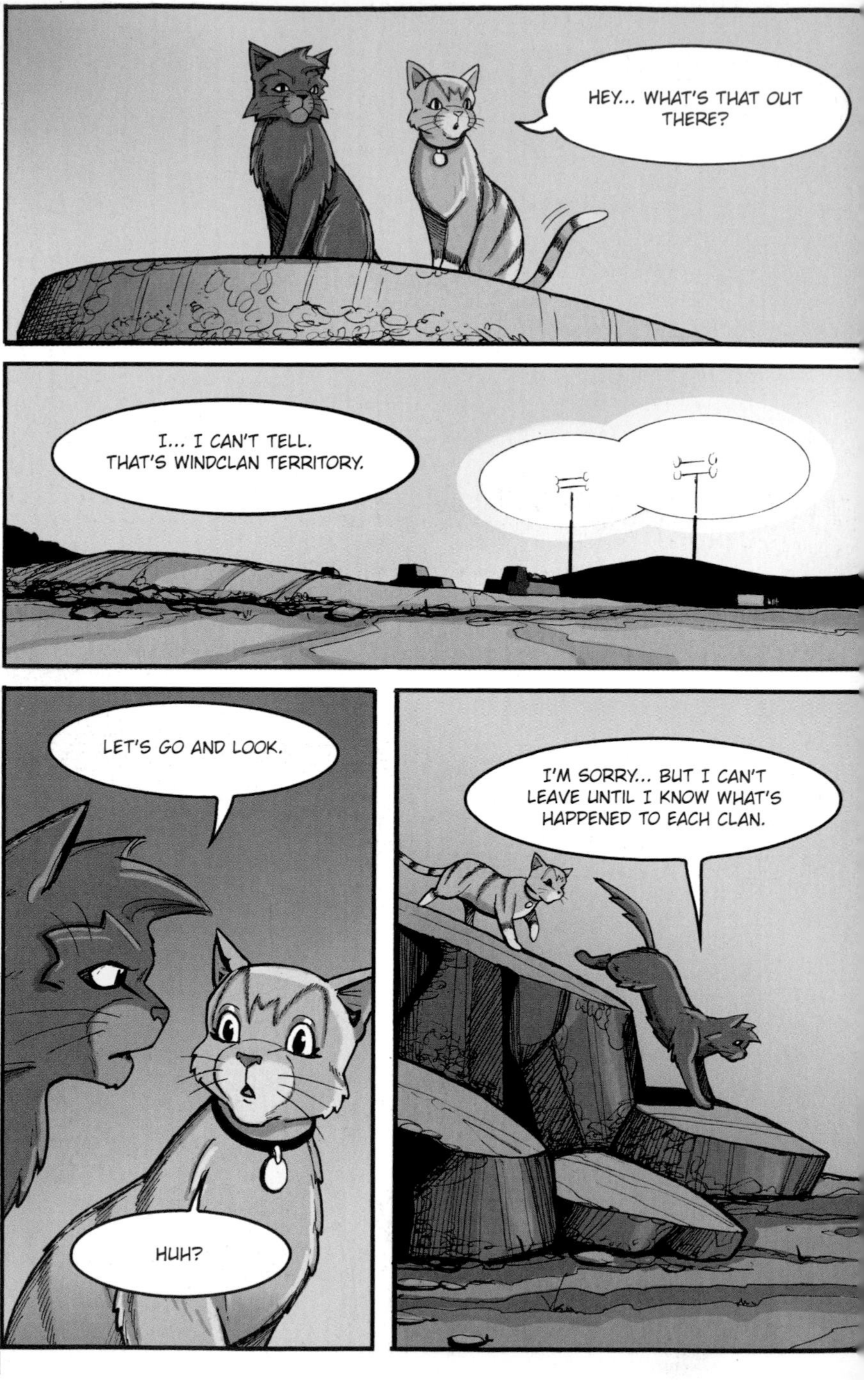
HEY... WHAT'S THAT OUT THERE?
I... I CAN'T TELL. THAT'S WINDCLAN TERRITORY.
LET'S GO AND LOOK.
HUH?
I'M SORRY... BUT I CAN'T LEAVE UNTIL I KNOW WHAT'S HAPPENED TO EACH CLAN.

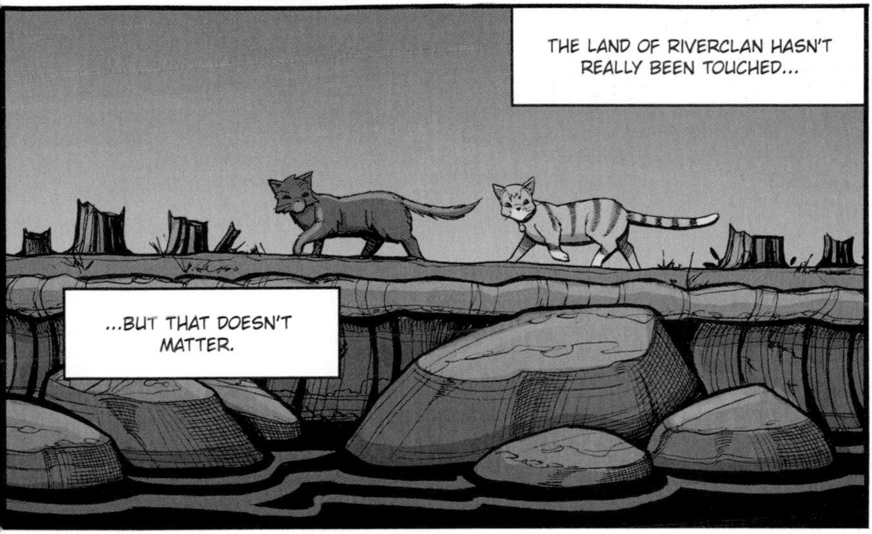
THE LAND OF RIVERCLAN HASN'T REALLY BEEN TOUCHED...
...BUT THAT DOESN'T MATTER.

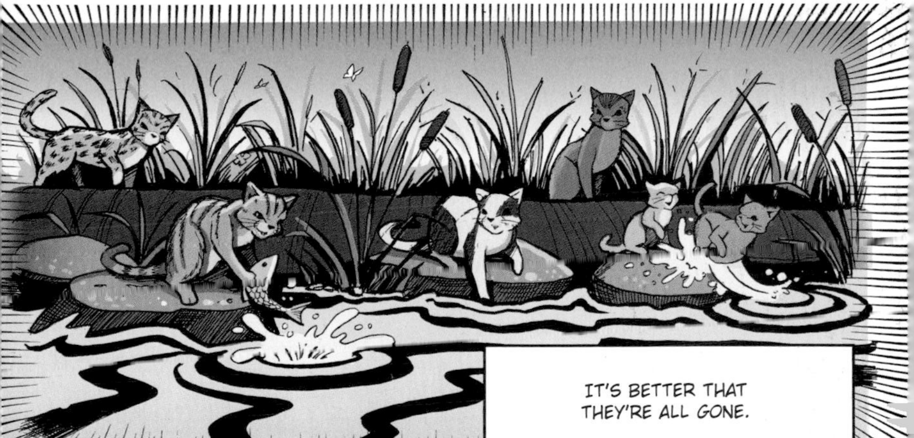
IT'S BETTER THAT THEY'RE ALL GONE.

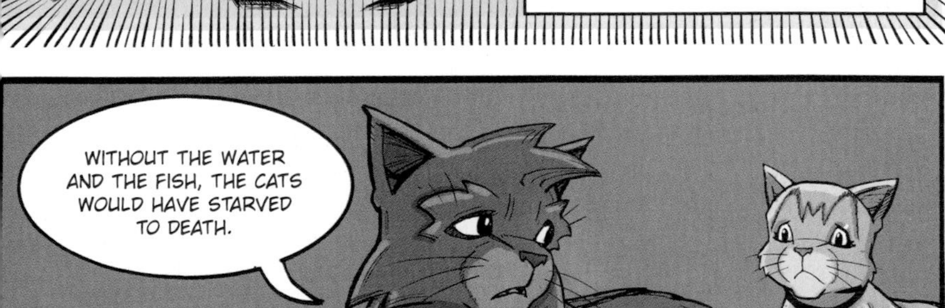
WITHOUT THE WATER AND THE FISH, THE CATS WOULD HAVE STARVED TO DEATH.

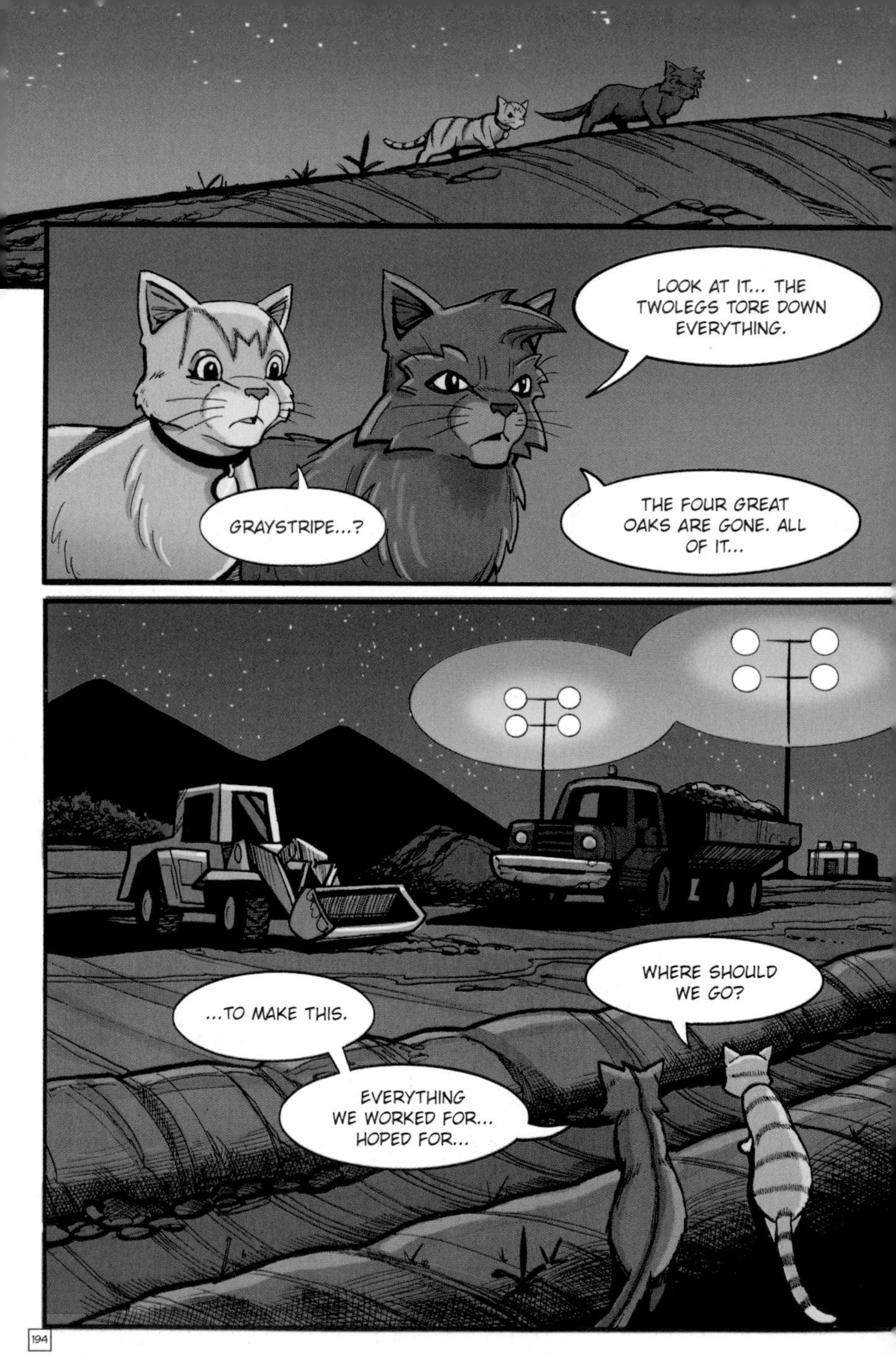
LOOK AT IT... THE TWOLEGS TORE DOWN EVERYTHING.
GRAYSTRIPE...?
THE FOUR GREAT OAKS ARE GONE. ALL OF IT...
...TO MAKE THIS.
EVERYTHING WE WORKED FOR... HOPED FOR...
WHERE SHOULD WE GO?

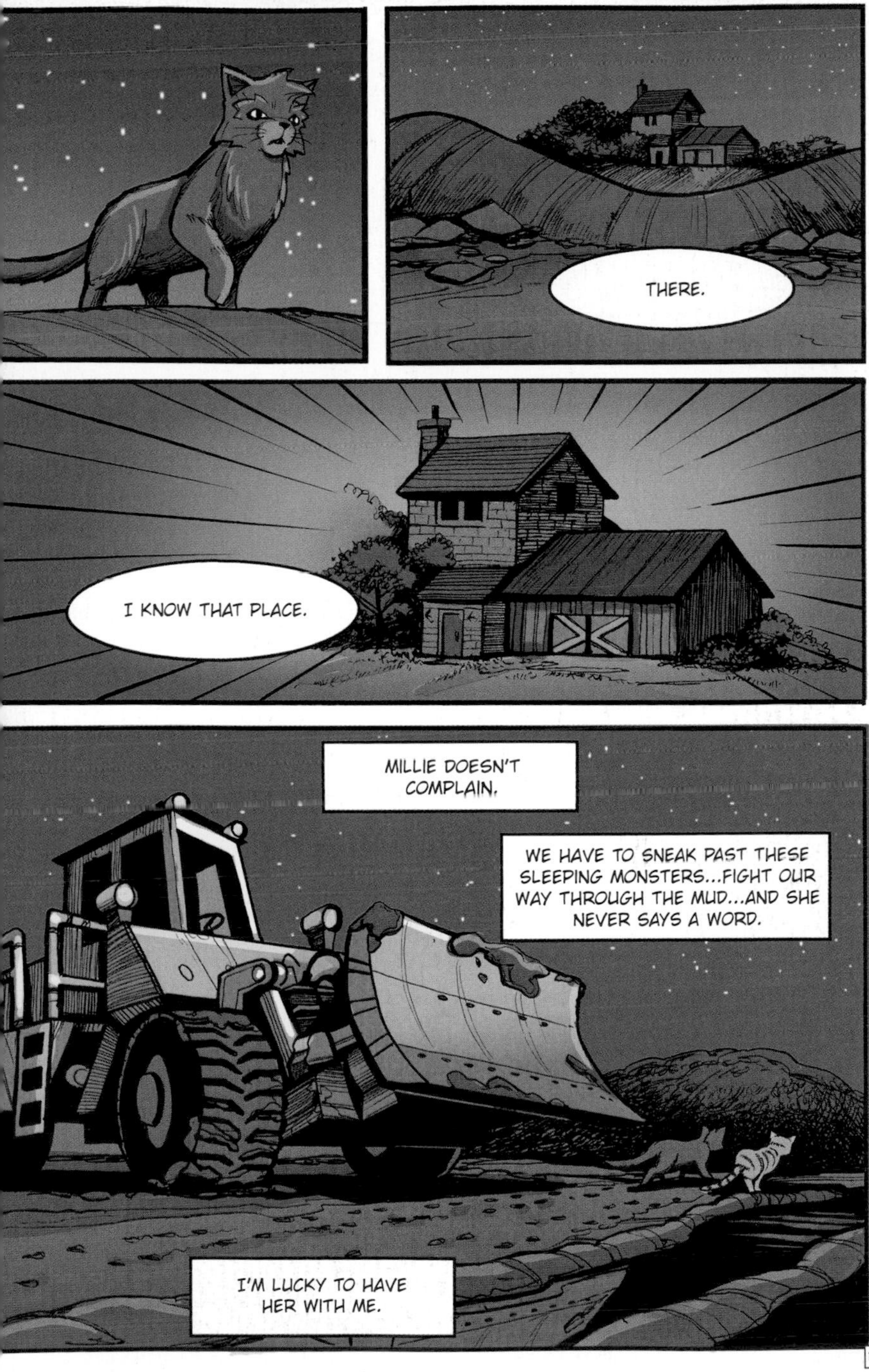
THERE.
I KNOW THAT PLACE.
MILLIE DOESN'T COMPLAIN.
WE HAVE TO SNEAK PAST THESE SLEEPING MONSTERS...FIGHT OUR WAY THROUGH THE MUD...AND SHE NEVER SAYS A WORD.
I'M LUCKY TO HAVE HER WITH ME.

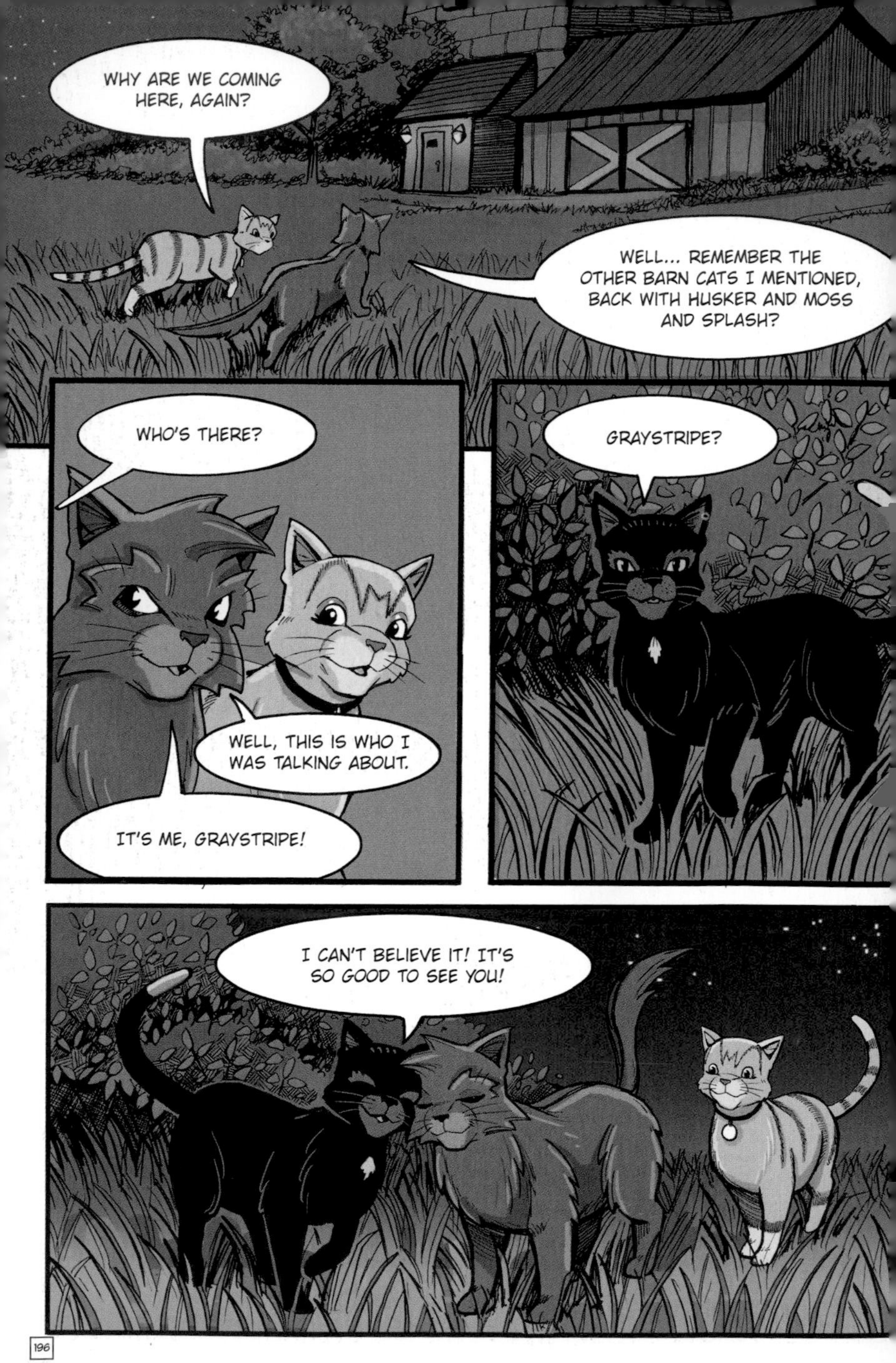
WHY ARE WE COMING HERE, AGAIN?
WELL... REMEMBER THE OTHER BARN CATS I MENTIONED, BACK WITH HUSKER AND MOSS AND SPLASH?
WHO'S THERE?
WELL, THIS IS WHO I WAS TALKING ABOUT.
IT'S ME, GRAYSTRIPE!
GRAYSTRIPE?
I CAN'T BELIEVE IT! IT'S SO GOOD TO SEE YOU!

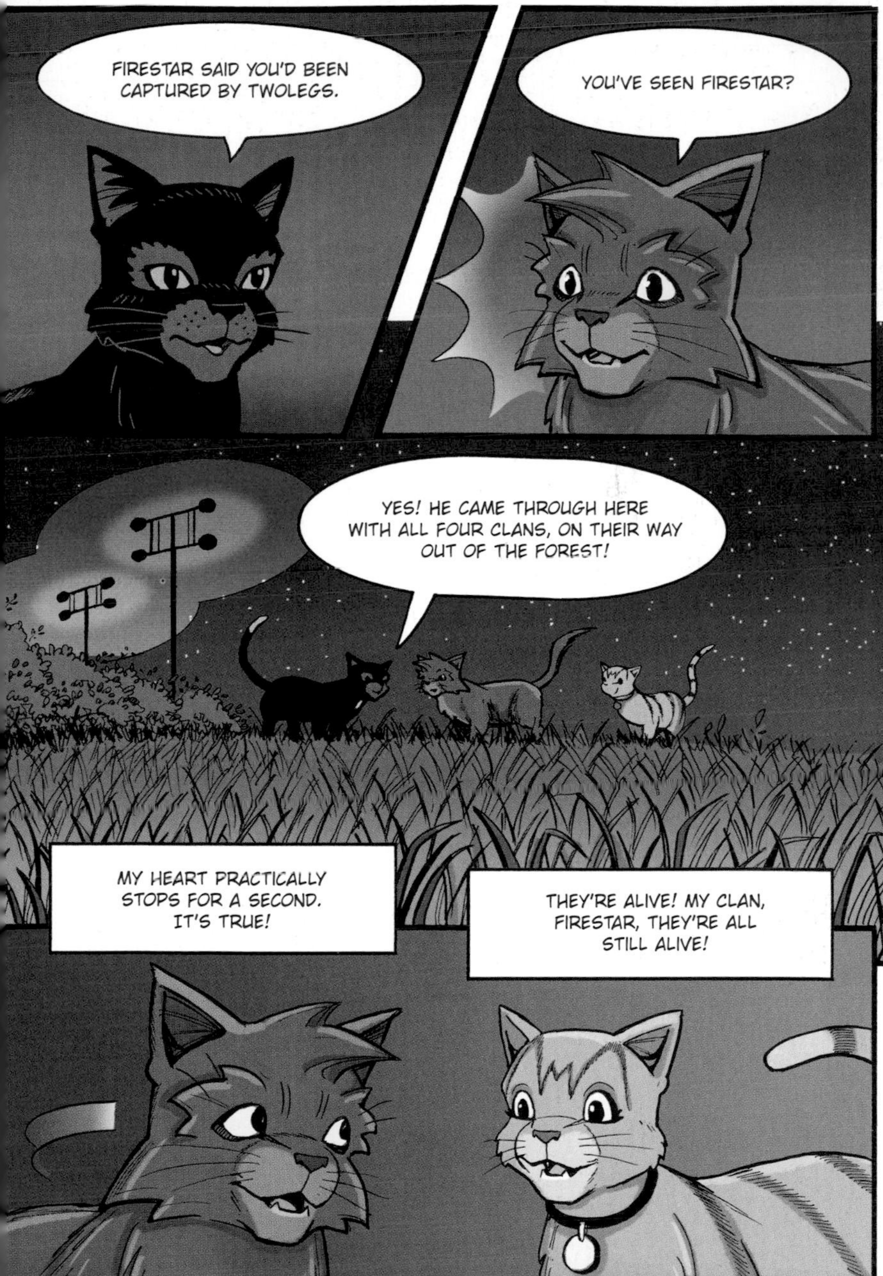

FIRESTAR SAID YOU'D BEEN CAPTURED BY TWOLEGS.
YOU'VE SEEN FIRESTAR?
YES! HE CAME THROUGH HERE WITH ALL FOUR CLANS, ON THEIR WAY OUT OF THE FOREST!
MY HEART PRACTICALLY STOPS FOR A SECOND. IT'S TRUE!
THEY'RE ALIVE! MY CLAN, FIRESTAR, THEY'RE ALL STILL ALIVE!

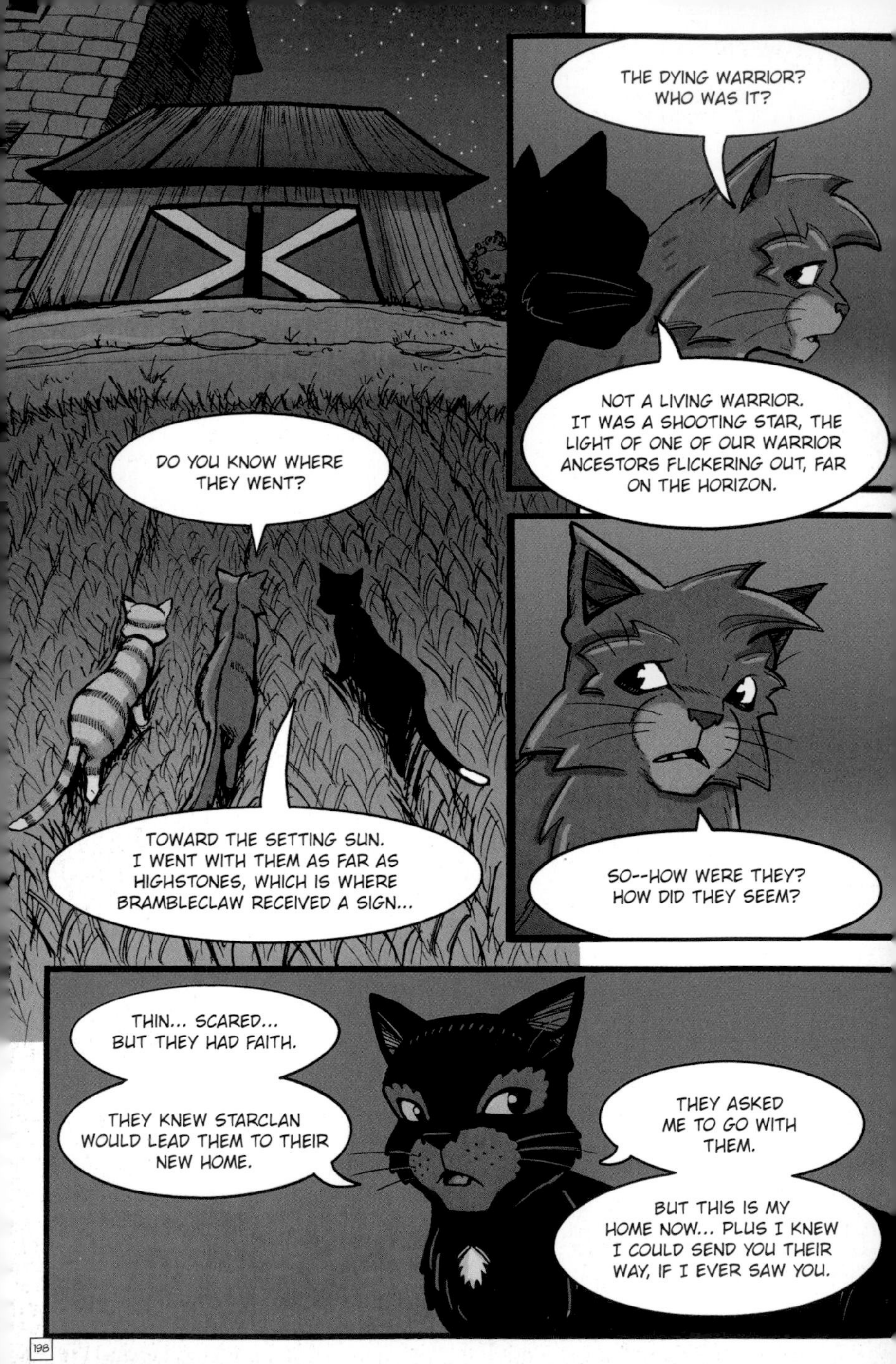
DO YOU KNOW WHERE THEY WENT?
TOWARD THE SETTING SUN. I WENT WITH THEM AS FAR AS HIGHSTONES, WHICH IS WHERE BRAMBLECLAW RECEIVED A SIGN...
THE DYING WARRIOR? WHO WAS IT?
NOT A LIVING WARRIOR. IT WAS A SHOOTING STAR, THE LIGHT OF ONE OF OUR WARRIOR ANCESTORS FLICKERING OUT, FAR ON THE HORIZON.
SO--HOW WERE THEY? HOW DID THEY SEEM?
THIN... SCARED... BUT THEY HAD FAITH.
THEY KNEW STARCLAN WOULD LEAD THEM TO THEIR NEW HOME.
THEY ASKED ME TO GO WITH THEM.
BUT THIS IS MY HOME NOW... PLUS I KNEW I COULD SEND YOU THEIR WAY, IF I EVER SAW YOU.

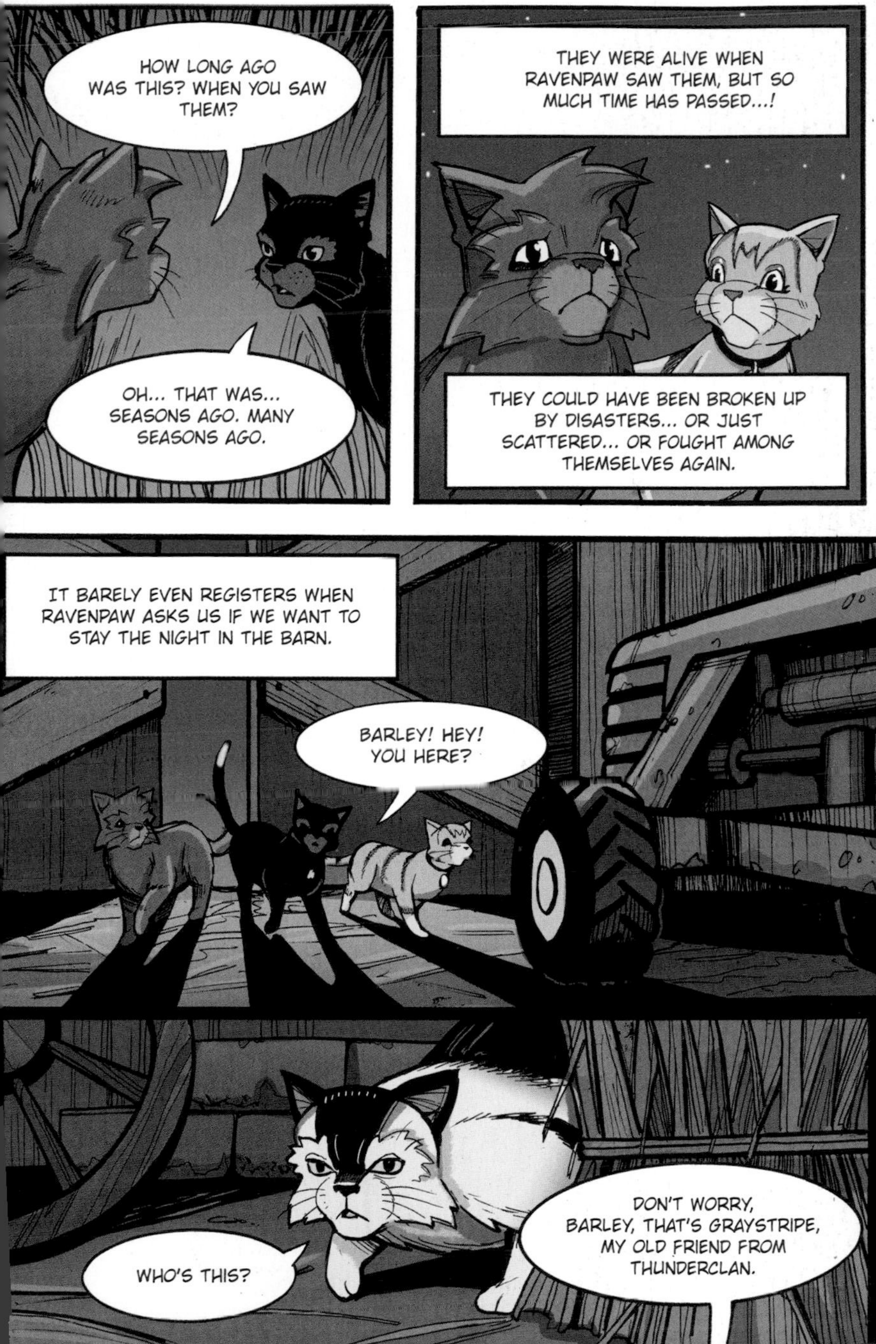
HOW LONG AGO WAS THIS? WHEN YOU SAW THEM?
OH... THAT WAS... SEASONS AGO. MANY SEASONS AGO.
THEY WERE ALIVE WHEN RAVENPAW SAW THEM, BUT SO MUCH TIME HAS PASSED...!
THEY COULD HAVE BEEN BROKEN UP BY DISASTERS... OR JUST SCATTERED... OR FOUGHT AMONG THEMSELVES AGAIN.
IT BARELY EVEN REGISTERS WHEN RAVENPAW ASKS US IF WE WANT TO STAY THE NIGHT IN THE BARN.
BARLEY! HEY! YOU HERE?
WHO'S THIS?
DON'T WORRY, BARLEY, THAT'S GRAYSTRIPE, MY OLD FRIEND FROM THUNDERCLAN.

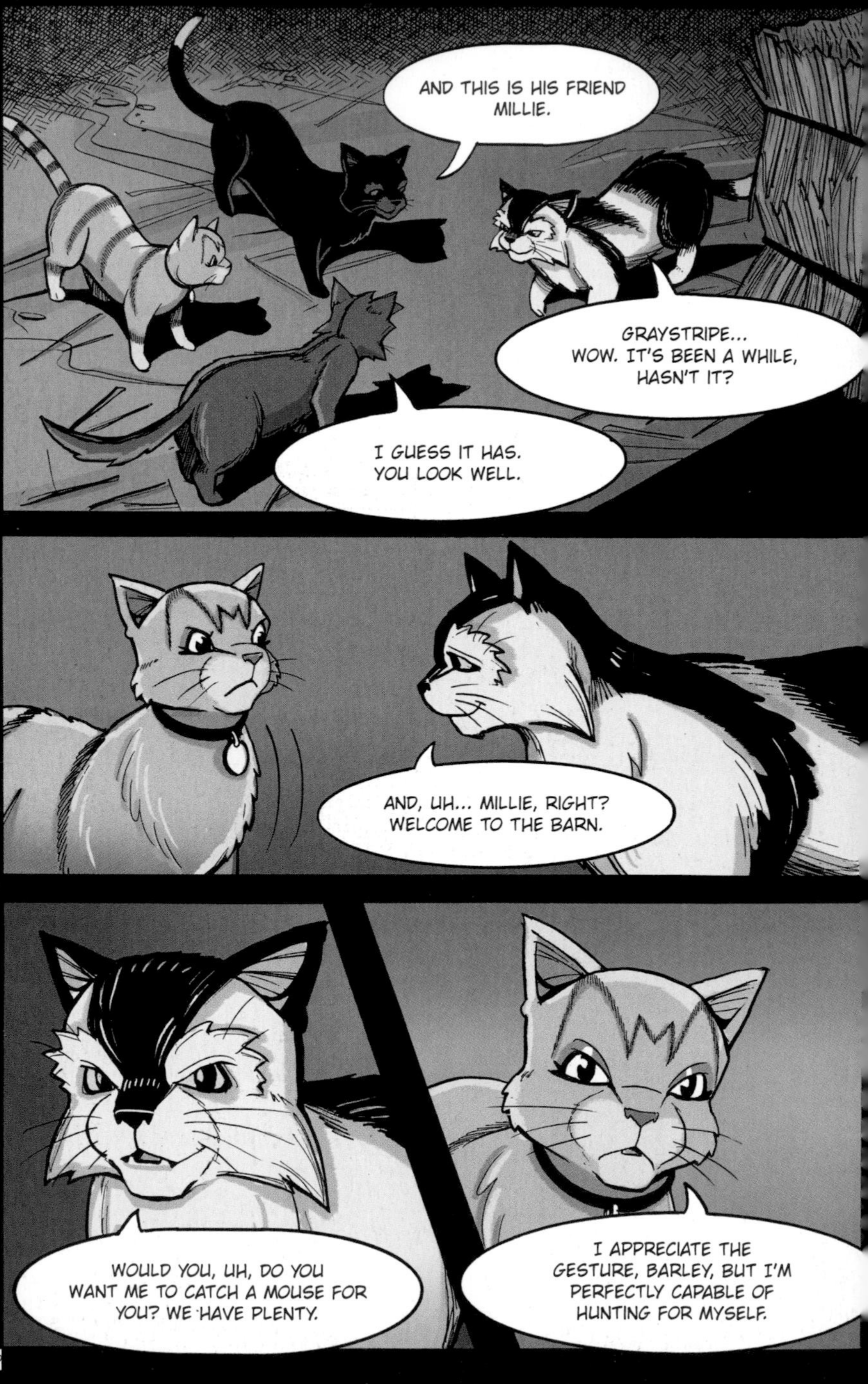
AND THIS IS HIS FRIEND MILLIE.
GRAYSTRIPE... WOW. IT'S BEEN A WHILE, HASN'T IT?
I GUESS IT HAS. YOU LOOK WELL.
AND, UH... MILLIE, RIGHT? WELCOME TO THE BARN.
WOULD YOU, UH, DO YOU WANT ME TO CATCH A MOUSE FOR YOU? WE HAVE PLENTY.
I APPRECIATE THE GESTURE, BARLEY, BUT I'M PERFECTLY CAPABLE OF HUNTING FOR MYSELF.

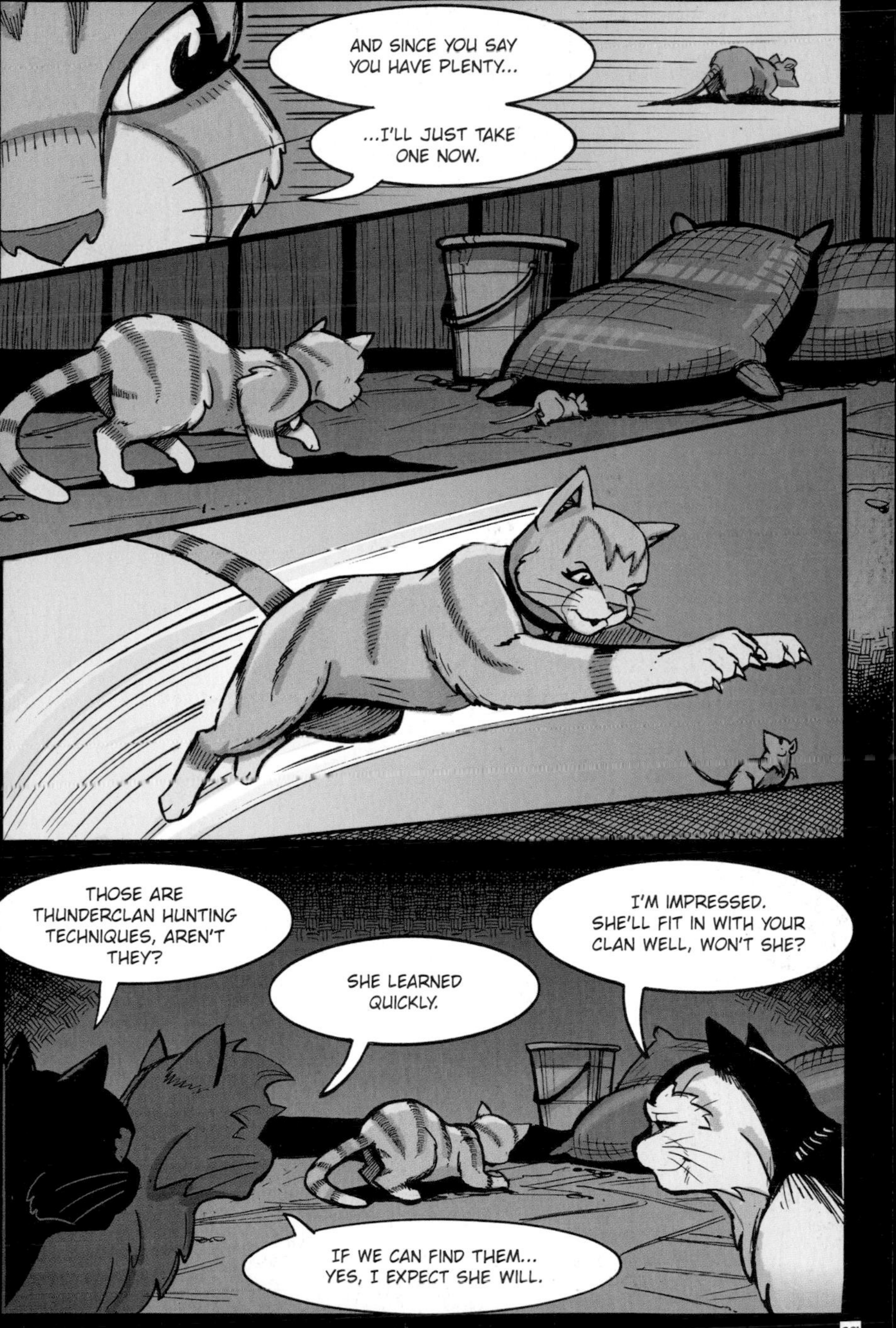
AND SINCE YOU SAY YOU HAVE PLENTY...
...I'LL JUST TAKE ONE NOW.
THOSE ARE THUNDERCLAN HUNTING TECHNIQUES, AREN'T THEY?
SHE LEARNED QUICKLY.
I'M IMPRESSED. SHE'LL FIT IN WITH YOUR CLAN WELL, WON'T SHE?
IF WE CAN FIND THEM... YES, I EXPECT SHE WILL.

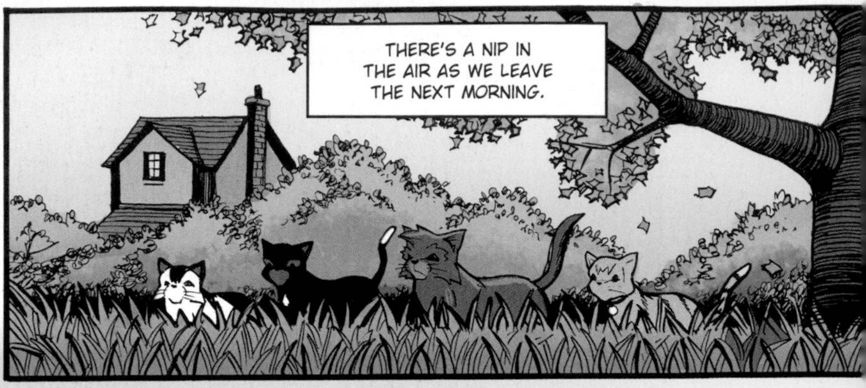
THERE'S A NIP IN THE AIR AS WE LEAVE THE NEXT MORNING.

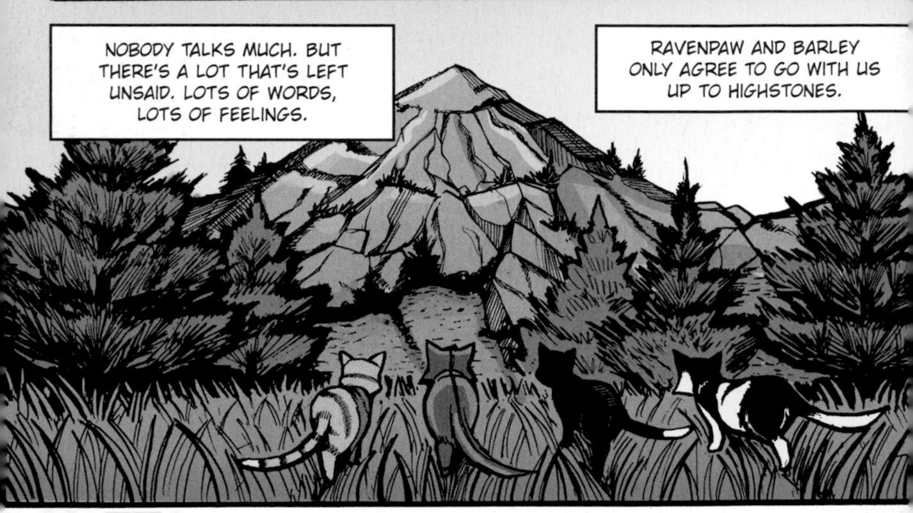
NOBODY TALKS MUCH. BUT THERE'S A LOT THAT'S LEFT UNSAID. LOTS OF WORDS, LOTS OF FEELINGS.
RAVENPAW AND BARLEY ONLY AGREE TO GO WITH US UP TO HIGHSTONES.

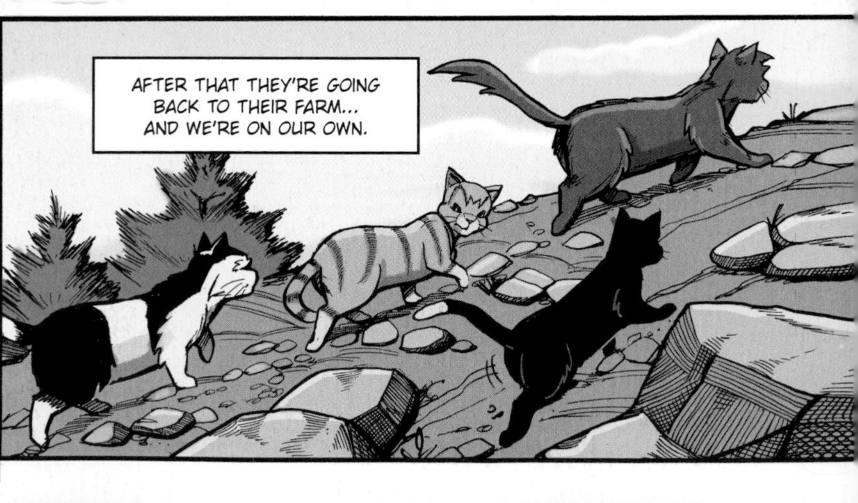
AFTER THAT THEY'RE GOING BACK TO THEIR FARM... AND WE'RE ON OUR OWN.

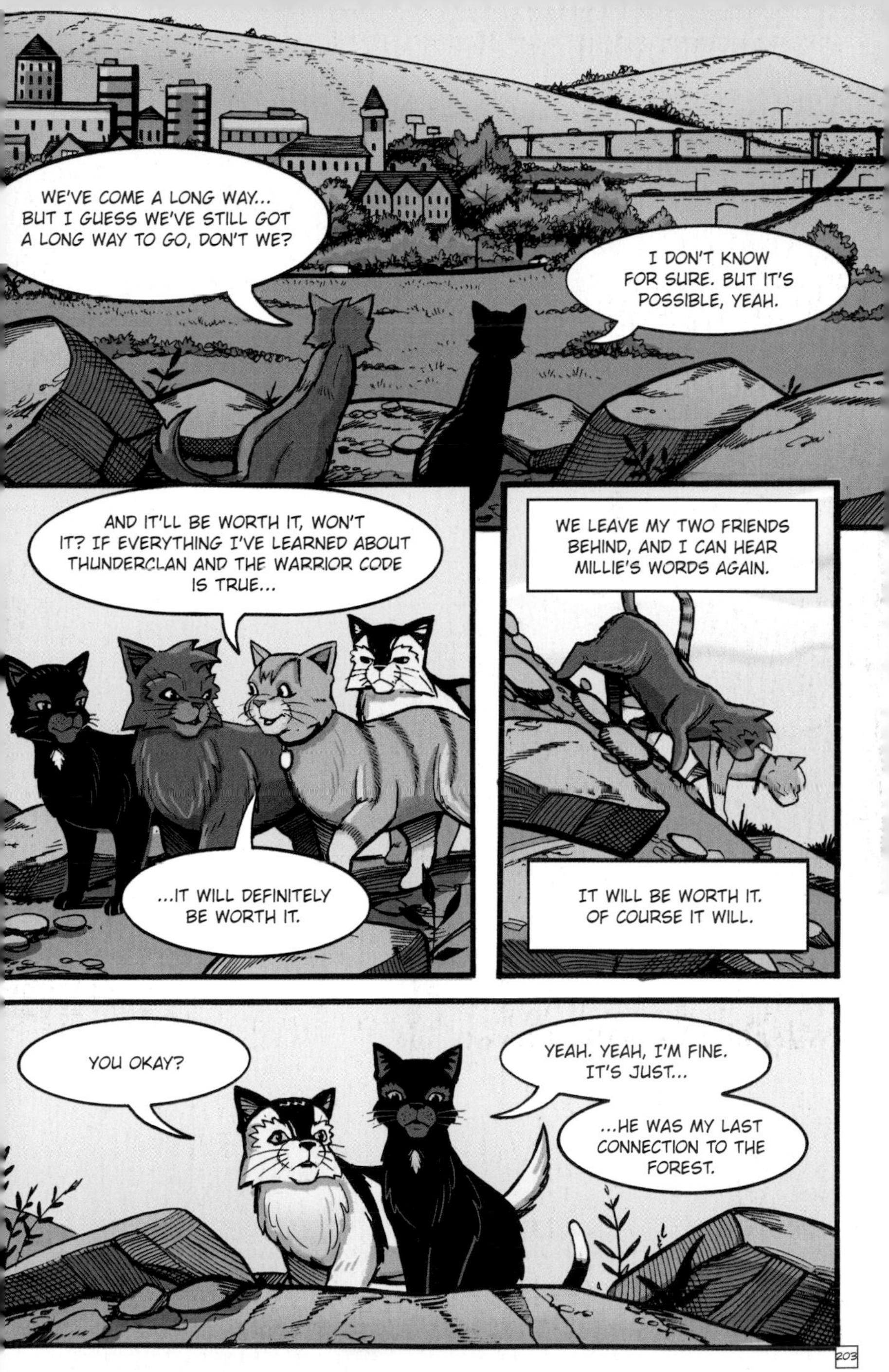
WE'VE COME A LONG WAY... BUT I GUESS WE'VE STILL GOT A LONG WAY TO GO, DON'T WE?
I DON'T KNOW FOR SURE. BUT IT'S POSSIBLE, YEAH.
AND IT'LL BE WORTH IT, WON'T IT? IF EVERYTHING I'VE LEARNED ABOUT THUNDERCLAN AND THE WARRIOR CODE IS TRUE...
...IT WILL DEFINITELY BE WORTH IT.
WE LEAVE MY TWO FRIENDS BEHIND, AND I CAN HEAR MILLIE'S WORDS AGAIN.
IT WILL BE WORTH IT. OF COURSE IT WILL.
YOU OKAY?
YEAH. YEAH, I'M FINE. IT'S JUST...
...HE WAS MY LAST CONNECTION TO THE FOREST.

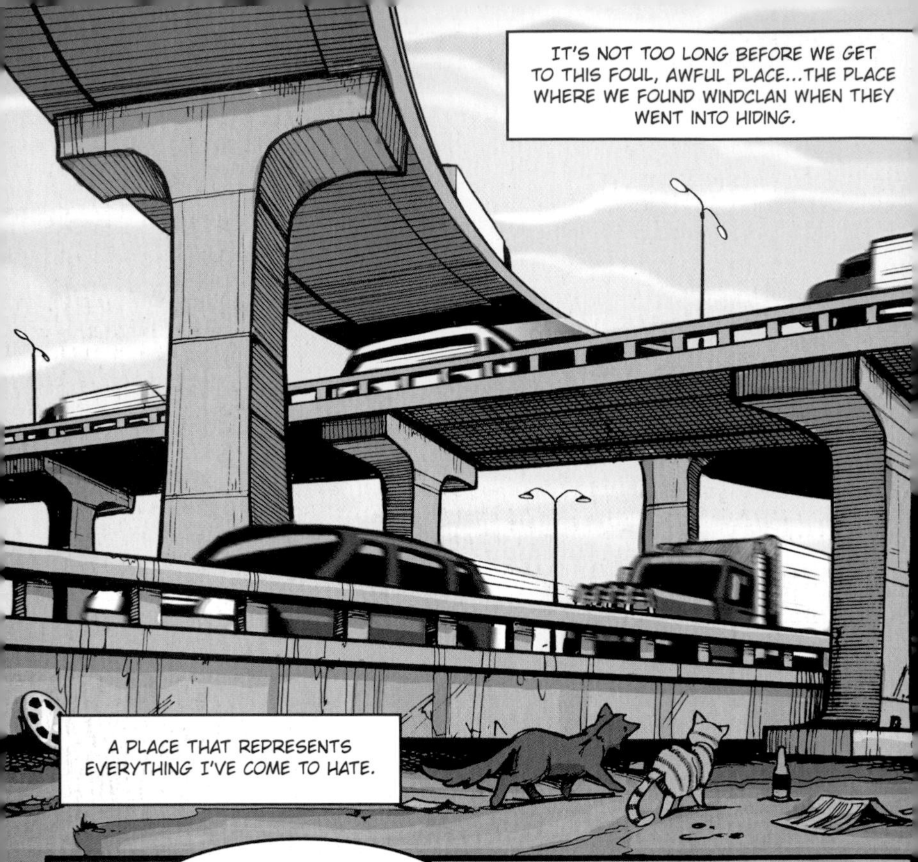
IT'S NOT TOO LONG BEFORE WE GET TO THIS FOUL, AWFUL PLACE...THE PLACE WHERE WE FOUND WINDCLAN WHEN THEY WENT INTO HIDING.
A PLACE THAT REPRESENTS EVERYTHING I'VE COME TO HATE.
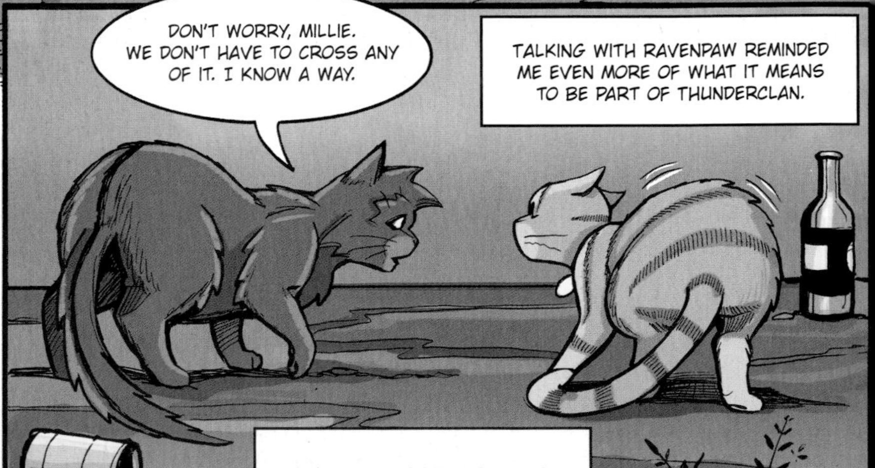
DON'T WORRY, MILLIE. WE DON'T HAVE TO CROSS ANY OF IT. I KNOW A WAY.
TALKING WITH RAVENPAW REMINDED ME EVEN MORE OF WHAT IT MEANS TO BE PART OF THUNDERCLAN.
IT'S TIME I EMBRACED THAT.

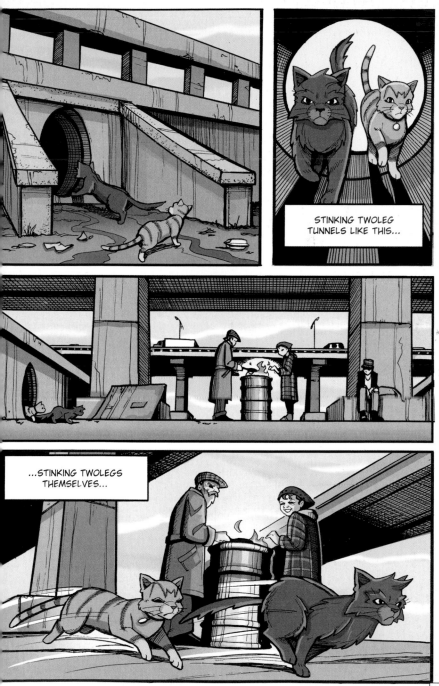

STINKING TWOLEG
TUNNELS LIKE THIS...

...STINKING TWOLEGS
THEMSELVES...

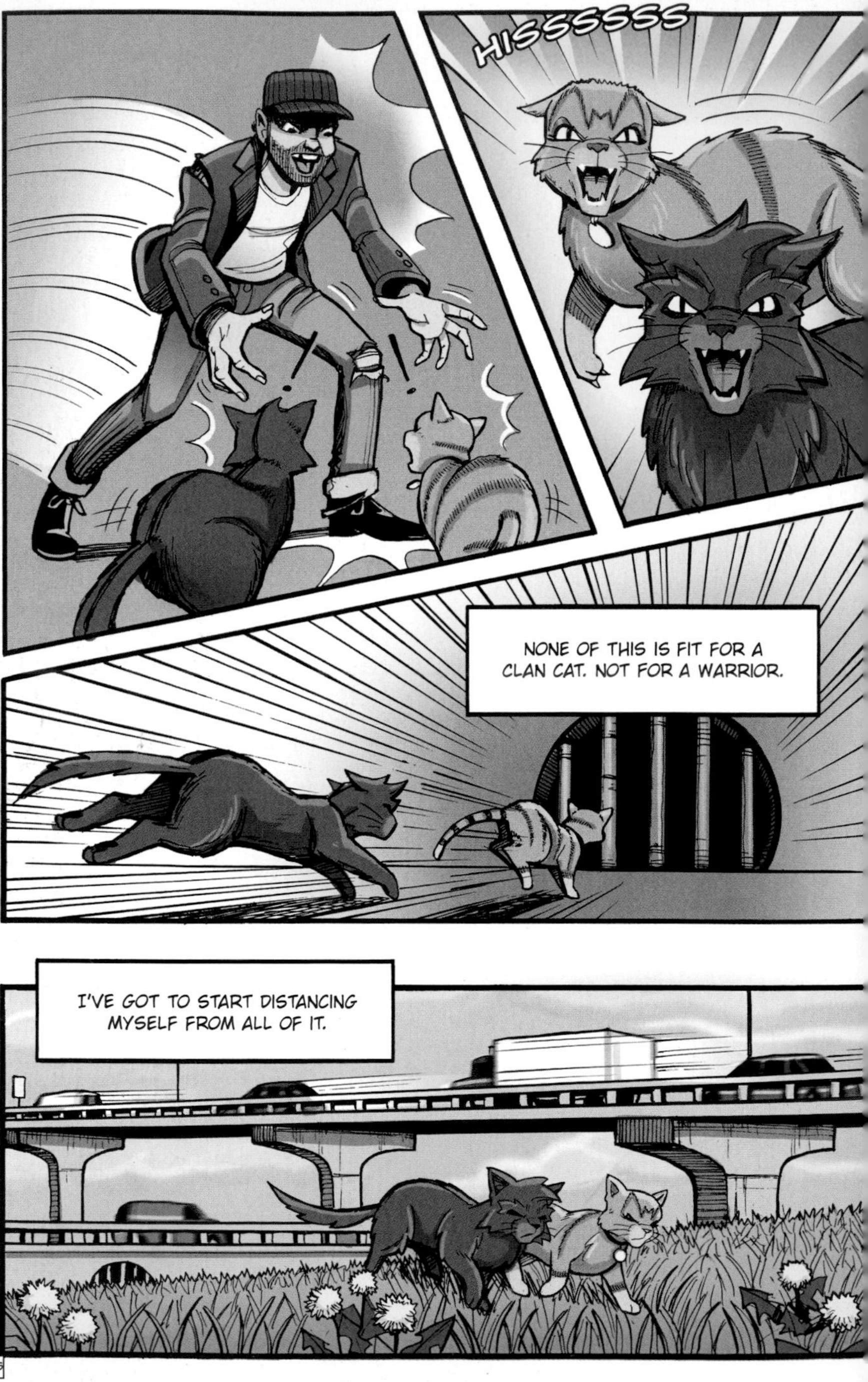
HISSSSSS
NONE OF THIS IS FIT FOR A CLAN CAT. NOT FOR A WARRIOR.
I'VE GOT TO START DISTANCING MYSELF FROM ALL OF IT.

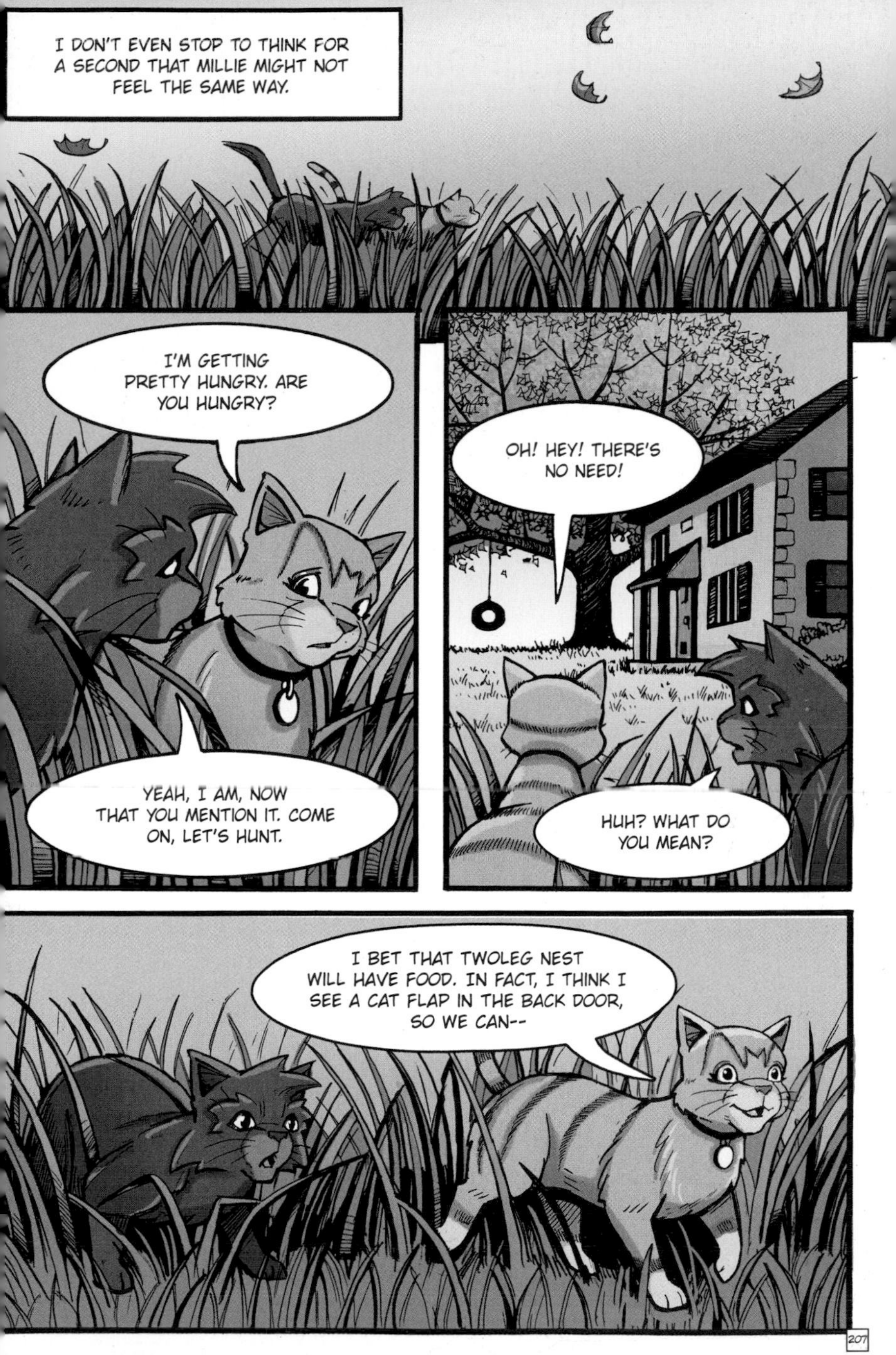
I DON'T EVEN STOP TO THINK FOR A SECOND THAT MILLIE MIGHT NOT FEEL THE SAME WAY.
I'M GETTING PRETTY HUNGRY. ARE YOU HUNGRY?
YEAH, I AM, NOW THAT YOU MENTION IT. COME ON, LET'S HUNT.
OH! HEY! THERE'S NO NEED!
HUH? WHAT DO YOU MEAN?
I BET THAT TWOLEG NEST WILL HAVE FOOD. IN FACT, I THINK I SEE A CAT FLAP IN THE BACK DOOR, SO WE CAN--

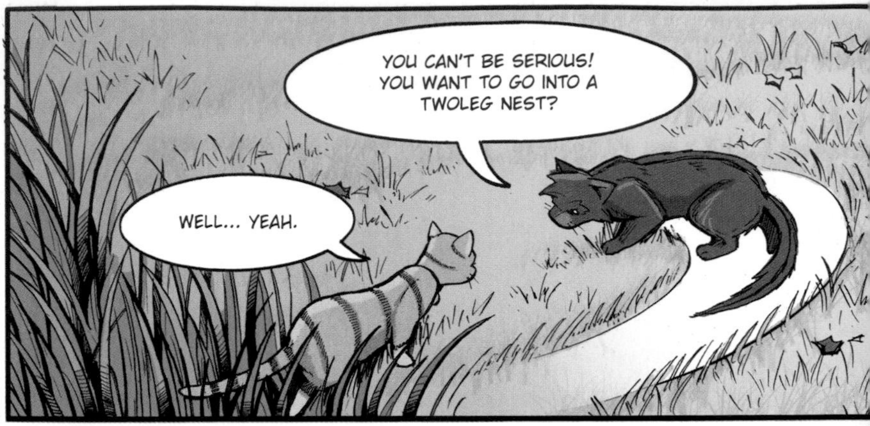
YOU CAN'T BE SERIOUS! YOU WANT TO GO INTO A TWOLEG NEST?
WELL... YEAH.

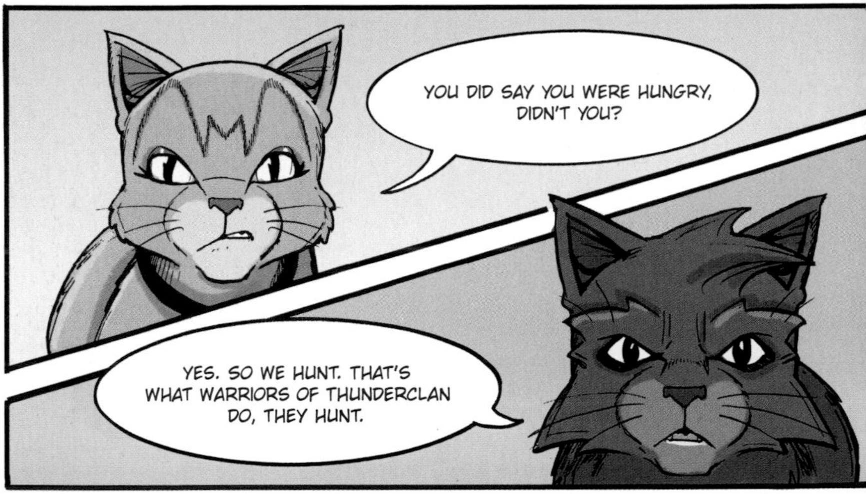
YOU DID SAY YOU WERE HUNGRY, DIDN'T YOU?
YES. SO WE HUNT. THAT'S WHAT WARRIORS OF THUNDERCLAN DO, THEY HUNT.

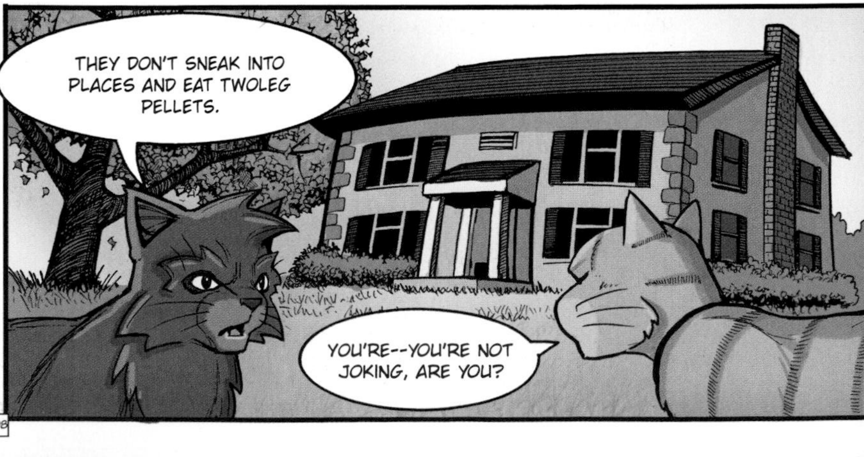
THEY DON'T SNEAK INTO PLACES AND EAT TWOLEG PELLETS.
YOU'RE--YOU'RE NOT JOKING, ARE YOU?

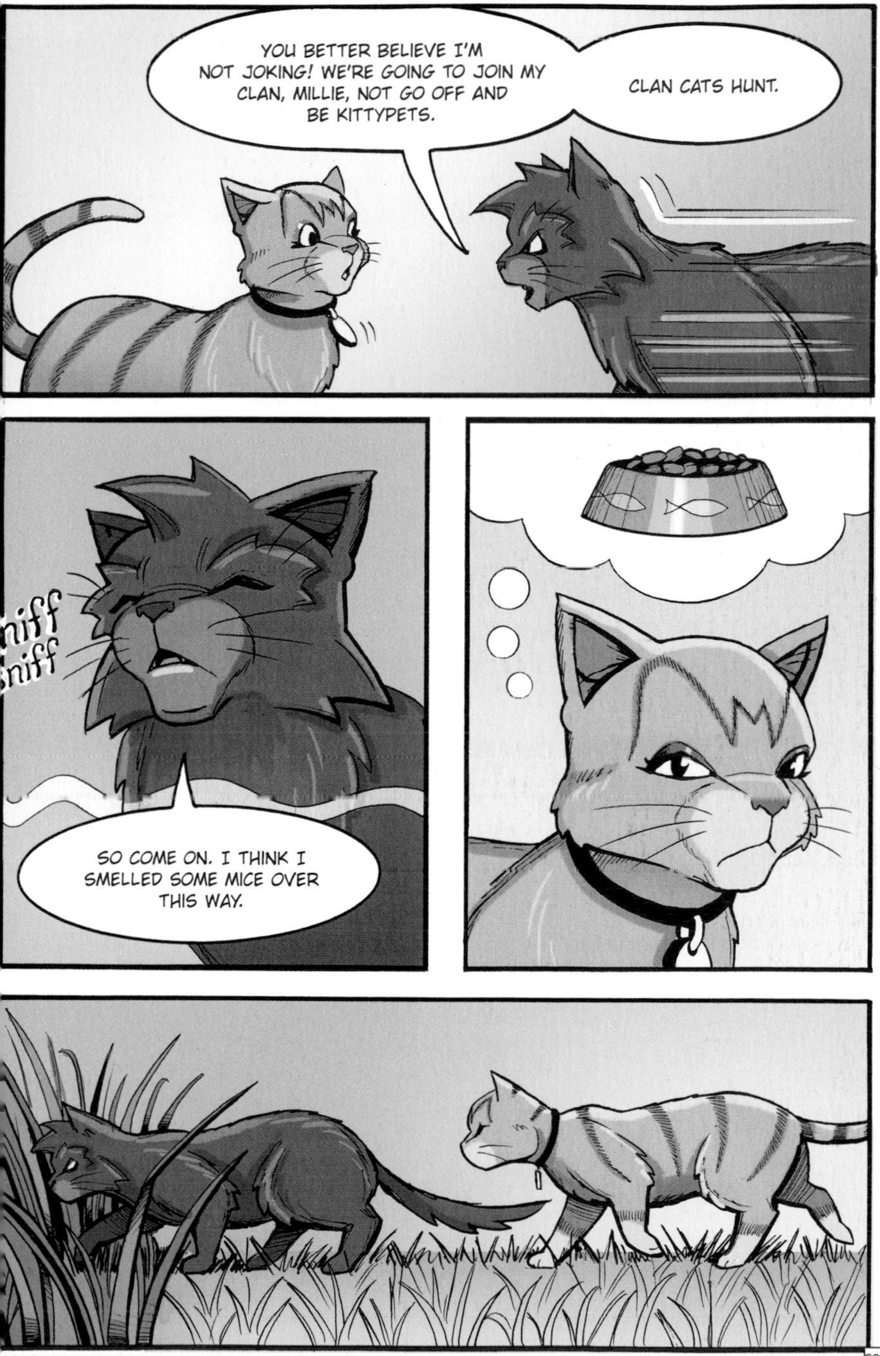
YOU BETTER BELIEVE I'M NOT JOKING! WE'RE GOING TO JOIN MY CLAN, MILLIE, NOT GO OFF AND BE KITTYPETS.
CLAN CATS HUNT.
SO COME ON. I THINK I SMELLED SOME MICE OVER THIS WAY.

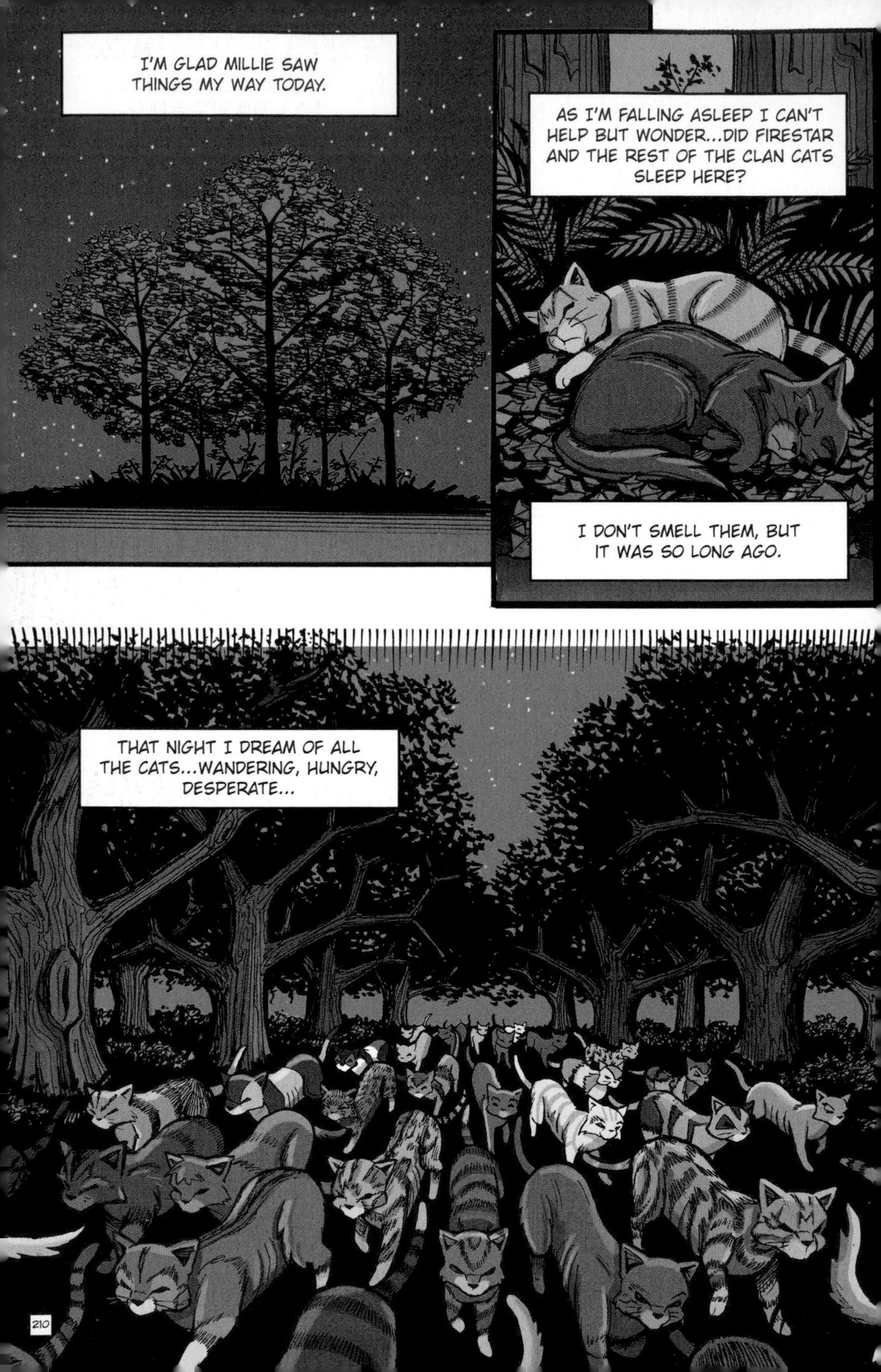
I'M GLAD MILLIE SAW THINGS MY WAY TODAY.
AS I'M FALLING ASLEEP I CAN'T HELP BUT WONDER...DID FIRESTAR AND THE REST OF THE CLAN CATS SLEEP HERE?
I DON'T SMELL THEM, BUT IT WAS SO LONG AGO.
THAT NIGHT I DREAM OF ALL THE CATS...WANDERING, HUNGRY, DESPERATE...

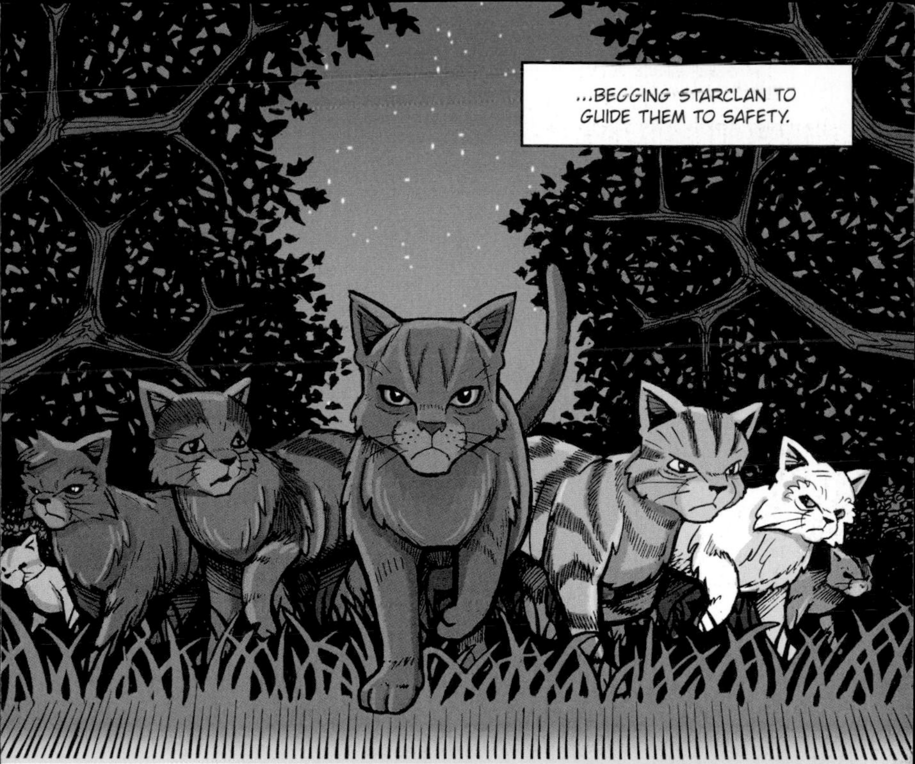
...BEGGING STARCLAN TO
GUIDE THEM TO SAFETY.

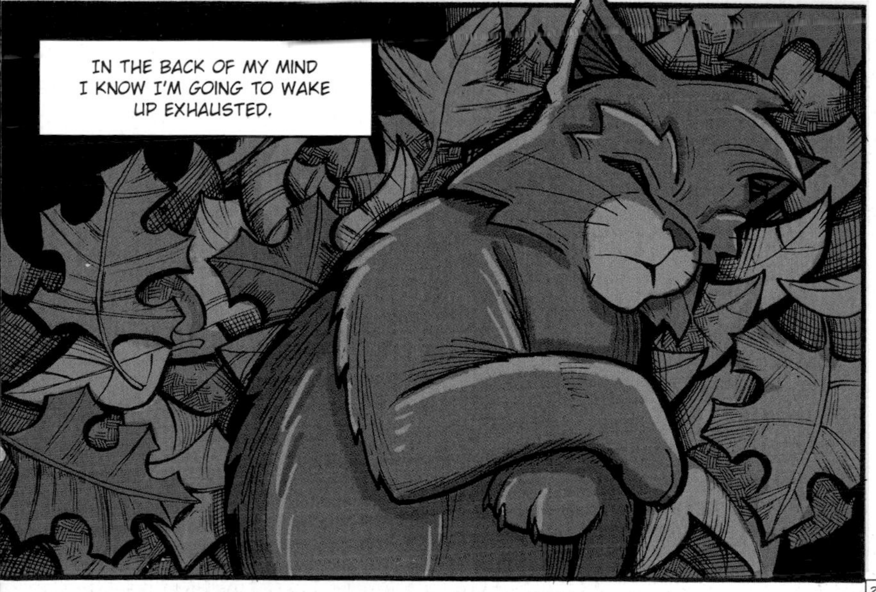
IN THE BACK OF MY MIND
I KNOW I'M GOING TO WAKE
UP EXHAUSTED.

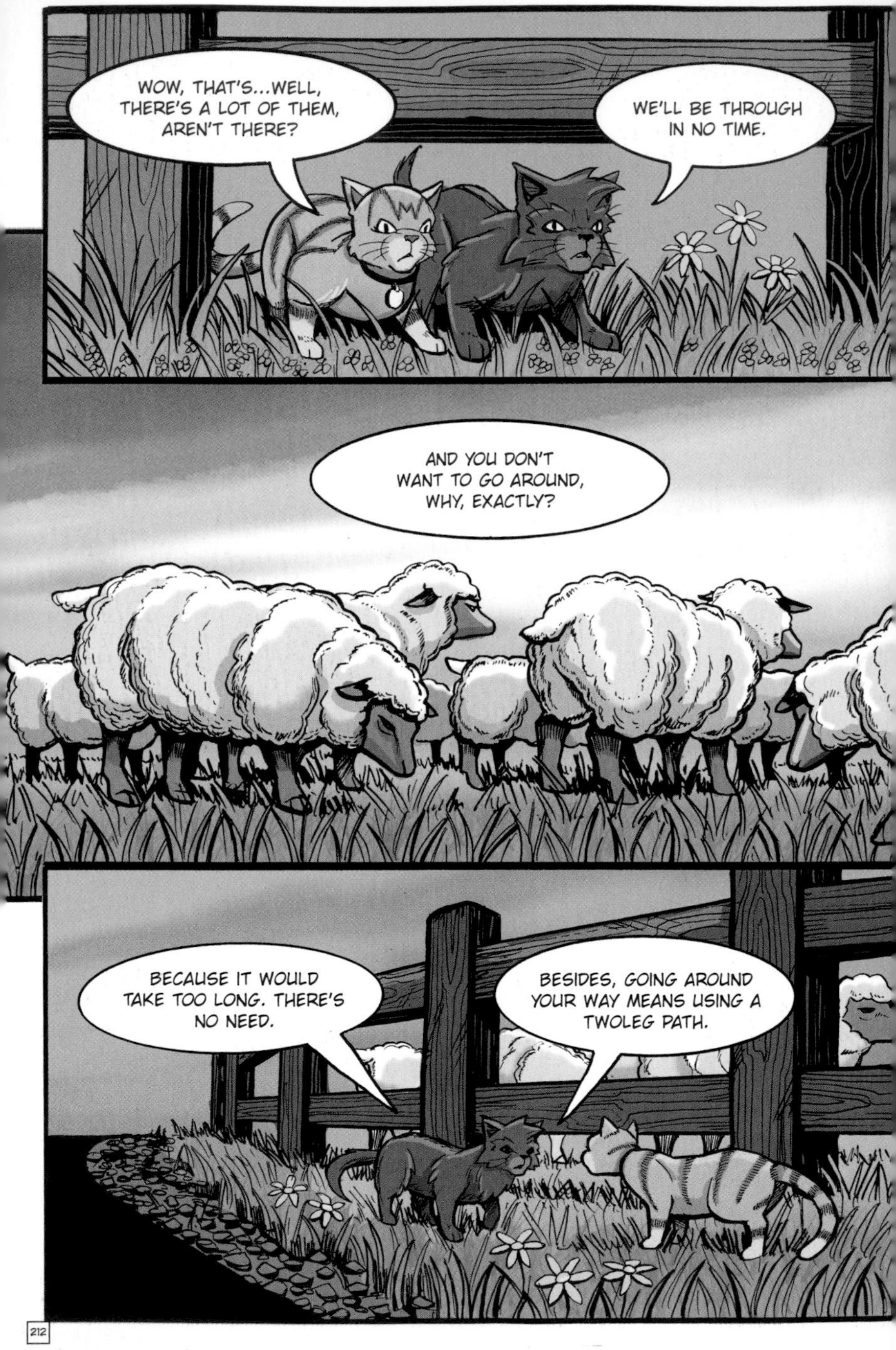
WOW, THAT'S...WELL, THERE'S A LOT OF THEM, AREN'T THERE?
WE'LL BE THROUGH IN NO TIME.
AND YOU DON'T WANT TO GO AROUND, WHY, EXACTLY?
BECAUSE IT WOULD TAKE TOO LONG. THERE'S NO NEED.
BESIDES, GOING AROUND YOUR WAY MEANS USING A TWOLEG PATH.

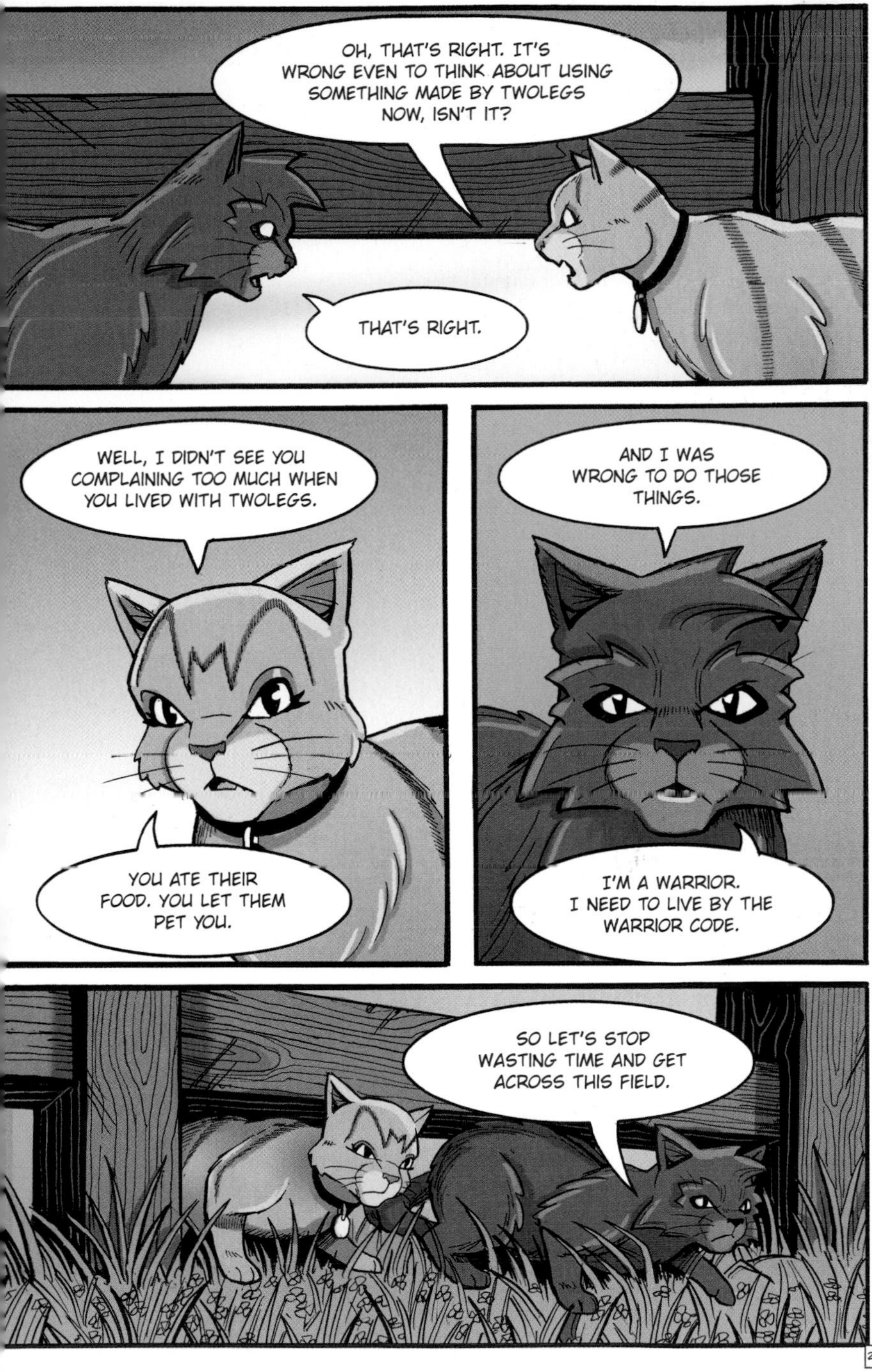
OH, THAT'S RIGHT. IT'S WRONG EVEN TO THINK ABOUT USING SOMETHING MADE BY TWOLEGS NOW, ISN'T IT?
THAT'S RIGHT.
WELL, I DIDN'T SEE YOU COMPLAINING TOO MUCH WHEN YOU LIVED WITH TWOLEGS.
YOU ATE THEIR FOOD. YOU LET THEM PET YOU.
AND I WAS WRONG TO DO THOSE THINGS.
I'M A WARRIOR. I NEED TO LIVE BY THE WARRIOR CODE.
SO LET'S STOP WASTING TIME AND GET ACROSS THIS FIELD.

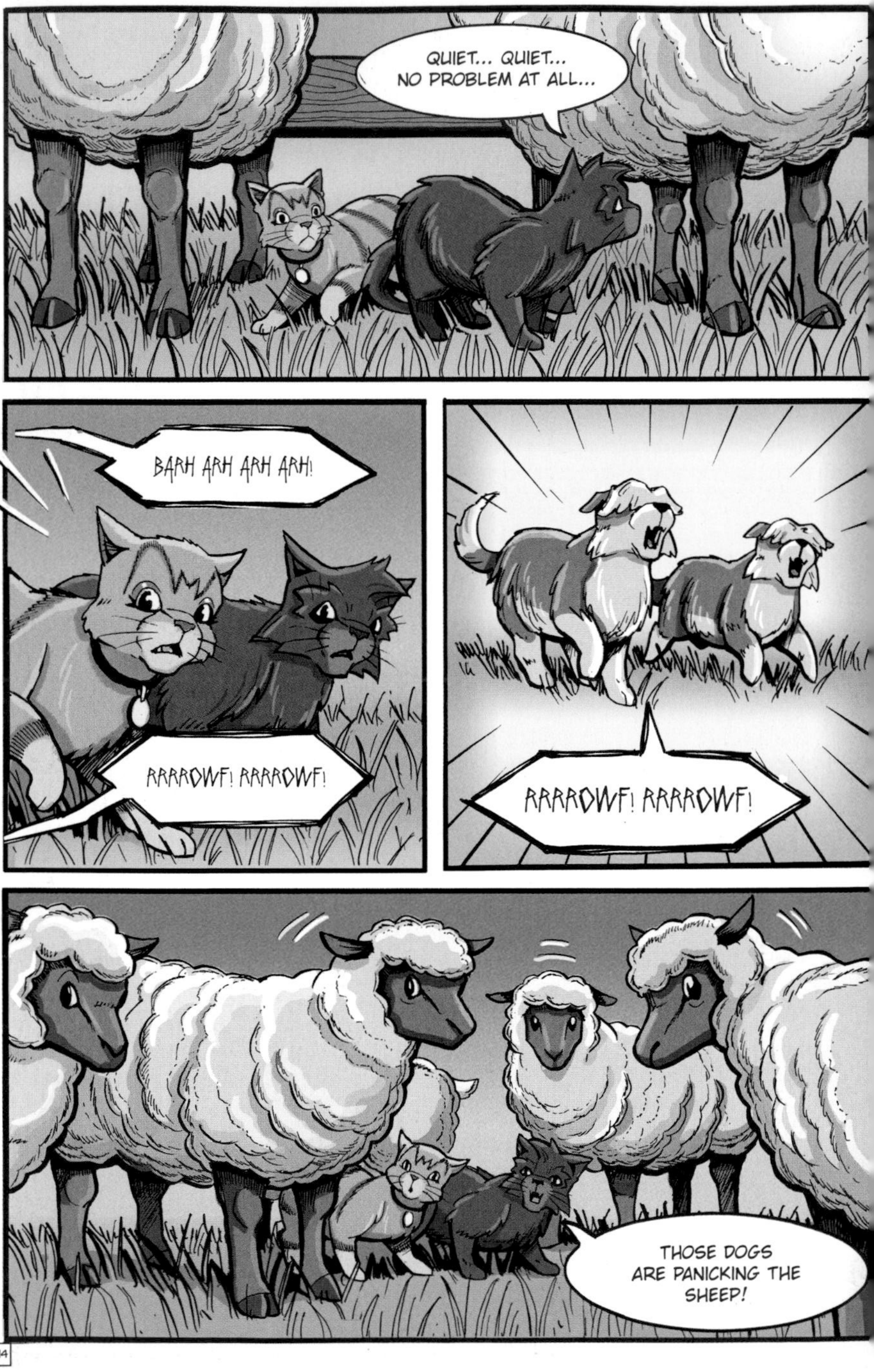

QUIET... QUIET... NO PROBLEM AT ALL...
BARH ARH ARH ARH!
RRRROWF! RRRROWF!
RRRROWF! RRRROWF!
THOSE DOGS ARE PANICKING THE SHEEP!

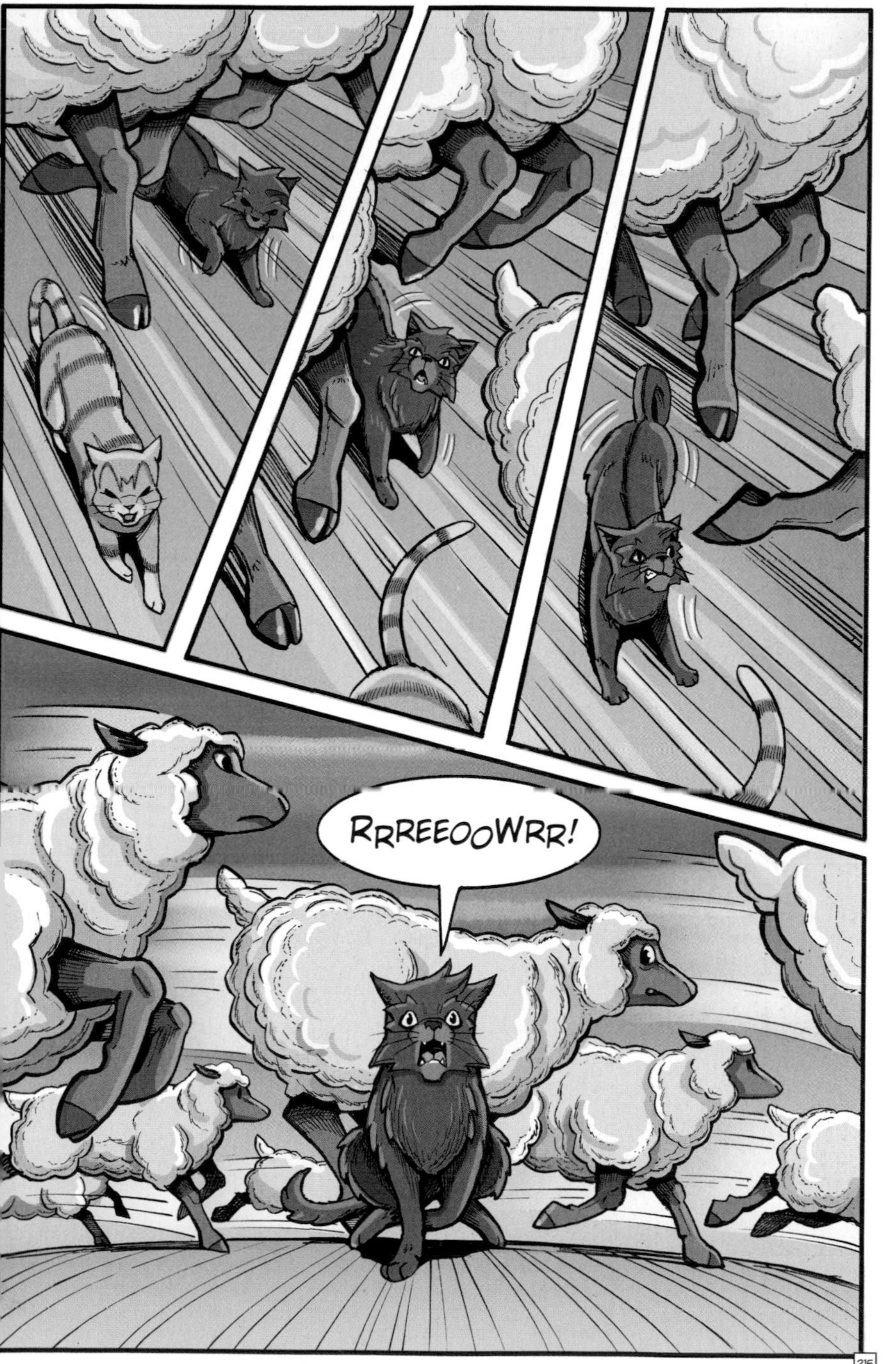
RRREEOOWRR!

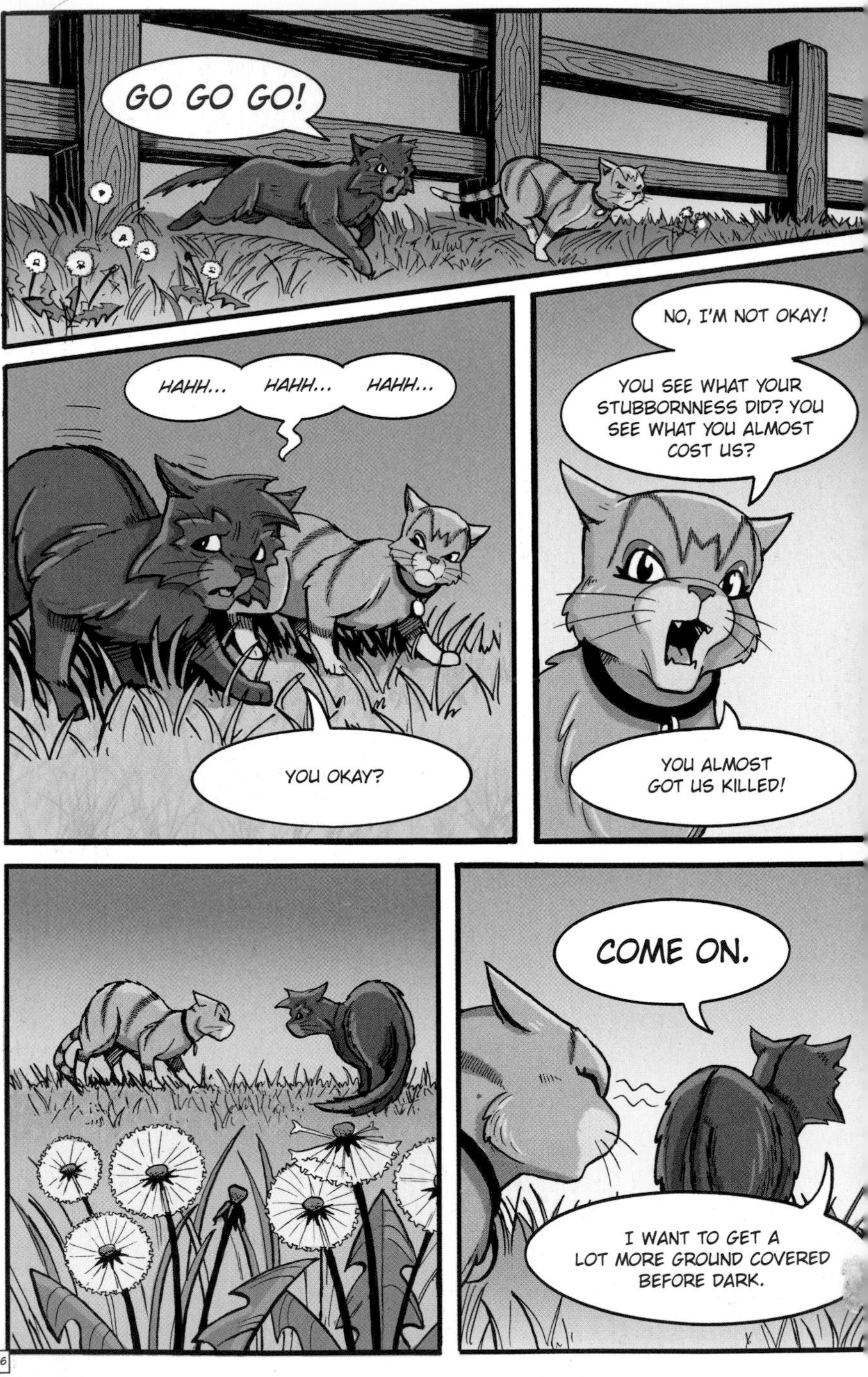
GO GO GO!
HAHH... HAHH... HAHH...
YOU OKAY?
NO, I'M NOT OKAY!
YOU SEE WHAT YOUR STUBBORNNESS DID? YOU SEE WHAT YOU ALMOST COST US?
YOU ALMOST GOT US KILLED!
COME ON.
I WANT TO GET A LOT MORE GROUND COVERED BEFORE DARK.

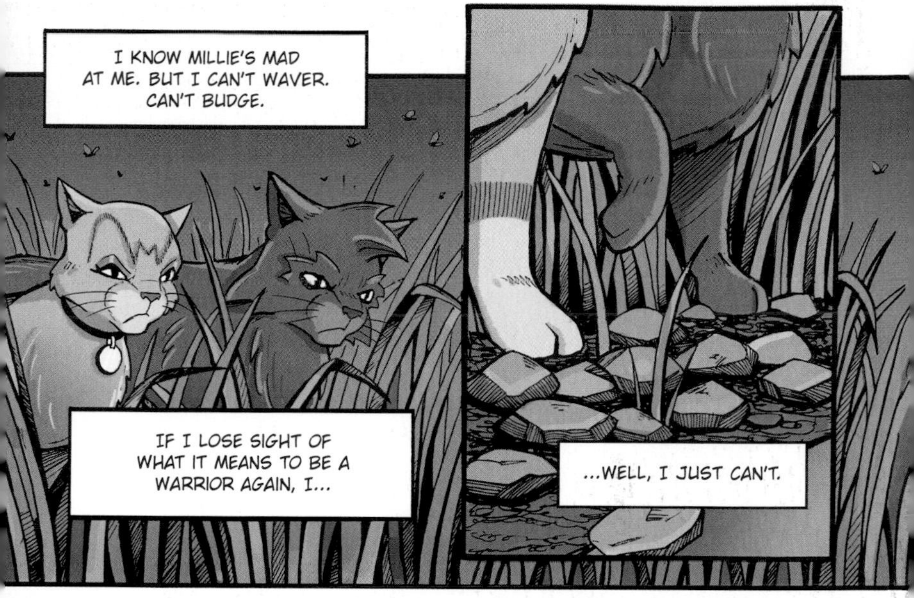
I KNOW MILLIE'S MAD AT ME. BUT I CAN'T WAVER. CAN'T BUDGE.
IF I LOSE SIGHT OF WHAT IT MEANS TO BE A WARRIOR AGAIN, I...
...WELL, I JUST CAN'T.

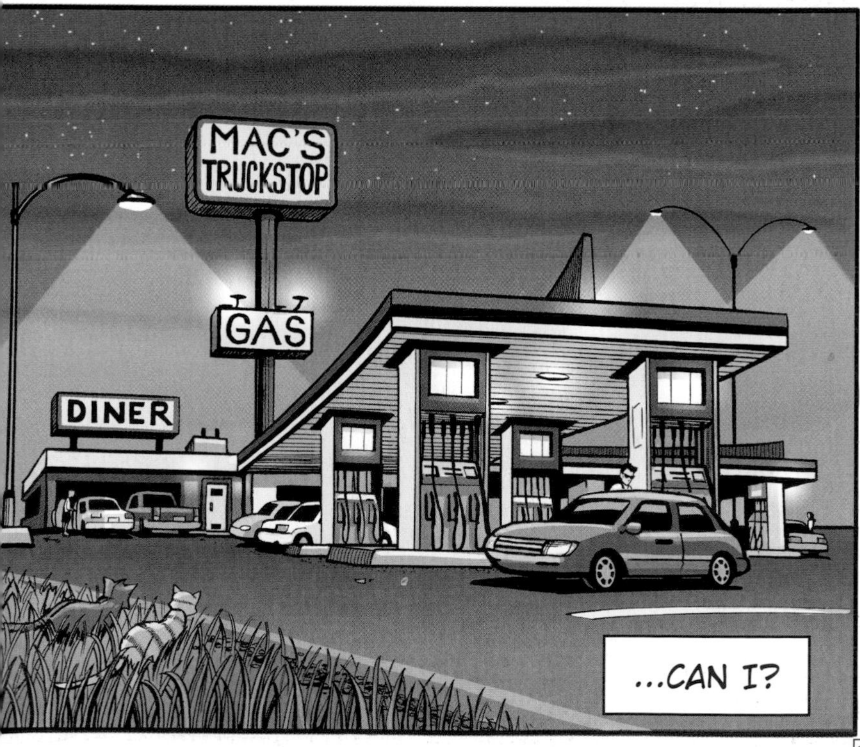
MAC'S TRUCKSTOP
GAS
DINER
...CAN I?

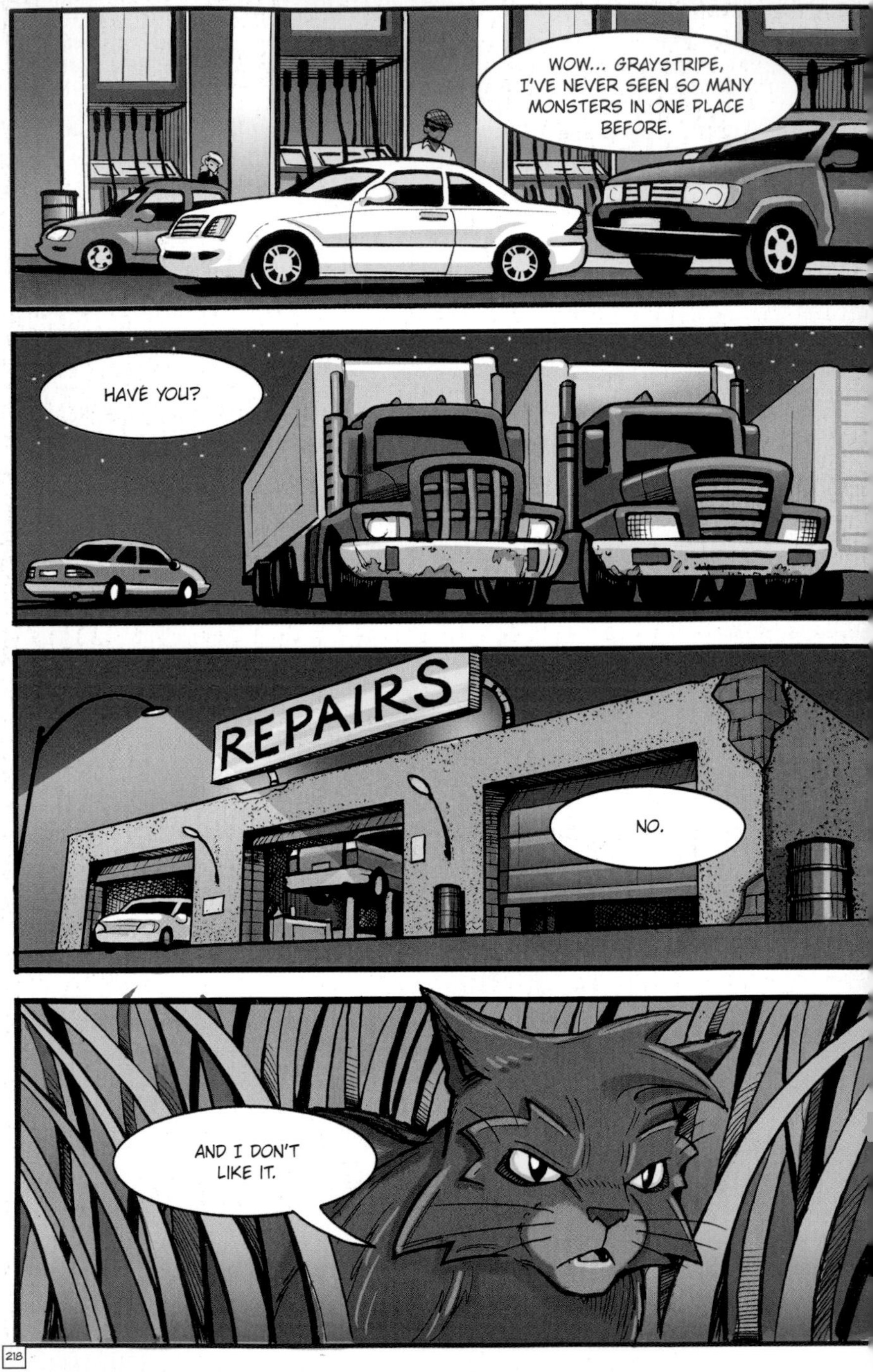
WOW... GRAYSTRIPE, I'VE NEVER SEEN SO MANY MONSTERS IN ONE PLACE BEFORE.
HAVE YOU?
REPAIRS
NO.
AND I DON'T LIKE IT.

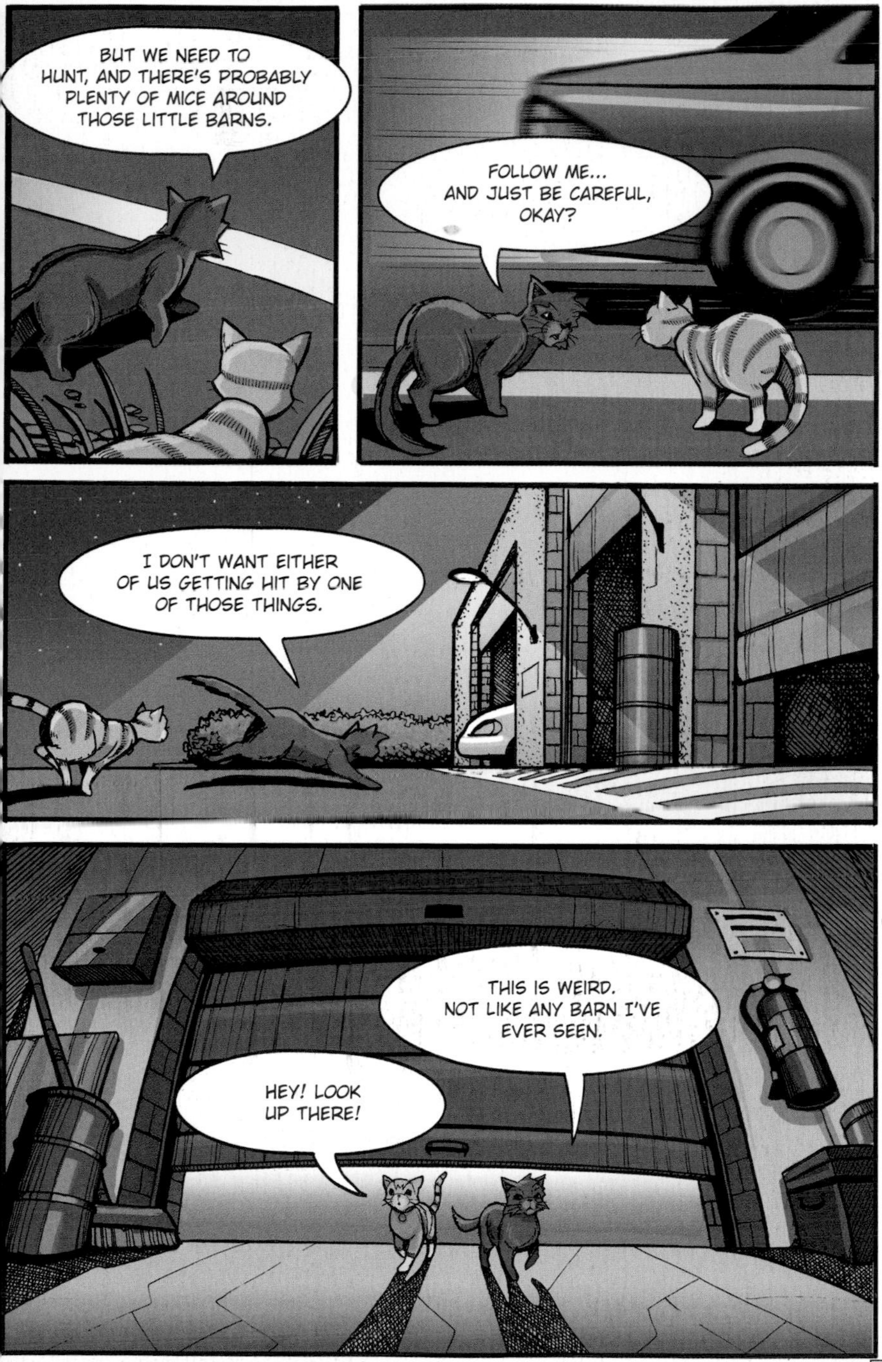
BUT WE NEED TO HUNT, AND THERE'S PROBABLY PLENTY OF MICE AROUND THOSE LITTLE BARNS.
FOLLOW ME... AND JUST BE CAREFUL, OKAY?
I DON'T WANT EITHER OF US GETTING HIT BY ONE OF THOSE THINGS.
THIS IS WEIRD. NOT LIKE ANY BARN I'VE EVER SEEN.
HEY! LOOK UP THERE!

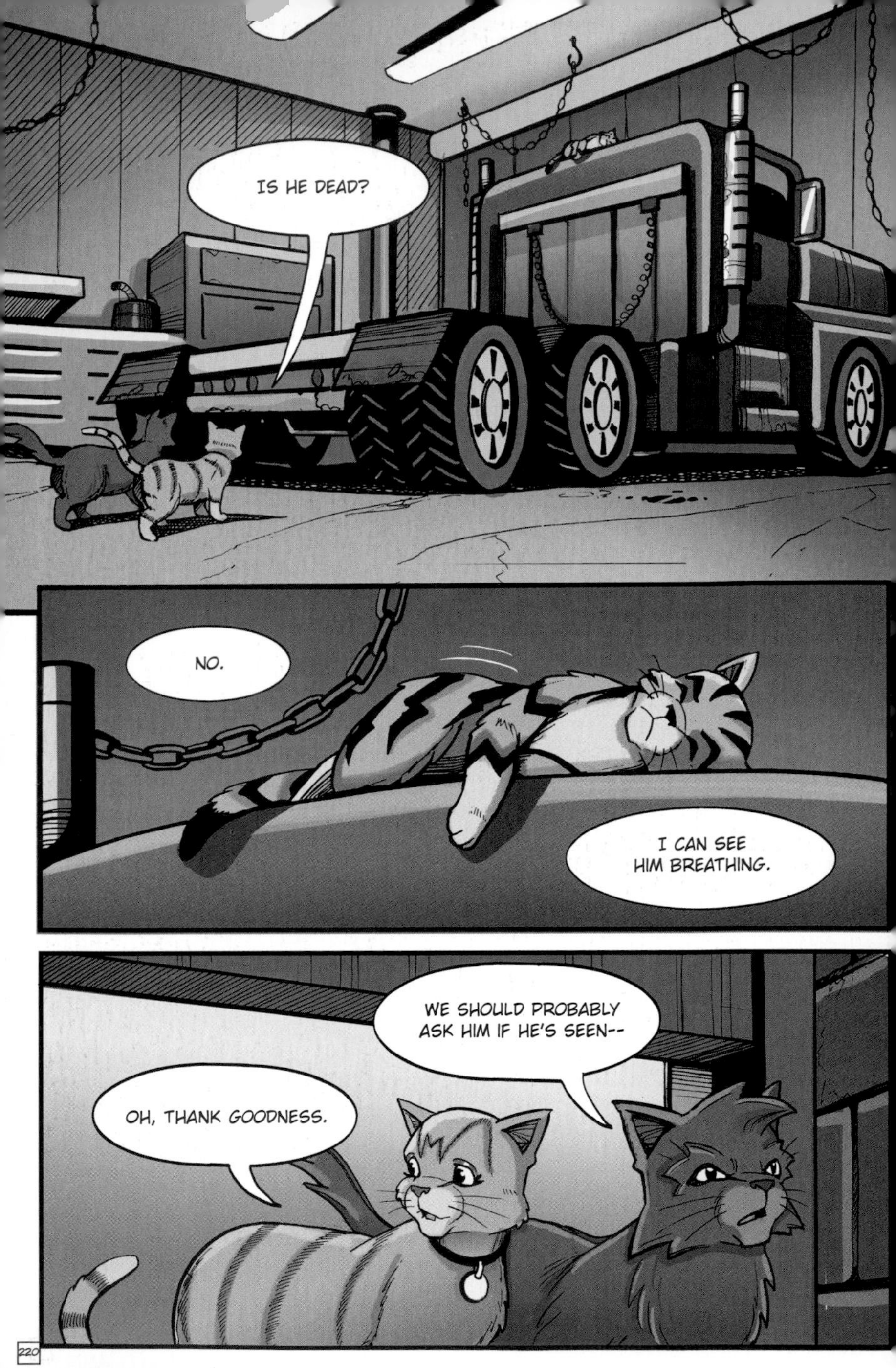
IS HE DEAD?
NO.
I CAN SEE HIM BREATHING.
OH, THANK GOODNESS.
WE SHOULD PROBABLY ASK HIM IF HE'S SEEN--

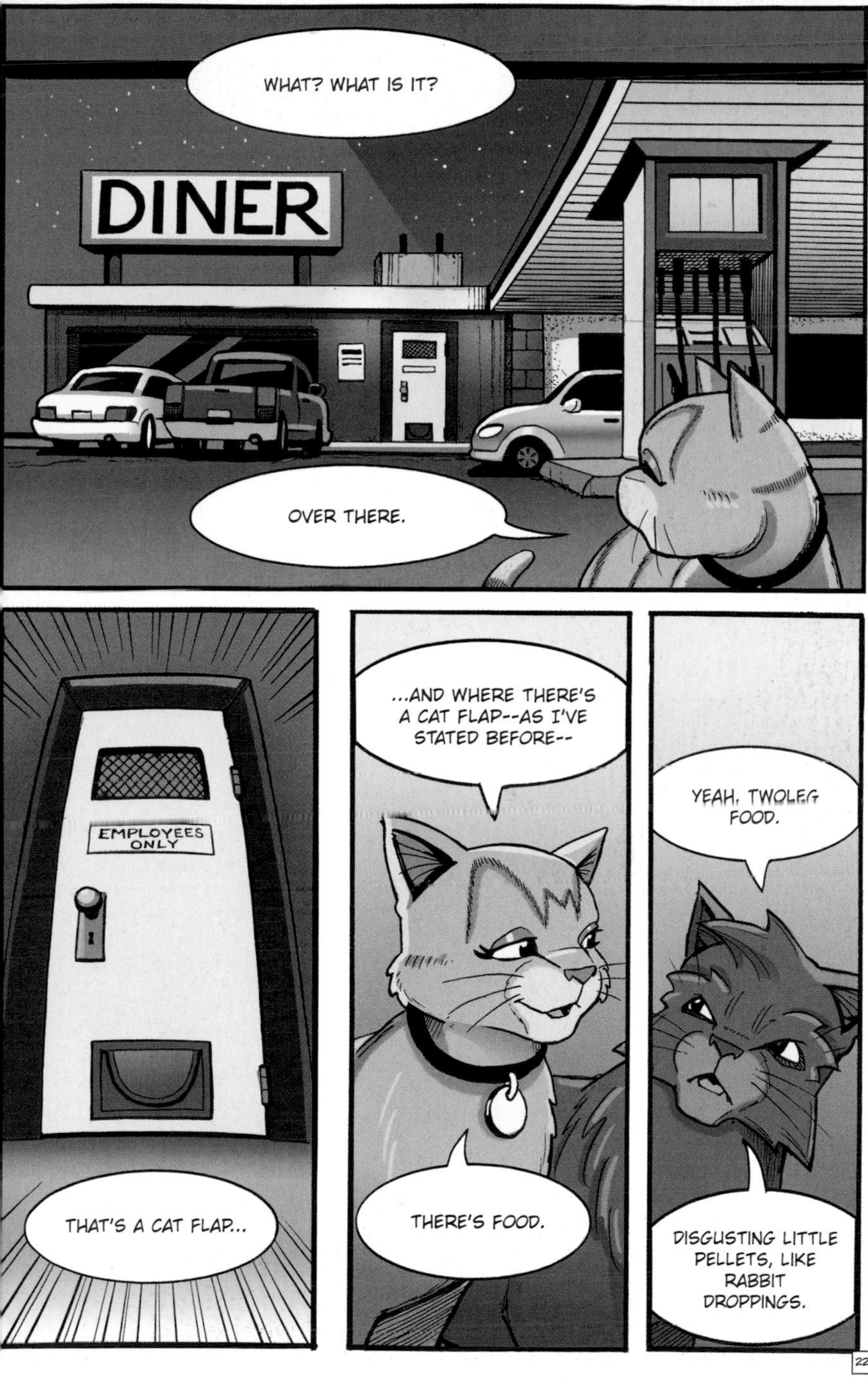
WHAT? WHAT IS IT?
DINER
OVER THERE.
EMPLOYEES ONLY
THAT'S A CAT FLAP...
...AND WHERE THERE'S A CAT FLAP--AS I'VE STATED BEFORE--
THERE'S FOOD.
YEAH, TWOLEG FOOD.
DISGUSTING LITTLE PELLETS, LIKE RABBIT DROPPINGS.

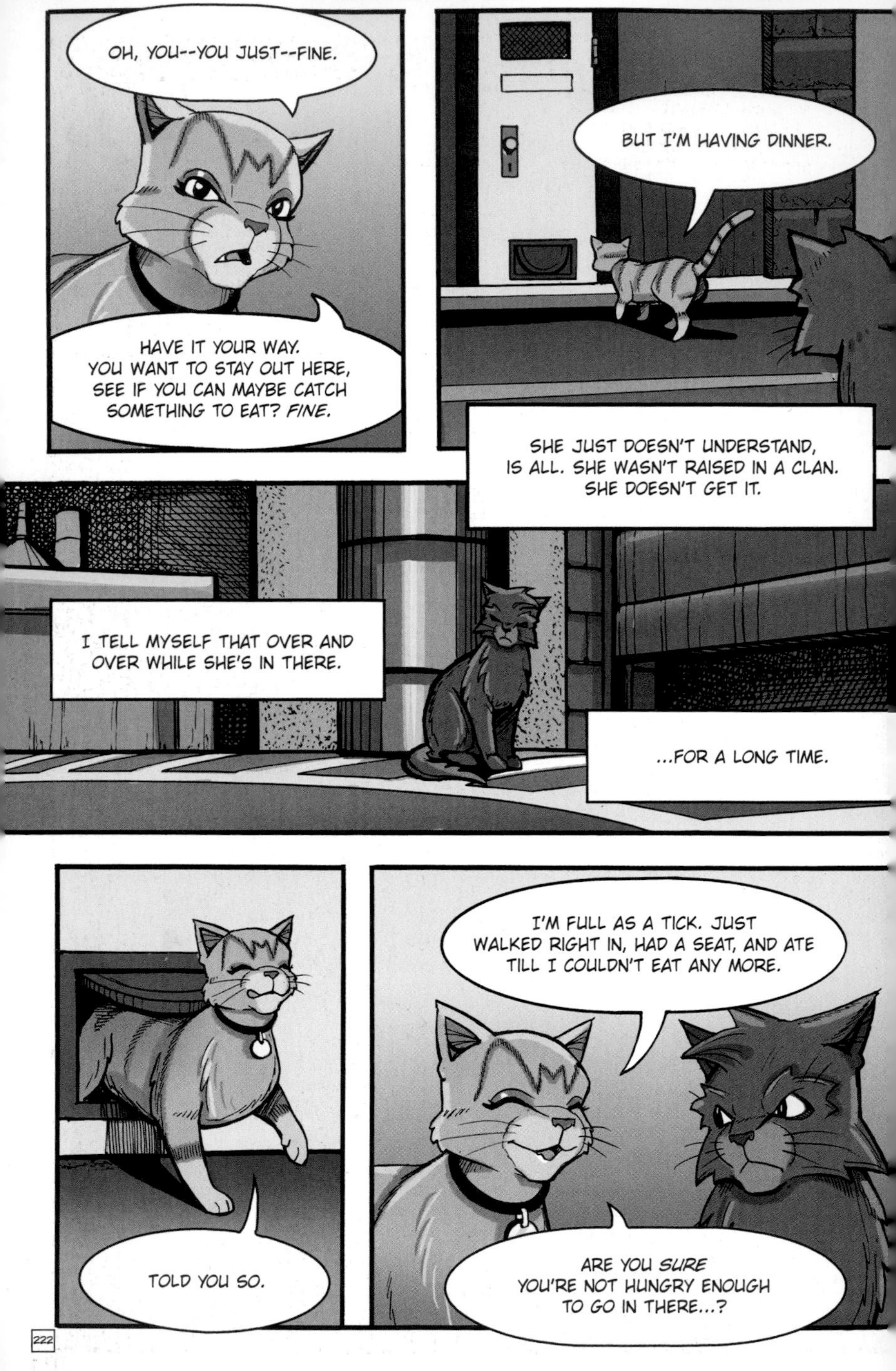
OH, YOU--YOU JUST--FINE.
HAVE IT YOUR WAY. YOU WANT TO STAY OUT HERE, SEE IF YOU CAN MAYBE CATCH SOMETHING TO EAT? *FINE.*
BUT I'M HAVING DINNER.
SHE JUST DOESN'T UNDERSTAND, IS ALL. SHE WASN'T RAISED IN A CLAN. SHE DOESN'T GET IT.
I TELL MYSELF THAT OVER AND OVER WHILE SHE'S IN THERE.
...FOR A LONG TIME.
TOLD YOU SO.
I'M FULL AS A TICK. JUST WALKED RIGHT IN, HAD A SEAT, AND ATE TILL I COULDN'T EAT ANY MORE.
ARE YOU *SURE* YOU'RE NOT HUNGRY ENOUGH TO GO IN THERE...?

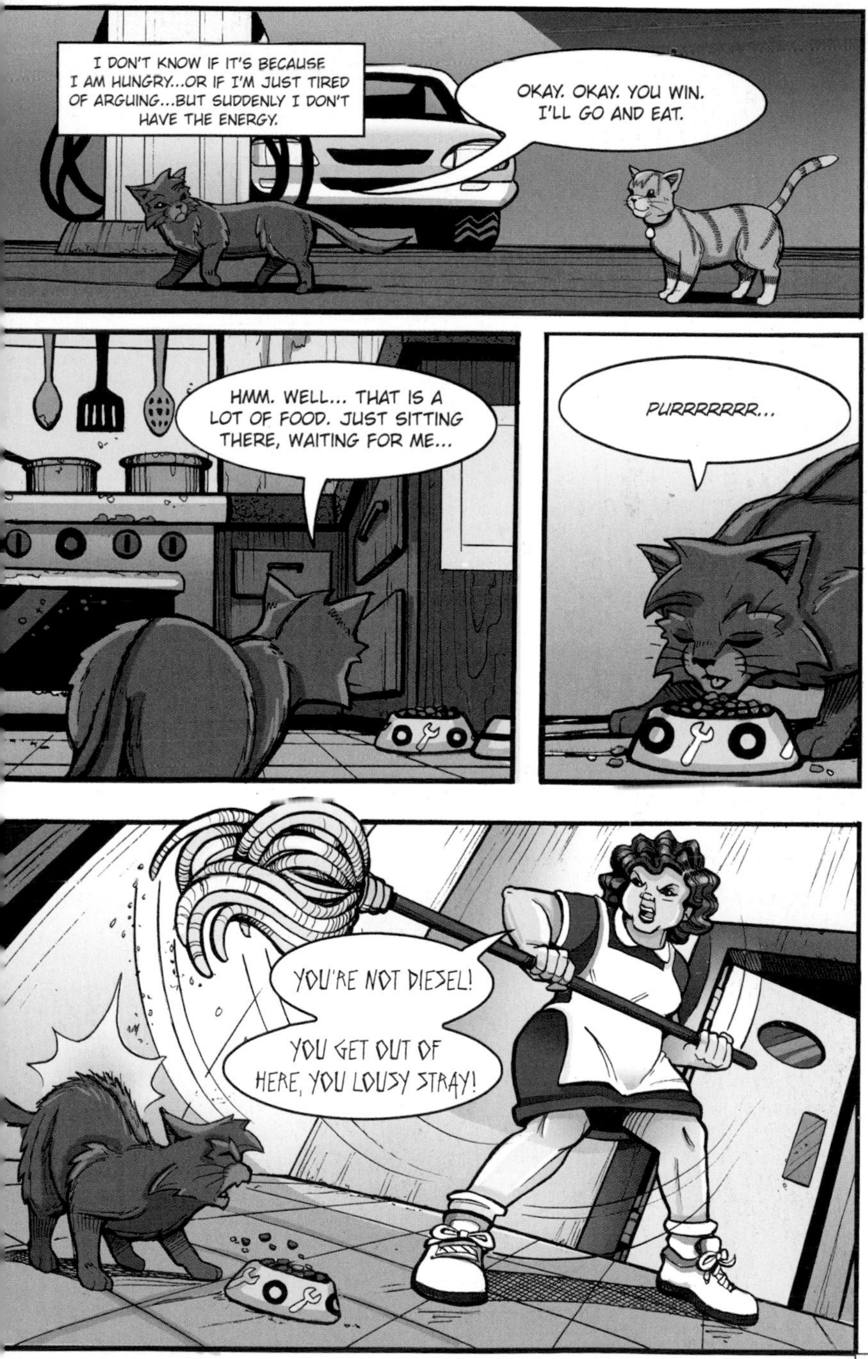
I DON'T KNOW IF IT'S BECAUSE I AM HUNGRY...OR IF I'M JUST TIRED OF ARGUING...BUT SUDDENLY I DON'T HAVE THE ENERGY.
OKAY. OKAY. YOU WIN. I'LL GO AND EAT.
HMM. WELL... THAT IS A LOT OF FOOD. JUST SITTING THERE, WAITING FOR ME...
PURRRRRRR...
YOU'RE NOT DIESEL!
YOU GET OUT OF HERE, YOU LOUSY STRAY!

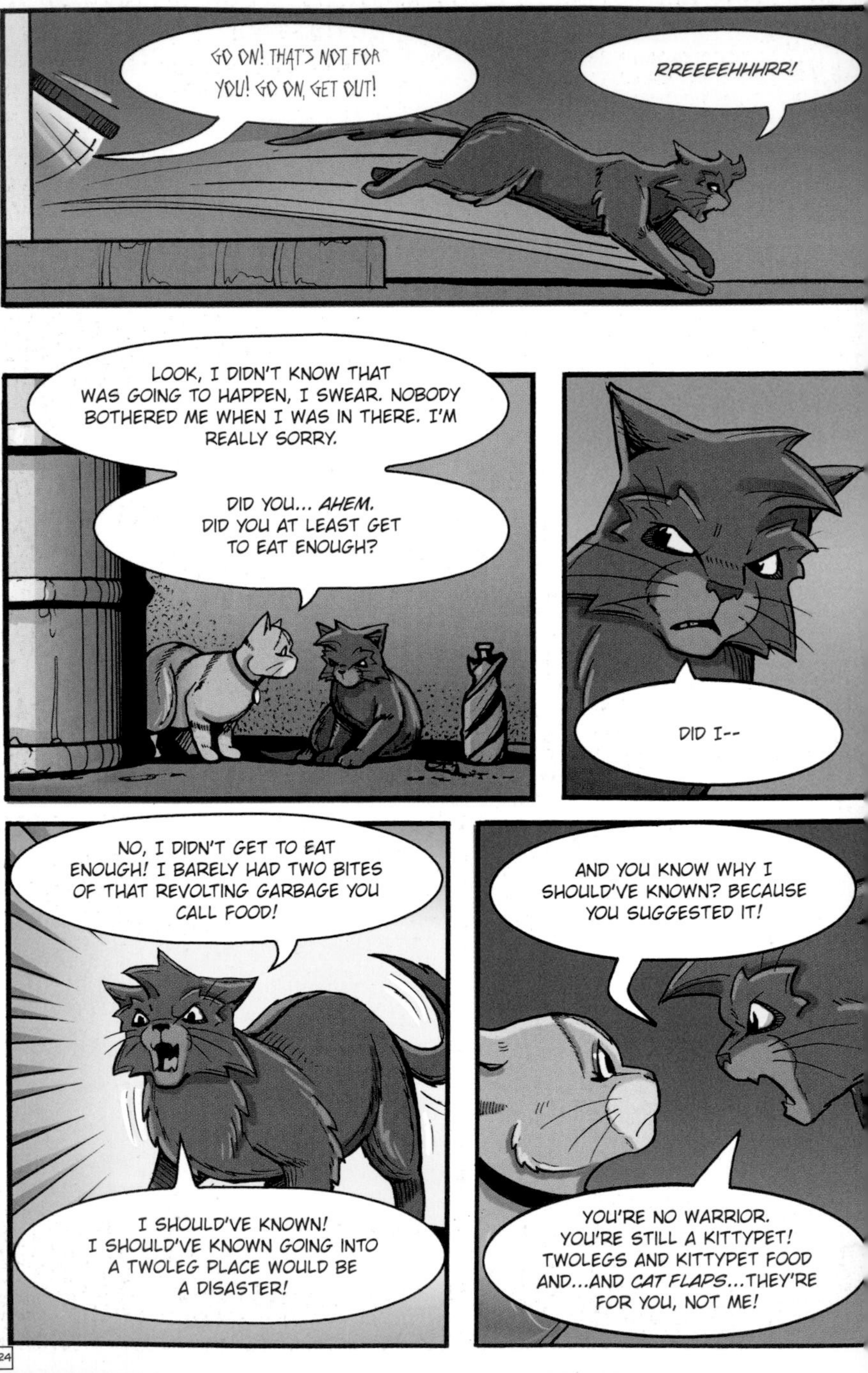
GO ON! THAT'S NOT FOR YOU! GO ON, GET OUT!
RREEEEHHHRR!
LOOK, I DIDN'T KNOW THAT WAS GOING TO HAPPEN, I SWEAR. NOBODY BOTHERED ME WHEN I WAS IN THERE. I'M REALLY SORRY.
DID YOU... *AHEM.* DID YOU AT LEAST GET TO EAT ENOUGH?
DID I--
NO, I DIDN'T GET TO EAT ENOUGH! I BARELY HAD TWO BITES OF THAT REVOLTING GARBAGE YOU CALL FOOD!
I SHOULD'VE KNOWN! I SHOULD'VE KNOWN GOING INTO A TWOLEG PLACE WOULD BE A DISASTER!
AND YOU KNOW WHY I SHOULD'VE KNOWN? BECAUSE YOU SUGGESTED IT!
YOU'RE NO WARRIOR. YOU'RE STILL A KITTYPET! TWOLEGS AND KITTYPET FOOD AND...AND *CAT FLAPS*...THEY'RE FOR YOU, NOT ME!

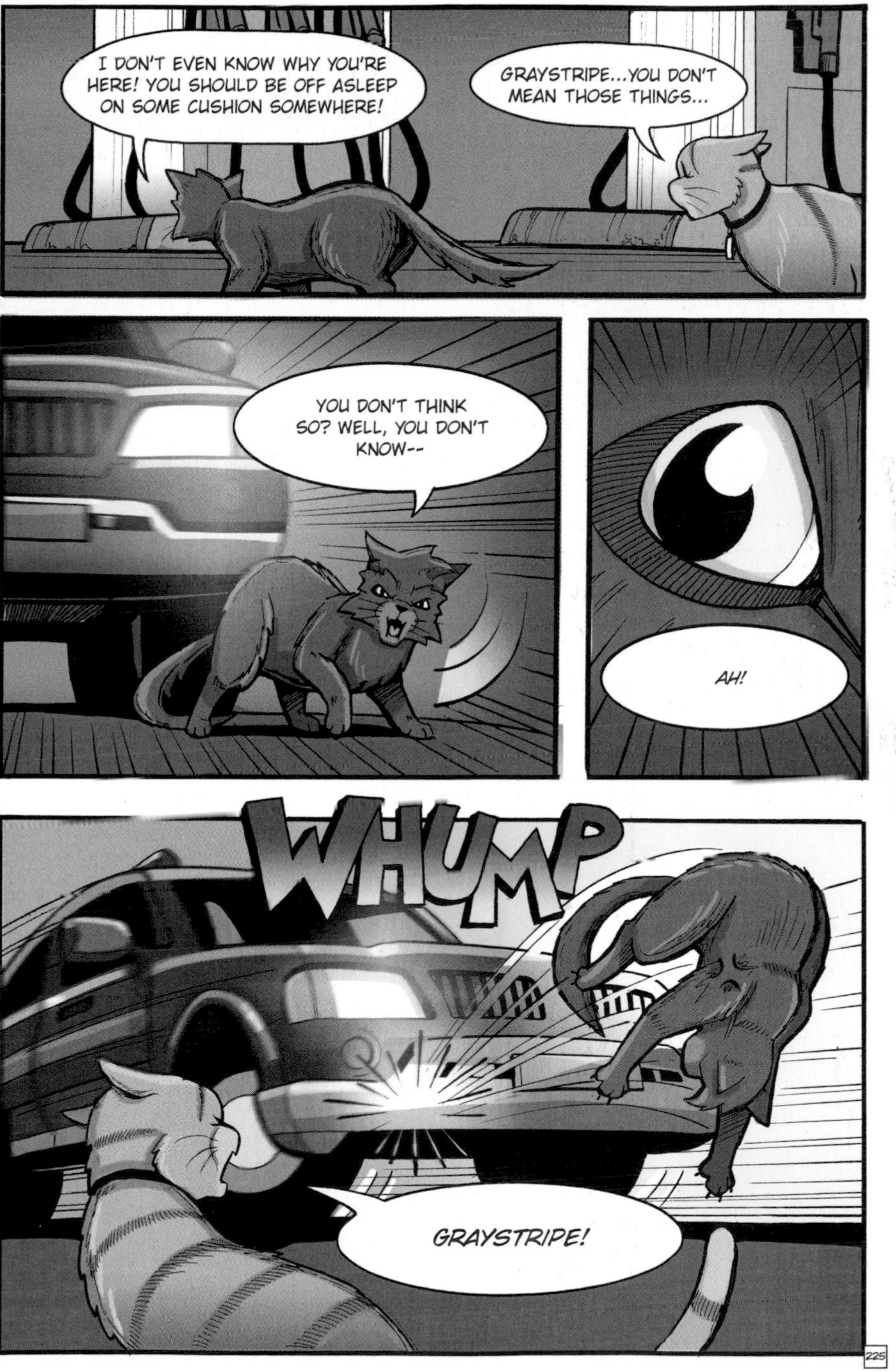
I DON'T EVEN KNOW WHY YOU'RE HERE! YOU SHOULD BE OFF ASLEEP ON SOME CUSHION SOMEWHERE!
GRAYSTRIPE...YOU DON'T MEAN THOSE THINGS...
YOU DON'T THINK SO? WELL, YOU DON'T KNOW--
AH!
WHUMP
GRAYSTRIPE!

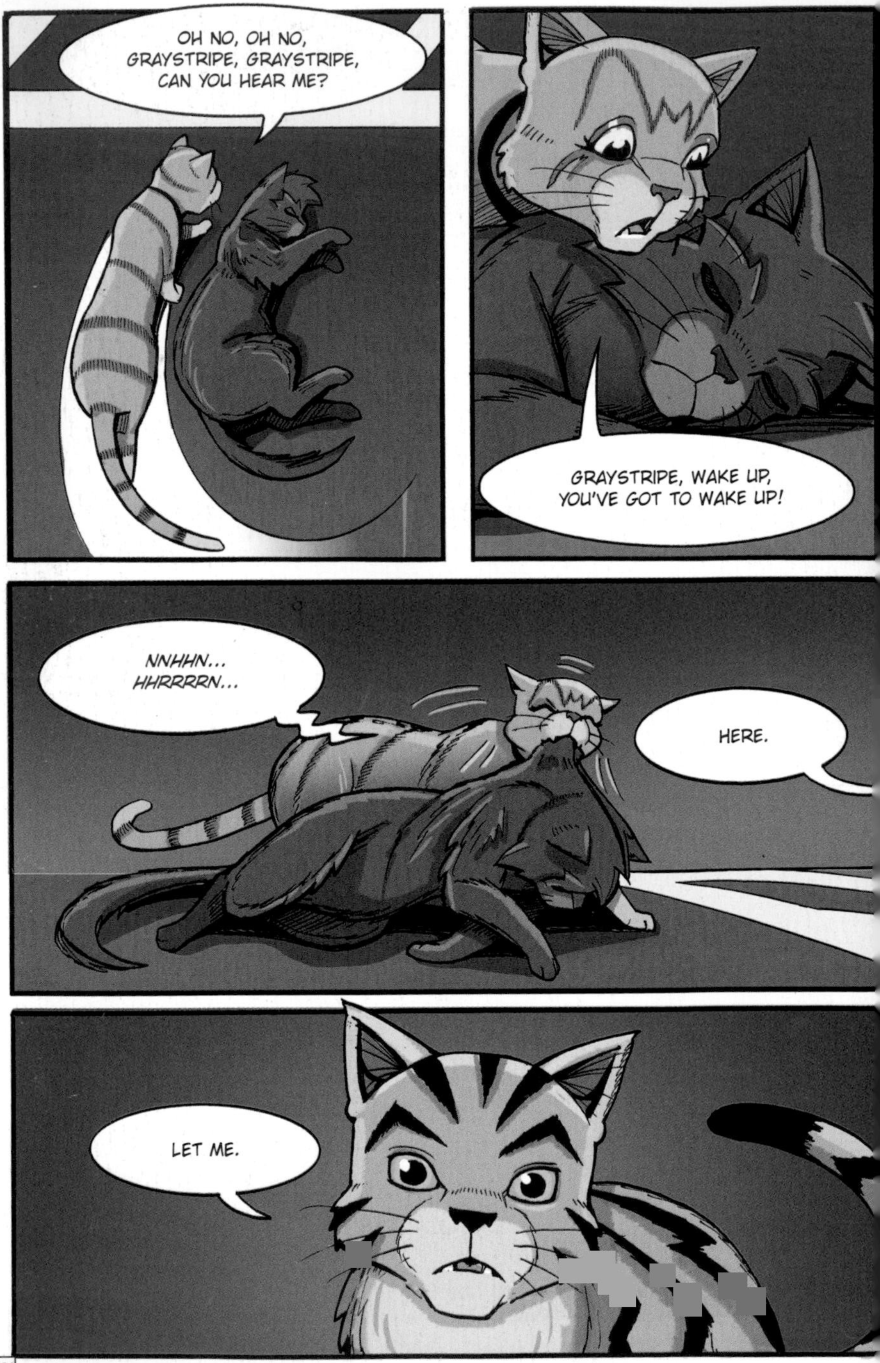
OH NO, OH NO, GRAYSTRIPE, GRAYSTRIPE, CAN YOU HEAR ME?
GRAYSTRIPE, WAKE UP, YOU'VE GOT TO WAKE UP!
NNHHN... HHRRRRN...
HERE.
LET ME.

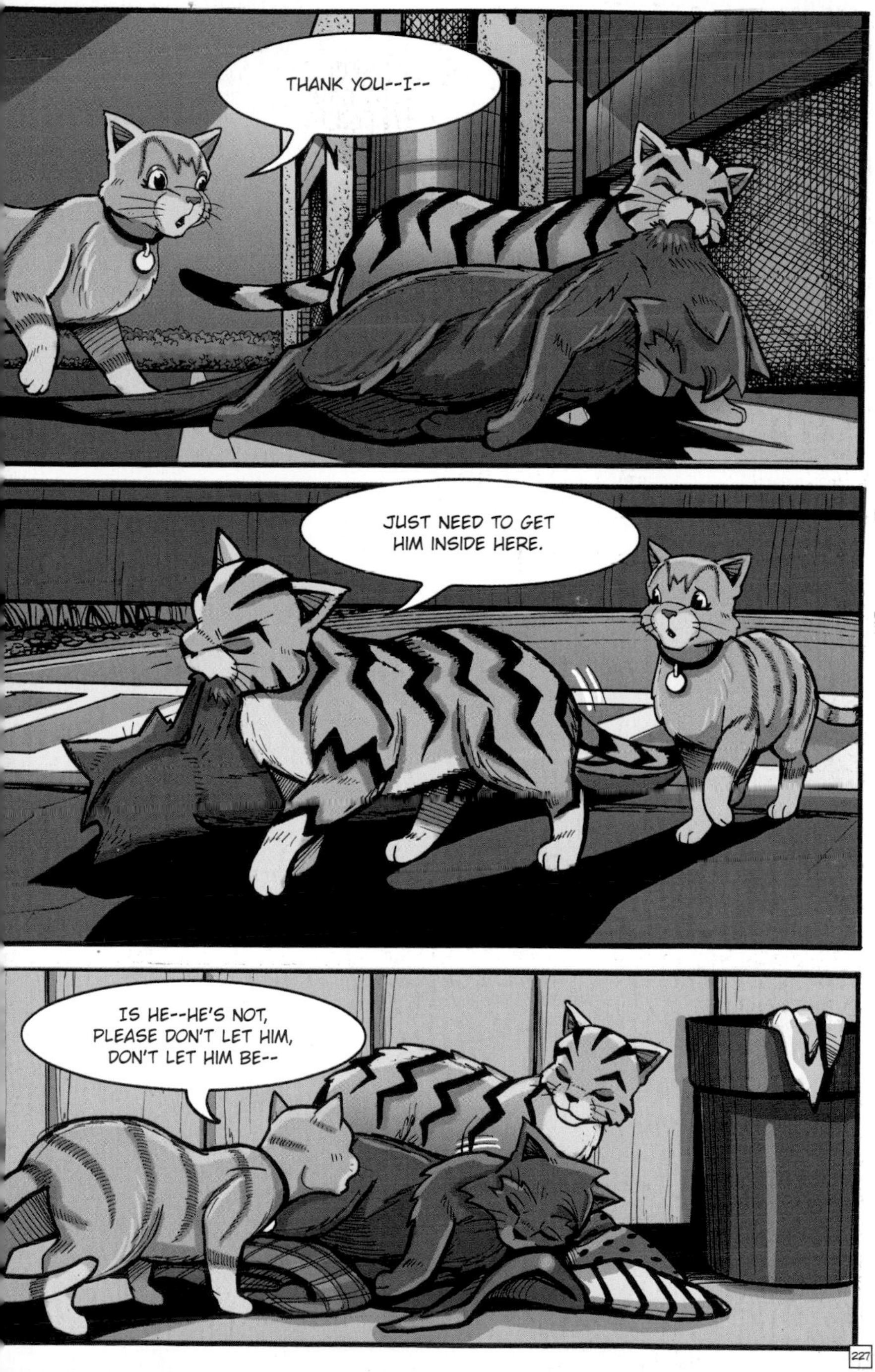
THANK YOU--I--
JUST NEED TO GET HIM INSIDE HERE.
IS HE--HE'S NOT, PLEASE DON'T LET HIM, DON'T LET HIM BE--

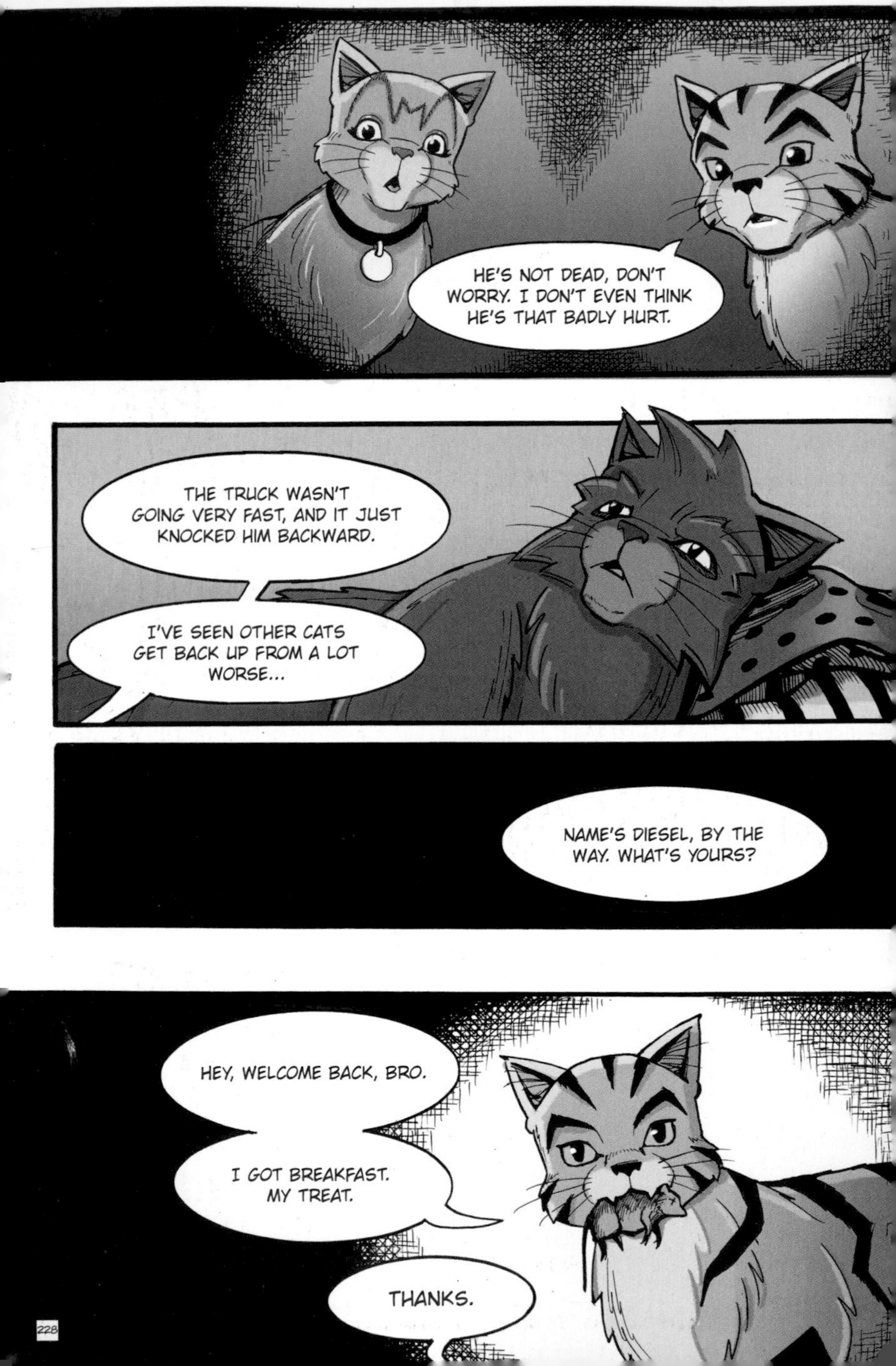
HE'S NOT DEAD, DON'T WORRY. I DON'T EVEN THINK HE'S THAT BADLY HURT.
THE TRUCK WASN'T GOING VERY FAST, AND IT JUST KNOCKED HIM BACKWARD.
I'VE SEEN OTHER CATS GET BACK UP FROM A LOT WORSE...
NAME'S DIESEL, BY THE WAY. WHAT'S YOURS?
HEY, WELCOME BACK, BRO.
I GOT BREAKFAST. MY TREAT.
THANKS.

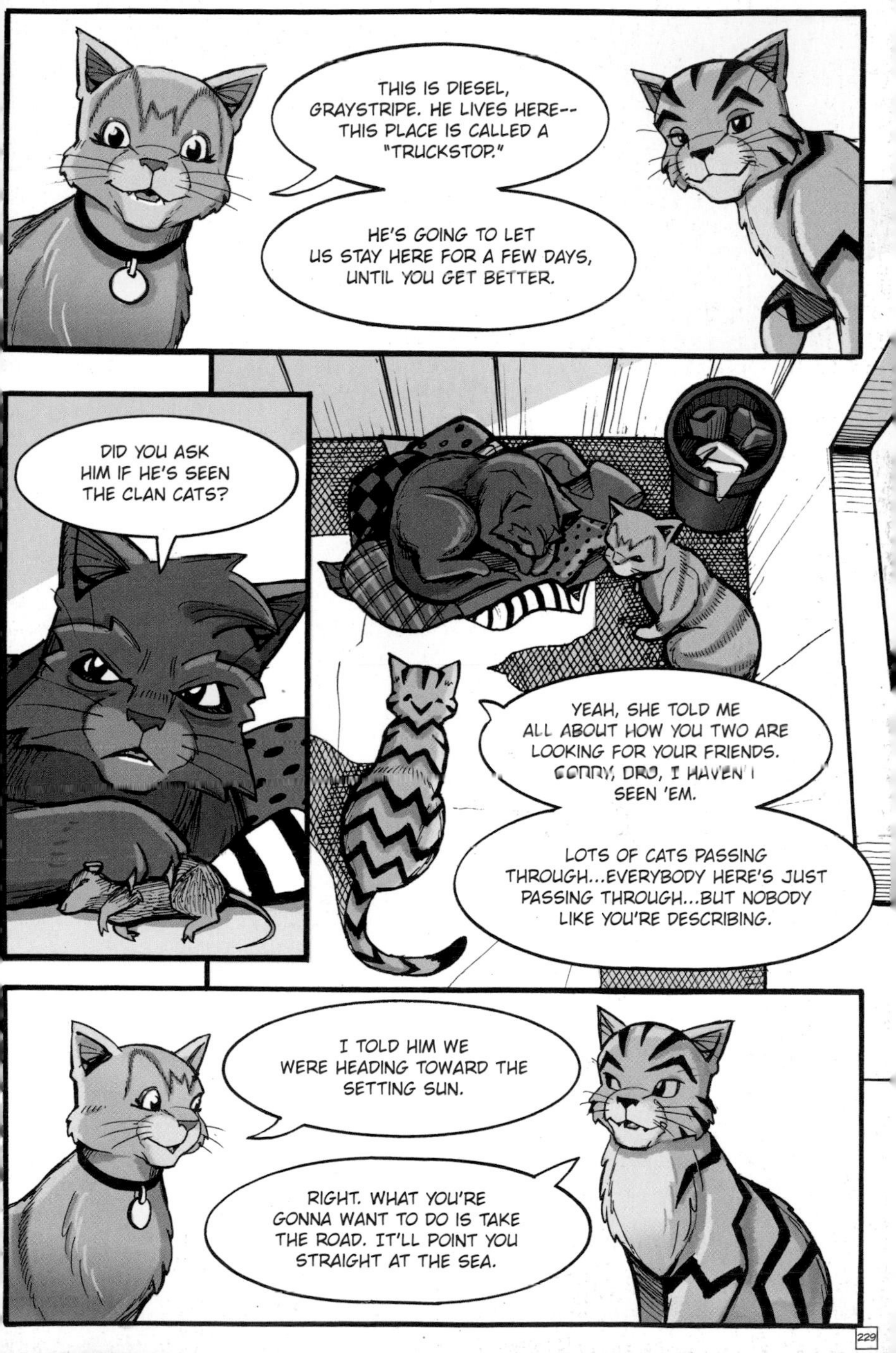
THIS IS DIESEL, GRAYSTRIPE. HE LIVES HERE-- THIS PLACE IS CALLED A "TRUCKSTOP."
HE'S GOING TO LET US STAY HERE FOR A FEW DAYS, UNTIL YOU GET BETTER.
DID YOU ASK HIM IF HE'S SEEN THE CLAN CATS?
YEAH, SHE TOLD ME ALL ABOUT HOW YOU TWO ARE LOOKING FOR YOUR FRIENDS. SORRY, BRO, I HAVEN'T SEEN 'EM.
LOTS OF CATS PASSING THROUGH...EVERYBODY HERE'S JUST PASSING THROUGH...BUT NOBODY LIKE YOU'RE DESCRIBING.
I TOLD HIM WE WERE HEADING TOWARD THE SETTING SUN.
RIGHT. WHAT YOU'RE GONNA WANT TO DO IS TAKE THE ROAD. IT'LL POINT YOU STRAIGHT AT THE SEA.

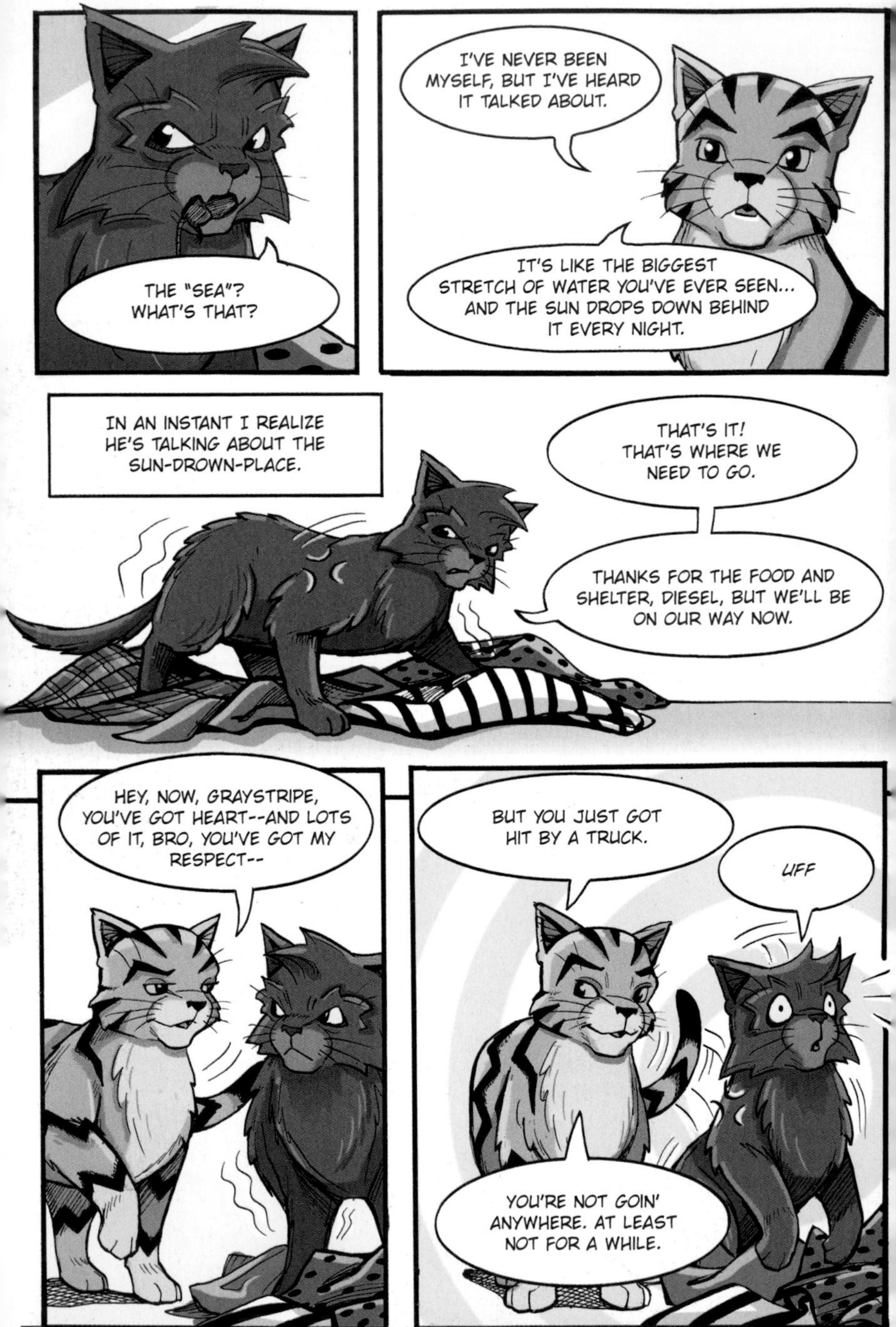
THE "SEA"? WHAT'S THAT?
I'VE NEVER BEEN MYSELF, BUT I'VE HEARD IT TALKED ABOUT.
IT'S LIKE THE BIGGEST STRETCH OF WATER YOU'VE EVER SEEN... AND THE SUN DROPS DOWN BEHIND IT EVERY NIGHT.
IN AN INSTANT I REALIZE HE'S TALKING ABOUT THE SUN-DROWN-PLACE.
THAT'S IT! THAT'S WHERE WE NEED TO GO.
THANKS FOR THE FOOD AND SHELTER, DIESEL, BUT WE'LL BE ON OUR WAY NOW.
HEY, NOW, GRAYSTRIPE, YOU'VE GOT HEART--AND LOTS OF IT, BRO, YOU'VE GOT MY RESPECT--
BUT YOU JUST GOT HIT BY A TRUCK.
UFF
YOU'RE NOT GOIN' ANYWHERE. AT LEAST NOT FOR A WHILE.

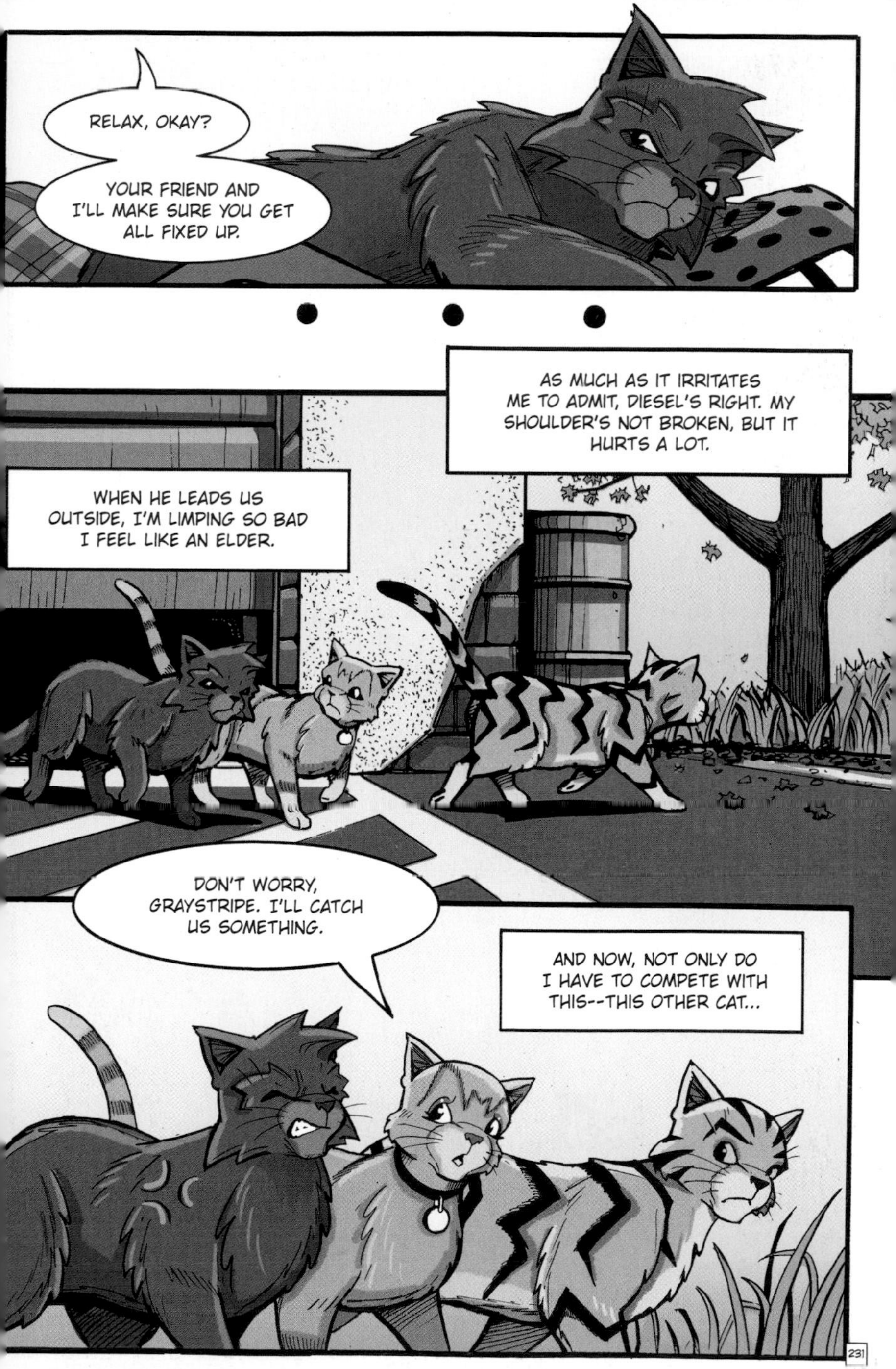
RELAX, OKAY?
YOUR FRIEND AND I'LL MAKE SURE YOU GET ALL FIXED UP.
WHEN HE LEADS US OUTSIDE, I'M LIMPING SO BAD I FEEL LIKE AN ELDER.
AS MUCH AS IT IRRITATES ME TO ADMIT, DIESEL'S RIGHT. MY SHOULDER'S NOT BROKEN, BUT IT HURTS A LOT.
DON'T WORRY, GRAYSTRIPE. I'LL CATCH US SOMETHING.
AND NOW, NOT ONLY DO I HAVE TO COMPETE WITH THIS--THIS OTHER CAT...

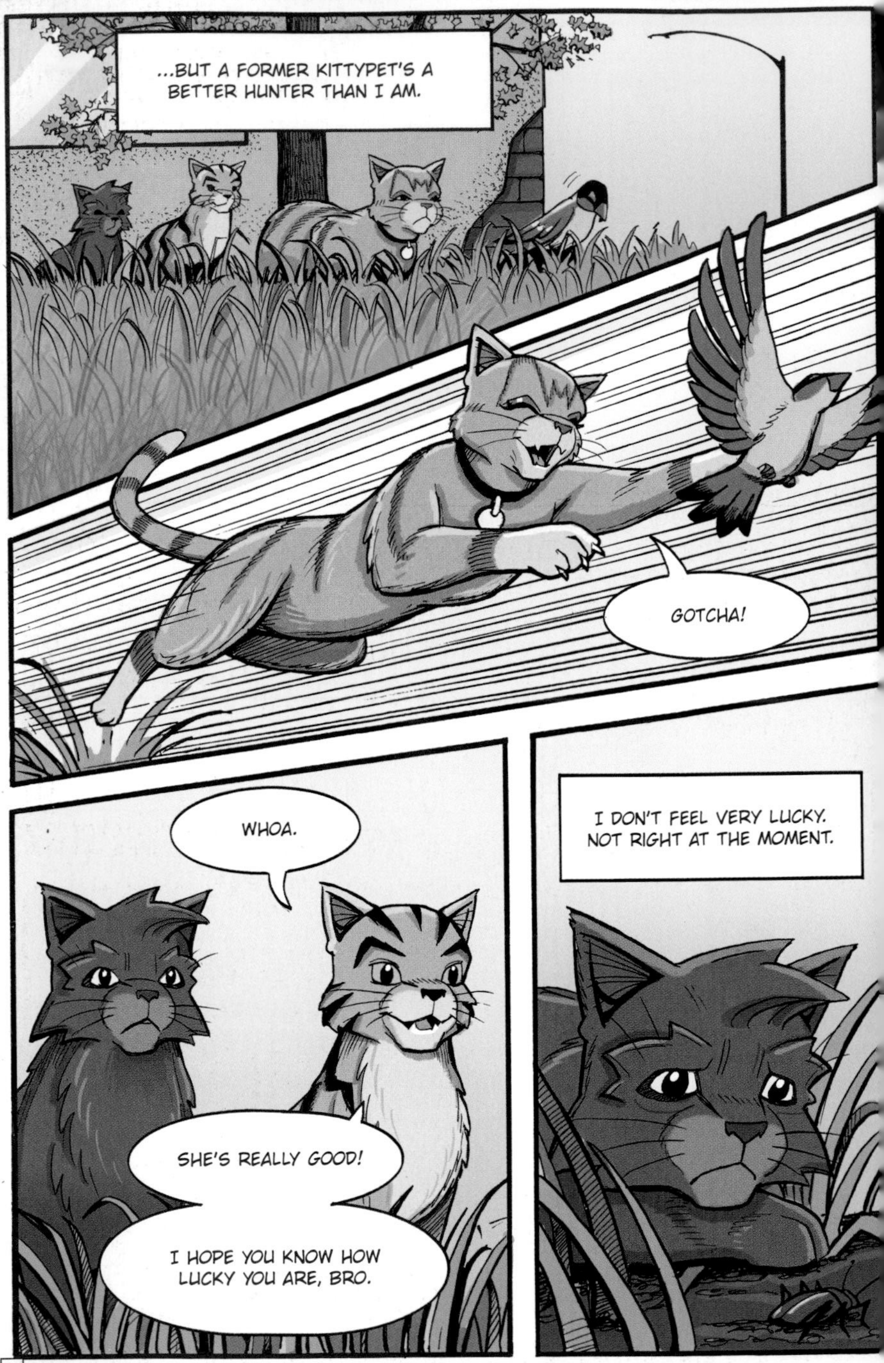

...BUT A FORMER KITTYPET'S A BETTER HUNTER THAN I AM.
GOTCHA!
WHOA.
SHE'S REALLY GOOD!
I HOPE YOU KNOW HOW LUCKY YOU ARE, BRO.
I DON'T FEEL VERY LUCKY. NOT RIGHT AT THE MOMENT.

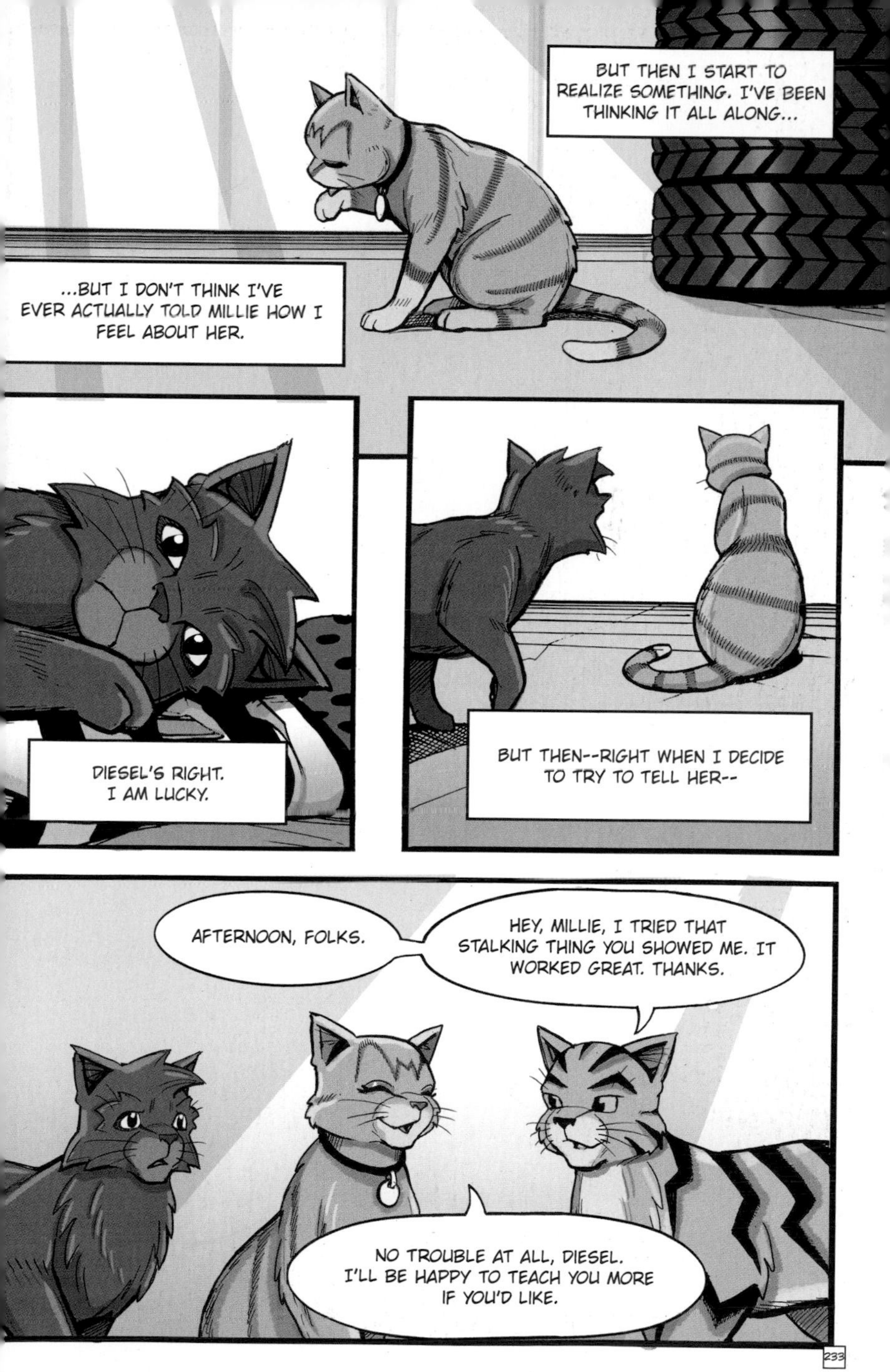
BUT THEN I START TO REALIZE SOMETHING. I'VE BEEN THINKING IT ALL ALONG...
...BUT I DON'T THINK I'VE EVER ACTUALLY TOLD MILLIE HOW I FEEL ABOUT HER.
DIESEL'S RIGHT. I AM LUCKY.
BUT THEN--RIGHT WHEN I DECIDE TO TRY TO TELL HER--
AFTERNOON, FOLKS.
HEY, MILLIE, I TRIED THAT STALKING THING YOU SHOWED ME. IT WORKED GREAT. THANKS.
NO TROUBLE AT ALL, DIESEL. I'LL BE HAPPY TO TEACH YOU MORE IF YOU'D LIKE.

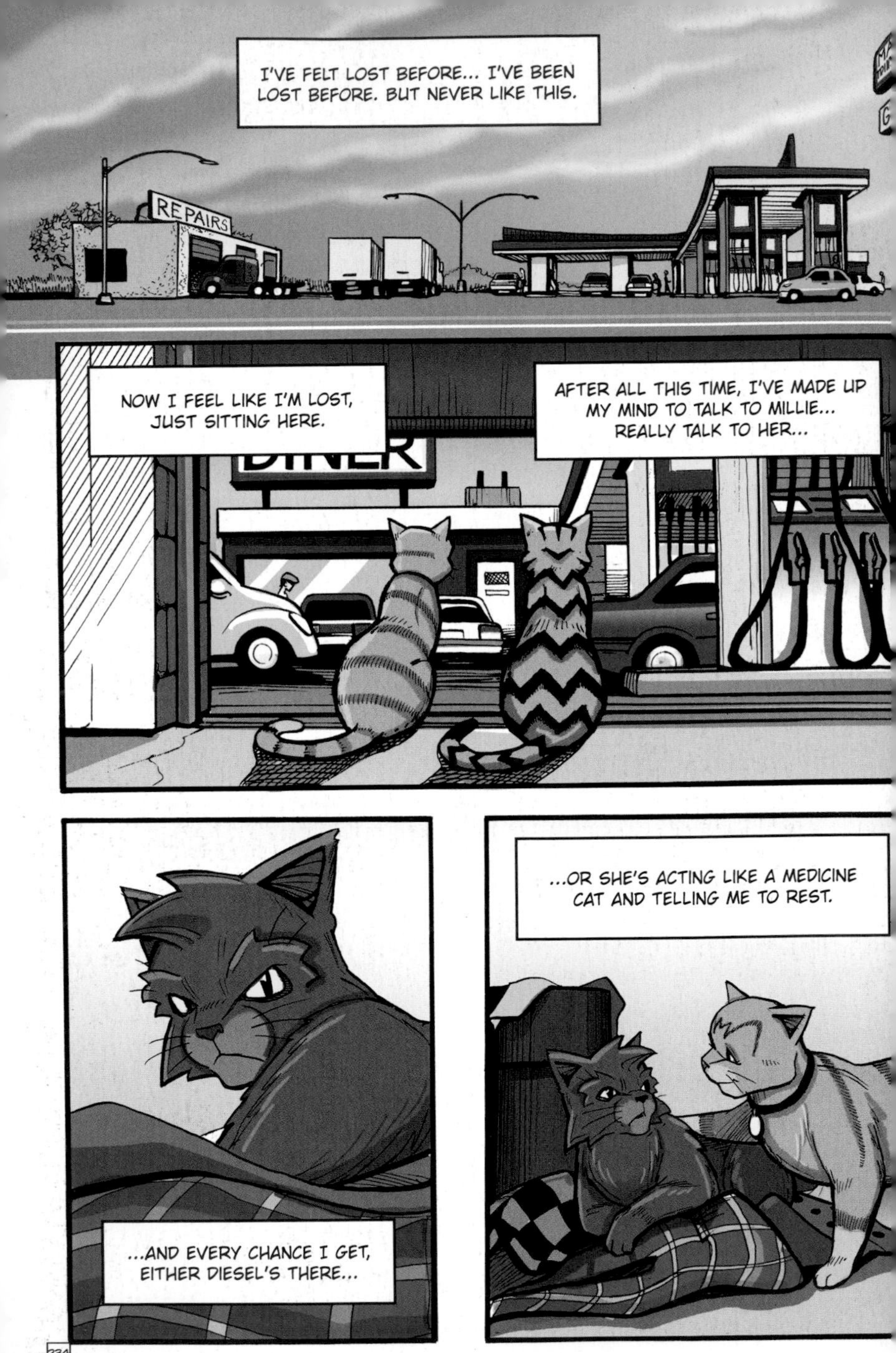
I'VE FELT LOST BEFORE... I'VE BEEN LOST BEFORE. BUT NEVER LIKE THIS.
REPAIRS
NOW I FEEL LIKE I'M LOST, JUST SITTING HERE.
AFTER ALL THIS TIME, I'VE MADE UP MY MIND TO TALK TO MILLIE... REALLY TALK TO HER...
...AND EVERY CHANCE I GET, EITHER DIESEL'S THERE...
...OR SHE'S ACTING LIKE A MEDICINE CAT AND TELLING ME TO REST.

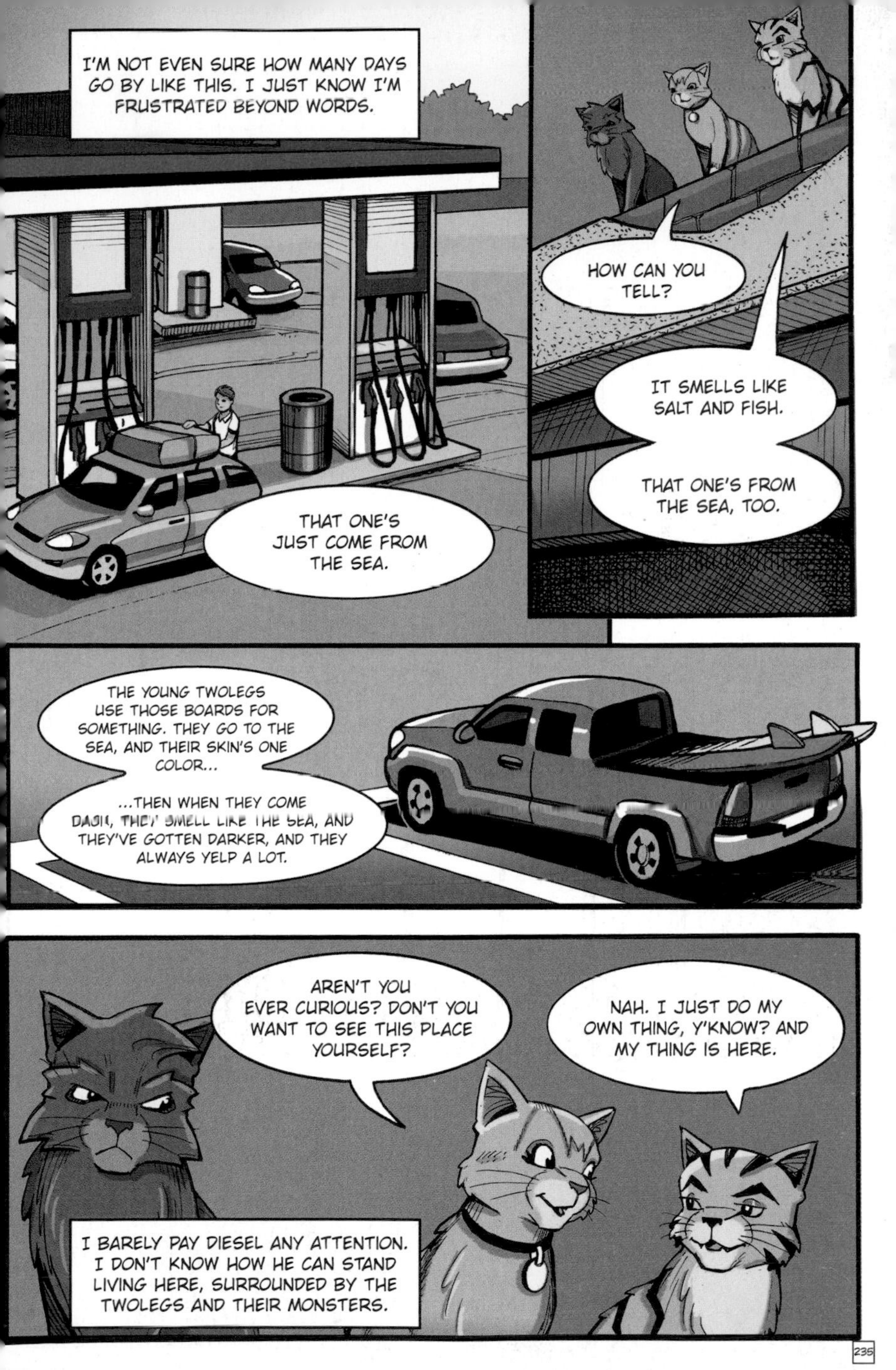
I'M NOT EVEN SURE HOW MANY DAYS GO BY LIKE THIS. I JUST KNOW I'M FRUSTRATED BEYOND WORDS.
THAT ONE'S JUST COME FROM THE SEA.
HOW CAN YOU TELL?
IT SMELLS LIKE SALT AND FISH.
THAT ONE'S FROM THE SEA, TOO.
THE YOUNG TWOLEGS USE THOSE BOARDS FOR SOMETHING. THEY GO TO THE SEA, AND THEIR SKIN'S ONE COLOR...
...THEN WHEN THEY COME BACK, THEY SMELL LIKE THE SEA, AND THEY'VE GOTTEN DARKER, AND THEY ALWAYS YELP A LOT.
AREN'T YOU EVER CURIOUS? DON'T YOU WANT TO SEE THIS PLACE YOURSELF?
NAH. I JUST DO MY OWN THING, Y'KNOW? AND MY THING IS HERE.
I BARELY PAY DIESEL ANY ATTENTION. I DON'T KNOW HOW HE CAN STAND LIVING HERE, SURROUNDED BY THE TWOLEGS AND THEIR MONSTERS.

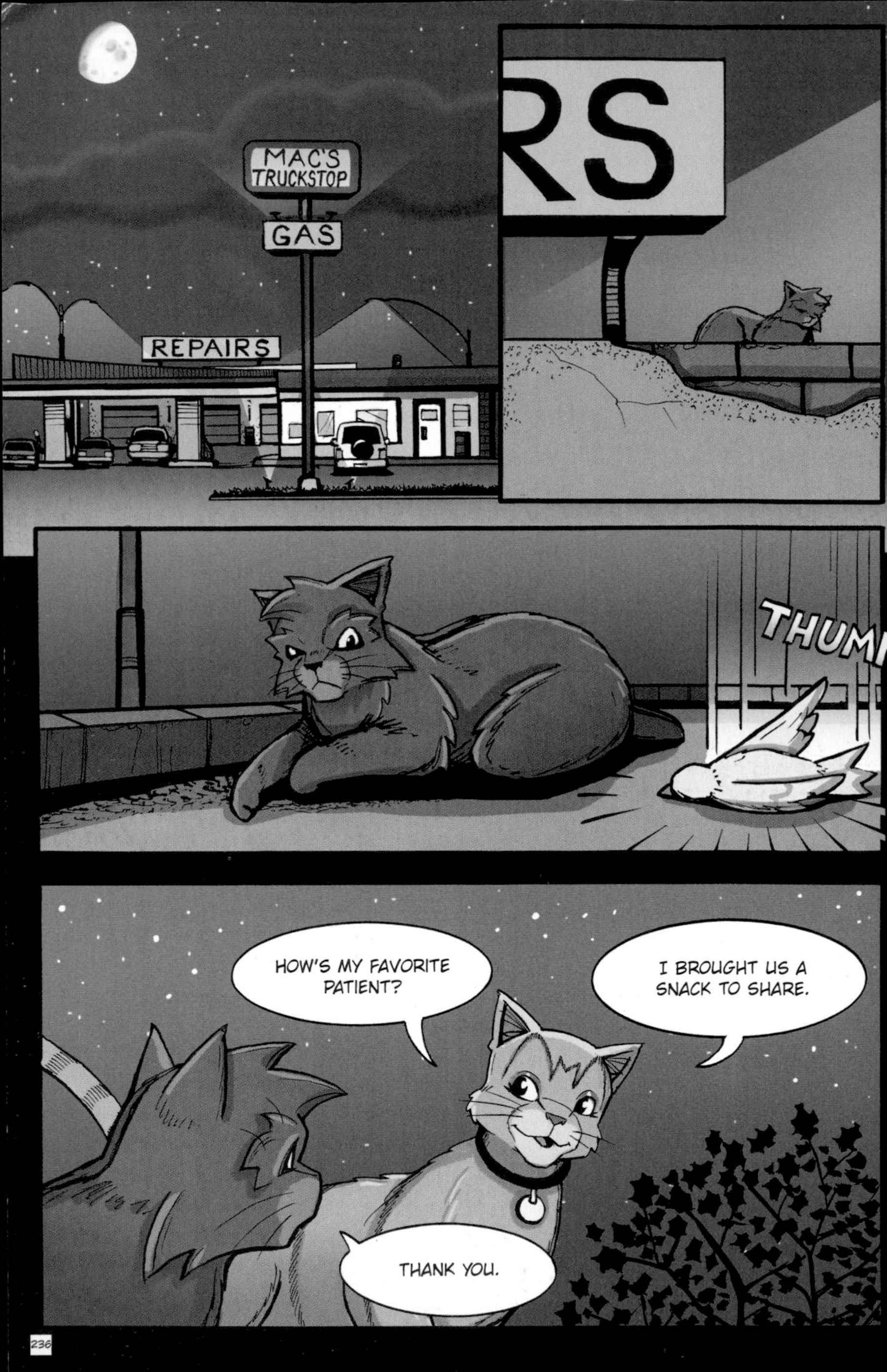
MAC'S TRUCKSTOP
GAS
REPAIRS
RS
THUM
HOW'S MY FAVORITE PATIENT?
I BROUGHT US A SNACK TO SHARE.
THANK YOU.

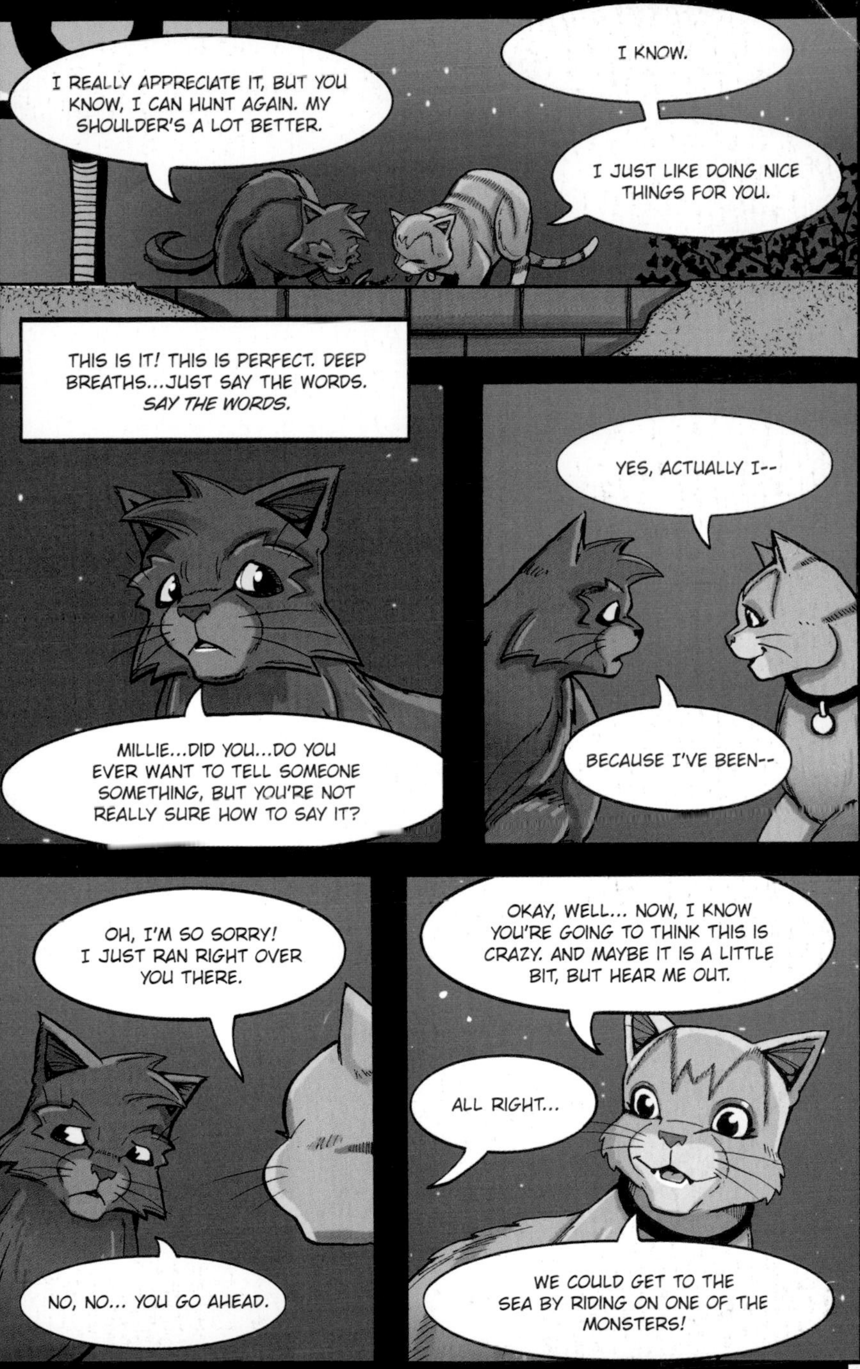
I REALLY APPRECIATE IT, BUT YOU KNOW, I CAN HUNT AGAIN. MY SHOULDER'S A LOT BETTER.
I KNOW.
I JUST LIKE DOING NICE THINGS FOR YOU.
THIS IS IT! THIS IS PERFECT. DEEP BREATHS...JUST SAY THE WORDS. *SAY THE WORDS.*
MILLIE...DID YOU...DO YOU EVER WANT TO TELL SOMEONE SOMETHING, BUT YOU'RE NOT REALLY SURE HOW TO SAY IT?
YES, ACTUALLY I--
BECAUSE I'VE BEEN--
OH, I'M SO SORRY! I JUST RAN RIGHT OVER YOU THERE.
NO, NO... YOU GO AHEAD.
OKAY, WELL... NOW, I KNOW YOU'RE GOING TO THINK THIS IS CRAZY. AND MAYBE IT IS A LITTLE BIT, BUT HEAR ME OUT.
ALL RIGHT...
WE COULD GET TO THE SEA BY RIDING ON ONE OF THE MONSTERS!

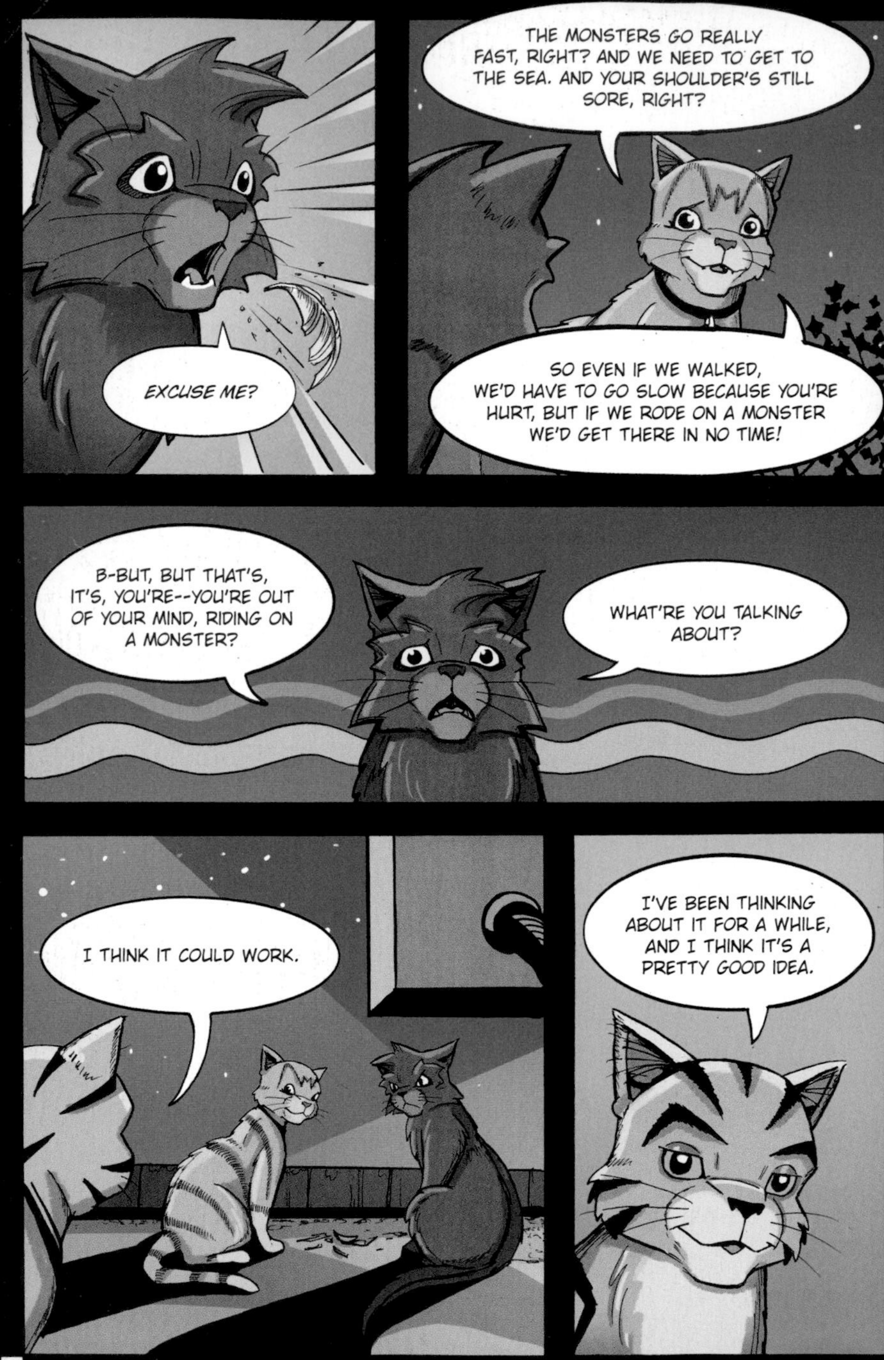
EXCUSE ME?
THE MONSTERS GO REALLY FAST, RIGHT? AND WE NEED TO GET TO THE SEA. AND YOUR SHOULDER'S STILL SORE, RIGHT?
SO EVEN IF WE WALKED, WE'D HAVE TO GO SLOW BECAUSE YOU'RE HURT, BUT IF WE RODE ON A MONSTER WE'D GET THERE IN NO TIME!
B-BUT, BUT THAT'S, IT'S, YOU'RE--YOU'RE OUT OF YOUR MIND, RIDING ON A MONSTER?
WHAT'RE YOU TALKING ABOUT?
I THINK IT COULD WORK.
I'VE BEEN THINKING ABOUT IT FOR A WHILE, AND I THINK IT'S A PRETTY GOOD IDEA.

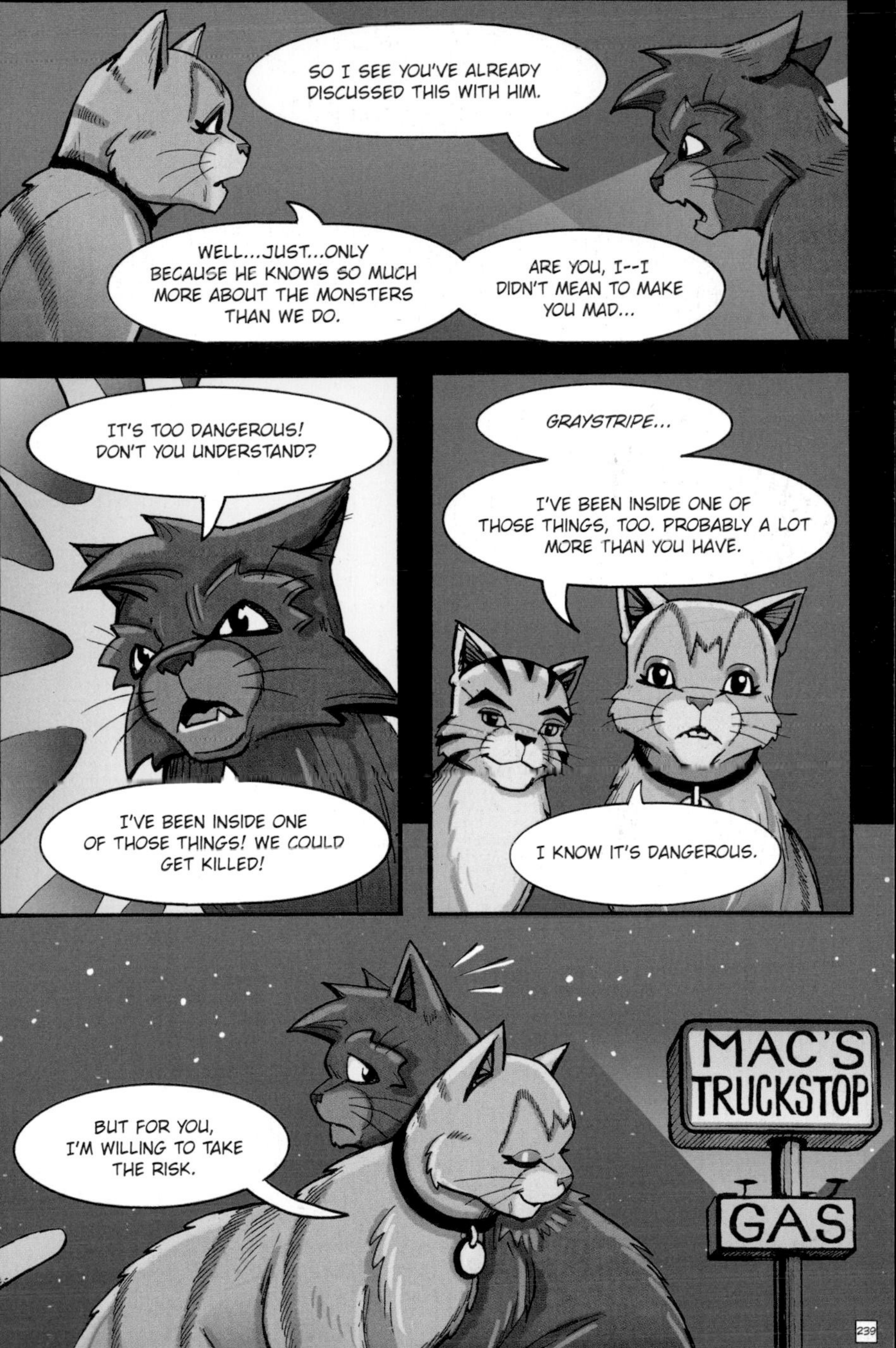
SO I SEE YOU'VE ALREADY DISCUSSED THIS WITH HIM.
WELL...JUST...ONLY BECAUSE HE KNOWS SO MUCH MORE ABOUT THE MONSTERS THAN WE DO.
ARE YOU, I--I DIDN'T MEAN TO MAKE YOU MAD...
IT'S TOO DANGEROUS! DON'T YOU UNDERSTAND?
I'VE BEEN INSIDE ONE OF THOSE THINGS! WE COULD GET KILLED!
GRAYSTRIPE...
I'VE BEEN INSIDE ONE OF THOSE THINGS, TOO. PROBABLY A LOT MORE THAN YOU HAVE.
I KNOW IT'S DANGEROUS.
MAC'S TRUCKSTOP
GAS
BUT FOR YOU, I'M WILLING TO TAKE THE RISK.

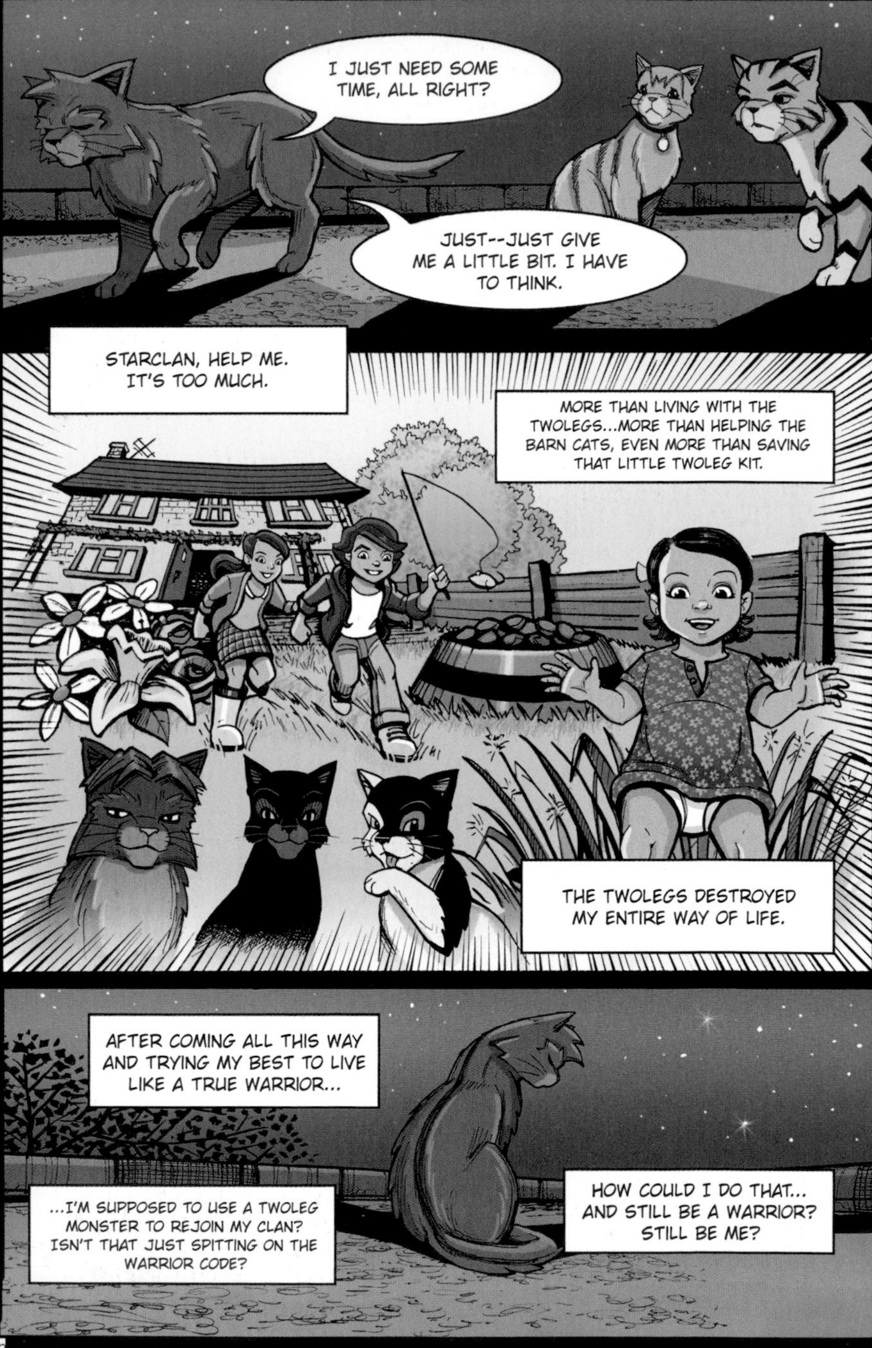
I JUST NEED SOME TIME, ALL RIGHT?
JUST--JUST GIVE ME A LITTLE BIT. I HAVE TO THINK.
STARCLAN, HELP ME. IT'S TOO MUCH.
MORE THAN LIVING WITH THE TWOLEGS...MORE THAN HELPING THE BARN CATS, EVEN MORE THAN SAVING THAT LITTLE TWOLEG KIT.
THE TWOLEGS DESTROYED MY ENTIRE WAY OF LIFE.
AFTER COMING ALL THIS WAY AND TRYING MY BEST TO LIVE LIKE A TRUE WARRIOR...
...I'M SUPPOSED TO USE A TWOLEG MONSTER TO REJOIN MY CLAN? ISN'T THAT JUST SPITTING ON THE WARRIOR CODE?
HOW COULD I DO THAT... AND STILL BE A WARRIOR? STILL BE ME?

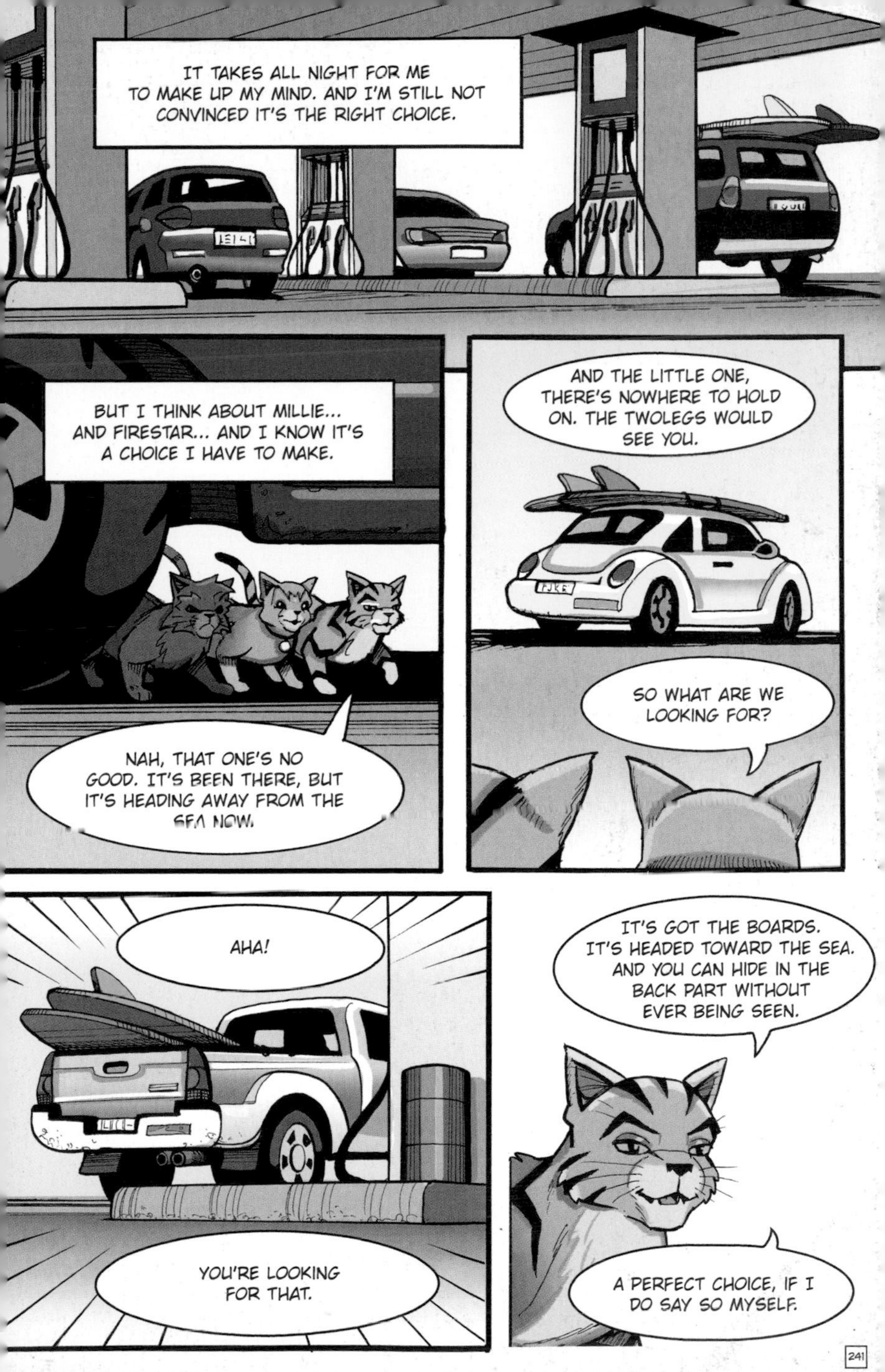

IT TAKES ALL NIGHT FOR ME TO MAKE UP MY MIND. AND I'M STILL NOT CONVINCED IT'S THE RIGHT CHOICE.
BUT I THINK ABOUT MILLIE... AND FIRESTAR... AND I KNOW IT'S A CHOICE I HAVE TO MAKE.
NAH, THAT ONE'S NO GOOD. IT'S BEEN THERE, BUT IT'S HEADING AWAY FROM THE SEA NOW.
AND THE LITTLE ONE, THERE'S NOWHERE TO HOLD ON. THE TWOLEGS WOULD SEE YOU.
SO WHAT ARE WE LOOKING FOR?
AHA!
YOU'RE LOOKING FOR THAT.
IT'S GOT THE BOARDS. IT'S HEADED TOWARD THE SEA. AND YOU CAN HIDE IN THE BACK PART WITHOUT EVER BEING SEEN.
A PERFECT CHOICE, IF I DO SAY SO MYSELF.

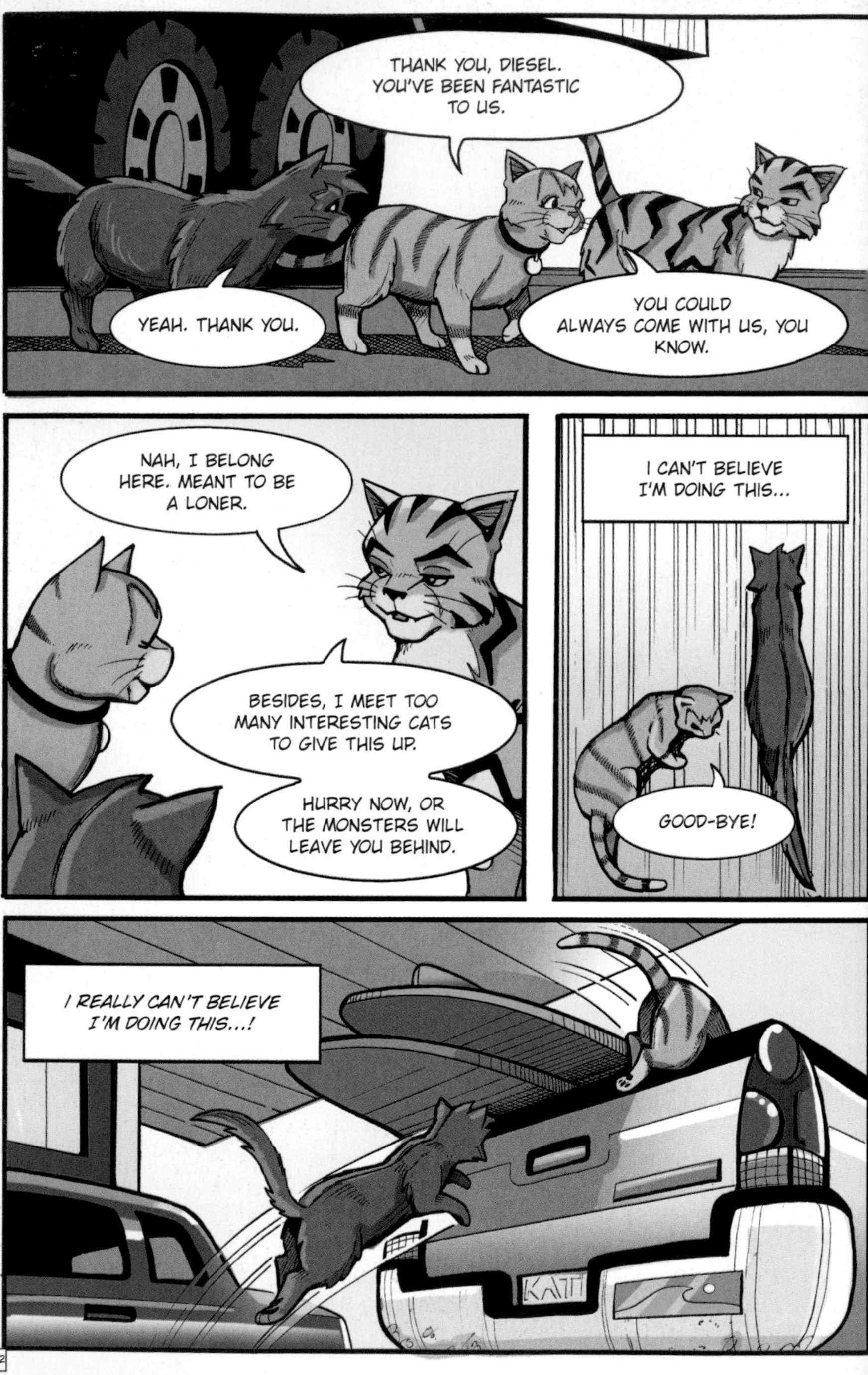
THANK YOU, DIESEL. YOU'VE BEEN FANTASTIC TO US.
YEAH. THANK YOU.
YOU COULD ALWAYS COME WITH US, YOU KNOW.
NAH, I BELONG HERE. MEANT TO BE A LONER.
BESIDES, I MEET TOO MANY INTERESTING CATS TO GIVE THIS UP.
HURRY NOW, OR THE MONSTERS WILL LEAVE YOU BEHIND.
I CAN'T BELIEVE I'M DOING THIS...
GOOD-BYE!
I REALLY CAN'T BELIEVE I'M DOING THIS...!

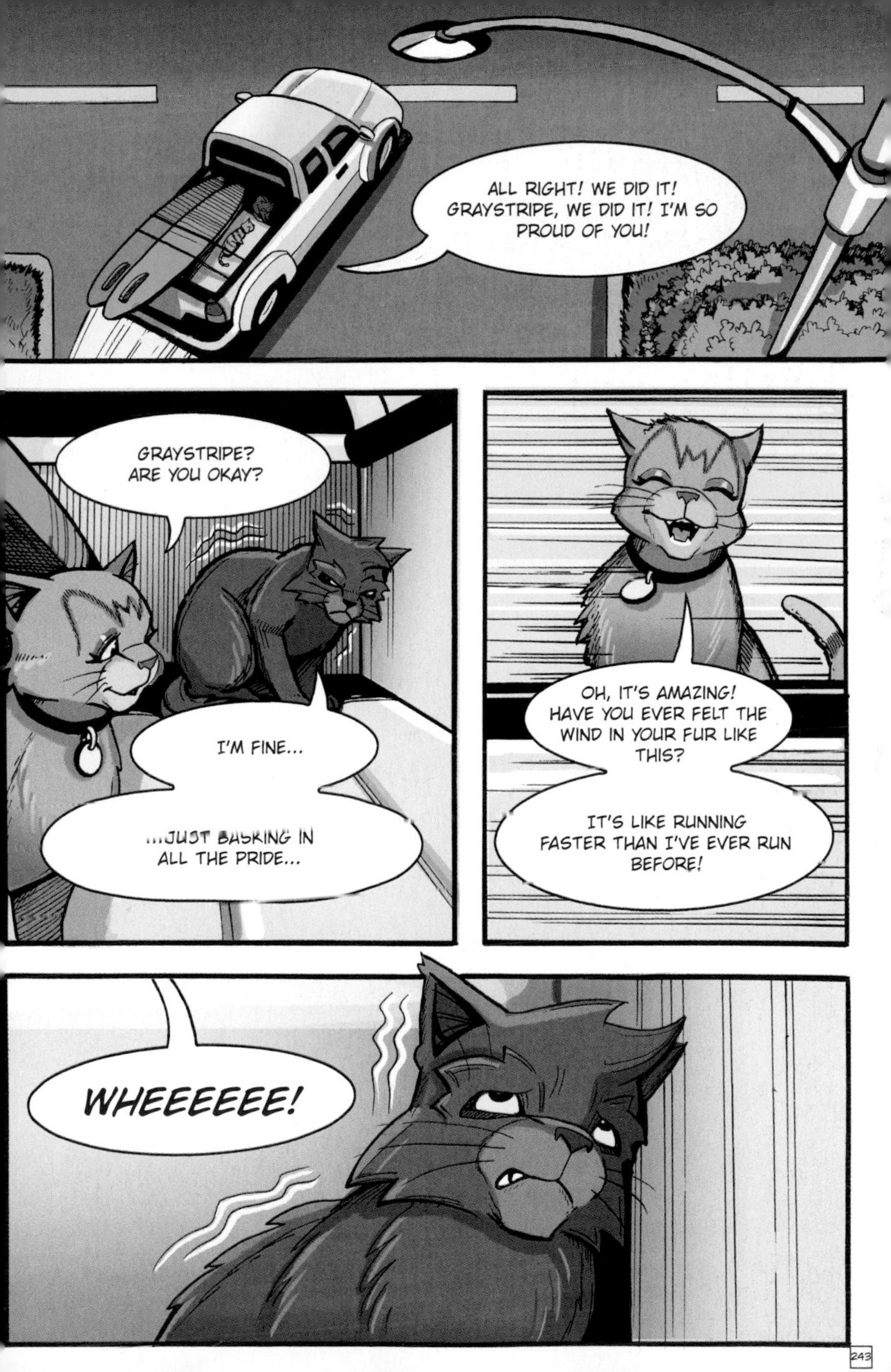
ALL RIGHT! WE DID IT! GRAYSTRIPE, WE DID IT! I'M SO PROUD OF YOU!
GRAYSTRIPE? ARE YOU OKAY?
I'M FINE...
...JUST BASKING IN ALL THE PRIDE...
OH, IT'S AMAZING! HAVE YOU EVER FELT THE WIND IN YOUR FUR LIKE THIS?
IT'S LIKE RUNNING FASTER THAN I'VE EVER RUN BEFORE!
WHEEEEEEE!

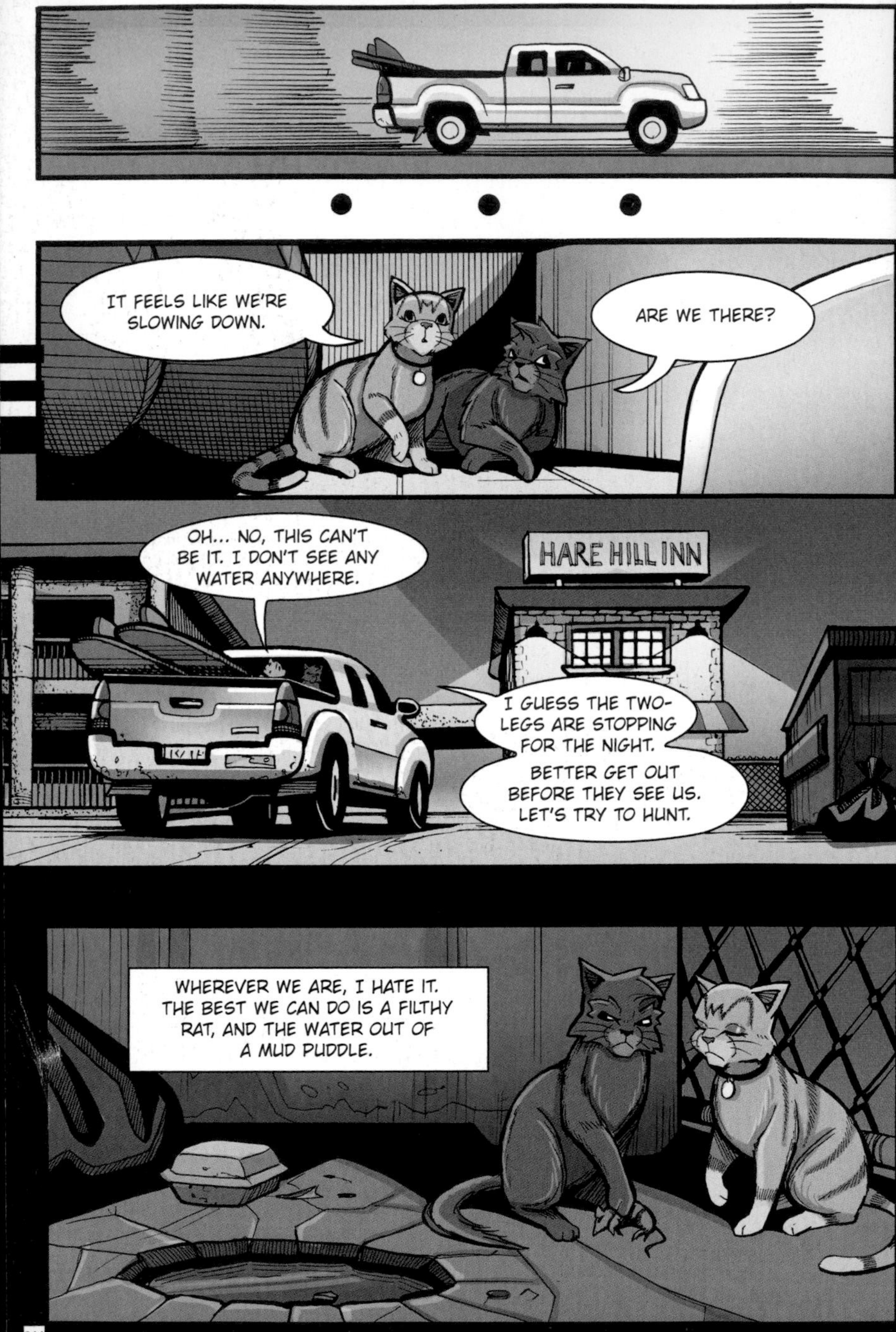
IT FEELS LIKE WE'RE SLOWING DOWN.
ARE WE THERE?
OH... NO, THIS CAN'T BE IT. I DON'T SEE ANY WATER ANYWHERE.
HARE HILL INN
I GUESS THE TWO-LEGS ARE STOPPING FOR THE NIGHT.
BETTER GET OUT BEFORE THEY SEE US. LET'S TRY TO HUNT.
WHEREVER WE ARE, I HATE IT. THE BEST WE CAN DO IS A FILTHY RAT, AND THE WATER OUT OF A MUD PUDDLE.

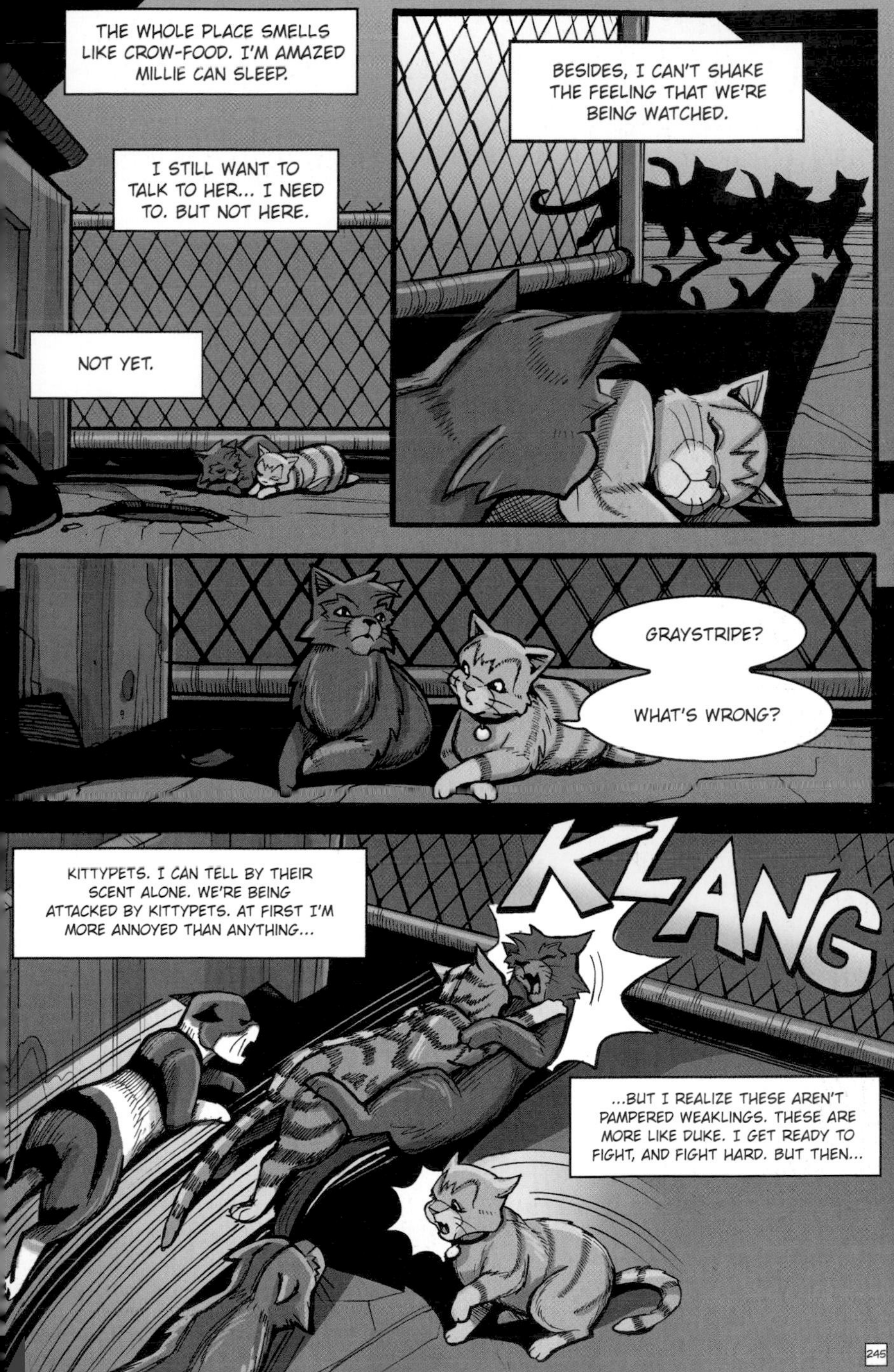
THE WHOLE PLACE SMELLS LIKE CROW-FOOD. I'M AMAZED MILLIE CAN SLEEP.
I STILL WANT TO TALK TO HER... I NEED TO. BUT NOT HERE.
NOT YET.
BESIDES, I CAN'T SHAKE THE FEELING THAT WE'RE BEING WATCHED.
GRAYSTRIPE?
WHAT'S WRONG?
KITTYPETS. I CAN TELL BY THEIR SCENT ALONE. WE'RE BEING ATTACKED BY KITTYPETS. AT FIRST I'M MORE ANNOYED THAN ANYTHING...
KLANG
...BUT I REALIZE THESE AREN'T PAMPERED WEAKLINGS. THESE ARE MORE LIKE DUKE. I GET READY TO FIGHT, AND FIGHT HARD. BUT THEN...

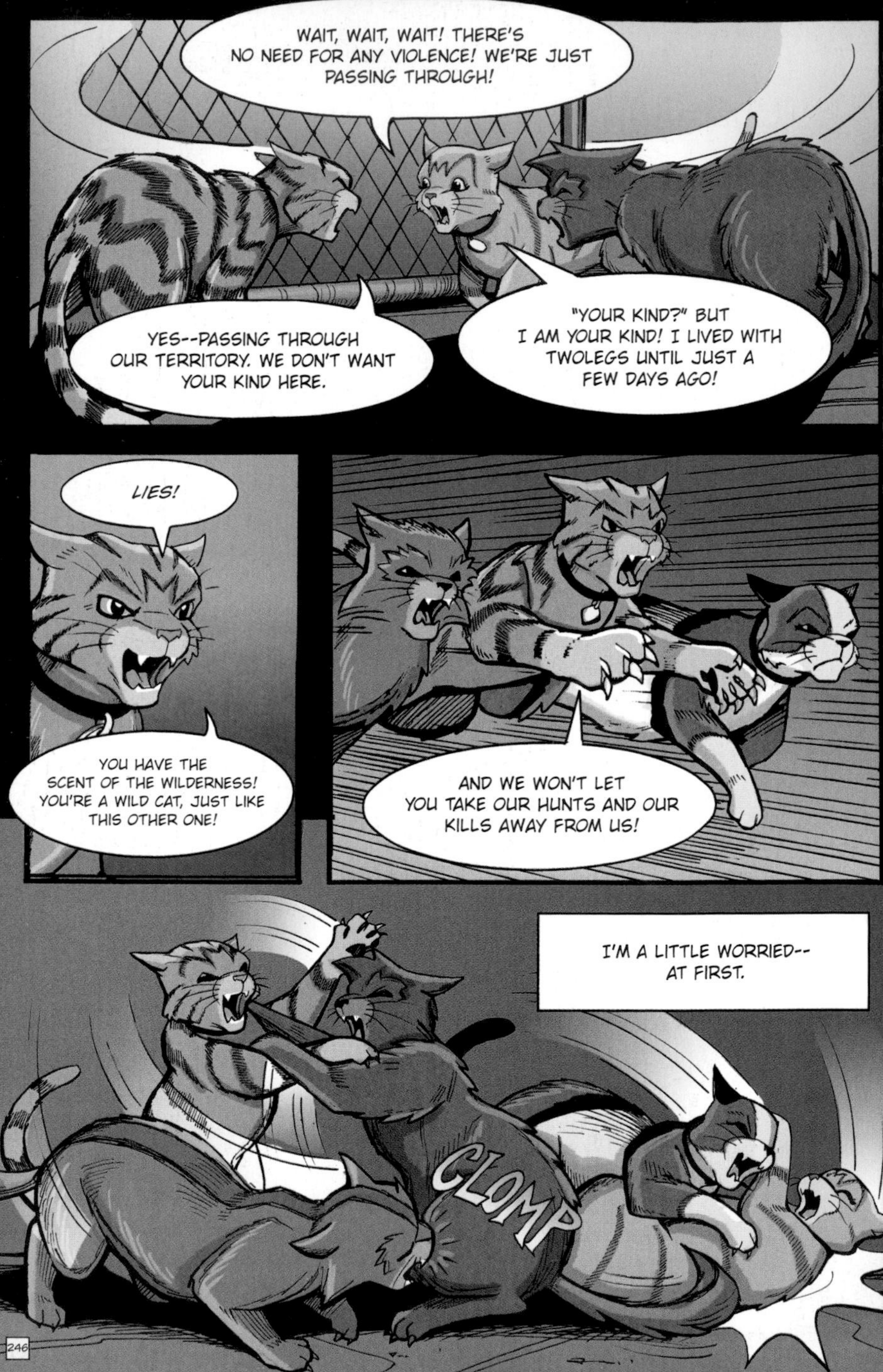
WAIT, WAIT, WAIT! THERE'S NO NEED FOR ANY VIOLENCE! WE'RE JUST PASSING THROUGH!
YES--PASSING THROUGH OUR TERRITORY. WE DON'T WANT YOUR KIND HERE.
"YOUR KIND?" BUT I AM YOUR KIND! I LIVED WITH TWOLEGS UNTIL JUST A FEW DAYS AGO!
LIES!
YOU HAVE THE SCENT OF THE WILDERNESS! YOU'RE A WILD CAT, JUST LIKE THIS OTHER ONE!
AND WE WON'T LET YOU TAKE OUR HUNTS AND OUR KILLS AWAY FROM US!
I'M A LITTLE WORRIED-- AT FIRST.
CLOMP

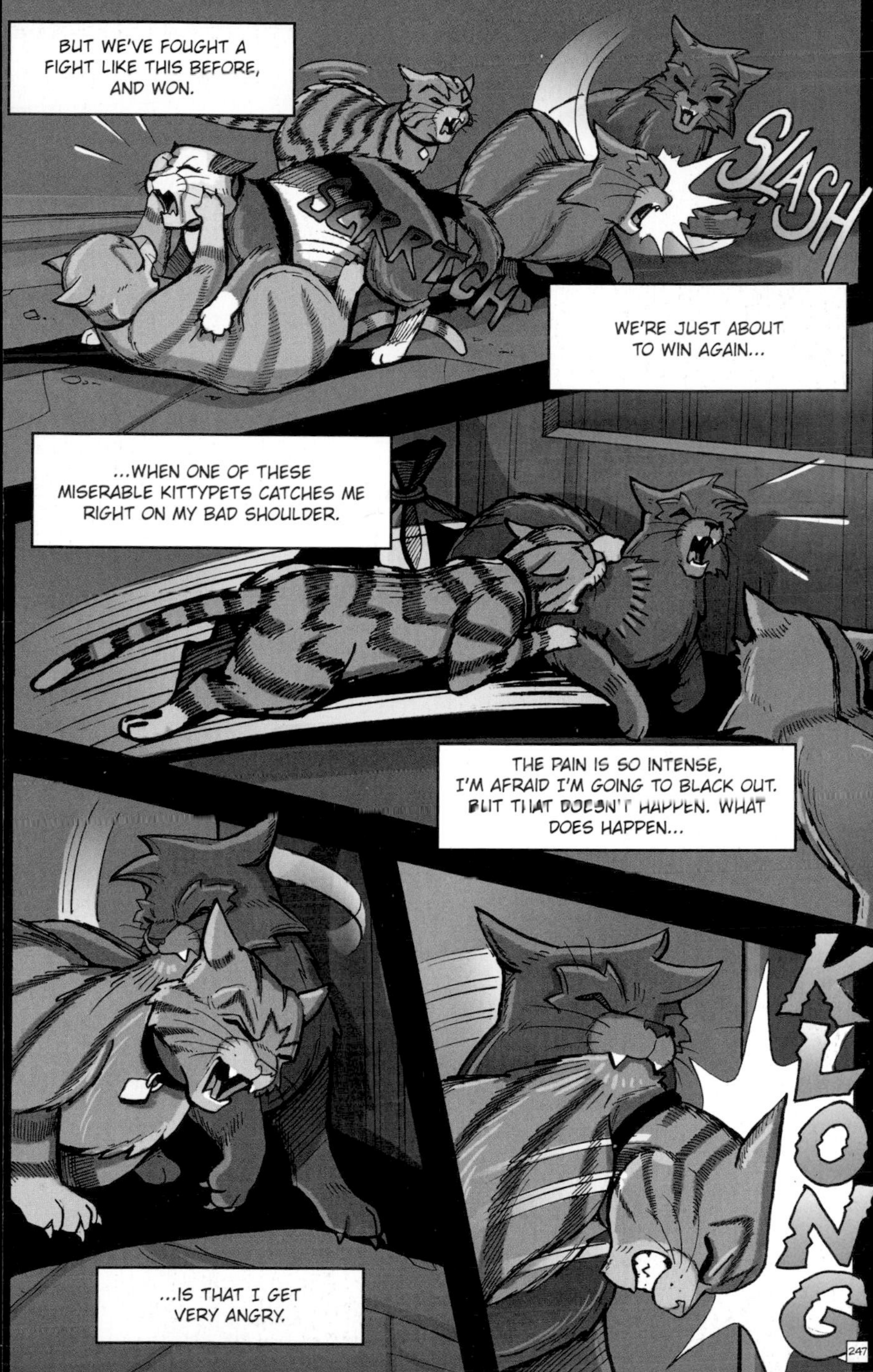
BUT WE'VE FOUGHT A FIGHT LIKE THIS BEFORE, AND WON.
SCRRTCH
SLASH
WE'RE JUST ABOUT TO WIN AGAIN...
...WHEN ONE OF THESE MISERABLE KITTYPETS CATCHES ME RIGHT ON MY BAD SHOULDER.
THE PAIN IS SO INTENSE, I'M AFRAID I'M GOING TO BLACK OUT. BUT THAT DOESN'T HAPPEN. WHAT DOES HAPPEN...
...IS THAT I GET VERY ANGRY.
KLONG

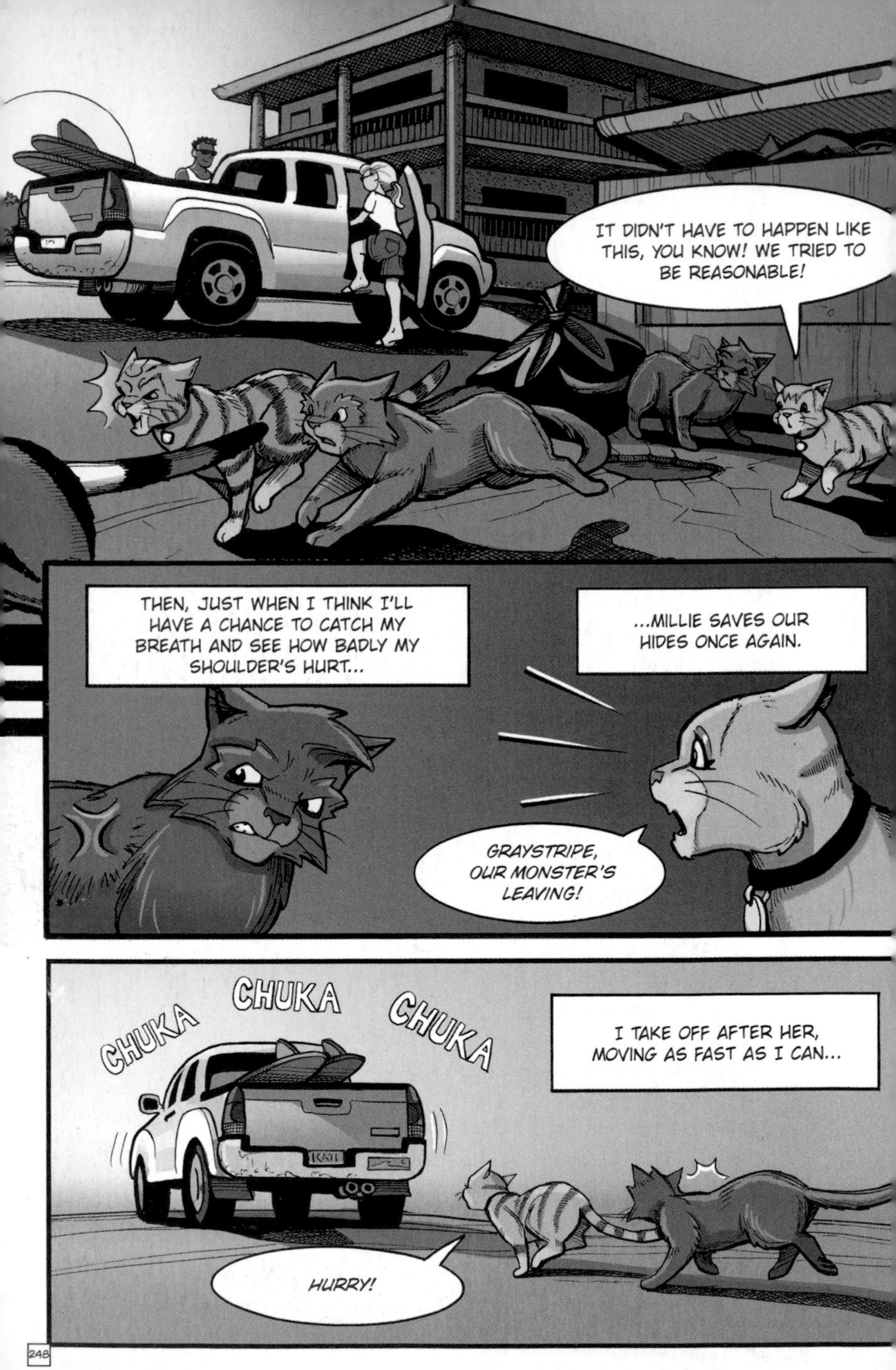

IT DIDN'T HAVE TO HAPPEN LIKE THIS, YOU KNOW! WE TRIED TO BE REASONABLE!
THEN, JUST WHEN I THINK I'LL HAVE A CHANCE TO CATCH MY BREATH AND SEE HOW BADLY MY SHOULDER'S HURT...
...MILLIE SAVES OUR HIDES ONCE AGAIN.
GRAYSTRIPE, OUR MONSTER'S LEAVING!
CHUKA
CHUKA
CHUKA
I TAKE OFF AFTER HER, MOVING AS FAST AS I CAN...
HURRY!

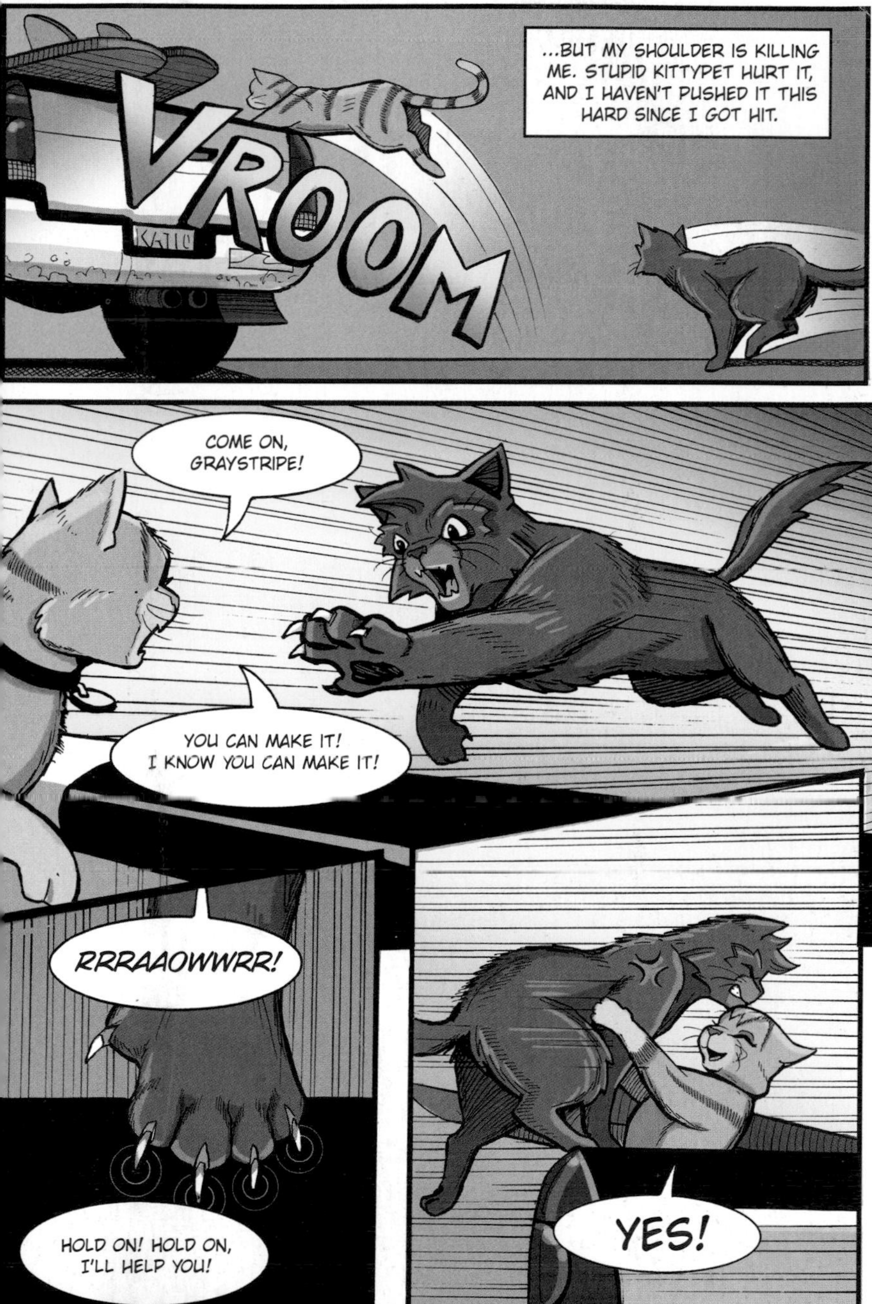
...BUT MY SHOULDER IS KILLING ME. STUPID KITTYPET HURT IT, AND I HAVEN'T PUSHED IT THIS HARD SINCE I GOT HIT.
VROOM
KATIO
COME ON, GRAYSTRIPE!
YOU CAN MAKE IT! I KNOW YOU CAN MAKE IT!
RRRAAOWWRR!
HOLD ON! HOLD ON, I'LL HELP YOU!
YES!

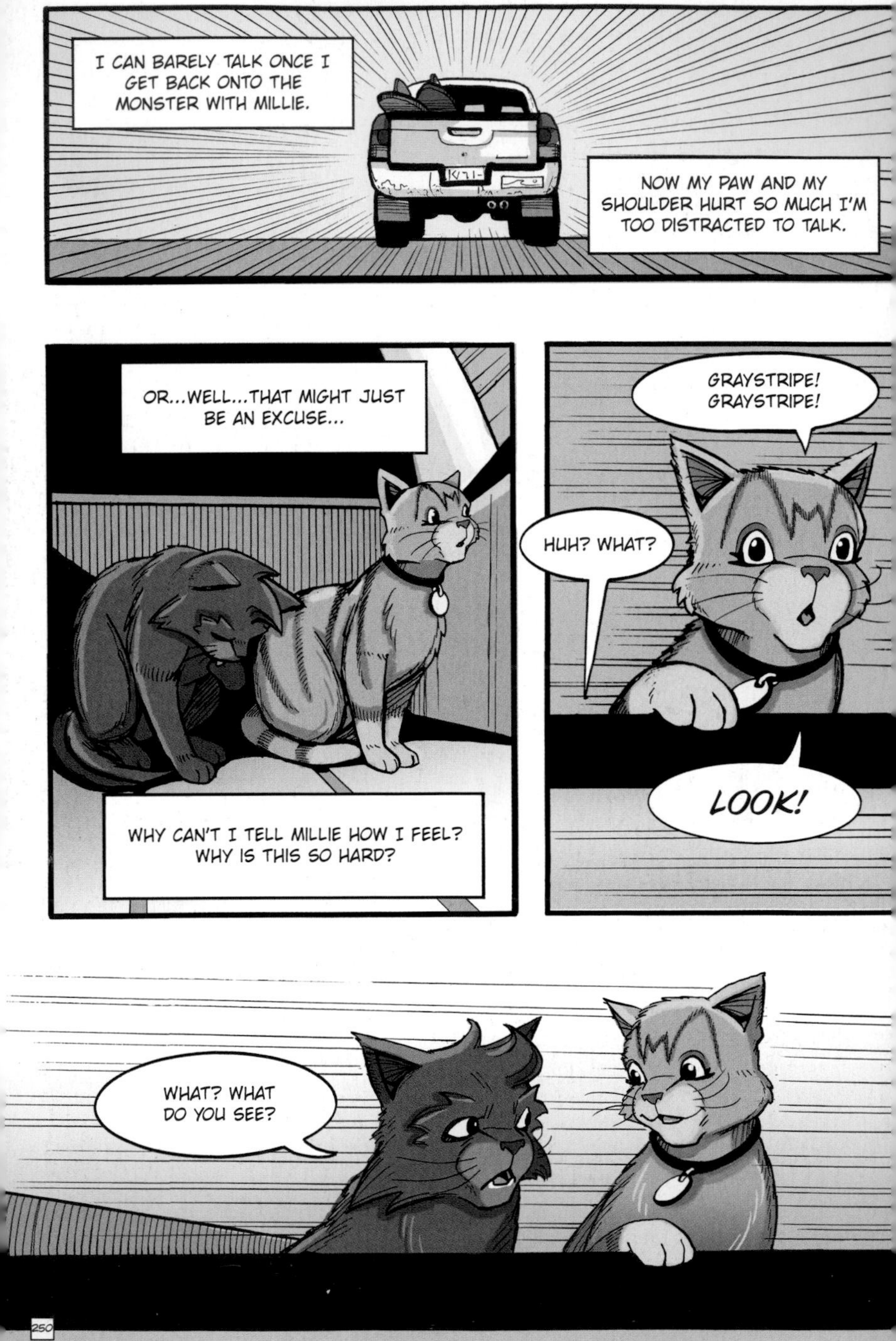
I CAN BARELY TALK ONCE I GET BACK ONTO THE MONSTER WITH MILLIE.
NOW MY PAW AND MY SHOULDER HURT SO MUCH I'M TOO DISTRACTED TO TALK.
OR...WELL...THAT MIGHT JUST BE AN EXCUSE...
WHY CAN'T I TELL MILLIE HOW I FEEL? WHY IS THIS SO HARD?
GRAYSTRIPE! GRAYSTRIPE!
HUH? WHAT?
LOOK!
WHAT? WHAT DO YOU SEE?

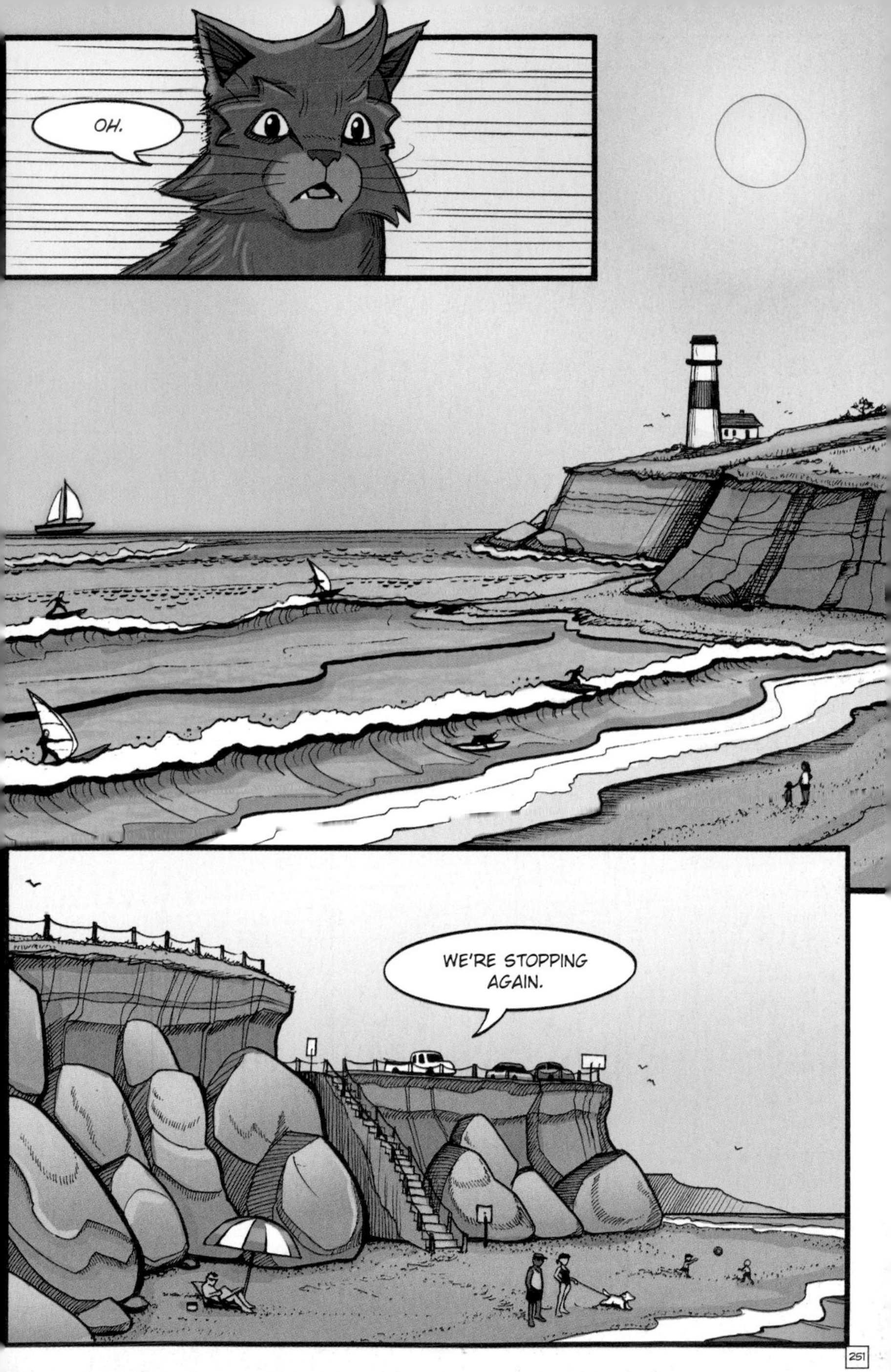
OH.
WE'RE STOPPING AGAIN.

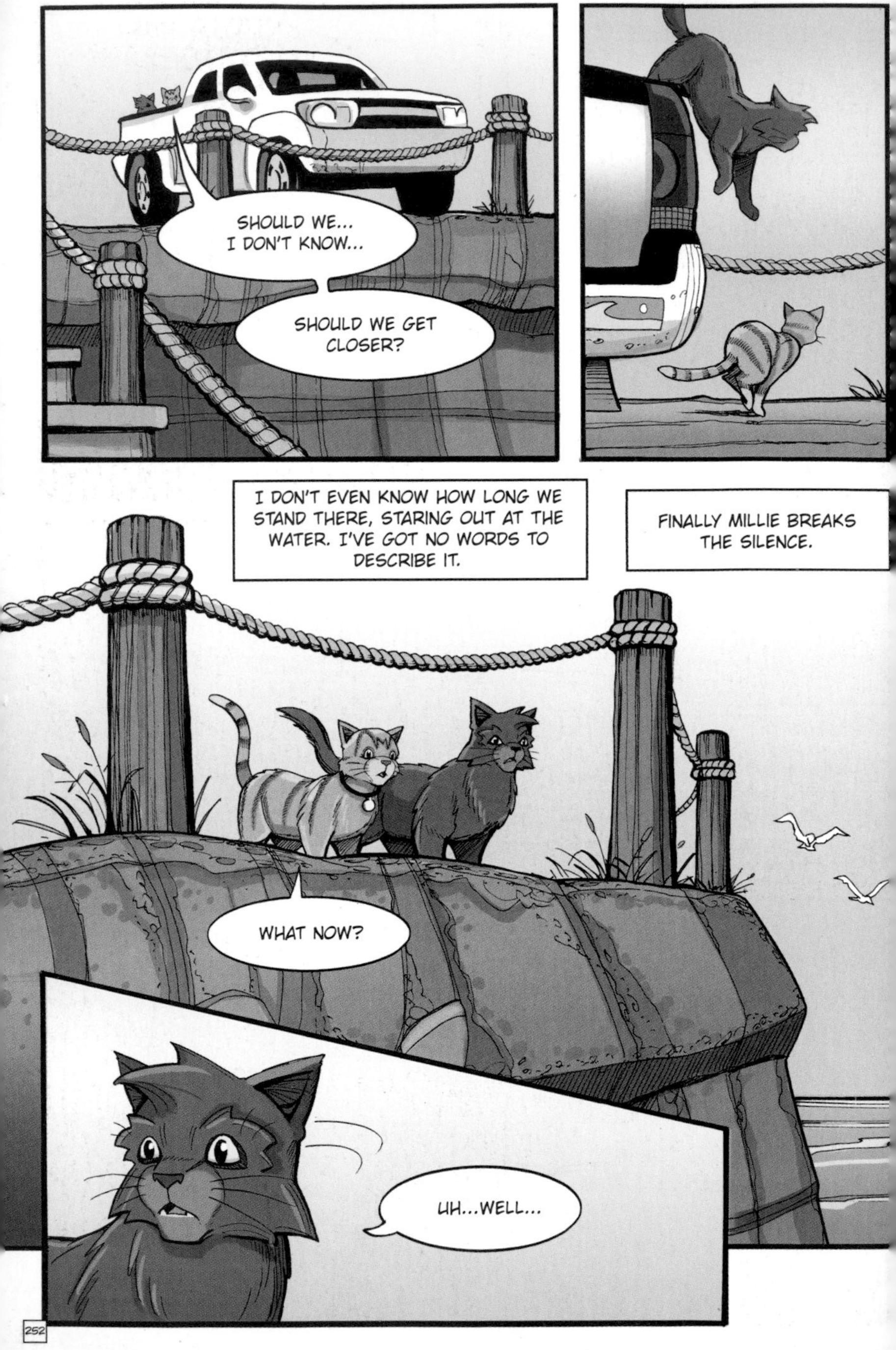
SHOULD WE... I DON'T KNOW...
SHOULD WE GET CLOSER?
I DON'T EVEN KNOW HOW LONG WE STAND THERE, STARING OUT AT THE WATER. I'VE GOT NO WORDS TO DESCRIBE IT.
FINALLY MILLIE BREAKS THE SILENCE.
WHAT NOW?
UH...WELL...

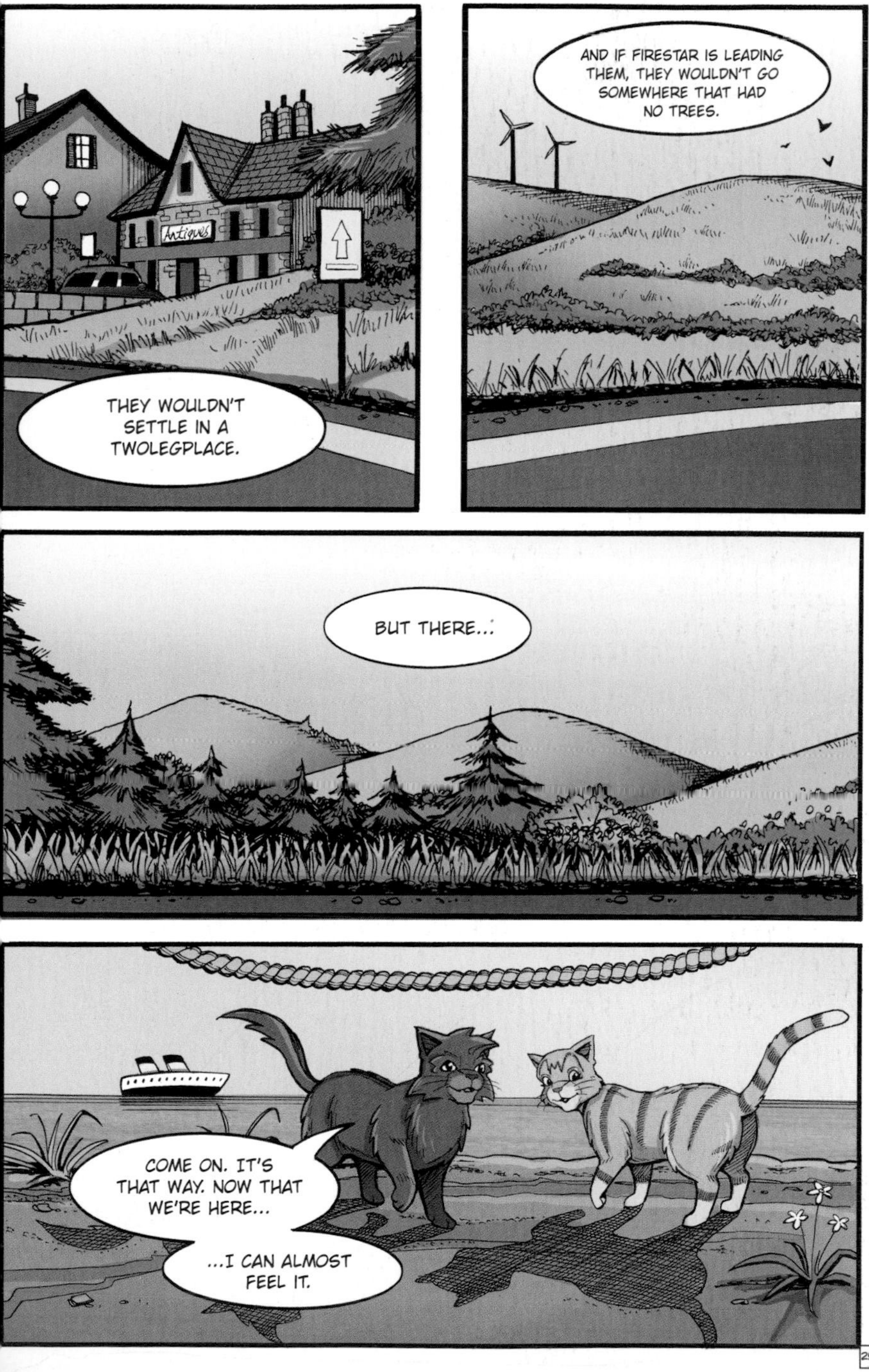
Antiques
THEY WOULDN'T SETTLE IN A TWOLEGPLACE.
AND IF FIRESTAR IS LEADING THEM, THEY WOULDN'T GO SOMEWHERE THAT HAD NO TREES.
BUT THERE...
COME ON. IT'S THAT WAY. NOW THAT WE'RE HERE...
...I CAN ALMOST FEEL IT.

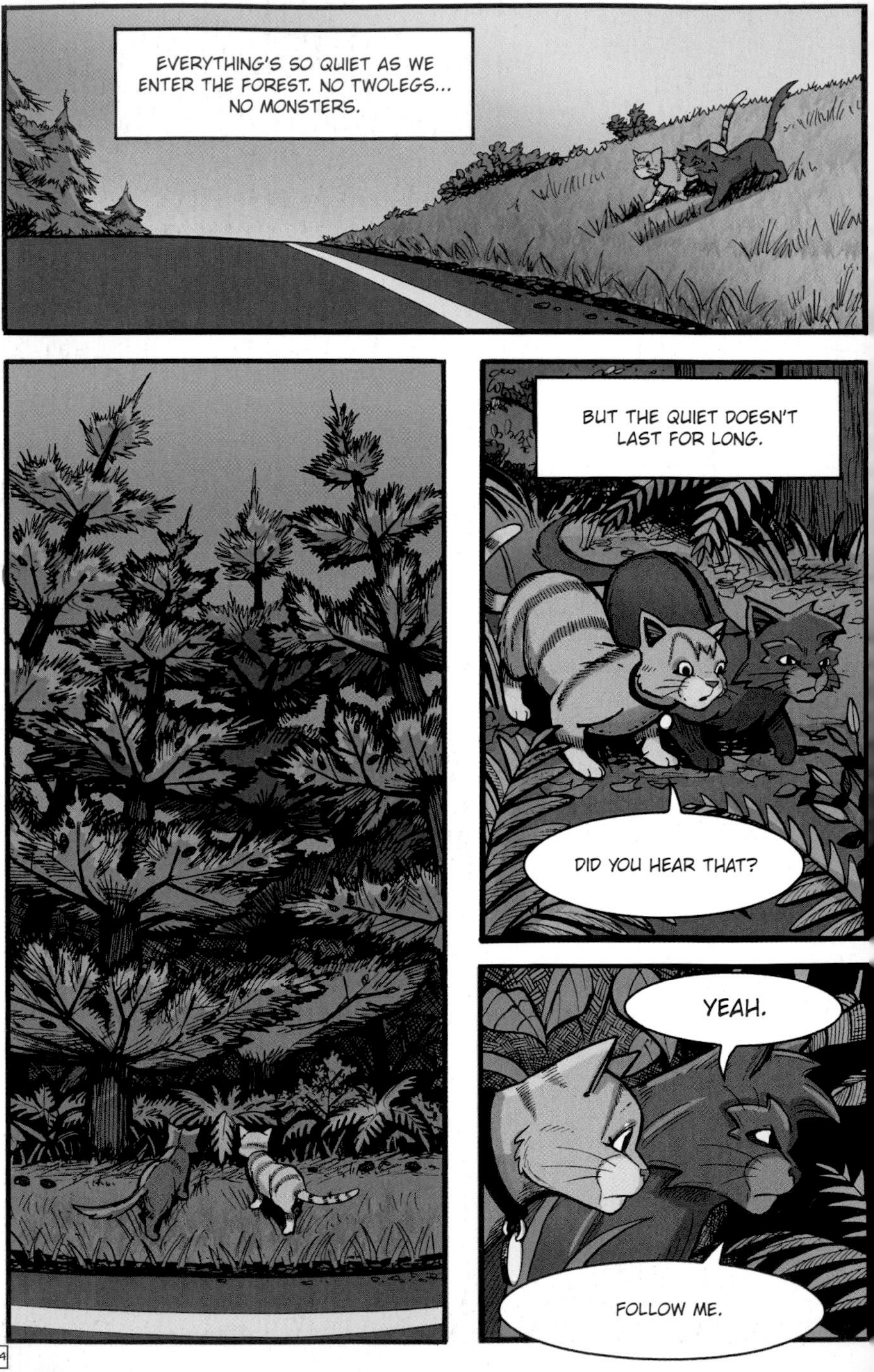
EVERYTHING'S SO QUIET AS WE ENTER THE FOREST. NO TWOLEGS... NO MONSTERS.
BUT THE QUIET DOESN'T LAST FOR LONG.
DID YOU HEAR THAT?
YEAH.
FOLLOW ME.

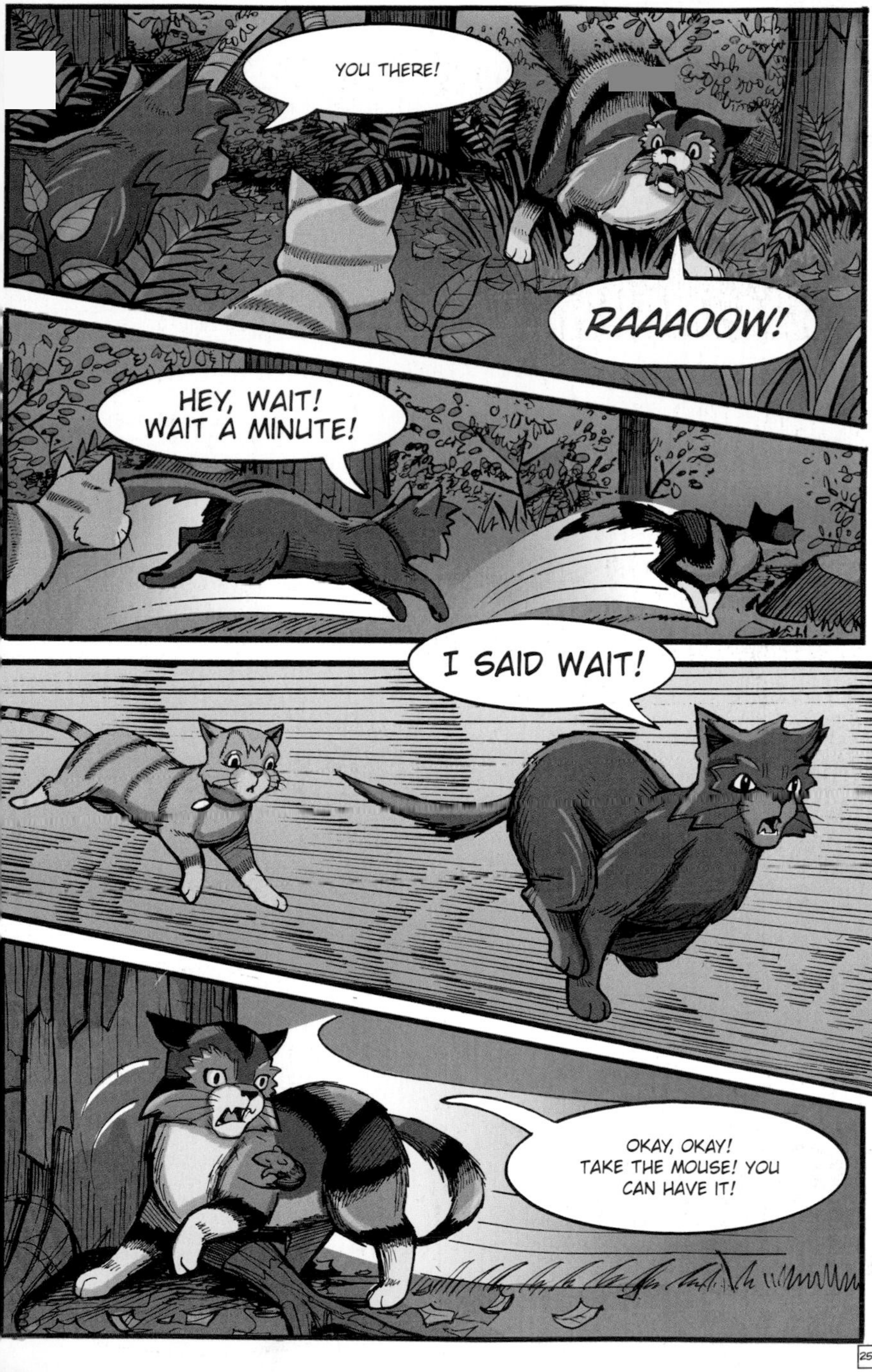
YOU THERE!
RAAAOOW!
HEY, WAIT! WAIT A MINUTE!
I SAID WAIT!
OKAY, OKAY! TAKE THE MOUSE! YOU CAN HAVE IT!

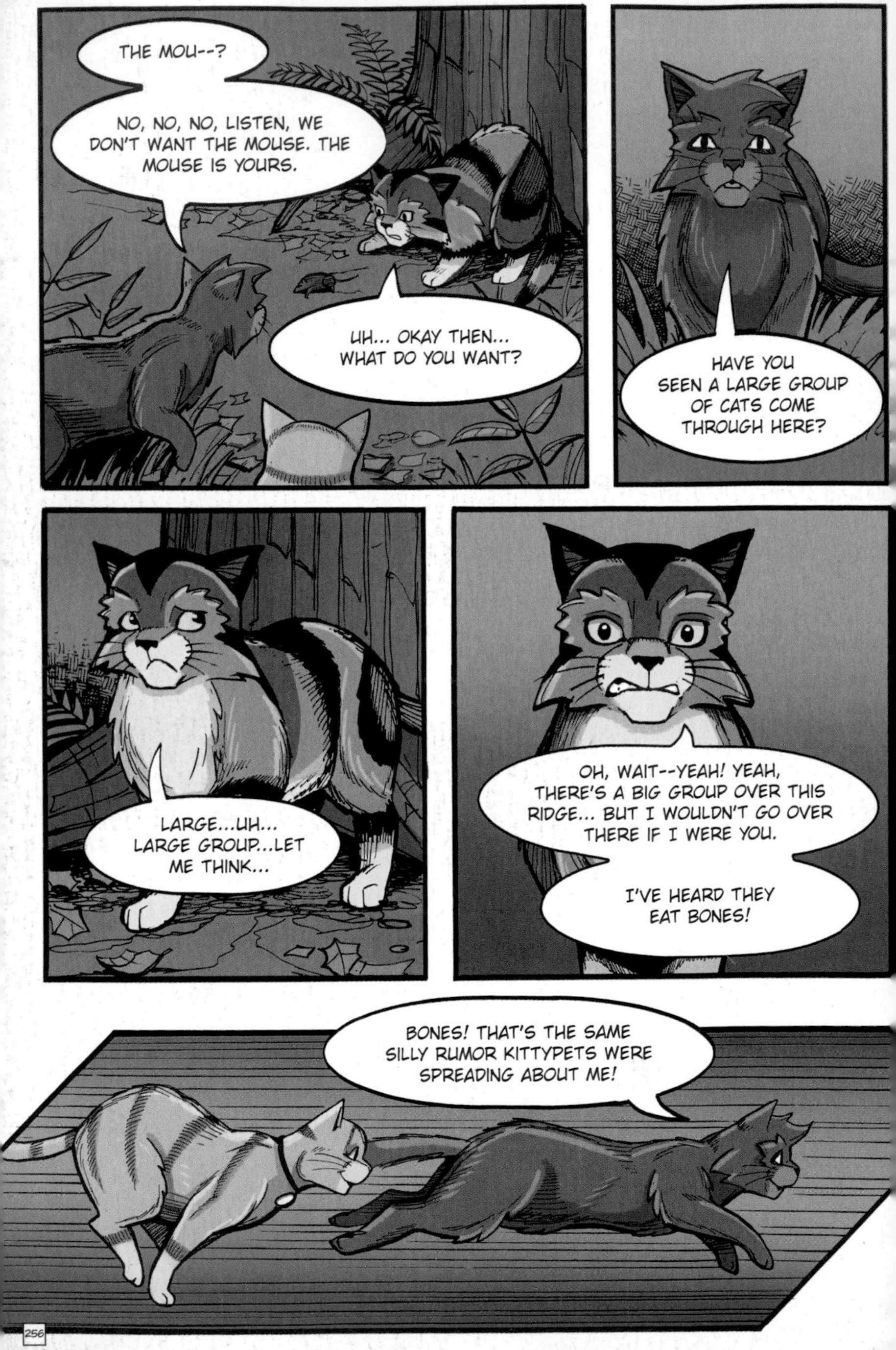
THE MOU--?
NO, NO, NO, LISTEN, WE DON'T WANT THE MOUSE. THE MOUSE IS YOURS.
UH... OKAY THEN... WHAT DO YOU WANT?
HAVE YOU SEEN A LARGE GROUP OF CATS COME THROUGH HERE?
LARGE...UH... LARGE GROUP...LET ME THINK...
OH, WAIT--YEAH! YEAH, THERE'S A BIG GROUP OVER THIS RIDGE... BUT I WOULDN'T GO OVER THERE IF I WERE YOU.
I'VE HEARD THEY EAT BONES!
BONES! THAT'S THE SAME SILLY RUMOR KITTYPETS WERE SPREADING ABOUT ME!

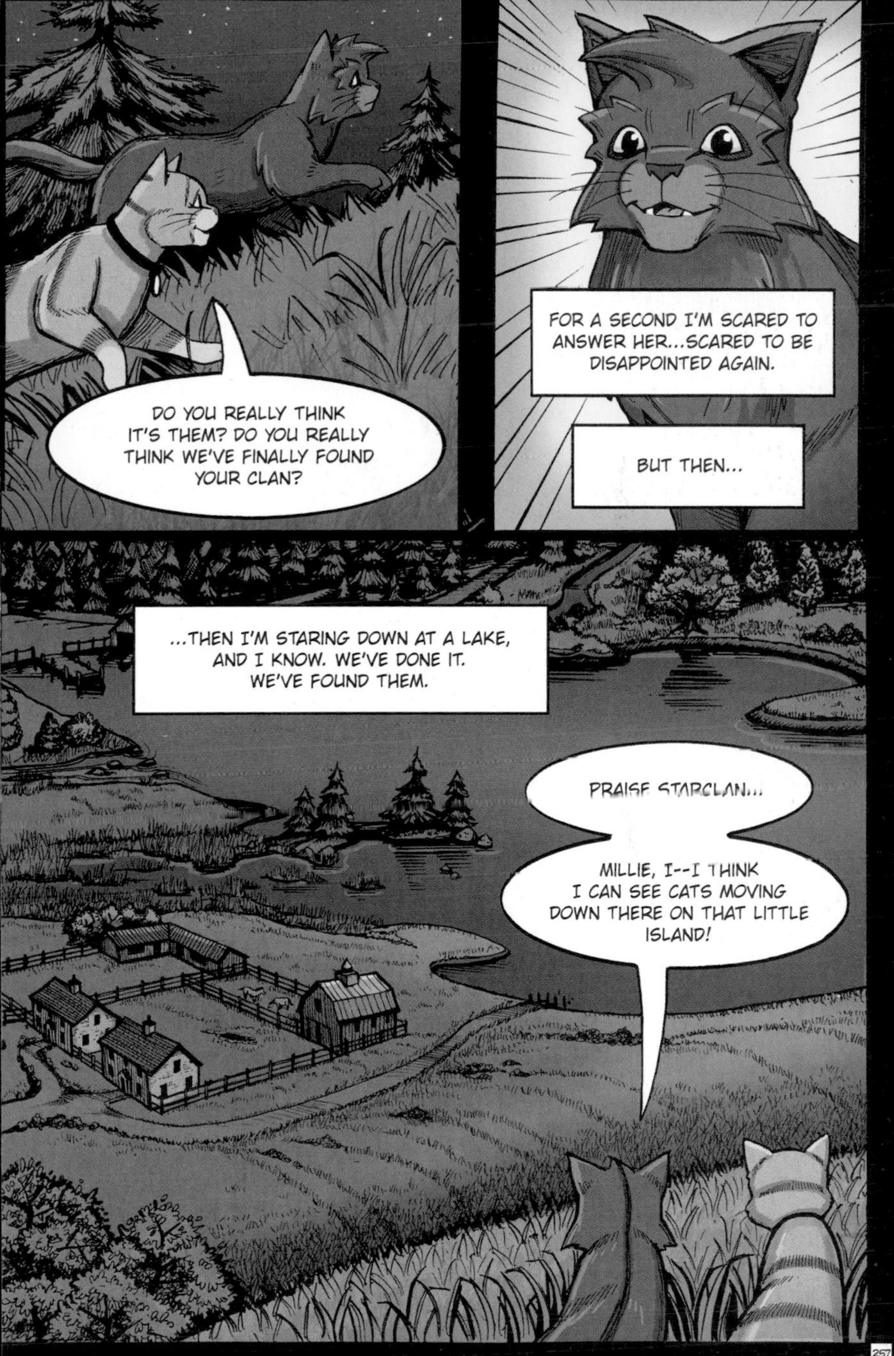
DO YOU REALLY THINK IT'S THEM? DO YOU REALLY THINK WE'VE FINALLY FOUND YOUR CLAN?
FOR A SECOND I'M SCARED TO ANSWER HER...SCARED TO BE DISAPPOINTED AGAIN.
BUT THEN...
...THEN I'M STARING DOWN AT A LAKE, AND I KNOW. WE'VE DONE IT. WE'VE FOUND THEM.
PRAISE STARCLAN...
MILLIE, I--I THINK I CAN SEE CATS MOVING DOWN THERE ON THAT LITTLE ISLAND!

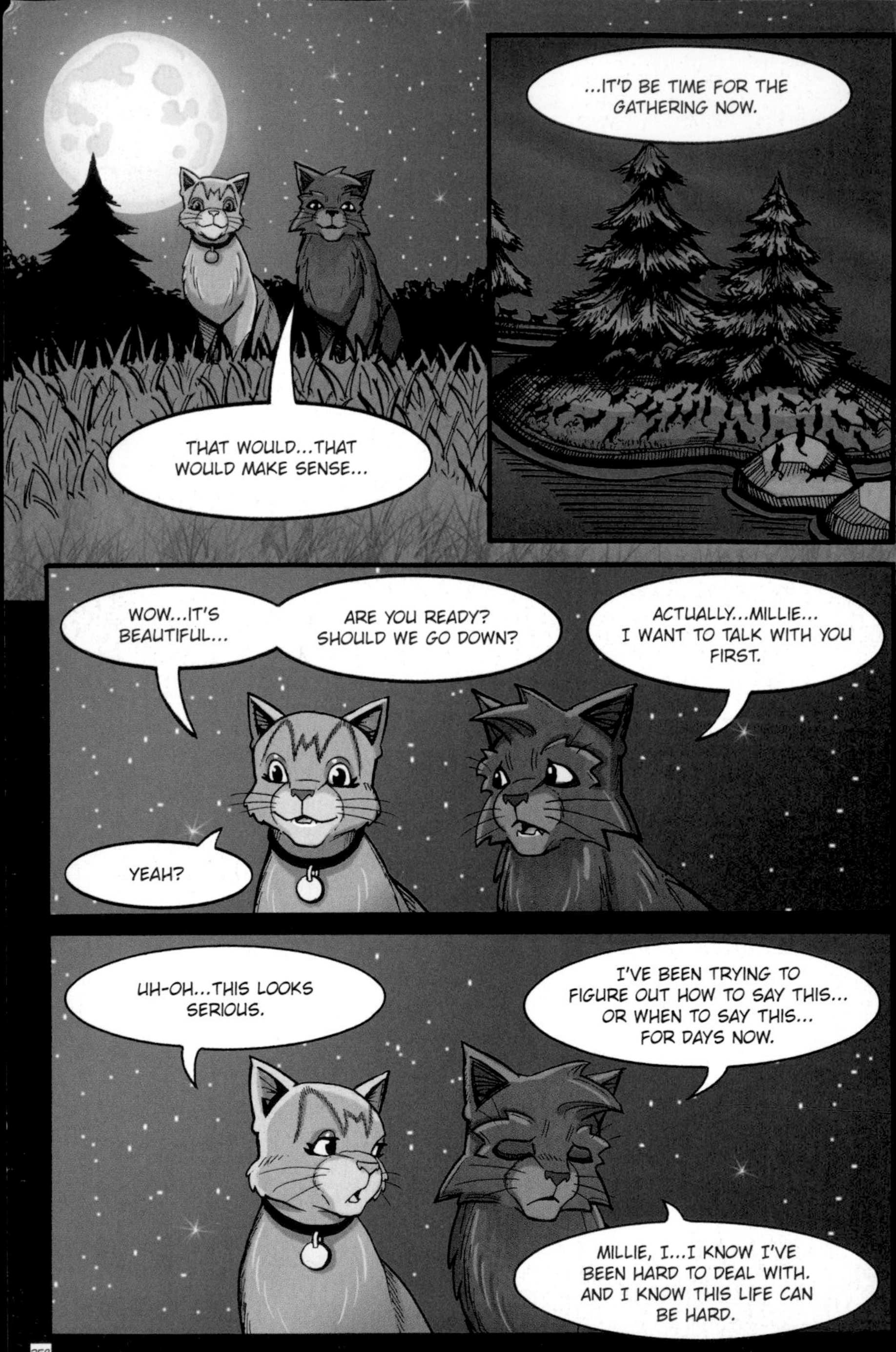
THAT WOULD...THAT WOULD MAKE SENSE...
...IT'D BE TIME FOR THE GATHERING NOW.
WOW...IT'S BEAUTIFUL...
ARE YOU READY? SHOULD WE GO DOWN?
ACTUALLY...MILLIE... I WANT TO TALK WITH YOU FIRST.
YEAH?
UH-OH...THIS LOOKS SERIOUS.
I'VE BEEN TRYING TO FIGURE OUT HOW TO SAY THIS... OR WHEN TO SAY THIS... FOR DAYS NOW.
MILLIE, I...I KNOW I'VE BEEN HARD TO DEAL WITH. AND I KNOW THIS LIFE CAN BE HARD.

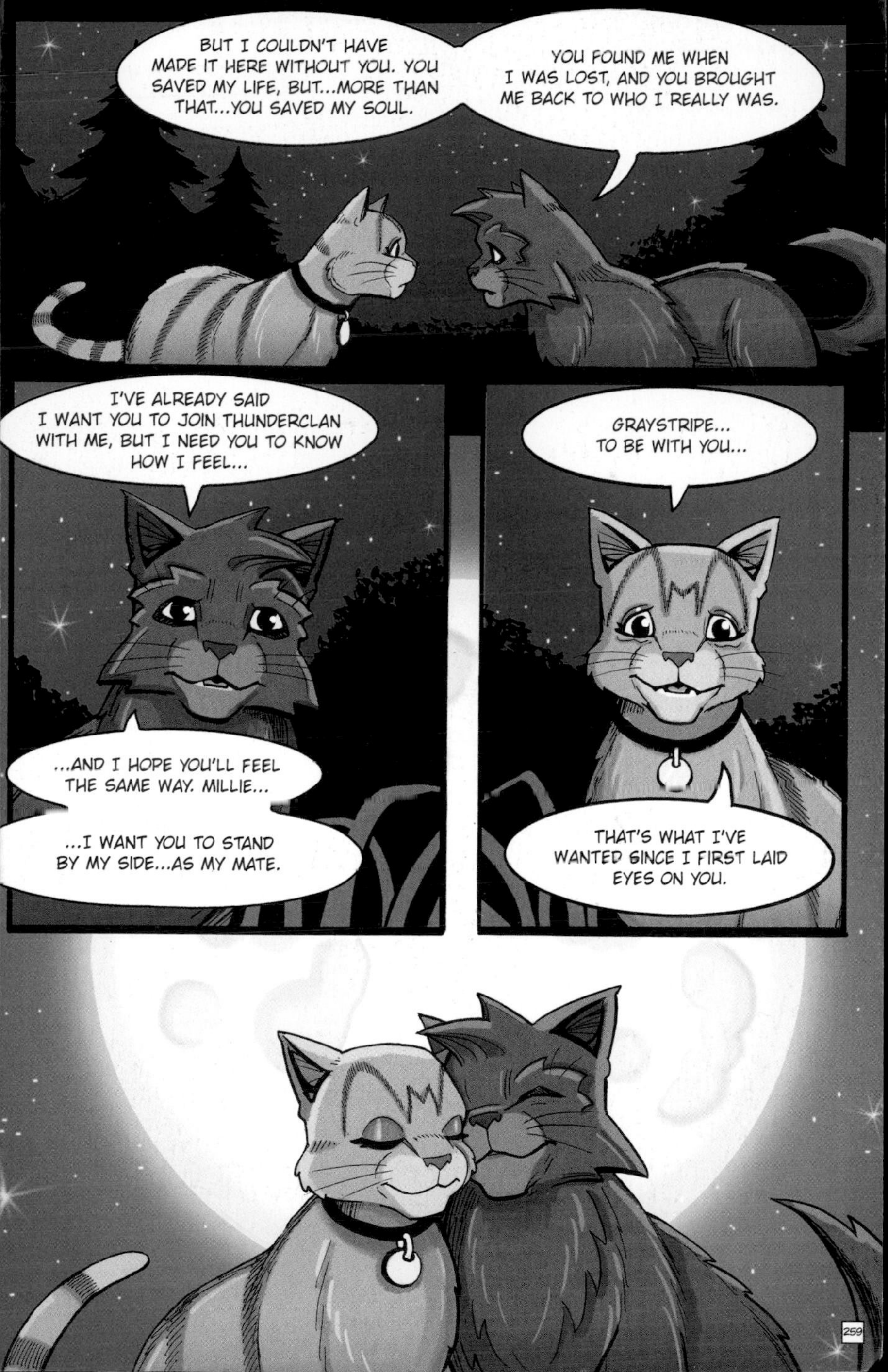
BUT I COULDN'T HAVE MADE IT HERE WITHOUT YOU. YOU SAVED MY LIFE, BUT...MORE THAN THAT...YOU SAVED MY SOUL.
YOU FOUND ME WHEN I WAS LOST, AND YOU BROUGHT ME BACK TO WHO I REALLY WAS.
I'VE ALREADY SAID I WANT YOU TO JOIN THUNDERCLAN WITH ME, BUT I NEED YOU TO KNOW HOW I FEEL...
...AND I HOPE YOU'LL FEEL THE SAME WAY. MILLIE...
...I WANT YOU TO STAND BY MY SIDE...AS MY MATE.
GRAYSTRIPE... TO BE WITH YOU...
THAT'S WHAT I'VE WANTED SINCE I FIRST LAID EYES ON YOU.

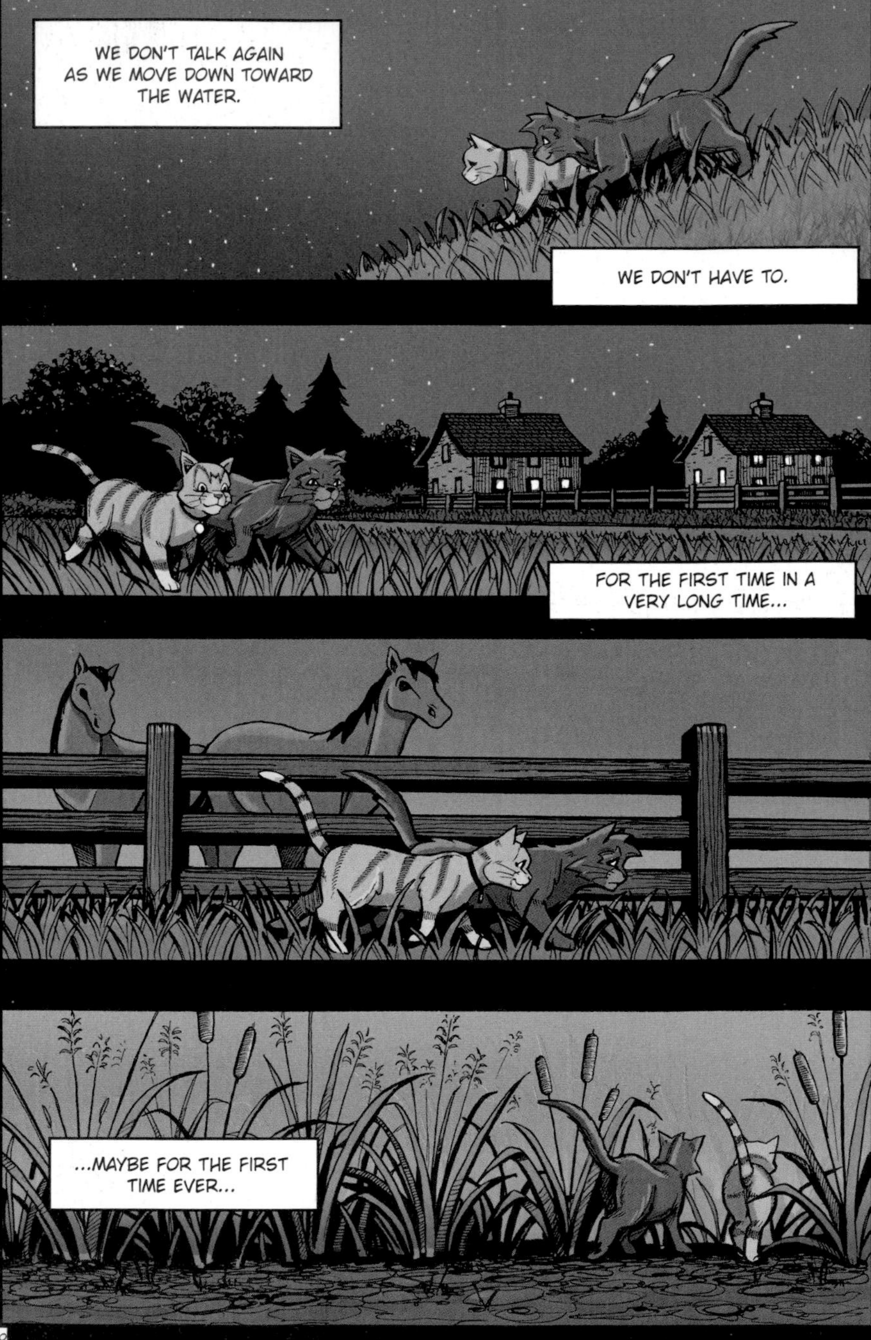
WE DON'T TALK AGAIN AS WE MOVE DOWN TOWARD THE WATER.
WE DON'T HAVE TO.
FOR THE FIRST TIME IN A VERY LONG TIME...
...MAYBE FOR THE FIRST TIME EVER...

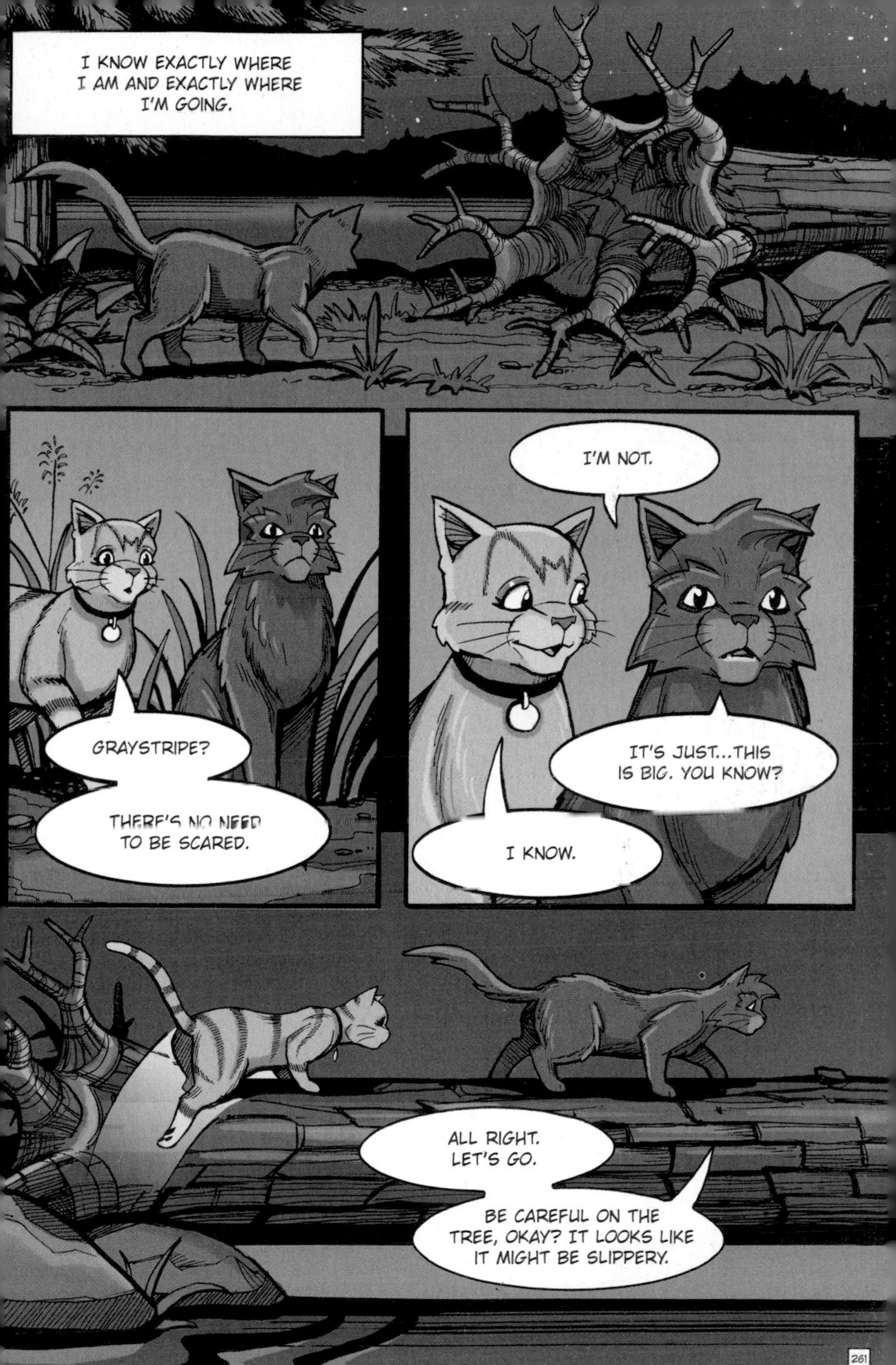
I KNOW EXACTLY WHERE I AM AND EXACTLY WHERE I'M GOING.
GRAYSTRIPE?
THERE'S NO NEED TO BE SCARED.
I'M NOT.
IT'S JUST...THIS IS BIG. YOU KNOW?
I KNOW.
ALL RIGHT. LET'S GO.
BE CAREFUL ON THE TREE, OKAY? IT LOOKS LIKE IT MIGHT BE SLIPPERY.

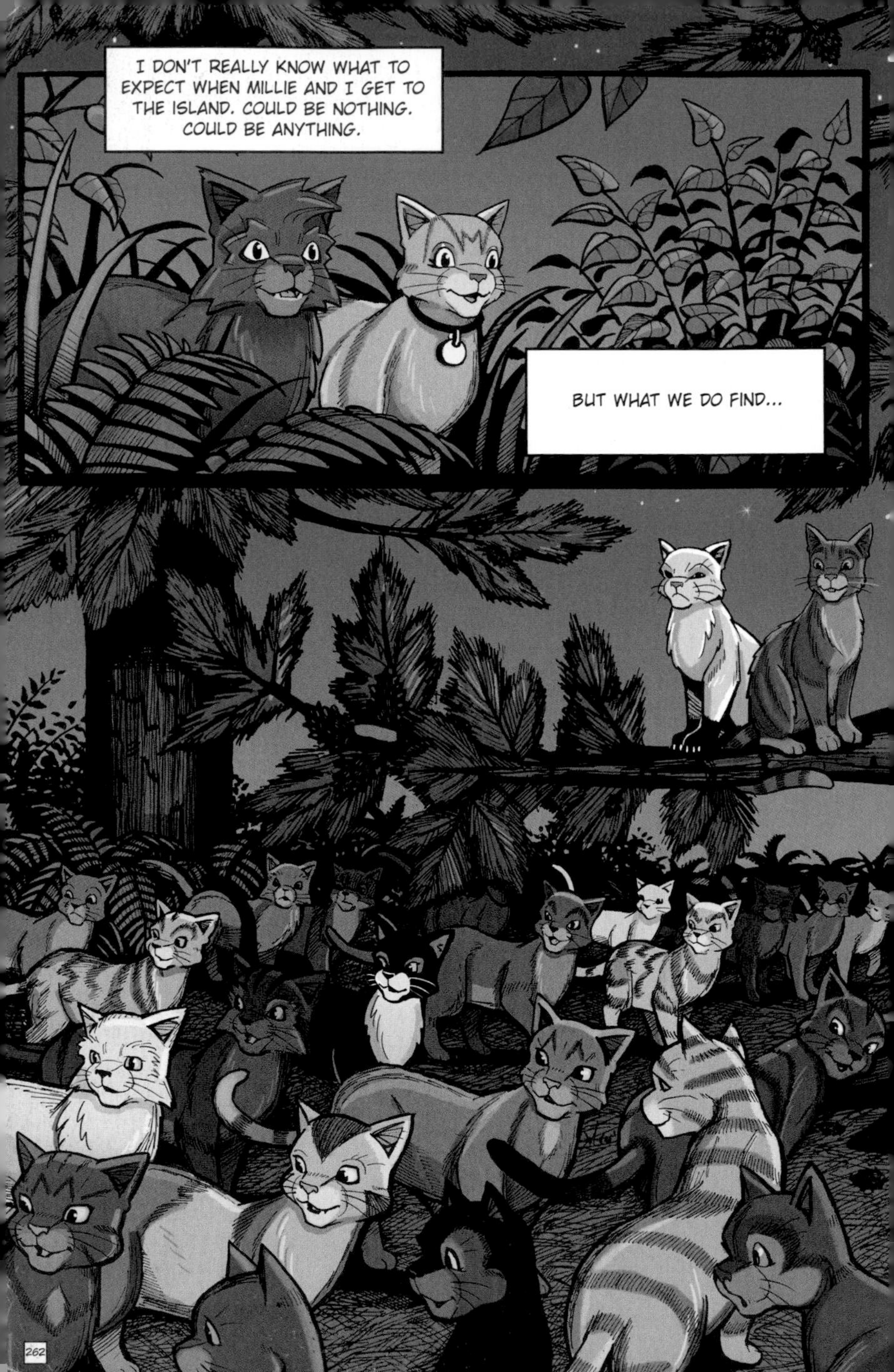
I DON'T REALLY KNOW WHAT TO EXPECT WHEN MILLIE AND I GET TO THE ISLAND. COULD BE NOTHING. COULD BE ANYTHING.
BUT WHAT WE DO FIND...

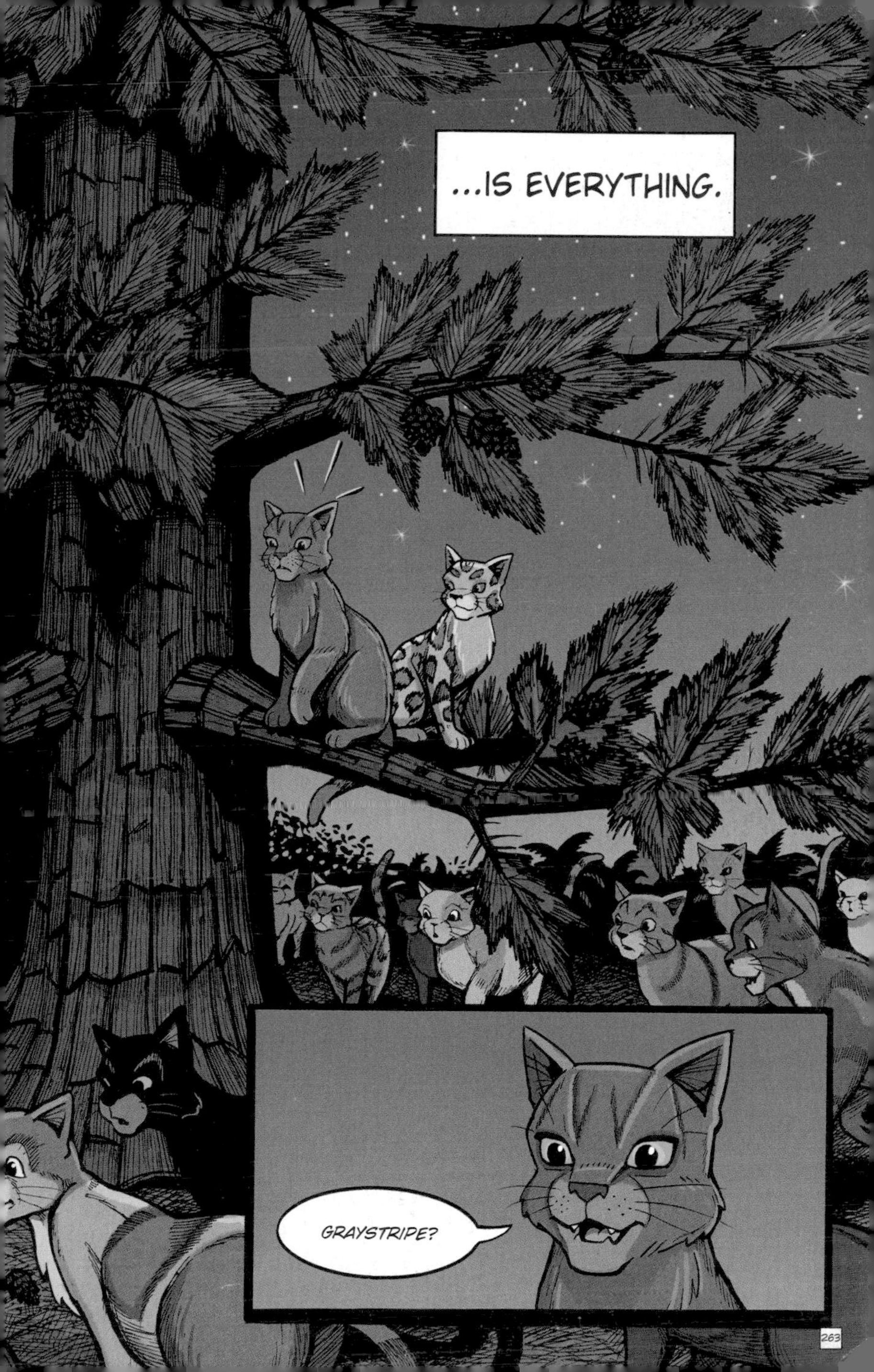
...IS EVERYTHING.
GRAYSTRIPE?

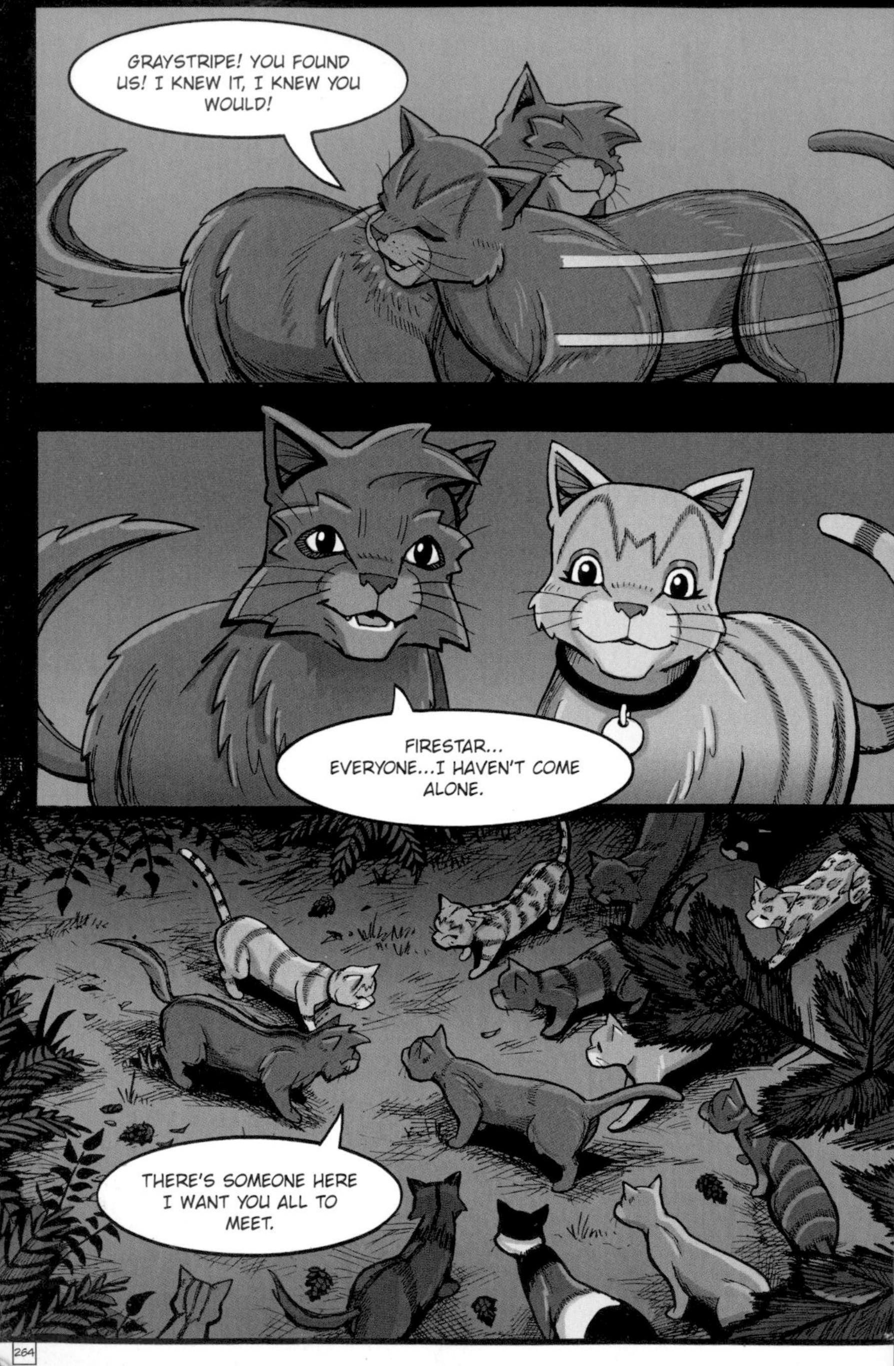
GRAYSTRIPE! YOU FOUND US! I KNEW IT, I KNEW YOU WOULD!
FIRESTAR... EVERYONE...I HAVEN'T COME ALONE.
THERE'S SOMEONE HERE I WANT YOU ALL TO MEET.

ERIN
HUNTER

is inspired by a love of cats and a
fascination with the ferocity of the
natural world. As well as having great
respect for nature in all its forms,
Erin enjoys creating rich mythical
explanations for animal behavior.
She is also the author of the Seekers,
Survivors, and Bravelands series.

Download the free Warriors app at
www.warriorcats.com.